A FOLLY BEACH MYSTERY COLLECTION VI

BILL NOEL

ANGELICA CRUZ

Front cover and design by Bill Noel

Author photos and original map by Susan Noel

ISBN: 978-1-958414-87-3

Enigma House Press

Goshen, Kentucky 40026

Engimahousepress.com

BILL NOEL'S
FOLLY
BEACH
SOUTH CAROLINA

Charleston
Sandbar Lane
Charles's Apartment
Indian Ave
Center Street
West Second St
Hudson Ave
Cooper Ave
Ashley Ave
Arctic Ave
East Second St
Huron Ave
Erie Ave
Chris's House
First Light

1 Rita's
2 Dude's surf shop
3 Sand Dollar
4 Haunted House
5 Loggerhead's
6 Snapper Jacks
7 St. James Gate
8 Surf Bar
9 Cal's
10 Mr. John's Beach Store
11 Landrum Gallery/Barb's Books
12 The Crab Shack
13 City Hall/Public Safety
14 Sean Aker, Attorney
15 Planet Follywood
16 Woody's Pizza
17 The Washout
18 Post Office
19 Pewter Hardware
20 Lost Dog Cafe
21 Bert's Market
22 The Edge

* From my imagination to yours

Boneyard Beach
Morris Island Lighthouse
Marsh
Folly River
Washout
Pier
Folly Beach County Park

ALSO BY BILL NOEL

Other Folly Beach Mysteries by Bill Noel

Folly

The Pier

Washout

The Edge

The Marsh

Ghosts

Missing

Final Cut

First Light

Boneyard Beach

Silent Night

Dead Center

Discord

A Folly Beach Mystery COLLECTION

Dark Horse

Joy

A Folly Beach Mystery COLLECTION II

No Joke

Relic

A Folly Beach Mystery COLLECTION III

Faith

A Folly Beach Christmas Mystery COLLECTION

Tipping Point

Sea Fog with coauthor Angelica Cruz

Mosquito Beach

Pretty Paper with coauthor Angelica Cruz

Adrift

A Folly Beach Mystery COLLECTION IV

Overkill with coauthor Angelica Cruz

Midnight

A Folly Beach Mystery COLLECTION V

Phantom with coauthor Angelica Cruz

MIDNIGHT

A FOLLY BEACH MYSTERY

1

———

"Few things can beat a peaceful walk on the beach," Charles Fowler said as we traipsed though soft, warm sand away from where we entered the shoreline at the Folly Beach Fishing Pier.

I'd met Charles more than a dozen years ago during my first week on the small South Carolina barrier island. We'd quickly become friends although we had as much in common as a walnut to a walrus. One thing that did draw us together was an interest in photography.

"True," I said.

"You could've picked a cooler day, though."

It was mid-August, and the humidity level was as high as the current upper-eighties temperature.

"Charles, you forget this walk was your idea?"

"There you go, splitting hairs. Let's walk closer to the dunes. I want to photograph some of those itty-bitty pink flowers."

The farther we got from the Pier, the nine-story, beachfront Tides Hotel, and the area where most vacationers on Folly first stick their toes in the Atlantic, the quieter, and according to Charles, the more peaceful our walk was becoming. I followed him as he angled closer to the dunes and the pink blooms on railroad vines snaking over the barrier separating the beach from private residences. It was refreshing seeing him bend to photograph blooms since his primary area of focus is normally discarded candy wrappers and vehicle-flattened drink cans.

My friend's photo shoot was interrupted by a dozen college-age young people illegally trampling over the dunes on their way to the wide expanse of sand while carrying coolers, a pop-up tent, folding chairs, and a volleyball set. I'm no psychic but would wager from the sounds of the exuberant guys the coolers weren't holding soft drinks and water.

Charles glared at the loud crowd like they'd disrupted him photographing the cover for *National Geographic*. He pointed his ever-present, homemade cane at them and said, "Did you invite the circus?"

That didn't deserve an answer, so I suggested we head farther away from the group that was now planting their tent in the sand for anything but a peaceful day at the beach. The guys who had carried the coolers distributed cans of beer to the others, despite the often-ignored law prohibiting alcoholic beverages on the beach, while two of the females were yelling for someone to get the tent finished while they opened the chairs and arranged them in a semi-circle. A hundred yards past the group, we reached a spot occupied by only the two of us, and Charles once again headed closer to the dunes to continue photographing native wildflowers.

A scream grabbed our attention. This time it wasn't coming from the beach, but from a large three-story house under construction near where Charles was photographing flowers. We turned toward the house but didn't see anything. Seconds later, three men wearing hardhats exited the door at the top of the stairs leading down to a concrete patio.

That's all it took for Charles to grab my arm, point to the men, and say, "What are we waiting for?"

He didn't wait for my answer. He was already at the newly constructed stairs leading from the beach to the house's yard. Taking two steps at a time, he was near the top of the stairs before I'd managed to cover three steps.

Before I reached the top of the stairs, two other construction workers exited the house and the five of them were staring at something on the patio. A sour taste grew in my stomach when I saw that the something was a woman; a woman face down, her arms twisted behind her, her head twisted in an unnatural position. I had no doubt she was dead.

Charles inched his way between two of the workers like he was one of the crew. I stood behind him but turned my head away from the gruesome sight. Two more workers emerged from the house and stood beside me.

"Anyone call 911?" I asked the man closest to me.

He looked at me like I didn't belong with the group. No surprise since I didn't. He pointed to the man probably in his sixties standing on the other side of the group. "Randy done called."

If I'd waited a few more seconds, I wouldn't have asked. The distinct sound of a Folly Beach fire engine came from the center of the small island about six blocks from where we were standing. The high-pitched siren from one of the city's patrol cars approached from the other direction on West Ashley Avenue, the island's longest street.

Charles nudged me with his elbow and pointed at a man in his thirties wearing a white T-shirt with Donnelly Plumbing in large red letters on the back. He said, "I'll ask Kyle what happened."

Before I could say okay or ask who Kyle was, Charles made a beeline to the plumber, leaving me beside the older gentleman who'd removed his hard hat and was holding it over his heart. He shook his head and mumbled, "Tragic, so tragic." He then put his hard hat back on, turned to me, and said, "I'm Lucius. You live in one of those houses?" He nodded toward the house on each side of the construction site.

I reached to shake his hand and said, "No, I'm Chris Landrum. My friend and I were walking up the beach and heard a scream. Came to see if there was anything we could do to help. What happened?"

He looked at the body on the concrete patio, sighed, and said,

"Don't know. I'm an electrician and was inside working on the electrical panel. Heard people out here yelling and came to see what was going on. You know as much as I do."

A member of the Folly Beach Department of Public Safety came around the side of the house, saw the woman on the deck, waved for us to move back, and knelt beside the lifeless body. Public Safety Officers double as firefighters and many are certified EMTs. I didn't know the officer. Two firefighters arrived next. I also didn't know them but did know the next person who appeared. I'd known Officer Rodney New since he'd joined the force three years ago. He took a quick look at the body, did a police gaze at the group standing around the patio, stopped when he saw me, rolled his eyes, pointed to the far corner of the house, and said, "Gentlemen, please move over there in the shade. I'll be with you in a minute."

The way he said it left no doubt it wasn't a suggestion.

Charles joined me as we headed to the shade and said, "Her name's Shelly Whitley, a carpenter. Husband's named Raymond. No kids, no pets. Hubby's a bartender in Charleston."

"Charles, you got all that from, umm, what's his name?"

"Kyle, yeah."

"He know what happened?"

"Not really. Said it looks like she lost her footing and fell off the roof." Charles looked toward the top of the house. "Got a peaked roof up there. Kyle said it was a bear building it. Sees how she could've fallen."

"Did he know if anyone saw her fall?"

"Nope."

"Nope he didn't know or nope to anyone seeing her fall?"

"He didn't know if anyone saw it."

Two more Public Safety Officers arrived while we were gathering beside the house. Officer New waved for Charles and me to follow him to the street where he slowly shook his head and said, "Chris, Charles, I know you're too lazy, and I might add, too old, to be working on this house, so what in blue blazes are you doing here?"

I'd finally reached the age of seventy, way too quickly, I might add. Charles was two years younger.

He said, "You know us well, Rodney. We were walking down the beach. I was taking photos of—"

Rodney interrupted with, "Unless you photographed the lady tumbling off the roof, skip the history lesson and tell me what happened."

I smiled and answered before he could go into a lengthy monologue about no telling what. "Rodney, we heard a scream then saw guys coming out of the house and staring at the patio. We came to see what the commotion was about. You know as much about what happened as we do. All I can add is her name's Shelly Whitley."

"Did you know her?"

"No, one of the workers told Charles who she was."

"Charles, I know I may regret it, but is there anything you can add? Anything relevant?"

Yes, he did know my trivia-collecting, irrelevant information-accumulating friend well.

"Umm, she was a carpenter, married to Raymond, no kids, no pets. Guess that's it."

"Thank you," the officer said, bordering on sarcasm. I don't see any reason to keep you two around. We'll be spending time with the workers; besides, I know where to find you if we need more."

I knew Charles wouldn't be happy being dismissed without learning more about what happened.

"Officer New," he said, "sure you don't need us to stay?"

I rest my case.

"Goodbye, Charles, you too, Chris."

I took Charles by the elbow and pivoted him toward the steps leading to the beach. He followed my lead, but not without a huff, a mumble, and possibly a muted profanity.

2

____

I 'd be lying if I said sleep came quickly. My mental image of the
woman on the concrete pad floated in and out of my consciousness. Thinking about her young life ending while she was
simply earning a living left me saddened. Her dreams about the
future, her life with her husband, the possible addition of children to
her family, vacations, gatherings with friends and relatives, all wiped
out by one wrong step on the vaulted roof. As the construction
worker had said, "Tragic, so tragic."

The summer sun peeking through the slats in my window blinds
woke me at least an hour later than my normal seven o'clock awakening. Other than the memory of staring at the lifeless woman on the
new house's patio, I remembered Charles saying I should call Cindy
LaMond, Folly's Director of Public Safety, aka Police Chief, to find out
more about the incident. Granted, Charles knows the Chief as well as
I do and has her phone number, so he could've made the call. I
reminded him of that yesterday before we went our separate ways. He
reminded me that the Chief thinks he is, in his words, an idiot, a pain
in her posterior, and not someone she'd confide in. He's partially
correct.

"Morning, Cindy."

"Let me put on my fortune-teller hat," she said after an audible sigh. "You called so I could tell you everything, everything in exhaustive detail about what happened yesterday at the construction site, the construction site where you and your shadow happened to be nosing in business that's none of your business. How am I doing so far?"

I was hoping for a response more along the lines of, *Good morning, Chris. How are you this fine morning?* While that was my hope, I'd learned years ago that a civil comment was seldom the beginning of many calls on Folly, especially on calls with Cindy. I'd known her since she'd moved here eleven years ago. I also counted her and her husband Larry good friends.

"You're right."

"Of course, I am." I heard paper rustling in the background. "The late Shelly Whitley turned thirty-two in July. She won't be turning thirty-three. She was married to Raymond Whitley, age thirty-five, who, with luck, will turn thirty-six in January. No children, and you can tell Charles, you know, the guy who cares more about people's pets than he does about people, that the Whitleys didn't have any critters in the house."

She hesitated so I figured it was time to say something. I didn't want to tell her Charles had already learned that much about the Whitleys, all but their ages. "And?"

"Gee, you want their Social Security numbers, blood types, and shoe sizes?"

I held back a chuckle. "I was more interested in what happened."

"Me too, but there's not much more. According to Randy Lee, the foreman, Shelly was working on the bonus room, at least that's what he called it. It's at the top of the house and has a vaulted roof. Apparently, she was on the slant, lost her footing, and fell to her death. Cause of death, most likely a broken neck. End of story, and sadly, end of Shelly."

"Anyone see her fall?"

"No one said they did. Each guy claimed to be in the house working on, well, whatever he was supposed to be working on."

"There's nothing to suspect it was anything but an accident?"

"I know you think you're a private detective and like to stick your nose in every death that happens here, but there's nothing to indicate it was anything but a terrible accident."

"Charles is the one who claims to be a detective."

Since retiring to Folly from a boring, mind-numbing career in the human resources department of a large health-care company in Kentucky, I'd stumbled across a few murder situations. Through fate and good, or many would say, bad luck, I and a few of my friends had managed to solve crimes that'd stumped the police. Charles, whose imagination knew no bounds had proclaimed he was a private detective. No, he has neither formal training nor a license to back up his claim, but those minor stumbling blocks were no barrier for my friend.

"If you say so."

There was no need to respond. She'd hung up.

One of Charles's quirks, one of many, was if I learned something he felt he needed to know and didn't tell him within seconds, if that long, I was violating one of the Amendments to the Constitution and probably one of the Ten Commandments. With that in mind, I knew it'd be a matter of minutes before Charles would be calling to hear what I'd learned from Cindy, that is, after asking why it'd taken me so long to tell him.

He always wanted to know what I'd learned, but often made it difficult. I called three times to no avail. He has a cell phone but leaving it in his apartment was something he managed to do more often than taking it whenever he ventured out.

My growling stomach reminded me I hadn't eaten. For most people, that was easily remedied by a trip to the kitchen. In my small cottage, a trip to the bedroom housing my computer would be as fruitful as walking to the kitchen for finding food. Fortunately, my abode was next door to Bert's Market, Folly's iconic grocery that's open twenty-four hours a day, three-hundred-sixty-five days a year and sells everything from beer to bananas.

I don't drink beer or like bananas, so a prepackaged sandwich was my focus as I took the short walk where I was greeted by Denise, one of the store's friendly and helpful employees. We spent a couple of minutes sharing the obligatory comments about the weather and the many vacationers invading the island before Denise said she had to get something out of the storeroom and left me searching for lunch.

I was deciding between a ham on rye sandwich or turkey on whole wheat when I saw Brad Burton heading my way. Brad retired from the Charleston County Sheriff's Office a few years ago and moved to a house on the far side of mine. When he was still working, we'd had several run-ins. He accused me of murder the first month I was on Folly; hardly the welcome I'd hoped for. I helped the police catch the killer, but it didn't affect how Detective Burton viewed me.

When his daughter was killed three years ago, Brad spiraled into deep depression. What brought him out isn't recommended by mental health professionals. His daughter's killer planted a bomb in Brad and his wife Hazel's house. Through divine intervention and his nosy neighbor, aka me, I saw the killer leaving the house and went to check on the Burton's. I managed to drag Brad out of the house seconds before it exploded. Fortunately, Hazel wasn't home at the time. Saving Brad didn't turn him into a member of my fan club, but he began tolerating me without sneering. His house was rebuilt last year, and I'd regularly run into him, mainly here in Bert's and occasionally talked with him when he crossed through my yard to get to and from the grocery.

"See you're shopping for lunch," he said as he pointed to the sandwich in my hand.

I guess his detective instincts hadn't evaporated when he retired.

"Yes, my chef has the day off."

"Cute." He nodded in the direction of the sandwich. "If it wasn't for Hazel, I'd be getting all my meals prepackaged from here."

"How's Hazel liking the new house?" I asked, not knowing what else to say.

He smiled. "She loves the house. It's me being there all the time that's driving her crazy."

I returned his smile. "I thought she would've adjusted to you being there by now. You retired, what, four years ago?"

"Five years next month." He shook his head. "She put up with me being in her space the first few years. After the house, umm, was destroyed, we were too busy with everything, busy enough it didn't bother her having me around. She keeps telling me I need to get a hobby." He smiled again. "Get a hobby, anything as long as it's out of the house."

"Having any luck?"

"I tried golf. Hated it. Can you see me surfing out there?" He nodded in the direction of the Atlantic.

"Umm, no."

"Right. Fishing is more boring than watching grass grow."

"Sorry. I know it's hard. If I didn't have photography to fall back on when I retired, I'd have gone bonkers."

When I moved to Folly, I'd opened a photo gallery on Center Street, Folly's figurative center of the island and its literal center of commerce. Unfortunately, my dream became a nightmare when I realized locals and vacationers would rather spend their money on necessities like food, lodging, and lottery tickets rather than photos. The gallery closed five years ago but my interest in photography hasn't lessened.

Brad rubbed his chin. "If memory serves me correct, catching killers and interfering in police investigations is another of your hobbies."

"Not really. I've occasionally been lucky to have been in the right place at the right time."

"Most of the time your, umm, hobby pissed me off." He hesitated then smiled. "I still owe you for my life and catching my daughter's killer, so I won't complain about one of the times you nosed in where you shouldn't have."

No comment struck me as the best response.

"Well," he said, "don't want to hold you up. Nice talking to you."

He pivoted and headed to the coolers on the side of the store.

That was the first time he'd ever acknowledged it was nice talking to me.

3

My ringing phone showed that Charles was calling. It'd "only" been nine hours since I tried to get him to answer this morning.

In the spirit of surrendering to non-normal phone etiquette, I answered with, "About time you called."

"Yeah, whatever. You on your way?"

Okay, I deserved that.

"Might I ask where and why?"

"Yes. Loggerhead's."

That answered where but still left why a mystery. I also knew the best, and possibly only, way to find out the reason I was summoned was to say, "On my way."

The early evening temperature was comfortable, so I walked three blocks to one of the beach's more popular dining spots. I reached the top of the stairs to the elevated deck and entrance to the colorful restaurant where I saw Charles on the packed deck at a table near the bandstand. He would've been hard to miss in his crimson University of Alabama long-sleeve T-shirt. Now that I knew where he was, the next unanswered question was who were the two people with him?

I weaved around several tables packed with loud groups enjoying the weather, the food, and from what I could tell from the number of glasses and bottles, the drinks.

Charles saw me approach, glanced at his empty wrist where most people wore a watch, his way of saying I was late, which, of course, I wasn't.

Instead of standing, Charles pointed to the man I would guess to be in his late-thirties, and said, "Chris, meet Kyle Manger and," as he nodded to the other person at the table, "Pat, umm—"

"Zellner. She's my girlfriend," Kyle said as he stood to shake my hand.

Kyle wore jeans, a black T-shirt with CREED on the front, and well-worn work boots. He was roughly five-foot-eight, thin, with black hair, and a short beard. It finally struck me that he was the man Charles had talked with at the site of yesterday's incident.

We shook as I said I was glad to meet him. I nodded toward Pat who remained seated, and added I was glad to meet her as well. She also wore jeans and a white T-shirt and was even thinner than Kyle. She nodded my direction but didn't say anything. Kyle returned to his seat and I took the chair beside Charles.

Becca, one of Loggerhead's servers, was quick to the table to ask what I wanted to drink. The other three were drinking beer but I opted for white wine. Kyle said they hadn't ordered, so I wasn't far behind.

Becca left for the bar and Charles said, "Chris, remember when we were at the house under construction, and I went to talk to Kyle? This is him. He's a plumber working where Shelly slipped off the roof."

It was beginning to make sense why Charles had two people at the table with him.

Kyle said, "We saw Charles over at the bar where he told us he was meeting you for supper. He invited us to join you. I didn't want to, but he insisted. Hope you don't mind."

"Of course not," I said as if I had a choice.

Kyle said, "I didn't remember seeing you there with Charles, but I was traumatized seeing Shelly lying there."

"Isn't that an amazing coincidence, Chris? Us being there and me running into Kyle tonight."

It would've been amazing if I believed it was a coincidence that Charles, the alleged private detective, had run into Kyle.

I didn't have time to tell him how amazing it was. Pat leaned toward Charles and said, "That's all he's talked about since he got home yesterday." She rolled her eyes. "Like I want to hear about some dead person."

I had no idea what Charles would say, but the odds were it would probably irritate Pat more than she already appeared to be.

I said, "I was shaken seeing her on the patio, and I didn't know her. I imagine it was traumatic for Kyle since they worked together. Sometimes talking about the experience can help."

"Whatever. Are we going to order or what? I'm starving."

Becca returned with my drink and asked if we were ready to order, hopefully in time to prevent Pat from starving. We each nodded.

Kyle and Pat ordered fish tacos, Charles a cheeseburger, and I chose a fried flounder sandwich. After we ordered, Pat tapped Becca on the arm and said she needed another beer. The rest of us said we were okay with our drinks.

"Chris, Kyle's a plumber," Charles said like it was the most logical thing to say after declining more drinks. Besides, I knew that from seeing him in the Donnelly Plumbing shirt at the job site.

"Me and Joshua are doing most of the plumbing on the project for Custom Builders Group. That's the company building the house."

"When you got here, Chris, I was asking Kyle how well he knew Shelly." Charles turned to Kyle. "You were saying?"

"Didn't know her well. She was usually working on a different floor from where I was."

That wasn't enough for Charles. "What'd you know about her?"

"He thought she was a looker," Pat said then glared at Kyle.

"Charles," Kyle said, ignoring Pat's comment, "she was the only gal on the crew. Couple of the guys thought she got off easy because she was female."

Charles said, "Did she?"

Becca set Pat's beer in front of her.

"I'll take another one," Kyle said.

Pat put her arm on Kyle's shoulder. "Maybe you ought to slow down. That's what, four?"

"Another beer," he said to Becca, as if she hadn't heard him the first time.

Pat removed her hand from his shoulder and grabbed her drink.

"Did she get off easier than the guys?" Charles said ignoring Kyle and Pat's tense exchange.

"Best I can tell there were five carpenters; six when it started, one got fired. I wasn't around them most of the time, so I didn't see any difference, but they did a lot of bitching about her slowing them down. Joshua and me had enough work to keep us more than busy. No time to see what was going on with the hammer swingers."

Pat said, "What about the guy you said was always hitting on her?"

"What about him?"

"Bet he didn't think she was goofing off."

Kyle's beer arrived.

"Don't know what he was thinking." He took a long draw on his drink then continued, "All I know is he has a reputation as a lady's man and I know from hearing him a couple of times he was doing his best to get her to have a drink or grabbing a meal with him." In a lower voice, he added, "and more." He slowly shook his head. "I heard her tell him she was married. He said, no big deal, her husband would never know."

Charles said, "What'd she say to that?"

Our food arrived before Kyle answered. Kyle took a bite of his taco, a sip of beer, and said something about the nice weather.

As I could've predicted, it took Charles fewer than ten seconds before he repeated his question.

Kyle took another bite, swallowed, and said, "Know the old saying *if looks could kill?*"

Charles nodded.

Kyle took a large draw on his drink, then smiled. "If that was true, Mason would be dead instead of Shelly."

Charles said, "Mason?"

"Mason Playboy Ryle."

"Where was he when Shelly fell?"

"Don't know," Kyle said as he brought his beer to his lips. "Know what's got me a little confused?"

"Probably the number of beers you've had," Pat said before taking another bite.

Kyle ignored her. "Know what Shelly told me a couple of weeks ago?"

Of course, none of us did, but it was Charles who said, "What?"

"It's so sad. Said she was terrified of heights. And look what killed her. Poor thing."

"Crap, Kyle," Pat said, "if it'd been any of the guys who fell off the roof, you'd said *oh well, shit happens.* It's a cute chick, so you go all mushy. Oh, so sad. Poor thing. Boo-hoo."

Charles pointed his fork at Kyle. "You thinking someone may have pushed her off?"

"Not really. I know how hard it was to work on that roof. Accidents happen. I think it's sad, no matter who it was." He turned to Pat. "Doesn't matter if it was a gal or guy."

Charles said, "So, you think it was an accident?"

Isn't that what Kyle said?

"Seems like it. But I'll tell you one thing, if someone pushed her, I'd put Mason at the top of the list."

Charles leaned closer to Kyle. "Why?"

"He's a hothead. He don't like being rejected."

"And you don't know where he was working the day of the, umm, accident?"

"Could've been anywhere. He's a carpenter. If I had to guess, I'd say on the top floor."

"Why's that?"

"A lot of the work's been finished on the other floors, but again, it's only a guess."

"Who do you think knew Shelly best?"

"You mean besides Mason?"

Charles nodded.

"Probably the boss man."

"Randy something?" I added, to rejoin the two-way conversation between Charles and Kyle.

Charles gave me the look that probably meant how did I know the name of the boss, or foreman.

"Randy Lee, old guy, he's foreman. I don't know for sure but suspect he knew her better than the others since he hired her."

Pat grabbed Kyle's arm. "Enough about what's her face."

Kyle reached for his beer. Charles and I didn't reach for anything but took the far from subtle hint. Shelly wasn't mentioned the rest of the evening.

4

The phone jarred me awake. A glance at the out-of-focus clock told me it was midnight. The equally out-of-focus screen on my phone read *Charles*.

I managed to hit the button to answer and said, "You better be dialing in your sleep or calling to tell me I won the lottery."

"Nope, but the call's your fault."

"Why are you calling?"

"I was peacefully sleeping when the sleep fairy whispered in my ear that you forgot to tell me at Loggerhead's how you knew the name of the foreman. See, it's your fault."

"And you couldn't wait until a decent hour in the morning to ask?"

"Of course not. So, are you going to tell me? You're keeping me awake."

My eyes were focusing better, so maybe I could remember and share the highlights of my talk with Chief LaMond. As I went through the story sharing what little she knew or felt comfortable telling me, I knew Charles wasn't fully awake since he didn't interrupt with a thousand questions. His only question was if I was sure Shelly didn't have any pets. I reminded him he'd said the same thing at the construction site the day of her death. He confessed he may not be thinking clearly. I told him I was certain he wasn't since he called at a time he knew I'd be asleep.

"Good point," he mumbled. "Meet me at the Dog at seven-thirty to tell me the rest."

There was no rest to tell, but it sounded like the best way to get him off the phone.

I said I'd see him there and tapped *end call*.

THE LOST DOG CAFE, called the Dog by most locals and many vacationers, was Folly's go-to spot for outstanding breakfasts, lunches, socializing, fact collecting, and gossip. Since I used my kitchen about as often as an albino rhinoceros knocked on my front door, the Dog was my informal dining room and had been for years. It was roughly five blocks from the house and less than a block off Center Street. It may be called Lost Dog, but there was seldom a shortage of canines on its two outdoor patios, none appearing lost and were hanging out with their owners. Charles didn't own a dog but considered every canine he encountered his.

My friend was sitting on the front patio petting a collie and telling it something in collie-speak. The dog's owner did what many people do when near Charles and their pets. The man in his seventies continued eating while ignoring Charles conversing with the canine.

I walked to the side entrance to the patio and pulled out the chair opposite Charles.

"Hey, Chris, meet Libby," he said as he nuzzled the friendly collie.

I rubbed Libby's head while Charles told her he'd talk to her again before leaving. If Libby was excited about it, she didn't let it show. Charles returned to the table and his bacon and eggs.

Kathy, one of the servers, arrived with a mug of coffee without me having to say anything. I thanked her and said I'd like an order of French toast, the item I ordered most every time I'd been here.

Charles watched Kathy head inside then said, "So, what'd you forget to tell me last night?"

"You mean when you called in the middle of the night?"

He smiled. "That'd be the call."

"I think I told you everything Cindy said."

"You dragged me over here this early after keeping me up most of the night to tell me nothing?"

Revising history is one of Charles's numerous quirks.

"You know that's not what happened, don't you?"

"Whatever. So, what'd you think of Kyle and cranky Pat?"

"Seems like a nice guy. Other than that, I don't think much either way. As for Pat, I agree with you. Disagreeable would be putting it kindly."

Charles reached over to the next table and gave the collie another pat on the head as her master paid and headed to the exit. He then turned to me. "Guess she's not disagreeable to Kyle. What about the guy hitting on her?"

"Hitting on Pat?"

"Get with the program, the guy Kyle said had been hitting on Shelly."

"Mason Ryle."

"That's the one."

"Why do I get the impression you think Shelly's death wasn't an accident?"

He shrugged. "Seems suspicious."

"Why?"

Kathy returned with my French toast, refills on our coffee, and asked if we needed anything else. We said no and she moved to bus the table that'd been occupied by the collie's owner.

Charles said, "Why what?"

"Why do you think the death was suspicious?"

"Duh. She had a conflict with at least one person on the crew. She was afraid of heights and was working on the top of the house. Umm, there was one more reason I thought of in the middle of the night, but it escapes me."

So does common sense, I thought.

"I don't think telling a co-worker you don't want to have a drink, a meal, or whatever with him is much of a conflict. And what does being afraid of heights have to do with someone killing her? It was her job to be there, and from what we've heard, there wasn't anyone near her when she fell."

"Wouldn't you avoid the edge of a roof if you were afraid of heights?"

"Yes, unless my job required me to be there. Besides, the roof was slanted so we don't know how close she was to the edge when she slipped."

"Okay, Mr. Pessimist, as Harry Truman said, 'A pessimist is one who makes difficulties of his opportunities and an optimist is one who makes opportunities of his difficulties.' I still think it's fishy."

Charles looked over my shoulder. "Hey, Marc. How's my city today?"

I turned to see Marc Salmon, one of Folly's City Council members, approaching the entrance. He walked to the railing separating the patio from the entry.

"Charles, Chris, good to see you. Charles, to answer your question, something I pride myself doing for my constituents, the city's doing fine, just fine."

Marc is a daily regular at the Dog. He usually meets Houston Bass, another member of the Council, to allegedly discuss city business. I say allegedly, because regulars know the two politicians are collecting and spreading gossip far more than city business.

"Now a question for you guys. Did you hear about the lady who died in a construction accident at a house in the six-hundred block of West Ashley?"

City business or gossip, you decide.

"Sure did," Charles said. "We got there right after it happened. Sad."

I said, "Why'd you ask?"

"I'm a member of the Council, have been for years, know a lot about what's going on around here, but whenever there's a death on the island, you and Charles know more about it than I ever do. Figured this time wouldn't be the exception." He chuckled. "From what Charles said, it wasn't. I hear it was an accident. That your take?"

"Yes," I said.

Charles said, "Not sure. What do you think?"

"No idea."

"Bet there is something you do know," Charles said.

"What's that?"

"Who's owns the house?"

Marc smiled. "Oliver Trescott, mid-sixties. Moved to our neck of the woods a while back. Came from Maryland, I hear. Got a building permit seven months ago. That lot's been vacant for years. It had an old concrete block house on it back in the dark ages. Construction on Trescott's mansion began in April. That's all I know."

"What about the company building it?"

"Custom Builders Group owned by Joe Argyle. He's built several of the larger homes over here, some on Kiawah too. Why?"

"Curious, that's all."

"If you say so. Gotta get in there. Don't want to keep Houston waiting. City business can't wait." He saluted in our direction and headed inside.

I said, "What was that about?"

"What?"

"Asking about the house's owner, the construction company."

"I'm simply collecting information. That's what detectives do, you know."

"In case you haven't been listening, there's nothing to detect."

"We won't know that until all the questions have been answered."

"To quote you, 'Whatever.'"

5

———

I finally got a peaceful night's sleep. No phone calls from my faux-detective friend, no dreams about someone falling off a roof. With sleep under my belt, or under my top sheet, I was up at six-thirty, in time to see the sun rising over the house across the street and the first few early workers driving past the cottage on the way to their jobs. I enjoyed watching vehicles pass the house while knowing I had nowhere I had to be. Cruel, I suppose, but wouldn't be surprised if some retired person took pleasure in me driving by his or her house during the forty-plus years I was a member of the workforce.

Two cups of coffee later, I realized the morning rush-hour was over and a cottage in dire need of a good cleaning was waiting for me. Before I lugged the vacuum cleaner from the closet, I saw Charles peddling his classic 1961 Schwinn bicycle up the road and turning into my front yard. He owned a motorized vehicle but preferred using his bike around the island and also used it to deliver packages for our friend Dude Sloan, owner of the surf shop.

Charles was wearing his black, long-sleeve, NYPD T-shirt he often wore when he was focused on performing what he called *private detecting*. I had no doubt his arrival wasn't a social call. He leaned the bike against the screened-in porch, took a cardboard tray out of the basket on the front of the bike, and said, "See you're waiting for me. Sorry I'm a little late. Had to stop at Bert's for this." He held up the container as if I wouldn't have known why he stopped at Bert's.

"How would I be waiting for you if I didn't know you were coming, late or not?"

"Excellent question. Glad you're in a mood to question things. I brought a bunch of them."

I opened the door, glanced in the carton, then told him to take it to the kitchen. I followed and grabbed two paper plates so we could divide the cinnamon-covered packaged donuts. He handed me one of the cups of coffee from the container, and no, I didn't tell him I'd already had two cups and wasn't ready for more.

While I was using all my culinary skills separating the donuts from their packaging, he said, "Knew you wouldn't have anything to eat, and I got these so we could have a breakfast meeting."

"Thoughtful. Would it be too much to ask the agenda for this, umm, meeting?"

"Shall we retire to the living room? The meeting will commence in there."

We did. Charles wolfed down two donuts, took a couple of sips of coffee, before removing a folded sheet of lined paper from his pocket, and spreading it out on his knee.

"Know what this is?"

"A written apology for disturbing my peaceful morning."

"Horrible guess. You have no idea, do you?"

"How would I?"

"Our suspect list," he said, leaned back in the chair, and nodded his head like that said it all.

"Gosh, how did I not know that?"

"Suppose you're not as good a detective as yours truly. I'll give you a hint. They're suspects in the killing of some young lady we happened to sort of became acquainted with on a walk the other day."

"I knew what you meant. What I didn't know was how or why you think she was murdered, thus the need for a list of suspects."

"Allow me to enlighten you," he said and took a bite of his third donut.

"Please do."

"Last night while you were, umm, heck if I know, but am certain it was nothing worthwhile, I was at Cal's having a beer."

Cal's was a country music bar owned by Cal Ballew, a friend who'd ended up on Folly after traveling the south for forty years singing his brand of classic country music at any venue that'd have him.

"How's having a beer at Cal's more worthwhile than me doing nothing?"

"Glad you asked. I was talking to Cal when he pointed to a guy sitting at the bar and asked if I knew him. He looked familiar but I couldn't place him until Cal said he worked for a construction company building a house out West Ashley. Then it clicked. It was Randy Lee. Since I'm such a friendly guy who likes to make everyone feel welcome on my island, I took my beer and sidled up to Randy who was looking bored and needed someone to talk to."

"Let's see if I have this right. You saw a bored guy and wanted to make him feel welcome. Nothing more?"

"Sure, but since he was there, I didn't see harm in learning what he knew about Shelly's death. Anyway, he seems like a nice guy. He let me buy him a couple of beers and is a talker. Did you know he lives in a thirty-three-foot-long travel trailer? Got it parked at the Oak Plantation Campground off Savannah Highway."

I told him I didn't know any of that while not wasting any time or words asking how he thought I would have.

"He told me he hangs out at Cal's almost every night; something about loving his travel trailer, but it gets cramped being stuck in it too long. Anyway, he's been with Custom Builders Group nine years, but only got promoted to foreman for the job over here."

"What'd he do before that?"

"Said he was a jack of all trades. Did electrical work, carpentry, and occasional drywalling. Little of everything, I suppose."

I nodded to the sheet of paper balanced on Charles leg. "And that list has something to do with Randy?"

"You're catching on." He tapped his forefinger on the sheet of paper. "These are the guys working in the house when Shelly fell, umm, was pushed."

"Your suspect list is everyone who was at the house?"

"Some higher up on the list than others, but yes."

I motioned for him to continue. After another bite of donut, he picked up the list, studied it like he was prepping for an exam, then said, "Let's see, we've already talked to Kyle Manger, remember the guy from Loggerhead's?"

"That was two days ago. My memory's not that bad."

"Just checking. Okay, then there's Mason Ryle, remember, Kyle told us about how he'd harassed Shelly?"

I nodded.

"Scott Rawlins, another carpenter according to Randy. He's one of the ringleaders who said Shelly got by easy because she was a she. Randy thinks Scott may have a drinking problem, but it never bothers him at work. Add Timothy Hale to the group. Another carpenter. He was hired at the beginning of the project. No issues that Randy mentioned. Let's see, Lucius Walker, a black guy who's an electrician with Bolt Electric. Randy said his first name is Latin and means luminous in a biblical reference."

"I met Lucius the day we were on the building site."

"See, you already know two of the suspects: Lucius and Kyle. That's progress."

"That's not—"

"Hang on, let me get through the list. Mitchell Baldwin, one more carpenter. Big surfer according to Randy. Then there's Luis Ortez, another electrician. Born in Puerto Rico but has lived in Charleston since he was six. Only been with Bolt Electric three months; guy before him quit. Finally, we have Joshua Bennett. Randy said he had several run-ins with Joshua."

"Kyle mentioned Joshua," I said.

"There you go, Chris. The odds are good one of them killed Shelly."

"Didn't you forget someone?"

Charles looked at the list and ran his finger down the names. "Don't think so."

"Randy? Wasn't he there?"

"Yes, but ... but he—" He looked back at the list. "Okay, you're right. See, you're a better detective than you think."

I shook my head. "I admit, that would be an appropriate list of suspects if there had been a crime. But, as I've tried to get through your thick skull, no one says Shelly's death was anything but a tragic accident."

"You're wrong, aspiring detective. One person has said it was murder."

"Who?"

"*Moi.*"

6

———————

In addition to Charles finishing the donuts, before leaving, he'd talked me into meeting him tonight at Cal's. So, here we are.

Cal's, formally named Cal's Country Bar and Burgers, is located on West Cooper Avenue across the street from and a little past the city's Department of Public Safety. It's the perfect example of a quintessential country music bar. Entering the door feels like you're walking in a tavern from the 1940s or '50s. The walls are dark green, a beat-up dark wood bar is on the right side of the room with a tiny kitchen behind it. The dozen tables along with their chairs look like they're on their last legs. Occasionally, one of the chairs can no longer support an overweight or overenthusiastic patron and collapses. So far, only the customers' pride has been hurt, quickly soothed by a complementary beer or two from the owner. The smell of stale beer and greasy burgers permeates the air as does the country classics from days gone by emoting from the Wurlitzer jukebox located on the small stage where Cal entertains his customers with sets on weekends.

Cal was behind the bar when Charles and I entered the near-empty venue. The seventy-six-year-old owner is six-foot-three, looking taller in his sweat-stained Stetson that'd travelled with him most of his life. Adding to the country-crooner look, he wore a white rhinestone trimmed coat that also had accompanied him throughout the south. In a break from tradition and a concession to his life on Folly, a red Folly Beach T-shirt peeked out from under the jacket.

Cal saw us, gave a quick, stage-perfected smile, and waved us over.

"Beer and white wine?" he said as way of a greeting.

"You bet, partner," Charles said and tipped his Tilley at the owner.

Cal grabbed a beer out of the cooler behind him, handed it to Charles, then poured a glass of Chardonnay for me, before saying, "What brings you two vagrants out? It sure wasn't to mingle with the crowd." He waved his hand around the room that held exactly three customers at a table by the twelve-by-twenty-foot laminate dance floor hugging the front of the stage.

Charles said, "We came to see you. What more reason would we need?"

Cal rolled his eyes. "Pard, you can't out-crap this old crap spewer."

The country crooner was from Texas, so I assumed—hoped— that was a Lone Star State saying.

Without tipping my Tilley, I said, "You're always the main reason we stop by. We're also looking for Randy Lee. He been in tonight?"

Cal looked at his watch. "Came in thirty minutes ago, started to mosey over to the table by the wall, snapped his fingers, shared a profanity, didn't clean it up by saying crap, told me he had to grab something at Bert's, but for me to keep a beer cold, he'd be back."

That was more than we needed to know, but bottom line, he'd probably make another appearance. A customer I didn't know came in and headed to the bar. I told Cal we'd be at a table in the middle of the room. Cal focused on the new arrival as Johnny Cash shared his thoughts from the jukebox on blues in Folsom Prison. Charles and I settled at the table in hopes Randy would return soon.

The next person through the door wasn't Randy. Brad Burton

looked around, then surprised me when he headed our way. In his detective days, he often had a slovenly appearance with his wrinkled suit, white shirt pulling out from his dress slacks, and a tie that was seldom centered on his torso. Since retiring, his casual wear maintained the unkept look. His green polo shirt was a size too small for his expanding stomach and his casual slacks were too long. Unlike every time I saw him at work, he was smiling.

He reached the table then looked around like he didn't know how he got here. He finally said, "Hi, Chris, Mr. Fowler."

I said, "Care to join us?"

"Umm, I don't want to interrupt anything."

"You're not," Charles said, "We were having a drink and killing time. Take a load off."

Charles had heard my stories about conflicts with Brad but had few contacts with the retired detective.

"If you don't mind."

"Not at all," I said, hoping I sounded sincere.

"Hey Brad, want a beer?" Cal yelled from behind the bar.

"Yes."

I'd only seen Brad in here one other time and said, "Come here often?"

"Two, three times a week. Hazel tries to kick me out of the house more, but I don't get much satisfaction hanging out in bars. At least in here there's good music, beats the stuff played in some of the other places."

Brad liking country music surprised me as much as knowing he was here that often. "It's a special place," I said as Conway Twitty sang "You've Never Been This Far Before."

Cal set a beer in front of Brad and said, "First time I've seen you three together: a retired detective and two private dicks. Who would've thought?"

That proved Cal didn't know about the bad blood between Brad and me, or if he did, he was trying to get an argument started.

I said, "Brad's the only one who's been a detective, a good one at that."

"I'll be back," Charles said as he pushed his chair back and headed toward the entry.

I turned and saw Randy Lee at the door. He looked around and headed to the bar. My friend followed. I thought, *Charles, please don't bring Randy over.* That would be just what I needed, him meeting Brad as Charles interrogated the foreman about Shelly's death.

I dodged a bullet, figurative speaking, when Randy took a seat at the bar, Charles took the stool beside him, and Cal headed behind the bar to see what Randy wanted. Problem averted, for now.

Brad watched Charles put his arm around Randy's shoulder. "I've heard Mr. Fowler knows everybody over here. That true?"

I smiled. "Everybody with pets." I said, slightly exaggerating. "He knows many who don't have pets, but I suspect a few fly under his radar."

"Also hear he, and you, I might add, still stick your noses in every murder on the island, and now have expanded your interference to deaths over on Mosquito Beach. Suppose that's what Cal was talking about when he called you two private detectives."

That was one topic I didn't want to get into with Brad. It dredges up too many memories, some a mere few feet away related to how hostile Brad had been with my involvement. That was even after Charles, and I'd learned the identity of the person who killed Brad's daughter and I'd saved Brad's life.

"Brad, we were lucky a couple of times, nothing more." Time to change the subject. "Have you figured out a hobby to get you out of the house?"

Brad showed an emotion I'd never seen from him. He chuckled. "Know what one of the tells is in an interrogation when a suspect is lying or feeling trapped?"

"Can't say I do."

"He changes the subject."

Perhaps Brad was a better detective than I'd given him credit for. "Like I did when I asked if you'd figured out a hobby?"

"Exactly."

"You're right, of course. I was serious when I said that I've been lucky a few times when—"

"Hey guys," Charles said as he appeared behind me, "look who I found at the bar?"

I knew who he'd found. There may be examples of worse timing, but I couldn't think of one.

"Hi, Randy," I said. "Meet Brad Burton. Brad, this is Randy Lee. He's foreman on a new house being built out West Ashley Avenue."

Brad stood and shook Randy's hand while adding the obligatory *nice to meet you* regardless if he meant it or not.

Charles said, "Randy said he wouldn't mind having a drink with us. I told him you'd pick up his tab, Chris. That okay?"

"Sure," I said, knowing Brad would detect the lack of sincerity, although he wouldn't know the reason.

After everyone was seated, Charles said, "Randy, tell them what you were telling me over there." He nodded toward the bar.

"Umm, I don't know. It wasn't anything more than a reaction I had."

"That's okay," Charles said and patted Randy's arm. "Go ahead."

"Well, umm, I was telling Charles I'd been thinking a lot about Shelly's death." He took a sip of beer, hesitated, then said, "I think I told you before, this was my first job as foreman. I knew when I took the promotion, I'd have to keep up with everything happening on the job, knowing not only what the crew's doing, but what needs to be done next to make sure materials were delivered and the right number of employees were where they need to be. Logistics is what the company's owner calls it. A pain in the ass is what I call it." He hesitated.

Charles, being as patient as a hungry newborn, said, "And?"

Randy looked at Charles. "And what?"

"What you were telling me about Mason."

"I was getting there."

Not quick enough for Charles.

Randy frowned at Charles, turned to me, and said, "I'm learning that in addition to the building things I have to keep up with, knowing how the crew relates to the other members is almost as important. I think I already told you that Mason had been giving Shelly a hard time. Truth be told, hitting on her would be more accurate. Anyway, since her death he's been acting strange."

Charles said, "Strange?"

If Brad still carried a badge, he'd probably be pulling it out about now while he figured out how to arrest Charles, and yes, me, for interfering in police business.

"Umm, before it happened, he struck me as even-tempered, calmer than most of the guys. He went about his business without making a fuss. Since her death, he's flown off the handle two times I know of. Blew his top over a minor delay in the truck getting drywall to the job site. Then this morning he jumped all over one of the electricians claiming the guy was slowing him down by not getting the room wired in time. Stuff like that." He snapped his fingers. "Almost forgot, there've been two times when I was talking to him about things that needed changing and he acted like he didn't hear me. I was looking him right in the eyes, not three feet away, and he ignored what I was saying."

I said, "Think he was distracted?"

Randy finished his beer before answering. "If he was, it was something in his head. We were in an empty room, nothing going on except me and him talking."

I was surprised when Brad said, "Where was Mason when Shelly fell?"

"Don't know. He was supposed to be in the owners' suite on the second floor." He sighed. "Company's owner said we couldn't call it the master suite anymore. Sexist, I suppose. Anyway, Scott, he's another carpenter, told me Mason wasn't there. He'd told Scott it was his break time."

Brad said, "Was it?"

"Could be. I'm generous with breaks. I've been on too many jobs where the foreman is so anal that he, on one job, she, wouldn't let us take a piss unless it was at an assigned time. I didn't want to be that way once I got in charge." He looked at his watch. "Guys, I've got an early morning. Thanks for the beer, Chris."

"It's not that late," Charles said. "Sure you have to go?"

Charles wasn't done fishing.

"Afraid so," he said as he glanced at his watch a second time. "Have to stop at the construction site to make sure everything's okay." He chuckled. "Seems like one of my guys make a habit of leaving some equipment on nearly every day. Don't want to have the house burn down on my first job as foreman."

"That's too bad," Charles said. "Which guy leaves stuff on?"

"No one in particular. Someday this one; someday that one. They're always in a hurry to get out of there when their shift ends. I often wake up in the middle of the night worrying and have to get dressed and check it out. Course I could do a better job checking all the stuff before I leave after work. It's hard breaking my habit of clocking-out and getting as far from work as I could back before I was promoted. Guess that's why I get the big bucks now. Thanks for the conversation and drink."

He started for the exit, stopped, turned back to the table. "Nearly forgot. One more thing about Shelly. Guy named Raymond, said he was her husband, stormed into the house this morning demanding to talk to the person in charge. My guys were quick to point their fingers my way. None of them wanted to deal with the guy." He shook his head.

Charles said, "What'd he want?"

"Wanted to know who he needed to see about life insurance the company had on his wife. I told him I had no idea, that he could talk to the owner of the company and gave him the phone number for Custom Builders Group."

I said, "How'd he take not learning more than that?"

"The boy was pissed. Before he stormed out, he said something about suing me, the company, the homeowner, and hell, probably God for creating gravity that yanked Shelly off the roof headfirst onto the concrete patio." He looked at his watch once more. "See you guys later."

Freddy Hart was singing "Easy Loving" when Cal returned and asked if we needed anything else. Brad said he could handle a second beer, Charles did the same, and I said I was okay. Cal looked around the near-empty room, said he figured he'd have time to get the drinks.

Charles said, "Looks like we have ourselves a good suspect, possibly two."

Brad glanced at me. "Tell me again how you and your friend aren't playing cop."

I didn't waste my breath repeating what I'd told him earlier. I shrugged.

Charles appeared oblivious to what Brad and I were talking about and said, "Brad, you were a detective, what do you think?"

I was surprised when he didn't shower Charles with a profanity-infused tirade about it not being any of my friend's business.

He said, "First, I didn't hear anything remotely indicating that Whitley's death was anything but an accident."

"But," Charles interrupted.

Brad stuck his right hand in Charles's face. "And, even if it was something more sinister, nothing he said about, umm, the carpenter, or the husband indicated they were responsible."

"Of course, you're right. That shows how great a detective you were back in the day," Charles said, nodding the entire time. "Let me ask you this, if you were the detective on this case, what would be your next step?"

"Mr. Fowler, if I were still with the police and investigating, I'd probably write up the death as an accident and close the file. Now if my boss, who happens to be a police officer, told me I had to pursue it, I'd look to see who, if anyone, had something to gain from her death."

Charles said, "How would you—"

Brad used his hand in the face motion once again. "Mr. Fowler—"

Charles interrupted. "Call me Charles."

Brad sighed then continued, "Charles, I wouldn't do anything. I'm a civilian. I'm no longer a member of a law-enforcement organization. I have no authority to do anything. And, in case you haven't noticed, neither does anyone else at this table. Now I've got to get home. Wouldn't want Hazed to think I've run away." He smiled. "On the other hand, she probably would be thrilled if I had." He stood, went to the bar to pay Cal, then headed home, or to run away.

7

———

The sun had set long before I walked home from Cal's. I approached Bert's Market where I saw Dude Sloan staring at the large mural painted on the side of the building featuring Bert, the market's namesake, shown dressed as a pirate with a devilish smile plastered, more accurately, painted on his face, and a hook replacing his hand.

I moved beside Dude and said, "Talking to Bert?"

My friend of more than a decade glanced at me. "No be silly. He faux. Admirin' hook."

Dude was in his late sixties, thin, five-foot-seven, with long hair, and wearing one of his ever-present tie dye T-shirts. He also has a speaking style slightly more articulate than a chimpanzee but was much smarter than many people assumed based on his verbal quirks.

"Contemplating getting a mural painted on your building?"

He's owned the surf shop for more than thirty years and is one of the island's most successful business owners.

"Contemplated it two revolutions around sun ago. Called drawer of this. He be Douglas Panzone. Pondered it. Poultry out."

Charles had known Dude way longer than I had and often served as a translator of Dudespeak. While I wasn't nearly as articulate, I figured he called the artist a couple of years ago since Dude's hobby, other than confusing listeners, was astronomy and the earth circles the sun once a year. The rest was merely guessing that he chickened out. It didn't matter, so I wasn't hung up on an accurate translation.

"I see," I said, although far from it.

"Talking about seeing, see about dead chick at house out W. Ashley?"

"Unfortunately, yes. Charles and I were nearby when it happened."

Dude nodded twice. "Figures."

"Why?"

"You plus Chuckster be private detectives. Always around bad stuff happening." He nodded again, like it was obvious.

"How'd you hear about it?"

"Mitchell," he said and nodded again.

"Who's Mitchell?"

Dude rubbed his chin. "Umm, piano, young dude."

"Mitchell Piano?"

He shook his head. "Mitchell Baldwin, like piano."

The name sounded familiar but took me a few seconds to remember why. It could have come to me quicker if I hadn't had to work my way through the piano reference.

"Is he a surfer who works on the construction project where the woman died?"

"Proof you be detective."

I translated that as a yes. "What'd he tell you?"

"Said one tick of watch she be on roof. Next tick she be on patio. Tim agreed."

I followed all of that except the part about Tim agreeing. "Tim?"

"Mitchell's bud. He be hodad."

It'd taken me nearly a decade but learned a hodad was someone pretending to be a surfer but isn't. I also vaguely remembered someone else on the crew at the house was named Timothy, or Tim.

"Does Tim work with Mitchell?"

Dude nodded. "Both be woodcutters."

"Carpenters?"

"Yep."

"When were they telling you about it?"

"Day this side of fall. Chick fall, not season."

"Did they say anything else?"

"Yep, Tim couldn't come up with lucre to get wetsuit."

"Anything more about what happened with the woman?"

"They be sorry she dead but not for good reason."

"What's that mean?" I asked, an often-used phrase when talking with Dude.

"Sorry because they had to do their work plus her work. Sorry, but wrong reason."

"Anything else?"

"Nope." He snapped his fingers. "Yep, told Pluto be at *casa* now. Gotta go."

Pluto was Dude's Australian terrier. I didn't ask how Pluto could tell time but simply told him it was nice talking with him.

Dude wasn't going to be the last person I talked to this evening. Charles called as soon as I got home.

"Okay, I'm convinced," he said as a greeting.

"Convinced of what?"

"Shelly was pushed off the roof."

"What convinced you?"

"Not what, who. Weren't you paying attention to Randy? Not only did he tell us about one guy who had reason to do her in, he gave us two."

I tried to remember back to what had been said in Cal's. Nothing came to mind implicating one, much less two people as having reason for killing her.

"Okay, help me understand, who are the two and what was said to convince you?"

"Fantastic suspect number one, Mason Ryle. He'd been hitting on Shelly, harassing her. That could get Mason in big trouble, right? Then after he killed her he was feeling guilty, letting his temper get the best of him; being distracted, not listening to Randy giving him instructions. Mason is torn up with guilt. Yes, he killed her."

"If he killed her, what about the second person you mentioned?"

"Raymond, her husband. It's obvious. He killed her for money. She hadn't been dead long enough to be buried and he's asking about life insurance the construction company had, then if that isn't enough, he's hinting he'll sue the company. Cindy tells us the spouse is the first suspect, always. She's got it right this time."

"If Raymond killed her, what about Mason? You know, your *fantastic suspect number one.*"

"You caught that. To be honest, I'm a little confused. Both couldn't have killed her, could they? Like been in cahoots."

"I suppose they could've been, as you said, in cahoots, or either one of them could have killed her. I only see one small problem with your theory."

"See, that's why we work so well together as detectives. What's the small problem?"

"There's no evidence her death was anything other than an accident."

"My friend, how many times have you and I stumbled on a situation, a situation where someone was dead, and the police were convinced the death was an accident or suicide or some space creature did the person in?"

"Space creature?"

"Okay, that was an exaggeration, but the point is, how many times?"

I got the point that occasionally Charles's imagination bordered on lunacy, but that wasn't what he wanted to hear.

"I suppose it's happened more than once."

"Way more than once. This is another one of those times. She was killed and we, okay, I know the killer."

"And you know it's Mason, oh wait, no, you know it's Raymond?"

"Did you miss the part where I said I was a little confused?"

"I get that you're confused."

"You making fun of me?"

"A little."

"Fair enough. Anyway, the point is I need your help. I'll let you think it over and we can get together tomorrow, figure it out, and then you can let Cindy know who killed Shelly."

He didn't give me a chance to say how absurd his plan was. He'd already hung up.

8

———

Rain filled the morning air as I sat on my porch sipping coffee and watching a steady stream of cars passing the house carrying sleepy commuters to work. I was again thinking how good it felt not being among that group when the phone rang. I figured it had to be Charles since he'd said we needed to get together today to *figure it out*. I still wasn't sure what *it* was other than an alleged murder fomenting in Charles's vivid imagination.

Instead of looking at the phone's screen to see who was calling, I answered with, "Good morning, Charles."

"That's by far the most insulting thing you've ever said to me," Bob Howard bellowed.

That'll teach me not to look at the name of the caller. Bob was the realtor who helped me find the cottage I was talking to him from. I met him when I first arrived on Folly and quickly learned he was loud, boorish, gruff, opinionated, and profane. Those were some of his better qualities. For reasons I can't explain, even though many people have asked me why over the years, we became friends.

"Sorry, thought you were Charles."

"No kidding. I figured that out after you said three words."

"Okay, let me start over. Good morning, Bob."

"Better, but it'll take me decades to get over being called your quarter-wit friend."

Like with many of my friends, it's best to ignore many of his comments. "Bob, why'd you call?"

"Crap, couldn't it be because I wanted to see how my friend's doing?"

I smiled. "No."

"You're damned right. So, here's the question. Are you and your eighth-wit friend sticking you noses in the untimely death of some carpenter-chick on a building site on your quirky island?"

"Bob, why would you ask that?"

"Hell's bells, how about because you two meddle in every death that happens over there. Why would this time be different?"

"I don't know what you've heard, but the carpenter-chick, as you call her, is Shelly Whitley. The police and those who were working there when it happened believe she accidentally slipped and fell off the roof. A tragic accident, nothing more."

"Remember, you're talking to your buddy Bob. I heard you say the police believe and the folks who were working there believe she slipped and fell. You're too old to be a cop and I know you and definitely Charles are too lazy to work anywhere. What do you think happened?"

"I have no reason to believe it was anything other than an accident. Charles and I were there seconds after she fell."

"If that's not the chocolate icing on the cake, I don't know what is. You simply happened to be there. I bet Charles interrogated everyone who was around. Am I right?"

"No interrogation, Bob. Everyone was shocked. We waited until the police arrived then left."

He chuckled and said, "So, the cops ran you off."

I sighed. "They asked us if we knew anything about what happened. We didn't and left—left without a police escort."

"Who's the builder?" Bob asked like it was a logical question after me telling him we left the site.

"Custom Builders Group."

"Joe's outfit."

"You know him?"

"Did you forget you're talking to one of the Lowcountry's most successful realtors? That is until I retired and bought one of the Lowcountry's most famous bars."

The first half of that was true. Bob had been a successful realtor in both commercial and residential real estate until he retired a few years ago and bought an aging, rundown bar in Charleston from his long-time friend Al Washington. Bob wouldn't admit it, but he bought the bar that was in debt more than it was worth to help his friend who had suffered serious health issues. If Al had remained owner much longer, he wouldn't have survived.

"Does that mean you know Joe Argyle?"

"Do I have to spell out damn near everything? Yes, I know him. He's one of the best in this market. He's built houses on Kiawah, Mt. Pleasant, and a few on your island."

"Have you heard rumors or anything negative about him or his company?"

Bob laughed. "Let's see if I have this right, you and your sixty-fourth-wit friend aren't sticking your nose into what happened?"

"Curious, that's all."

"You know the word curious comes from the Latin word *nosy*?"

"You made that up."

"Yep, like you made up not nosing in police business."

"So, you don't know anything negative about Joe or his company?"

"Like he kills one of his employees at every house he builds?"

"That would qualify."

"I don't know him well. He's got a good reputation and I sold one of his houses a while back in Mt. Pleasant. The owner ran out of money before he ran out of people he owed it to and had to sell. From my times in the house, it appeared well-built and passed the inspection with flying colors."

"That's it?"

"I'm a lowly bar owner. I don't think Joe Argyle has ever been in Al's. He's never called me to say he was planning to kill one of his employees. Tell you what, though, if he does, you'll be the first to know."

"Thanks."

"Do you think he had something to do with the, umm, accident?"

"Not really."

"Was he at the house when the woman fell?"

"I don't think so. No one there mentioned him. How's Al?"

"Sassy, obstinate, getting lazier each day. Why?"

"I was wondering more about his health."

"I know. Don't want to talk about it. I worry about him. He's old you know, not young or in good shape like me."

Al was eighty-three, only five years older than Bob. And Bob was in as good shape as many people in the ICU at Roper Hospital, plus he carries roughly a ton more pounds than recommended for someone with his six-foot-tall frame.

"Tell him I said hi."

"Hell, tell him yourself when you come over to get a cheeseburger at my world-famous restaurant and bar."

"I will."

"Good, and I'll check around to see if there're any rumors about Joe Argyle, not that it matters to you since you're not nosing in police business."

He hung up before I thanked him and denied I was anything but curious.

9

There was a break in the rain, so I walked to Bert's to grab breakfast. Before I reached the double-door entry, I received my second phone call of the day. This time I looked at the screen.

"Morning, Charles."

"Looks like I'm going to have to cancel our appointment."

"Appointment?" I said, although I suspected I knew what he was talking about.

"Duh. To figure out the killer."

"And you're canceling?"

"Aloysius called."

"Aloysius?"

"Remodeler. I've helped him before on a couple of projects. You remember?"

I didn't remember. "Okay, he called, and?"

"Needs help with the sunroom addition he's sticking on a house out East Cooper."

Charles hasn't been burdened with a real job since he was in his mid-thirties but picks up enough "off the books" income to meet his modest expenses by making deliveries for Dude, helping a couple of restaurants with clean-up during busy season, and lending a hand to contractors. By lending a hand, that's about all he can offer since he's shared he has difficulty pounding a nail or sawing wood. His talent is in hauling lumber and holding wood or drywall in place while someone who can drive a nail does his thing. Apparently, Aloysius is one of those contractors.

"Shall we reschedule our appointment for tomorrow?" The one I didn't know had been scheduled for today.

"I'll call you."

"Okay," I said to a phone that'd already ended the call.

With the appointment I didn't know I had canceled, my agenda for the day was blank, but I still needed something healthy and nourishing for breakfast. What better place to find something than the pastry cabinet, I rationalized?

I grabbed a cinnamon roll from the display, took a step back, and nearly stepped on Randy Lee's foot.

"Morning, Randy. Sorry for almost stomping you."

"That's okay, Chris, right?"

I nodded.

"I spend my day running into my workers or them running into me. Feet are often trampled. Nearly a dozen workers spending the day working in a house gets crowded. That's one reason I wear steel toe shoes. Add a bunch of power tools and it can get quite harried."

"I imagine so," I said, not knowing what else to say about his observation. I noticed two boxes of donuts in his hands. "You must be hungry?"

He smiled, the goal of my comment. "We're running behind finishing the house. We were scheduled to do some work on the exterior today and this rain screwed up those plans. And don't even mention cops. They stole a day and a half from us. Each of us had to answer question after question from the local cops and then some detective from Charleston had us tell him the same thing. Add to that, we couldn't work on the upper level for four hours while guys in white suits looking like astronauts were doing no telling what up there."

I was glad to hear the police had taken the death seriously and didn't automatically buy the explanation about the carpenter slipping and falling. Of course, I didn't share that with the frustrated foreman.

"That's too bad."

"Sorry for bitching. I'm pissed we're behind. The owner expects, no, demands, that we have his house ready for him to move in next month. He bought the property a decade ago, and now he wants us to have the place ready for His Highness to occupy." He hesitated, looked around the store, then back at me before saying, "You don't know the owner, do you?"

"Don't think so."

"I shouldn't have said that about him. After all, he's paying my salary. The guys have been working extra hours to get us back on schedule. That's why I'm getting these. Donuts are great for bribing construction workers. Not quite food for the soul, but they cheer up a bunch of workers. I know they did when I was in their shoes."

"They're fortunate to have a concerned foreman."

"I guess. It's my first gig with that title, so I want to do everything I can to keep them happy while bringing the job in on schedule. Speaking of on schedule, I better get back before they start a revolt."

"Good talking to you, Randy. One more quick question. Have you heard anything else from Shelly's husband?"

"Not directly, but Joe, my boss, was on-site late yesterday and told me Raymond came to his office yesterday morning demanding to know about insurance. Joe told him the company didn't carry life insurance on its employees. If they wanted any it was their responsibility to buy it through the company benefits plan."

"How'd Raymond react to that?"

"Joe said an exploding stick of dynamite wasn't as loud as Raymond's eruption. Joe thought he was going to have to call the cops."

"Did he calm down?"

"Yeah, enough to tell Joe he'd be hearing from Raymond's lawyer."

"How did Joe react?"

"Said he didn't. By then one of the other guys in the office, a big bruiser, used to be a wrestler from what I understand, heard the commotion, and came in the office to see what was going on. He and Joe escorted the irrational guy out of the building."

"Sounds like that may not be the end of it."

"You've got that right. I told my guys to keep an eye out and let me know if they hear or see Raymond around our project. Gotta go."

I watched him head to the register and wondered what would happen next. The sound of thunder reminded me I'd better get home before the rain returned. A day puttering around the house without any appointments had a lot of appeal.

10

The next morning, I awakened to the sound of silence. Most of yesterday and a couple of times during the night, rain pelting my metal roof and periods of rolling thunder disturbed my peaceful day and night of rest. Having lived in the Lowcountry more than a dozen years, I knew flooding would be an issue for houses on several streets as well as in the low-lying areas in nearby Charleston. Fortunately, my cottage was on high enough ground to avoid most of those problems.

The morning silence was interrupted by the phone. It was better than even odds that Charles was the person on the other end, after all, he wanted to reschedule our getting together to figure out something. I'd learned my lesson yesterday and glanced at the screen on the phone before answering. Virgil appeared rather than Charles.

I'd met Virgil Debonnet about a year and a half ago. He'd been a stock market analyst until bad investments, bad habits including gambling and drugs, and bad luck cost him his marriage, his magnificent house on Charleston's Battery, the city's premiere residential location, and his wealth. Despite losing more than most people ever had, he's one of the most optimistic people I've known.

"Morning, Virgil."

"Have you heard?"

"I need a hint. Heard what?"

"The electrocution."

I waited for him to elaborate. The wait was futile. "Virgil, what electrocution?"

"Some guy at a house under construction out West Ashley Avenue."

"Where are you?"

"The Dog."

If Virgil knew more, getting it out of him on the phone appeared remote.

"I'll be there in fifteen minutes."

"Good, you can buy breakfast."

Ten minutes later, I was parking at a space at the far end of the restaurant's gravel parking area. Virgil was sitting at a small table on the front patio. He waved when he saw me heading his way. I entered the side entrance to the patio and joined him at the table.

Virgil was in his early forties, my height at five-foot-ten, thin, with black hair. He wore sunglasses that seldom left his face, a long-sleeve, button-down light-blue shirt untucked over navy-blue chinos. He also had on his pride and joy, resoled Guccis.

Before I had a chance to say anything, Amber Lewis set a mug of coffee in front of me.

"Virgil said you'd be joining him. French toast?"

"Why not."

Amber smiled. "I can give you several reasons, beginning with the big one, eventually, clogging your arteries and then a heart attack."

I'd met Amber my first week on Folly. She was my favorite server on the island; always in the know about gossip, and unlike many servers, listens to her customers. We'd dated for a while and after deciding to go a different direction, we'd remained close friends.

"I appreciate your concern. I'll risk it today."

"It's your heart," she said, pivoted and headed inside to place my deadly order.

I turned to Virgil. "Okay, spill it."

He raised his glass. "Don't suppose you mean my orange juice."

I sighed. "Virgil."

"Okay. I got here a half-hour ago and heard two guys talking. They were standing by the entrance. Each had a to-go cup of coffee so I figured they'd already eaten and were heading, well, heading somewhere. Anyway, I heard them saying something about a construction worker getting himself electrocuted overnight. Said he was working on a house under construction. Now, don't ask me what the guy was doing working overnight."

That wasn't much more than Virgil had shared over the phone. "Did they say anything else?"

"They did, but they were walking to their truck and I couldn't hear anything else. I thought about following them to their vehicle but figured that since I'd never seen them before that'd be rude."

"On the phone you said the house was out West Ashley Avenue. Did they say that?"

"Hmm, if that's what I told you, they must have. I haven't heard anyone else saying anything about it. Why, you know the house?"

"I've only noticed one being built out that way. If it's the same house, it's where the woman fell to her death from the roof the other day."

"Wow, that's one whale of a coincidence."

"Yes, it is. You sure they didn't mention the person's name?"

"Not that I heard. They may've said it after they left the entry over there, but I didn't hear it if they did."

Amber arrived with my heart-unhealthy breakfast and a refill on my coffee. She headed to the far end of the patio where the only other two patrons were seated.

A Folly Beach Department of Public Safety cruiser pulled into a spot in front of the restaurant where a minivan had departed. Trula Bishop stepped out, yawned, then headed to the door.

Trula had joined the police force about seven years ago. She was in her forties, five-foot-five, and African American.

I said, "Good morning, Officer Bishop."

"Oh, hey, Mr. Chris, umm, you too, Mr. Virgil. Didn't see you there. My eyes are a bit fogged after being up all night."

Trula stepped away from the door to let two customers get in, then moved to the railing separating the patio from the entry.

"Officer Bishop," Virgil said, "since you were up all night, were you out there where some guy got electrocuted?"

"Afraid so. Tough scene."

I said, "What happened?"

"Hard to tell. The guy was working near the electrical panel. The floor was wet because of all the rain, water seeped under some of the equipment. Looks like a wire was hot and he didn't know it. You can guess the rest."

"Any way to tell when it happened?" I asked.

"Midnight."

Virgil said, "How do you know?"

"There was a clock radio plugged in a socket beside the panel. Was one of those old-fashioned ones, real clock hands, not digital. Don't remember when I saw one of those last. Anyway, the workers listened to it while they were working. The power to that area got blown when the man was killed."

Virgil said, "What was the guy doing working out there at midnight?"

"No idea, and he's in no condition to tell us."

"Was anyone else there when it happened?"

"If there was, he or she didn't hang around."

I said, "Who found him?"

"Two guys on the crew. Apparently, they were behind schedule and came in early to catch up. Got there a little before sunrise. It wasn't the way they wanted to start their day."

I said, "Who were they?"

Bishop took a small notebook from her pocket, flipped through a few pages, and said, "Mason Ryle and Scott Rawlins. Why?"

I told her I'd been at the site when the woman fell off the roof and had met a few of the workers. I was afraid I knew the answer to my next question, but asked anyway, "Who was the man?"

"Name's Lee, Randolph Lee. He was the foreman."

I told her I knew Randy; that I'd talked to him a couple of times.

"Why was the guy out there at midnight?" Virgil asked for a second time. "Seems weird."

I shared what Randy had told me about having to occasionally check to make sure all the equipment was turned off since some of the workers failed to.

"That's strange," Trula said and jotted a note in her small notebook. "When I asked Ryle and Rawlins if they had an idea why he was there, they said no. I would assume if the foreman had to visit the site after hours, he would've made a big stink with the crew about taking care of their equipment. I know I would've."

"Me too," added Virgil.

I agreed with both of them but didn't say it.

Bishop looked at her watch. "Guys, I've got to pick up a to-go order for two guys at the fire station. Good talking to you."

She headed inside and Virgil turned to me. "Chris, if you ask me, that sounds mighty suspicious."

I knew what he meant, but instead of agreeing, I said, "Why? People pick up to-go orders all the time."

Virgil's sunglasses prevented me from seeing it, but from the wrinkles on his face, I'd put money on him rolling his eyes at me. I wouldn't have blamed him.

11

———————

The first thing I had to do after getting home was call Charles and tell him about Randy's death. Yes, I could've made the call from the Dog, but figured doing it in private might avoid having to debate my friend in front of others.

"Figured out who killed Shelly?" Charles said instead of hello or any of the other civil responses to a phone call.

"No, haven't thought about it this morning."

"You're failing to meet the minimum requirements of a private detective. Do I have to give you a refresher course?"

"I've been busy."

"What could be more important than catching a killer?"

Instead of leading him further down the yellow brick road, it was time to share what was more important, knowing once he heard, he'd agree.

"Learning about an electrocution."

"How's that more—whoa, electrocution?"

"Randy Lee was electrocuted at the job site around midnight."

"Oh crap, he seemed like a nice guy. Did you say midnight?"

That's what Trula Bishop said."

"Where'd you see Trula?"

This is a textbook example of where a partial answer is better than a complete one. "Ran into her this morning."

"What else did she say? How did it happen? Why was Randy out there at midnight? Who found him?"

All excellent questions, I thought. Answering them would allow me to slip past telling him I'd been at the Dog with Virgil.

"Trula didn't know much. Mason Ryle and Scott Rawlins found Randy this morning. They didn't know—"

Charles interrupted, "Mason the harasser, the guy who'd hit on Shelly?"

"Yes. May I continue?"

"Was clarifying."

I didn't ask how many guys named Mason he knew working at the construction site.

"According to Trula, the floor was wet and Randy either stepped on or grabbed a hot wire. And remember, Randy told us he often went to the site at all hours of the night to make sure the equipment was turned off and stored safely. I suspect that's why he was there that late."

I waited for Charles's response. None was forthcoming.

"Charles, you still there?"

"You know what this means, don't you?"

I was certain I knew what Charles thought it meant but asked anyway.

"Means there's a murderer on the loose. Done killed Shelly, now Randy."

"We don't know that. Construction site accidents happen all the time."

"Chris, oh Chris, since you don't read anything more complicated than road signs, let me tell you what I read a couple of weeks ago. Did you know five construction workers died during the building of the Empire State Building?"

"Were they murdered?"

"Let me finish."

I mentioned for him to continue.

"That's five accidental deaths out of, umm, guess how many construction workers built it."

"A bunch."

"A big bunch, 3,400."

"And how does that archaic fact relate to a house on West Ashley Avenue?"

"There are, what, maybe ten people working on the Ashley Avenue house? Now, two of them are dead. I suppose one of them could've been an accident. But two, get real. Shelly and now Randy were murdered. Period. No, make that an exclamation point."

"You could be right, but I still don't see anything other than the odds on it being more than two unfortunate accidents."

"Did Trula tell you anything else?"

"No."

"I'll call Kyle Manger to see what he knows. Before I go, put these words in that brain under your Tilley, *they were murdered.*"

I didn't have time to tell him where I'd have liked to put the words. He'd hung up.

I didn't want to give Charles the satisfaction of knowing I wasn't far behind him thinking two deaths at the site appeared extraordinarily high for such a small project. Perhaps Cindy could shed light on what was going on. Before I could punch in her number, the phone rang, and the Chief's name appeared on the screen.

"Morning, Cindy. What did I do to deserve a call?"

"Absolutely nothing. But seeing that it's noon and you haven't pestered me about what happened overnight out West Ashley Avenue, I was afraid something terrible happened to you."

"It's nice you care about my health."

"Hell yes, who'd buy me meals if you kicked the proverbial bucket?"

"You're all heart."

"Enough foolishness. First, did you hear about this morning's death?"

"Yes, Vigil told me he'd heard about it at the Dog, and then I ran into Officer Bishop and asked about it."

"Figured you'd heard."

"Think it was an accident?"

"Looks like it. Seems the deceased often went out there after hours to make sure everything was okay. It'd been raining and for some reason he grabbed a hot wire, and you know the rest."

"Anything suspicious about it?"

"Okay, Mr. Charles in training, other than it being the second death at the house in less than a week, I didn't see anything that set off alarm bells."

To share the Empire State Building statistics or not, that is the question. Knowing I'd have to reveal how I knew its history, I chose not.

"So, that's the end of it?"

"Almost, the Sheriff sent over one of his detectives to take a gander, but I'd be shocked, pun intended, if he finds anything. The guy couldn't be old enough to have graduated from middle school. I could be wrong, but if he's been a detective longer than it takes your buddy Dude to say a three-word sentence, I'll be surprised."

"I appreciate you letting me know."

"Hell, I only called so you wouldn't be calling during my exciting luncheon meeting with our mayor."

"I still appreciate it. Enjoy your exciting meeting."

12

Early-morning walks are one of the pleasures of my retirement, probably because I had little time to take them during decades in the workforce. Today would be one of those times. I grabbed a cup of coffee from Bert's before making my way a block to Center Street.

With the sun casting its glow along the upper levels of stores and businesses along the west side of the street, the temperature in the upper seventies, and the sidewalk occupied by a mere handful of people on their way to a couple of restaurants open for breakfast, I told myself I'd made the right choice on how to spend part of the day.

While I had control over how I spent the morning, I couldn't help but think about the tragic events over the last few days. Shelly Whitley went to work the other morning thinking it was simply another day of work. I didn't know how much she loved her job or if she only endured it to earn a paycheck to afford her lifestyle. If, like most people, she had thoughts of what she would do after work, or on the weekend, or on the vacation for which she may have been saving part of her earnings. I doubt it entered her mind that it would be the last day of her life, the last day she'd see her husband, the last day her dreams of the future would exist. When

Randy Lee left his travel trailer to return to the job site to make sure the equipment was turned off and stored properly, I imagine his thoughts were on how irritating it was he had to make the long drive back at midnight rather than thinking it would be his last night going there.

These weren't the thoughts I wanted to have as I approached the spot where Center Street dead-ended at the entrance to the Tides Hotel. Rather than pushing them out of my mind, they were intensified when I saw Lucius Walker, reminding me he was the first person I'd met at the construction site the day Shelly fell to her death. He was headed my way carrying two boxes of donuts.

"Good morning, Lucius?" I said as he got closer.

"Oh, hi, umm, sorry, I forgot your name. That was a terrible day when we met."

"Chris Landrum, and I agree."

"Chris, got it."

I pointed to the boxes in his hands. "You hungry?"

He started to respond, hesitated, then smiled. "Funny. No, they're for the guys at the job site. Boss man used to get them for us. Made the workday a little more pleasant." He looked at the sidewalk and slowly shook his head. "Now he's gone. Figured I could pick up where he left off."

"That's kind of you. I hated to hear about Randy's accident."

He stared at me, his gaze narrowed, then he said, "Yeah, right."

"What's that mean?"

"Nobody's asked me, but if they did, I'd tell them I didn't think it was an accident."

"Why not?"

"I'm an electrician, have been going on twenty-five years. I know my way around everything electrical. Know what's safe, what ain't. Randy knew what he was doing. He was foreman on this job, but he was also a certified electrician. Unlike me, he could also do carpentry work with the best of them, even did some plumbing in a pinch. He shook his head. "There's no way in hell he would've stepped in a puddle and grabbed a wire that had a chance of being hot. No way."

"It was late, and he was probably tired. He may not have noticed the water or picked up the wire without thinking."

Lucius sighed. "Randy was in his sixties. Know how electricians live that long? They don't make that mistake."

"You say you haven't told anyone your theory?"

"May've mentioned my suspicions to a guy or two on the job, but like I said, no cop asked me. Since it was after hours when it happened, none of us were there, so we couldn't have seen anything. Seems to me, the cops figured it was an accident and closed the books on it."

"Let's say you're right and it wasn't an accident. Any thoughts on who may've been there and, umm, caused him to be electrocuted?"

"Not really. From what I could tell, he got along with everybody out there. Sure, there were minor blowups. Always are on a job with a group of workers sharing the same space, but nothing stands out. Don't know diddly-squat about his life outside work."

"Let me ask something else. Do you think there's any connection between Shelly Whitley's death and Randy Lee's?"

"Don't see how there could be. Looks to me like she simply slipped on the roof and fell."

I didn't remind him that most people thought Randy's death was an accident, the same as Shelly's.

"You're probably right. Did any of the others out there have a problem with Shelly and Randy?"

"It don't sound like you think her death was accidental."

"It strikes me highly unlikely that there could be two accidental deaths at one construction site in that short period of time."

"That's because Randy's wasn't accidental."

"Lucius, I'm good friends with Folly's Police Chief. If I asked her, would you be willing to tell her what you told me about your theory about Randy?"

"I have to get along with the other guys. I've already had to put up with some comments and snubs because I'm black. I can't afford to get anyone else down on me, so no. Sorry." He looked at the boxes in his hands. "I got to get these out there. Good talking to you."

He didn't wait for me to respond before heading in the direction of the new house.

He said he didn't want to talk to Cindy about Randy's death. I didn't say I wouldn't.

"Morning, Cindy," I said as she answered her phone on the second ring.

"Where are you?"

"In front of the Tides."

"I'll be there in thirty seconds."

She wasn't far off. Her city owned Ford pickup truck pulled in the hotel's lot in less than a minute.

She smiled and said, "Thanks for offering to buy me coffee in Roasted."

Roasted is the coffeeshop located in the oceanfront hotel.

"My pleasure," I said even though I knew I hadn't made the offer.

We entered the hotel through the door closest to Roasted and were greeted by Penny, the shop's personable manager. We each ordered coffee and moved to one of the two small tables in the center of the room.

Cindy took a sip, glanced around the room, then said, "So what did I do to deserve a phone call and cup of coffee?"

I was tempted to say she hadn't done anything for the coffee but knew nothing positive would come from it. Instead, I said, "I was curious if you'd learned anything more about Randy Lee's death."

She tilted her head. "You were curious about that rather than being curious about how I was doing, what I fixed Larry for supper last night, how my meeting went with the mayor, how my aching feet feel after walking a thousand miles around town yesterday, how—"

"Cindy," I interrupted, "of course I was curious about all those things. So, learn anything more about Randy Lee's death?"

"Good, pizza, bad as usual, sore, no," she said, stared in her cup, then took another sip.

"Taking talking lessons from Dude?"

"He be my idol," she said and smiled.

I returned the smile before saying, "So, nothing new about the death?"

"Last night the baby detective called and said it's clear as day, no question about it, an accident. Case closed."

"What's Cindy LaMond say?"

"I would agree with him if there weren't two alleged accidental deaths there in less than a week."

"Before I called you, I ran into Lucius Walker, he's an electrician on the project. He thinks it's highly unlikely that a trained electrician would've been killed by that kind of accident."

"I thought Randy Lee was foreman on the job."

"He was, but according to Lucius he was also a licensed electrician."

"Good to know. Other than *highly unlikely*, did he have any proof or idea who may've wanted Lee dead?"

"No."

"That figures. The problem with highly unlikely is that it doesn't eliminate likely."

"You're right. I assume by the detective saying case closed, the Sheriff's Office won't be doing any follow-up."

"You assume correctly."

I smiled at the Chief. "I also assume the highly skilled, competent, and lovely, I might add, Folly Beach Director of Public Safety isn't closing the case."

"You're a highly perceptive, intelligent citizen. A total suck-up at times, but still all those other things. I can't do much but will keep my eyes and ears open and have already told my guys to do the same."

"Good."

"This is where I tell you not to butt in; to leave it to the police."

"You know—"

She pointed her coffee cup at me. "But I know I'd be wasting my words and energy telling you, so let's leave it at be careful."

"Always, Chief."

13

———

When Charles answered the phone, I tried the same line on him that Cindy had used on me. "Where are you?"

"At the spa getting a facial and pedicure."

There was a better chance my friend would be skinny-dipping at the North Pole than being at a spa. I tried again.

"Where are you?"

"Okay, you caught me. I'm delivering sandals to a couple staying at a house out East Cooper. Dude said they absolutely had to have them in the next fifteen minutes or, well, he didn't say or what. You calling each of your friends to see where they are?"

"Good guess but wrong. I'm only calling you. I just met with Lucius Walker and figured you'd want to know what he said."

"Lucius, the guy from the deadly house?"

"How many guys named Lucius do you know?"

"Got it. What'd he say?"

"Head to the end of the Pier after you finish the emergency sandal delivery."

Fifteen minutes later, I saw Dude's local-delivery person. He was wearing a crimson and blue University of Kansas, long-sleeve, T-shirt, tan shorts, his summer Tilley, and tapping his cane on the wooden deck as he approached me on a bench at the Atlantic end of the thousand-plus-foot-long structure. He stopped twice to talk to dogs that were accompanying their masters on a walk along the Pier.

"Sorry I'm late. Had to wait for the couple, who happened to be from Chicago, to try on the sandals. It's their first trip to the ocean and wanted to make sure the sandals fit so they could walk for 'hours and hours' on the beach. I was beginning to think I'd have to wait *hours and hours* for them to unpack the shoes, try them on, and model them for each other. The best news is the sandals fit, and here I am."

"Fascinating," I said, not disguising my sarcasm.

"Well, what'd he say?"

I gave Charles a blow-by-blow description of my conversation with Lucius. I was surprised when he only interrupted twice with questions. First was when he wanted to know where Randy received his apprentice training to become a certified electrician. He huffed and puffed when I told him I didn't know. His second question was no-doubt critical to the conversation. He asked what kind of donuts Lucius was taking to the crew. That I could answer.

After I managed to get through my description of the conversation with Lucius, I shared what Cindy and I'd talked about. He was either totally engrossed in my description or fell asleep early in it because he didn't ask anything.

He finally said, "See, told you so."

I suspected I knew what he meant. "You did say you thought the two deaths were suspicious."

"Not suspicious, murder. Clear as day."

"For what it's worth, I'm beginning to agree with you."

"You are?"

"Yes."

"You never agree when I say we need to help the police."

"Can't say that again, can you?"

"Trying to confuse me?"

I didn't think that would be too difficult but didn't say it. "No, I agree with you that we need to get involved."

"With me and the Chief, you mean."

"She's not certain. For that matter, neither am I."

"I am, and the best thing in all of it is Folly's top cop wants us to find out who killed them."

"That's not exactly my interpretation of what she said. She did say she knew we'd have a hard time not sticking our noses where they didn't belong."

"My friend, that's police-speak for the Chief asking, correction, begging us to catch the killer. Us as in you and me. Plain as day."

"How do you, umm, we plan to do that, Mr. Private Detective?"

"Excellent question, Assistant Detective." Charles turned and watched three surfers sitting on their boards waiting for a wave large enough to get excited over.

"You have an excellent answer to go with that excellent question?"

He stopped watching the surfers, turned to me, and said, "Nope."

"That helps."

"Nope."

"Okay, since you're the one with the detective agency, what's your plan?"

"After all the years you've known me, you know coming up with plans ain't my strong suit. You're the college-educated member of the agency. You're the one always making lists, coming up with catching the bad guys strategies, outlining stuff we need to do, all those other textbook learning ways to catch bad guys. I'm the chief stumbler." He patted me on the arm. "So, what's the plan?"

I would've laughed at his analysis, but knew he was serious; off base by a mile, but still serious.

"You have to understand, I haven't given any thought to who might've killed the workers. First, we're not certain their deaths were anything other than accidents. They—"

"I'm certain."

I ignored his comment. "Granted, two deadly accidents in a short span of time on such a small project would appear to defy odds, but still, we have no proof of anything more sinister." I hesitated, then added, "Even if we assume you're right, we know little about the victims. Without knowing more about them, we have no way of knowing who would've wanted them dead. We don't even know if Shelly and Randy had contact with each other outside work. If they didn't, I have a hard time seeing how they could've done something on the job that made someone want to kill them."

Charles smiled. "See, you've already started one of your lists of things we need to do."

I have? "Okay, repeat it for me."

He sighed, held up his forefinger, and said, "Number one, learn everything there is to know about Shelly and Randy." He added his middle finger to the number. "Two, see if Shelly and Randy had a relationship outside work." The ring finger was added to his count. "Three, catch the person who killed them." He closed his hand into a fist and raised it in the air. "*Voila*, another successful crime, umm, crimes solved."

I stared at him and said, "Wow, silly me, I thought it would be difficult."

Charles looked at his watchless wrist and said, "Gotta go. Time for me to start stumbling around. Got a killer to catch."

14

I remained on the Pier after Charles left on his quest to stumble into something that would help him, help us, learn who killed the construction workers. What that was, I didn't know. I wouldn't call him the *chief stumbler* in his imaginary detective agency, but he did excel in getting to know strangers. Minutes after meeting them, they were telling him things they wouldn't share with their family or closest friends. Using that innate skill on potential suspects, he could get them saying things that could lead him closer to solving murders. They seldom suspected they were being interrogated, although in a couple of instances, his, umm, nosiness nearly got my friend killed.

He was right about a couple of things. If we had a ghost of a chance at helping the police, we needed to learn more about the victims. Add to that, who are the logical suspects? From everything I've heard, only workers were present when Shelly met her untimely death. Did any of them see or hear anyone else in the house that morning? Clearly, if no one else entered, and if Shelly was pushed, the killer was one of her fellow workers. Those, of course, were two large ifs.

Then there's Randy Lee. According to Lucius Walker, Randy's

death couldn't have been accidental. I didn't rule that out. It had been midnight, dark in the house, he would've been tired, and not paying as much attention to his surroundings as he normally would have been. If Lucius was correct, the suspect pool was unlimited. We had no clue as to who may've wanted to harm Randy. My knowledge of the man was limited to him telling me it was his first job as foreman and that he bought donuts for the employees. Neither reasons for him to be killed nor if he was murdered, a clue as to suspects.

I stared at the group of surfers that'd increased since Charles was here. I appreciated the distraction since I had no idea what to do next and according to Charles, I was charged with developing a plan to catch the killer or killers of two people where no one except Lucius, Charles, possibly Cindy, and in weaker moments, I thought crimes had been committed.

Over the years, some of my best thinking occurred near this spot on the Folly Pier. I couldn't explain why, but regardless, it'd been the case. Today wasn't one of those times, so I headed home.

I was opening my front door when I heard someone behind me say, "Hey, neighbor."

I turned and was surprised to see Brad Burton crossing his front yard and heading my way. His long-sleeve, white dress shirt looked big on him, mainly because it wasn't tucked in and fell nearly to the bottom of the tan shorts he wore.

"Brad," I said.

"Glad I caught you. Was headed over but didn't know if you were home."

"I am now. Can I interest you in a soft drink?"

"Don't want to put you out."

He wouldn't be if I had any drinks in the refrigerator. With luck, I would, besides, I was curious to know why he was looking for me.

"Don't be silly. Come on in."

He followed me in as I wondered what condition I'd left every-thing, then stopped wondering about appearances considering how disheveled my neighbor looked. He followed me to the kitchen, the most underused room in my cottage. I opened the refrigerator and was relieved to see four Diet Pepsis and two regular Pepsis.

I gave him the two options and he chose the regular soft drink. I grabbed the diet version and motioned for him to have a seat at the table.

He took a sip, looked around the kitchen like he expected someone to jump out and steal his drink, then said, "Have you heard about what happened to Randy Lee?"

"Yes, so sad."

"What'd you hear?"

To tell or not to tell Lucius Walker's theory of what had happened. Brad had no hesitation to accuse me of nosing in police business, so why not. I told him about meeting Randy's coworker on the street and what he'd theorized about Randy's death not being an accident. I was pleased when Brad didn't berate me for, for what? All I did was repeat what someone had shared.

Not only did he not criticize me, but he also said, "You think he's right?"

"I don't know. In addition to Randy being foreman, he was a certified electrician. That should've made him more careful around electrical equipment, but on the other hand, it was late, dark, and he probably was tired after working all day and then having to return to the job site."

Brad nodded slowly. "Doesn't it strike you strange that there are now two deaths from the small crew on the project?"

"Yes, combine that with some of the crew saying Shelly would've been more careful on the roof. They think it was unlikely she would've put herself in position to slip."

"Does seem unlikely, doesn't it?"

"Yes, but accidents happen."

Instead of focusing on what had happened, I was puzzled about why Brad was sitting in my kitchen talking about the deaths. I didn't have to wait long for an answer.

"Back when I was a detective, this kind of situation would keep me up at night. Each of the deaths can easily be explained. Each could be chalked up to an unfortunate accident. Tell you what, though, I don't like the odds on them being accidents."

"Think your old office is taking it seriously?"

He shrugged. "I don't know much about the young guy who caught the deaths. I suppose he's good, but he hasn't been a detective long. He has other cases, so it's a lot easier to write these off as accidents than to look for something that might not exist. That's especially true since no one is breathing down his neck about them being murders."

"If you were still on the job, what would you be looking for?"

He took a sip of his drink, grinned, and said, "You're not playing detective by any chance?"

"Interested, that's all."

He slowly nodded. "Let's for a moment assume both people were murdered. The first question would be did the same person kill both of them? Logic would tell me yes. It'd be unlikely that there'd be two murderers killing people who worked at the same small construction site." Brad scratched the side of his face, looked at his drink, and continued, "Then the next question would be why were they killed? If it isn't already confusing, it'd get there fast. For example, were they killed for the same reason? If so, what was the reason and what was the connection between the victims other than being coworkers? Next, did Randy Lee figure out who killed Shelly Whitley and the killer did him in so he couldn't tell the police who it was? Finally, if they weren't killed for the same reason and it wasn't because Randy figured it out and was killed so he couldn't divulge the name of the killer, why were their lives ended?"

"Brad, you're right about it getting complicated."

"That's why I retired." He tapped his finger on the table. "And that's why an amateur has no business meddling in police business."

"I get your point."

"But it's not going to stop you, is it?"

He took another sip, stood, saluted me, said he had to go, and was out the door before I had a chance to lie to him about meddling.

15

———————

Brad was right about me wanting to learn what happened to the two workers but wanting to and learning were separated by a gap wider than the Grand Canyon. The next morning, I decided a walk would be the best way to get my brain working, possibly come up with something I could use to get closer to the answer to the question, and if not, the day was pleasant with a temperature in the upper seventies and exercise would do me good.

It was later than my normal early-morning walking time, so foot traffic along Center Street was busier than I would've preferred. I crossed Center Street and headed west on Ashley Avenue. There wasn't a sidewalk but enough space to walk without worrying about being hit. I'd gone a couple of blocks when I noticed Chief LaMond's pickup off to the side of the road with the chief leaning against the fender and talking to two men. The men looked vaguely familiar, but I couldn't recall where or when I'd seen them.

"Morning, Chief," I said as I approached her vehicle.

"You walking to the County Park," Cindy said with a smile, knowing the odds on that were slim since County Park was on the west end of the island nearly two miles from where were standing.

"Nothing that exciting."

"Nothing that strenuous, you mean. I'm aware of your aversion to exercise." She smiled, glanced to the two men she'd been talking to, turned to me, and said, "Chris, you know Tim Hale and Scott Rawlins?"

"Guys, you look familiar, but I don't recall from where."

The younger of the two, probably in his early twenties, stepped forward and held out his hand. He was six-foot-two, thin, with long black hair.

"I'm Tim Hale. Pleased to meet you."

I shared the same sentiment and told him my name.

The other gentleman, probably in his early sixties, was a half foot shorter than Tim, muscular but with much of it turning to fat, with long gray hair pulled into a ponytail, put a large paper bag he'd been carrying on the ground and offered me his hand to shake.

"Scott Rawlins."

He didn't appear pleased to meet me, or if he did, he didn't mention it.

Cindy said, "Tim and Scott work on the construction site where the two deaths occurred. They were walking back to the house. Walking is good, you know." She smiled then looked at her watch. "Have to go guys, thanks for the information. Umm, Chris, have fun jogging to the County Park."

That's why they looked familiar. They were standing around Shelly Whitley's body when Charles and I first approached the construction site.

"Nice lady," Scott said as Cindy got in her truck and pulled out on the street.

"I've known her several years and agree. She giving you jaywalking tickets?" I smiled hoping they knew I was teasing.

Tim returned my smile. "Not this time. We were heading back to work with lunch for some of the guys when she stopped to ask if we remembered anything we hadn't told the cops about the deaths."

"What happened to your coworkers was horrible. I've heard both deaths were accidental. You agree?"

"Afraid so," Tim said as he shook his head. "Both seemed like mighty nice folks. Poor Randy hired me the day they started building the house. He didn't know me from Adam but said he needed another carpenter and gave me a chance. He didn't have to. I appreciated it."

"I agree about Randy." Scott said and turned to Tim. "He hired me, what, a week after he hired you?"

"Yes."

"He was always fair with us. That's not something I can say about many of the foreman I've worked for over the years. About the only negative thing I can say about him is he favored Shelly."

"What's that mean?" I said, although I'd heard the same thing about him treating her with kid gloves.

"He took it easy on her. Mind you, it wasn't a big deal, irritating, that's all."

Tim patted Scott's arm. "Randy had a soft spot for Shelly, but like Scott said, it wasn't a big issue. He made up for it by giving us more freedom when it came to breaks, lunch time, leaving early if we had doctor appointments or other stuff we needed to do. Damn terrible what happened to him."

Scott said, "It was sort of our fault he got electrocuted."

"How?"

"He was so, umm, what's the word, conscientious about everything, he often went out to the site after all of us left to make sure everything was buttoned down like it was supposed to be. If we, especially some of the younger guys, did everything we were supposed to do, he wouldn't have had to go out there in the middle of the night to check our work."

Tim looked at Scott. "Younger guys like me, you mean?"

"Tim, you may be the baby on the job, but I've never seen you do anything wrong. You may've not noticed, but I've seen you straightening up after Mason left a mess and once left the circular saw turned on when he went on a break."

"Guys," I said, "I know it's only a rumor, but I heard someone in town say he heard Shelly was pushed off the roof and it wasn't an accident. Is that possible?"

"Anything's possible," Scott said, "but I wouldn't put credence in it. I ain't heard anyone say there was somebody else up on the roof when she fell. Tim, did you hear of anyone being up there?"

"Not that I heard. I agree with Scott, anything's possible, but I don't see how."

Scott said, "Do the police think something like that happened?"

"If they do, they haven't said anything to me," I said. He didn't ask if Charles or I thought it was possible. "How well did Randy know Shelly?"

Scott said, "He gave her the easier jobs, like I said. Is that what you mean?"

"I meant did they know each other outside work? If there was any truth to someone killing them, it seems there could be some connection between the two."

Tim said, "I don't know about you, Scott, but I never heard anything that made me think they had any contact off the job site. Shelly was married, married to a jerk, but still married. Randy lived by himself in a small RV somewhere off Folly. I never heard him say nothing much about his personal life."

"Chris, I agree with Tim. I never heard either of them mention anything about the other one that wasn't about work."

"That's what I figured. There's probably no truth to the rumor. Tim, what do you mean about Shelly's husband being a jerk?"

"That's my impression. The couple of times I saw him at the job site, he was bossing her around. Stuff like *be home by five,* or *don't forget to pick up bread on the way home.* It wasn't what he was saying but how he said it. He was almost yelling. Who yells about getting bread on the way home?"

"Did either of you see him there the day she died?"

Tim shrugged. "Not me. How about you, Scott?"

"No, but I was stuck in one of the bedrooms most of the day trying to get the walls finished. Didn't see much of anything so he could've been there. Why?"

"Curious, that's all."

Scott looked at the bag of food on the ground and said, "Would like to talk longer. It's easier than work, but we'd better get back. Nice meeting you."

16

I realized the next morning that the only thing in the house I had to eat was a Hershey's Bar with almonds. It covered two food groups, but I suspected it wasn't on the list of breakfast recommendations by the American Heart Association. A walk to the Lost Dog Cafe would achieve two things. It would get me some much-needed exercise and a plate full of calories to negate any advantage from the walk. That equaled out, didn't it?

The temperature had fallen short of the seventy-degree mark, so I chose to sit inside. Amber met me at the door and pointed to a table on the far side of the room and said my coffee would arrive momentarily. Before I reached the table, Marc Salmon motioned me to his usual spot in the center of the room.

He was by himself, so I said, "Where's your table mate?"

Marc looked at his watch. "He should be here in the next five minutes," the councilmember said and looked toward the entry. "Update, make that the next five seconds."

Houston was making his way around a table of two adults and three kids, patted me on the back, said it was good seeing me, then took the chair opposite Marc.

I started to head to my table, when Marc said, "Hear anything else about the two deaths?"

"Nothing you don't already know, I suspect."

"Give me a call if you do. I'm always interested in knowing what's going on over here. City business, you know."

City gossip, I know, but said he'd be the first to hear if I learned anything. He said he'd look forward to it, then turned to his fellow gossip. Not hearing an invitation to join them, I continued to the table Amber had pointed me toward, the one where she'd already set a mug of coffee.

She was back at the table before I had time to take a sip.

She glanced at Marc and Houston's table and said, "You giving the council members advice on how to run the city?"

"It's my observation they're the ones giving the advice."

She tapped my arm. "You know them well."

Before I agreed, Sean Aker entered the restaurant, looked around, and headed my way.

Sean is a local attorney I'd used when I was starting my photo gallery. When he was accused of killing his law partner nine years ago, Charles and I muddled our way through catching the real killer. Sean said he owed us big time and we'd taken advantage of his legal assistance on several occasions.

"You look like you could use some company," he said as he eyed the other chair at the table.

Sean was approaching fifty, thin, too thin in my opinion, well-toned and athletic; all things I'm not.

I took the hint. "You're always welcome at my table, Counselor."

Amber had drifted to a table on the opposite side of the room to deliver the check to its occupants then returned with coffee for Sean.

Sean looked at me. "You ordered?"

I said no.

"He'll have French toast and bring me a cup of fresh fruit parfait."

It was sad when my attorney knows what I order for breakfast most every time I'm in the Dog. It also goes a long way to explain why Sean's thin and I'm not.

Amber said, "Why am I not surprised?"

She headed to the window opening to the kitchen to place our orders before I could respond to her question that, to be honest, needed no response.

Sean sipped his drink, nodded, and said, "So, what's this I hear about you and Charles sticking your noses in the deaths at a house being built on West Ashley?"

"Where'd you hear that?"

"Let's see, first, Marlene told me she got it from a good source. As you know, Marlene is never wrong."

Marlene is Sean's receptionist and only other employee in his law practice.

"I don't know where—"

"Hang on, she wasn't the only source." He nodded in the direction of the councilmember's table.

"Got it," I said. "Anyone else?"

He chuckled. "Not yet, but if you-know-who over there knows, it'll spread like water at a dam break. Now, if you're done asking about my sources, can I get back to the question?"

I'd already forgotten the question, but suspected it was him nosing into Charles and my nosing.

"Charles and I were at the job site when Shelly fell. We also met Randy Lee, the foreman who was electrocuted. We were curious about what happened."

Sean interrupted, "And you don't buy the deaths were accidents?"

I shrugged and said, "Don't you think it seems like it could be more than a coincidence that there are two deaths in fewer than a handful of days on a construction site with only ten or so workers?"

"Do you have anything more than a hunch?"

"Not really."

"And that's not going to stop you from trying to find out more?"

"I didn't say that."

"Didn't have to. You think I haven't paid attention to what you two have done over and over catching killers? You think I don't owe you my freedom after what you did when I was accused of murder?"

"What happened to those construction workers appears to be tragic accidents. If that's what they were, there's no amount of, umm, curiosity Charles and I exhibit that'll change the facts."

"But if they weren't accidents, do you think you two can do more than law enforcement agencies are able to achieve getting to the bottom of whatever happened?"

"Don't know."

"Well said." He tapped his fingers on the table. "If there's anything you need from me, or anything I can do to help, let me know. I've told you several times, but it bears repeating, I owe you big time."

"I appreciate it."

Amber slipped a plate of French toast in front of me and handed Sean his parfait. "Sorry it took so long, guys. It's been a busy morning."

We thanked her as she left to greet newcomers at the table next to ours.

"Sean, do you know anything about the owner of the house under construction?"

"Who is it?"

"Oliver Trescott, think he's from Maryland or somewhere up that way," I said as I poured syrup on my French toast.

"I don't have any dealings with him, and don't recall hearing his name. Why?"

"I didn't figure you would. I heard he bought the property several years ago and didn't do anything with it until less than a year ago. I'm reaching for anything to help get a handle on why the deaths may be something other than accidents."

"Is this Trescott character over here now?"

"Don't know."

"Have you heard anything about him that would indicate he knew the victims?"

"No."

"Other than working on the house, did the victims have other connections, say outside work, or conflicts with anyone on the job?"

"If they did, no one's mentioned it," I said and took a bite of French toast.

"Who's building the house?"

"Custom Builders Group, owned by Joe Argyle."

Sean ate a spoonful of parfait, then smiled. "I know Joe, helped him with a minor squabble a couple of years ago. Other than that, and even then, it wasn't any fault of his, I got the complaint against him dropped. He's a good guy. From what I've heard, he does a good job for his clients."

"Glad to hear it."

I ran out of things to ask Sean and apparently, he ran out of questions I couldn't answer. The conversation transitioned to some of his hobbies. I couldn't add much to the conversation since I had near zero interest in any of them, including skydiving, surfing, and scuba diving.

He finished breakfast, took a final sip of coffee, and said, "I'd better get to the office before Marlene sends her bloodhound out to round me up."

Marlene's bloodhound is a Shih Tzu that's more at home sitting on her lap at the office, but I took Sean's hint and told him I enjoyed having breakfast with him. I enjoyed it more when he picked up my tab, a rare occurrence from my friends.

17

Charles agreed to meet me at Loggerhead's for supper, especially after I said I was buying and that I'd met Tim and Scott, two more of the workers at the ill-fated house. I hung up when he tried to make me feel guilty for not telling him about meeting them immediately after it happened.

Ed, Loggerhead's owner, met us at the top of the stairs on the deck and said there was a fifteen-minute wait for a table. I told him we'd be at the bar and were assured someone would come for us when a table was available. The weather was perfect, and the crowd was two-deep at the bar, so I was surprised the wait was only fifteen minutes. I inched my way through the crowd to get the bartender's attention and ordered a beer for Charles and white wine for me.

Before I managed a sip, Charles started on his lecture about me not calling him the second I left Tim and Scott. I told him I would've if I learned anything worth sharing.

"That doesn't matter, you should've called when—" He hesitated and looked over my shoulder in the direction of the railing over-looking the parking area on the side of the building. "There's Kyle Manger. Who's that with him?"

I turned to see who he was talking about. Kyle was leaning on the railing and the man facing him was waving his right hand around like he was swatting at a swarm of no-see-ems. He was in his mid-thirties, roughly five-foot-ten, obese, and had a straggly beard that could house a family of field mice. I didn't know who he was but could tell he was irritated about something.

"Don't know."

Charles nodded, glanced back at the men, and said, "Guess we'd better go see."

"They don't look like they're in a mood to meet strangers."

"Kyle's not a stranger."

"Why don't we give them a few minutes to resolve whatever has the other guy so animated?"

Kyle either had to go or had enough of whatever the other man was saying. He pushed away from the railing and headed toward the ramp leading to the parking area. Charles told me he'd be back and followed Kyle down the ramp.

I was beginning to wonder if Charles had deserted me when he reappeared, retrieved his beer from the counter, looked toward the other man who was now leaning over the railing staring at who knows what, and said, "You'll never guess who that is." He tilted his head in the other man's direction.

"You're right. Why don't you tell me?"

"Raymond Whitley."

"Shelly's husband?"

"In person."

"What was he doing here with Kyle? Were they friends?"

"Friends, no. Kyle had seen him at the job site a couple of times. That's when he learned about Raymond and Shelly being hitched. Saw him here tonight and wanted to express condolences." Charles looked at Raymond. "Kyle said it was a mistake, actually said it was a 'big-ass mistake.'"

"Why?"

"As soon as he told Raymond who he was, the guy started in about life insurance he was fighting the builder about, how the builder claimed there wasn't any, how the builder was trying to screw

Raymond out of what was his. Then Raymond topped it off by saying he was going to sue the builder, all the guys working on the job, and probably the company that made the shingles on the roof that he claimed made Shelly slip and fall." Charles set his beer on the counter then said, "He's leaving." He then made a beeline for Raymond.

At the same time, Bobbie, one of the servers, tapped me on the arm and said our table was ready. I followed her to the table near a seating area made from a converted VW bus. I figured Charles, being a private detective, could find me once he'd finished with Raymond.

As predicted, Charles did find me, but not as predicted, he wasn't done with Raymond.

"Chris, you'll never believe who I ran into over by the bar."

Yes, I would since Charles intentionally went to meet Raymond. This wasn't the time to correct him.

"Who?"

"Would you believe this is Raymond Whitley? He's Shelly Whitley's husband, you remember the lady who tragically fell from that new house she was working on."

I turned to Raymond. "I'm terribly sorry about your wife. You have my deepest sympathy."

He shook my hand, said, "Thank you. Your friend Charles invited me to share a table with you for supper. Hope you don't mind."

"Raymond was going to eat by himself, but I figured he may not want to be alone during such a dreadful time. I told him we'd buy his supper."

We meant yours truly.

"Glad you could join us."

"Did you know Shelly?"

Bobbie returned before I could respond. Charles and I said we were fine with our drinks; Raymond said he'd have another beer.

Charles said, "No, we didn't have the pleasure. As I said over there, the only way I knew who you were was when I saw you talking to Kyle. We'd met him here and knew he worked with Shelly. I asked him who you were. I'm so sorry about what happened. I didn't know her, but everyone who did said she was a wonderful person."

"How well do you know Kyle?" I asked, in hopes of learning what they'd been arguing about.

"Met him a couple of times when I picked Shelly up after work. Wasn't often. I'm a bartender at the Twin Rivers Bar in downtown Charleston. Most days I'm going to work when she's getting off."

Bobbie arrived with Raymond's drink and Charles and I ordered cheeseburgers and Raymond went with a patty melt.

"Did you know the man who got electrocuted out there the other night?" Charles asked as if it was a logical question after someone ordered a patty melt.

"The damned incompetent bastard," he said and took a swig of his drink.

Charles said, "Why?"

"His fault she's dead. No wonder he killed himself. Too stupid not to step in a puddle while grabbing something electric. He doesn't know a damned thing about building a house."

I said, "Why'd you say it was his fault your wife was dead?"

"He knew she was scared of heights, but that didn't stop him from making her work on the roof, of all places. Not any roof, mind you, but a slanted one." He took another long draw on his drink.

"Did she tell you she thought Randy Lee was incompetent?"

"Said he was reckless; said she wouldn't be surprised if someone got hurt out there." He looked at his drink, shook his head, and continued, "Didn't think it would be her. Know what the damned company told me?"

Charles said, "What?"

"Said they didn't have life insurance on Shelly. Got nothing for all her work and then giving her life for them to make a ton of money on the house. Tell you one thing, they ain't getting away with it."

Bobbie delivered our food and asked if we needed anything else. Raymond said another beer, again, Charles and I said we were okay. By now, I was wondering how many beers Raymond had consumed since arriving at Loggerhead's.

I knew Charles wouldn't let the interruption disrupt his interrogation. I wasn't disappointed when he said, "What'd you mean by they wouldn't get away with it?"

"I'm getting a lawyer and suing their ass off. They ain't getting away with not paying me anything."

"Good luck," Charles said. "Were you at work when she fell?"

Raymond narrowed his gaze at my friend. "Why?"

"It had to be horrible hearing what'd happened and wondered if you were working when you got the call."

"Oh. I wasn't scheduled to go in until four that day. Most days I work from four until eleven or so."

From the look in his eyes, I could tell Charles wasn't done with his questioning. "Were you with friends when you got the word? You know, someone who could help you with whatever you needed to do."

"No, was driving around."

I had no doubt Charles was thinking no alibi. I wondered if he would risk asking Raymond where he was when Randy Lee was killed.

To keep Raymond from getting suspicious about what Charles was searching for with his questions, I asked him how long he and Shelly had been married.

"Seven years last month."

"Any children?"

"She always said she didn't need any kids, that one big one was enough." He smiled for the first time since he sat down.

"Any pets?" Charles asked, as only he could.

Raymond looked at Charles as if he'd asked if he'd seen any Martians lately, before he said, "No."

I was confident Raymond wouldn't be confessing to killing his wife or Randy Lee, so I tried to keep him talking about things he was familiar with and away from mentioning the construction site, the construction company, or lawyers. I asked a couple of questions about his job. Fortunately, he appeared to want to talk about humorous things that'd happened on the job rather than anything negative.

After about forty-five minutes he kept nodding his head, and a couple of times I worried he would fall asleep. He finally jerked his head up, stood, and said he'd better be going.

We said we enjoyed having him at the table with us. He claimed the same then thanked us—me—for buying his supper and drinks.

18

———

The crowd had increased from two to three deep at the bar, so I figured some of them were waiting on a table. I didn't want to take up valuable real estate longer than we had to, and besides, two musicians had begun their set at a volume that made it difficult to hear anything Charles was saying. Much of what he had to say could go without hearing, but occasionally he would impart something important.

I yelled over the music, "Ready to go?"

"What?"

That answered my question whether Charles knew it or not. I waved for Bobbie to bring the check, paid, and pointed to the stairs leading off the patio. Charles followed me down the stairs and to West Arctic Avenue.

"You ready to head home or want to walk up Center Street?"

He didn't answer until we'd walked a block and were standing in front of the Sand Dollar, Folly's iconic private bar where membership was limited to people who could afford a one-dollar membership fee. Four Harley's were parked diagonally in front of the bar and a man was seated on the bench near the entry. He was holding a leash with an aging brown and white pit bull on the other end. The dog looked as exhausted as its owner.

Of course, Charles had to squat to pet the dog and say a few words only he and the pit bull understood. One belly rub later, Charles said goodbye to the dog, stood, and said, "Well, where're we headed?"

"It's early so I thought we could walk up Center Street and enjoy the music."

On any given night in the summer, bands and solo musicians could be heard playing their brands of music from several restaurant patios and decks.

Charles said, "What're we waiting for?"

Which I translated as he'd love to walk with me. At Folly's sole traffic light at the corner of Center and Ashley, we stopped to listen to competing bands from Coconut Joe's and across the street from the rooftop bar at Snapper Jack's.

A familiar voice coming from behind us said, "You two are doing what I spend a bunch of time doing every day."

I turned and said, "Evening, Virgil."

Charles said, "What are we doing that you spend so much time doing every day?"

He looked at the traffic signal. "Watching it change from red, to green, to yellow, to red, to—"

"That's fascinating," I said not wanting to see how many color changes he was going to relive. "We were on our way up the street enjoying the music."

"Holy moly, that sounds more exciting than watching the light change. Mind if I tag along?"

Charles said, "You're always welcome."

Virgil glanced at me, probably wondering if the decision was unanimous. I nodded. A block later, we were walking side-by-side in front of the gift shop Native.

Virgil put an arm around each of our waists and said, "Who could've guessed, the crime fighting trio is back together?"

When I first met Virgil, he'd proclaimed Charles and me to being a crime fighting duo, with no encouragement from Charles or me, I should add. Since he'd been a financial analyst before he lost everything, math was one of his strengths, so, again with no encouragement, he added himself to the duo and came up with trio.

I'd learned it'd serve no purpose to try to correct his analysis, so I said, "Anyone up to a drink?"

Virgil, who now lived in perpetual poverty, said, "You buying?"

Charles, who lived as a perpetual bum, said, "Chris is."

I said, "Where?"

"Planet Follywood," Virgil said. "I like their back-in-the-old-days vibe."

We crossed the street and entered the long, narrow restaurant. I wouldn't have put it like Virgil had, but there was no doubt the restaurant had the feel of the classic beach bar. The aroma of long-eaten fries remained in the air. Colorful murals drew attention to the walls and posters promoting future events competed with posters for long-past happenings. Loud music was coming from the patio out back, so I suggested we remain inside so we could hear each other rather than compete with the rock music outside. Four seats were vacant at the bar at the back of the room. We took three of them. Two men were watching a rerun of a television show from the nineties, the sound muted. Charles and Virgil opted for beers; I stuck with white wine. It didn't take Virgil long to get to what I figured the real reason for wanting to tag along.

"Guys, where are we on catching the killer, or is that killers?"

"Funny you should ask," Charles said. "We shared a meal with the guy who killed both of them."

"Wow! You tell the cops? They arrest him? How'd you figure it out?" He hesitated. "Oh yeah, who is it?"

I deferred to Charles to figure out the questions, and the answers.

Charles looked at me, then turned to Virgil as our drinks arrived. "Umm, no. We haven't told the cops."

Virgil took a drag off his beer before saying, "Why not?"

This time I didn't wait for Charles. "Because we don't know who killed the two people. We don't know for sure they were murdered."

"Of course, we know they were," Charles said. "The police know it. Your good buddy Brad Burton knows it. And we, okay, I know it."

"Holy moly, Detective Charles, don't keep me in suspense. Who did it?"

"Raymond Whitley, slam-dunk case."

"Whitley, Whitley," Virgil said. "He kin to the lady killed?"

"Her husband."

"Ah, that explains it. Everyone knows the spouse is always the leading suspect. How'd you figure it out?"

Good question, I thought. I looked forward to Charles's slam-dunk answer.

I'd have to wait. The man seated to our right paid and slid off the stool. Two men then took the next two vacant seats. I recognized them and whispered to Charles not to say anything else about the deaths.

Of course, I received an exasperated sigh and, "Why not?"

Instead of answering, I leaned back and turned to the newcomers. "Hey, Scott, Tim."

The men glanced my direction, started to speak, but I could tell they didn't recognize me.

"I'm Chris, Chief LaMond introduced us the other day on the side of the street."

"Oh yeah," Tim said. "You're the old guy she teased about walking to the County Park."

"Whoa, Tim, Chris ain't that old."

Thank you, Scott, I thought.

Tim said, "Yeah, you said that because you're nearly as old as Chris."

Charles had enough age talk. "Tim, Scott, I'm Charles. The other guy here is Virgil. Nice meeting you."

Virgil smiled at the newcomers, and said, "Want a drink? We're buying."

"Sure," Tim said.

Virgil motioned the bartender over and told her to put Tim and Scott's drinks on "our" tab.

She left to get their drinks, and Charles said, "You two are working on the new house out West Ashley?"

Scott said, "Umm, yes. How'd you know?"

"Chris and I were out there when the lady, what's her name, Chris?"

"Shelly," I said, knowing Charles knew her name.

"Yeah, Shelly. We were there when she was killed."

Scott said, "What do you mean killed?"

"I hear someone pushed her off the roof."

"No way. Everyone working out there knows she slipped. Tragic accident, nothing more."

Charles said, "That right, Tim?"

"Makes sense. That roof has a dangerous pitch to it. Easy to slip. So sad."

Virgil must've felt left out, he pointed his drink at the newcomers, then said, "I hear her husband may've had something to do with her death."

Scott said, "Don't know about that, but I'll tell you he's a damned prick."

"I agree," Charles said. "We just had supper with him."

"Oh," Scott said. "He a friend of yours?"

"Just met him. What about the foreman. Think he was murdered?"

"Nah," Scott said. "Another unfortunate accident."

Virgil said, "What do you think, Tim?"

"Have no reason to think it wasn't an accident. It is getting to me, though."

Charles said, "What is?"

"Starting to scare me to go to work there. Two accidents in less than a week. Two dead coworkers. Not that I believe it, you know, but someone out there told me there's something wrong with the house. Cursed," he said.

Charles said, "Who said it was cursed?"

"Don't recall, for sure. There's a lot of talk going around. Guys are starting to think who's next? Damned scary."

Scott said, "Foolish talk. You're young, you'll learn some day that things happen. Don't need no reason. No such thing as cursed houses."

"Hope you're right," Tim said. "Enough house talk. You guys come here often?"

"Occasionally," Charles said. "You two live over this way?"

"Not far off-island," Scott said.

Tim said, "James island. Little farther away than Scott. How about you guys?"

We each told them versions of living on Folly. They then asked what we did. We answered and I figured they were tired of talking about the deaths and the cursed house. They finished their beers and I thought they were going to order another, but instead, Scott said they'd better be going.

After they left, Virgil returned to his question to Charles, the one about how he figured the husband was the killer. Charles outlined his weak case against Raymond. Virgil must have thought it was as weak as I did.

He said, "Sounds possible."

Charles stared at him. "He did it. Mark my words."

Virgil said, "Sure it isn't because the house is cursed?"

"Of course, it isn't, unless you count it's cursed by a murderer running around bumping off workers."

"Suppose it's up to us to find out what kind of curse," Virgil said.

Charles said, "You bet."

I changed the subject, and the deaths weren't mentioned again. At least, not tonight.

19

After having supper with Raymond Whitley, then talking with Scott Rawlins and Tim Hale at Planet Follywood, I didn't have a better idea what'd happened to Shelly Whitley and Randy Lee than I had before the evening. Charles, often quick to jump to conclusions, claimed Raymond had killed both his wife and Randy based on the financial gain he may achieve. The problem with that theory is that it may be a reason for Raymond to have killed Shelly but doesn't explain Randy's death. Money, of course, was often a motive for murder, but it seemed to me there was one significant flaw in that thinking about Shelly, and the same being true about Randy's death. There was no proof that either person had been murdered. I wasn't a judge or jury, but it seemed like that would be a hole large enough to float the aircraft carrier Yorktown through in the prosecution of anyone for murder.

With my mind focused on the lack of proof, I realized it'd been several days since I talked to Barb Deanelli, the lady I'd been dating the last few years.

I couldn't solve whatever was going on with the deaths, but I could do something about talking with Barb. She owned Barb's Books, a used bookstore located on Center Street. The mild August weather was hanging around, so the three-block walk to the store would let me see Barb, plus would give me some exercise.

The tingling of the bell over the entry door announced my arrival at the attractive, neat, and welcoming bookstore. Barb wasn't behind the counter and it took a few seconds before she stepped out of the small office behind the sales area. Barb was four years younger than me, my height, and thinner—much thinner.

"Hello, stranger. I figured you'd run off with a young, sexy chickadee."

I smiled. "You're describing yourself. Why would I want to run off with someone else?"

She returned my smile. "You've been hanging around some of your friends too long. The ones who have trouble recognizing the truth. Anyway, what brings you in this morning? I know it's not to buy a book."

"To see you. You're right, it's been a while and I wanted to rectify that situation."

"Could I entice you with a cup of coffee?"

"Absolutely."

I followed Barb to the well-appointed, professional appearing office which could pass for an attorney's office, which made sense since she'd been a successful attorney in Pennsylvania prior to moving to Folly. She fixed each of us a cup of coffee before moving her chair close to the door so she could keep an eye on arriving customers.

She took a sip of her drink then said, "Anything exciting going on in the life of a retiree?"

"Did you hear about a construction worker falling off a roof at a construction site out West Ashley Avenue?"

"I'd be an abject failure and humiliated as a Folly resident if I hadn't heard of it. Why?"

"Charles and I were walking by the house when it happened."

She frowned. "Why does that not surprise me? Did you happen to be by the same house a few days later when another worker was electrocuted?"

"No."

"I'm shocked, no pun intended. How did that slip past you and your friend?"

I shrugged and smiled. "It happened past my bedtime."

She took another sip, looked toward the front of the store, then said, "I heard a couple of things about the deaths. Someone said they suspected foul play, but most people figure they were accidents. Let me guess. Charles thinks they were murdered?"

"Why think that?"

"Simple. Charles thinks all deaths that happen in the 29439 ZIP Code are murders."

"You can add these two to the list."

"Do you agree?"

"I'm not nearly as certain as Charles, but they appear suspicious."

"Why?"

I shared what'd been said about Shelly's husband's desire to benefit financially and how Randy was a licensed electrician and how unlikely it seemed he would make such a fatal mistake around electricity. I also said it struck me as suspicious that the deaths came so close together considering the small number of overall employees on the job.

Barb listened patiently, something I wasn't used to from my friends, took another sip, then said, "If I was still an attorney defending someone accused of killing those two people, I'd shred those arguments quicker than a wood chipper can shred a twig."

"I don't disagree. All I'm saying is it appears suspicious."

"What do the police think?"

The doorbell stepped on an answer.

"Hold that answer. I'll be back."

Three minutes later, she returned, shook her head, and said, "She wanted two books on this week's bestseller list. I didn't have either. Said she'll have to order them online."

"Sorry. What was your question again?"

"What do the police think about the deaths?"

"They're leaning toward accidental."

"And they have the resources to investigate, collect evidence, analyze items that may give them clues to what happened."

I knew where she was going with her well-constructed reasons for me to leave it to the law enforcement authorities.

"Yes."

"Do you have anything, anything remotely applicable, indicating the police are wrong?"

I started to tell her about Brad Burton's suspicions but decided this wasn't the appropriate time to bring him up. She knew my history with the former detective.

"You're right."

She chuckled. "Of course, I am."

"You said you'd heard a couple of things about the deaths. What was the other thing?"

"You do listen. I'm impressed. There's a story going around that the job site, or the house that's being built, is jinxed or cursed."

"Who said that?"

"Heard it from three customers, but it could be that only one person is saying it and the others are simply repeating the rumor."

"Do they really believe it's cursed?"

"Two of them laughed it off. The other one said she's certain it's true."

"Based on what?"

"No idea. I didn't ask. I'm not a believer in cursed buildings." She smiled. "If I was, I never would have moved into this space your gallery failed in."

"Thanks a lot."

She leaned over and planted a kiss on my cheek, and said, "You're welcome."

The bell over the door chimed.

"I'd better get to work, unlike those of us who spend all their time slaving over retirement."

I walked her to the front of the store and told her I'd talk to her later.

She said, "Great. Try not to get yourself killed."

20

———

On my way home from Barb's Books, a black Dodge Ram pickup truck pulled beside me. The passenger side window rolled down and the driver said, "Hey, stranger, want a ride?"

The driver wasn't a stranger. I'd met Imani Marshall, aka Noelle Ward, two Christmases ago when she'd been one of the residents in a small, decaying apartment building that'd been torched by an arsonist. She's African American, thin, with a short afro haircut. After the fire, Barb had generously invited Noelle to stay in her condo until she found somewhere to rent.

"Sure," I said and slid in the passenger seat. I hadn't seen her more than twice since she moved out of Barb's unit after staying three months.

She said, "Where're you headed?"

"Home."

She smiled and looked over at me, or I assumed I was the subject of her gaze, although I couldn't tell since she wore oversized sunglasses. "In a hurry to get there?"

"No."

"I'm headed out to the old Coast Guard property. Want to tag along?"

The Lighthouse Inlet Heritage Preserve, commonly called the old Coast Guard property, is at the east end of the island and is one of Folly's most popular attractions. It offers visitors an unobstructed view of the Morris Island Lighthouse that was decommissioned in 1962.

"Sounds good. Seems like forever since I've seen you. How's your new apartment?"

"Perfect, it's the dump I was looking for."

I smiled. "I don't often hear that."

Noelle has a well-paying job with an advertising agency in downtown Charleston but is writing her first novel and wanted to live on Folly so she could become immersed in the environment of a small, barrier island, similar to the imaginary island in Georgia where the novel is set. To get in character, she had gone so far as to purchase a nine-year-old Dodge Ram like her protagonist and moved to an apartment that would be considered by some, meager, or in her words, a dump.

"True."

"Why're you heading to the Preserve?"

"Research. I've got Gabriel slinking around in a large coastal park like the Preserve while he's looking for the bad guys."

"Gabriel is the teenager who told your private eye that he saw bank robbers, but the police didn't believe him."

She turned and faced me again. "Wow! You remembered that after what, two years?"

"A little less than that, but yes, you're the only novelist I know, so I remembered much of what you told me. How's the book coming?"

When we first met, Noelle confided that she was in the process of writing a novel, in fact, that's why she wanted to go by Noelle rather than Imani. She'd told me potential readers were more likely to choose a book if the author was Noelle. I couldn't remember the last time I'd read a novel, so had no reason to doubt her logic.

"Well, I don't think you can call me a novelist until I write a novel.

I'm two-thirds through the draft. All I need to do now is figure out how the PI Gabriel hired is going to catch the bad guys."

"That going to be a problem?"

She laughed. "Nah. I'm an ad writer; spend my workdays making up stuff about products. Surly, I can make up a good ending."

We were approaching the end of East Ashley Avenue where it dead-ended at the entrance to the Preserve and Noelle started looking for somewhere to park. In season, traffic looking for places to park outnumbered legal parking spots and was always a challenge for those wishing to visit the Preserve. We turned around at the end of the street and drove a couple of blocks back Ashley Avenue and pulled off on the sandy berm in front of two houses. The temperature had to be in the upper eighties, and I was beginning to sweat as we walked toward the Preserve. Noelle had to be hotter in her black T-shirt and black jeans, but she didn't mention it. Being in her early thirties probably helped.

We walked past the stanchions blocking unauthorized vehicles from entering the Preserve, when Noelle said, "Heard something about you and your friend, umm, Charles, right?"

"Yes, it's Charles. What'd you hear?"

"You're playing like my imaginary PI and snooping around in the death of those two folks working on a house being built."

"Where'd you hear that?"

"A friend of mine works out there. Name's Mason."

"Mason Ryle?"

"One and the same."

"How do you know him?"

"Ran into him a couple of times at the Crab Shack. We're about the same age so we started talking." She chuckled. "He was doing a little flirting. I figured I'd get some ideas on having a character like him in the book, so I played along."

"You're dating?"

She tilted her head left and then right. "He thinks so, but not really."

In the spirit of Charles, I said, "What's that mean?"

"I've met him a few more times at the Crab Shack and at Rita's. Had a couple of drinks, that's all. Never left the restaurants with him if you know what I mean. He thinks he's a lot more charming than he is. More smarm than charm. He'll be perfect as a character in my book."

That sounded like the Mason I'd heard about who'd hit on Shelly.

"What'd he say about us other than we'd been snooping around?"

She stopped, looked off to the right, and said, "Let's go that way."

I followed her down a narrow path headed toward the ocean. I was going to repeat my question, when she said, "Mason said you and Charles were at the job site when the lady fell, then you'd been talking to the foreman, don't know his name, but he was the guy who died a few days after the lady."

"Randy Lee."

"Sounds right. Mason also said you'd talked to one of his coworkers with a girlfriend named Zellner. I don't remember the guy's name but remembered hers because it's a horrible name. Guess it's the ad copy writer in me, but I wouldn't use names like it in my book."

"His name's Kyle."

"That's a better name. Mason said a couple of the others said you'd talked to them. Seems that none of them liked you butting into their business."

"Did Mason say why it bothered them?"

She nodded. "He said it looked like you were thinking the deaths weren't accidents, like the police said."

"So, why'd that bother them? Wouldn't they want to know if someone killed two of their coworkers? Wouldn't they want the murderer caught?"

We'd reached where the path opened to a wide, sandy beach. Noelle looked each direction and stared at the ocean as if she were taking a mental picture.

"Is this what you came to see?"

"Yes. Got a perfect scene in the book for this spot."

"Good," I said, not knowing what else to say.

She removed her sunglasses and wiped sweat off her forehead then returned the glasses to her face. "Seems to me the guys don't want you looking into what happened out there because one of them, or maybe more than one of them, may've been involved in the deaths." She shook her head. "Mind you, I've got a vivid imagination, and I could be looking at it from the point of view of someone trying to create a mystery where there's not one."

"So could Charles and I." *Especially Charles*, I thought.

She tapped me on the arm. "I know from experience, if there's a killer out there, a real one, not one in my imagination, you and your buddy will figure it out."

"I don't know about that."

She chuckled, took a couple of photos of the beach with her cell phone, and said, "Yes you do. I told you so. Ready to head back to the big city?"

"Whenever you are. I'm just tagging along."

As we walked back to her truck, she said, "Seen Barb lately?"

"I was coming from her store when you kidnapped me."

"Hum, there's a plot in there somewhere. Maybe that'll be in my second novel."

"Good."

She unlocked the truck's doors, shook her head, and said, "Suppose I have to write the first one before I start talking about the second book."

She pulled in my drive, turned to me, and said, "If I can offer a suggestion, be careful out there. My extensive research on killers says if someone kills two people, killing number three comes pretty easy."

21

———

I'd managed to push the deaths to the back of my mind and was enjoying a peaceful meal at Snapper Jack's Seafood Restaurant and Bar until I noticed Scott Rawlins at a table at the far side of the room seated with someone who looked vaguely familiar. Scott looked my way, smiled, then gave a tentative wave. I returned the smile and nodded at him.

I'd refocused my attention back to my food and was gazing at the television above the backbar when Scott approached.

I smiled and said, "Scott."

"Thought that was you," he said as we shook hands. "Heard anything more about the deaths at our construction site?"

"No," I said thinking it was a strange question to ask someone he barely knew. "Why, did something else happen?"

"No, nothing like that. Mason and I were talking about it, so it was on my mind."

I looked at Scott's dinner companion, and it dawned on me where I'd seen him. "Is that Mason Ryle?"

"Yeah. We were putting in overtime and finished after everyone else, so thought we'd grab a bite before heading home." He looked over his shoulder at Mason before turning back to me. "You sure you haven't heard anything new about the deaths?"

Even if I had, it wouldn't have been a good idea to share it with Scott or any of the other workers who might've had something to do with the deaths.

"No," I said for the second time. "Why do you ask?"

"Nothing really. We were talking about how weird it was that two of the crew died so close together. Mason thinks there's some sort of curse on the house. He's not the only one. One of the other guys don't think it's the house but something about the old house that was on the property."

The curse on the house had been mentioned but this was the first time I'd heard about the previous house.

"Who mentioned the old house?"

"Don't recall. Could've been Lucius Walker."

"Why Lucius?"

Scott chuckled. "He's shared ghost stories with some of us. Think he believes in that kind of crap. I don't." He again looked back at his table. "Don't want to interrupt your meal. Better get back to my food. Good talking to you."

We shared a couple more pleasantries before he returned to his meal with Mason. My peaceful meal of not thinking about the deaths had ended. This was what, the second or third time someone had brought up the house being cursed? I didn't believe in curses, but at this point, it made as much sense as two fatal accidents at the house under construction. What was I missing?

I finished my meal as Scott and Mason headed to the exit where they went opposite directions. I wasn't far behind and nearly collided with Mason.

"Sorry," I said. "Wasn't paying attention to where I was going."

"No biggie, happens all the time at work."

"You're Mason Ryle?"

"Yeah, and you're Chris Landry. Scott and me were talking about you in there." He pointed his thumb to the restaurant we just left.

"Chris Landrum," I corrected. "Something good, I hope."

He shrugged. Not a good sign about what they were saying about me.

His shrug appeared to be the end of his comments, so I said, "I remember seeing you at your worksite the day Shelly Whitley fell."

"Bad day."

I waited for more, but he stopped and stared at me. Foot traffic was heavy on Center Street, so I inched around the corner to the side of the restaurant to get out of the way of a group of vacationers waiting for the traffic light to change so they could cross Ashley Avenue. Mason didn't say anything but did come with me.

I said, "Noelle Ward, a friend of mine, told me she knows you."

He came close to smiling but failed. "Yeah, we're dating. How do you know her?"

Not her version of their relationship, but I wasn't about to challenge him. "We met a couple of years ago. I met her after her apartment building burned."

His gaze narrowed. "So, it's true what they say about you."

I smiled hoping to receive a similar response from him. "Depends on what they say."

"You're a busybody, nosing in other people's business." His gaze turned to a stare.

How do I respond?

"I don't know what you're referring to."

"Word around the job is you're butting in, trying to talk to all us guys. Throwing accusations around that instead of accidents causing Shelly and Randy's deaths, you're stirring up rumors they were murdered." His hands balled into fists. "Then you're saying they were not only murdered, but one of the crew, one of us, did it."

"I don't know who's saying that, but I'm doing no such thing. I do know some people, even a police officer or two, who are thinking the deaths look like too big a coincidence to be accidents."

"You saying you don't have a reputation around town as being the busybody who caught the guy who left a body in a boat a few months back?"

"I'm not denying that. All I'm saying is I have no reason to think the deaths on your job site are anything other than accidents. If they weren't accidents, I have faith the police will figure out what happened. If it turns out the workers were murdered, the person or persons responsible will be caught."

He pointed a finger in my face, took a deep breath, and said, "I'm telling you one thing, it's none of your damn business what happened and I'm not the only person thinking that. You can call it whatever you want, but don't be nosing around any of us." He stomped his foot on the pavement, turned, and left me staring at his back as he headed west on Ashley Avenue.

22

What brought that on? I was clueless, but if nothing else, it piqued my interest in learning more about what was going on with the guys working on the new house. If Mason's goal was to get me to, as he said, stop nosing around the construction workers, he'd failed—failed badly. If anything, I was more determined than ever to find out what was going on.

It was still early, so I decided walking up Center Street would either help me get my mind off the strange conversation with Mason or change my focus enough to allow some incredible insight into the deaths to reach my consciousness. I also smiled to myself when I realized the true reason was to enjoy the walk.

Charles wasn't with me, so I didn't have to stop and converse with each canine I encountered. Three blocks later, I'd crossed Center Street and was in front of Woody's Pizza and surprised to see Brad Burton on the restaurant's deck leaning against the railing separating it from the sidewalk. Brad was by far the oldest of the dozen or so patrons huddled on the deck and looked as out of place as a Chihuahua in a horse show. He was drinking a Palmetto Amber Ale while staring at the street like he was watching a movie.

"Hey, Brad," I said as I stepped on the deck and moved beside him.

"Oh, hi. Have a slice."

One slice of what appeared to be a pepperoni pizza and remnants of two other slices were on a plate in front of him and a glob of tomato sauce on the front of his 1988 Cooper River Bridge Run T-shirt that was stretched to the limit around his midsection. I'd wager my house he'd not participated in the 1988 or any other 10-kilometer bridge run.

"Thanks, but I had supper at Snapper Jack's. Did Hazel throw you out?"

He laughed. "Not this time. She's gone to Charleston with a friend. They're having supper at Peninsula Grille, and I'm having an exquisite meal at Woody's. Sure you don't want this slice? I need it like I need an IRS audit."

I again declined but was glad to see he was in a relaxed, talkative mood, something I'd seldom, if ever seen from him.

"Know what I was thinking about when you walked up?"

The small area was getting more crowded the longer we talked. It'd be nice to move somewhere where we could hear each other better, but Brad appeared glued to the stool he was perched on.

"No, but I noticed you were staring off into space like something was on your mind."

"Was thinking about what Hazel said about me needing a hobby. I think I told you the hobby wasn't for me, but to get me out of the house."

"Yes, you shared that. Decided on one?"

"Chris, I spent more years being a cop than I'd like to admit. Never got into golf, or playing cards, or bowling, or, hell, anything else that'd be considered a hobby." He took a sip, looked at the uneaten slice of pizza, then back at me. "All I know is police work."

The crowd noise made it difficult hearing everything he said, but I didn't detect him mentioning a hobby he wanted to pursue.

"I can understand that. So, what—"

He pointed the beer bottle at me and said, "I've been thinking that since all I know is being a cop, why not use some of those skills looking at the deaths out at that new house?"

That was the last thing I'd expected him to say, and it left me momentarily without a response. After all, I couldn't count the times Brad had berated me for sticking my nose in police work, rudely reminding me police business is for the police, not some busybody civilian.

"When you were a detective, you accused me of meddling in police business, pointed out it was not my business, and more. Isn't that what you're talking about doing?"

He gave me what I call a police stare, or in this case, a former police stare. I was afraid he would erupt and revert to the old cop he'd been. I rationalized that he probably wouldn't yell at me on the crowded patio. On the other hand, with the sound level as high as it was, I doubt anyone would notice if he did.

Instead of yelling, he looked around, finished his drink, and said, "Up for a walk? If I sit here longer, I'll eat this slice and regret it in the morning."

"Sure."

I followed him off the deck and another block up Center Street to the Folly Beach branch of the Charleston County Public Library where he pointed to a bench by the front door. The library was closed so this would be a quiet a spot for us to talk.

"Chris," he said, as I joined him on the bench, "I'm not talking about going Rambo and trying to catch the bad guys. I don't even know if there are bad guys. But after decades on the job, I've learned enough to tell when someone is trying to pull something over on me, or to see patterns where most civilians wouldn't. Some of that could possibly assist the police." He stared across the street at Our Lady of Good Counsel Catholic Church.

I didn't want to point out that wasn't much different than what I'd been berated for, so I said, "There's no doubt you were an outstanding detective, and could provide valuable assistance, but is that what you really want to do as a hobby?"

He smiled. "I haven't forgotten how I almost arrested you the first time we met, or how I accused you of doing exactly what I'm suggesting on more than one occasion. I also know you think I was slovenly in performing my duties during that time."

"That's not—"

He no longer had a beer bottle to point at me; instead, he held his hand in front of my face, palm facing me. "In hindsight, you were right. Those last years, I was going through the motions, nothing more. If I'd been my boss, I would've fired me." He again looked at the church. "When we were in your kitchen, I said it seemed strange that there were two deaths at that house mere days apart. I think I shared that if I'd investigated what'd happened when I was working, it'd keep me awake at night." He again hesitated.

"Is it bothering you now?"

"A bunch. Remember when we saw Randy Lee at Cal's?"

I nodded.

"He said something about how one of the other guys had been acting strange after the woman's death."

"Mason Ryle," I said, since he was fresh on my mind after my confrontation with him earlier tonight.

"Yeah, Ryle."

"Randy also said the woman's husband came around threatening to sue over her death."

"Yes."

"I also remember saying that night that it didn't appear to be unusual enough to classify the death anything other than an accident."

"Yes, but—"

"That's what I would've said my last few years on the job. I was stuck with several murders, pressured to wrap them up as fast as possible. Her death would've been easy to close as an accident. One less case to worry about."

"That's what the police are saying now."

"I understand where they're coming from, but now we have Randy's electrocution. Chris, it doesn't compute."

"I mentioned earlier that I had supper at Snapper Jack's. Two of the guys from the construction site, Mason Ryle and Scott Rawlins, were there. I'd never met Mason, Scott came to my table to say hi and told me who he was with, so I introduced myself after we'd finished eating and were out on the street. Scott had already gone, so I was standing with Mason. I didn't ask him anything about what'd happened at the house, but he suddenly turned borderline hostile. He accused me of butting into the business of some of the construction workers and claiming the two deaths weren't accidents. I'm not certain why, but he was angry."

Brad smiled. "Sounds familiar."

I returned his smile. "True, but he then came close to threatening me to stay away from them. The point is, even if I were butting in, why would Mason have reacted so strongly?"

"I'm no expert on the topic but have faced countless hostile suspects. I'm no shrink, but my antenna told me the ones who get the most hostile are often guilty. Is there any reason you know of to accuse Mason of the deaths?"

"Nothing you'd call evidence. We've heard he'd hit on Shelly only to be rejected. Plus, Randy said Mason was acting strange after Shelly's death. Finally, Mason was one of the two guys who found Randy's body, although that could've been a coincidence."

"That's all pretty sketchy; nothing I could hang an arrest on."

"True."

"It's a start," he said and looked at his watch. "I'd better head home. Wouldn't want Hazel thinking my new hobby was barhopping."

"That'd definitely get you out of the house."

He smiled and said, "Out of the house and into the doghouse." He stood to leave, turned to me, and added, "Tell you what. Why don't you let me know if you hear anything that could get us off sketchy and closer to an arrest?"

I said I would and watched him amble down Center Street.

A while back, I'd gotten to know a Wiccan family that'd moved to

Folly. Their sixteen-year-old son Desmond and his dog had saved Charles's and my life. After that, Desmond told me he'd bet I never thought I'd be friends with a witch. That paled in comparison to having Brad Burton as a friend.

23

———————

My day began with the sun gazing through the slats in my bedroom shades and Charles on the phone saying, "Guess who I ran into last night?"

"The President of Botswana," I said, suspecting I was wrong.

"You're a sucky guesser."

"Who?"

"You."

"You ran into me?"

"No, you're the sucky guesser."

I wiped sleep out of my eyes, sighed louder than I should have, and said, "Who did you run into last night?'

"Thought you'd never ask. Tim Hale."

It took me a few seconds to remember who that was. I blamed it on still being asleep. "And you're calling before seven a.m. to tell me because?"

"Splash water on your face, wake up, before you head to the Dog, and I'll answer your question."

I hung up on him.

Twenty minutes later, I was sitting at a table in the Dog and staring at Charles stuffing a half-slice of toast in his mouth while shaking his head in disgust at me for taking, in his words, *two hours* to get there. Amber had wisely handed me a mug of coffee before I reached the table and asked if I wanted my normal breakfast. I told her of course. She sighed, but not as loud as I had on the phone with Charles and went to place my order.

"Where did you run into Tim Hale?" I asked to move our conversation past me being Charles-late.

"I was minding my own business sitting at an outside table at the Crab Shack enjoying the music. I saw Tim, remember, we talked to him and Scott at Planet Follywood?"

"Yes."

"Well, I went over to say howdy."

I had trouble getting past Charles claiming he was minding his own business, but it wouldn't do any good saying anything about it, so I said, "Was he by himself?"

"Was until I said howdy. He didn't argue when I invited myself to join him. He was a little standoffish at first. Normal, I suppose since he'd only seen me once. Anyway, I told him again how sorry I was for the loss of his coworkers."

"What'd he say?"

"He'd miss Shelly."

"Did you mention you thought she was murdered?"

"Nah, I didn't want him to think I was accusing him. Think I said she slipped."

"Were they close?"

"Don't think so. Didn't ask, but when he was talking about her, umm, accident, he didn't tear up. He did say her husband was a jerk, but we already knew that."

Amber slipped my French toast in front of me and refilled my mug. She asked if we needed anything else. Charles said he was okay.

I said I was fine and after she headed to the next table, I said, "What'd he say about Randy Lee's death?"

"He was more emotional about that than what happened to Shelly. Guess Randy hired Tim when they started building the house."

"Did he think anything was suspicious about the deaths being close together?"

Charles smiled. "Yep, thinks the house is cursed. Think he told us that at Follywood. Think he's afraid to work there."

"Did he say he was afraid?"

"Said he'd quit the job if he didn't need the money."

That's two or three workers who've said the house was cursed.

"Why does he think it's cursed?"

"Told me he grew up in the Lowcountry, not far from here. Told me he wasn't sure but had heard Charleston and the surrounding area has the most hauntings anywhere in the country. Don't know about that, but he believes it." Charles chuckled. "Think I could've said boo and he would've jumped out of his britches."

"I know Charleston is saturated with ghost tours, but why would a house under construction have ghosts or a curse on it?"

"There's still hope for you as a private detective. I asked him the same question."

"What'd he say?"

"He didn't know."

I took a sip of coffee then smiled. "Takes a mighty good private detective to get that much information out of him."

"Smartass."

"Yep."

I felt someone pat me on the shoulder.

"You talking about me?"

"Hey, Virgil," Charles said. "Why would we be talking about you?"

"Heard you say smartass, so I came to mind."

I laughed. "Not this time. Care to join us?"

"Hoped you'd ask." He took a seat and waved for Amber.

"Morning, Virgil," she said. "Coffee?"

"Miss Amber, you bringing me a cup of your fabulous elixir would make my day."

Maybe Charles's smartass comment referred to Virgil after all.

She left to conjure up his elixir and Virgil said, "Still think Shelly's evil husband killed her now that the other guy bit the dust?"

Charles said, "What do you think?"

"Course I'm not as good a detective as you two but did until what's his name got himself killed. Now, don't know. Either of you know Mitchell Baldwin?"

"Carpenter on the house," I said.

Virgil said, "That's the one."

Charles said, "I already forgot about him. You're the one with the bad memory. How'd you remember him?"

"I wouldn't have if Dude hadn't called him Mitchell Piano."

Virgil took off his sunglasses, a rare event, rubbed his eyes, returned the glasses to their rightful place, then said, "What are you two talking about?"

I said, "It's not important. What about Mitchell?"

"I was at Loggerhead's last night, enjoying a brewski. Abel bought it for me, generous guy."

Charles, of course, couldn't let that bit of trivia go. "Who's Abel?"

"That's not the important part of my story. Abel had to get home to his wife and his Pekinese pup, so I was—"

Charles interrupted, "What's the pup's name?"

Virgil pointed his mug at Charles. "Still not the important part of my story."

Charles said, "Continue."

"Thanks. Anyway, Mitchell plopped down on the stool Abel vacated to go home to his pup, the one I don't know the name of." He turned and looked at Charles.

"Did Mitchell have anything to say about the deaths?" I said, hoping to drag the conversation back to something more interesting than the name of a dog none of us had seen.

"Mitchell's not a big talker. Charles, he's in his early twenties so he might not have enough accumulated in all his years to have much to say. I had to use all my interrogation skills you taught me to get anything out of him."

Charles smiled like Virgil had awarded him a gold medal for private detecting, and said, "Got an answer to Chris's question?"

"I'm getting there."

His arrival would have to wait a few minutes longer. Amber returned with Virgil's elixir, aka coffee, and asked if he wanted anything to eat. He looked over at me and shrugged, his way of asking if I was buying. I nodded, he told her a breakfast burrito, and she left to seat a couple who were waiting by the door.

Charles said, "Virgil—"

"I know, I know," Virgil interrupted. "Mitchell said the crew was getting antsy. None of them could come up with a story from another job they worked on where someone got killed at work, much less, two people. Said the owner of the construction company has been on the job site nearly every day since Randy was killed. He's trying to hold everything together; can't lose more workers."

"Does Mitchell think the deaths were accidents?"

"Said he wants to but wondered what the odds were on that happening. Heck, there were only a couple of handfuls of workers on the job. That's, umm, let's see, two out of, anyway, a good percentage of the entire work force out there."

Charles said, "If they weren't accidents, does he have an idea who may be responsible?"

"Nothing I'd call a big clue. He can't see any reason one person would've killed both workers. Said they weren't close, didn't wave any red flags. But he couldn't figure out why two people would've killed them, especially on the same job."

Charles said, "He say anything about the crew thinking the house was cursed?"

"Said some of them believed it, but he doesn't believe in cursed houses, so he thinks the guys who do are full of crap."

Virgil's burrito arrived which ended any significant discussion about the deaths, assuming anything he'd said before was significant. I wouldn't wager much on it.

24

After our less-than-informative breakfast with Virgil, Charles and I walked to the end of the Folly Pier. I said it was to get exercise to work-off the needless calories I stuffed in my mouth at breakfast; Charles said it was to ponder what we'd learned and to figure out what was going on at the house under construction.

We'd commandeered one of the blue tables near the Atlantic end of the structure, when Charles said, "Did Virgil tell us anything about the deaths we didn't already know other than he couldn't calculate the percent of workers on the job that'd been killed?"

"The guys are getting antsy and more appear to think the house is cursed."

"All but Mitchell, the skeptic."

"Let's try this again. Did we learn anything other than the far-fetched idea that the house is cursed?"

"The owner of the construction company has been there more than he was before the deaths. Think it means anything?"

I said, "I don't know what. My understanding is he has more than the West Ashley house under construction, so he'd be at the other job sites at different times."

"Yeah, but—"

The distinct siren of one of Folly's fire engines interrupted Charles. We couldn't see where it was going from our vantage point, but it sounded like it turned west on either Ashley or Arctic Avenue.

Charles laughed then said, "Guess they're heading to another death at the construction site." He then air quoted. "Accidental death."

I didn't see humor in his comment. A police patrol car followed the fire engine.

"Charles, that's nothing to joke about."

"You're right. Want to check it out?"

"If they're on Ashley, they could be going two miles to the end of the road. You ready to walk that far?"

"Putting it that way, no way. Stop avoiding my question, what'd we learn from Virgil that'll help us figure out who killed the workers?"

I thought we'd covered it already but knew he had something on his mind, or he wouldn't have brought it up again.

"Charles, what do you think Virgil said that'd help?"

"Heck if I know."

Okay, maybe he didn't have anything on his mind, something he'd been accused of more times than I can count.

Other than three seagulls on the top of the structure's roof arguing about something, the next sound I heard was the approaching siren of an ambulance coming toward us on Center Street. It then turned west on one of the perpendicular streets.

Charles looked in the direction the ambulance had gone, turned to me, and said, "Now, ready to see what's going on?"

"It could be going miles."

"Okay, here's a plan. Let's walk up the beach, let's say, umm, to where Shelly fell off the roof. If all the commotion isn't happening there, we can head back."

That I could manage. "What're we waiting for?"

We worked our way from the Pier to the beach and traipsed west. There was no sign of emergency vehicles, smoke, or any other indication anything was wrong, that was until the construction site came into view.

Two guys wearing hardhats were being escorted to the edge of the property by one of Folly's Public Safety Officers, while at the side of the house, three firefighters were standing beside a red forklift. The object of their attention appeared between the forklift and the house.

Charles stopped and said, "You're right, I shouldn't have teased about another death out here."

"We don't know anyone is dead. Construction accidents happen all the time. The forklift could've run over someone's foot."

Two more construction workers appeared and were escorted to where the first two were standing. I recognized the latest arrivals as Kyle Manger and Tim Hale. The other two were facing the house so I couldn't tell who they were.

Charles said, "Are you going to stand here all day or go see whose foot got run over, or worse?"

He didn't wait for my answer. He started up the steps leading from the beach to the patio when Officer Rodney New intercepted him. He waited for me to catch up with Charles.

"Guys, please don't tell me you were walking on the beach, minding your own business, and got to this spot for the second time when something happened at this house."

"Rodney," I said, "we were on the Pier when we heard the sirens."

Charles interrupted, "I wanted to make sure nothing bad happened out here. We know a few of the workers and were concerned about them."

"Un, huh, sure, Charles," muttered the leery police officer.

I stepped between Rodney and Charles, if for no other reason, so he wouldn't kick us off the property before we found out what'd happened.

"Rodney, another accident?"

He shook his head, looked back at the forklift, and said, "Only if you think the forklift started on its own, put itself in reverse, and pinned a man between it and the wall."

Charles said, "Is he dead?"

Rodney again looked back toward the forklift, where two paramedics were lifting a stretcher and sliding it in the back of their ambulance, then turned to us. "No, but he's in bad shape. I'll be surprised if he makes it."

I said, "Do you know who it is?"

"Not sure. Heard one of the workers say Mason."

Charles said, "Mason Ryle?"

"Don't know, just heard Mason."

"Anyone see it happen?" I asked.

"You mean other than the person on the forklift?"

I nodded.

"I haven't talked to any of the workers over there with our guys. My understanding is they were off-site having lunch and when they got back, they found Mason behind the forklift."

Out of the corner of my eye, I saw Chief Cindy LaMond beside the forklift looking in our direction. She said something to one of her firefighters and headed our way. Her expression was far from *glad to see you*.

"Officer New," Chief LaMond said, "go help the guys with the workers. I'll take care of these two."

Rodney headed to the gathered workers and Cindy focused on Charles and me.

"Mr. Landrum, Mr. Fowler, what in hell are you doing here?"

The only time she refers to us by our last names is when she's irritated or angry.

"Chief," Charles said, "we know some of the workers and when we heard your emergency vehicles headed this way, we wandered over to see if there was anything we could do to help."

"Touching," she said, "although I know that's a load of crap."

I said, "What happened?"

"Don't know for certain. One thing I do know, it wasn't an accident like the other deaths on this property."

Charles said, "You mean three non-accidents. Like as in murders."

Cindy glared at him, took one step closer to the two of us, and said, "Gentlemen, as I see it, I have two choices. I could arrest you for trespassing and pissing off a police chief, or I could politely ask you to shuffle down those stairs, savor the ocean breeze, and get your butts back to the center of town. Which choice do you think I should make?"

Charles said, "Chief LaMond, we'd love to stay and continue this cheery conversation, but Chris and I have to get, umm, somewhere. Don't want to be late."

"Wise choice, Mr. Fowler."

After we *shuffled* down the stairs, Charles looked at the house and said, "What time you think we ought to meet at Loggerhead's?"

"Silly me. I didn't even know we were meeting there."

"Who's there most every night?"

I could name several regulars, then the "correct" answer came to me. "Kyle Manger."

Charles smiled. "Gold star for aspiring detective Chris."

"Seven."

"Seven what?"

"Pay attention to your questions. That's when we're meeting at Loggers."

25

———————

I arrived at Loggerhead's at six-thirty knowing Charles would already be there or arriving any second. The temperature was in the low eighties with a cloudless sky; the patio packed. While I didn't see always-early Charles, I found Kyle Manger leaning against the patio's railing staring at the beer in his hand. I maneuvered around a large group of young people I assumed to be college students since several were wearing University of Georgia T-shirts.

Kyle was still staring at his beer like it was the most fascinating thing he'd ever seen as I inched closer. He was still wearing his Donnelly Plumbing shirt and the dirt on his jeans made me think he'd been working under the house.

"Hey, Kyle."

That jarred him out of his trance. "Oh, hi, umm, hi."

"Chris."

"Sorry, I knew that. This has been one hell of a day."

"You okay?"

"Will be. I'm a lot better than Mason."

"My friend and I were out by the construction site today when all the commotion was going on. All we heard was a worker was injured. Was that Mason?"

"Thought it was you out there. Yeah, Mason Ryle was the—"

"Hi, Kyle," Charles said as he barged between us interrupting whatever Kyle was going to tell me.

"Kyle," I said, "you remember Charles?"

"Sure. Weren't you with Chris at the job site today?"

"Yeah," Charles said. "What happened?"

Kendra, one of the servers I'd known for a couple of years, patted me on the arm. "Chris, can I get you something to drink?"

Charles interrupted before I answered. "Kyle, you had supper?"

"No."

"Want to more join Chris and me? Chris is buying."

"Sure, why not."

After Charles's generous invitation, I ordered a glass of white wine, Charles a beer, and an even more generous Charles ordered another beer for Kyle. Kendra said she'd get our names on the list for a table and headed to the bar to get our drinks.

Charles said, "Kyle, you were telling us what happened."

"Like I told Chris, Mason Ryle was hurt, hurt bad, when the forklift backed up pinning him between the machine and the wall."

"That's horrible," Charles said like he hadn't already heard the same thing from Officer New. "How'd it happen? Don't those machines start beeping when they're backing up so anyone behind them can get out of the way?"

"Don't know what happened. The rest of the guys and I were off having lunch. And yes, they're not required, but the forklift out there has one of those irritating alarms beeping whenever it backs up."

I said, "Did anyone see the accident?"

"Someone must've."

"Who?" Charles said.

"Whoever was driving the forklift. It didn't back up on its own."

"Who was driving it?"

"Don't know."

Charles said, "You don't think it was an accident?"

"Don't see how it could've been."

Faux detective Charles said, "Did someone out there have a beef with Mason?"

"I wasn't close to him since we worked for different companies. He didn't strike me as the most likable fellow, but I don't know anyone who." He hesitated, snapped his fingers, and continued, "Shelly's husband was pissed with him."

"Because he'd been harassing or flirting with her?"

"Yeah."

Charles said, "Did you see Shelly's husband today?"

"No, but I wasn't near the house over lunch, so he could've been. I usually eat my energy bar with Joshua in his truck, but he wasn't there today. He's the other plumber on the job. This morning was frustrating because of a couple of plumbing issues, so I took a long walk on the beach during lunchtime."

I said, "Have you heard how Mason is?"

He shook his head. "All I know is he was unconscious when they loaded him in the ambulance."

Charles said, "That's too bad. Where was Joshua today?"

"Called in sick. That's why I was having such a hard time with the plumbing. Doing a job needing two guys by myself sucks." He shook his head. "It ain't as bad as getting squashed by a forklift."

Kendra arrived with our drinks, apologized for taking so long saying the bar was backed up, then added that our names were on the list for a table. We thanked her and Charles continued his interrogation.

"How come Mason didn't leave the job site for lunch?"

"He usually eats there. Has one of those big silver lunchboxes, you know, like you see old pictures of coal miners carrying to work. Don't know for sure but guess that's what he did today."

"What about the other guys?"

"Charles, you ask more questions than that damned detective."

"What detective?" Charles said, adding one more question.

"Young guy. Think his name was Fisher. He kept us from getting any work done for two hours, and even then, we couldn't go anywhere near the forklift. Some lab guys combed over the site like they were looking for gold."

Charles repeated, "What about the other guys?"

"What about them."

"What did they do during lunch hour?"

"How would I know. Like I said, I was walking on the beach and didn't see any of the others out there."

I could tell he was getting agitated with Charles, so I said, "Kyle, I know you didn't see where the others were, but we were wondering what they usually did during lunch." I smiled. "Most of us are creatures of habit and do the same thing most days."

Kyle glanced at Charles before turning to me. "Sorry guys, this has been a day for the freakin' record book. It's got me shook."

Charles put his arm on Kyle's shoulder. "I know what you mean. I've had more than one of those days lately. Chris is right about us doing the same stuff every day. What do the other guys normally do during lunch?"

Kyle took a long draw on his new beer, looked over the railing at the parking lot, then turned his attention back to Charles. "Lucius, he's the black guy, doesn't seem to be with any of us more than he has to be. Every couple of weeks, Joe, the company owner, takes a few of us to one of the restaurants for lunch. Lucius always declines to go. That's probably more than you wanted to know. The answer is I don't know where Lucius was."

I said, "Was Joe on-site this morning?"

"I was trying to get the plumbing connected under the house most of the morning, so I don't know if he was there all morning but saw him once when I went to the truck to get PVC couplings. He was talking to Tim and Scott."

Charles said, "What do Tim and Scott usually do for lunch?"

"Umm, let's see, know he doesn't do it every day, but Tim often sits out on the beach. Told me once it reminded him of growing up out that way."

"How about today?"

"He was there when I walked away. Was back at work when I

came back since our lunchtime was over and I was running late getting back. Now Scott's another story."

"Why?" Charles said instead of letting Kyle tell it on his own.

"Ever since Randy Lee got himself electrocuted, Scott's been sucking up to Joe. I haven't heard Scott say it but would put money on him trying to get Joe to make him foreman."

Charles said, "How do you know?"

Kendra returned to tell us our table was ready, so we followed her to a table near the center of the patio. She said it wasn't her table and Ellie would be with us shortly.

Kyle said something about how great the weather was and how much he enjoyed eating outside. I smiled to myself knowing Charles wouldn't let him get distracted that easily.

Charles being Charles, said, "Eating outside is great. So, how do you know Scott wants the job?"

"I like watching people; watching how they interact with each other. Scott follows Joe around like a lonely puppy nearly every time Joe's there. I'd be embarrassed if it were me acting like that. He's always out of money, so the promotion could help. That, plus I overheard him once say something to Joe about how he thought he'd be good at the job."

"That's it?" Charles asked.

A server I hadn't seen before approached our table and asked if we were ready to order. Charles said we were and to put it all on one check. Mine, of course. Charles and I went with chicken fingers and fries. Kyle selected the flounder platter after Charles told him to order anything he wanted before reminding him I was paying.

"Anything else about Scott?" Charles asked after our server headed to the kitchen.

Kyle smiled. "Anyone ever tell you that you ask a lot of questions?"

Anyone ever not tell him that, I wondered.

"Sorry, I'm a curious guy," Charles said, then proved it by repeating, "Anything else about Scott?"

"No."

I said, "Anyone else there this morning?"

Kyle rubbed his chin then said, "Umm, Mitchell was the only other regular there. Luis Ortez was at another job for Argyle and I already told you Joshua was sick."

Charles said, "What does Mitchell usually do at lunchtime?"

"Don't rightly know about every day. I remember one day he grabbed his surfboard off his truck and went surfin'. Said there were boss waves; couldn't pass them up." He chuckled. "Don't know how he works the rest of the day all soggy and salty. Other times, I don't know." He hesitated before continuing, "How come you two are asking about all of us? Seems weird."

"You probably don't know this, but Chris and I have helped the police a time or two solve crimes."

"So, you're playing cop?"

"Not really, simply curious," Charles said. "That's three incidents in what, the last couple of weeks? Don't you think that's strange?"

Kyle sighed. "Yeah, two accidents and someone hurting Mason on purpose."

Charles said, "Ever think if Mason doesn't live it could be three murders?"

"Not really. Who would've wanted to kill three of us? That doesn't make sense."

"That's what we're trying to figure out," Charles said. "If the first two deaths weren't accidents, do you know anyone who would've wanted two and almost three dead?"

"Know what some of the guys think about it?"

I said, "What?"

"The damned house is cursed."

We'd heard that, but it didn't answer Charles's question. I waited to see how long it took for Charles to repeat it.

In less time than it'd take an egg to break while being run over by a semi, Charles said, "Who would've wanted all three dead?"

"No idea."

Our food arrived and remained our focus for a few minutes until Charles said, "Sure you don't know anyone who—"

Kyle pointed his fork at Charles. "Guys, I honestly appreciate this meal and our conversation, but it's been a damned horrible day at work. How about no more talk about it?"

Charles said, "Just a couple more—"

"You're right, Kyle. No more questions."

"Thanks."

26

Cindy LaMond called the next morning interrupting my peaceful first cup of coffee with something I'm certain I'd never heard her say.

"Good morning, Sunshine."

I recognized her voice, but not the sentiment. "You on drugs or hallucinating?"

"That's none of your business. Want to meet me for breakfast? I'm buying."

Now I knew I must be talking to a Cindy impersonator. "Sure, whoever you are. When and where?"

"Now. Blu," she said, and the phone went dead.

Hanging up on me was more like the Cindy LaMond I'd come to love.

Blu was the upscale restaurant in the Tides Hotel. Fifteen minutes later, I was greeted at the hotel by Jay, a friend who works as the hotel's unofficial greeter, bellhop, fount of knowledge about everything Folly that hotel guests might ask about.

"Good morning, Chris," Jay said as he looked at his watch. "Chief LaMond told me to escort you to her table."

"Thanks. I think I can find her on my own."

"She said it wasn't so you don't get lost, it was so you wouldn't scare any of our guests."

Further proof Cindy was back to being Cindy.

"Lead the way."

The Chief was at a small table against the window overlooking the ocean. She greeted me with a smile and slight wave. Jay said he'd leave me in her hands and headed back to the lobby.

"Good morning, Cindy."

"It's not nearly as bad as most of them. Want to know why?"

"Of course."

"Because I'm hiding here rather than my regular breakfast spot at the Dog. Few people would think to look for me in this classy joint."

A middle-aged server arrived with coffee before asking if I was ready to order. I told him Cindy's pancakes looked good and I'd have the same with a side order of bacon.

He went to put in my order and Cindy said, "Sure that's all you want? Remember, I'm buying."

"That's kind of you. What'd I do to deserve such a treat?"

"Not a speck of anything."

Again, that's the Cindy I know. "Thank you anyway."

"Suppose you're wondering why I invited you."

I smiled. "It'd crossed my mind."

"I wanted to apologize for being so cranky with you yesterday at the construction site."

She apologized nearly as often as she bought me a meal.

"That's okay. You know some of my friends, so you know I'm used to being around cranky people."

"I'll pretend you're not comparing me to Bob Howard."

"Never, Cindy. Never."

"Good. That'd really make me cranky."

"Me, too."

"Know why I was so pissed yesterday?"

"Stumbling on Charles and me?"

"That should be it, but it isn't. Hell, I'm used to seeing you two at crime scenes. No, it was the third time I'd been to that house. Not because someone wanted to give it to me, but because the first two times there was a dead body. Each looked like an accident. Yesterday's wasn't. Add to that, you and your buddy tried to tell me the first two were murders rather than accidents."

"I don't think we were saying that. All I know is they appeared suspicious."

"I'm thinking you're right, but know who doesn't?"

"Detective Fisher?"

"Bingo."

"Why are you leaning that way?"

The server interrupted Cindy's answer when he slid my plate of pancakes in front of me along with a side order of bacon. He asked if Cindy wanted anything else. She said she didn't, and the server left us so we could eat in peace.

She watched me take a bite of pancake and said, "What was your question again?"

"Why do you think the first two, umm, deaths weren't accidents?"

"Nothing beyond a gut reaction based on what the law of averages would attribute three deaths in nine days at one small construction job?"

"Three deaths?"

She frowned. "That's the other thing I wanted to tell you. Mason Ryle died before the ambulance got to the hospital."

"I hate to hear that. Did he say anything before he died?"

"Like who killed him?"

I nodded.

"That'd be too easy. He never regained consciousness."

"I assume getting caught between the forklift and the wall caused his death."

"Massive internal injuries, the docs said, but he's being autopsied to make sure."

"Did any of the guys working out there say anything that could help find whoever was driving the forklift?"

She shook her head. "Detective Babyface Fisher interviewed everyone working there yesterday. He called me later to report that he learned nothing, *nada*, bupkis. Most claimed they were at lunch and nowhere near where it happened."

"Do you think the detective was thorough enough to learn anything significant?"

"He's been a detective six months. He wants to do a good job, I get that, but from what he said, I wouldn't bet my worn-out tennis shoes on him succeeding in identifying Ryle's killer. Add to that, he still doesn't believe the first two deaths were anything but tragic accidents. Therein lies most of my frustration."

"Fisher might be right about where the others were at the time of the, umm, murder."

"Why?"

I told her about Charles and I having dinner with Kyle Manger at Loggerhead's. I ignored her cold police stare and went on telling her what Kyle said about where everyone was or claimed to have been when Mason was killed.

"What's it going to take to get you and your witless buddy to stay out of police business?"

"All we did—"

She waved her fork in my face and said, "Never mind. Don't waste your vocabulary. I know as well as I'm sitting here that you were going to say you were simply having a meal with one of the workers and talking about what happened yesterday. No butting in police business, no interfering in an investigation, blah blah blah."

I smiled. "Cindy, you're a mind reader. No wonder you're the top chief in South Carolina."

"Don't press your luck. I already said I was buying breakfast." She looked out at the ocean, shook her head, then turned to me. "Besides, from what you told me, you learned more about what happened than Detective Babyface came close to learning. With that said, can I ask two favors?"

"Of course."

She held up her forefinger. "First, will you share anything significant you learn while you and Charles are not butting into police business?" She held up her middle finger. "Second, will you try, try really hard, not to get yourselves killed while you're not butting in?"

"Yes, ma'am."

The rest of our breakfast conversation revolved around how busy her husband Larry's business was at Folly's small hardware store and how hard she was working on losing a few pounds she'd gained over the winter from spending too much time in her office writing reports the council had requested. Trying to keep from breaking the second promise I'd made her, I didn't ask how her pancake breakfast was helping her lose weight.

27

———————

On the walk home, I saw Charles heading my way. He would've been hard to miss in his bright red Maryland Terrapins long-sleeve T-shirt and navy-blue shorts. I waited for him in front of Dude's surf shop.

"Ready to go?" he said instead of an appropriate greeting.

"Where?"

"It's Saturday so I thought a pleasant walk out Ashley Avenue would get us, especially you, some much-needed exercise."

I ignored the exercise cut and said, "What's Saturday have to do with anything?"

"We could stop on our walk at the cursed house. Being the weekend, there probably aren't workers there and we could, umm, check out where Mason was injured."

"Aren't you curious about where I've been?"

"Yes, but thought you'd tell me while we walked," he said before crossing the street on his—our—exercise walk.

Charles was right about it being a great day for a walk. The temperature was in the low eighties with a cloudless sky. It was still early, so traffic was much lighter than it would be later.

"Where?"

"Where what?"

"Where you have been without me. Must've been important or you wouldn't have mentioned it."

Charles is more perceptive than most give him credit.

"Having breakfast with Cindy."

"Why?"

"We were hungry," I said knowing it would irritate him. One must take pleasure whenever possible.

"And?"

"She told me Mason died on the way to the hospital."

"Crap. Did he say anything on the way; anything like who tried to kill him?"

I shook my head and said, "He never regained consciousness."

"What else did you learn?"

"Fisher, the detective who caught the case, will investigate Mason's death, but still believes the first two were accidents. Cindy says he's been a detective only six months and she doesn't have much faith in his ability to catch whoever is responsible for Mason's death."

"It's coming clearer, she wants us to solve the murders."

"I didn't say that."

"You didn't have to. It's as clear as today's sky."

Charles was righter than he thought, but I wasn't about to tell him what Cindy had said about us getting involved.

We'd reached the Ashley Avenue side of Loggerhead's when Charles pointed to the restaurant. "Did we learn anything last night when we were with Kyle?"

"Nothing useful. No one saw the forklift strike Mason. Kyle wasn't certain but told us where he thought everyone was when it happened."

"Don't forget him saying several of the guys are beginning to believe the house is cursed."

"You believe that?"

"It's as good a theory as any but even if it's cursed, someone, like a real, live person, hopped on that forklift and rammed Mason."

We were within sight of the house under construction. The lack of vehicles parked in the lot or on the street near the house told me Charles was right about no workers being there.

"See, no one here," Charles said as if I wouldn't have figured that out on my own.

"So, what's your plan?"

"Follow me and ye shall see."

We were near the spot where we'd seen the forklift surrounded by first responders, when Charles stopped, bent down, and rubbed his hand in the sandy soil.

"Charles, you think the killer dropped a confession?"

"That'd be great, but I doubt it. I was looking for anything that'd give us a hint of who was here."

"You know the ground around here was trampled by the first responders, and, most likely, some of the construction workers. I can't imagine anything useful still being here."

Charles stood, wiped his hands on his shorts, walked to the back yard, then looked at the roof. "Do you think Shelly could've slipped and fell on her own?"

"That's a steep pitch, so it's possible."

"But we've heard from a couple of people that she was afraid of heights. I know if it'd been me and I was afraid of being up there, I'd be more than careful. It'd take a push to get me to fall."

"I agree, but that still doesn't eliminate it being a freak accident."

"Yes, but—"

A black Mercedes E 450 backed into the drive and a distinguished-looking gentleman slowly exited. He was in his mid to late sixties, six-foot two with styled gray hair and wearing a white polo shirt and gray dress slacks. He clearly wasn't here to work. He glanced at the house before heading our way.

"Who might you two be?" he said in a northern accent.

"Hi, I'm Chris Landrum and this is my friend Charles Fowler. And you are?"

"Chris, Charles, this happens to be my property, so please tell me why you're trespassing?"

"You're Oliver Trescott," I said. "One of the city council

members told me your name." I hoped that'd give some, although slight, idea that we weren't simply thieves getting ready to steal equipment.

"That's correct. Again, why are you here?"

"Charles and I were here when the young lady fell from the roof. We were also nearby yesterday when the man was killed by a forklift. We're good friends with Folly's police chief and had been talking with her about what'd happened, so we wanted to come by to look more closely at the scene of the, umm, unfortunate deaths. We apologize if you don't want us here."

"I'm confused. Are you working with the police or simply damned nosy nellies snooping around?"

Charles responded before I could say anything. "Mr. Trescott, I'm a private detective. Chris and I have helped the police bring more than one murderer to justice."

He glared at Charles then said, "What's your friend's number? I'd like to confirm what you've said."

I gave him Cindy's cell number knowing nothing good would come from his call to her. He put the phone on speaker and dialed. Four rings later, Cindy's voicemail kicked in. To my surprise, Trescott hit *end call*.

He put the phone in his pocket, smiled, and said, "I suppose you wouldn't have given me the chief's number if you were getting ready to break in. Sorry for giving you such a hard time. I'm pretty upset about what's been happening."

"I understand, Mr. Trescott."

"Please call me Oliver. Let's stand over there in the shade."

We followed him to the shady side of the house where he said, "You know more about what's going on than I do. All I was told when Joe Argyle the owner of the construction company called me last night was someone had been killed."

I said, "Were you aware of the other two deaths in the last few days?"

"I knew about the guy who got electrocuted but not about someone falling."

We filled him in on the facts as we knew them but avoided speculating that all three victims were murdered.

"That's awful. Joe's going to hear from me for not telling me about the other death."

"The councilmember who told me about you building said you were from Maryland."

He nodded. "Just outside D.C."

Charles said, "How long have you been over here?"

"Got here a few months ago. Been back and forth several times. Took me longer than I anticipated to get my businesses where I could leave them. I'm staying in a condo at the Oceanfront Villas until the house is finished."

"What kind of businesses do you have?"

"Had," he said followed by a smile. "I finally managed to retire. I had a couple of holding companies, owned a seven-story office building, and a couple of retail buildings."

Charles said, "That's a lot to keep up with."

"That's why I was happy to retire. What do you two do besides trespass?"

"We didn't mean to—"

Oliver laughed. "Kidding."

Charles smiled. "Good, Chris is retired; worked at a big insurance company in Kentucky; then had a photo gallery on Center Street. I worked for him before retiring."

I chose not to correct Charles's stretching of what he'd done, and said, "Someone told me you'd owned this property for years before starting this house."

"Bought it nearly a decade ago. Got a deal I couldn't pass up." He chuckled. "Some called it a steal. There was a small old concrete block house here. The owner came into hard times and had to unload the house. I was lucky to hear about it and grabbed it fast. I had the old house torn down right away and planned to start this one then."

Charles said, "Why didn't you?"

"My businesses were growing faster than I could keep up with.

Had to hire a passel of others and as you may know, when you have a bunch of employees you need to stay tethered to your work."

"I know what you mean," Charles, the person who never owned anything, said.

Oliver added, "Didn't even get a building permit until this year."

Charles said, "You married?"

He smiled. "Yeah, my wife is a retired schoolteacher. She's the reason this is such a large house, and expensive, I might add." He looked at his watch. "Guys, speaking of my wife, I promised to take her shopping on King Street. I'd better go, or I might be moving in by myself."

"We enjoyed talking with you," I said.

"Maybe I'll see you around."

We watched him climb in his Mercedes and pull out on West Ashley Avenue.

"Interesting fellow," Charles said. "I forgot to ask him about the house being cursed."

"It was wise not to mention it."

"Not that wise. As Woodrow Wilson said, 'Wisdom doesn't necessarily come with age. Sometimes age just shows up all by itself.'"

Whatever, I thought.

28

———

Brad Burton was standing in my yard when I returned from the encounter with Oliver Trescott. I'd talked with the retired detective more in the last two weeks than I had during the entire time he'd lived next door. I was still surprised to see him.

"Hi, Brad. You going to or coming from Bert's?"

"Neither. I was coming to see if you were home then I saw you heading this way."

Sweat was running down the side of his face.

"Want to come in where it's cool?"

"Affirmative."

He followed me to the kitchen. "Want something to drink? I've got beer, wine, Pepsi, Diet Pepsi, coffee, and a faucet full of water."

"I'll go with Diet Pepsi." He patted the front of his Patriots Point Naval and Maritime Museum T-shirt. "Hazel says I'm getting fat."

Hazel was right, but I had enough sense not to agree with anyone about getting fat. Okay, I probably should say not agree with anyone in front of the person being accused of getting fat. Instead of commenting, I busied myself getting Brad's drink out of the refrigerator and grabbing one for myself.

I nodded toward the kitchen table then set his drink on it. He took the hint and sat.

"Brad, I suspect you weren't waiting for me so you could share Hazel's thoughts on your weight."

He took a sip, leaned forward, and said, "I heard last night Mason Ryle had been killed."

I nodded. "Charles and I were near the construction site after it happened."

"Dare I ask why?"

"We'd been on the Pier and heard sirens heading out West Ashley, so we took a chance on them going to the house. Sadly, we were right."

He took another sip, stared at me long enough to make me worry about what he might say next.

"Know who I concluded had been the person responsible for the first two deaths out there?" He held up his hand to stop me from answering. "The person I thought was responsible until yesterday afternoon?"

"Mason Ryle?"

"Yes. If I was still on the job, I wouldn't have had enough evidence to arrest him, but from everything you'd said, and stories going around, he would've been my prime suspect."

"For what it's worth, he was mine as well. Let me throw out an idea and get your take."

"Let's hear it."

"You still could be right about Mason."

"He killed the first two victims and someone else killed him?"

"Yes."

"Good point although it strikes me as unlikely. When you were out there, did anyone or anything appear suspicious?"

"We didn't get to talk with any of the workers who'd gathered around the body." I smiled. "You'll appreciate this. The police escorted us off the property before we could speak with anyone."

Brad returned my smile. "Wise cops."

"We talked to one of the construction crew that evening. Ran into Kyle Manger at Loggerhead's."

Brad stared at me. "Accidentally ran into him?"

"Sort of. We were looking for any of the workers and knew a couple hung out at Loggerhead's."

Brad shook his head. "Butting into police business."

I repeated, "Sort of."

"Don't keep me in suspense, did you learn anything helpful?"

I was beginning to like Brad's new hobby.

"The incident happened during their lunch break. Kyle gave us his best thoughts about where everyone was when it happened. It didn't help much since he said none of the guys stayed at the site, other than Mason, that is."

"Did he strike you as being candid or evasive?"

"I didn't get the impression he was hiding anything."

"Did Kyle think the other employees stayed together during lunch or did any of them spend the break apart from the others? In other words, could one of them have returned without the others knowing?"

"It sounded like they go their separate ways during lunch."

"Little help."

I agreed.

"He did say he talked with a detective and had the impression the guy didn't think the first two deaths were anything but accidents."

"Did he identify the detective?"

"Some young guy, thought his name was Fisher."

Brad looked at the ceiling then at me. "Len Fisher. I talked to a buddy of mine in the Sheriff's Office. He said Fisher was recently promoted to his vaulted status. Also said Fisher will be good someday, but he said he wouldn't bet on him solving whatever happened over here."

I had difficulty grasping that Brad still had a *buddy* in the department. A couple of years ago, another detective in the Sheriff's Office shared that Brad had the reputation as being a COF, or for those who aren't conversant in acronyms, a Cranky Old Fart. And that wasn't the worst thing he was called.

I shook that image out of my head and said, "That's not encouraging."

"Add to his lack of experience, Fisher is on the team investigating the murder case of that former politician who's been in the headlines the last couple of weeks. The Mayor is getting pressure from all sides to get that one solved. As you can guess, when the Mayor gets pressure, he passes it along to the local cops. The guy was killed in the county, so the Sheriff's Office is getting all the pressure."

"Fisher is focusing on that case?"

"The Sheriff will deny it, but I've been there and know what's happening."

"Not good news."

"While I still have a friend in the Sheriff's Office, do you have a list of guys who are working out there? I can see if my friend can run background checks on them."

"Isn't that something Fisher would've already done?"

Brad grinned. "Should've and would've are two different things. And don't forget, he's only looking for the person who killed Mason. There could be some connection with one or both other victims."

I grabbed a legal pad from my office, returned to the table, and wrote down the names of as many workers on the job site as I could remember. I tore the sheet out and handed it to Brad and warned him that I may not have the spelling correct.

"I understand. This is a long shot at best. Also write down the approximate age of each guy."

I did but shared I was worse at guessing ages than I was at spelling names.

He thanked me for the drink and list of names.

He smiled as I walked him to the door. "Chris, I know murder is a horrible thing and shouldn't be taken lightly, but this hobby is a hell of a lot more fun than golf."

29

———————

B y the time the sun finished its long day illuminating Folly Beach, I was also finished, more accurately, exhausted. Breakfast with Cindy, followed by meeting Oliver Trescott, then the session with Brad Burton had depleted my daily ration of energy. I'm in my recliner in the living room staring at a mind-numbing documentary on Abraham Lincoln. If I had the energy to follow the history presented on the screen, I'd learn some interesting facts about the sixteenth president, possibly even a quote I could throw at Charles. But when I realized the show had ended and I was staring at a drug commercial I knew no more about Lincoln than I did when I plopped down in the chair three hours ago.

I also realized after talking with many of the construction workers at the ill-fated house, the house's owner, Chief LaMond, Brad Burton, and several others, I was no closer to learning the identity of the person who killed the three workers than I was to accumulating Lincoln trivia. If I was honest with myself, I wasn't even certain the first two workers were killed. Sure, Charles and I thought their deaths weren't the result of accidents, Brad Burton was on the same page, and even Chief LaMond had her doubts, but to my knowledge there was no evidence.

If there were three murders, shouldn't there be something tying the victims together? If they weren't connected, is it conceivable that there's a serial killer out there who chose the three victims, because —because what? Could it simply be they worked on the house? If that's the case, wouldn't the remaining workers be in danger? Taking that logic one step further, not only would the remaining workers be in danger, but wasn't it likely the killer is one of them? Otherwise, how would he have gotten away with killing three people at the job site without being seen? Someone who didn't belong at the house would've drawn the attention of one or more of the workers. Whoever pushed Shelly had to know when and where she'd be so he could shove her and get away with it without anyone seeing him. The same is true with Mason's death. How would the killer have known where each of the other employees would be during lunch so he could get away with getting on the forklift, backing it into Mason, then escaping? Electrocuting Randy Lee would've been easier to do without witnesses, but how would the killer have known Randy would be at the house at midnight? Unless the culprit is the luckiest serial killer who ever lived, I'd wager he's one of the workers. The only outlier to that theory is Shelly's husband Raymond. He could've known where she was scheduled to work the day of her death. He could've learned from her the lunchtime habits of the others including where each normally chose to spend that time. Finally, she could've told him about Randy's habit of returning to the job site some evenings to make sure everything was in order.

Yes, the killer could be one or more of the workers or Raymond Whitley, but other than not knowing who, I keep coming back to why kill the three people? The optimist in me said the answer to that question was within my reach and all it'd take was one more piece of information before it's revealed. My realistic side laughs at my optimistic tendencies. For good reason, I conclude.

I know little about the victims. I'd never met Shelly and only had limited encounters with Randy and Mason, so how could I possibly know the reasons for their deaths? In addition to knowing little about the victims, I know near nothing about the possible suspects.

The last question I had before falling into bed was, is it possible the house is cursed?

No way.

Or was there?

I WAS AWAKENED, not by a eureka moment realizing I knew the identity of the killer, but by the ringing phone. The first thought I had before reaching for it on the bedside table was *not another murder*, followed by the realization of how sad it is for a retired bureaucrat to have the thought of murder bubble to the surface.

"Good morning, Christopher," said the voice on the other end of the call.

Virgil is the only person who uses my given name. He knows I prefer the shorter version, but with Virgil being Virgil, I've learned to accept his quirks.

"Morning, Virgil."

"Didn't wake you, did I?"

I lied and said no.

"Good. Got something interesting for you. Was talking to Mitchell, you know the carpenter at the death house."

"I know him."

"Well anyway, was talking to him last night at Loggerhead's. He told me a couple of things I knew you and Charles would find interesting."

"What?"

"Umm, are you getting hungry? I know I am."

"Want to meet for breakfast?" I asked knowing the answer as well as I knew my name, short or long version.

"Great idea. Tell you what, why don't you head to the Dog?"

"Are you there?"

"Yep, see you."

I may not know the identity of the killer but was certain I'd be buying Virgil Debonnet breakfast.

He was seated at a table on the side patio. He stood and waved for me as I approached as if I wouldn't have seen him otherwise. Heather, one of the restaurant's friendly servers, met me with a mug of coffee before I had time to get seated.

"Virgil told me to keep an eye out for you. Said you were buying his breakfast so I should treat you well. French toast?"

I said yes, thanked her, said hi to Virgil, then took the seat opposite him.

"Glad you could make it," Virgil said. "I called Charles first, but he didn't answer, so I called you."

There's nothing like being second, especially if it's second behind Charles. I didn't share that with Virgil.

"Anyway," Virgil continued, "Mitchell doesn't usually say much, but was in a talkative mood last night. Think it corresponded to the number of beers he had. Anyway, I knew you'd be interested in what he said."

I motioned for him to continue.

He took a bite of his breakfast burrito, a sip of water, then said, "Remember the last time I told you what he said when I saw him at Loggerhead's?"

No. "Remind me?"

"Some of the guys on the construction site were getting antsy. Some were even saying the house was cursed."

"That I remembered."

"Anyway, Mitchell said five or six of them are ready to walk off the job."

"Because they think the project is cursed?"

"Yes."

"Do they really believe that's possible?"

"Just reporting what Mitchell said. Don't you find it strange that three out of what, ten, workers are now dead?"

"No doubt it's unusual."

"Three people out of ten having the same first name would be unusual. Three people getting themselves killed out of ten is beyond unusual."

"Did Mitchell say why the house is cursed?"

"He didn't know."

"Is he one of the guys who're talking about walking off the job?"

"He wasn't certain but is leaning that way. Said the only reason he wouldn't was because the company had been good to him. He figures the job would shut down if many of the guys quit. He didn't want to leave Custom Builders Group in a bad way."

"Did he say who else was considering quitting?"

Virgil smiled. "Think so, but I'd been at Loggerhead's awhile before I saw Mitchell. A couple of guys have been nice enough to buy me drinks. Who was I not to show them how appreciative I was for their offer? It's possible I may've had a beer, umm, or two, too many. Life experiences tell me that made it sort of hard remembering names Mitchell had thrown out, if you know what I mean."

I was afraid I did.

"Remember any of them?"

Heather arrived with my breakfast. Virgil waited for her to leave then said, "Let's see. Think he mentioned Kyle and Tim. Give me a sec, there were more."

I took a sip of coffee and gave him a second which turned into a minute, possibly longer.

Virgil snapped his fingers. "Got it. He said the Puerto Rican guy, what's his name?"

"Luis Ortez."

"That's it, Luis."

"Anyone else?"

"Yes, but their names escape me." He smiled. "Probably forever."

"Did he really think some of them would walk off the job because they thought the house was cursed?"

"Don't know if they would or not, but the way he was talking, I wouldn't be surprised. Any of that helpful in figuring out who did the three folks in?"

Not really, I thought but said, "You never know. Every piece of information can be critical in figuring it out."

He smiled and said, "That's what I thought, Christopher."

If only if it was that simple.

30

———————

The next three days, I focused on getting my mind off the deaths. I took long walks on the beach, intentionally staying west of the Folly Pier to avoid seeing the "death house" as some were calling it. I even cooked myself two suppers in my kitchen. Okay, my definition of cooking meant sticking Stouffer's TV dinners in the microwave, but hey, that's still cooking, isn't it?

During this same period, Charles found himself busier than he had been at any point during the last thirty-something years. A builder he occasionally provided manual labor for had asked him to help with a room addition on a house on East Erie Avenue. In addition to making deliveries for Dude's surf shop, these off-the-books, aka cash, jobs helped my friend earn enough money to live.

I was close to putting the deaths out of my mind when Brad Burton appeared at the door. I invited him in, offered him something to drink, then grabbed two Diet Pepsis from the refrigerator while he was making himself at home at the kitchen table. Sweat rolled down his cheeks.

"Been jogging?" I asked as I set his drink in front of him.

"That's a joke. It's hot out there in case you didn't notice."

I smiled. "That's why I'm in here."

I waited to hear what I'd done to get another rare visit from the retired detective. I didn't have long to wait.

"My buddy in the Sheriff's office got back with me first thing this morning. Figured you'd want to know what he learned."

Apparently, my avoiding what'd happened at the construction site was coming to an end.

"Sure."

Brad took a small notebook out of his pocket. The book looked old enough to have been used by Columbus to document his trip to the new world.

"Roman, that's my friend, didn't find much. He didn't have access to all the databases available to his office, something about being afraid the sheriff would know if he'd been snooping without it being tied to a case. Something about signing in and passwords. I was never big on using the office technology but assumed Roman knew what he was doing." Brad turned a few pages then set the book on the table and said, "Rawlins, Scott, sixty-one. He has one DUI from three years ago. Also, his wife accused him of abuse a couple of years ago. They divorced and she never pursued the charges. That's all he found on Rawlins."

"Interesting," I said, then grabbed a notebook from the kitchen counter. "With my memory being what it is, I'd better take notes."

Brad smiled. "I know the feeling. Now we have Walker, Lucius, fifty-three. Roman found nothing on him. That doesn't mean much. The databases he had access to only covered South Carolina. Walker could be a mass murderer from Georgia and Roman wouldn't find anything about it."

"I understand. Anything about the others?"

"Be patient. Manger, Kyle, thirty-seven, has a juvenile record but it's sealed and Roman had no way of gaining access. Ortiz, Luis, fifty-three. Nothing to show about him, again, that doesn't mean anything for the same reasons I gave for Walker."

"Okay."

"Same was true for Bennett, Joshua. Nothing there. That brings me to Hale, Timothy, twenty-two. A speeding ticket last year."

"That's all?"

"All for Hale, now Baldwin, Michael, that's another story. He's twenty-seven. Three years ago, he was convicted of firearm possession. Served a year."

"Isn't that severe for having an unlicensed firearm?"

"Yeah. I suspect there was more, and he pled guilty to the possession to get off lighter than he would for whatever the other charges were."

"Your friend couldn't find out what the other charges involved?"

"Nope."

"Anything else?"

"You didn't mention him, but I had Roman check on the owner of the construction company. It got a little interesting there. Argyle, Joseph, fifty-seven. He'd been sued three times for not fulfilling promises he'd made to people he built houses for. All three were settled out of court. That doesn't necessarily mean he did anything wrong. Everybody is suing everybody nowadays."

"Did your friend find out anything about the house's owner, Oliver Trescott?"

"Nothing, not even a speeding ticket, but he hasn't lived here long, so that doesn't mean squat."

I looked down at my notes then said, "Is that it?"

Brad smiled. "Saved the best for last. Whitley, Raymond, thirty-five. The boy got one DUI a year ago, add public intoxication two years ago, then here's the kicker. He was convicted eleven years ago for spousal abuse, gave the state two years of his life."

"Do you think he killed his wife?"

"He'd be at the top of my list."

"Who else would be on your list?"

He tapped his finger on the notebook. "Everybody I talked about since I came in your front door."

"If you were still on the job, what would you do next?"

Brad looked at his watch. "Go to lunch."

31

———

Brad headed home, and I headed to the living room to review my notes to see if anything he learned about the others provided a clue to what was going on. I'd love to say I found some hidden nugget that pointed to one of the names as being the killer. If it was there, it evaded my search, so I was relieved when I heard another knock on the door and didn't have to find something in my notes where nothing existed.

I opened the door and stood face to face with a stranger. He wore a navy blazer, a white dress shirt, and a red and blue rep tie, so I figured he wasn't here to rob me. The five-foot-seven, stocky gentleman with wavy black hair looked no older than a teenager, which should've given me a clue as to his identity.

"You Chris Landrum?"

"Yes."

He flashed a badge and said, "I'm Detective Fisher, have a few minutes?"

I nodded and said, "Come in."

I pointed to the couch and he detected the hint and sat. Before moving to the recliner, I asked if he wanted something to drink. He declined and I sat opposite him.

"Mr. Landrum, I'm investigating the death of Mason Ryle. I believe you know who that is."

"Sure, he was the worker killed at a construction site on West Ashley Avenue."

"How well did you know him?"

"I'd seen him a couple of times at the site, but only talked to him once, and that was on the sidewalk outside a restaurant."

His right foot tapped the floor like a nervous tic. "What reason did you have for being at the new house? You're not a contractor or anyone required to be there, are you?"

I explained how a friend and I had been walking on the beach and heard the commotion at the site.

"Twice?"

Umm, twice not counting the day we saw Oliver Trescott there. "Yes."

"That strikes me as beyond coincidences, especially knowing how far that is from your house."

Was he accusing me of something? I didn't know how to respond, so I kept my mouth closed and looked at the detective.

He pointed his finger at me and said, "You have nothing to say to that?"

"No. If I may ask, why are you here?"

"Do you know Scott Rawlins or Kyle Manger?"

"I've met them, but don't know them well. Why?"

He jotted something in a notebook he took out of his coat pocket then stared at me. Instead of answering my question, he said, "Did you know Shelly Whitley or Randy Lee?"

"Never met Ms. Whitley. I talked to Randy Lee once. Why?"

He again wrote in the notebook. I don't know what, but it took him as long as it would to write the Gettysburg Address.

He finally turned his attention back to me. "How about Pat Zellner?"

It took me a few seconds to recall who that was. "She's Kyle Manger's girlfriend. I met her once when she and Kyle were at Loggerhead's." I watched him as he jotted that down in his notebook.

"Detective, I've answered all your questions, so don't you think it's time you told me why you're here?"

"Mr. Landrum," he said as his foot continued to tap the floor, "your name's come up a couple of times at the office. I believe you know my colleagues Detectives Adair and Callahan."

They were detectives with the Sheriff's Office whom I'd dealt with on murders that I got involved in solving over the years.

"Yes."

"They've shared stories how you and a few of your friends had interfered in investigations they'd been involved with."

"Yes, and with my help they—"

He interrupted, "Mr. Landrum, those days are over, do you understand?"

"I'm not certain what you're getting at."

"You know why I asked about Pat Zellner?" he said as his voice got louder.

"Not really. Like I said, I only saw her once."

He pointed his notebook at me. "She said you and some other guy, a friend of yours, I suppose, cornered her and her boyfriend at the restaurant and started interrogating them like they were public enemy number one and two."

"Detective, all we did was ask—"

His face started getting red as he leaned toward me. "I'm not done, sir. Who gave you the right, the audacity to stick your nose in police business? Who said you could play cop and harass law-abiding citizens who were having a peaceful meal?"

"Did either Detective Adair or Detective Callahan tell you how I, and to be honest, a few of my friends, helped take murderers off the street? Did they tell you how they weren't making any headway on those cases until I got involved?" I leaned forward and matched his glare.

"They mentioned how you butted in, how you kept valuable information about the cases from them." He took a deep breath, his shoulders relaxed, and he leaned back on the couch. "Mr. Landrum, all of that is ancient history. In addition to Ms. Zellner telling me how you harassed her and her boyfriend, she added she felt intimidated by how you pounced on them. Furthermore, do you deny talking with Scott, umm," he glanced down at his notes, "Scott Rawlins?"

"No. We had a pleasant conversation about what was happening at his job site."

"That's not the way he saw it. He wasn't as upset as Kyle, and especially Pat, but said he felt uncomfortable when you were interrogating him."

No sense in having him interrupt whatever I would say, so I shrugged and remained silent.

He leaned forward one more time and said, "I don't give a rat's patootie about what you did regarding investigations last year, or for that matter a dozen years ago, but consider yourself warned. If I hear anything else about you nosing in the murder investigation of Mason Ryle, I'll stick you in jail quicker than you can say crap. Do you understand?"

"Loud and clear."

"I'm serious."

"I don't doubt it."

He started to push up off the couch.

"Detective, I'm not butting in, but could you answer one question?"

I imagined feeling handcuffs on my wrists as I said, "You didn't mention the other two deaths. Are you investigating Shelly Whitley and Randy Lee's deaths?"

He sat back down on the couch. "Why would I? They were accidents, nothing more."

"Just curious."

He glared at me for what seemed like an eternity before saying, "I sincerely hope this is the last conversation you and I have." He gave me a faux smile and added, "If it isn't, you have a lot more to lose than I have. No need to walk me to the door. I can find my way out."

I remained in the recliner and watched him leave, ending with a slamming door.

32

———

The rest of the day, much of the evening, and part of the next morning was spent trying to figure out why Detective Fisher was so upset with me. If I were stereotyping him, I'd say he was overcompensating because of his youth and short stature. What else could it be? If he'd talked with the other two detectives in his office like he said he had, they would have told him my efforts had helped them catch killers. Sure, they'd say I did butt into police business, but didn't the ends justify the means? Regardless, I didn't doubt Fisher would honor his threats if he caught me nosing in the case.

The rest of the morning, I tried to figure out why Kyle and his girlfriend had been so down on me. She was irritated that Kyle and I had been talking so much about Shelly, but me harassing her, never. Had Scott Rawlins shared anything negative about me? If he had, I don't recall Fisher mentioning it. Other than Kyle having an obnoxious girlfriend, I hadn't given much thought to him being the killer. Maybe I should. If nothing else, he appeared to want me to stop looking at what might have happened.

The thing Fisher said that worried me the most was his denying that the other two deaths could be anything other than accidents. Did he honestly believe three deaths in such a short period of time weren't related? Or was I doing what I've been accused of by more than one person, that by looking at every death on Folly Beach as being a murder.

After concluding absolutely nothing, a walk up Center Street and lunch at one of the restaurants sounded much more productive than pacing the living room, achieving nothing.

I was in front of the Crab Shack when I saw Noelle Ward on the corner, looking across the street at the mural painted on the side of Planet Follywood. I assumed that's what she was staring at because I couldn't tell for sure since she was wearing sunglasses. She was in her typical garb of black jeans and a dark gray T-shirt.

I tapped her on the shoulder and said, "Researching?"

She'd told me once she liked watching people so she could get ideas on how they could act in her novel.

She smiled. "Caught me. I was watching people staring at the mural. You can tell a vacationer visiting the island for the first time by how long they gaze at the thing. Who knows, I might add a mural to one of the buildings in my fictional town. Are you walking around catching random researchers?"

"Was on my way to get lunch. Have you eaten?"

"Yes, but it was yesterday. Where are we going?" she asked, placing the emphasis on we.

"You're standing beside it."

She smiled and said, "The Crab Shack it is."

We were greeted at the door by Britany, one of the Shack's longer tenured servers. She asked if we wanted inside or outside. I glanced at Noelle who said outside. I figured it was so she could observe the foot traffic along Center Street. Britany escorted us to a large table on the corner of the deck and said a server would be with us shortly.

"Are you off today?" I said after our server delivered water to each of us.

"I had a presentation to a group of bigwigs last night. It ran until eleven and my boss said I could have the day off." She chuckled. "He didn't have to say it twice."

"Did you get the account?"

"Yes. If we hadn't, my boss wouldn't have been so generous about me taking off."

"Yours is a tough business."

"You can say that again. But know what's tougher?"

I said I didn't as the server returned and asked what we wanted to eat. We each ordered a flounder crunch sandwich and iced tea then the server headed to the kitchen with our orders.

"What's tougher?"

"Writing a danged novel. Wouldn't you think making stuff up would be easy?"

"Noelle, I can't imagine anything about writing a novel being easy, except maybe giving up and deciding not to do it."

She laughed. "You're not far off. My granny used to tell me I was the most stubborn person she knew. I suppose that stubborn streak is what's keeping me going on the book."

I was going to brag on her making the effort when someone from the sidewalk said, "Hey, Chris. Having lunch?"

I turned and saw Brad Burton leaning on the railing separating the sidewalk from the restaurant's deck. I resisted offering him a smart aleck remark about what else would I be doing at lunchtime sitting at a table in a restaurant. Instead, I said, "Yeah, want to join us?"

He looked around and said, "Don't want to interrupt anything."

Noelle said, "You're not, come join us."

Brad smiled and headed to the entrance.

I said, "You know Brad?"

"Not yet," my lunch companion said. "He looks interesting, sort of street person chic."

I laughed. "You may not want to share that observation with him."

"Why?"

Brad reached the table before I could answer.

"Thanks for the invite," he said and turned to Noelle. "I'm Brad Burton, live next door to Chris."

Noelle shook his hand and told him who she was.

Britany brought our tea, said our server was slammed so she'd be taking care of us, then asked what Brad wanted to drink and if he was ready to order. He looked at me and I told him what we'd already ordered. He told Britany he'd have the same and she left to get his started.

"Noelle," Brad said, "what do you do for a living other than hanging around with old guys like Chris, and I guess me?"

"I work at an ad agency in Charleston."

I waited for Brad to ask her why she wasn't working today, but he didn't.

I said, "Brad, Noelle's writing a novel."

"Really? What about?"

"It's a murder mystery set on an imaginary island in Georgia."

I said, "Noelle moved here since her imaginary island is similar to Folly."

Brad's brow scrunched up as he said, "What do you know about writing about murder?"

I said, "Brad's a retired detective from the County Sheriff's Office."

"Cool."

"Young lady, there's nothing cool about it," Brad said.

"Sorry, I didn't mean murder was cool. I think you had a fascinating job, a tough job, a job not many people could handle."

Brad nodded. "True. So, what makes you think you know enough to write that kind of book? Were you ever a cop, ever study police science?"

"No, but in my book the protagonist is a private detective and doesn't have to follow all the procedures police must follow."

Brad turned to me. "Sort of like your buddy Charles?"

I smiled. "I suspect Noelle's private detective will do the job much better than Charles."

Brad said, "I hope so."

Our food arrived and hopefully would distract Brad enough so we could get on a more positive topic. We each took a couple of bites, before Brad said, "Chris, hear any more about what's going on at the construction site?"

"Not really," I said then wondered if I should share the visit I had from Detective Fisher.

I didn't have to decide, Noelle said, "You mean where Mason Ryle was killed?"

"Yeah," Brad said. "Did you know him?"

"Yes, we shared a few drinks and a couple of meals together."

"You were dating?"

"No, nothing like that, although I heard he told a couple of his friends we were."

Brad said, "You don't know anyone who had anything against him, do you?"

"No, but I don't think he was the most liked guy out there."

"Did you know either of the others who were killed?"

"No. Mason never said much about the others. If I was writing this story in a novel, I'd start having my private detective look at the rumors about the house being cursed."

I said, "Why?"

She nodded slowly, then said, "Cursed is another way of saying evil. You've had three deaths there. Sure, two are supposed to be accidents, but regardless, three deaths at one place strikes me as evil. After all, doesn't a mystery story have to have some mystery? Adding a curse gives more depth to the plot."

Brad pointed a fry at Noelle. "Young lady, that's bullshit."

Her head jerked back then she said, "Could be. I'm simply saying that'd add to the intrigue of the mystery. Besides, if I were writing this story, I wouldn't have a new house cursed. Most cursed places are old, have squeaky floors, spiderwebs, a rat or two scampering about, and dust flying around."

"That's my point," Brad said. "There's nothing real in a novel. It's all made up so the writer can wrap everything in a nice package with a red bow tied around it at the end of the story. Real life murders don't fit in that box."

Noelle leaned toward Brad. "I'm not telling you what happened out there. Truth is I have no idea, but what I do know is most good novels have enough truth in them to be believable. Otherwise, they're no good."

"Noelle," I said, "did Mason say anything to you about believing or others out there believing the house was cursed?"

"Yes, otherwise I wouldn't have brought it up."

I said, "Two or three of the other guys have told me the same thing. Some of them are considering quitting the job because they're afraid they might die next."

"That's crap," Brad said. "I was a cop longer than Noelle here has been alive. Before I became a detective, I saw countless ways man inflicts harm on others. After being promoted to detective, it was my job to catch the ones who inflicted the harm. Chris, Noelle, in all those years, not a single person was killed because of a curse, or voodoo, or any other supernatural force. People kill people, period."

I didn't see much hope for a pleasant lunch if the deaths at the construction site remained the focus of our conversation.

"Noelle, Brad's probably right. He's also right about you and I not having the information and skills needed to solve whatever happened out there. It's in the capable hands of the Sheriff's Office, and I'm certain they will get it sorted out. Before Brad joined us, you mentioned that you had landed a big account at work. That sounds exciting and interesting. Do you mind sharing what it is?"

She spent the next few minutes sharing the details of her presentation and how much the new account meant to her agency. Watching her come alive while talking about it told me she not only was good at her job but loved the work as well. Even Brad got into it and asked a couple of pertinent questions. Best of all, nothing else was said about the three deaths and a battle between my lunch mates was averted.

33

To prevent another battle, I wanted to share with Charles Detective Fisher's visit and what Brad had learned about the construction workers. The weather was perfect, so instead of calling, the five-block walk to Charles's Sandbar Lane apartment would do me good. He'd anticipated being done with the room addition he was helping with, so there was a better than average chance he'd be home.

Charles's classic, 1961 Schwinn bicycle leaned against his apartment building and his Toyota was in the gravel parking lot, so the odds were now more than better than average that he was here.

"To quote Virgil, *holy moly*! What'd I do to deserve a visit to my humble abode." Charles said after seeing me on his front step.

"I thought you could only quote Presidents."

"I'm multitasking. Do I have to guess why you're here, or are you going to enlighten me?"

He often had me guess things I had no way of knowing the answer, but to prove I have better manners, I said, "No need to guess. I thought I'd stop by to tell you who I've talked to since we talked."

"Then why are you standing out there?" He waved me into the tiny apartment.

The apartment felt even tinier since it contained more books than are in the Library of Congress, or so it appeared. He has floor-to-ceiling bookshelves on three of the living room walls holding the quantity of books that'd be more comfortable on more bookshelves than he owned. In addition, there were foot-high stacks of books in two of the corners. He motioned to a wicker rocking chair in another corner, I assumed for me to have a seat. I moved another stack of books from the chair while he plopped down on his navy-blue velour recliner.

"I didn't know you were coming, so I didn't fix hors d'oeuvres and my wine cellar is empty."

No surprise there since in all the times he knew I was coming, he'd never had hors d'oeuvres.

"That's fine. I just ate. I wanted to let you know I had a visit from Detective Fisher. He came—"

"The detective on our murder cases?"

Yes about the detective; wrong about it being our murder cases. Rather than parse words, I nodded then continued telling him what I'd wanted to before he interrupted. I made it through Fisher's visit with a minimal number of questions. That ended when I ended my story with Fisher slamming the door on his way out.

"What's Kyle talking about? Each time we talked with him we were polite, never accusing him of anything. He never said anything about us bothering him, much less, harassing him."

"I agree."

"Then what's got him riled?"

"The detective didn't say, but I had the impression the main complaints came from Kyle's girlfriend."

"Obnoxious Pat?"

I nodded. "Remember how upset she was at Loggerhead's?"

"Yeah, but she was pissed at Kyle more than at us."

"I agree. She's the one who said Shelly was a looker and irritated that Kyle was taking up for her."

Charles stared at the front door, nodded, then said, "What if Kyle's the killer?"

"Why say that?"

"He knows you and I are closing in on him. He wants the cops to force us to step aside."

"Why do we think Kyle is the killer?"

"Don't you remember, he hinted that Mason was the killer? Then, I remembered this, he told us there had been a sixth carpenter on the job and he got fired. See, a fired guy would want to kill the guys who were left working on the job. Kyle wanted us to suspect the fired guy."

"But—"

"Finally," he interrupted, "he's trying to get us off the case. See, he's *numero uno* on my list."

"Before we make a citizen's arrest, let me tell you what Brad learned about the other guys working there."

He shook his head. "First, Virgil attaches himself to my private detective agency, now Brad? Am I going to have to put him on the payroll?"

If Brad were put on the payroll, he'd be the only one, and that's including Charles. Instead of adding to the rapidly deteriorating discussion of Charles's imaginary agency, I said, "Let's start with Scott Rawlins."

I quickly listed what Brad's friend in the Sheriff's Office learned about each worker. I made it through the names with few questions, few for Charles.

"Are you sure Brad said the person who got this for him is a friend?"

I smiled. "I know. I was as surprised as you are that Brad has friends, especially friends working in the Sheriff's Office."

"Anyway, it still looks like Kyle's the killer for the reasons I said earlier."

"He might be, but why not see what we can learn about some of the others?"

"Like who?"

"Scott Rawlins. We know he'd been accused of abuse, so he probably has a temper. When Shelly was killed, he claimed to be alone in the owner's suite. That's on the top floor of the house. No one would have seen him if he pushed her."

"Yes, but—"

"He's sucking up to the construction company's owner trying to get promoted to foreman, the vacancy that became available with Randy Lee's death. Finally, he said he thought Shelly's husband could have killed her."

"Trying to blame the husband. That doesn't mean anything."

"That's the same argument you used when accusing Kyle of killing them."

"Moving right along. What about Michael Baldwin and the talk about the house being cursed?"

"Add to that, Brad learned that he'd spent time in jail for firearm possession."

Charles said, "That'd be a good reason for him killing without using a gun. Oh yeah, isn't he the guy spreading gossip about the house being cursed? Them dying from a curse would let him off the hook."

"He's not the only guy there who mentioned a curse."

"True, but he's the only one pushing that rumor who's spent time in the hoosegow. Think it is?"

"Cursed?"

"Yeah."

"I don't believe in curses or cursed houses, but it doesn't matter what I think. Some of the guys are scared, and I suspect only staying because they need the job."

"What about Tim Hale?"

"Brad didn't find anything about him, and from what we've heard, he wasn't close to Shelly."

"What about when Mason was squashed?"

"Kyle said Tim was sitting at the beach staring at the ocean when Kyle took his walk on the beach. When he returned, Tim had gone back to work."

Charles held both hands out to his side and said, "See, more proof that Kyle did it."

"Because he was walking on the beach?"

"Yep. No one saw him and he could've easily come back and fired up the forklift."

"That's possible."

"You don't believe it, do you?"

"Kyle is still a good suspect, but again, we need to look at the others as well."

"Whatever. Who's next?"

"Joshua Bennett," I said. "We were told he had some run-ins with Randy so he could have had a reason to kill him. Killing the others, I don't know. And remember, he wasn't at work the day Mason was killed."

"That doesn't mean he couldn't have snuck back and did Mason in."

"Unlikely, but yes, that's possible," I said. "I think we can eliminate Luis, umm, Ortez. He was working at another project the day Mason was killed. That brings me to Lucius Walker. I think he was the first person who told me he thought Randy's death wasn't an accident."

"Because Randy was an electrician and wouldn't have grabbed a hot wire while he was standing in water."

"Yes."

"So, he could be using backward psychology on us. Thinking we wouldn't suspect the person who killed Randy if he said Randy had been murdered."

"Reverse psychology," I said.

"Whatever."

"That's possible."

Charles shook his head, walked to the kitchen, returned with two cans of Coke, handed me one, then said, "I'm seriously confused."

It would've been way too easy to say he was way beyond confused, so instead, I said, "What's bothering you?"

"Okay, let's agree that there were three deaths."

"No question."

"The first two have been called accidents by the police."

I nodded.

"So, look at the possibilities. One could be an accident; two murders. Two could be accidents; one murder. I'm certain all three were murders. Follow, so far?"

A second nod.

"Add to that, there could be one, or two, or three murderers."

"Yes."

"So, how in holy hell are we supposed to catch one, or two, or three killers?"

"That's a great question."

He chuckled. "In all the years we've known each other, that's the first time you gave one of my questions that much credit."

Most likely because it was the first great question he'd asked, I thought, but said, "You always have good questions, but let me throw one more person in the mix, Shelly's husband Raymond. Brad learned he was married before he and Shelly got married. He was convicted of spousal abuse eleven years ago and served time for it. Brad thinks he's the most-likely killer."

"Okay, he killed his wife and I suppose could've killed Randy because he saw something or heard something that's implicated Raymond."

"Possibly."

"Then why kill Mason? Besides we haven't heard anyone saying that Raymond was on the property when Mason was killed."

"True, but if we assume one person killed all three, no one appears to have a motive for killing the three. The only thing we know they had in common was each worked on the house."

Charles took a sip of Coke, leaned back in his chair, and said, "So, Mr. Logical Thinker, what's our next step?"

"Try to learn more about our most-likely suspects."

"Who would be?"

"Kyle, umm—"

"See, I told you he was the killer."

"Tell you what, for now why don't we say he's the top suspect. In the unlikely event he's not guilty, we should see who else may be."

"Okay, for now. So, who else should we add to the list?"

"The most logical candidate would be Raymond Whitley, then I'd add Scott Rawlins."

"Because he appears to have the most to gain by Randy's death?"

"Yes," I said.

"Anyone else?"

"Nobody jumps out at me, but we shouldn't eliminate any of the others. We don't know any of them well enough to make a guess if they're involved. How about you?"

Charles's phone rang interrupting whatever he'd planned to say. He answered, said okay twice, then ended the call.

He shook his head. "I thought I was done with the room addition. Now he wants me to meet him out there and clean up."

Our meeting had officially ended.

On the walk home, I thought it'd be wise for me to tell Cindy about Detective Fisher's visit before she heard it from the Detective.

She answered the phone with, "What are you pestering me about this time?"

"Chief LaMond, I was calling to see if I could buy you breakfast in the morning?"

"I'd prefer supper at Halls Chophouse but since you're so tight, I suspect breakfast is the best offer I'll get."

Halls Chophouse is one of Charleston's finest restaurants.

I swallowed back a chuckle and said, "Is that a yes?"

"Absolutely. Seven-thirty at the Dog."

The phone went dead.

<h1 style="text-align:center">34</h1>

Cindy's pickup was in the small parking area in front of the Dog when I arrived. Amber met me at the door, leaned close, and whispered, "I've already told your breakfast date we don't have filet mignon and caviar on the menu, but she'll probably tell you that's what she wants. Said you're picking up her check."

I thanked Amber for the warning and headed to the booth in the back of the room where Cindy was reading what looked like a police report. I slid in the booth and waited for her to finish whatever she was doing before speaking. Amber set a mug of coffee in front of me.

Cindy slipped the paperwork in a manila folder, sighed, and said, "Remember when Brian became mayor and appointed me chief?"

Brian Newman was the long-time chief before running for mayor after the previous occupant slinked out of town under a cloud of controversy.

"Of course."

"Why in all that's holy didn't you tell me to say no? Why?"

I smiled. "Because I knew you would be a fantastic leader and the city needed you. So did Brian."

"It'll take way more sweet talk than that to make me believe you."

This is where I would ask most people I know what the problem was. It wouldn't work on Cindy. She'd tell me when and if she chose to.

Amber returned and asked if we were ready to order.

I said, "Do you have filet mignon this morning?"

Cindy slapped me with her napkin and gave Amber a dirty look. "You told him, didn't you?"

Amber laughed. "Who me?"

Cindy said, "Get this old geezer French toast and I'll have whatever costs the most on your breakfast menu that doesn't even have caviar on it."

"Yes, ma'am," Amber said and laughed again as she left to put in our orders.

"Okay Mr. Tightwad who invited me to the cheapest meal you could find, why the invite?"

I took a sip of coffee, then said, "I had a visitor at the house the other morning."

"Do you want me to guess or are you going to tell me who?"

"Detective Fisher."

She rolled her eyes. "Don't suppose he arrested you, or you wouldn't be buying me breakfast."

"Some of the people who work on the new house on West Ashley, plus the girlfriend of one of them, claimed Charles and I were harassing them about what happened at the job site."

"You were, weren't you?"

"No. Charles and I ran into Kyle Manger, he's one of the plumbers on the job, and his girlfriend Pat Zellner on the patio at Loggerhead's. We had a pleasant conversation, and everybody left happy, or so I thought."

"Was that the only time you saw the girlfriend?"

"Yes."

"Did she seem okay or pissed about anything?"

"She got irritated when Kyle kept talking about Shelly and her death, but I didn't detect any problem with Charles or me."

"Did you talk with Kyle any other times?"

"Yeah, a couple more times at Loggerhead's."

"So what, that's three times in a week or so. Don't you think he could feel you were, umm, harassing him?"

"I suppose so."

"Did Fisher mention anyone other than Kyle and Pat?"

"Yeah, he said Scott Rawlins told him we were also pestering him, or something like that."

"Were you?"

Breakfast arrived before I could respond. Cindy told Amber she could use more coffee, since she didn't serve bourbon at breakfast. She also told Amber she'd need something strong if she had to put up with me much longer. Amber said she knew what Cindy meant, chuckled, and headed for the coffee pot.

Cindy watched her go, and said, "Well, were you?"

"Pestering Scott?"

Cindy said, "Yes."

"No."

"Okay."

"Okay what?"

"I believe you. I had two phone calls after I got home last night."

Do I ask from whom? Why ask knowing she'll tell me? I waited.

"Well, aren't you going to ask who they were from? Larry certainly did. I told him they were from my boyfriend. Don't know if I should feel good about his reaction or not. He laughed." She took a sip of her refreshed coffee, then added, "Well, aren't you going to ask?"

"Cindy, who called you last night?"

"The first call was from someone you know, Detective Fisher."

"What'd he want?"

"Wanted to share a fascinating conversation he had with one of my city's residents. I think you know him. He's the geezer sitting across the table from me."

I sighed. "Why didn't you tell me that before I went through the conversation with him?"

"It's too much fun watching you squirm. Besides, I wanted to hear your version of what happened."

"How'd it compare with his version?"

"You used fewer profanities and didn't sound nearly as angry as he did. Two things you need to know. First, I've known you a long time. I trust you're telling me the truth, even if it can get you in trouble. If you say you and Charles didn't harass Pat what's-her-name, you didn't harass her."

"Thanks. We didn't harass her and our conversations with Kyle were always pleasant even though we were talking about death, not a pleasant topic. To be honest, it strikes me as strange that he's trying to make us be the problem. Charles thinks he's saying bad things about us, so we stop asking questions about what happened."

"Do you think he had something to do with it?"

"Wouldn't rule him out, but it's only a gut reaction. What did Fisher want you to do?"

"I think he wanted me to cuff you to Charles then ship you off to Provo, Utah, or some other far-away place."

"What'd you tell him?"

"Said I'd keep my ears open and if I heard anything negative about you two, I'd, umm, didn't tell him what I'd do."

"Thank you."

She pointed her mug at me. "You're welcome." She set her mug down and tapped the manila folder beside her. "Know what I was reading when you got here?"

"Whatever's in that folder."

"Wow, maybe you are a detective like hallucinating Charles thinks you are."

"You know—"

"Was reading a report about something that happened out by the County Park last night a little after midnight. That was call number two. I still don't know why Officer Bishop thought I needed to know, but she did."

"What happened?"

"A pickup truck driven by one Scott Rawlins drifted off the road and had an encounter with a palmetto tree. Officer Bishop caught the call and found Rawlins in an alcohol-infused state. He wasn't falling down drunk but blew enough to get him a night behind bars as opposed to standing in front of a bar which got him in trouble to begin with. His passenger, umm," Cindy looked at the paper in the folder. "Timothy Hale was more sober, so Bishop let him call someone to come get him. There wasn't much damage to the truck, but enough to where it wasn't drivable."

"Isn't it unusual for one of your guys to call you for something that minor?"

"Yes, that's what I mumbled to Bishop after she dragged me out of my sleep. She said she knew both guys worked at the house where three had died. She said it was pure luck that Rawlins didn't run into a house killing its residents and both guys in the truck."

"You see anything connecting the three deaths with the wreck?"

"Not really. I think Bishop was making a CYA call in case some connection is found."

"Speaking of the three deaths, does Detective Fisher still think the first two were accidents?"

"Yes."

"I think he's wrong."

"For what it's worth, so do I."

35

On the walk home, my mind kept wandering back to why Kyle felt the need to complain to Detective Fisher about Charles and me. Could it be as simple as he believed the talks we had had about the deaths were inappropriate? Could it be because his girlfriend raised a stink about it since she was there when Charles and I were talking with him about Shelly's death? Clearly, it irritated her when her boyfriend expressed sympathy for his dead coworker. Or could it be because he was the killer and thought Charles and I were getting close to figuring it out and wanted to have the detective warn us off? The fact was, we were nowhere near figuring it out and because of his efforts to deter us, I was more intent on getting to the bottom of what had happened.

I stopped in Bert's to grab one of their deli sandwiches for lunch when I saw Lucius Walker with a box of donuts.

I said, "Feeding the crew again?"

"Oh, hi, umm—"

"Chris."

He smiled. "One of these times, I'm going to remember your name. Yeah, I'm trying to stay on everyone's good side with a bribe. You'd be surprised how well crews from different companies work together if they like each other. Even if the like is from a box of donuts."

"You're a wise man."

He smiled again. "Wise, not a bit. Just been around the block more than a time or two."

"Speaking of work, how's the project going?"

"Lot of bitchin' going on this morning. Couple of the guys didn't show up leaving those there in a pickle. That's another reason I got these." He glanced at the donuts.

"Who didn't show?" I asked, figuring I knew who one of them was.

"Mitchell and Scott. Funny thing about it is neither called in sick, or anything although Tim told the company owner that Scott wasn't feeling well when he left work yesterday."

I doubt Scott would've used his one call from jail to call work but didn't share that with Lucius. Tim knew what'd happened, so he was covering for Scott saying he was sick.

"That's too bad."

"That's one more thing slowing progress. I can't imagine what would happen if some of the guys walk off the job."

"Because of the rumor that the house's cursed?"

"Not a rumor, it's a fact."

"You believe it's cursed?"

"Yes sir, I sure do."

There wasn't much I could say to that, so I said, "How many of the guys do you think would walk?"

"Six are talking about it, but when it comes to losing money for food, housing, and car payments, I'm not sure how many would actually do it."

"Are you one of the six?"

"Afraid so, except there's one thing that's holding me back."

"What's that?"

"I believe in things being cursed, truly do, but from everything I heard from my relatives when I was a youngster, ghosts, goblins, and things that curse buildings do it in old places. My grandpa was the community expert on that kind of stuff. Not saying it can't happen, but it seems unlikely that a new house like what we're building would've had time to get itself cursed." He smiled. "Guess I'm sounding like one of those kooks who go around spreading ghost stories." He looked at his watch. "Chris, umm, see I got your name right this time. Anyway, I need to get back. Don't want any of those guys to starve."

I told him I enjoyed talking with him then he headed to the register. I grabbed a Southwest wrap from the deli and followed Lucius to pay.

Sean Aker called as soon as I stepped in the house.

"Did I catch you at a bad time?"

A socially acceptable way to begin a conversation. I was surprised I recognized it since they came so seldom.

"It's a good time. What's up?"

"Think you could stop by the office in the morning?"

"Sure. I could come sooner if you want me to."

"No, I'm heading out in a few minutes to meet a potential client in Charleston. It could take the rest of the afternoon."

I chuckled. "You mean you might actually get a client? Won't that screw up your life of leisure?"

"Marlene has this archaic idea that I should pay her for sitting on her hands in the reception area every day. The sacrifices I make for my staff."

"You're all heart."

"Aren't I though? Gotta go. See you in the morning. Get here around eleven, that'll give me time for my morning nap."

"Okay. I wouldn't want to have Marlene wake you up."

"Smart ass," he said and ended the call.

Okay, at least he began the call with a civil opening.

36

On the walk to Sean's office, I found Virgil leaning against City Hall. He was in his typical garb of a frayed-cuff long-sleeve dress shirt, navy slacks, his beloved resoled Guccis, and, of course, sunglasses.

"Morning, Virgil. What are you doing?"

He grinned. "Supporting local government."

I smiled. "I think City Hall can stand on its own."

"Don't put money on it. What're you doing out this early?"

I didn't think ten-thirty was early, but told him I was on my way to see Sean Aker.

"You been arrested again?"

"Not this time. He called and wanted me to stop by this morning. Want to come with me?"

"I know Sean's an okay guy, but going through my divorce, the forced sale of my mansion, my boat, hell, my everything, I've had my fill of lawyers. You're on your own. Besides I'm working."

"Supporting city government?"

"In addition to that, I'm heading to the hardware store to get some plumbing stuff for an apartment I'm working on."

Virgil lived in a tiny apartment in a run-down apartment building and did odd jobs for the landlord in lieu of paying rent, something that otherwise would be difficult to do since he was unemployed.

I smiled. "That sounds exciting."

"Yeah, right. I am glad I saw you this morning. Last night I was at the bar at Rita's enjoying a cold beverage, or two. Guess who I ran into?"

"Pope Francis."

Virgil rolled his eyes. "No, he was at Planet Follywood. Mitchell Baldwin was at Rita's, and believe it or not, he recognized me."

"You're glad you ran into me so you could tell me you saw Mitchell?"

"I doubt that's newsworthy. What he told me might be in the breaking news category."

"What did Mitchell tell you?"

"Thought you'd never ask. He said Scott, umm, Rawlins, I think that's right."

"There's a Scott Rawlins on the crew with Mitchell."

"You're right and wrong."

"Care to explain?"

"Scott quit yesterday, no notice, didn't show up to quit. He called Joe, the owner of the construction company and said he was history."

"He give a reason?"

"No, but Mitchell said it had to be because he thought the house was cursed and he was afraid he'd be next to turn up dead."

"Why was Mitchell so sure that was Scott's reason?"

"He and Scott talked about, as he put it, 'the curse problem' the day before yesterday and Scott apparently was convinced the house was a disaster waiting to happen. That's all he shared with me. Now here's something that isn't news yet but could be soon. Mitchell said he may do the same thing the next day or so."

"The same reason?"

"I don't know what kind of bee they have in their construction bonnets but yes, Mitchell and some of the others are scared. Scared enough to quit their jobs."

"He say anything else?"

"Only 'you're welcome' after I thanked him for buying my beers."

"I should have asked the question better. Did he say anything that could help catch the killer?"

"Nope. I'd better get to the hardware store. You'd be amazed how royally pissed a tenant gets if he can't flush his toilet."

I wouldn't, I thought, but instead said, "Thanks for letting me know about Scott. Good luck with the toilet repairs."

He saluted, headed in the direction of Pewter Hardware, and I headed to Sean Aker's office.

The office was on the second floor above one of Folly's gift shops.

"Good morning, Marlene. Is Sean Aker, Esquire in?" I asked as I petted the Shih Tzu sitting in her lap.

"Don't you mean is he awake?"

"Yes," came the voice of the attorney who was standing in the doorway to his office.

"Thank you, Marlene," I said with a tinge of sarcasm.

She laughed and said, "I believe Mr. Aker, Esquire is available to see you."

I followed Sean into his office. A scuba dive tank was propped against a wall in the corner of the room, a surfboard in another corner, and a packed parachute on one of the two side chairs in front of his desk, all tools required for some of his hobbies. I sat in the unoccupied chair.

Sean pushed aside a manila folder, leaned back in the chair, and said, "Thanks for stopping by."

"I always jump when my attorney summons me."

"I wish you could teach Marlene that trick. She's convinced I work for her, and don't do enough of it."

"We all need someone to keep us on the straight and narrow."

"Whatever. I suppose you're wondering why the invitation."

"I am."

He leaned forward in his chair. "In the last three days, I've received two calls from attorney friends who work in law offices in downtown Charleston. Someone you may be familiar with has been attorney shopping in some of the hoity-toity firms over there." He tapped his pen on a legal pad in front of him.

"Care to share who?"

"I told the attorneys I wouldn't divulge their names, and that doesn't matter anyway, since neither of them took the case. The shopper was Raymond Whitley."

"The late Shelly Whitley's husband."

"Correct."

"Why did the attorneys contact you?"

"They knew my office was a mile from where Shelly took her last breath and figured I may know something about the situation out there."

"Why didn't they take the case?"

"First, they said Raymond was a sleaze." Sean hesitated, smiled, and held his hand in front of me. "I know, I know, we attorneys represent people of the sleaze persuasion all the time, but they said in addition to that, they didn't see where he had much of a case. They said they could've taken it on but saw years of battles with the contractor's insurance company, and even if they won, it wouldn't have been worthwhile, especially if they had to deal with Raymond."

"You think Raymond will find an attorney to take the case?"

"Absolutely, he just didn't talk to two who were hungry enough."

"Is his case good enough to win?"

"Possibly, especially if you and your buddies can't prove her death was murder and not negligence on the part of the construction company."

"You mean if the police can't prove it was murder."

"I said what I meant," Sean said as he tapped his fingers on the desk. "You're not going to try to convince me otherwise, are you? Anyway, I thought you'd want to know what's going on."

"Thanks. While I'm here could you do me a favor?"

"Is it going to cost me a ton of money, or worse, incur Marlene's wrath?"

"No to the cost, but I'm not sure about Marlene."

"Let's hear it."

"I was told Oliver Trescott bought the property the house is being built on about a decade ago. There was an old concrete block house on the property at the time. After Trescott bought it, he tore the structure down and didn't do anything with the property until he got a building permit for the current house seven months ago."

Sean took notes on the legal pad then looked at me. "Okay, so what's the favor?"

"Could you see what you could find on the transfer from whomever to Trescott when he bought it and if there's anything else that's happened with the property since then?"

"Hmm, it'll be easy for me to check the registry of deeds to see what they have on the transfer. Beyond that, I doubt I could find much. Why is this important?"

"I don't know that it is. It strikes me a little strange that Trescott bought it that long ago and didn't do anything with it until recently."

"That's not unusual, happens all the time. Someone inherits a property and doesn't touch it for years. Someone gets a good deal on a vacant lot and waits until they have enough money to do something with it. Someone buys a property, and something changes in his or her personal life to where nothing can be done with the property."

"I understand. I know it's a long shot, but at this point, I don't know what else to do."

What I didn't tell him was the stories about the house being cursed made me wonder about the history of the property. Hadn't Lucius' grandfather said things that're cursed are old and not new? I didn't believe houses were cursed, but Virgil just told me Scott Rawlins had quit because of the rumors, and Mitchell Baldwin may not be far behind. I also know Lucius Walker believes the rumor. I have no idea how those stories may be related to the deaths, if at all, but I was honest when I told Sean I didn't know what else to do.

37

"Know where I am?" Charles asked as the phone interrupted me sipping my morning coffee on the front porch.

"Madrid, Spain."

He sighed into the mouthpiece. "Why do I keep asking you anything?"

"If you continue asking questions I couldn't know the answer to, I'd assume you're a glutton for punishment. So, where are you?"

"That's better. On the walking pier at the Folly River Park."

The Folly River Park is a small community park at the corner of Center Street and East Indian Avenue.

"You called to tell me that because?"

"It's a beautiful August day. The temperature is tolerable, and there's a group of kayakers going in circles in the river in front of me. Figured you'd want to be here."

I hated to admit it, but he had good points. "I'll be there in a few minutes."

"On your way, why don't you grab me a cup of coffee from Bert's. While you're there, how about picking up a couple of sweet things, things that'll go good with coffee?"

Clearly, he wanted more than my company. Instead of answering, I hung up on him and realized it felt better than the other way around.

Twenty minutes later, I'd reached the walking pier while carrying two cups of coffee and a bag containing two cinnamon rolls. Charles was standing on the far end of the pier, leaning against the railing, and watching a small fishing boat pass in front of the structure. He was wearing a long-sleeve, Kelly green Notre Dame T-shirt, his Tilley, and tan shorts.

He looked back at me and said, "You're late. You done missed some vacationers taking kayak lessons going around in circles; now they're somewhere out in the marsh."

I didn't share any sorrow for missing that exciting spectacle. I sat on the wooden bench and took his roll out of the bag.

He looked at the roll, took a sip of coffee, and said, "You're forgiven."

"You're so kind."

"Smartass."

I smiled and said, "You bet."

"Where've you been the last few days? Thought we'd be spending time catching the killer."

"Do you know who it is?"

"No."

"Then how're we going to catch him?"

"Guess our plan has a couple of holes in it."

"Couple of big ones. I did learn more about the house and its crew." I proceeded to tell him about Scott and Tim's wreck." After he berated me for not telling him sooner, I shared what Virgil had said about talking with Mitchell and that Scott had quit without giving notice.

"That's because he's the killer. He knows we're getting close and took off. By now, he's probably in California, or Canada, or in, well, you get my point."

If we were getting close to revealing him as the murderer, he knew way more than we did. "He told Mitchell it had something to do with the rumor that the house is cursed. Mitchell told Virgil he may be quitting sooner rather than later."

"Why?"

"Same reason."

"They're grown men. Don't they know there's no such thing as a cursed house?"

"Apparently not."

"Well, they should. That brings me to why I invited you here."

"You mean other than me bringing you food and drink."

"Of course. That was a bonus."

"For you. Okay, why invite me?"

"Aloysius called last night."

"Aloysius?"

"The remodeler I helped with the sunroom."

"Okay, he called, and?"

"He got a call yesterday from Joe Argyle, you know, the guy who owns the company building the death house."

I nodded.

"Joe asked him if he knew any carpenters who'd be available to work immediately."

"Aloysius called you?"

"He knows my skill set, the one that lacks, umm, skill in carpentry. He thought since I help contractors, I might know someone. I didn't. That's not my point."

"What's your point?"

"Joe told Aloysius he was in a tight spot with the death house. Of course, he didn't say death house. Anyway, he said he'd lost three employees, and unless he found replacements soon, he may have to shut down the job until more workers are found. Said there are only two carpenters left and according to rumors, one is considering bailing. Something about if he didn't have carpenters, the plumbers and electricians wouldn't be able to work since some of their work couldn't be done until the carpenters finished doing stuff."

"What'd you tell Aloysius?"

"I only know a couple of carpenters and they're happily employed."

"Doesn't Argyle's company have other jobs in the area? Couldn't he free up workers to help over here?"

"He must have at least one other job," Charles said. "Remember one of the other guys was at another job the day Mason was killed?"

"Yes, Luis Ortez. Besides, Argyle must've explored all his options before he called Aloysius."

Charles took the final bite of his roll and mumbled, "What do we do now?"

"Sit back and wait for the kayakers to come back from the marsh."

"I meant about catching the killer."

"I know."

Charles said, "Well?"

"No idea."

This is our time together catching the killer.

It'd been several days since I'd seen Barb, so I called her on my way home to see if she wanted to meet me for supper. She did and we agreed on a time and location.

38

———

I'd agreed to meet Barb at Pier 101 Restaurant & Bar located at the Folly Beach Fishing Pier with outstanding views of the ocean and the beach. Pier 101 is the second iteration of the restaurant since I'd moved to Folly. Many folks hated to see Locklear's, its predecessor, go, but many had returned to the new restaurant because of its menu and location. I was one of those returnees. It was often crowded this time of year, so I arrived a half-hour early so I could get our name on the waiting list.

I was waiting for Barb at the outside bar when she reached the top step to the Pier's deck and looked around. She joined me, asked how long I'd been waiting, then ordered a beer. I told her I'd been here a half hour and there should be a table for us relatively soon. As if I coordinated it with the management, the receptionist approached to tell me the table was ready. Barb acted impressed although we both knew it was luck.

We took our drinks as we headed to the table along the side of the patio overlooking the ocean. Lauren, one of the restaurant's college-age servers, was quick to the table and asked if we needed anything else to drink. We declined and she said she'd give us a few minutes to decide on our dinner selections.

Barb took a sip of beer, leaned back in her chair, and said, "This has been one busy day. You can tell it's the middle of the season."

I would've been thrilled to have had one busy day during the time Landrum Gallery was housed in the bookstore's current space, but instead of sharing that, I said, "Then take a deep breath, enjoy the late afternoon sun, the view, and me."

She smiled. "You were doing fine until you got to the last part of that."

"The *me* part?"

"You got it." Her smile turned to a laugh. "Sorry, teasing. You're almost as good to look at as the view."

I didn't ask why almost. At my age, I'll take any compliment or near compliment I can get.

"I was talking to Noelle the other day. She told me again how much she appreciated you offering her your condo's spare bedroom after her building burned."

"She was a delight to have around. I haven't seen her for a few weeks. How's her book coming?"

I told her Noelle's novel is nearly finished, at least the draft. I also told her how I was with her when she met Brad Burton and how they clashed on her lack of law enforcement experience or training when she offered her thoughts on the deaths at the house on West Ashley.

"He's right, you know. He has what, forty plus years working in law enforcement and she, along with a couple of guys I know, managed to get involved in one real-life criminal investigation."

I would've felt better if she hadn't interjected Charles and me into the conversation.

I limited my response to, "True."

Lauren returned to see if we were ready to order. Barb said she'd like a big, juicy hamburger then asked if the fries were the "big, chubby ones; not those skinny ones some restaurants serve." Lauren assured her they were, so Barb said she'd have an order of them with her burger. I said I'd have the same.

Lauren headed inside and Barb said, "I'm not going to ask if you're getting involved in the deaths out there. Wouldn't want you to lie to me, so, has anything new happened to help you get a better idea who might've committed the crimes?"

"Did you hear about the guy getting pinned between a forklift and the house?"

"I'd have to be deaf, dumb, and in Mozambique to not have heard about it. Nobody thinks it was an accident like the other deaths, do they?"

"No, but the Sheriff's Office detective thinks it's the only murder out there."

"And you and, I suppose, Charles think the other two deaths weren't accidents."

"Correct, and neither does Cindy."

"Then let me ask this, do you think they were killed by the same person?"

"That appears the most likely scenario."

"Okay, so let's go with that assumption. What did the three have in common?"

"Great question."

"Of course it was. Did you expect anything less?" She then laughed.

"Never. But, to your question, I keep coming up with nothing in common other than working on the house. From everything I've heard, they didn't know each other outside work. Their ages ranged from thirty to sixty-two. They didn't live near each other; didn't have the same friends. One was married. I've talked with several others who worked with them and none of them said there were conflicts among the victims." I shrugged.

Lauren delivered our food, asked if we needed anything else to drink, we each declined, and she went to the next table to ask the same question.

"Then why they were killed must be answered before the police, yes, the police and not you and Charles, can focus on who did it."

"That's much more difficult since the police aren't looking for anyone other the person who killed Mason Ryle."

"The guy between the forklift and the building?"

"Yes."

She slathered a fry in ketchup then stuck it in her mouth. She put her hand in front of her face and mumbled, "I love chubby fries."

I envied her metabolism. I could eat far less than she did and gain weight. She could out eat most people I know and never gain an ounce.

She took a sip and said, "Unless there's a serious nutcase out there killing people for no reason, there has to be something in it for him or her other than the perverted thrill of killing people."

"I agree, and since the first two deaths were made to look like accidents and the third murder committed while others working on the project were nearby with nobody seeing anything unusual, I would tend to eliminate the *serious nutcase* explanation."

"Back in my days practicing law, I defended a couple of guys who would qualify as nutcases. Don't confuse that with them being dumb. Some are, of course, but they can also be smart, wily, cunning, and able to plan near-perfect crimes. With that said, those are few and far between. What would the killer gain by these three alleged murders?"

"I don't know."

"Okay, let me throw out a couple of possibilities. Three deaths on such a small project would bring a heap of negativity on the construction company. I'm sure OSHA is investigating. Seldom does anything good come out of their involvement. Companies get shut down, fines get levied, and negative publicity often results." She took another bite then continued, "What do you know about the company?"

"Custom Builders Group is owned by Joe Argyle. I've heard good things about it. They've built several houses over here and more in Charleston, Mt. Pleasant, and Kiawah. I've not heard anything negative about him or his company. But there is one thing." I hesitated and took a sip of wine.

"But what?" Barb said doing a no-patience Charles imitation.

"This may sound silly, but several of the workers think the house is cursed. Charles told me about one of the carpenters quitting out of fear."

"Why do they think it's cursed?"

"I think they attribute the high number of, umm, deaths in such a short period of time to a curse. I've not heard anyone saying why they think the house is cursed, but it may directly affect the builder."

"Meaning?"

"Charles was contacted by a builder he occasionally does work for. Aloysius, he's the builder, asked Charles if he knew any carpenters who could use work. Apparently, Joe Argyle contacted him to ask the same thing. Argyle told Charles's acquaintance that unless he could replace a couple who've quit and one he fired, he might have to temporarily shut down the project."

"So," Barb said, "Custom Builders Group would be hurt by the deaths, more than possibly getting a bad reputation for safety standards, or anything OSHA does."

"True."

"Okay, what about the person they're building the house for?"

"His name's Oliver Trescott. Bought the property a decade ago. Moved here earlier this year from the D.C. area. I've met him once; seems like an okay guy."

"You don't know any reason a killer would want to cause harm to the homeowner?"

"None I know of."

"Unless you can learn what's in it for the killer, there's little, if any chance you'll be able to find him, or her." She gave a slight nod. "Need I remind you, doing any of this is the job for the police, and not two gentlemen I'm familiar with."

"I know."

True, I knew that, but it wasn't going to stop me from trying. Barb also knew that, so there was no reason to revisit what I should do, and what I will do. A change of subject was in order, and Lauren returning to see if we were ready for another drink provided that change.

"Yes," I said and ordered a second glass of wine for me, another beer for Barb.

The deaths weren't mentioned the rest of the evening; not here, not on the brief walk to her condo, and not during the next two hours there.

39

"**D**id I catch you at a bad time?" Sean said as I answered the phone while taking a box to the trash container by the back door.

"No, you're fine."

"Good, if you're out and about this morning, think you could stop by the office?"

"Sure, but what are you doing there on Saturday?"

He laughed. "Marlene's off and I didn't want her to catch me doing legal work."

"That'd ruin your reputation with the rest of your staff. I can be there anytime, so what's good for you?"

"Around eleven."

"See you then."

"Call when you're downstairs. I keep the door locked on the weekend."

I was surprised he called, but not as surprised as I was knowing he was working on a Saturday. At a few minutes before eleven, I called and was told he'd be down shortly. Good to his word, two minutes later he opened the door and motioned for me to follow him upstairs. Instead of going in his office, he pointed at one of the chairs in the reception area and asked if I wanted something to drink. I said no, and he sat in Marlene's chair.

"I hate getting cooped up in my office all the time. That's one of the reasons I spend so much time at the Dog or walking around. Of course, Marlene assumes I'm goofing off when I'm away from the office."

"Aren't you?"

He smiled. "Most of the time. Marlene's a wise lady. Anyway, I didn't ask to take up your time to discuss my claustrophobia. Hang on." He walked into his office and returned with a legal pad and returned to Marlene's chair.

"I had to be in Charleston yesterday afternoon, so I went by the ROD office to see—"

I interrupted, "The what?"

"Sorry, the Register of Deeds office, it's in the County Office Building on Meeting Street. It's where land titles, liens, and other documents related to property transactions in Charleston County are maintained."

"The property on West Ashley Avenue?"

"You're catching on."

"What'd you learn?"

"Not much." He looked at the legal pad then said, "Ten years ago, this month in fact, David and Sarah Halloran sold the property to IH Financial Group, a holding company out of Connecticut."

"Oliver Trescott, the current owner told me he owned a couple of holding companies in addition to several properties."

"Then you know more than I learned from the ROD office."

"Do you know the Hallorans?"

"Don't think so, or if I did, I've forgotten about it. Do you?"

I shook my head. "This is the first I'm hearing about them. Was there anything else related to the sale in the records?"

"There was a handwritten note on the paperwork that said, *Reginald Salyer, Realtor*."

"The buyer or the seller's realtor?"

"No idea."

"Was anything else included?"

"Nothing other than the lot's description."

"I appreciate you looking into it."

"Don't suppose that helps much. I looked to see if there was any mention of the property being cursed."

"Didn't figure there was. With that out of the way, why are you working on a Saturday, other than not to confuse Marlene?"

"Got a client who's going to make an offer on an office building on James Island. He got all antsy about it early this morning, so I told him I'd research something for him before his meeting with the owner Monday."

"Thanks for the help."

"Sorry I couldn't find out more. Any hot leads on who killed from one to three people out there?"

"If there are, I don't know about them."

"Try not to get yourself killed looking."

"Excellent advice, Counselor."

It was another perfect August morning. Puffy white clouds dotted the sky, and the temperature was in the upper seventies, so instead of heading home I walked three blocks to Loggerhead's then up the ramp to the patio. Ed asked if I wanted a table. His twisting my arm worked. It was still before noon so there were a couple of vacant tables. He pointed to a small one by the railing overlooking the parking area and said a server will be with me as soon as he found one.

He succeeded because Shelia, a server who'd waited on me a few times over the last couple of years, was at the table before I'd settled.

She said, "White wine?"

"Not today. A diet Coke."

She said she thought she could handle that and headed to the bar.

As I was waiting for my drink, I called Bob Howard. Instead of the phone's cranky owner, I got his cranky voicemail "greeting" that said, "You know who you've not reached, so if you insist on talking to me, leave a message at the sound of the tone, and I might return your call. Have a nice day."

"Bob, this is Chris, your sweet voicemail message warmed my heart. Got a question. Do you know a realtor named Reginald Salyer? If you do, give me a call. I may answer."

Shelia set the drink in front of me while I was having the warm and fuzzy conversation with Bob's voicemail. I took a sip and replayed the conversation with Sean Aker to see what, if anything, I'd learned new. Other than the name of a realtor, the only thing I didn't know was the name of the holding company listed as the purchaser. I assumed it was one of Oliver Trescott's.

Shelia returned to ask if I was ready to order. I said yes and she left with my order for a cheeseburger, and as my effort to cut back on calories, I didn't order fries. Okay, I agree, that wasn't much of an effort considering I ordered a cheeseburger. It's the thought that counts, or so I told myself.

Forty-five minutes later, all I'd achieved was consuming a cheeseburger. I was no closer to learning who killed the workers out West Ashley Avenue. The deck was now crowded with several groups waiting on a table, so I paid and headed home.

As soon as I opened the door, I knew something was wrong. Two magazines I'd left on the small table by my recliner were on the floor. The wise thing for me to do would be to step outside, call 911, and wait in the yard until an emergency responder arrived. So, of course, I didn't follow my wise counsel.

I slowly walked though the living room and looked in my second bedroom, aka my office, and immediately wished I hadn't. A window-pane was broken, and the window was pushed up enough for someone to climb through. Two of the four drawers in my filing cabinet were open with their contents spread haphazardly on the floor. I'd left three files on the desk beside my computer. They had joined the other files and papers on the floor.

I backed out of the room and headed to my bedroom. I took a sigh of relief when nothing appeared to be disturbed. The kitchen was my next stop and it appeared undisturbed. All that was out of place was the back door, which was partially open. I glanced in the bathroom on the way back to the office. Seeing no one hanging around with a knife, gun, or hand grenade, I returned to the office and was more relieved than I'd been in the bedroom when I saw my camera bag untouched in the corner. My computer was switched off just as I'd left it. I doubted someone who'd leave the back door open would've turned the computer off when he or she was done snooping through it.

I went to the refrigerator, poured myself a glass of white wine, made sure the front and back doors were locked, moved to the recliner in the living room, and called Chief LaMond.

40

———————

en minutes later, Cindy was pounding on the front door
and yelling my name.

"Are you okay?" she asked as I opened the door and
waved her in.

"Yes. Thanks for coming."

"Don't read too much into it. I'd do most anything to get out of the
office and the pile of paperwork that's growing faster than Jack's
beanstalk. Tell me again what happened."

"There's not much to tell. I'd been at Sean Aker's office then went
to Loggerhead's for lunch, came home to find evidence someone had
been here."

She nodded, then said, "Then you got out of the house as fast as
your aging legs could carry you because whoever broke in could still
be here. Then after you were safely outside, you called me."

"Well, that's not—"

"Hold on," she interrupted. "That's what a normal, careful, sane
person would do." She put her forefinger on the side of her head, and
continued, "Using my psychic powers and outstanding chiefly skills,
let me guess. You came in, saw someone had been here and instead of
getting out of here faster than a roadrunner, you went through each

room to see what'd been taken or disturbed, never thinking the burglar could still be here ready to put a bullet in your thick skull. How'd I do?"

I translated that to say she cares about my safety and is glad I was okay.

"Cindy, want to see what's been done?"

"I knew it. I'd ask you to pat me on the back, but as reckless as you've been, you'd probably miss." She sighed, looked around, and said, "It's your tour."

She followed me into the room I use as an office. I left everything as I'd found it, so it didn't take all her *psychic powers and outstanding chiefly skills* to see what physical damage and disruption had occurred.

She pointed to the broken windowpane. "Since I've known you, how many times has Larry had to replace glass in that window after someone broke in?"

I smiled. "Enough times I'm beginning to think you're the one breaking it so I can keep Larry in business."

"Right, three or four times replacing the glass in that small window is going to keep Pewter Hardware in the black." She laughed and continued, "Before I leave, I'll call him so he can come over and take care of it, again. He probably keeps a supply of panes that size just for your window."

She sat in the folding chair I keep in the office for my rare guests in that room. I took the desk chair and pulled up in front of her.

"If you're done marketing for your hubby's store, want to hear what was taken?"

She took a small notebook out of her pocket and said, "Okay mister aggrieved citizen, what was taken?"

"Aggrieved?"

"The mayor's still insisting I need to increase my vocabulary, something about it helping me communicate with our diverse and highly educated vacationers and citizens. I'm going with the idea of learning a word a day to keep the mayor away. Now, am I going to have to call you yesterday's word of the day which means trouble-maker, or are you going to tell me what's missing?"

One of Cindy's talents is making people feel comfortable regardless of the situation. I think it helps her communicate more effectively with people than springing new words on them. I know I'm way more relaxed since she'd arrived.

"Nothing."

"Nothing is missing?"

"Correct. To be honest, I can't say some of the papers from the filing cabinet aren't missing. It'd be almost impossible to tell what if any of them are gone. Those two drawers hold files and papers from my first couple of years here. Nothing recent."

She pointed at the filing cabinet. "Did you touch those two open drawers?"

"They're how I found them."

"How about the window?"

"I haven't touched it since I got home."

"Good. I'll have one of my guys come over and see if there're any prints on the window or the filing cabinet." She looked back at the door. "You sure nothing else has been disturbed other than those magazines in the living room."

"I can't be a hundred-percent sure, but nothing appears to have been moved."

"It looks to me like one of two things. It wasn't a burglar since your TV, computer, and camera are still here, or it was a burglar and he cut his scavenger hunt short when he or possibly she heard you coming in the house."

I smiled and said, "So your *outstanding chiefly skills* told you it was, or it wasn't a burglar?"

She nodded, then said, "When you opened the front door, did you hear anything?"

"Like someone opening the back door and running out?"

"That'd be what we highly trained, professional law enforcement officials call a clue."

"I wasn't thinking about it, but it's not that far from the front door to the back door, so I think I would've heard someone leaving."

"If that's the case, then I would assume whoever was in here was looking for something, and not something to hock."

"I agree."

"You said you were at Sean's before coming home, right?"

"Sean's and then Loggerhead's."

"What were you doing at Sean's on Saturday?"

"I'd asked him to try to find out who sold the property on West Ashley to Oliver Trescott. He looked it up yesterday and was in the office today working up some information for a client, so he called and asked me to stop by."

Cindy leaned back in the chair and said, "So, you're still butting in business you have no business doing."

"I'm only asking questions since I'm interested in finding out more about the house to see if there is some possible connection to the three deaths. As you know, the only thing the victims have in common is they were working on the house."

"Has it entered your pea-sized brain that you might be getting too close to learning something that the person who killed Mason Ryle, and possibly killed the other two people, doesn't want you to know?"

"Chief—"

"Hang on, I'm not done."

I motioned for her to continue.

"And, that person broke in here looking for anything you may've had that could point to him or her."

"Yes."

"Yes, what?"

If Charles or a couple other of my friends asked that, I would've told them if they paid attention to what they'd asked me, they would know what I was saying yes to. Folly's top cop wasn't one of those people. Instead, I said, "Yes, I'd thought about it being the person who killed the three workers."

"Good, because if I had to guess, that'd top my list." She looked at the papers on the floor and continued, "You're not going to back off, are you?"

"No."

She sighed and shook her head.

I said, "Now that you're here, let me ask a question."

"If all you wanted to do was ask me a question, you simply could've called. You didn't have to break in your house to get me to come over."

"You know I—"

She stuck her palm in front of me and said, "That was an attempt at levity."

"Hilarious. The question is do you know the Hallorans, David and Sarah?"

"Who're they?"

"The couple who sold the house to a holding company that's probably owned by the current owner, Oliver Trescott."

"Wasn't that a decade or so ago?"

"Ten years this month."

"That's not long after I moved to Folly. Hell, at that time, I didn't know where the public restrooms were, much less who owned houses. Do you think the sale of the house is somehow related to the three deaths?"

"I'm grabbing at straws. What I know is the only thing tying the victims together appears to be the house. Do you know if Detective Fisher is looking at it that way?"

"Since he's only looking at one being murdered, I doubt it. You still think all three were killed?"

"Yes, don't you?"

She nodded and said, "But with nothing more than playing the odds on what would be the chance that the other two had fatal accidents days before Ryle was killed." She leaned forward in the chair. "Now it's time to ask you a question."

"And it is?"

"During all your snooping, have you and Charles learned anything the police might be interested in?"

"Don't know how much it'll help, but one of the workers told Charles that Scott, he's one of the carpenters, quit and the rumor's going around that Mitchell Baldwin, may be next."

"Why?"

"The rumor about the house being cursed appears to be picking up steam. Charles also said the guy he occasionally helps on construction jobs, contacted him, and asked if he knew any carpenters looking for work. Apparently, the owner of the company building the house contacted him saying unless he finds more workers, he may have to shut down the job."

Cindy leaned back in the chair. "All because of a damned curse, excuse me, rumor of a curse?"

I nodded.

She sighed and said, "Anything else?"

"Sean told me Raymond Whitley, Shelly's husband, is shopping lawyers in Charleston so he can sue the builder for negligence causing her to fall."

"Are you saying Raymond snuck up on the roof and pushed his wife off to get a bundle of money from the contractor?"

"Unlikely, but possible."

She looked at her watch. "I'd love to sit here and talk about ghosts, or curses, or whatever, and deranged husbands pushing their wives off roofs, but I'm already late for a meeting with two of my guys. There's some matter of life-or-death they have to talk to me about."

"Life-or-death?"

"No biggie. They always talk that way. They probably want longer breaks or other such life-or-death issues." She looked around the room. "Need help picking up all this stuff?"

I told her I could handle it.

Before she left, she repeated that she'd have someone stop by and take fingerprints, she'd have Larry call me to schedule repairing the window, and for me not to get killed before I could buy her more meals.

That was further proof of her saying she cares about me and wants me to stay safe, or so I told myself.

41

The next morning, I started thinking about yesterday's *unwelcome* visitor and thought I should warn Charles since he was as involved as I was. I called him and after four rings, and an out of breath Charles answered.

"Are you working out at the gym?" I asked, knowing the odds on that being true were about the same as me winning the lottery.

"Did you call to make a joke?"

"Okay, then where are you?"

"Six-hundred block of your street making a delivery for Dude. Why?"

"What are you doing after you make the delivery?"

"Have two more to make. What's all the interest in my location?"

Instead of getting into it over the phone, I said, "Meet me for lunch at the Crab Shack."

"If you insist," he said and hung up.

The phone rang seconds later.

"Noon," I said.

"What in the hell are you talking about?" Bob Howard asked.

"Sorry, I thought it was someone else."

"Who do you know named Noon? Sounds like some kind of freakin' New Age, crystal healing, whatever name."

"It's a time, not someone's name. Now, why did you call?"

"A bit cranky this morning, aren't we—meaning you."

"I'm fine."

"Fine and cranky. Anyway, your message said you wanted to know if I knew Reginald Salyer. Yes."

I waited for more, but hearing nothing, I said, "What do you know about him?"

"Don't know him well. He was in the business nearly as long as I was. From what I could tell, he seldom handled upscale housing, in layman's terms, expensive houses. His bread and butter was hawking starter homes and foreclosures."

"Anything else?"

"Hell, Chris, you think I'm Wick-e-opedia?"

A little sucking-up is often appropriate when talking to Bob. "No, but you were one of the most successful realtors in the area, and I figured if anyone knew something about Salyer, it'd be you."

"Damn right. That was a little too syrupy, but right. Okay, you dragged it out of me. When good ole Reggie was in his prime, he had the reputation as not being reliable."

"What's that mean?"

"I think it's a quaint, nonjudgmental way of saying he couldn't be trusted. His word couldn't be taken as gospel."

"Did you have dealings with him during those years?"

"Only once. He was handling a foreclosure. My client looked at it but decided on another property. And before you ask, no, Reggie didn't do or say anything to me that I found to be inaccurate. I don't know if his reputation was based on fact, or gossip."

"Anything else?"

"Tell you what, why don't I call him and see if I can entice him into coming to Al's for lunch. He's retired now like you and since you're both worthless members of society, he probably could find time. You can happen to be here at the same time and talk with him. And best of all, I can make money off both of you. A win-win."

"That's a great idea."

"That's still too syrupy, but truthful. I'll let you know."

I ARRIVED at the Crab Shack at eleven-thirty. After telling the server all I needed to drink was water, I saw Charles pulling up to the side of the building and parking his Schwinn in the bike rack at the corner.

"Sorry I'm late," he said, although I hadn't told him what time to meet me. "Dude had me deliver one more thing. This has been a prosperous day. I made enough money to buy both of our lunches. I won't but I could."

"That's almost generous of you."

"Sarcasm, right?"

"Close enough."

The server arrived with my water and asked Charles what he wanted to drink. He told her to bring him the same as I was having. She left to try to find water for Charles then he said, "I figure you wanting to have lunch with me wasn't the only reason you called."

"True. Someone broke in my house yesterday."

"Whoa, you waited this long to tell me?"

"I called this morning, and you were making deliveries for Dude."

"Excuses, excuses. Okay, apology accepted. What happened?"

I shared what little I knew about the break-in and added, "I wanted to let you know so you could be careful. Have you seen or heard anything around your place that could be suspicious?"

"Not really. I know nobody's been in my place because everything's a mess."

Charles's apartment suits his needs, but too many would be considered a hoarder's paradise, so I knew what he meant about it not being neat. If anything was straightened up, Charles hadn't done it.

The server returned and took our orders, and Charles leaned back in his chair and said, "Sounds like someone thinks we're about ready to learn who killed those folks."

"That's what Cindy thought."

"Then who is it?"

"No idea."

"If you ask me, I think it's Kyle for all the reasons I already told you. He's tried to get us off the case from the beginning. He and Shelly had their conflicts, so he had reason to shove her off the roof."

"All of that may be true, but is it enough for him to go on a killing spree?"

"Sure it is, but, umm, what about Scott? He wanted to be foreman so killing Randy would've sped up the process. And now he's quit and probably decided we were getting close and plans to skip the country."

"Now I'm confused. Do you think it's Kyle or Scott?"

"Yes."

"Yes, what?"

"Could be either."

"There you go, you've figured it out."

"Picking on me again?"

"Yes."

"Figures, so what's our next step?"

"Eating lunch," I said as the server slid lunch baskets in front of us.

The phone rang before we'd finished. The screen said Bob.

"Hello, Mr. Howard."

"That's better than calling me a moon rock, or New Age guru. Just got off the phone with my good buddy Reggie. Guess where he's having lunch tomorrow?"

"Al's."

"You're getting to be as good a detective as your quarter-wit friend Charles."

I glanced over at Charles, and said to Bob, "Okay if he comes with me tomorrow?"

"You bet, that's more bucks in my pocket. Bring more if you can find anyone else who'd want to eat with you," he said and hung up.

Charles looked at me like what are you getting me into. I shared what I'd learned about Reginald Salyer, aka Reggie, and about his invitation to lunch tomorrow at Al's.

Charles gave me a thumbs-up and said, "That'll put us one step closer to solving the crimes."

42

I was in front of Bert's on the way home when the phone rang. This time I looked to see who it was before answering.

"Hello, Brad."

"Are you home?"

"I'm about fifty yards from the front door and heading that way. Why?"

"Mind company? I wanted to bounce a couple of ideas off you."

I told him to come on over, then shook my head thinking how much he detested me and my meddling when he was a detective. Has he changed that much or am I different than I was not that long ago? Or, has Hazel's pronouncement that he get a hobby the reason for his changing?

He was knocking before I had time to give his metamorphosis more thought. I invited him in and asked if he wanted something to drink. I was pleased when he declined since I wasn't sure what I had. He had a manila folder in his hand so I suggested we sit in the kitchen so he could spread whatever he had in the folder on the table if he wanted to.

"I suppose you're wondering why I invited myself over."

"Yes."

"I got a call this morning from Len Fisher, the detective on the Mason Ryle case. I take it you've met."

"He came knocking on my door a few days ago. Said he'd heard I was asking questions about the murder he was investigating and said if he heard I was continuing to butt in, he'd have me arrested." I smiled and continued, "His people skills need some work. What'd he want?"

"Today was the first time I'd talked to the guy, so I was surprised when he called. He said some of the guys in the office had told him I used to be with the Sheriff's Office, had retired, and now lived next to you."

"So?"

Brad rubbed his chin, looked at the folder on the table, and said, "He said since we lived so close, I might know something that would strengthen his case against you. For some reason he's mighty upset with you."

"Why?"

Brad chuckled. "It wasn't that many years ago that I spent a good portion of my time pissed at you. Whenever I caught a murder over here, I kept running into you. If I asked you about it, you kept saying all you were doing was asking a few questions. And how many times did those, umm, questions get you in the middle of my investigation?"

"Brad, you know—"

"Yes, your involvement helped take some bad guys off the streets. And yes, you saved my life because of your butting in. The point is, he's got a burr under his saddle about you."

"What'd he want you to do?"

"He didn't use these exact words, but from what I could tell, he wants to get evidence that you're meddling so he can come down on you like a load of bricks. He wants you in jail."

"Again, what does he want you to do?"

Brad smiled. "Said I should keep my trained detective eyes on you and let him know if you are still snooping in his case."

"What'd you tell him?"

"I figured someone in the office told him about our, umm,

disagreements over the years, so I said I knew what he meant about you snooping and said I'd try to see what I could find."

"What are you going to do?"

"Seeing what I can find out about your snooping." He laughed. "I didn't tell him I'd let him know what I learned. If he assumed I would, he's got a lot to learn before he becomes a good detective." He shook his head. "Young know-it-alls. Now that brings me to why I'm here." He opened the folder and took out two sheets of lined paper with scribbling on them. They were either written in code or the quality of his writing equaled his ability to run a marathon. He then took a pen out of his pocket and set it on the paper. "I've been giving a lot of thought to the murders. What's making it so difficult to get a handle on, it's not known how many of the deaths were murder, right?"

"Yes. Your new detective buddy Fisher is stuck on the idea that only Mason Ryle was murdered and the other two were accidents. I'm convinced all three were killed. You still agree?"

"Yes, but what perplexes me is motive. The vics have nothing in common other than working at that house. Have you learned anything to dispute that?"

"No and that makes me think the murders have something to do with the house."

Brad pointed the pen at me. "You're not falling for that ludicrous idea your friend, umm—"

"Noelle?"

"Yeah, her idea the house is cursed and that's somehow killing the workers?"

"I don't believe in curses, but there still could be something about the house that's involved with the deaths."

Brad shook his head. "Like what?"

"I don't know, but it should be considered."

"Whatever. Remember I first thought the dead woman's husband would've been my top suspect if I was working the case?"

"Yes, Raymond Whitley."

"I changed my mind."

"Why?"

"Because I think the same person killed all three, and if that's true, I don't see how it could've been him. Sure, he could've somehow gotten in the house and pushed her off the roof without anyone seeing him. Remote, but possible. He also could've electrocuted the next guy since it was at the deserted house at midnight. But that brings me to the third death. All the workers were eating lunch. Some close to the house, some not so close. You can't tell me the husband could sneak up to the house, start a loud forklift, back into the guy, then climb off and walk away without anyone seeing him."

"Brad, if you're right, and I think I agree with you, the killer is one of the workers."

"Yes. And that brings me to this." He tapped the papers he took out of the folder. "These are the guys who are working on the house. Since we don't know the reason for the crimes, we have to approach it by seeing who couldn't have done it and take it from there."

I liked his use of *we*.

"Makes sense."

"Were any of the guys not working the day the woman was pushed or the day of the forklift incident?"

"I haven't heard about any of them not being there the day of Shelly's death."

"That didn't help, did it?"

"No. About the day Mason was killed, I heard Joshua Bennett was out sick."

"Good," Brad said and marked through his name on his list, or I assumed it was Joshua's name since I couldn't read Brad's writing. "Anyone else not there?"

"Luis Ortez was working on another job the day of Mason's death."

Brad marked through Ortez's name. "That all?"

"That's all I know about."

"See if I have this right. That leaves the following guys there when Shelly and Mason were killed: Lucius Walker, Tim Hale, Mitchell, umm."

"Mitchell Baldwin."

He wrote Mitchell's last name on his paper, then said, Kyle Manger, and Scott Rawlins. "Anyone else?"

"That covers it."

"Anything you've heard sound suspicious about any of them?"

"Scott Rawlins quit the other day."

"Why?"

"I heard he was worried he might be the next victim."

"What made him think there'd be more deaths?"

I was prepared for an outburst when I said, "He thought the house was cursed."

Brad stared at me and didn't say anything.

I continued, "Like I told you before, I don't believe in curses, but if he's a believer, that's what counts. I also heard Mitchell Baldwin was considering quitting for the same reason."

"Who started the damned rumor about the place being cursed?"

I realized I didn't know. Several of the workers had mentioned it, but I had no idea how or when it started.

"That's a good question. I don't know." I then shared Charles's call from the contractor he'd done some work for, then added, "Whether the curse rumor is true or fiction it still could endanger the project. Getting it closed down could be a motive for the killings."

Brad stared at his list of workers, then looked at me. "Good point, but why wouldn't the construction company be able to find more workers, even if he had to pay more, to complete the job?"

"That seems like his best option. He couldn't afford to permanently shut it down or even shut down for an extended period."

"None of that gets us closer to knowing the identity of the killer."

"No, but it narrows the list."

He again looked at his list. "Okay, unless we learn otherwise, that leaves: Manger, Walker, Baldwin, Hale, Rawlins." He looked at me. "Agree?"

I agreed with his list and then debated telling him about my efforts to learn more about the previous owners of the property. What would it achieve, other than him thinking I was joining the list of people thinking a curse was the reason for the deaths? What I did share was the break-in at the house. He said it was interesting but didn't elaborate.

He looked at his watch. "Think I'll take a walk out to the construction site and see if I can talk to a few of the workers."

"Want me to go with you?"

"Thanks for offering, but no. Haven't most of them seen or had contact with you?"

"Yes."

"I'll approach it from the angle that I haven't heard anything about what's going on and see if I can learn something that way."

"Good luck."

"I'll let you know if I succeed."

He left the house with a bounce in his step. His new hobby apparently was giving him a purpose in life.

The twenty-minute drive from Charles's apartment to Al's Bar, a block off Calhoun Street near downtown Charleston, consisted of my friend asking me no fewer than five times what I thought we were going to learn from Reginald Salyer, and me responding no fewer than five times that I didn't know. I told him if I knew what we would learn, we wouldn't be making the trip. Traffic was always heavy around the Medical University of South Carolina, a couple of blocks from Al's, so Charles decided silence was the best way for me to safely finish the trip. Occasionally, he exhibits a glimmer of wisdom. Al's doesn't have a parking lot, so the closest vacant on-street parking spot was a block past the bar.

Al's shared a concrete block building with a Laundromat in a pre-gentrified, aka rundown, section of town. At one point, the building had been white but that was a long-gone memory.

It took our eyes a minute to adjust from the sunny day into a near pitch-black bar. The only illumination came from Budweiser and Budweiser Light neon signs behind the bar and a few rays of sun sneaking in the large plate-glass window that had its lower half painted black to give diners privacy. Roy Acuff's version of "Blue Eyes

Crying in the Rain" was playing on the jukebox near the front door. When Al owned the bar, he'd salted the jukebox with country classics in deference to Bob, a huge country music fan. To put it mildly, the country tunes weren't well received by the primarily African American clientele, but Al's friendship with Bob was stronger than the objections and the songs remained.

We were warmly greeted by Al Washington, the bar's former owner, who'd agreed to stay on after Bob bought the struggling business to serve a role like a Walmart greeter. The unpaid position gave the eighty-three-year-old something to do plus it helped bridge a divide the width of the Atlantic Ocean between the bar's diners and the pasty-white new owner.

"Chris, Charles, it's great seeing you," Al said as he gave each of us a hug. "Blubber Bob," an endearing term, I assumed, "has been pestering me every five minutes about if you were here yet." Al chuckled. "It's like he couldn't see everyone entering since he's sitting forty feet from the door."

"It's good to see you too, Al. How're you feeling?"

"I'm still here."

"Al, you're looking good," Charles said, probably feeling left out of the conversation.

Al laughed. "That's why we keep the lights off."

"Al, damnit," boomed Bob Howard's voice from the back of the room, "earn your astronomical salary and let those skinny honkies get over here and spend money."

Al turned to me and said, "What's not to love about that guy?"

I said, "We'd better get back there. Wouldn't want you to get fired and lose your astronomical salary."

"Good idea. I'd hate to lose the nothing he's paying me."

We each gave Al another hug and headed to Bob's table; the table everyone knows is Bob's because he'd installed a plaque on the top of it telling anyone who could read that it was his. Only two other diners were in the room plus Bob with his stomach pinned between the chair and the table. He wore a green T-shirt, tan shorts, and a four-day old beard. With the lack of illumination in the room he resembled an out-of-season Santa, although his demeanor was anything but Santa-like.

Bob looked at his watch then said, "Reginald said he'd be here in about ten minutes. Want something expensive to drink while you wait? Lawrence, get over here and wait on these two."

Lawrence was Al's part-time cook and ever since Al's arthritis kept him from getting around the room like he used to, the cook doubled as server.

"Morning, Mr. Chris, Mr. Charles, what can I get you?"

"It's good to see you, Lawrence. I'll have a glass of white wine. Charles, want a beer?"

Charles said yes and Lawrence headed to the front of the bar to get our drinks.

Bob watched him go and said, "Reggie might act surprised when he sees you. I didn't tell him anyone else would be joining us. I figured he might not have accepted my generous offer if he knew you'd be pestering him for information. I did tell him I was interested in a deal he'd been involved in around a decade ago and gave him the name of the holding company that bought the property."

Lawrence returned with our drinks and Bob glanced at the entry. "He's early."

I turned to see someone headed our way. The man was roughly my age, thin, and dressed like a used car salesman in a light-blue suit, white shirt, and a red tie. Bob had said he was retired, but you wouldn't know it from his appearance. He carried a file folder that matched the color of his tie.

"Reggie," Bob said, "good to see you." Bob leaned toward the newcomer without getting out of his seat and they shook hands. "Meet my friends Chris Landrum and Charles Fowler."

We all shook hands and Reginald, aka Reggie, took the seat beside Bob and across from Charles and me.

Lawrence delivered our drinks and asked Reggie what he wanted. He looked at the beer bottles in front of Bob and Charles and said he'd have the same.

Reggie glanced around the room and said, "You own this place?"

"Yes, it's a goldmine," Bob said.

Reggie hesitated like he couldn't tell if Bob was serious then said, "Quite different than when you were a successful realtor."

Lawrence was quick to the table with Reggie's beer then asked if we were ready to order.

Bob said, "We've got the best cheeseburgers in the state, and possibly the country. I'd go with that if I were you. That's what Chris and Charles are having."

It was the first time I was hearing about my menu choice, but he was right since they're good, although I couldn't vouch for them compared to everywhere else in the state.

Reggie said, "Sounds good."

"And fries, too," Bob added.

"Sure."

Lawrence headed to the kitchen to start on our order, and Bob started on Reggie.

"Thought you'd retired?"

"I have," Reggie said.

"Then what's with the sartorial splendor?"

I suspected anyone wearing long pants and a shirt with a collar would meet Bob's definition of sartorial splendor.

"It's a hard habit to break. After dressing like this for forty-three years, I'm more comfortable this way than how, hmm, you're dressed."

"Did you find out what I called about?" Bob said, apparently tired of the conversation about clothing.

Johnny and June Carter Cash were singing "Jackson" as Reggie tapped on the red folder. "Everything I know about it is here."

"Good," Bob said. "Chris and Charles are investigating some deaths over on Folly and were asking about the property that was sold a while back. I told them you were the expert and if anything could be found, you'd find it."

I'd never seen Bob's sucking-up skills in action. It wasn't bad for someone who spews insults most of the time.

Reggie looked at me then at Charles. "You law enforcement?"

Before I could say no, Charles said, "Private detectives."

Bob nearly choked on his beer.

Reggie said, "Oh."

Bob pointed at the folder and said, "Let's hear what you've got."

"This goes back a few years, so I'll have to refer to the paperwork to refresh my memory," Reggie said then opened the folder. "I was the seller's agent. The property on Folly Beach was oceanfront as I recall. I didn't know the seller until I got a call from a friend of mine at the Folly police department. Anyway, he called and said there was a family that needed a realtor and needed one fast."

Charles said, "Why the rush?"

"A sad story. The owner's wife had died a year earlier after a protracted battle with cancer. They had two kids. The husband was unemployed at the time. I don't recall what he did for a living when he was working. Couldn't find anything in the file about that. Anyway, he spent all his savings and borrowed past his limit to pay for healthcare for his wife." Reggie looked toward the front window like he was remembering something from the past. "Don't know if I have all this right, but it seems like the medical expenses, hospital and docs cost, plus medicine put him a couple hundred thousand in debt, a massive amount back then."

Lawrence returned with our lunch and set a plate in front of us, and a smaller plate piled high with fries in front of Bob. The cook/server knew how to keep his boss happy.

We each took a bite and Bob said, "Well, Reggie, isn't it the best you've ever had?"

"It's good."

"Good, hell," Bob said, "it's the best."

Reggie had taken another bite and put his hand in front of his face before saying, "I think you're right."

Reggie might not know Bob well but knew him enough not to argue over something that couldn't be proven.

Charles, who has the patience of a starving chipmunk said, "So what happened with the guy and his house?"

Reggie turned to Charles, "The world was closing in on the poor guy. The bank was hours from foreclosing on the house. Credit card companies were calling almost hourly. The utility company had shut off his electric. He was in a world of hurt." He shook his head. "That's why my buddy on the police department wanted me to get involved. He wanted to see if the guy could get out of any of it." He hesitated and took another bite of maybe the best cheeseburger Reggie had ever eaten.

"What happened?" Charles asked after waiting as long as he could for Reggie to continue.

The smooth sounds of Sammi Smith singing "Help Me Make It Through the Night" filled the air combined with the aroma of the burgers. I hadn't heard anything yet that'd help learn who killed the workers.

"Charles," Reggie said in a raised voice, "by the time I met with the homeowner on a Monday afternoon, he already had a court order to be out of the house by midnight Thursday or the police would forcefully remove him along with his belongings. He was in a panic when we met. He was bouncing off the walls screaming about being left with nothing and two kids. What'd he think I could do with only three days until he was kicked out?"

"Hell, Reggie," Bob said, "stop turning this into a soap opera and tell us what happened."

Reggie glared at Bob then turned to Charles. "I knew a guy down in Savannah who handled some distressed properties and brokered some deals with out-of-state holding companies. He owed me a favor or two. He gave me the name of an outfit out of Connecticut that invested in undervalued properties. I called them and with luck got the right person on the phone; somebody who could wheel and deal. The guy had a cousin living in Columbia. My contact had his cousin come see the property. The house didn't look like more than a tear-down, but it was beachfront. Property values over there weren't escalating like they are today, but he still saw it had potential."

Bob leaned toward Reggie. "Unless you speed up this story, you'll be buying supper here."

Reggie straightened his tie and turned back to Charles. "The out-of-state company offered nearly what the owner owed but said they would make sure the bank didn't come down on him for the rest. I don't know what they did, but it worked. To make a long story shorter, for Bob's sake, the family was out on Thursday like they had to be." He looked at his cell phone, and added, "It'll be ten years in a couple of days."

Bob said, "Reggie, you've given us a blow-by-blow description of everything that happened except the important parts. What's the name of the family, the company that bought the property, and, well, that's enough for now."

Reggie flipped through the papers in the folder and said, "Family's the Hallorans. Like I already said, the father is David. Sara's the mother and the kids are named Austin, age thirteen, and Hannah, sixteen."

Bob sighed before saying, "The company that bought it?"

"The property was purchased by IH Financial Group."

Sean had already told me about the sellers, the Hallorans, and the buyers but hadn't mentioned the children's names.

"That is sad," I said.

Charlie Rich was singing "Behind Closed Doors," Bob was stuffing his mouth with fries, and Charles said, "What happened to them?"

"I'm afraid it gets sadder," Reggie said as he closed the folder. "I heard most of this from my friend on the police force. He left Folly's force and hired on in North Charleston. Died last year in a truck versus car accident. Anyway, I don't know where my friend got the information, but I have no reason to doubt it. He said the family moved to a tiny apartment in a bad section of North Charleston. The dad took to heavy drinking and blamed all his bad fortune on the holding company that bought the property. I didn't see where he had a case since he had no choice but to be out. At least the company kept him out of bankruptcy. Anyway, he died less than two years after moving. Alcohol got him."

Charles said, "What happened to the kids?"

"No idea," he said and took the last bite of cheeseburger.

Lawrence returned to see if we needed anything else. Reggie said no and asked for his check, saying he had a doctor's appointment. He didn't offer to buy lunch for Charles and me, and, of course, neither did Bob. We said our appropriate goodbyes and Bob told him to come by anytime and bring his friends with him. Reggie said he would in a tone that screamed *no way.*

Charles and I stood to shake his hand and Bob leaned his direction to gracelessly stick out his hand to shake.

"Well, what'd we learn?" Charles asked as soon as we returned to the car.

"Not much. That's a sad story about the family who sold the house to the holding company, but I don't see how it's connected to anything going on now."

"We learned the name of the family and the company that bought it."

"Sean had already told me that much. All I heard new were the kids' names."

I felt Charles's eyes beaming at me before he said, "When did Sean tell you their names?"

"Couple of days ago."

"And I didn't learn about it until now?"

"I didn't see where it was important. The family name wasn't familiar."

"That's still no reason to keep it from me. I could've known them."

"Did you?"

"No."

"You're still right. It still seems irrelevant since I don't see any connection between what happened a decade ago and now. Do you?"

"Not really."

Nothing else was said until I crossed the bridge to Folly, when Charles broke the silence with, "Why don't we meet at Loggers at, umm, let's see, how about four-thirty? Maybe one or more of the workers from the house will be there and we can, umm, do something."

I doubted anything productive could come from that, but it was a nice day and sitting outside would beat being holed up at the house, so I told him I'd see him there.

44

The problem going to a restaurant with outdoor seating in good weather is good weather makes everyone want to be outside, or so it seems. Today was no exception. When I arrived at Loggerhead's, every patio table was occupied, and the bar was packed. Today was one time I was glad Charles arrived thirty minutes early for everything. He was seated at the far side of the bar talking to someone I didn't recognize.

"Chris," he said as I moved beside him, "meet Lonnie. He works at Crosby's."

Crosby's Fish & Shrimp Company is the go-to spot for most people on Folly who seek fresh food from the sea.

"Nice to meet you, Lonnie."

"Likewise," he said and looked at his watch. He took the last sip from his beer and turned to Charles. "Gotta head out. Nice meeting you, Charles, you too, Chris."

Charles watched him go, turned to me, and said, "Good timing. You show up late and get a stool beside me."

I ignored his comment as the bartender asked what I was having. I told him white wine before turning to Charles. "Okay, here we are. Seen any of the construction workers?"

"No, but they're probably getting off about now. You need to be patient like me."

I didn't laugh but should have. Charles claiming to be patient was by far the funniest thing I'd heard all day, possibly all week.

I said, "Have you thought about what Bob's friend said today? Any new ideas?"

"Not really, but it doesn't matter. I still think the killer is Scott, possibly Kyle, or could be Mitchell."

"You think it's Scott because he quit?"

"That and he was itching to become foreman which would've given him a reason to kill Randy."

"Why Kyle?"

"That's an easy one. He's the one who sicced the cops on us, well, mainly on you to try to get you, us, off the case. Besides, I don't like his girlfriend. Don't know what he sees in her."

That wasn't much, but I couldn't disagree. Couldn't prove it either.

"Then, what about Mitchell?"

"Virgil said he's pushing the *house is cursed* stories. If people think a curse killed those folks, it'd get Mitchell off the hook. Deflection, my friend."

"Okay, let's say it's one of those three. If you had to choose one, who would it be?"

"Kyle."

"Why?"

"He's worked the hardest to keep us off his trail. Who would you choose?"

"I'm not certain it's one of those three, but if I had to choose one of them, I'd agree with you."

Charles took a sip of his beer, then said, "How do we prove it?" He hesitated, looked over my shoulder, and added, "Hold that thought and my seat."

He hopped off the stool and weaved his way around the crowd gathered in front of the bar. He stopped but I couldn't see who he was talking to until he was on his way back with his arm around Kyle Manger's shoulder.

"Hey, Chris, look who I found."

"Hi, Kyle," I said and slid my stool a few inches farther away from Charles's.

Kyle shook my hand, moved between Charles and me, then said, "Charles said you were buying drinks. I appreciate it."

I would too if someone else was buying the drinks, although that seldom happens.

He leaned over the bar and told the bartender he'd have a beer.

Charles said, "Kyle was telling me he just got off work."

No surprise, since that was the reason Charles suggested we meet here.

Kyle said, "Chris, this has been a bear of a day. Every time I turn around, I'm forced to stop working on what I need to do until one of the carpenters gets his work done."

I said, "I understand they're having a hard time getting carpenters."

"Yeah, they're down to two. One got fired a couple of weeks ago, Scott quit, and, well, you know what happened to Mason."

"That's rough," Charles said. "How come Scott quit?"

Charles was beginning his fishing expedition.

"Don't know for certain," he said before taking a long draw on the beer that'd been set in front of him. "Heard it had to do with the rumor about the house being cursed. Damned stupid reason for giving up a good paying job if you ask me."

Since he brought it up, I thought it was a good time to add something to the cursed rumor.

"I hear Mitchell is thinking about quitting for the same reason."

"Yeah, I heard that, but I wouldn't put too much stock in it. He told me he didn't believe in silly curses." He took another sip before saying, "I'm glad I ran into you two. I want to apologize."

Charles said, "What for?"

"Sort of what my girlfriend did."

I waited for him to continue, but he didn't.

Charles didn't wait. "What'd she do?"

"I'm sort of embarrassed about it. After the deaths out at the house, that detective, believe Fishell's his name, he—"

"Detective Fisher," Charles corrected.

"Yeah, that's it. He came to talk to me about the deaths. Where I was when it happened, what I saw, stuff like that. Pat was with me, so he included her in the discussion. Pat's a wonderful gal but can get riled up. When you first met her, here, in fact, we were talking about the death of Shelly and Pat got all pissy. Think she was jealous, stupid since Shelly was dead. Anyway, she went off on you two with the detective."

"What do you mean?"

"She started ranting about how you'd harassed us, wouldn't let us eat in peace, claimed she felt intimidated by your questioning when all you were doing was talking." He slowly shook his head. "I barely got a word in edgewise. I apologize."

I said, "That's okay. I hope she doesn't really feel that way."

"I don't think she does. I know she's calmed a lot since then." He smiled. "Calm as long as I don't mention Shelly."

Charles said, "I understand. But while I'm thinking about it, where did the rumor start about the house being cursed?"

"I don't know who started it. It was going around with some of the guys as soon as Shelly fell, then after Randy got himself electrocuted, nearly everyone was talking about a curse. Why?"

"Just curious. Being that it's new, I was wondering how the idea of a curse got started. Aren't they usually in old houses?"

"You're asking the wrong guy about that. Curses ain't something I think much about. Now I don't know about it being a curse, but something sure must be wrong out there. Three dead people in such a short period of time and all of them working on one job. That's hard to believe." He took another drink then added, "Speaking of Pat getting pissed, I'm supposed to meet her for supper near her apartment. If I don't leave now, I'll be the one getting her wrath."

Charles reminded him I would pick up his tab. Kyle thanked me, patted Charles on the back, and headed to the stairs.

Charles watched him go, took another sip of the beer I was

buying, and said, "Well, now what do you think of our number one suspect?"

"He seemed sincere with his apology, and I can see how Pat clouded Detective Fisher's impression of what happened when we met them here."

"That mean you no longer have him at the top of your list?"

"I'm leaning that way. How about you?"

"Yep."

45

The next morning, I awoke to the sound of rain bouncing off my metal roof. With nowhere I had to be, this would be a good day to stay in the house and get caught up reading photo magazines that'd come in the last few weeks. I fired up my Mr. Coffee machine, found some three-day-old donuts on the counter, and parked myself at the kitchen table to wait for Mr. Coffee to do its thing. The coffee maker was acting like I was feeling: slow and aging.

It finished perking a carafe of coffee, I poured a cup, grabbed one of the magazines and the donuts, and moved to the front porch to watch people who still had jobs drive past the house. While I was glad I didn't have to go to work, I suspected few, if any, of them felt slow and aging.

Neither the articles about how to take great landscape photos or the commuters driving past held my attention, so I began revisiting yesterday's meeting with Charles and Kyle. I mainly focused on something Charles asked the plumber. That was where did the rumor start about the house being cursed? There's one way to find out.

I grabbed my phone and tapped in Charles's number.

"Are you calling to invite me to breakfast?"

"No."

"Good, it's too yucky to go anywhere. Now that I talked you out of going to breakfast, why'd you call?"

"Yesterday, when we were talking to Kyle, you asked him how the rumor started about the house being cursed."

"Yeah, so?"

"Why'd you ask him that?"

"I've been thinking about the rumor. Didn't it have to start somewhere?"

"Yes," I said then took a sip.

"You thought Scott was trying to push blame onto Shelly's husband. Why? To deflect blame away from himself. Then early on, Kyle talked about a carpenter getting himself fired. Why? To deflect blame away from himself."

"Your point?"

"Okay, let's say the killer starts getting everyone blaming the deaths on a curse, wouldn't that deflect the blame away from him?"

"I guess so, but while the first two deaths could've been accidents and, I suppose, attributable to a curse, someone got on that forklift and pinned Mason between it and the house. A curse didn't drive it."

Charles said, "Did I say my theory was foolproof?"

"No."

"It doesn't appear more farfetched than yours about something related to the sale of the house, or whatever that was about."

"I'll give you that," I said. "Okay, let's say the person killing the workers started the rumor that the house was cursed. How do we find out who it was?"

"Ask each worker out there. We've already talked to Kyle. That leaves, umm, several more. I've got us this far, now it's up to you to figure out how to ask each of them. That's something to do on a rainy day. Call when you get it figured out."

I assured him I would and ended the call.

Charles's logic made sense but trying to ask everybody who works there the question appeared to be a daunting task. And, by asking each of them, we would be asking the person who started it. If my theory is correct, asking a murderer who'd already killed three people sounded dangerous.

The phone rang before I could figure out a good way to interrogate the group without turning a murderer loose on us.

"This is your good buddy Bob. Hungry for a cheeseburger?"

"I was there yesterday. Why would I want to go out in this weather for a cheeseburger?"

"Figured you wouldn't, but thought I'd ask."

"So, you called to not invite me to Al's for a cheeseburger?"

"That sounds like a trick question, so I'll ignore it. I called to tell you I got a call last night around ten-thirty from my friend, over-dressed Reggie Salyer. After I got him off the phone, I would've called you, but knew it was past your bedtime. Being the kind, gentle, and considerate person I am, I waited until now."

I waited for him to continue, but he didn't, so I said, "You waiting for applause?"

"Smartass."

Kind, gentle, and considerate?

"Yep."

"Well, aren't you going to ask why he called?"

"I figured you called to tell me."

"You'd be more fun to talk to in the middle of the night. Reggie remembered something else he'd heard about the Halloran family. He said it was only a rumor, so not to take it as gospel."

I sighed. "What did he tell you?"

"That's better. Remember he said the father died?"

"Yes, a couple of years after being forced out of their house. Died caused by his drinking."

"Yes. What Reggie didn't remember to tell us was that the son, believe his name's Austin, had a nervous breakdown or two after his dad died. Reggie didn't know any of the details, but heard the kid was in and out of mental hospitals for three or four years."

"Is that it?"

"Yes. Reggie said he didn't know if that'd mean anything but wanted to let me know so I could share it with you and your quarter-wit private detective friend."

"I don't know if it will help or not, but I appreciate you letting me know."

"Good. Now you owe me another meal at my upscale and wildly popular bar."

"Of course," I said to a dial tone.

There was one thing I did agree with Bob on. I had no idea if that additional bit of information about the Halloran family helped.

46

By late afternoon, the rain had stopped and steam from the evaporating water was giving the road in front of my house an eerie appearance as the sun peeked out from behind clouds. All in all, it looked like a pleasant evening in the making. After being stuck in the house all day, I needed to stretch my legs and decided a walk out West Ashley Avenue should meet that need. Yes, I was also headed in the direction of the house under construction. *Probably not a coincidence*, I thought, as I left my cottage.

A red pickup truck with a Bolt Electric logo on the door was the only vehicle at the job site. I started to cross the street and see if Lucius Walker was the Bolt employee still at work when I heard, "Yo, Christopher" coming from the vacant lot beside me.

I turned and saw Virgil step out from behind a row of shrubs and walk my way.

"Hi, Virgil, what're you doing out here?"

"Honing my private detective skills. I've got a lot to learn to be near on par with you and Charles."

"Hiding behind shrubs is how you're, umm, sharpening your skills?"

He looked across the street at the job site, then at me. "Not standing behind any old shrubs, but the one that gives me a clear view of you-know-what. What brings you out this way?"

Probably the same thing Virgil was doing, but instead of sharing that, I said, "Been thinking a lot about the deaths and wanted to walk by to refresh my memory about the roof Shelly fell from, and where the forklift was when Mason was killed."

Virgil smiled. "See, I'm on the right track."

Lucius Walker was leaving the house carrying a small tool kit. He got in his truck, backed out, then headed toward town. Fortunately, he didn't notice us standing across the street.

"How long have you been here?"

"Got here after the rain stopped. There were four guys finishing for the day. They were loading tools and some scrap wood in their trucks, waving bye to each other, then headed out."

"Did you learn anything significant from watching?"

"Yeah, when four o'clock rolled around, they split like cockroaches when lights come on."

"How was that significant?"

"Christopher, you have to remember, I'm not as good as you and Charles. I doubt it was significant. I'm establishing a profile of the employees. For example, as you saw, that electrician guy didn't rush to leave like the others."

"And you found that significant?"

"Maybe it was; maybe it wasn't. He could've stayed later to set a trap in the house so when the others get here tomorrow, someone could fall for the trap and get himself killed. Probably something electrical since he's an electrician. That would be one more reason to think the place is cursed. On the other hand, he could've stayed late to finish up something that had to be done today."

I didn't think Virgil's observation meant anything, but since I had no idea what was going on, it was as good as anything I'd learned.

I said, "What's your plan now?"

"Head back to town, stop at Loggers, see if I can charm someone into buying me a beer."

"Why don't I go with you and buy you a beer? No charming necessary."

"That sounds like a splendid plan."

The crowd at the outside bar wasn't as busy as it had been the last time I was here. The earlier rain must've kept a few customers away. We took two vacant stools at the bar. Good to his word, Virgil ordered a beer, and I went with a soft drink.

Our drinks arrived, we each took a sip, and I said, "Are you still doing maintenance at your apartment building?"

"So far, I think I'm a better amateur plumber than private detective. I've handily defeated every clogged drain and toilet that've been thrown at me. They don't stand a chance against plumber Virgil."

"Speaking for all the tenants in your building, I'm glad to hear that."

He smiled and nodded before the smile faded. "Now in my other career as an assistant private detective in Charles's agency, I still have much to learn."

Him claiming to be an assistant private detective proves he has much to learn.

"Have you come to any conclusions about the deaths?"

He took a sip, looked around the rapidly filling bar, then said, "Calling it a conclusion may be giving it too much credit, but I've been thinking about how so many of the guys are calling the house cursed."

"What about it?"

"Most of them are smart guys. It takes a lot of knowledge to be a plumber, an electrician, even a carpenter. I could be wrong, but I don't believe places can be cursed. I'm not nearly as smart as most of them, so if I know there's no thing as a cursed house, why do they think there is? See what I mean?"

I nodded. "I don't understand it either."

"Seems to me, there's a killer on the loose. Seems to me, he works at the house. Seems to me, there must be a reason he's killing off his fellow employees. And, I don't have a clue why he's doing it."

"Me either."

He took a couple more sips, tapped the bottle on the counter, and said, "Still got the curse thing on my mind. You remember back when you, Charles, and I were at Planet Follywood talking with Tim and Scott?"

"Sure."

"One of us asked the guys who started the rumor about the house being cursed. I think it was Tim who said talk was going around about it, but he didn't know who started it."

"I vaguely remember that. What about it?"

"I was up here last night. Sitting at the far end of the bar to be more specific." He nodded his head a couple of times. "Saw Mitchell, you know, one of the carpenters, and started up a conversation. He'd had a rough day at work; something about an upstairs room needing to move a wall that they'd already built. I didn't understand what he was talking about, but he was PO'ed." He took another drink and stared across the deck.

"What about Mitchell?"

He smiled. "Sorry, got off track, didn't I? Anyway, that danged curse was on my mind last night like it is now. I asked him if he believed it. He said he guessed so. Pretty noncommittal if you ask me."

If that was all Virgil was going to share, he was off track again.

"Is that it?"

"No, I was trying to remember the sequence of the conversation. Oh, yeah, since the curse was on my mind, I asked him who started talking about it first. He said he didn't know but figured it must've been Tim Hale. After he said that, I asked why he thought that. Said he may be wrong, but Tim was the first person who mentioned it to him. See what I mean?"

I didn't see how that proved that Tim had started the rumor.

"I understand why he said that, but that doesn't prove Tim started it."

"I agree, but that's the best I could get out of him. It's something to think about though."

"Yes," I said, more to encourage Virgil than as a viable possibility.

"So, what do you and Charles know about Tim? I haven't heard his name mentioned as the possible killer."

"All I know is he was hired at the beginning of the job and the only thing that came back on his background check was a speeding ticket."

Virgil smiled. "Not quite the stuff serial killers are made of."

"True."

Virgil snapped his fingers, looked at his watch, and said, "Christopher, have to go. I was supposed to unclog a sink in unit thirty-four before Sammi's husband gets home and yells at her for not having supper ready."

I said I'd get his tab.

He thanked me and headed to Sammi's sink-clogged apartment.

47

I was awake before sunrise the next morning thinking about what Virgil had said about Tim Hale possibly being the first person who mentioned a curse on the West Ashley Avenue house. That didn't prove, didn't even suggest, that Tim was the person who'd started the rumor, but it reminded me of something Kyle had told me the day Mason had his deadly encounter with the forklift. I'd asked where the crew members were when the death occurred. He said he'd taken a walk on the beach, and that Tim either often or occasionally sat on the beach. Was that all he'd said? It seems there was more, but for the life of me I can't recall what.

Often, a good way for me to remember something that for whatever reason had slipped my memory was to do or think about something else. Maybe after a cup or two of coffee, Kyle's words would come back to me. I padded into the kitchen, started Mr. Coffee, and sat at the table to watch the liquid brain-starter drip into the carafe.

Had Virgil said anything else that could help me figure out who'd ended the three lives. He said Lucius Walker could've stayed late to boobytrap something in the house to add another victim to the growing list. That seemed unlikely although a possibility.

Now back to thinking about what Kyle had said. Some of it was coming back to me. Hadn't he said Tim was sitting on the beach when Kyle started his walk but wasn't there when he returned? Was that significant? Probably not, because Kyle had also said when he returned from the walk, their lunch break was over, and Tim was back at work.

Finally, it came to me. Kyle said Tim had shared that when he sat on the beach it reminded him of growing up out that way. I wonder if Tim could've said growing up there, as in where the house was being built, rather than *in the area*. Hadn't Bob's acquaintance Reggie said the Hallorans had two children, a boy and a girl, Austin and Hannah? If I remember correctly, Reggie had also mentioned the two kids and said the boy was about thirteen years old, the girl a couple of years older?

What were the chances that Timothy Hale was Austin Halloran? Tim was about the same age as Austin since it's been about ten years since his father was forced to sell the house. Even if he was the same person, what would be his motive for killing three people? If his motive was revenge, none of the victims could have known about or been part of forcing the Hallorans out of their house. Also, how easy would it have been for Austin to change his name?

On my second cup of coffee, I then remembered what Bob had said Reggie told him about the son having one or more nervous breakdowns and spending time in mental health facilities. I suppose he could still be suffering issues and in a confused state, sees logic in killing people at the site that was so traumatic for him.

Was it merely a coincidence Tim was hired at the beginning of the job or had he planned it? If killing the other workers was his plan, what better place to be than on the crew?

While there were still many unanswered questions, Tim being Austin appears to be the most logical scenario for what'd happened at the job site.

I wonder if Reggie remembered anything else about the family, especially Tim. Of course, the best way to find out was to ask. I didn't have Reggie's number, so going through Bob would be the best way to contact the retired realtor. He wouldn't be at Al's yet, but should be awake, or so I hoped.

"Bob, this is Chris, did I catch you at a bad time?"

"You always catch me at a bad time. You calling to make a luncheon reservation?"

"Not this time. Could you give me Reggie's phone number?"

"I could, but I need a lot more information than that before I give it to you."

"Like what?"

"Like why in the hell do you want his number? He can't fix you any great cheeseburgers. He can't sell you any real estate that I can't. And he ain't going to give you any gossip on me because I have too much on him and he knows it. So, why want his number?"

I told him I was looking for more information about the Halloran family.

"You're still nosing in those deaths."

No reason to deny it.

"Yes."

"Tell you what, let me call him. He's more likely to tell me things than he would be to tell you. Tell me what you want to know."

That wasn't my preferred way to approach Reggie, but Bob probably knew how to get information from him better than I did. I told him I was more interested in learning more about the son, Austin.

"Don't suppose you're going to tell me why, are you?"

"Not yet, but it could be important. Thanks for offering to make the call."

"Yeah, whatever. I'll call you after I talk to him. I'll also expect a customer for lunch as payment for my valuable information."

"If it's valuable, you can count on me for that lunch."

He apparently got what he wanted to hear since he'd hung up.

My next call was going to be more difficult.

"Brad, this is Chris. Catch you at a bad time?"

"If you called ten minutes earlier, it would've been bad. I was in the middle of a stack of hotcakes Hazel fixed. Never disturb me when I'm eating hotcakes."

"I'll keep that in mind. Got a question."

"Does it have to do with you meddling in the deaths out at that house?"

"Yes."

"Good. What is it?"

"When you were giving me the information your buddy in the Sheriff's Office found out about the guys employed at the construction site, you said Timothy Hale had a speeding ticket. Did you say how many years back that was?"

"Hang on a second. I have that information somewhere in my office."

I heard him tell Hazel who was on the phone and he'd help her clean the living room when he got off the phone.

"Here we go. Let's see, Timothy Hale, one speeding ticket a year ago."

"And that's all you got on him?"

"Yes, my buddy said he was a little surprised. Said twenty-two-year-old guys don't usually stop with one speeding ticket. He had a good point. Back in the dark ages when I was a patrol officer, I'd get the same kids two, three, or more times speeding. Of course, there were always exceptions, but they were rare. What's the deal with Timothy Hale?"

"Not sure there's anything. I'm following up on some of the things I've been told. I'll let you know if it comes to anything."

"You better. Now I have to clean the living room. Sure you don't need me to drive you somewhere?"

I dreaded the next call but knew that if I didn't make it and something happened, I'd never be able to live it down.

"Cindy, good morning."

"What's good about it? I've got three guys out sick. Another one turned in his resignation ten minutes ago, and I have a headache."

"Sorry. That sounds like a rough morning."

"Are you going to make it rougher?"

"Maybe, so let me start with a question."

"No, you're too old to replace the officer who quit."

I smiled then said, "Then let me try another question."

"Well, what is it?"

"How difficult is it to change your name?"

"Legally or illegally?"

"Either."

"Legally, there are some hoops to jump through, but it's possible."

"How about illegally?"

"Find a good forger. He can forge documents you normally have. Things like a birth certificate, driver's license, even a passport if your friendly, neighborhood forger is really, really, good."

"Would the illegal documents get by if someone gets a speeding ticket, for example?"

"Possibly, but that'd depend on the cop issuing the ticket. If he, or she, ran the information through an on-board computer, there'd be a problem. But many forces don't have access to that technology in their vehicles, so most likely, it wouldn't get flagged. You planning to change your name?"

I then told her my theory about Timothy Hale being Austin Halloran, the son of the man who had to sell the house and who later drank himself to death. I was surprised when she didn't interrupt several times, scream at me calling me a nutcase at best, and telling me to mind my own business. Her headache probably prevented her from exploding. After I finished sharing my story, she had me repeat a couple parts of it, said something about needing a dozen pain pills, and telling me she'd share my story with Detective Fisher. I thanked her and asked if she was okay.

"No, but it's early, so the day can get worse."

I managed to say I was sorry before she hung up on me.

The other call I needed to make was to Charles.

He didn't answer and his voicemail kicked in after six rings. I told him to call when he got a chance, then realized Cindy's headache had worked its way through the phone and into my skull.

48

I spent the rest of the day nearly as frustrated as I'd been early this morning. The phone remained so silent that I hoped for a robocall. Charles hadn't returned my call and Bob Howard hadn't gotten back to me with whatever he'd learned from Reggie. A walk next door to Bert's to get something from the deli for supper was my only venture out of the house. Nothing on television interested me and I went to bed a little before ten.

The phone jarred me out of my sleep. I focused my half-asleep eyes on the clock on the bedside table to find that it was nearly midnight. Surely, Bob or Charles wouldn't be calling this late. I grabbed the phone to discover I was wrong. The screen read *Charles*.

I mumbled, "What were you thinking calling me this late?"

"Get to the house on West Ashley," he said, barely above a whisper. "Don't park close."

I couldn't believe I heard him correctly. "Now?"

"Hurry."

I heard what sounded like a door opening in the background, then the phone went dead.

It took me a couple of minutes to shake my head awake and get my bearings. I glanced at the phone like I couldn't believe the call. It read *11:47*.

I dressed and slowly walked to the car. My legs were a little wobbly but stepping outside in the cool air awakened me more.

Mine was the only car on the road as I drove out West Ashley Avenue. Once the construction site came into view, I pulled off the road and parked. The house appeared deserted. No lights were visible, nor were lights on in the house on either side of the one under construction. An old red pickup truck was parked in front of the house on the far side of my destination.

I slowly approached the house regretting I hadn't brought a flashlight. The light on my phone would have to do. Illumination from a full moon helped some as I walked slowly around the house. Charles was nowhere in sight.

On my second time around the house, I noticed the sliding glass patio door was open about a foot. Surely, the workers would've done a better job of closing the house up after they left for the day. I stuck my head into the house and listened.

Nothing.

I took a deep breath, and opened the door another foot, stepped in, and said, "Charles?"

No answer, so I tried again, this time louder. Still no answer.

Do I venture further into the dark house or back out and call the police?

If I called the police, what would I tell them? I was sneaking into a house under construction and not hearing any sounds I decided to call the police. Umm, no.

I called Charles's' name one more time. Hearing nothing, I went from room to room on the first floor. No Charles. I was approaching the stairs when I heard a sound coming from upstairs. At first, I thought it may be a mouse or a bird that managed to get in the house. Then I heard it again, and the thought entered my mind that it could be Charles and he may need help.

I walked up the steps to the sound of each stair tread squeaking as I put weight on it. At the top of the stairs, I saw what I thought was someone on the floor. My phone light wasn't bright enough for me to see who, so I took three steps closer to the person, only to find two people lying beside each other. Neither was moving.

The closer I got, I realized the person closest to me was Charles. The other person was facing the other direction so I couldn't tell who it was.

I quickened my pace then bent over Charles to see if he was alive.

I nearly tripped over my friend's body when behind me, someone said, "They're alive. For now."

I turned to see Tim Hale. He was dressed in black, had a pistol in one hand, and a gasoline can in the other."

"Tim, you startled me. What's going on?"

I was certain I knew the answer, but anything I could do to keep him talking increased my chances of leaving the house alive.

He looked at his watch, set the gas can on the floor beside a pile of six-foot-long two-by-fours, took a flashlight out of his pocket, and pointed it at me. He then said, "Eleven fifty-seven. Know what tomorrow is?"

I'm not certain why, but something popped in my head that Sean Aker had told me. He said it'll be ten years in a couple of days to when the family had to be out of their house.

"The tenth anniversary of when your family was evicted from the house that was on this site."

He sighed and said, "Knew you were figuring it out. Saw the way you looked at me whenever you saw me. That's why I broke into your house, but I didn't find anything about me." He shook his head like he was shaking thoughts out. "Who told you about the anniversary?"

I figured I knew what he had in mind for us but didn't want to say anything that'd endanger Reggie or anyone else. "A friend. Tim, or should I say Austin?"

With his voice breaking, he said, "How do you know that?"

"A lawyer told me." I hesitated then said, "The police also know."

His hand holding the pistol began to shake and he said, "It doesn't matter."

"Tim, why kill the three people? What'd they do to you? Did they know your identity?"

He pointed the flashlight at the other person on the floor. "Because of him."

I still couldn't see the person's face.

"Who is it?"

"The man who killed my Dad. The man who stole my happy place. The man who ruined our family."

"Oliver Trescott?"

He nodded.

"I understand that, but why kill three innocent people."

"I wanted him to suffer like Dad did; like my sister did; like I did."

"Let me guess. You started the rumors that the house was cursed so Trescott would watch progress on the house get slowed down and possibly stopped. You hoped he'd hear the rumors you'd started and connect them to his buying the house. Then as your final act, he would die when it burns." I nodded toward the gas can.

He looked at the can, then up at me, "I hated to sacrifice three people. I liked them, but, well, you know, it had to be done. The bastard sent me away from my happy place into a dingy, tiny apartment."

"Tim, why did it take you this long to get revenge?"

"I was a kid when it all happened getting shuffled around from foster home to foster home after Dad died. I loved the old house that was here. I'd spend hours sitting out back watching the ocean, the tide, the shrimp boats out there. Anyway, I didn't even start looking for the person who bought the house until a couple of years ago. I was, umm, indisposed, stuck in a nuthouse for a couple of years and couldn't look."

I heard Charles moan and saw his hand move. Tim also heard him and stepped back so he could see Charles and me without having to turn around.

"Why'd you change your name?"

"That wasn't easy," he said and smiled.

I waited for him to continue. When he didn't, I said, "Were you afraid Trescott might recognize your name from when he bought the property?"

He shrugged. "I've pictured this house going up in flames ever since the first day on the job here. He put me in hell, so he has to burn in hell on earth." He laughed although I didn't detect any humor. "I felt sort of silly working so hard to get the construction right knowing it would all be gone." He looked at his watch again. "All gone today." He looked in the direction of Trescott. "He killed Dad, he ruined my sister's life, and look what he did to me." He pointed his handgun at Charles. "Think I'd be grateful if you'd go over there and lie down beside your friend. If you're good, I won't have to smack you with one of those boards. I've got work to do."

"Tim, you don't have to do this. The police will understand why you've done what you did."

"I may be a mental case, or so that's what the shrinks said, but I'm not stupid. Did you know Trescott killed my Dad, ruined my sister's life, ruined mine, too?"

His gun hand was shaking more than it had been a few minutes ago. Repeating himself made me wonder if he was on the verge of losing touch with reality. If that were the case, would it make it easier for me to escape or would he shoot me sooner?

"Yes," I said in the calmest voice I could muster. "I know what he did to all of you was terrible. He—"

He interrupted, "You know I loved sitting out back watching the ocean, and those shrimp boats were something to see. All the birds flocking over them to get leftover shrimp." He jerked the pistol in my direction. "Get down there. I've work to do. Didn't you hear me the first time? Why aren't you on the floor?"

I didn't see any good options. He appeared to be bouncing between wanting us dead and reliving his time here as a child. I moved closer to Charles, bent down, and started to lie beside my friend, when I heard someone downstairs say, "Mr. Chris, you there?"

Tim took a step backwards and jerked his body around until he was facing the stairs.

I grabbed a five-foot-long piece of two-by-four lumber that was behind Tim and pushed myself off the floor.

Tim heard me and turned around. Before he pointed his gun at me, I swung the board at the side of his head. It connected with a thud, vibrated my hand holding it, knocked me off balance, to where I nearly landed on Charles.

Before I got to my feet, Tim uttered a profanity, shook his head, then managed to point the gun at me.

I kicked his leg. The blow struck hard enough that he fell sideways landing on his arm holding the weapon. This time I was able to push up enough to regain my balance. I grabbed his arm holding the gun and twisted it.

He started to get up when the voice I'd heard earlier from downstairs said, "Police. Don't move."

Tim wisely followed the order.

Officer Trula Bishop kicked the gun out of Tim's hand and told him to turn over with his hands behind his back. Again, Tim obeyed her orders. The officer quickly cuffed him and asked me if the other two people were okay.

I was surprised when I turned back to Charles. He was in a seated position and rubbing the back of his head.

He shook his head twice and said, "Where is it?"

I said, "What?"

"The train that ran over me?"

And I thought Tim was losing it.

Charles looked up at Trula, and said, "Hey, Trula. What're you doing here?"

Trula said, "Mr. Charles, stay seated. We need to have your head checked."

I'd thought that for more than a decade but remained silent while Trula radioed for an ambulance and if the dispatcher had the nerve to call her this late, Chief LaMond.

By now, Trescott began moving and Trula told him to remain still that medical assistance was on the way.

The next hour was a blur. An ambulance left with both Charles and Trescott, after Charles swore he was fine countless times. For once, he lost, and was loaded on a stretcher. Cindy arrived and castigated me for dragging her out of bed in the middle of the night, before having me tell her what was going on. Then I had to repeat it again when Detective Fisher arrived. I was relieved when he listened to my story without reminding me how he'd threaten to have me arrested if I messed in his business. Clearly, his mind wasn't operating on all cylinders. I suspected I'd hear more about it later.

Before Cindy told me I was free to leave, I asked Trula why she came in the house looking for me. She said she was on patrol when she noticed my car up the street from the job site. Trula then noticed the red pickup truck on the property that wasn't there an hour earlier when she drove by. Fortunately, she put two and two together and walked the property until she found the sliding door open, came in, and yelled my name.

I thanked her for saving three lives, especially mine.

49

Charles called from the hospital about ten-thirty that morning and asked when his cab, aka me, would arrive to take him home. Apparently, he was being discharged after they couldn't find anything wrong with his head. Clearly, he hadn't been seen by a psychiatrist. I told him I'd be there within an hour.

An hour and a half later, I'd learned that Oliver Trescott was in a little worse shape than Charles and had been admitted, and we were in my car and pulling out of the hospital's parking lot and headed to Folly.

"Charles, how'd you end up out there?"

"I was sipping on a beer at Logger's, minding my own business, if you can believe that, then—"

"I can't."

"Can't what?"

"Believe you were minding your own business."

"You want to know what happened or call me a liar?"

I smiled and said, "You were minding your own business, then what?"

"Looked across the street at the Oceanfront Villas, and who do you think I saw getting in a red pickup truck?"

"Tim and Trescott."

"You passed private detective quiz number one."

"Then what?"

They pulled out of the lot and crossed Arctic. I leaned over the railing to see what direction they went when they reached Ashley Avenue."

"They turned left."

"Yes, but that was so easy it doesn't count as a quiz."

"Okay," I said, "How about me saying you left Loggerhead's and walked out West Ashley to see if they were going to the house?"

"Quiz two passed."

"Then what happened?"

"The truck was empty, so I headed around the house to see where they were and what they were doing. I couldn't figure any good reason for them being there. The sliding glass door in back was open. I listened and thought I heard them upstairs. I called you and learned I was wrong about where Tim was." He shook his head. "Only Trescott was up there. Know how I learned that?"

"Tim was downstairs."

"How about behind me? He stuck his gun in my back and told me to get upstairs. I did, and that's when the train ran over me, or in looking back, it could've been a piece of lumber that made contact with my head. Then the next thing I knew was you talking to Tim, or whatever his name is." He looked out the window, then turned toward me. "Now it's your turn. What happened?"

"After you called, I went to the house. Like you, I found the door open and came in. Came upstairs and met Tim with the gun and the gas can."

"How'd you know all that stuff I heard you talking to him about. Tim equals Austin, on-and-on."

"If you'd returned my call yesterday, you would've known."

"You would've told me about who you thought Tim was, but I probably wouldn't have believed you."

"You do now, don't you?"

"Every syllable."

After I delivered Charles to his apartment and got home, my next-door neighbor called.

"Chris, think I've got it figured out. Ready to hear who the killer is?"

"Before you say who, let me tell you a story." And I did.

After Brad finished saying "You're kidding," three times, he finished with, "Damn, you have all the fun."

Later that afternoon, Cindy called to ask how Charles was and to tell me that Tim, or whatever his name is, had been charged for the three murders plus a handful of other charges relating to kidnapping and assaulting Trescott and assaulting Charles. He would also be undergoing a psych evaluation.

On a cheerier note, she ended the call by giving me a message from Detective Fisher. Apparently, he told Cindy that if he ever caught me meddling in another one of his cases, he wouldn't arrest me. He'd shoot me.

I told her to tell him for me, "You're welcome."

She laughed and said, "For solving his murders. I might not forward your kind words."

PHANTOM

BILL NOEL AND ANGELICA CRUZ

1

Across the street, the sound of Mac Calhoun, a popular local entertainer, beginning his set on the patio of Rita's Seaside Grille, filled the air as I walked along the sidewalk in front of the Folly Beach Fishing Pier's parking lot. It was a little after sunset, and I was heading home after having supper at Loggerhead's Beach Grill a block behind me. I moved to the side of the walk to allow a man heading my direction to pass. After all, how could I not defer to someone who was at least 6'3" wearing a red and black turban and matching smoking jacket? Having lived on the small South Carolina barrier island for fourteen years, it took more than someone's unconventional attire to surprise me.

I smiled at the gentleman. He returned the smile then we turned our attention to the street beside us as we heard the roar of a car accelerating as it approached. Through its lowered passenger-side window, I caught a glimpse of the driver's arm extended toward the window. The driver was wearing a black ball cap pulled low over his face, a long-sleeve black T-shirt, and although the sun was no longer a factor, aviator sunglasses. None of that caught my attention as much as the black handgun pointed at us.

The music from Rita's faded into the background as two gunshots assailed my eardrums.

Before I could react, the vehicle sped out East Arctic Avenue. Its brake lights didn't illuminate until it was two blocks away. I took a deep breath, realized I was still standing, and the strangely attired man who'd smiled at me seconds earlier was no longer smiling, nor standing.

My first, and naïve, thought was he'd been startled by the gunshots, tripped on the edge of the sidewalk, and had fallen. Blood pooling beside his unmoving body reinforced what I'd reluctantly realized. I knelt close to the man and felt his neck for a pulse. Nothing.

A young couple who had been seated at the back of Rita's patio had noticed the two of us on the sidewalk, left the restaurant's back exit and headed across the street. I yelled for them to call 911 and looked around to see if anyone else was nearby. While the man was calling, the woman said she was a nurse and leaned over the turbaned gentleman.

I tried to stand to get out of her way, but my legs were so wobbly I was afraid I'd fall. I scooted a couple of feet back and remained on my knees. The nurse bent over the man a couple more seconds then leaned back and said there was nothing she could do for him.

She stood, patted me on the shoulder, and said, "I'm Charity and that's my husband Thomas. You okay?"

I nodded to the man standing behind his wife before saying, "I wasn't hit, but I'm far from okay. I'm Chris Landrum. Thanks for coming over."

The City of Folly Beach's Department of Public Safety, housing both the fire and police departments, is fewer than three blocks from where we were and in seconds, I heard sirens from one of the fire engines and the high-pitched sound from a police vehicle approaching.

Charity started to respond when the fire apparatus stopped in the street beside the body and two firefighters who also served as EMTs exited the vehicle. They looked around then rushed to the man on the sidewalk. I motioned for Charity and Thomas to move with me into the Pier's parking lot a few feet away from the activity on the sidewalk.

A Department of Public Safety SUV came around the corner from Center Street which intersects Arctic Avenue and stopped diagonally behind the fire engine closing off vehicular traffic on East Arctic. Officer Trula Bishop exited the SUV, went to the firefighters kneeling beside the victim, and said something. She spotted me and headed in my direction.

"Mr. Chris," she said the same way she'd addressed me since she'd arrived on the island seven years ago, "are you okay? What happened?"

I lied and said I was okay then gave her a capsule summary of what little I knew and motioned Charity and Thomas over and introduced them to the officer. Trula asked the couple the same thing she asked me and learned little new about what'd happened.

"Charity and Thomas, sure you didn't see the car the shots came from?"

Thomas said, "Officer, we didn't see or hear anything before I looked over and saw the man on the sidewalk with Mr. Landrum knelt over him. Charity was facing the other direction and didn't see anything until I pointed it out. She's a nurse and said we needed to check on the man. Didn't do much good, though. Sorry."

Trula said, "Thanks for checking on him. Were you finished with your meal?"

"Just got our drinks when Thomas saw the guys."

"Tell you what," Trula said, "why don't you go back and finish your supper. I don't want to spoil your meal. I'll have someone come over and get your information in a little while."

I wondered if their supper hadn't already been spoiled. Mine had been and it'd been a half hour since I'd eaten.

As is the case surrounding most police or fire activity, a crowd began gathering on both sides of the street and since the police vehicle had the road blocked, several people were inching closer on the street. A second police vehicle arrived from the other direction driving the wrong way on the one-way street. Officer Rodney New hopped out of the patrol vehicle, glanced at the man on the sidewalk, then came over to Officer Bishop and the rest of us. I'd met Rodney a year ago when he joined the Folly force after working with a sheriff's office near Asheville, North Carolina.

Bishop told him to herd bystanders away from the scene and tape off the area. He nodded and returned to his vehicle for a roll of crime scene tape. She watched Rodney go to his vehicle and the young couple enter the back gate to Rita's patio, and said, "Think you'd be more comfortable in my SUV?"

I'd recently turned seventy-one but at this moment my legs felt twice that age. "Trula, that'd beat me collapsing in the parking lot."

One of the firefighters approached and asked Officer Bishop if she wanted him to call the police chief and the coroner's office. She nodded then put her arm around my waist and escorted me to her vehicle.

"Mr. Chris, you know who he is?"

"No. To my knowledge, the first time I saw him was when he was walking toward me."

"Tell me again, how close you two were when you saw the firearm?"

"Couldn't have been more than a foot apart."

"Nearly side by side?"

Then it struck me. What if he wasn't the target?

2

The sight of another police vehicle speeding toward us going the wrong way on East Arctic Avenue drew our attention.

"The boss arrives," Trula said as a silver four-door Ford F-150 pickup truck slammed on its brakes, turned into the Pier's lot, and pulled up to the sidewalk.

Cindy LaMond, Folly's Director of Public Safety, slowly exited her official vehicle then walked over to the subject of everyone's attention plus her two firefighters and one public safety officer. They huddled a couple of minutes before the officer pointed to Bishop's vehicle. The Chief barked some orders then approached us.

I had known Cindy since she moved to Folly from East Tennessee thirteen years ago to join the police force. She was promoted to Director of Public Safety six years ago. I count Cindy and her husband, Larry, among my closest friends.

Cindy pointed to me and said, "Officer Bishop, have you arrested that vagrant for shooting the gentleman splayed out on our sidewalk?"

Bishop, like many of us, had learned to accept the Chief's dark sense of humor, and said, "Thought I'd give you the honor."

"I'll take him off your hands, and you can help the other guys see if there were witnesses or if anyone can tell us more about Mr. Turban."

Bishop gave her boss a quick salute and headed toward Rita's and the Tides Hotel while Cindy and I moved to her vehicle. I barely had time to get situated when she said, "You've lived on Folly what, a hundred years? Has anyone been killed over here in all that time where you, an aging retired bureaucrat, haven't been nearby when it happened or stuck your nose in our investigations?"

Unfortunately, Cindy was right about my getting involved in police investigations. Not only did I and a few of my friends get involved, we helped the police bring some bad folks to justice.

"Fourteen years," I said, although I suspected she knew I hadn't lived here a hundred years.

"Hell's bells, I'm not writing a history book, my point is, here you are again, smack dab in the middle of a murder."

"Cindy, I was walking down the sidewalk, minding my own business, when the man was shot."

"I'll accept that for now. Start from the beginning, what the hell happened?"

I shared how there wasn't much "beginning" since the fatal shot was fired seconds after I first noticed the man.

"Any idea who he is?"

"No."

"Recognize the killer?"

"No."

"Okay, easier question, was it a male or female?"

"It was dark inside the car, and all I noticed was a ball cap, sunglasses, and a long-sleeve shirt." I took a deep breath, exhaled, and added, "And a black handgun."

"Kind of vehicle?"

"By the time I noticed it, shots were fired and the man who'd been standing inches away was on the sidewalk, blood oozing out of his body. So no, I have no idea what kind of car it was."

"Then I don't suppose you got its license plate number?"

I stared at her, not thinking that questions deserved a response.

She reached over and squeezed my arm, before saying, "You good?"

"Not really."

"Anything I can do to help?"

"Catch the person who did this."

"Gee, why didn't I think of that?"

Another comment that didn't deserve a response.

Officer New tapped on Cindy's side window. She saw who it was and lowered the window.

"Chief, guy's license says he's Wesley Thomas, age sixty-five, lives on Pawleys Island. Also found a Tides Hotel keycard in his pocket."

"Anything else?"

"Thirty-five bucks and a Kia key fob."

"Someone from the Sheriff's Office should be here shortly. When a detective arrives, give him or her the wallet, keycard, and fob. Until then, help Officer Bishop see if you can find anyone who knows more about what happened."

"Yes, Chief."

The Charleston County Sheriff's Office investigates suspicious deaths on Folly since Cindy's force isn't equipped nor staffed to conduct murder investigations.

"Chris, any thoughts on where the car came from? I doubt the driver was out for a joy ride, saw two older gentlemen, and decided to shoot one of them."

"If it were waiting for, what did Officer New say his name was?"

She glanced at a notebook where she'd jotted down the victim's name, and said, "Wesley Thomas."

"If the shooter had been waiting for Thomas or me, he would've been parked in the Tides lot or one of the on-street spots this side of Center Street until Thomas was close then pulled onto the street. If he was parked on Arctic on the other side of Center Street, his vehicle would've been pointed the wrong direction, and there's nowhere on Center Street where he could've been parked and seen us."

"I agree. You think you may've been the intended victim?"

I closed my eyes, sighed, and said, "Don't see why, but it entered my mind."

I didn't tell her that thought held a prominent spot in my mind.

"Have you acquired any enemies recently, pissed off any of our fine citizens, or killed anybody's pet aardvark?"

"No, no, and who has an aardvark?"

She shook her head. "Merely an example of something bad you could've done."

Her phone rang before she could add other examples of bad things I could've done to anger someone enough to try to kill me.

"Yes, Detective," she said, listened for a few seconds, then added, "We'll be here."

She tapped *End call*, rolled her eyes, and said, "Good ole Detective Adair, your favorite and mine. He's in North Charleston dealing with who knows what and won't get here for an hour or longer."

Kenneth Adair was one of the Charleston County Sheriff's Office detectives and was the lead investigator on a handful of cases where I and some of my friends had stuck our noses where they didn't belong. The only thing that had kept us out of jail for interfering in a police investigation was that we solved the crimes, something the detective hadn't managed to do. Chief LaMond also wasn't a fan of Adair, but for different reasons. The detective treated Folly's police like they existed to provide help when he needed it and seldom thought it was important for the communication between his department and Folly's to go both ways.

Officer Rodney New returned escorting a lady in her mid-forties, with a frown on her face that practically went from ear to ear. Cindy lowered her window and New said, "Chief, this is Val Laramie. She's a guest at the hotel and said she saw the victim yesterday."

Cindy stepped out of her vehicle, gave Ms. Laramie one of her sugary smiles, and said, "Thanks for coming over with Officer New. Tell me about Mr. Thomas."

Ms. Laramie gave New a look like he'd dragged her away from eating a hot fudge sundae, then turned to Cindy, and said, "Not much to tell. My friend and I were checking in yesterday around five. We're from Wheeling, West Virginia, and had been looking so forward to visiting Folly. Anyway, the man your officer described was in front of us in line, and that's about it."

"Was he by himself?"

"Was then, but I have no way of knowing if there was someone with him."

"Was he wearing a turban?"

"Yes."

"Remember anything else about him?"

"Not much. He seemed friendly. He kept asking the clerk questions, not about the hotel, but about her life, now long she'd worked there, even asked if she was a surfer. Stuff like that. Tell you the truth, it irritated me since we had to wait until he was done before we could check in. Did I mention we're from West Virginia and anxious to get out there and walk on the beach? We—"

Cindy interrupted and said, "Anything else?"

"That covers it."

"You've been helpful, Ms. Laramie. Please give Officer New a number where we can contact you. You'll be hearing from a detective later this evening or in the morning."

New offered to walk her back to the hotel.

"Helpful?" I said to Cindy.

"Not really, but I didn't want her to think she'd wasted time coming over with Officer New. After all, she'd taken time from walking on the beach to talk with us. She's from West Virginia, you know."

"That's what I heard—twice."

Cindy looked toward the Tides then at the body on the sidewalk, and said, "Looks like I'm stuck here until not-so-humble Detective Adair arrives. Why don't you head home? Think you can do that without getting shot?"

I started to say I could try, when Officer Bishop approached Cindy's vehicle and pointed to a heavyset woman, in her sixties with short white hair, standing thirty feet away beside a palmetto tree near the hotel's entrance.

Officer Bishop said, "Chief, that's Alice Clay. She's a guest at the hotel and claims to know something about the shooting."

"What?"

"It would be best if she shared it with you."

"Then bring her over," Cindy said and exited the vehicle. I remained seated but since Cindy had left her window down, I could hear what would be said.

"Alice, this is Chief LaMond, you can share what you told me in the lobby."

"Chief, like I was telling your officer, I saw the shooting."

That got my attention, and I leaned closer to the window.

"Where were you at the time?"

"In my room. It's number 517."

"You mean you were standing outside your room on the open walkway to the elevator where you could see over here?"

The Tides Hotel is Folly's only beachfront hotel, with all guest rooms facing the ocean, their entry doors facing the city.

"No."

"Help me understand, Ms. Clay. Were you standing in your doorway and saw the shooting?"

"No, I was sitting on that nice sofa in the room and reading your local newspaper, *The Folly Current*, I believe. You see, I arrived this afternoon and wanted to see what was occurring in your quaint little burg."

"And you saw the shooting?"

She smiled and said, "Yes."

"Where did you see it, Ms. Clay?"

She pointed to the side of her head.

For the first time in the thirteen years I've known Cindy LaMond, she was speechless.

3

———

Cindy glanced at me as I leaned toward the driver's side window, then turned her gaze to the "witness," and said, "Ms. Clay, I'm confused. How were you seated in your room yet claim to have seen the man get shot?"

"Chief, I understand your confusion. You see, I have visions, can see things before they happen."

"Why don't you join me in my vehicle where you'll be more comfortable than standing out here?" She turned to me. "Chris, why don't you move to the back seat so Ms. Clay can join me in front?"

From what I'd heard seconds earlier, I suspect Cindy wanted a witness to whatever was going to be said rather than allowing me to stay to keep her company.

Ms. Clay walked to the passenger side of the pickup as I exited and reentered through the back door. Before Ms. Clay entered, Cindy looked at me and rolled her eyes.

"Thank you, Chief. This is much more comfortable. Please call me Alice."

"Okay, Alice, let's go through everything you think you saw."

"Everything I saw," Cindy's new passenger corrected with a smile. "Sorry, everything you saw."

"A man walking. A large, black thing moving, a car, a truck, could've been I-don't-know what. It was dark so my image of it's fuzzy." She smiled and added, "My visions are not always one-hundred percent accurate. I saw it more like a phantom rather than a man-made vehicle."

Cindy said, "Okay, then what?"

"When it got near the man, there was a blinding white flash, then the phantom slid away. Death remained."

"You saw the man get shot?"

"I saw death."

"Did you see a man wearing a turban?"

"Don't know. Remember, it was dark."

I leaned forward and said, "Did you see two men?"

Cindy glared at me and turned to Alice.

"I don't recall a second man."

Cindy said, "Anything else about the shooting itself?"

"Sorry, I didn't hear what you might call a gunshot. The white flash was all. The flash then death."

"I see," Cindy said in a tone that implied the opposite. "How long have you had these visions?"

"Lordy, couldn't tell you exactly. I moved from Ohio to Kure Beach, North Carolina, six years ago after I retired from teaching literature at a high school in Cincinnati. Kure is south of Wilmington. That's more than you wanted to know, but I've had visions long before moving."

Cindy said, "How often do you have them?"

"Probably one or two a week, sometimes more, sometimes less."

"Are they always accurate?"

"Hard to tell."

"Why is that?"

She rubbed her chin and said, "Okay, here's an example. On the drive down, I visioned a wreck on the Interstate on the opposite side of the road. Two of those big eighteen-wheelers collided. It was horrible. Anyway, since I kept driving, I wasn't nearby to see if it happened. See what I mean?"

"Believe I do. How long will be you staying at the Tides?"

"Leaving a week from tomorrow. I'll be here to celebrate Halloween next Sunday."

Cindy glanced at me then turned to Alice. "Is Halloween one of your favorite holidays?"

She nodded and smiled.

"Alice, is there anything else you can tell us about your vision about the death?"

"Chief, I hope you don't think I'm some sort of nut. My visions are real, honest."

"I'm sure they are. If you think of anything else that may help us understand what happened, please give Officer Bishop a call. Let me give you her number."

Cindy gave Bishop's number to Alice then thanked her for the information.

Cindy watched the seer of visions slowly walk to the Tides then turned to me. "Your reaction?"

"She seems sincere about what she saw."

"So do many residents in psychiatric hospitals."

"I don't suppose it was an accident that you gave her Officer Bishop's number instead of yours."

She smiled. "I'm not Chief because I'm stupid, although others might argue that point." Her smile faded. "Didn't I tell you to go home?"

"Yes, but that was before you asked me to stay so you'd have a witness to the story Ms. Clay was going to tell about seeing the murder while she was sitting on a sofa in her hotel room."

Her smile returned. "I repeat, I'm not Chief because I'm stupid."

I took that as a hint to head home.

4

———

The walk home was a blur except when vehicles approached. I caught myself holding my breath and subconsciously ducking. I didn't recall ever feeling more relieved as I entered my cottage and was surrounded by a sense of security. I grabbed a Diet Coke and waited in my recliner for a visit from Detective Adair.

Minutes felt like hours, and I gave up my vigil at midnight. Sleep was slow to come, and when it did, it was filled with nightmares. Wesley was smiling at me before dropping dead, and then I was the one lying on the sidewalk looking up at his face as I took my last breath.

I stumbled out of bed before sunrise after realizing I wouldn't be getting any rest. I padded into the kitchen and awakened my aging Mr. Coffee machine before realizing coffee was the only thing in the kitchen I could call breakfast. After my second cup, I decided a trip to the Lost Dog Cafe with its fully stocked kitchen would meet my need for nourishment. The Dog had been my go-to breakfast and lunch spot since I'd arrived on Folly.

The temperature was in the low sixties, which provided enough chill to clear any remaining cobwebs from the unsettled night as I made my way five blocks to the popular restaurant. Along the way, I realized the sounds of nearby moving vehicles didn't bother me as they had on my way home last evening.

I approached the Dog and noticed Charles Fowler, my best friend since I'd moved to Folly, leaning on his classic Schwinn bicycle at the bike stand near the side of the restaurant. He was wearing a purple sweatshirt with Bellevue University in gold letters on the front. I'd done my best over the years to stop asking about his unlimited supply of college and university sweatshirts and T-shirts to prevent hearing more than I wanted to know about the schools they represented.

Charles patted my back and said, "Figured you'd be here. Bellevue University is in Bellevue, Nebraska. They're the Bruins. The school was—"

I interrupted with, "How long have you been standing there?"

Charles looked at his bare wrist where most people wear a watch. "Shade under ten minutes."

"Why'd you think I'd be here?"

He shrugged.

I figured that was the most I was getting out of him, so I said, "Can I interest you in joining me for breakfast?"

"Thought you'd never ask," he said and followed me into the colorful restaurant.

Amber, one of the servers and nicest people on the island, was in front of the large coffee urn at the side of the room and said, "Grab a seat and I'll get your coffee."

The restaurant was only half full and we took my favorite booth along the back wall where we were stared at by countless canines in photos dotting the walls.

Amber arrived with our coffee, and said, "What can I get you?"

Charles nodded my direction and said, "He'll have French toast and I'll partake of the Loyal Companion."

Amber headed toward the kitchen without checking to see if that's what I wanted, although French toast was a safe guess since it was my breakfast choice most every visit.

Charles watched her go and said, "Sorry I canceled on Logger-head's last night. Was a long day."

"Wish I had."

Charles looked up from his coffee. "Why?"

"Something happened on the way home."

He shrugged.

"Someone was shot beside Rita's," I said and waited for what would rival the Spanish Inquisition.

"What, who, and why didn't you tell me sooner, like last night? Start from the beginning."

"In the beginning, God created—"

"Smart ass. After you left Loggerhead's?"

"I was on the sidewalk in front of the Pier's parking lot when a car sped up behind me. The driver shot a gentleman walking past me. He died before the EMTs got there. That's all."

"Not even close to 'that's all.' I need to know everything if we're going to solve it."

Charles, without any formal training or licensing, claims to be a private detective, and further claims I'm his assistant in the imaginary agency.

I said, "You know, that's up to the police. It doesn't concern you or me."

"Chris, oh, Chris, tell me again where you were when the person was shot?"

"He was walking past me."

"What makes you think you weren't the target?"

Before I responded, Amber set our meals in front of us, refilled our mugs, and said, "Need anything, holler."

I said we would as Charles took a bite of bacon. With his mouth full, I had time to think about what he'd said and came to the same conclusion I'd arrived at last evening. There was as good a chance of me being the target as there was the man who had been standing beside me. Do I share that?

I didn't have to, since the next thing he said was, "Do you know who he was?"

"Wesley Thomas. He lived on Pawleys Island."

"Did he say anything to you?"

"No, not verbally but his attire spoke volumes. He would've stood out in a crowd."

"Why?"

"He was tall, wore a black and red turban, and a matching smoking jacket."

Charles took another bite, swallowed, and said, "Wonder if he's one of the fortune tellers?"

"One of what?"

"Fortune tellers. Saturday, I saw Darrin at a house on East Arctic that he and Stormy are renting for some of the fortune tellers that're meeting at the Tides this week."

"Darrin?"

"Remember Darrin Roserun? We met him a couple of years ago. He and Stormy are friends with Shannon and the kids. They own a metaphysical shop in Charleston."

"I knew the name sounded familiar. I suppose it's possible Wesley was one of the attendees. That might answer another question about a lady who came forward after the shooting."

"What lady?"

"She was sort of a witness to the incident, think her name was Ms. Clay. She told Cindy she had a vision of the shooting, even though it was vague."

"I'm sure Cindy loved that. Since we have an inside angle, guess we're the guys to solve the murder."

It'd been wishful thinking Charles wouldn't return to his original point.

"Not sure what inside angle you're talking about, but I have faith the police will solve it."

"When are you going to face facts? It's our mission to solve it."

While I wasn't willing to agree, I still had the nagging question: Was Wesley the target, or was I? If I happened to be the intended victim, why? And who was the shooter?

Charles kept saying something about the fortune tellers congregating at the Tides and how it was up to us to catch whoever fired the fatal shots, regardless of the intended victim, but I was too distracted to follow everything he was saying.

We'd finished our meals, and Amber brought the check, then started clearing the plates. She glanced at Charles and then at me before saying, "Looks like you were in a deep conversation. Please tell me it's about your costumes for Halloween and not about last night."

Charles said, "What'd you hear about last night?"

"It's not something I heard. I was meeting a friend at Rita's and saw the emergency vehicles. Asked the server if there was an accident and she told me it was a shooting. I didn't see either of you and breathed a sigh of relief. Finally, something bad happened here and you weren't involved." She again glanced at Charles, then turned to me. "Right?"

"Wrong. Chris was standing beside the guy when he was killed."

Amber put her hand on my arm and said, "Are you all right? Do you know who the man was?"

"I'm a little shaken. I didn't know him. Charles thinks he could've been a part of a group meeting at the hotel."

"I read about that last week in the *Charleston City Paper*. The event is being sponsored by Stormy Rose, Darren and Stormy's metaphysical shop. There was a copy behind the counter. Let me see if it's still there."

Amber returned with the weekly paper and handed it to me, then said, "I need to get back to work."

Charles watched as I scanned the article, then said, "Anything interesting?"

"Don't know yet, besides we're assuming Wesley has something to do with the meeting."

"What are the chances someone dressed like that isn't connected with fortune tellers?"

"You know Folly as well as I do. We have our share of quirky residents and visitors, but I tend to agree with you about why Wesley was here."

Charles smiled like he'd solved a Rubik's Cube, stood up, took the last sip of coffee, and said, "Got to go. Can't be late making Dude's deliveries," he added as he headed to the exit.

Charles was not on anyone's payroll and hadn't been for a thousand years. He made a meager living, but enough to cover his minimal expenses, by making on-island deliveries for our friend Dude Sloan's surf shop, assisting contractors doing unskilled labor on projects, and in season, occasionally assisting local restaurants doing clean-up work, all jobs off the books. He also covered some of his food expenses by generously allowing me to pay for many of his meals.

I enjoyed the final bites of French toast in silence before leaving the money on the table, and nodding to Amber as I headed out. The walk home was pleasant but the events from last night were still bouncing around inside my head, making me realize I needed more answers about what led to a man's death.

Instead of going into the house, I sat on my screened-in front porch and opened the *City Paper* to the second page where there was a photo of Darrin and Stormy Roserun standing in front of Stormy Rose. The first part was an introduction to the shop and its owners, how long they'd been in business, and some of the items and services they offer. The second part included short bios on some of the people coming to Folly for the meeting. Reading about Tarot card readers, crystal balls, palm readers, and something called scrying reminded me I never knew there were so many different methods of telling fortunes. Then again, what I don't know about the subject could fill the large conference room where the meeting was being held at the Tides.

Fortunately, the phone ringing prevented me from confusing myself more about the various methods of fortune telling. Barb's name appeared on the screen.

Barb Deanelli moved to Folly six years ago and opened Barb's Books, a used bookstore located in the space that had previously housed a photo gallery I'd owned before conceding I couldn't make enough to make the business worth my time and closed it. Barb and I've dated for the last five years.

I smiled and said, "Hi, Barb."

"So, when were you going to tell me what I've heard from a dozen people this morning, not one of them being you?" she said with no smile reflected in her voice.

I guessed without taking much of a leap she was referring to yesterday's shooting and said, "About the shooting?"

"The shooting that came within inches of killing you."

"I should've called last evening, but I was so shaken I didn't know which way was up. Sorry."

"Apology almost accepted. Now to the main reason for the call, are you doing okay?"

"Better than I was last night. Thanks for asking."

"Anything I can do to help?"

"Your call helps."

"Suckupery has never been one of your strengths."

"That a term you learned in law school?"

Before moving to Folly from Pennsylvania after a highly contested divorce, Barb had been a successful defense attorney. She was also my friend Dude Sloan's half-sister.

To my relief, she laughed, and said, "Made up the word, but did learn the fine art of sucking up while in school. Now, enough of your deflection, you sure you're okay?"

"Yeah, although it was one of the most traumatic experiences I've had."

"That's going some, considering how many tight situations you and Charles have managed to get into. Do you know anything about the man killed?"

"Not much. Name's Wesley Thomas, lived on Pawleys Island, and was staying at the Tides. Speculation is he was here for a fortune tellers' conference, convention, meeting, or whatever."

"Are the police certain he was the intended victim?"

"As opposed to being me, you mean?"

"Yes," she whispered.

No, I wasn't sure, but there was no reason to upset Barb more than she already was if you think the shots were intended for anyone other than Mr. Thomas."

"Please let me know if anything else happens, or if you need to talk with someone about any of this."

"I will, Barb, and again, I apologize for not calling last evening."

"Again, apology almost accepted," she said and ended the call.

5

---

fter finishing the article in the *City Paper*, I found myself thinking about the same thing that'd consumed much of my time since yesterday evening: the shooting and my proximity to it. Fortunately, my ringing phone interrupted my fruitless thoughts. Chief LaMond's name appeared on the screen.

"Afternoon, Cindy."

"Glad you didn't say good afternoon, or I would've called you a liar."

"What's wrong?"

"Gee, let's see. How about a visitor to the island where I'm allegedly responsible for public safety getting himself murdered within sight of one of the island's most popular restaurants, in front of Folly's Fishing Pier, and yards from our largest hotel? How about your director of public safety having no, zero, zilch idea who killed the visitor or why? Those enough reasons why the day ain't so good?"

"How about how one of your favorite and wonderful citizens could've been killed?"

"If that was supposed to make me feel better, you failed. Anyway, my call wasn't about me, how are you?"

That was more like my close friend who happened to be Folly's chief law enforcement official.

"Still a little shaky, but, of course, I'm much better than Wesley Thomas. I was going to call later to see if you had any additional information. I'm also confused why Detective Adair hasn't appeared on my doorstep."

"We've confirmed Mr. Thomas was here for some sort of gathering sponsored by a couple who own a shop in Charleston."

"Darrin and Stormy Roserun."

"Very good, Mr. Pain In My Posterior."

"Don't think I'm the pain, you called me. So, what about Adair's interview?"

"When he managed to arrive at the crime scene, everyone was pissed. When he asked about witnesses, I mentioned your name." She chuckled. "He didn't take it well. Said something like you should be banished from the island, or maybe from the earth. Then said you were my problem, and I should interview you again to see if any additional details had emerged."

"Doesn't seem professional, him normally being by the book."

"Don't get me started on his professionalism."

"Sorry to disappoint you, but I don't know anything I didn't share last evening."

"It was a shot in the dark. With that said, try and stay out of trouble. I need to spend time worrying about Halloween pranks pulled by the youngest of our residents, not homicides and not senior citizens pretending they're cops."

"Cindy, thanks for calling to check on me. I'm fine."

"Call if you think of anything that'll help the police, I repeat, help the police solve this unfortunate event."

The phone went dead. Instead of getting more frustrated thinking about the identity of the intended victim, I decided to go next door to Bert's Market. When I bought my cottage, I hadn't realized how fortunate I was to have moved next to the iconic Folly Beach institution, especially since I fixed food in my kitchen as often as polar bears waving Portuguese flags parade down Center Street. Bert's was known for being open twenty-four hours a day, 365 days a year, and selling everything from fishing lures to headache cures.

Denise, a long-term personable employee, greeted me with a smile and a cheerful salutation. On my way to the cooler to resupply my refrigerator with Diet Cokes, I heard the booming voice of Preacher Burl Costello say, "Brother Chris, how are you this fine day?"

I'd met Preacher Burl several years ago when he moved to Folly and founded First Light Church, a nondenominational house of worship. Or, more accurately, a place of worship. since it holds services on the beach near the Pier.

"Preacher, I'm well, and you?" I said, overestimating my condition.

"Shopping for my afternoon trek with Sister Roisin. I wouldn't want to be lost in the great outdoors without sufficient provisions." He laughed as he reached for a couple of donuts.

"Getting lost on this island would be challenging."

"True, but it's a great excuse to acquire junk food."

I nodded and said, "How is Roisin and the rest of the Stone family?"

I'd met the Stone family two years ago, and shortly after meeting them, Mike, Shannon Stone's spouse, and father to Roisin, age thirteen, and Desmond, age eighteen, was murdered. They'd resided on Folly less than a year when Mike was killed and were known as practicing Wiccans. The surviving members of the family, especially, Roisin, had established an excellent relationship with Preacher Burl.

"Sister Shannon is coping with her loss like most would, up some days, down others."

"How is morose Desmond?"

"Brother Desmond puts on a good front, but I get the impression he is having issues."

Losing the Stone family patriarch almost two years ago would be rough on anyone, and Preacher Burl had maintained a close relationship with the family during that period.

"I'm sorry to hear that about Desmond. Let me know if there's anything I can do."

"I certainly will." He looked at his watch and added, "I need to get going. Don't want to keep Sister Roisin waiting. Shall I tell the Stones you will be stopping by?"

"What makes you say that?"

"I've been a preacher a long time and a judge of human character even longer. I see how you speak about the Stone family." He then patted me on the arm.

"I'll reach out."

As Preacher Burl paid for his survival food, I couldn't help but chuckle thinking about a Christian minister being a good friend with a family of Wiccans. Burl had brought up a good point. I was concerned about the family since I was the person who'd unfortunately discovered Mike murdered in the family's driveway. Perhaps the family's beliefs and lifestyle might also give me insights into the latest murder. If nothing else, insight into the culture of the group holding meetings at the Tides Wesley Thomas had been on Folly to attend.

Before I made my way out of Bert's, Charles called.

"Hi, Charles, finished your deliveries?"

"Nope, but I'm taking my union's mandatory break, so I was using it to see if you have any new information."

"Your union?"

"The DBDDU."

"What's DB whatever?"

"You never cease to amaze me about what you don't know. It's the Dude's Bicycle Delivery Driver's Union."

"How could I have overlooked that organization?"

"My thought exactly."

I said, "No."

"No what?"

"I have no new information."

"Then how are we going to catch the killer if you don't learn about the victim?

"Charles, how many times have I told you it's not our job?"

"You're right, it's not our job, it's our duty."

"How do you figure?"

"My break's over, so I'm not going to quibble over duties and merely a job. What are your plans?"

"Going to call Shannon Stone and see if she has time to see me this afternoon. Want to join me?"

"I would, but I have several more deliveries. Take notes so you can tell me everything that's said."

The line went dead before I told him I wouldn't be taking notes.

"HEY, CHRIS," Shannon Stone said as she answered the phone.

"I was calling to see if you could spare a few minutes this afternoon."

"Where are you?"

"Leaving Bert's."

"Tell you what, I'm on the beach walking Lugh and we're about a half-mile from the Pier. Why don't you go out on it, and I'll wave when we're nearby. You can join us as we head home. Will that work?"

"Sounds good."

The beautiful afternoon and the sound of the surf drew me to the Pier, my favorite place for contemplating and relaxing. Anglers flanked both sides of the structure, which surprised me since it was mid-October. Then again, even if the fish weren't biting the anglers couldn't complain about the scenery.

A relaxing fifteen minutes later, I spotted a familiar face and her canine. Shannon was attractive, trim, and in her late thirties with her red hair glowing in the sun, and Lugh, an Irish Wolfhound about the size of a Clydesdale, followed close beside her.

She spotted me, waved, and waited as I left the Pier and walked down the steps to the beach.

"Merry meet, Chris," she said with a smile as bright as her red hair.

"Thanks for meeting me, and you too, Lugh," I said as I patted the massive canine's head. "Your boy seems bigger than the last time I saw him. When will he stop growing?"

"He's full size now, might get a bit chunkier but then don't we all. Shall we continue?"

"My pleasure."

We headed east down the beach in the direction of the Stones' cottage when she said, "I heard a nasty rumor you were present at a shooting."

"I regret to say it's true. Actually, that's the reason I wanted to talk to you."

"Let me use my mystic powers to start this conversation." She closed her eyes and put her finger to her lips. "You want to know about the fortune tellers, sorcerers, and others here for the week."

"Impressive, what can you tell me?"

"As you know, our family is close with Darrin and Stormy, and I know two of the out-of-town guests."

"If you don't mind, could you tell me a little about them? If you assume I know nothing about their craft or whatever, you won't be far off."

"Of course, I don't mind. What do you want to know?"

"Did you know Wesley Thomas?"

"No, but Stormy and my friend Chloe did."

"Chloe?"

"Chloe Meriweather is from Marian, South Carolina. She's a firefighter and reads Tarot cards. She also makes gris-gris bags. She visited the house once and purchases herbs from my online shop so that's how I got to know her."

"Gris-gris bags?"

"A talisman, it's usually a small cloth bag filled with herbs and additional items used for protection, luck, or other issues."

"Know anything else about her?"

"Not really, although I've heard good things. Spencer Ford is the other participant I know. We met a year ago at his store Ford and Fortune Mystical Shop in Charlotte, North Carolina. He travels the Southeast and Mexico looking for items for his shop. When I first heard about the shooting it worried me because the description sounded much like Spencer."

"How so?"

"Same build and wears a turban."

"Spencer wears a turban?"

"Yes, when he's working, he wears one matching his suit. He believes it adds to the mystery he's portraying and practicing."

"Does he use Tarot cards?

"His medium is scrying. Scrying can be done in a crystal ball or as Spencer does it lighting a candle and staring into a dark mirror for answers or communication."

"Interesting."

"It sounds odd and many who claims to do these things are frauds, but some are genuine and gifted."

"On that note, do you know Alice Clay? She approached Chief LaMond after the shooting saying she was in her room and saw the whole thing, although her description was vague."

"I know the name but haven't met her. Anything else I can help your troubled soul with?"

"I didn't know my soul was troubled. I was simply looking for information."

"I didn't mean to imply anything. I see a deeper level of concern in your eyes. Anytime you have questions, call or, better yet, come by the house. Our door is always open for you and, of course, Charles."

"Thank you."

"If you want, I can introduce you to Spencer and Chloe or any of the attendees. Consider me your witch among witches."

"Better not let Roisin hear you say that."

"Yes, my little nymph doesn't like me calling myself a witch."

6

The first thing I realized when I rolled out of bed the next morning was that the horrific event which had occurred two days earlier wasn't the dominant thought on my mind. It was there, but more mundane items were rising in importance. With much cooler weather approaching, I needed to get filters for my furnace, a task I usually don't think about until the furnace starts growling at me because of its clogged filter. I was also reminded there was nothing in my kitchen a normal person would call food.

A six block walk to Pewter Hardware with a stop along the way at Bert's Market would allow me to meet both needs. A handful of construction workers wearing yellow safety vests and hardhats were gathered in front of Bert's coffee urn, so I headed to the pastry cabinet and grabbed a chocolate croissant before joining the workers at the popular urn.

One of the workers turned to a colleague and said in a voice loud enough to have been heard above the roar of a chainsaw, the volume he probably used on the job, "Hear it was a damned psychic. Served him right. Who invited the faker here anyhow?"

The recipient of the comment, poured his coffee, looked around to see who might've overheard the comment, then leaned closer to the man whose comment probably reached everyone in the store plus those in cars driving past Bert's, and said, "Lou, all I heard was someone was killed. Don't know who or what he was, but it's horrible."

His loudmouth buddy laughed and said, "If the guy was really a psychic, his crystal ball would've told him not to be where he was that got him shot. Damned fraud."

"Still a shame," a third man said as the group finished getting coffee and headed to the exit.

I drew my coffee, paid for the croissant, and continued walking to the hardware store while wondering if the opinionated worker's view was shared by many others. To my knowledge, I'd never met anyone who claimed to be a fortune teller, but I didn't have an opinion either way about the profession.

Pewter Hardware was located on East Indian Avenue beside the Folly Beach Post Office and less than a block off Center Street. The store was tiny and could fit inside the tool department at Lowe's, but it was stocked to meet most home improvement or repair needs of Folly's residents.

I was the only customer and was greeted by Brandon Tigert, the sole full-time employee other than Larry LaMond, the store's owner.

"Morning, Chris, what brings you out this early?"

Brandon was in his early fifties and an admitted "reformed hippy" who often wore an old T-shirt with a peace symbol under his tan Pewter Hardware shirt. Today was one of those days.

"Furnace filters."

He smiled. "Furnace growling at you again?"

Knowing everyone's business is one of the greatest and occasionally most frustrating features of living in a small town. I returned the smile. "Not this time. For once, I thought of it before being yelled at by the inanimate object. Where's Larry?"

Brandon was in front of the shelf holding furnace filters, pulled a package of three out, then headed to the register. "This is your size, isn't it?" he asked, proving another positive feature of small-town living.

I nodded and he added, "Larry headed to the Post Office twenty minutes ago, but since that trip usually takes him five minutes, I have no idea where he is. Is the rumor true?"

"I need a hint, what rumor?"

"You were nearby when one of those so-called psychics was killed."

"Sadly, yes. Do I hear doubt about you believing in psychics?"

"Know what else I heard?"

"What?"

"You were the person shot at."

"Where'd you hear that?"

"You know Chester Carr?"

"Sure."

I met Chester nearly a decade ago. He was now in his mid-90s, and it'd been more than a year since I'd seen him.

"He was in yesterday afternoon buying lightbulbs and told me whoever was doing the shooting was aiming at you."

"What made him say that?"

"Wasn't anything you could take to the bank. He said since you get yourself in the middle of every bad thing that happens here, he figured one of the bad guys from your past wanted to get even."

"That all Chester said?"

He nodded. "Told you it wasn't anything you could take to the bank."

I paid for the filters with something he could take to the bank and said, "What about you and psychics?"

"Not going to let it go, are you?"

"Curious, that's all."

He frowned and said, "I wouldn't go around shooting at any of them, if that's what you're asking."

"That never entered my mind. Like I said, I was curious since the man shot is supposed to be one, and I hear they're holding a meeting at the Tides."

"Let's say I'm not a believer. My ex-wife went to one a couple of times. Big waste of money if you ask me."

Although I'd known Brandon ever since I'd moved to Folly, this was the first time he'd mentioned his ex-wife, although Larry had shared a little about her and Brandon's daughter.

"Did she have a bad experience meeting with a psychic or fortune teller?"

"Not really. All the con artist revealed was stuff that could apply to nearly anyone. Nothing unique to her." He looked at the door like he was wishing another customer would come in to distract me. No one entered, and he said, "Think Chester's right?"

He was done talking about psychics.

"That the shot was meant for me?"

He nodded.

Good question, wish I knew.

"I doubt it, but thanks for your concern. I'd better let you get back to work."

He looked around the empty store, then at the counter that had nothing on it but a computer screen, a pad of Post-it notes, and a ballpoint pen. He smiled and said, "Yeah, as you can see, I'm snowed under."

I smiled and said, "Good talking to you," then headed to the door.

Before I opened it, he said, "If I were you, I wouldn't ask Larry about fortune tellers, mystics, or whatever they're called."

"Why?"

"He ain't as calm as I am about them. If you bring it up, expect to get an ear full. Consider yourself warned."

"Got it."

7

I'd left Pewter Hardware and headed toward Center Street when I heard a familiar voice calling me from across the street and up a small hill leading to the Folly River Park, a small city park bounded by Center Street, East Indian Avenue, and the Folly River. Larry LaMond was seated on a swinging bench at the top of the hill and waved me over.

My friend was 5'1", weighed no more than a hundred pounds and was in his mid-60s. His Pewter shirt was untucked and would've reached mid-thigh if he stood. He remained seated and said, "Hope you spent a lot in there." He pointed to his store.

"Sorry, not that much. What're you doing hanging around out here? Brandon said you went to the Post Office and didn't know where from there."

"Did you have to wait behind a big crowd to pay for whatever's in that bag?"

I shook my head.

"Think my highly trained, experienced employee can handle the morning rush. I spend a thousand hours a week in there and it's getting harder to do without escaping occasionally."

"You've earned that escape."

"How are you doing?"

"Okay, why?"

"Cindy told me about the shooting. The way she tells it, you could be dead instead of that other guy."

I was one of a handful of people on Folly who knows how unconventional their marriage was considering Larry had spent eight years in Coastal State Prison in Georgia for burglary and Cindy was Folly's police chief. He'd used his jockey-like stature and climbing ability to earn a reputation as an accomplished cat burglar, that is, until his luck ran out. After leaving prison, he moved to Folly and took a job in its tiny hardware store before buying it a few years later. Cindy and her predecessor as chief who's now Folly's mayor knew about Larry's checkered past and had learned to respect his conversion to the right side of the law.

"Larry, I don't know who the intended victim was, but am fortunate to be here. Does Cindy have any leads?"

"None she's told me about. If you ask me, the shooter was gunning for the quack who was killed."

"Why say that?" I asked, then remembered what Brandon had said about me being warned.

Larry looked around, leaned forward in the swing, then turned to me, before saying, "Let me tell you a story. In my former life when I was spending a year in a county jail in Georgia, long before my time in Coastal State, I had a bunkmate named Joseph Beal. That was his real name, but he went by Derek Avalon, claiming it made him appear mysterious. Anyway, he'd earned the privilege of being my bunkmate because he'd been convicted of being a con artist. Seems he'd been with a travelling circus for years before going out on his own where he said he could make way more money than with the circus."

"Let me guess, Joseph was a fortune teller."

"Know what you just did?"

"What?"

"Used one of Joseph's cons."

"Listening to what you said about your time with Joseph and

what you said earlier about the dead man being a quack, then putting it together and guessing Joseph was a fortune teller?"

"Exactly, except Joseph would talk about several things with the person he was conning so the person wouldn't remember what he'd said. Joseph would then spew some mumbo jumbo like he was talking in tongues, rubbed a crystal ball or flipped over cards, then acting out of breath, he'd tell the mark, as he called the sucker, what he learned from what was already said."

"His marks, his victims, fell for it?"

"Yes, according to Joseph, people who came to him for a reading wanted to believe, so they were more gullible than any skeptic. He ripped off people from all over the country without knowing a thing about them, simply by listening. Another trick was when he used the Barnum Effect."

"As in P. T. Barnum?"

"Exactly, the guy who said, 'a sucker is born every minute.'"

"How does that apply?"

"Chris, don't you have a college degree in psychology?"

I nodded.

"Then I bet you can figure it out."

"Larry, I went to college with Sigmund Freud. Okay, not that long ago, but way more years ago than I can remember. Help me out."

"The best I can do is say people believe what they want to believe. I could make up a bunch of general statements like you have a need for other people to like you, or you tend to be critical of yourself, general stuff like that. Then if I used some of Joseph's hocus pocus and told you those things, the odds are you'd believe me. But look at it like this, those things are true of most every Tom, Dick, and Harriet. Did that make Joseph, excuse me, Derek a psychic, a palm reader, or a fortune teller? Hell no. It made him a con artist." He slapped his thigh with his hand, exhaled, and added, "They're all frauds, period. It's horrible they decided to have a big powwow on Folly. I'm not the only one who thinks that."

"What do you know about their event?"

"No more than what I read and what Cindy told me."

"You said a few others feel the way you do?"

"More than a few."

"Who are some of those folks who are against the meeting?"

He looked toward the Post Office, then down at the ground, before saying, "You're a good friend. You know, we've been through a couple of near disasters over the years, and I'd trust you with my life."

"I feel the same about you, but?"

He glanced at me, "But the folks who shared their feelings did it for my ears only. They don't feel comfortable with others knowing. You understand, don't you?"

"Yes."

"But you think one of them may've shot that man."

"I have no idea who did it. What do you think?"

"The people I've talked with have strong feelings about the group, but I've known most of them for years, and I'm certain, okay, as certain as I can be, none of them would've shot the guy. I think one of the other frauds did it."

"Why?"

He smiled. "You're the detective. That's for you to figure out."

"That's Charles who claims he's a detective. I'm just the guy who was standing by the guy when he was shot."

"Did you forget you're talking to your buddy? I have more faith in you figuring out who did it than the detective from the Sheriff's Office." He lowered his voice and added, "Even more faith than our police department solving it. And, if you tell Cindy I said that I'll be the one shooting at you. I won't miss." He glanced over at the hardware store and said, "I'd better get back and help Brandon with the throngs of customers."

Before he headed down the hill to the store, he added, "Mark my words, it was one of the people attending the event that shot the guy."

8

———

Larry's words stayed with me as I headed home. I'd never known him to have such an intense opinion on anything. The old saying that you shouldn't talk about politics, religion, or money should be amended to add fortune telling. I understood why Larry felt the way he did and wondered how many others agree with him.

Two blocks from home, I had the feeling I was being watched. I turned to find Charles walking his bike a dozen feet behind me. He was wearing a navy-blue sweatshirt with what could be described as a yellow worm wearing a light blue jersey with UCSC on it.

I took a deep breath and said, "What are you doing?"

"Seeing how long it would take you to notice me."

"Why?"

"Practicing my private detective surveilling."

That'll teach me to ask.

"Oh."

"Bet you're wondering what the critter is on my shirt."

Not really, but knew that wouldn't stop him from telling me, so I said, "What is it?"

"None other than the University of California Santa Cruz's famous mascot Sammy the Banana Slug."

"Who knew?"

"My surveillance tells me you're not very observant for someone who was shot at the other day."

"Point taken, so you don't have to try sneaking up on me again. I was on the way home. Want to join me?"

"What's in the bag?"

"Furnace filters."

"Planning a career as a furnace repairman?"

I glanced at him and remained silent, something he should practice more often.

He shrugged and fell into step beside me before saying, "Have any snacks?"

"What do you think?"

"What I figured. Go replace your filter and I'll grab some stuff at Bert's."

I'd finished changing the filter before Charles arrived carrying two bags.

"You were going to pick up a few snacks, so why two bags?"

"Can't have enough brain food. I was hoping you'd have convinced Burt's to run a tab. The receipt's in the bag with the Doritos. You can write me a check if you don't have enough cash on you."

"Thanks," I said, making no effort to hide the sarcasm or to grab my checkbook.

We took our snacks of Doritos, Oreos, and soft drinks and went to the living room.

"Did you have many deliveries for Dude?" I asked as I plopped down in the recliner.

"One delivery but it had nothing to do with the surf shop."

"Meaning?"

"Dude won a month's supply of homemade dog treats and samples of food from the pet store near Walmart."

"That's a long bike ride."

"That's why I drove and also drove when I took the winnings to Martha and her menagerie."

Martha Wright is an octogenarian who lives with a house full of dogs, cats, a parrot, a raccoon, and my least-favorite critter, a snake named Squeezy. She also puts out food for strays that happen to wander through her yard. She moved to Folly eight years ago after her husband died. As she put it when I met her five years ago, "Tommy hated the ocean, so when he went to the Pearly Gates I went to the beach." Her oceanfront house on East Arctic Avenue hints at her wealth.

"That's nice of Dude. Why didn't he keep his winnings for Pluto?"

"He told me, 'Pluto be simple pup. Highfalutin' food not good for his tummy.'"

Pluto is Dude's Australian Terrier.

"Oh."

"Enough small talk, have you figured out who shot the all-knowing wizard."

"If Wesley was all-knowing, he would've avoided walking down the sidewalk."

"Unless he wasn't the target."

"You don't have to remind me. Speaking of Wesley, I had an interesting conversation with Larry before you started surveilling me."

"About?" Charles said then grabbed an Oreo and stuffed it in his mouth.

"He thinks the killer is one of the fortune tellers, and apparently he's not the only one thinking that."

"Cindy?"

"He didn't mention her but said there's a handful of locals who have an issue with the group being here."

"He give names?"

"He didn't feel comfortable saying, since apparently they told him in confidence."

"Wonder if Dani is one of those."

"Who?"

"Dani Crow, a woman renting a room from Martha."

"I didn't know Martha rented rooms."

"You know she has trouble getting around. She's used a cane as long as we've known her, but she's getting worse. Dani helps with chores."

"What do you know about Dani?"

"I met her a few months ago when she was walking four dogs near the Pier, I recognized them as part of Martha's pack, and had to make sure she wasn't dognapping."

"Of course, you did."

"She wasn't dognapping."

I sighed. "Good, now what about Dani?"

"She's in her fifties, long gray hair about the color of Martha's pooch Lady and has the greenest eyes. She moved in with Martha six months ago after they met at The Wild."

"The Wild?"

"Chris, oh, Chris, you have so much to learn. It's a pet store on Folly Road. Dani takes care of the animals when Martha is away. She also works at Woody's."

"She didn't know Martha before that?"

He shook his head.

"Didn't it seem impulsive asking a stranger to move in?"

"That was my thought, so that's why I asked Dani about it. She said she was surprised, but Martha said Mr. Squeezy fell in love with Dani when they met, and the rest is history."

I said, "How do you know if a snake loves someone?"

Charles moved up in his seat as if he were getting ready to give me the entire rundown on snakes' likes and dislikes.

I put my hand up and said, "That's rhetorical. Anything else about Dani?"

Charles smiled and said, "Glad you asked. I saw her this morning. She asked if we were investigating the shooting."

"Why would she think that?"

"We're the closest thing to Sherlock Holmes or Miss Marple on Folly."

Ignoring the Holmes and Marple reference, I said, "What made her think we're investigating the shooting?"

He chomped on another Oreo, wiped crumbs off his lips, and said, "Could be because I told her I, and yes, you, are detectives and help the police catch bad guys."

Why am I not surprised, I thought, but said, "Did she know Wesley?'

"Since she brought up the shooting, I asked her. She got upset and told me in no uncertain terms she would not be associated with the likes of an evil, swindling fraud. That's why I mentioned her after you said what you did about Larry."

"So, what's her interest in the visiting group and if she didn't know Wesley, why would she think he's evil or a fraud?"

"Being a great detective, I asked if she had any idea who might've killed him. She dodged my question and said the killer had to be one of 'those people' and the God-fearing locals would not stoop so low."

"Why bring it up at all?"

"Good question. Guess we have our first suspect unless you add Larry to the list."

"First, there's no way Larry would have any part of the killing. And second, because Dani dislikes the fortune tellers doesn't mean she's a killer."

"As an astute private detective, I say whoever shot Wesley didn't like him."

"True, but what do we know about any of this, except a stranger was shot in front of me?"

"Excellent point. Let's go to the horses' mouths."

"Meaning?"

"We finish our snack and go to the Tides to meet the fortune tellers."

"We simply walk in and start interrogating a group of people we know nothing about."

"Bingo."

9

______

Living fewer than three blocks from the Tides didn't give me much time to convince Charles his idea of going to meet the fortune tellers might not be the wisest decision he'd ever made. Not only was there a chance one of them was a murderer, but if Larry were right, confronting a con artist could lead down a dangerous path. On the other hand, Shannon Stone's words and actions negated most of my negative thoughts about legitimate fortune tellers. The Wiccan family's views on life and religion differ from much of the population, yet they have been nothing but welcoming, open, and educational when sharing their beliefs with me. Besides, what's the worst that could happen when meeting the visitors?

As if reading my mind, Charles tapped his ever-present cane on a light pole, stopping at the edge of the hotel's parking lot, and said, "Try and not get us turned into toads."

I'm not certain how serious he was, but his comment made me smile.

Halfway across the lot we were greeted by Jay Vaughn, the Tides concierge and all around go-to guy for anything you could need.

Jay approached Charles, grabbed his arm, and said, "You think it's safe walking next to this trouble magnet?" Jay laughed as he patted me on the shoulder.

"Someone has to keep him out of harm's way."

"How are you, Mr. Vaughn?" I said and smiled as I grabbed his extended hand.

"Busy as usual, but the conference we're hosting has attracted some interesting folks."

Charles looked at the entry, then turned to Jay and said, "That's why I dragged Chris over here. I think we should introduce ourselves to your interesting guests. You know, being neighborly."

Jay said, "I'll be happy to make introductions. A few of them are having drinks on the patio before heading back to the house Darrin and Stormy Roserun rented for some of the attendees who aren't staying with us."

Charles pointed his cane at the entrance and said, "Show the way."

Jay led us through the lobby to the patio outside BLU, the hotel's restaurant. Three people were gathered in the lounge area, and it didn't take a detective to know they were participants in the conference.

A lady sitting on the sofa looked to be in her mid-fifties, with shoulder-length black hair and dressed as if she'd stepped out of a painting of seventeenth century Scotland. Charles didn't see her or anyone else since his focus was on the small black and tan dog at the woman's feet.

Another female was seated in a chair facing the sofa. She was petite, with long gray hair, ice-blue eyes, and dressed like a stereotypical witch. She had on a long black dress, black pointed-toe boots, with her hair pulled back in a black lace scarf. The third person in the group was a tall gentleman, around 6'2', wearing a dark-blue turban and a matching suit.

He stood as we walked toward the group, his smile calming any apprehension I had earlier. He said, "Who are your friends, Jay?"

"Mr. Ford, I'd like to introduce two of the best men on Folly

Beach, Chris Landrum, and Charles Fowler. They wanted to meet members of your group. Hope you don't mind."

I extended my hand, "Pleased to meet you, Mr. Ford."

"Please call me Spencer, and you must be Charles," he said as he extended his hand to my friend. They shook, and he added, "If I may speak for everyone, it would be nicer if we used first names." Spencer looked at each of us and received nods.

Jay stepped closer and said, "I wanted to break the ice with introductions. I'd love to stay and talk, but if you'll excuse me, I need to get back to work."

With that, Jay headed to the door leading to the lobby, and Charles was already talking to the dog who was looking at him like he was the best thing since YumYum Bones dog treats.

Spencer, noticing the connection between Charles and his new friend, cleared his throat and said, "Charles, allow me to introduce my good friends Otter Bran and his constant traveling companion Tori Bran."

Stepping forward, I shook Tori's hand. "Nice to meet you, and, of course, Otter."

"The pleasure is all mine, Chris and Charles."

"Oh yes, nice to meet you." Charles glanced up at Tori. "What a good boy. I know a dog named Pluto that could be his big brother."

I said, "Tori, you'll have to excuse Charles, there's not a dog he doesn't want to be best friends with."

"I think it's wonderful, more people should show their true feelings instead of masking them."

The third human member of the group, dressed entirely in black, stood, took a step forward, gave a slight bow, and said, "Good afternoon, I'm Heidi Strongmire."

I said, "Pleasure meeting you."

Spencer returned to his seat and motioned for Charles and me to grab a couple of vacant chairs from the other side of the patio.

Once everyone was settled, Charles decided it was time to acknowledge the two-legged attendees but was cut short by one of BLU's servers who'd apparently noticed additions to the group. She came to get Charles and my drink orders and see if the others needed refills. We ordered water and the others said they were okay with their drinks.

No one spoke in the brief time it took her to return with our water. The silence was broken by Charles with, "So, are all of you witches or fortune tellers?"

He then took a sip of water while surveying the three faces. Instead of me trying to crawl under the chair, I remained silent. After all, it might be refreshing being a toad.

"Charles, do I look like a witch?" Heidi asked with a minimal smile, but her expressive eyes glowed.

Charles said, "You look like what I picture witches to look like."

Instead of turning my friend into a toad, Heidi laughed and said, "I am a witch, but lucky for you, not one who casts evil spells. My specialty is telling the future by using a crystal ball and reading auras. Much less witchy, I'm also a tour guide in Okefenokee Swamp in Georgia." She then pointed in Tori's direction.

Tori took the hint and said, "I'm not a witch. I practice palmistry, reading palms. My mother taught me the art and was one of the best. I'm also a seamstress with a shop in Black River, North Carolina." She reached down and rubbed Otter under the chin. "He's a Norwich Terrier and spends his days napping in sunny spots in the shop or hunting mice." Tori nodded to Spencer.

He waited for Charles to break away from focusing on Otter and said, "I'm also not a witch, warlock, or Wiccan. I'm the co-owner of Ford and Fortune Mystical Shop in Charlotte, North Carolina. My specialty is reading the future by scrying."

"Using a candle and a dark mirror." I said, smiled, and leaned back in the chair.

Charles turned and stared at me so quickly he could've given himself whiplash.

Spencer said, "Impressive, are you a witch?"

"No, but I know Shannon Stone who I believe is a friend of yours. She was telling me about you and another attendee."

"So," Spencer said, "I take it you two are not new to what we do?"

"We met the Stones a couple of years ago and got to know a great deal about them. They're delightful people."

"Even Desmond?" Spencer said.

I smiled. "Once you get to know him."

Spencer chuckled and said, "Then you do know the Stone family."

"Like Jay said, we're eager to meet the participants in the gathering. About how many are attending?"

Tori patted Otter's head. "Not as many as the Roseruns wanted but attendance has been pretty good, considering what happened to Wesley."

"Did you know Wesley?"

"I never met him. Stormy was friends with him, and I believe Spencer talked to him a couple of hours before he left his earthly existence."

"One doesn't often meet someone who has the same fashion sense in headwear," Spencer said and touched the side of his turban. "I only spoke to him briefly as we were waiting for the elevator. I was on my way to find Tori and he was 'going for a stroll' as he put it."

Charles said, "Did he say where he was going or if he was meeting someone?"

Heidi put her glass on the table hard enough to make Otter stand up looking for the intruder. "Why is it your business?"

I said, "Charles doesn't mean harm. I was walking past Wesley when he was shot."

"That's awful," Heidi said and glanced at her glass before continuing, "It explains why your aura is not a natural color. It's not you, just what has attached to you. That's what—"

"Heidi," Tori interrupted, and patted Heidi's knee. "Chris didn't ask for your take on his aura or any of us to comment on his future."

Charles said, "What do you see in his future?"

I said, "Charles, we need to go. It's been a pleasure meeting all of you. I hope the rest of your stay on Folly is enjoyable and you have a productive meeting."

Spencer stood and said, "Of course, we will be seeing you again."

Charles said, "Did you scry that?"

How Charles has made it this long without someone rearranging his nose is beyond me.

Spencer said, "No, my friend, simply a judgement on human nature and that everything happens for a reason." He turned to Tori and said, "Ready for me to walk you to the house?"

"Yes. I want to change before we go eat." Tori turned towards us. "Half of the attendees are staying at a house the Roseruns rented; the other half are here in the hotel."

The four of us walked through the lobby, while Spencer carried Otter. Once outside, he lowered Otter to the pavement and the dog started leading the way toward East Arctic Avenue.

I would normally have gone the same way to my cottage, but today I couldn't. The thought of a car speeding past me and the image of the lifeless man on the sidewalk inches from me, made me continue up Center Street rather than following the sidewalk on East Arctic. Charles fell in step, putting himself between the road and me. While he might be the head inquisitor and pot stirrer, he's still a good friend.

Half a block from the hotel, Charles stopped and turned to face the street as a golf cart illegally driving on Center Street came up behind us. Folly has no shortage of golf carts either owned by residents or rented by vacationers, and they're a great way to get around the island if wanting to go more than a handful of blocks. I'd never seen one like the one creeping next to my best friend. It was silver, had four seats, and a faux Mercedes-Benz grill.

The driver appeared in his sixties with thinning brown hair. He slowed down and crept along matching our walking speed, then yelled, "You would think good citizens wouldn't keep company with lie mongers and evil doers!" He then accelerated and continued up Center Street.

I watched the cart turn on West Hudson Avenue and said to Charles, "Who was that?"

Charles was red in the face, smacked his cane on the sidewalk, and said, "Donald Braxton, a retired lawyer that lives close to me on

Sandbar Lane. He works part time at Taco Boy, can you believe as a bartender?"

"You know him?"

"Nope, just know who he is and what he does."

We continued in silence while the early-evening breeze off the ocean did its best to wash away the strange occurrence, as well as my thoughts on Wesley's murder, and the apparent dislike for the visitors to Folly. I wasn't sure what Charles was mulling over since he was quieter than usual. We reached my cottage where he grabbed his bike, hopped on it, and headed home.

10

———————

I hadn't been in the house for more than fifteen minutes when the phone rang, and the screen read *Pewter Hardware*. I answered with, "Hi, Larry."

A voice sounding nothing like Larry said, "Chris, sorry to disappoint you, it's Brandon."

"Sorry, I was surprised, not disappointed. What's up?"

"I tried to call Charles, but he didn't answer, so I called you."

Not only is this the first time Brandon has ever called, but I wasn't the person he wanted.

I didn't tell him Charles had been here earlier, but said, "What can I do for you?"

"Think you could spare a few minutes to meet?"

"Sure. Want me to come by the store?"

"It'd be better if it was after I get off. Could we meet around seven-thirty?"

"Think so. Where?"

"How about Lowlife Bar."

"That works."

"One more thing, could you try to find Charles and see if he can join us?"

"Sure."

I didn't have as much trouble finding Charles as Brandon had. He answered on the second ring and said something about how much I must've missed him. I ignored his comment and shared what I knew about my brief call from Brandon and Charles agreed to be at Lowlife Bar at seven-thirty.

Knowing Charles's penchant for arriving thirty minutes early to, well, to everything, I arrived at the popular restaurant and bar a little before seven. Lowlife Bar was located on the lower level of a three-story building on East Hudson Avenue behind the Circle K gas station and convenience store. Brian Ross, a friend and one of the bar's personable bartenders, greeted me in front of the entry and said Charles was inside and asked him to tell me I was late.

"You know I'm not late, don't you?"

Brian chuckled and said, "Knowing Charles, I figure you're a half hour early."

"You're a wise man. Do you know Brandon Tigert?"

Brian nodded and said, "He stops in occasionally. Why?"

"He's meeting Charles and me at seven-thirty."

"If I see him, I'll point him in your direction."

Charles was seated on a bar height stool at one of the tables in front of a large-screen television. He would've been hard to miss in his red sweatshirt with *Ole Miss* in navy blue on the front. He'd changed from his shirt with the slug, but I wasn't about to ask why.

"You're late," he said, words he often used whenever I arrived, incorrectly used, I should add.

"That's what I heard."

"Good, Brian scolded you. Now, what does Brandon want?"

"No idea. Why don't we wait for him to tell us?"

"If you're sure you don't know."

I assured him I didn't.

"Think it has to do with you getting shot at?" he said, skipping over my assurance.

Brian stopped by the table and asked if I wanted anything to drink. I said a glass of red wine and he said he knew where to find one, and asked Charles if he needed another beer. He didn't.

"Sure you don't know what Brandon wants? Don't think I've seen him when he wasn't working."

I was again prevented from telling Charles I didn't know why, when I saw Brandon at the entry wearing his Pewter Hardware shirt. He smiled when he saw us and walked around a table to get to ours.

He nodded at me, turned to Charles, and said, "I'm glad you could make it."

I'm certain he was glad I made it, at least I think he was.

Brian arrived with my wine and asked Brandon what he could get him to drink.

"How about a Hamm's?"

"You've got it," Brian said and headed to the bar.

Charles said, "What's Hamm's?"

"Beer," Brandon said and pointed at Charles's beer can. "Better than Miller."

"If you say so. Okay, what'd you want to meet about?" asked Charles, who had the patience of a starving chipmunk.

Brian returned with Brandon's beer and Charles looked at him like he'd interrupted peace negotiations between two nuclear powers. Brian, who'd known Charles for years, ignored my friend and said for us to wave if we needed anything.

Before Brandon could take a drink, Charles said, "Okay, what's the deal?"

"Don't know if you knew this, but years ago I was married, divorced before I moved to this part of the country. Umm—"

"Think Larry mentioned it," Charles interrupted.

"Anyway, I have a daughter, name's Stevie. She turned twenty-seven a couple of months ago."

Charles said, "Like in Stevie Nicks?"

Brandon smiled. "Yeah. My wife and I were in our hippie phase when she was born. Thought Stevie was better than loading her down with Petunia or Dandelion."

Charles smiled and said, "What about her?"

I said, "Why don't we let Brandon tell why he asked us here?"

"Guys, I'm starving," Brandon said. "Mind if I get something to eat?"

Charles looked around the room, saw Brian behind the bar, and waved him over. I suspect he wanted to get the ordering out of the way so he could interrogate Brandon. Brian arrived and Brandon said he'd have a Green Chile Queso and Charles and I said we were fine with our drinks.

Brian hadn't had time to make it to the kitchen when Charles said, "What about Stevie?"

"She showed up last Wednesday."

Charles said, "Where's she been?"

I didn't kick Charles under the table but instead said, "Charles."

"Okay, okay. Brandon, go ahead and tell us."

He looked down at his can of beer, then at each of us, before saying, "This is hard and a little embarrassing. I haven't talked about Stevie with anyone in, I don't know how many years."

I nodded and Charles, to my surprise, remained silent.

Brandon continued, "The last time I saw her was eleven years ago. Sure, I'd sent birthday cards since then, but I didn't do that every year. I haven't talked to her mother since Stevie graduated from high school, let's see, guess that's been nine years." He slowly shook his head. "Time flies, don't it?"

Charles glanced at me, then said, "Sure does."

"They were living in Minnesota. Stevie told me the other day she moved to Atlanta five years ago."

Brian arrived with Brandon's queso, who proved he was starving when he took two bites before continuing his story. I was proud of Charles who'd remained silent.

Brandon took another sip then said, "Suppose you're beginning to wonder why I'm telling you this."

"Yes," I said, and Charles nodded. I was beginning to wonder what Brian had put in Charles's beer to silence him. I needed to get some of whatever it was.

"Stevie wasn't alone when she showed up. She had a guy with her, said he was her fiancé." Another bite of queso later, Brandon added, "How shall I put it? He struck me as shifty."

"Shifty, how?" Charles asked after reaching his silence limit.

"Don't know how to say it. You ever know someone who smiled like people think he ought to, said things people expected him to say, yet didn't strike you as meaning any of it?"

I nodded and Charles said, "You bet."

"That was the impression I had of Albert."

Charles said, "That his name?"

"Yeah, Albert McGrady."

I said, "If you haven't seen her for years, why is she here?"

Brandon stirred the food around on his plate, took a sip of Hamm's, and said, "Told me they were on vacation and wanted Albert to meet me." He shook his head then added, "To meet the man she hadn't seen for more than a decade. That make sense to you?"

"I can see her wanting you to meet him if they're getting married," I said.

"I suppose, but to be honest, I don't think that's it."

Charles said, "Why do you think she brought him?"

"There's one thing I haven't told you. After Stevie went through all the stuff about being on vacation and wanting Albert to meet me, she said she hated to ask but wanted me to lend her, lend them five-thousand dollars."

Charles said, "What for?"

Brandon finger quoted and said, "A sure thing Albert has a chance to invest in."

Charles leaned closer to Brandon, and said, "What's the sure thing?"

"Albert jumped into the conversation and said it had to do with something in the 'emerging international currency market' and I 'probably wouldn't understand the details,' his words, not mine."

"I'm beginning to understand your feelings about him," I said.

Charles said, "What'd you tell her about the money?"

"At first, I didn't know what to say. I finally managed to say I didn't have five-thousand bucks lying around and asked when she needed it."

"What'd she say?"

"She seemed surprised that I didn't pull out my checkbook and write her a check and said they wouldn't need it for a few days."

I said, "What're you going to do?"

Brandon smiled, took another sip of beer, and said, "That's why I wanted to meet with you. Charles, you're a private detective. I've watched you over the years, and how you, and you too, Chris, managed to catch bad guys. I could be wrong, but I have a hunch my daughter's fiancé would be in that group."

I said, "Have you talked with Larry about this?"

"That's what I don't want to do. Larry met Stevie the second time she came in the store, Saturday morning, I believe. Albert wasn't with her. We were busy, so all I did was introduce her to Larry but didn't say anything other than she was on vacation. Larry is my boss. We have a great working relationship. For that reason, I don't want to talk to him about it. If I did, he'd tell Cindy and she'd feel like she had to do the police thing. She'd want to talk to Stevie and Albert. She'd want to dig into her sources and computer programs to investigate Albert." He looked at his beer can, then slowly turned back to me. "What would that say to Stevie? I'll tell you what, she'd never trust me again, never want to see me again. Guys, I can't risk it. I can't."

This was no time to debate Charles's status as a private detective, so I said, "How do you think Charles could learn if Albert is on the up-and-up?"

"To be honest, I don't know. What do you think, Charles?"

Brian returned to see if we wanted anything else. Charles and I requested another drink and Brandon said he was okay.

Brian left and Charles said, "Brandon, I'd be glad to look into it."

"I can't pay you much."

"Good, because I don't want anything. Where are they staying?"

"Tent camping at the campground at the James Island County Park."

Charles leaned toward Brandon and said, "Staying in a tent?"

I thought that was what tent camping meant but didn't say anything.

"Yeah, but said they'd be here every day. Said she wanted to be close to the ocean and the beach as much as she could. Something about not having things like the ocean in Atlanta."

I said, "How long will they be here?"

"Until after Halloween, but nothing specific."

Charles said, "How can I meet her?"

"Don't know, but since you're a detective, you'll figure it out."

"I will. You have her picture?"

"Yeah, but it's her high school graduation photo."

"Mind if I borrow it?"

Brandon took out his wallet, flipped through a few of the transparent plastic inserts, and pulled out a wrinkled photo of a young lady with a beautiful smile, long black hair, and no resemblance to Brandon. He handed Charles the photo and said, remember, she's nearly ten years older now."

"Don't have a photo of Albert, do you?"

"No, but you find Stevie, you'll find Albert."

I said, "Did she say when you'd see her again?"

"All she said was she'd see me soon. I wouldn't be surprised if she didn't pop in tomorrow."

Brandon finished eating and said, "Fellas, I'm bushed after working all day. Gotta head home before I fall asleep here at the table."

Charles tried to wring more information out of the exhausted hardware store employee but was told two or three different ways that he'd already shared everything he knew about his daughter and Albert. Charles finally gave up and told Brandon I'd get his meal.

Brandon headed home, and Charles said he'd better get home and to sleep so he could, "scour the beach tomorrow for Stevie and sleezy Albert."

I didn't offer to assist with his scouring, and wished him a good night's sleep, before heading home.

11

---

he next morning, the temperature was pushing seventy degrees under a cloudless sky, so it would be an ideal day for a walk. One thing I didn't want to do was *scour* the beach in search of Stevie and Albert. That was private detective Charles's task, one I didn't envy him over.

I was on the sidewalk a few feet from Barb's Books, the inclement weather sanctuary of First Light Church, and Folly's newest attraction, an escape room appropriately named Escapade Folly. It was still early for the bookstore or Escapade to be open, and I doubted Preacher Burl Costello was in the sanctuary, so I continued up the sidewalk when from the other side of the street, someone yelled, "Yo, Chris, wait up!"

Junior Richardson was jaywalking across Center Street and heading my way. Junior was in his late fifties, 6'2", overweight, with a straggly black beard. He looked like he could be a pirate in Escapade's Pirates of Folly room.

He was slightly out of breath when he reached my side of the street, but managed to say, "You good?"

"Why, do I look like I escaped from one of the rooms in there?" I said and nodded toward Escapade Folly.

"Funny. No, I heard about the shooting."

"I'm fine. Thanks for asking."

"I heard someone was shooting at you and hit a visitor. Killed him."

"Who said that?"

"Some guy in the bar last night. Don't know his name."

Junior's father owns Cal's Country Bar and Burgers, Folly's quintessential country music bar. Cal had toured the south for more than forty years singing his brand of traditional country music in any venue that'd have him. His touring ended on Folly more than a decade ago when he bought and rebranded a rock and roll bar after its owner was convicted for killing an attorney. Many folks applauded the idea of killing a lawyer, but the justice system didn't take kindly to the action.

Junior had never met Cal until a few years ago when he found him after searching for years. He'd owned a successful chain of fried chicken restaurants before selling it and going in search of his father. He now helps his dad in the bar, where Cal calls him his executive chef.

"Hear anything else about it?"

"Heard the guy shot was one of those psychics here for some sort of meeting. Anyway, I'm glad whoever did it wasn't shooting at you."

"Don't know for certain he wasn't. I'd hate to think someone had me in his sights and killed a visitor, although I'm glad he missed me."

"I'll second that."

"Have you heard of any locals who have negative feelings about the fortune tellers?"

"Why? Do you think one of our folks killed the man because he told fortunes?"

"It's possible. Sorry, am I keeping you from something?"

"Not really. Was heading to the bar to work on inventory. You can keep me as long as you want. The longer the better. I hate counting crap."

It was still early, and the sidewalk was nearly empty, but I led him over to the wall to keep from blocking the walk from anyone who happened by.

"So, you haven't heard anything else about the fortune telling group?"

"You're beginning to sound like Charles. Don't tell me you're taking it on yourself to find the killer."

"Nothing like that. I'd heard some of our residents have strong feelings against the group."

"Around closing last night, I heard a couple of guys bitching and groaning about *Devil worshipers* at the hotel. To be honest, I didn't put much faith in what they were saying. Didn't hear it all since Dad had me fixing burgers for three gals."

"Why didn't you think much about what they were saying?"

"Around closing time, we occasionally have a few customers who've had more to drink than is good for them. We cut them off if we suspect they're driving anywhere when they walk out the door. One of the things they were bitching about was having to walk five blocks to their apartment. My point is they were drunk, walking, and not making much sense."

"You don't know who they were?"

"No."

"Remember anything they were saying about the fortune tellers?"

"Like I said, I was more concerned with getting the food out to the ladies than what two drunks were mumbling about. They did seem hung up about the group being Devil worshipers, said it three times that I heard, and I didn't hear half of what they were saying. Stupid, if you ask me."

"Why?"

"When I had my restaurants in Arkansas and Oklahoma, one of my managers was a fortune teller, or a psychic as he called himself. To be honest, I never totally understood the difference between a psychic, a medium, and a fortune teller. He tried to explain it once, something about a psychic predicts the future and a medium talks with dead folks, or something like that. Anyway, he, name was Andrew, was one of the best managers I ever had. I never heard about him bothering any of his employees or customers about whatever paranormal stuff he practiced. Never saw him wearing a fez or turban, or any of those other clothes people associate with psychics."

"He seemed as normal as any of your other managers."

Junior laughed and said, "More normal than some of them. My point is if Andrew worshiped the Devil or a can of sardines, he never let it show or interfere with his job. I never had a complaint about his work or how he interacted with his employees or customers."

"I'm glad to hear that. Do you know Donald Braxton?"

"Bartender at Taco Boy?"

"That's what I hear."

"Why? Is he a fortune teller?"

"Far from it would be my guess. He drove by Charles and me the other day in his golf cart. He was spouting off about how horrible it was how that we were associating with *lie-mongers* and *evil-doers*."

Junior patted me on the shoulder and said, "What made you think he was referring to the fortune tellers. Hell, that would describe a gaggle of folks you and Charles associate with."

"Thanks."

"Kidding. Tell you what, I'll keep an ear out for anything I hear about Braxton, and I'll try to see if I can get the names of the two spouting off in the bar."

"I appreciate it, Junior. Speaking of Cal's, you and your dad ready for your big Halloween party?"

"Why'd you have to bring that up? I shouldn't have told Dad last year how Halloween was my favorite holiday."

"Why?"

"He's gone bonkers over it. Don't get me wrong, I love him for it, but it's driving me crazy. Tell you what, if you can find a blank space on the walls or an empty spot on any flat surface in the place, it won't be that way by Halloween. Remember how much decorating we did last year?"

"It was amazing. I hadn't seen that much Halloween stuff in those mega-Halloween stores that pop up this time of year."

"This year will make last Halloween look like we didn't decorate."

"I look forward to seeing it."

"Great, so you'll be there Sunday?"

"I wouldn't miss it."

He looked at his watch and said, "I've stalled as long as can. Those cans of pickles aren't going to count themselves. Again, I'm glad you weren't the person shot the other night."

"Me too, Junior. Me too."

12

―――――

Watching Junior turn down West Cooper Avenue heading to where cans of pickles were more excited about being counted than Junior was about counting them, I reflected on how this small island contains so many different people and personalities. I also wondered about what he'd said about some of his customers referring to the visiting fortune tellers as Devil worshipers.

My thoughts were rudely interrupted by a burst from a shrill siren. I turned to the street behind me to be greeted by Chief Cindy LaMond laughing at me from her official vehicle.

I sighed then smiled before saying, "Careful before one of Folly's officers gives you a ticket for disturbing the peace."

"Or for startling a geezer," she added through the lowered window. "I don't worry about them since they're busy avoiding Detective Adair. Oh wait, that's what I'm doing."

Enough foolishness, I thought, and said, "Good morning, Cindy."

"You busy?"

"Busy walking around."

"Hop in."

I joined her in her vehicle. I'd lived my entire life and never been in a police vehicle until I moved to Folly. Now, it seemed like a regular occurrence.

"Buckle up. I don't want you to fall out." Her smile appeared more forced than usual.

"What did I do to deserve this honor?"

"Absolutely nothing. I needed to get out of the office."

"Mayor on your case again?"

"Not this time. Wanted to check on my citizens and clear my head. That's where you come in."

"You're giving each citizen a ride-along?"

"Don't make me regret hijacking you," Cindy said as she turned on East Ashley Avenue and approached my cottage. I waited for her to turn into my drive. Instead, she continued driving.

I expected her to say where we were going, but she remained silent.

I said, "What's going on?"

"You've managed to get yourself mixed up in more issues than this country girl can shake a stick at, but somehow you've managed to help us more times than I'll admit."

I waited for her to continue, and we traveled two more blocks before she glanced at me and said, "How much do you know about the conference at the Tides?"

"Not much, Shannon Stone's friends the Roseruns invited a group of fortune tellers to Folly for the weeklong meeting. Charles and I met a few of the participants yesterday. Why?"

"Because I knew you wouldn't leave the death of Wesley Thomas to the authorities—you know, we folk whose job it is to catch bad guys." She smiled and added, "And, you're a good judge of character and I wanted your thoughts."

"Afraid I can't add much. We only talked to three attendees. Now I have a question. Do you know any locals who would have an issue with this meeting or those attending?"

Cindy looked straight ahead. I could see her jaw clench but quickly recovered as she slowly continued driving east. The police radio crackled but no words came through the speaker. She glared at the radio and shook her head, before saying, "Some folks have issues with anything different than what they believe. You saw it firsthand when the Stones moved here."

"True."

"So, to answer your question, no. I haven't talked to anyone about what problems they might have with the group but know there must be some." She shook her head. "Detective Adair is handling the investigation and is being what I would generously call a stick in the mud."

"That's nothing new, is it?"

"He called wanting me to get a complete list of the conference goers because he'll be spending the day on Pawleys Island talking to friends of our deceased visitor."

"Isn't that something he should've already done?"

"A competent detective would've."

Her use of the word *competent* wasn't lost on me, and I said, "What about him talking to some of the other participants or even dear, sweet Alice Clay, after all, she saw the shooting?"

"By the time he got here, Ms. Clay had disappeared, not like a phantom, although after listening to her, that's possible. Anyway, he didn't talk to her and said it was too late to contact the group's organizers. He didn't talk with anyone and left that to me and my guys. At least today, he's following up with some of Wesley Thomas's friends."

"Lucky you."

"Yeah lucky. Ready to head back to town?"

"Whenever you are."

"I suppose so. I need to go to the Tides and try to find some of the people who are sitting around predicting the future."

"I don't suppose you're inviting me to interrogate them with you?"

"Wow, they teach you how to predict the future?"

I ignored her comment, and said, "It's a beautiful day, and a walk will do me good. Why don't you let me out here and I'll walk over to the beach and head back to town?"

"Think you can walk that far?"

"Sure," I said expressing more confidence than I felt.

Cindy pulled over on the shoulder, put on her four-way flashers, turned, and looked at me with either sadness or concern on her face.

"Chris, please take care of yourself and be careful. I don't want to lose you."

"I'm fine." As the words left my mouth, a knot rose in my throat. Did she think the bullet was meant for me?

"If you need anything, you know my number."

"Thanks. Have fun doing Adair's job."

Cindy shook her head as I stepped out of the truck. I waved as she pulled back onto the road, made a U-turn, and headed to the Tides.

I hadn't paid much attention to where Cindy dropped me until I faced the stairs over the dunes leading to the beach. A little over a year ago, on this spot and with the aid of a friend, I escaped from a man who had murdered three others and tried to poison me. I now climbed the stairs quicker than usual, and by the time I'd walked a block or so on the packed sand close to where the tide kissed the shore, the image of that night had drifted away only to be replaced by the recent murder. Who would want the visitor dead or was the killer aiming at the Folly resident who'd been standing next to him?

The rhythmic sounds of the waves brushing the shore pulled me out of the dark thoughts and memories. I hadn't gone far when the sight of two young kids dressed as Superman and Batman tagging each other and running back and forth stopped me in my tracks. It brought me a much-needed smile.

After passing the children, there was a long stretch of nature with me soaking up the day, making me regret not grabbing my camera before leaving the house. The next group of beachgoers appeared to be a large family searching for shells. When a gift from the sea was found, the finder would run to the others to show the bounty.

The breeze had picked up and the shorebirds were running along the tide break grabbing whatever they felt would make a good meal, reminding me I only had a cup of coffee and one powdered donut earlier. Lunch moved to the forefront and where I would find it became my top priority.

Twenty minutes later, I was leaving the beach and heading

towards Loggerhead's to rest my weary legs and fill my growling stomach. I called Charles to see if he wanted to join me. The phone rang several times then went to voicemail. I didn't leave a message.

I was in the middle of the Tides parking lot when I heard someone yell, "Mr. Chris, wait up!"

It was easy to recognize the cheerful, carefree voice as coming from Roisin, Shannon Stone's mini-me daughter.

I turned and saw not only Roisin, dressed in an emerald green dress with her red hair pulled in a ponytail, but she was flanked by the Roseruns. Two years ago, I'd briefly met them at Roisin's dad's funeral, although unlike the robes they wore to the service, today's attire was more mainstream.

"Good afternoon, Roisin, how grown up you're looking."

"Mom said before a blink I'll be wearing her clothes."

Darrin cleared his throat and held out his hand. "Mr."

"Landrum, but please call me Chris."

"Chris, this is my wife Stormy and I'm Darrin Roserun. It's a pleasure to see you again, this time under more favorable circumstances."

Darrin was wearing a black, button-down shirt, black jeans, and black cowboy boots. He was in his late forties, stood six feet tall, with black hair and violet eyes, Stormy took a step forward and shook my hand. Her ankle length black lace dress flowed around the black leather high heel boots. Even with the heels, she was a foot shorter than her husband. With her dirty blonde hair and brown eyes, she looked strikingly like Stevie Nicks, not the Stevie Charles was supposed to be finding.

"Nice seeing you again."

Roisin said, "We're going to Loggerhead's for lunch. Want to join us?"

"I don't want to impose."

"Don't be silly," Darrin said. "We'd be glad to have you join us."

As we walked up the stairs to the restaurant's deck, Roisin asked if we could sit outside. None of us came up with a reason not to, so she ran to the host station to share our request.

"We can sit anywhere," the enthusiastic teenager said, and added, "Someone named Kylie will be out to take our drink order."

We picked a table overlooking West Arctic Avenue with the view of the ocean partially obstructed by the large Charleston Oceanfront Villas condo complex. There was a small cauldron holding a variety of wrapped candies sitting beside the umbrella shaft in the center of our table. As soon as we were seated, Kylie came to welcome us and get drink orders, then left us to browse the menu.

Kylie was quick to return with three waters and a Coke for Roisin, then took our orders before heading to the kitchen. The awkward silence was broken by the ever-observant teen making sure we saw the Halloween decorations hanging around the tiki bar including a string of lights shaped like ghosts, jack-o'-lanterns, and witch hats. Along the back wall three giant fake spiders were clinging to a web and looking like they were waiting for lunch. I smiled as I told myself I was sitting at a table with one and possibly three Wiccans. There was no doubt Halloween was four days away.

Roisin looked at me, turned to Darrin, then to Stormy, and said, "Stormy, tell Mr. Chris about Stormy Rose."

Stormy patted her on the arm and said, "I'm not sure Chris would be interested in our shop."

I didn't wait for Roisin to respond, and said, "I'd be interested in your shop and also the conference being held this week." I felt my inner-Charles applaud my smooth inquisition.

Darrin and Stormy glanced at each other, smiled, and nodded. Stormy said, "Twenty years ago, Darrin and I opened Stormy Rose, a metaphysical shop in Charleston. That was a couple of months after our wedding. We offer most every tool and accessory one needs to perform and honor his or her religion or spiritual practices." She chuckled and added, "Starting a marriage and a business the same year, was not an easy endeavor."

Darrin said, "Quite an understatement but Stormy had the vision and the powers that worked for us. The store has tripled in size since opening. The last two years our online store has grown rapidly, not only helping our bottom line but more importantly, giving customers not fortunate enough to have a shop like ours in their community, a place to have their needs met."

Roisin smiled and said, "Mom has a space in the store where she offers herbs and sometimes does card readings."

"What about the attendees at the meeting?"

"Have you met any of our guests?"

"Yes, Spencer, Heidi, Tori and Otter, and sort of met Alice Clay."

Darrin said, "Sort of met Alice?"

"Sunday night—"

"Oh, forgive me," Stormy interrupted. "You were there when Wesley was killed. How did that slip my mind?"

Darrin put his hand on Stormy's shoulder, then turned to me and said, "That had to be terrible."

"It was."

Roisin sat up straighter in her chair and said, "Mr. Chris, you have met some really nice people but there are more."

"Like whom?"

Roisin squirmed in her chair and pointed towards the Tides parking lot. "See that purple car and camper?"

I turned and looked toward the Tides. I'm not sure how I missed it earlier. There was a purple Mini Cooper with a small camper attached the same color as the car.

"That belongs to Happy Bishop. Mom calls him a young hippy." She laughed. "Happy Hippy is what she calls him. He reads Tarot cards and has a bunch of colorful tennis shoes. His travelling companion is Raven Moon."

"What's her specialty?"

"Catching mice," Roisin said and laughed again. "She's a black Maine Coon cat with golden eyes and is huge." She held her arms out to her side. "Three feet long and weighs twenty pounds."

"Sort of like Lugh in cat form?" I said. "Happy Bishop might pass her off as a dog to Charles."

Roisin rolled her eyes and said, "You're silly, Mr. Chris."

I shrugged then smiled. "Only around you."

She smiled.

I turned to Stormy and Darrin. "Shannon told me a little about Chloe Meriweather, something about her being a Tarot card reader."

Stormy cleared her throat, "Yes, Chloe is here. She's a nice lady. Loves helping people. She's a professional firefighter and in addition to reading Tarot cards, makes gris-gris bags to help others." She stared at me then said, "This probably seems like a freak show to you. We seldom come across someone who is genuinely interested without passing judgement or wanting to burn us at the stake." She smiled but I didn't detect humor in her eyes.

"Neither crossed my mind, but I've heard others calling the participants frauds and con artists."

Darrin said, "Stormy was not directing that comment at you. Shannon has always held you and your friend Charles in high regard, not to mention how much Roisin likes you. But to your point, not everyone who claims to see things or do readings has the gift. Truthfully, some are doing it for the money, others have convinced themselves they can tell fortunes."

"I hate to seem ignorant, but how do you know the difference?"

Stormy leaned forward and said, "Fakers give overly broad descriptions and events. The faux fortune teller then reads your body language. Most clients give more away than they think. When the reading ends, the person believes the reader revealed something personal when they just said things that could mean anything or could've been gleaned from the client's body language."

"Please don't take offense, but does that apply to any of this week's attendees?"

"That's a valid question," Darrin said. "The truthful answer is we don't know. Additionally, one or more appear not to be what they have presented themselves to be. For, you see, we hadn't met a few prior to their arrival, and now that we have … not important."

Stormy patted Darrin on the arm, then turned to me, "Darrin is the skeptic in our marriage. I'm not saying all participants are what they say they are, but the reality is no true fortune teller or medium is accurate a hundred percent of the time, so it's difficult to determine the validity of their abilities."

"That makes sense," I said. "Have any of them said who they think may've shot Wesley Thomas?"

Darrin said, "Of course, no one knows who fired the deadly shots, but the overall feeling is it was someone from here who doesn't think Wesley, or members of the group in general, are good for the island."

"No one said it could be a member of the gathering?"

Stormy said, "If anyone believes that it hasn't been mentioned, at least, not to Darrin or me. Why, do you think it's one of our people?"

"I have no idea."

"For what it is worth, I agree with Darrin. I can't imagine anyone attending the conference taking another's life."

Yet they already said they didn't know all the participants before they arrived, but I didn't share that observation.

With our lunch finished and the conversation turning dark, I had the impression the Roseruns were glad when Kylie brought the check. I reached for it but was too slow. Darrin grabbed it and said, "Allow me. I see what the Stones have been talking about, sharing how respectful you are of their beliefs and how much they admire you for that."

"Even Desmond?"

Stormy laughed loud enough to startle a grackle walking across the deck's railing, "Sorry, yes."

I smiled and said, "That seems un-Desmond like."

"True," Darrin said, stood, pulled the chair out for Stormy and Roisin, then extended his hand to me, and said, "I look forward to seeing you again."

"It's been a pleasure and thank you for lunch. Best of luck with the conference."

Roisin hugged me. "Mr. Chris, don't get yourself in trouble."

"I'm the adult, so shouldn't I be telling you that?"

"Perhaps, but I'm not the one who catches bad guys."

13

After a morning and early afternoon filled with talking, walking, and lunch at Loggerhead's, I got home where it seemed reasonable to sit in my recliner and let an edition of *Outdoor Photographer Magazine* stare up at me resting my eyes. The next thing I remembered was awakening and glancing at my watch to see it was nearing suppertime; a perfect excuse to head to Cal's Bar and Burgers to see firsthand what Junior had described as his dad going "bonkers" decorating for Halloween.

I grabbed my Tilley and headed out the door. Sunset was still an hour away and the temperature was in the upper sixties, so there was no reason to drive the short distance.

I was thankful I chose walking since there wasn't a parking spot available near the bar located catty corner from the entrance to Folly's Department of Public Safety. As I stepped through the door, Conway Twitty's haunting rendition of "The Rose" echoed throughout the crowded room.

The music wasn't what grabbed my attention. I did a double take seeing Cal's was taken over by the ghost of Halloween past, present, and future. Five ceramic jack-o'-lanterns were on the bar, exhibiting both scary and funny faces. The dozen tables had ghost centerpieces holding battery-powered candles. The dark-green walls were covered with artificial webs occupied by large, fake spiders and bats. On either side of the jukebox on the corner of the small stage were black coffins with skeletons dressed in cowboy and cowgirl attire, reminding me of a horror movie version of Roy Rogers and Dale Evans.

The most notable addition to the room was next to the stage. There was a six-foot tall, mahogany and glass rectangular-shaped box, holding an animatronic woman with long black hair, a gold coin headband, wearing a red, long-sleeve billowy blouse with a black vest, and what looked to be a black skirt. She fit my image of a gypsy. Instead of taking my usual route to the bar, I turned to get a better look at the device. There was a small table in front of the mechanical gypsy holding a crystal ball with the gypsy's hands resting on either side of the globe. Carved in the wood above the glass were the words *Lady Lilith*, stenciled in gold above *Your Fortune 5 ¢*.

Junior appeared beside me and said, "Pretty, isn't she?"

"Not sure I'd call her pretty, but it's not something you see every day."

"I found it last week at an antique auction."

"You don't strike me as someone who attends antique auctions."

He smiled and said, "It was online. This time of year, I search various sites for anything having to do with Halloween. This was my biggest purchase, biggest ever."

"Size or cost?"

"Both. Don't tell Dad, but this 1920's fortune teller vending machine cost more than two thousand bucks."

"That's a lot of nickels," I said as I pointed at the sign.

"True, but sometimes you have to grab what speaks to you." He chuckled and added, "Even if others will think you're crazy."

"There're many words I could use to describe you, but crazy isn't one of them."

Before Junior replied, I felt a hand on my shoulder and turned to see Cal. His Stetson was pushed back on his head, exposing a huge smile.

The seventy-seven-year-old bar owner said, "Great to see you, my friend. I was beginning to think you forgot about your buddy Cal."

"Never. Been busy."

"Busy getting shot at, I hear."

I started to respond, but Cal squeezed my shoulder again and pointed at Lady Lilith and at the decorations around the rest of the room, and said, "Getting ready for the Halloween party Sunday. You coming? Before you answer, no costume is needed since I know you're as fond of wearing costumes as a honey-covered cricket at an ant hill."

Some things don't deserve a comment, so I said, "Wouldn't miss it. Everything in here looks spooky, just right for the party."

"Pard, I'm not close to being done decorating; still got some surprises." Cal turned to Junior, "Need you in the kitchen. The lady at the end of the bar is hankerin' for a burger."

"Sure, boss," Junior said and turned to me. "I'm assuming you'd like one?"

"Absolutely."

Junior headed to the kitchen and Cal pointed at the fortune telling device. "Don't tell Junior but that thing gives me the willies. I'll be happy Monday when she flies back to wherever she came from."

"Isn't giving people the willies what Halloween decorations are supposed to do?"

Porter Wagoner's version of "Green, Green Grass of Home" filled the air interrupting Cal's rant about the new addition to the decorations.

He looked toward the jukebox and said, "I ever tell you about me and Curly?"

"Curly?"

"Curly Putman, guy that wrote 'Green, Green Grass of Home.' He also cowrote 'My Elusive Dreams' for Tammy Wynette, and one of the biggest country hits ever, when he and Bobby Braddock wrote 'He Stopped Loving Her Today.'"

"Great songs, so what about him?"

"Crossed paths with him going around music row in Nashville

hawking his songs to any publishing company that'd listen. That was a couple of years after my hit 'End of the Story' back in '62. Curly hadn't had much luck. Anyway, we shared a couple of beers and stories at a seedy rundown bar. He was down and thinking about chucking his dreams and heading back home to Alabama. He sang me a couple of songs he was working on. I thought they were way better than average and encouraged him to not give up." Cal smiled as he looked at the ceiling, then back to me. "Long story short, Curly took my advice, stayed in Nashville. The rest is musical history."

It didn't take a detective to detect Cal was finished talking about the creepy Halloween addition to his bar.

"Then the world can thank you for some memorable country music," I said and smiled.

Cal shrugged and looked at a table against the wall and said, "That couple over there is about to leave. When they go, grab the table. I'll bring your wine and clear the table."

With that, my friend hurried behind the bar to help another customer.

Moments later, the young couple headed to the exit, and I headed to the table and looked around the room. All the tables were occupied as were the bar stools. I recognized several patrons, but many were strangers. The fortune tellers' conference came to mind as I looked around to see if anyone appeared to see dead people, or, at least, were talking to them. I smiled to myself, realizing the absurdity of that thought.

Cal returned and handed me a glass of red wine before clearing the table.

I took a sip and said, "Busy tonight."

"Busy last night, too. Figure some of them were from the conference at the Tides people are talking about."

"Who's talking about it."

"Couple of regulars were in earlier and pointed to the back table and said something like people like that shouldn't frequent such a good Christian place."

"Good Christian place?"

"Yep," Cal said and nodded. "I told them everyone is welcome in my bar."

"That was kind of you."

"I've seen too much discrimination on my travels over this here country. It rubs me the wrong way, it sure does."

"Mind if I ask who it was?"

"Norman Colter and Donald something."

"Did you know the people they were talking about?"

"Names, no, didn't catch them, but it was two chicks. One was a Black gal wearing a polo shirt with a Marion Fire Department logo. The other had her back to me and never looked up."

Junior brought my hamburger to the table and told Cal he was needed at the bar. They left me to enjoy supper. I was ready to order another drink when a glass of wine was placed next to my empty plate.

Without looking up, I said, "Thanks, Cal."

"Think that's the first time you've called me Cal," Charles said, then added, "I'm guessing you've forgotten my name along with inviting me to join you for dinner."

Charles plopped down in the chair opposite me. He was wearing a white sweatshirt with a bright green furry blob with golden eyes and long claws surrounded by the words *McDaniel Green Terror*.

"I called you earlier, but you didn't answer and if you had answered, the invitation would've been for lunch, not supper."

"You do know at the end of all that ringing, a recording tells the caller to leave a message."

Instead of arguing about the non-recorded lunch or supper invitation, I said, "Let me make it up and buy you a burger."

The words had barely left my mouth when Cal sat a burger in front of Charles.

Charles smiled and took a bite of the sizzling burger as Cal headed back to the kitchen.

Against my better judgement, I pointed to the green blob on Charles's sweatshirt.

He said, "McDaniel College in Westminster, Maryland. The Green Terror is their mascot. Seemed fitting for the holiday."

"Interesting," I said, not as enthusiastically as Charles would have liked.

"While I was walking around looking for you, it gave me time to think about our case. We have no solid anything yet. Could you be slipping in your old age?"

"Our old age?"

He snapped his fingers and said, "You're right, age has nothing to do with it. We haven't had enough time to solve Wesley's murder."

Instead of pointing out the flaws in his comment, I said, "I talked to the Roseruns today and they don't think the murder was committed by any of the conference attendees." I then waited for Charles to grill me on when, where, and why I'd talked with the Roseruns.

I was surprised when he took another bite of burger, nodded, and said, "If they thought it was one of their guests, think they'd tell you?"

"Don't see why not."

"Did it enter your mind that the killer might be one of the Roseruns?"

"You're saying they organized this conference so they could murder the turban-wearing psychic."

"Stranger things have happened."

"True." I was still uncomfortable talking about the murder while thinking I might have been the intended victim, so I said, "Have you found Stevie?"

"Nope, been busy tracking you down." Charles then looked around the room like this was the first time he'd noticed the decorations. "Cal went all out this year. That's good since no one has opened a haunted house and the Tides ain't doing another masquerade party."

"You know why?"

"Heard they're booked solid with meetings through mid-November. Cal's is going to be the spooky place to be. We'd better get here early to get a table."

"I'll leave that to you."

Charles looked at his watch-less wrist and said, "Time flies when you're having fun, I need my beauty sleep. Got a big day tomorrow."

"Making deliveries for Dude?"

"A few deliveries, but my other job needs attention. A private detective's work is never done."

"It's good you're not a detective," I said and smiled.

"Wrong," he said then grabbed his Tilley and cane before adding, "Want me to walk you home?"

"No, why?"

"Seems like you're hell-bent on getting yourself in trouble. Try not to get shot going home."

"Good night, Charles, I'll get the tab."

My friend threw up his hand in the form of a wave as he walked away.

Cal replaced Charles in the chair opposite me. He said, "Chased him away?"

"Said he has an early morning. You doing okay with tonight's crowd?

"Finer than armadillo hair."

"I'll take your word on that. Sending invitations to your Halloween party?"

"Just verbal. You know how people talk. I expect the whole town will be here."

"Not sure you have the room for Folly's entire population."

"Know I won't with the other decorations Junior and I'll be bringing out. This is only a tease, my friend. Wetting folks' whistles for the grand reveal." He smiled and stood. "Guess I better get back to work."

I told him I'd see him on Halloween.

Whispering Bill Anderson's hit "Walk Out Backwards" escorted me out of the bar.

I was three blocks from home when I noticed a black car driving slowly behind me. Brushing it off as someone looking for a place to park, I kept walking, but when I'd gone another two blocks and it was still behind me, my anxiety level soared. Perhaps I should've let Charles walk me home. When I was in front of Bert's Market, the car accelerated. I stopped watching the taillights disappear out East Ashley Avenue. It wasn't until I was in the house and locking the door that I realized I was shaking.

Who needs Halloween frights when life can be as scary—or worse?

14

The next morning, I was heading up Center Street to the Post Office, when I glanced in the window of Barb's Books and saw Charles in an animated discussion with the owner. Barb was holding a book in each hand and Charles was pointing to the one in her right hand. It appeared he had made his choice, so I didn't feel bad about butting into their conversation, a practice Charles performs with regularity.

Barb is a couple of years younger than me, my height at 5'10", but unlike yours truly, thin. She was wearing one of her trademark red blouses and black slacks, contrasting drastically with Charles's ever-changing shirts, today featuring a gray sweatshirt with Green River College Gators and a cartoonish version of an alligator's head on the front.

Barb saw me in the entry, honored me with a smile, pointed to Charles's sweatshirt, and said, "Slater's the Gator, Green River College's mascot."

I considered saying, "See ya later, Slater," and leaving, but wasn't excited about being made fun of after I walked out. Instead, I said, "Charles, you pestering this lovely shop owner?"

"You mean the one who is thoughtful, kind, and curious enough to ask about my shirt unlike someone else in here?"

Barb continued to smile and said, "He's doing something you've never done in my store."

"Buying a book?"

She said, "Excellent guess."

Charles took the book from Barb and waved it in front of me, before saying, "*Finance for the Twenty-First Century*. Know why I'm getting it?"

"To learn about finance in the twenty-first century?"

"Smartass," he said and turned to Barb. "Sorry, just popped out."

"Don't feel bad, I often hear that when people are referring to Chris."

I ignored their comments, and said, "Okay, Charles, why?"

"Guess who I ran into this morning on the beach?"

"Someone who quizzed you about twenty-first century finances?"

"Close. Stevie Tigert and Albert McGrady."

The reason for Charles's purchase was coming into focus.

"And Albert told you about needing money to invest in, as Brandon called it, the 'emerging international currency market.'"

Barb held up her hand like she wanted to ask a question or be excused to go to the restroom, and said, "Okay, you've lost me."

"Charles often has that effect on people."

She looked at me, rolled her eyes, and said, "You're the one who spouted off something about an emerging currency market."

Two ladies entered the store and Barb turned her attention in their direction and asked if she could help them find something. They said they were killing time while their husbands finished arguing about craft beers versus the well-known national brands as they sipped on their favorites in the nearby Crab Shack. Barb told them to take as long as they needed.

She then turned back to Charles and me. "You two want to continue your enlightening conversation in the office? I might have something to add to what Charles was saying." She smiled. "Or was getting ready to say."

That intrigued me enough to nod and headed to the office in back of the store, followed by Charles, and Barb.

The office had been a hangout for a few friends when Barb's Books' space was Landrum Gallery, but its current professional appearance with a glass-topped desk and a high-end ergonomic desk chair looked more like a law office than a guy's clubhouse. Barb stood in the doorway so she could see if newcomers entered the store or the ladies killing time needed assistance. I took the desk chair, and Charles leaned against the counter that was holding a Keurig machine and a laser printer.

I turned to Charles. "How did you find Stevie and her fiancé on the beach?"

"Used my well-honed detective skills, of course."

"And?"

"Asked every young couple I saw if they were Stevie and Albert."

"How many couples did you ask before your well-honed skills kicked in?"

"Seven."

And that was after he had a photograph of Stevie, I thought.

Barb said, "How'd you get from saying 'Are you Stevie and Albert?' to hearing about the 'emerging currency markets' or whatever? More importantly, why were you looking for them in the first place?"

"Barb, have you forgotten I'm a private detective?"

She glanced at me, turned to Charles, and said, "Of course not."

"After I asked if they were Stevie and Albert, they looked at me like I was a street person getting ready to hit them up for money." He shrugged. "Or maybe Slater the Gator scared them. Anyway, I gave them one of my charming smiles, and they confessed to being the couple I was looking for."

"Good job, Mr. Charm," I said.

"Smarta ... umm, aleck," he turned and smiled at Barb, then back at me. "I told them I'd been talking with Brandon at the hardware store, and he told me his lovely daughter and her fiancé were visiting and she'd shared that they wanted to walk on the beach while they were here. I added I'd known Brandon for oodles of years and wanted to meet his daughter, so that's why I was asking."

Barb said, "That's sweet, Charles, but how'd you get from that to talking about the currency market?"

He slowly shook his head. "That didn't take much detecting. Albert jumped into the conversation and said something about them being here to get Stevie's father to lend them money so he could invest it in a 'sure thing,' he finger quoted in case I didn't grasp how much a sure thing it was."

"What'd Stevie say to that?" Barb asked.

Charles turned to the bookstore owner who was focused on us rather than the two customers who were still killing time, and said, "She put her arm around Albert's waist, smiled and said something about how great he was at finding such a wonderful opportunity."

"That sounds like her."

This time, Charles and I quickly turned our attention to Barb. I said, "What do you mean?"

Barb smiled and said, "That's what she told me."

"When did you meet her?"

"She's been in a couple of times since she and Albert arrived last week."

Charles said, "How'd you know who she was?"

Barb smiled and said, "Used my well-honed detective skills."

Charles tilted his head and said, "You making fun of me?"

"Yes."

Charles glanced at me before turning back to Barb and said, "You do it sweeter than Chris."

To move the conversation back to something productive, I repeated what Charles had already asked, "How'd you know who she was?"

"She asked how long I'd had the store. I told her and she asked if I knew her dad. I told her how I'd talked with him several times when I was in Pewter Hardware. Told her I didn't know him well since the only time we'd talked was when I was there buying something."

I said, "Was Albert with her?"

She shook her head. "No, she said he was walking around town and wasn't much into shopping."

"Say anything else about him? How long they'd been together? If he seemed on the up and up?" Charles said clearly on a private detective fishing expedition.

"Said they were engaged so I figure she thinks he's on the, as you said, *up and up*."

Charles nodded and said, "All she said was he was good at finding good opportunities?"

"Yes. I probed a little about the opportunity you mentioned and she either didn't want to talk about it or didn't know much about it other than it was 'fantastic.'"

I said, "Did she say what they did in Atlanta?"

"I didn't want to appear nosy but did ask what kind of jobs they had since she'd mentioned how Albert was so good at finding opportunities. She changed the subject, so I took the hint and asked if there were books I could help her find. She said no, pulled a few out, flipped through them, but didn't buy anything."

"Yet she was in twice?" Charles said.

"Yes."

"That's strange."

Barb chuckled and said, "Not really. Your buddy here has been in, oh, a hundred or so times, and has never bought anything."

"Yeah, but he comes in to see the fetching bookstore owner."

Barb smiled at Charles, and said, "You sweet talker you. One more question, why were you really looking for Stevie and Albert?"

Charles glanced at me, then turned to Barb. "Brandon has concerns about why Stevie is here since he hasn't seen her in years. He's leery about her fiancé after he asked Brandon for money. Brandon knows I'm an outstanding private detective and asked me to see what I can find out about Albert and him wanting money. That's why I'm buying this. I'm not quite an expert on the emerging international currency market."

I pinched myself to keep from laughing at the person whose

knowledge of the currency market seemed limited to using my currency whenever he was in the market for a meal or drink.

Barb, proving why she had been a successful defense attorney, slowly nodded, looked at the book in Charles's hand, and in a sincere voice said, "Perhaps you can pick up a few nuggets."

He mimicked her nod and said, "That's my plan. I suppose I'd better get home and begin researching the international currency market. If you don't mind, next time Stevie or Albert are in, see what you can learn about their plans and when they're going to leave. Brandon said they were staying through Halloween but didn't know how long after that."

Barb smiled at him and said she'd see what she could learn.

Charles turned to me. "Why don't you go ahead and pay Barb for the book? That'll give you a reason to hang around longer so you can spend more time with the fetching bookstore owner."

Proof Charles has a good grasp of the local currency market.

15

———

After paying for Charles's book and reassuring Barb I was okay, or at least, better than when I'd talked with her the day after the shooting, I finally made it to the Post Office. With a handful of junk mail and two bills in hand, I was on my way to the trash container strategically placed beside the building to forward the junk mail to the landfill, when I saw William Hansel heading my way.

William was my height and age, and like most of my friends, weighed less than I did. I'd met him my first week on Folly and for a time had rented a house across the street from the tenured professor of Hospitality and Tourism at the College of Charleston.

"Chris," he said in his deep bass voice, "I'm glad I ran into you."

"Great seeing you," I said and glanced behind him in the direction he was coming. "You walk?"

He smiled and nodded. "Ah, you noticed. Yes, I'm determined to get in better shape. My muscles are disappearing at a rapid rate."

It wasn't as if his house was miles away. It was a few blocks from the Post Office, but most of the time I'd seen him out, he was driving his several-year-old Buick.

"We all could use more exercise," I said. "I'm doing the same thing."

"My friend, would you happen to be trying to prevent me from saying why I was glad I ran into you?"

"Sorry, no. Why?"

"Tell you what, why don't you allow me to retrieve my mail and then you can join me in getting some much-needed exercise while I share my apprehensions?"

William often sounded like he was lecturing a class. I'd grown accustomed to it, even though it was far from how most of my friends communicated.

I told him it sounded like a good idea and waited while he entered the Post Office. Less than a minute later he exited and took the same route I had taken to the trash receptacle.

He clapped his hands as if he were dusting postal cooties off his hands, smiled, and said, "Shall we traverse some of our island's terrain?"

I translated that to mean *Ready to walk?* and said, "Lead the way."

We crossed Center Street and when we reached the parking area for the library and community center, William slowed and said, "As you probably surmised, there's something I wish to speak with you about." He nodded toward a wooded area behind the building. "Why don't we see if there's seating available over there?"

"Fine with me."

I followed him past the low fence enclosing the David C. Israel Memorial Garden to one of the benches in the small park adjacent to both the community center and the Lost Dog Cafe.

I sat beside William who looked around, smiled, and said, "I doubt that would qualify as a walk far enough to restore my muscles to their previous strength."

"As much time as you spend in your garden tilling and doing whatever gardeners do, I suspect you're not in as bad a shape as you think."

"Physiologists would differ, but, seeing that there aren't any in the vicinity, this is a good spot to rest and converse."

"What's on your mind?"

"I came across a disturbing rumor yesterday. I heard you were the target of an assassin Sunday evening, and while I'm relieved the miscreant missed, a gentleman standing beside you failed to survive. I also know how rumors don't often reflect what truly occurs, so I wanted your version of the event."

I patted him on the shoulder before saying, "I'm also relieved I wasn't the victim, but to be honest, I'm not certain who was the target."

"Knowing your propensity for, how shall I say it, infusing yourself into matters that should remain the purview of law enforcement, you've been the ire of several evil individuals over the years. This goes back to when you aided in the apprehension of the people who killed my friend, what, thirteen years ago? With that in mind, what brings you to believe Sunday's incident may not have had you as the target?"

"To my knowledge, I haven't been involved in any issues recently that would warrant an attack. Do you, or the people who shared the rumor with you, know anything about the victim?"

"I'm not certain I've heard his name."

"Wesley Thomas. He was here to take part in a meeting at the Tides."

"Was it by chance the group activity of the fortune tellers described in last week's *City Paper*?

"Yes. Have you heard anything about them?"

"As you well know, I'm not a proponent of spreading gossip, but because you're one of the few individuals I trust to maintain confidences, I've previously shared things that wouldn't have left my mouth if you weren't the recipient."

"I appreciate that."

"My knowledge of the group is limited. According to the article, it's comprised of fortune tellers, psychic readers, palm readers, mediums, and other offshoots of predictors and readers of those who have left us. Are you familiar with the term Hoodoo?"

"No. I've heard of Voodoo, is Hoodoo different?"

"Yes, Voodoo is an actual religion originating in Africa. Hoodoo is a spiritual religious tradition created by enslaved African Americans in the United States. I doubt many Caucasians are aware of it, but since I'm African American, I've had exposure to Hoodoo since early youth. In fact, some of my ancestors on my mother's side practiced it."

"William, I hate to sound ignorant, but is it still practiced?"

"There are pockets, mainly in the South. When people were enslaved and brought to this country from Central and West Africa, their native religion had to be suppressed and many were forced to convert to Christianity. In fact, it was criminal to practice religious traditions coming from Africa, so many of the new Christians, fused some of their previous beliefs and traditions into Christianity. The merged religion was often called Afro-Christianity."

"Again, I'm being ignorant, but what does Hoodoo have to do with fortune telling?"

William smiled and said, "Sorry, I find myself wandering a bit from answering your question. Some of those who practice Hoodoo believe in spirit possession, divination or seeking knowledge of the future, and even using charms for spiritual protection against harm. Some believe in conjuring or the calling of spirits to appear. I suppose my point is many of these Hoodoo beliefs are similar, some possibly identical to what individuals who are meeting at the Tides believe and practice."

A couple walked past us on their way to the library housed in the building with the community center. William watched them as they turned in front of the building. He glanced at his watch, then turned back to me, and said, "This may not have anything to do with what happened to the participant in the event at the Tides, but my grandmother, the relative who practiced Hoodoo, on more than one occasion shared how she and her fellow followers had to hide their beliefs out of fear for their lives. She often said, 'What people don't understand, can hurt us.' That leads to the second rumor I heard last evening at a meeting of Preserve the Past. The gentleman speaking said there was no shortage of Folly residents who are, and I'll clean it up for you, severely agitated by the, umm, Devil worshipers being here."

Preserve the Past is a local organization created to preserve the Morris Island Lighthouse. William was one of the strong proponents of the goals of the organization and has been a member since before he and I met.

"Did he say why they were so opposed?"

"To be honest, he wasn't making much sense, but called the group satanic on more than one occasion."

"Do you mind sharing who was saying it?"

William looked at the gravel at his feet, took a deep breath, then slowly lifted his head. "I'll share it but do so reluctantly. You understand it may have nothing to do with what happened to Mr. Thomas."

"Yes, but it might."

"Norman Colter. Are you acquainted with the gentleman?"

"Don't believe so, but last night Cal mentioned him as one of his customers who was talking against the group being here."

"He's been on Folly five years or so. He doesn't say much, so I was surprised he was freely sharing his opinion about the group."

"What else can you tell me about him?"

"That covers it. The only time I see him is at the meetings. Sorry I can't be more help." He looked at his watch for a second time, then added, "I hate to end our conversation at this point, but I do need to be heading home."

"I understand," I said, although I didn't. "I'm glad I ran into you."

He chuckled. "And took this long excursion with me."

I smiled. "I already feel muscles regaining some of their strength."

"I don't know about that but repeat how glad I am that you are still among the living."

"I agree."

William headed home and I remained on the bench enjoying the pleasant October weather. The ringing phone interrupted my enjoyment of the day. Cindy's name appeared on the screen.

"Hi, Cindy. Beautiful day, isn't it?"

"I wouldn't know. I'm Super Glued to my chair staring at a mountain of paperwork I'm supposed to do something with. All I have to do is figure out what that is. Anyway, I didn't call to ask your help figuring it out, but if you volunteer, I'd accept."

"Afraid I wouldn't be much help. So, why did you call?"

"Checking to see if you remembered anything more about the car the killer was driving."

"Afraid not."

"Would it jog anything in your feeble memory if I said it could've been a four-year-old black Nissan Sentra?"

"You could've said it was a four-year-old Martian spaceship and I couldn't dispute it. Like I told you that night, I only focused on the gun and the body on the sidewalk. Why do you think it could be a Nissan?"

"You know Hazel Ott?"

"Don't believe so. Is she the shooter?"

"Doubt it. She's an eighty-seven-year-old widow who lives in a condo across from Harris Teeter. Yesterday afternoon, she reported her car had been stolen from the parking lot. Since—"

"Cindy," I interrupted, "that's three days after the shooting. Didn't she notice it missing before yesterday?"

"Ms. Ott, or as she said, 'Call me Hazel, sweetie,' says the only time she drives it is to cross Folly Road from her condo to go to Harris Teeter. She takes those hundred-yard trips on Wednesdays, so she didn't miss it until yesterday."

"She called you sweetie?"

"That's the only thing you got out of what I said?"

I ignored her comment, and said, "Don't suppose you've found her car?"

"Wrong. Her Nissan must be psychic like some of your friends at the Tides."

"Am I supposed to understand what you're talking about?"

"We found it in the Harris Teeter parking lot, as if it knew that's where it always went and drove there by itself."

"Could Ms. Ott have driven it there, walked home, and forgot she did it?"

"Nope."

"Why not?"

"Two reasons. First, she said she'd never walked across Folly Road since she moved into the condo six years ago. Second, after we found the car, we checked for prints. There wasn't a single one on the steering wheel, the gear shift, the door handle, or even the radio."

"Someone wiped it clean and that's why you suspect it was used in the shooting?"

"Excellent amateur detective detecting."

"How'd the thief, alleged killer, steal the car?"

"Seems that dear, sweet Hazel had a horrible time finding her keys whenever she gets ready to make her weekly trip to the grocery. A year or so ago, she found the perfect solution to the problem."

"Don't tell me she leaves the key in the ignition."

"Okay, I won't."

I started to laugh, until I realized we were talking about a vehicle someone possibly used to murder a visitor to my island or missed me and accidentally killed the person walking beside me.

"You think it's the vehicle used in the shooting?"

"Yes, but we're far from having proof. We know the person who took it from Hazel's parking lot wiped it clean of prints. It was left a few hundred feet from where it was taken, making me believe the shooter left his or her vehicle at Harris Teeter, walked across the street to Hazel's lot, stole her car, shot Wesley Thomas, returned to the grocery's lot, got in his or her vehicle and went wherever."

"Why didn't the killer simply return Hazel's Nissan to where he got it, so she wouldn't think it'd been stolen?"

"Excellent question. The short answer is hell if I know. A longer version, and one I'm going with until I learn differently, is the shooter didn't know Hazel only drove the car once a week and thought she might've reported it stolen when the killer still had it. It'd have been safer to return it to the Harris Teeter lot so he would be close to his car."

"How'd the killer find it in the first place?"

"Same short answer. The longer version, and pure speculation, is the killer didn't want to use his vehicle while shooting Wesley and walked around large parking areas looking for an unlocked vehicle, and stumbled across not only an unlocked car, but one with the keys in the ignition. A car thief's dream."

"Any witnesses to either the auto theft or cameras catching whatever happened?"

"No such luck."

"Any thoughts on who it could've been?"

"Yes, we've narrowed it down to a fortune teller or a local."

"Excellent police work."

"I give all the credit to Detective Adair."

"That's what I was afraid of."

"In addition to the identity of the shooter, there's still one other thing we don't know."

"If Wesley Thomas was the intended victim or if it was the person you're talking to?"

"Yes. Please be careful."

"I will," I said, while wondering how that would be possible without locking myself in the house or getting in the car and driving, umm, driving where?

"Don't hesitate to let me know if you need anything."

"Catching the killer would be a good start."

"It's on my to-do list, on Detective Adair's list as well, but I wouldn't hold my breath for that to happen."

On that optimistic note, I wished her well in figuring out what she's supposed to do with the pile of paperwork on her desk. In a profanity-laced response, she shared what she'd like to do with the stack of paper and ended our call.

16

———————

I stood to head home when my phone rang again. Hoping it was Cindy calling back to tell me the killer had turned himself in, my hopes were crushed when Charles's name appeared on the screen.

"Caught the killer?" I said, realizing occasionally a glimmer of his disjointed phone etiquette slips through my lips.

"Nope, that's our job."

"It's Detective Adair's job, along with other law enforcement officials."

"So, what time are you going to Harris Teeter?"

I concede, Charles is better at confusing phone calls.

"I wasn't aware I was going?" I said and wondered if he had my phone tapped during my conversation with Cindy.

"By my calculation, you're out of certain necessary items telling me today would be the perfect day to be heading to the grocery."

Knowing Charles, the easiest option would be to go with his plan. Besides, he was right since my cupboard was bare—again.

"And what time would I be going to get those necessary items, whatever they are?"

"You're really going?"

I smiled and said, "Sure."

"In that case, I'll go with you to help you decide what you need. Swing by my apartment in an hour."

Before he said anything else, I ended the call. The short walk home gave me time to compile a list of items I needed plus some thought on what Cindy had said about the car stolen from the condos across the street from Harris Teeter. It was frustrating that I didn't have any helpful recollections about the vehicle or its driver.

Charles was leaning against his apartment door and tapping his foot on the step as I pulled into his shell and gravel parking lot. His black sweatshirt with a large gray *C* with a snarling orange camel running behind it on the front was anything but subtle and made me chuckle.

My friend approached the passenger door, tipped his Tilley to me, and said, "Like my shirt?"

I glanced at it and said, "The one with a rabid camel on it?"

"I'll have you know this is Gaylord, Campbell University's fighting camel."

"How did I rate the honor of taking you and Gaylord grocery shopping?"

"I needed a few things I couldn't get at Bert's, and figured having a chauffeur would be nice. My battery died yesterday, and peddling the two and a half miles to Harris Teeter is not happening since I used all my pedal power going up and down the beach looking for Stevie and Albert."

That was all he said until we were beside Crosby's Fish and Shrimp on Folly Road. He cleared his throat but didn't speak until I looked over at him.

"Do you think Wesley was the target?" he asked as he stared out the windshield and didn't turn to see my response.

"I've no reason to believe otherwise, but it still worries me."

He continued staring out the windshield and in a lower voice said, "You need to be extra careful. I don't have time or desire to train another best friend."

"I will. What brought that up?"

"Face it, you've got yourself in many tight spots since I've known you, and more than a few people wouldn't mind seeing you disappear."

"You need to rephrase that to *we* have gotten into a few tight spots and the number of people we've helped see the inside of a jail cell keeps growing."

"You're right, we need to find the killer fast and ask who he was aiming at."

The longer I waited to tell him about what Cindy had learned about the car that most likely was used in the shooting, the worse it'd be for me. Might as well get it out of the way.

"Charles, you know Hazel Ott?"

"She have a dog?"

"I have no idea, so do you know her?"

"Don't think so, why?"

I told him what Cindy had learned about Ms. Ott's vehicle and her theory about it being the car the killer had driven. I was surprised how few sighs and eye rolls he gave me throughout the story.

I finished and as we were waiting for the light at Sol Legare Road to turn green so we could turn into Harris Teeter's parking lot, he said, "Think her car's in the parking lot?"

"I doubt it. I suspect the police had it towed so they could let the techs do their thing."

As we pulled into the grocery's lot, I was surprised to see so few empty parking spaces. As if Charles was reading my mind, he said, "Thursday is senior discount day," then pointed to a vacant spot near the end of the row where a car was pulling out. "There's one."

A rusting faded red Pontiac Tempest was backing at a snail's pace out of the space next to the one I pulled into. The car crawled past us and all I could see were knuckles on the steering wheel and a fancy red hat in the driver's seat. I thought of Hazel Ott using her car once a week on Wednesday. I suppose she doesn't want to deal with Thursday crowds. I shared that with Charles. He didn't respond, probably still irritated I didn't call as soon as Cindy had told me about the discovery. I didn't bring it up again.

Inside the store, we each grabbed a cart. I headed to the bread aisle to make my selections, as I watched Charles disappearing around the corner. I was busy marking off items I needed. I grabbed a package of cookies from the snack aisle, and was surprised Charles wasn't nearby since it's one of his favorite spots in the store. I walked past several ladies discussing why one spaghetti sauce was best, then saw Charles talking to a slender, athletic-looking woman with shoulder length black hair. I couldn't judge her age but was certain she wasn't a senior taking advantage of the discounts.

I approached the duo and said, "Charles, who's your friend?"

"Chris, meet Karen Johnson, who appreciates a fine fighting camel."

Karen held out her hand, smiled while looking at my face, which I'm certain had a puzzled look. "Nice to meet you. I saw Charles's shirt and had to say hi."

I smiled and said, "Because of a rabid looking camel?"

Karen laughed while shaking her head. "I'm from Durham, North Carolina, fifty miles from Campbell University, home of the Fighting Camels. I wanted to see if Charles was a fellow North Carolinian."

Charles, having been silent for way too long, said, "I told Karen about my collection of T-shirts and sweatshirts."

I said, "Are you on vacation?"

"No, moved here a couple of years after retiring from the Army. Live over in The Standard."

Charles said, "The Standard, isn't that the apartment complex near the Charleston Crab House?"

"Yes, are you both from here?"

I said, "I moved to Folly about fourteen years ago."

"What about you, Charles?"

"Been here since Moses was a baby. Live on Folly and love every minute of it."

"After what I heard the other day, I'm not sure it's the safest place around."

Charles said, "What'd you hear?"

"A friend of mine was having supper with her boyfriend over

there and saw a ton of police vehicles near the Tides. She has a nosy streak in her and went to see what was happening. Seems that someone had been shot and killed."

Charles said, "Chris was there when it happened."

Her head jerked in my direction as she said, "How terrible. Was the person a friend of yours?"

"Never met him. I was walking near him when it happened."

"They catch the shooter?"

"Don't think so," I said.

"Hope they catch him soon," she said then glanced at her watch. "Oh, time's gotten away from me. It was nice meeting you both and glad you're safe, Chris."

"The pleasure is all ours," Charles said.

"Nice meeting you," I said as Karen shook our hands before she disappeared around the corner.

I wondered if her friend saw the car or shooter but didn't want to chase her through the store to ask.

I looked in Charles basket and said, "That all you're getting?"

"No, I'll meet you at the checkout. Got to grab a couple more things."

I searched for the remaining items on my list, and some that weren't on it. I was headed to the registers when my phone rang. The screen read Shannon Stone.

"Afternoon, Shannon."

As if by magic, Charles appeared at my side leaning in to hear the conversation.

Shannon said, "Blessed be, Chris, hope I didn't catch you at a bad time."

"Yes and no, I'm grocery shopping so you know it's not a good time."

She laughed and said, "Totally agree. I'll not keep you. I wanted to invite you and Charles to a small get-together I'm having tomorrow evening."

"A Halloween party?"

"Nothing like that. The kids and I are having several of the attendees from the conference over. It'll be a quiet gathering so we can get to know each other better."

"Sounds nice, would we be the only, umm—"

"Non soothsayers?"

"Something like that."

"Maybe, I'm not sure if Roisin is inviting Preacher Burl."

"What time and what can I bring?"

"Six-thirty and simply bring yourself. I'm going to call Charles now."

"No need, I'll tell him. He's standing next to me."

"Good, then until tomorrow."

I put the phone in my pocket and headed to the register. Charles followed, looking like he was going to burst.

He finally said, "Who was that?"

"Shannon Stone inviting us to a gathering at her house tomorrow evening."

"Us, nobody else?"

"She's having people over who are attending the fortune tellers' conference."

"That way we won't have to figure out how to get them together to question them about Wesley."

"Shannon invited us to a quiet gathering, not your version of the Spanish Inquisition or the witch trials."

"Don't be silly, I'm smoother than that. Remember, I'm a private detective."

That was something he'd never let me forget. As we walked to the car, I could hear Charles's faux detective mind thinking of questions to ask the attendees. The ride to his apartment was quiet, that is, quiet for Charles being present.

When we arrived, my friend slowly got out the passenger door and opened the rear door to retrieve his bag of groceries and hesitated. I was ready to ask what was wrong, when he said, "This town is much better with you in it. I, umm, we are going to find out who shot poor Wesley. All you have to do is follow my lead tomorrow night."

"Thanks for that. Tomorrow night, let's agree we're guests and that's it."

"Agreed, guests with questions."

17

I put away the groceries, grabbed a cold Diet Coke, then headed to the screened-in front porch to enjoy the late afternoon. It didn't take long for the day to reduce my anxiety.

Traffic was light and consisted of several golf carts going to and from Bert's Market. Three of the carts carried the large family I'd seen on the beach the other day. They were laughing and joking among the riders on each cart. Large families aren't as common as they used to be, and among my friends, none of us have a large family, part of the reason our *island family* is so important.

My peaceful thoughts were interrupted by a commotion in the gravel lot between my house and Bert's. A man and woman were in a heated discussion. Not wanting to be Charles-like, I remained seated but continued listening.

"I'm not saying you're wrong," the woman shouted, "but walking up and confronting people can get you in trouble."

"Dani, I'm a decade older than you, and when I'm in the right, I need to let those who are doing evil things know it."

The voice was familiar, but I couldn't remember from where.

"We have the same concerns but approach it differently. I want it so those people are never permitted back on Folly."

"There are enough of us to make our feelings known about those Satanists, but I'm not sure we have enough to take it to the management at the Tides to restrict who can hold conferences there."

"We can't fix anything now and Paul is expecting his afternoon banana."

"Who's Paul?"

"You wouldn't understand."

"Whatever. Don't forget tomorrow."

The wheels of the golf cart flung gravel as it backed onto the road and sped past my house. I didn't get a good look at the driver but there was no mistaking Donald Braxton's fancy cart.

I left my drink on the porch and headed towards Bert's in time to see a petite woman, her long, gray hair framing her face, wearing jean shorts, and a gray shirt with a picture of the Pier on it. She was walking my way.

As she approached, she made eye contact, smiled, and said, "Afternoon."

"Good afternoon. A pleasant day for a walk."

"It is, which way are you heading?"

"The Pier."

She nodded as if I'd said the right thing, and said, "No prettier spot on the island." She chuckled and added, "Then again, I haven't been everywhere."

"You visiting?"

"No, I live out East Arctic Avenue."

"That's great."

"Yes, I found a wonderful woman who's renting me a room in her house shared with her extensive animal collection."

"Martha Wright?"

Her smile faded as she said, "How'd you know?"

"I've known Martha and her critters for years," I extended my right hand, and added, "I'm Chris Landrum."

Shaking my hand, she said, "Dani Crow. Nice meeting you. I know your friend Charles, umm, Fowler, is it?"

"Yes, it seems everyone knows him."

"He mentioned you two were looking into the drive-by shooting. Have any suspects?"

"The police are investigating the murder. Charles and I are simply concerned citizens."

"So, the cops have suspects?"

"I'm not certain, but again, that's a question for them. Did you know the victim, Wesley Thomas?"

Dani's expression turned into a scowl as she said, "No, I did not. Did you?"

"No, but I was next to him on the sidewalk when he was shot."

"Chris, don't get me wrong, I'm not saying he deserved to die, but when you lead an evil life, sometimes death comes sooner."

"Evil life?"

"What him and others do at that thing at the Tides is plain evil."

"Everyone has his or her opinion—"

"You think I'm wrong?"

"I was about to say I'm surprised you'd judge them as being evil without having met them."

"I never met the Devil but know he's evil."

Dani's stance and facial expression reminded me of a boxer getting ready to land a punch.

Not wanting to antagonize her more and perhaps tick off the killer, I took a step back and said, "Didn't mean to upset you. Everyone's different. If nothing else, we should respect that."

Her expression softened and she said, "I suppose so. Sometimes I get too passionate about my feelings."

"I understand. It was nice meeting you. Tell Martha I said hi."

"I will. Enjoy the Pier, and as a suggestion, watch your step." She turned and walked away before I could respond. Perhaps it was for the better.

On the way to the Pier, I kept rehashing the conversation with Dani. Wasn't her disgust for the fortune tellers extreme for someone who'd never met them? Yet, she's not alone. It appears the list of suspects who may've killed Wesley is growing. Larry had said there were several citizens who shared his viewpoint. What other locals might have an axe to grind or a bullet to fire?

By the time I escaped the never-ending circle of who and why, I was near the far end of the Pier. The sun sinking low in the late afternoon sky and the cascading colors reflected in the clouds brought me back to a more peaceful mental place. Pleasant thoughts kept me company as I stopped, leaned against the railing, and gazed at the never-ending waves rolling in. I couldn't tell where it went, but an hour slipped by as I stared at the sea. A glance at my watch combined with a rumble in my stomach confirmed it was suppertime.

Pier 101 Restaurant and Bar was the closest restaurant, but it was already crowded, so I decided to grab a to-go order. I placed my order with a server who didn't look old enough to be driving. As I waited for the food, I looked around the room and was impressed how crowded it was on the Thursday evening three days before Halloween. I was also amazed how many people were in costumes ranging from an exotic belly dancer to two frightening zombies.

"Your grilled chicken wrap, dude," the server said as he set the bag on the host stand while giving me a fake smile.

"Thank you, dude," I said with my version of a fake smile as I handed him my money.

I grabbed the bag and walked out the door and down the stairs to the parking lot, wondering when I'd last called anyone dude, other than Dude Sloan, the original hippy surfer.

I was approaching the spot where Wesley died. I took a deep breath and continued toward home when I noticed a lady standing on the sidewalk staring at the concrete path near her feet. She looked familiar, but I couldn't place her. As I got closer, I realized it was Alice Clay, the psychic who told Cindy she "saw" Wesley's murder. I didn't want to interrupt whatever she was doing, so I walked across the parking lot and away from her.

"Excuse me," she said. "Please wait."

I stopped and turned to see Alice walking toward me. I said, "Can I help you?"

She stopped inches from me and was holding what looked to be a deck of oversized playing cards, and said, "Thanks for stopping."

I smiled and said, "Sure."

"The reason I stopped you is—"

I continued to smile and said, "Let's start over, I'm Chris."

She smiled and said, "Alice, I wanted to tell you I've seen you before."

"Yes, last Sunday night when you were talking to Chief LaMond about the shooting, I was in the back seat of her vehicle."

"Oh sure, but that's not what I'm referring to. I see things, visions, and that's where I saw you."

"What did you see?" As soon as the question left my lips, I regretted asking.

She stared at me and slowly said, "Was you, but not really you, talking to death."

"I'm sorry, I don't understand."

She continued to stare but I had the eerie feeling she wasn't seeing me.

"Visions can be quite confusing for those who do not experience them."

That was a major understatement. I wished Charles or even Dude were here to translate where this conversation was going.

Instead of saying anything, I nodded.

"I'll try to be clearer. I was in my hotel room looking out at the ocean when I saw you, well it was not exactly you. The face and hair were different, but I'm sure it was you. Yes, I'm sure."

"What happened in your vision?"

"You were talking to death, and death wanted you and some other man to go with him."

"Death is a man?"

"No, death is death, but I feel it's masculine, at least during that vision."

"Do you realize this sounds strange?"

"That, my friend, is your opinion but I needed to tell you, to warn you."

"Were you waiting for me?"

"No," she said and began shuffling the large cards in her hands which started trembling.

"Are you all right?" I asked and looked around in case I needed assistance. No one was nearby.

"No. I need to lay my cards down and rest." She shook her head and added, "I'm not crazy."

I lied saying, "I don't think you're crazy, but it looks like you need help."

"Thank you, but you will be the one who needs help," she said and abruptly turned and walked towards the beach.

I watched her disappear around a storage building and again looked around to see if anyone else witnessed the strangest conversation I've ever been a part of, and that's going some considering some of my friends.

As the sun sank over the horizon, I started home again with dinner getting cold in my hand, and a warning from one strange character. Cindy had asked me if I remembered anything to call her. I wondered what she'd she say if I told her according to Alice, I'd been holding court with death. I'll never know since she won't be hearing it from me.

18

———————

With everything going on, staying around the house this morning was doing nothing for my mental health, so a walk on the beach should help. If nothing else, I'll get some exercise. With luck, I won't encounter Alice Clay. I got coffee at Bert's and made the short walk to the Second Street East beach access point.

I wasn't the only person who thought being at the ocean was a promising idea. As I looked toward the Fishing Pier and beach in front of the Tides Hotel, I counted more than thirty groups either walking while clearly focused on their destination, a few sauntering in and out of the surf, and several groups of vacationers resting on colorful beach towels soaking in the late October sun despite the temperature hovering in the mid-sixties.

Instead of walking through the crowded area near the Pier, I ventured left where the beach was less crowded. In addition to the cool temperature, the wind blowing off the ocean added even more of a chill in the air. A hundred yards or so from where I'd begun my beach walk, I saw a couple seated on cushions and staring at the breaking waves and a fling of sandpipers scampering in and out of the water. The female was in her mid-twenties, thin, with long black hair. What got my attention was that she was wearing an orange sweatshirt with *Pewter Hardware* in yellow on the front.

Larry sold those sweatshirts at the store, so it didn't necessarily mean the couple was Brandon's daughter and her fiancé, but by Brandon having told me they wanted to walk on the beach every day while they were visiting, I took a chance and approached them. The closer I got, I saw a resemblance to Stevie from the photo Brandon had given Charles.

I smiled and said, "Beautiful day, isn't it?"

The female looked up, returned my smile, and said, "We were saying the same thing. I thought it would be too cold with the wind, but the sun's doing a decent job warming us."

The man, who was a few years older than the lady, had long, black sideburns, a short beard, and black hair thinning on top, nodded, and mumbled, "Nice day."

He didn't appear the least bit happy to see me stepping between them and partially blocking their view of the ocean, so I focused on the female, and said, "Would you happen to be Stevie Tigert?"

She glanced at her companion before turning to me and saying, "How'd you know?"

I felt awkward looming over the seated couple but didn't feel comfortable sitting. I said, "It was a guess. I've known your father ever since I moved to Folly years ago. I was talking with him the other day and he shared you and your fiancé were visiting and the two of you wanted to walk on the beach every day. He was excited you're here."

She gave me a warming smile and said, "We don't get to see the ocean in Atlanta where we live."

Her companion startled me when he hopped up giving me a better look at his bodybuilder physique and height that exceeded mine by at least six inches. He was wearing jeans and an untucked, long-sleeve blue dress shirt. I was relieved when he smiled, stuck out his hand, and said, "I'm Albert McGrady, and you're?"

I shook his hand and said, "Sorry, I'm being rude. I'm Chris Landrum."

Albert said, "Care to join us, Mr. Landrum?"

"Please call me Chris. I don't want to interrupt your time at the ocean."

"Nonsense," Stevie said as she reached behind a Styrofoam cooler beside her and grabbed a multi-colored towel and placed it beside her. "We'd love to get to know some of Dad's friends." She pointed at the towel. "Have a seat."

I slowly lowered myself on the towel as Albert said, "Want something to drink? We have bottled water and Cokes."

"I'm fine, but thanks."

He opened the cooler, grabbed a bottle of water, handed it to Stevie, then pulled out a Coke for himself, before returning to the cushion where he'd been when I arrived.

"Where'd you live before moving here and what'd you do before that?" Stevie said before taking a sip of water.

I gave her a summary of where I'd lived and my previous occupation, then, now that that line of questioning had been opened, I asked them what they did for a living. I learned Stevie had worked retail sales at a HomeGoods in an Atlanta mall, as well as a server at Applebee's and IHOP.

She shook her head, and added, "Tried being a temp in a real estate office, but hated, really hated, being stuck in an office eight hours a day."

I turned to her companion and said, "How about you?"

While he was taking a long draw on his soft drink, I smiled to myself, thinking how Charles would be proud of me for interrogating the youngsters.

"Didn't go to college, allergic to school. I was a long-haul trucker for a few years, drove for Schneider and Walmart. Was a baggage handler at the Atlanta airport. Before that, bartending."

Neither of them shared their current occupations. That's where I differed from Charles. I didn't want to appear too inquisitive and didn't ask what they do now, but did say, "I think you may've met one of my friends the other day. Name's Charles Fowler."

"Guy with the cane?"

"That's Charles."

She laughed. "He came up to us about the same way you did, except we were walking. He asks lots of questions."

I smiled. "That he does, but he's a good person and has been my best friend for years. Think you also met another of my friends, Barb Deanelli."

Stevie said, "Bookstore lady?"

I nodded.

"How do you know her?"

"She's the half-sister of another of my friends, plus she and I are dating."

"She's got a nice store."

Albert leaned across Stevie's lap and said, "Hell, Chris, does everyone know everyone here?"

I couldn't tell how he meant the comment, so I smiled, and said, "Seems like it, but not really. When do you have to be back in Atlanta?"

Stevie said, "Don't know for certain. Thinking about heading out next week."

"Why'd you ask?" Albert said, still not revealing his mood.

I again smiled and said, "Thinking if you were going to be here over the weekend, you might like to attend the Halloween party at one of our bars. It's the biggest Halloween event around here."

"Don't you all trick-or-treat?"

"It's not permitted for safety reasons."

Stevie glanced at Albert before turning to me and saying, "Would we have to wear costumes to the party?"

"Only if you want to. A few will, but last year, it was only a handful. I know I wouldn't be going if costumes were required."

"Will Dad be there?"

"Don't believe he was last year, but I bet if you asked him to go, he would."

She smiled. "Good idea."

Albert said, "Since everyone knows everyone here, I guess you heard about the man getting shot over by the hotel the other night?"

That was one topic I wanted to avoid and the reason I was on the beach today instead of being at home moping. "Afraid so, but he wasn't from here."

Albert glanced at Stevie then turned back to me and said, "I heard he was a witch."

"Albert," Stevie said. "We don't know—"

"I bet Chris knows."

"All I know is the gentleman was here for a conference of fortune tellers. Most of them aren't Wiccans."

"Don't know either way," Albert said, "The guy telling me about it said the dead guy was a witch and, to be honest, sounded glad he was shot."

"That's too bad," I said. "Do you know who told you?"

"Don't know his name. I was walking down the street where Stevie's dad works, and this guy rolled up behind me on a big-ole golf cart and out of the blue asked me if I was one of those people here for the Satanic meeting."

Stevie said, "You didn't tell me about that."

"It was nothing. We talked a minute, that's all."

I said, "Can you describe the man or the golf cart?"

"Cart was bigger than most I'm familiar with, silver, with what looked like a fake Mercedes front end. The guy was older, but that's about all I can remember." He shrugged. "Yeah, that's about it."

I didn't share it, but that sounded like Donald Braxton. "You sure that's all he said?"

"Soon as I told him I wasn't here with any group and had no idea what he was talking about, he started telling me about the man getting shot because of his Devil worshiping."

"What else did he say about the group or the man who was shot?"

"To be honest, I wasn't paying much attention. Thought it was uncalled for accusing me of being a witch, so all I wanted to do was get away from him."

"What happened then?"

He didn't say anything else. Stomped on the accelerator and zoomed past me. Pretty rude guy."

"I guess I was in the bookstore and missed all that," Stevie said and grabbed another beach towel from behind the cooler and wrapped it around her bare legs. Albert noticed and patted her on the shoulder and said, "Getting cold?"

She nodded, Albert squeezed her arm, and said, "Let's walk a little more to warm up then head back to the campground."

Stevie stood and began collecting their items. I took the hint, stood, and folded the towel I'd been sitting on, while Albert picked up the empty drink containers, put them in the cooler, and said, "Where will the Halloween party be and what time will it start?"

I gave him the details, said I hoped to see them there, then waved bye as they headed toward the Pier.

I shook my head thinking how they'd avoided answering my question about what they currently did for a living. I then smiled, thankful that Albert hadn't asked me for any money or started a discussion about the emerging international currency market.

19

———————

What to do after I was left standing on the beach while watching Stevie and Albert heading toward the Folly Pier on their warming walk, was resolved when the phone rang.

"Morning, Charles," I said while thinking it'd be nice if he'd ever tried such a pleasant salutation when I called him.

"Well, why aren't you here?"

"It'd help if I knew where you were and why I should be there."

"Thought you'd want to see Dude, Pluto, Happy, and Raven Moon. You on your way?"

Of course, I knew Dude and his Australian Terrier, Pluto. I'd only heard of one man named Happy in my seventy plus years, so I assumed it was one of the fortune tellers, and if I remember correctly, he has a cat named Raven. With luck, I knew the cast of characters with Charles, but still would have a tough time seeing them without another hint.

"Where are you?"

"The Bark Park, of course."

The Bark Park was Folly's popular dog park located a few blocks from where I was standing.

"On my way."

Charles huffed then said, "About time, you're late."

I saved my huff until after I'd ended the call.

The Bark Park was easy to find since it was in the lot adjacent to Folly's water tower, visible from many spots on the island. Charles and the group with him were also easy to find, but for another reason. They were standing outside the fence enclosing the Park and looked like they'd escaped from a circus train.

Charles was wearing a yellow sweatshirt with Michigan in blue on the front. My friend was kneeling and petting Dude's pet wearing an orange dog sweater with *Pluto* in script on the back. Dude was wearing one of his many tie-dyed shirts with a glow-in-the-dark peace symbol on it. The gentleman with them would've appeared boring in his attire if he didn't have on stoplight red tennis shoes and holding a leash attached to a large, black cat with long tuffs on its ears, looking like a gargoyle.

Looking around and not seeing a circus train they escaped from, I approached to hear Dude say, "Yo, Chrisster, be joinin' us?"

"Sure," I said, not knowing if Charles had told the others he'd invited me.

"Meet my new buds," Dude said, put his hand on Happy's shoulder and added, "Be Happy. Honest, that be his real name."

Happy was in his early fifties, my height, with grayish brown hair. He smiled, shook my hand, and said, "My parents were hippies, thought Happy would be a good name if they wanted me to be a happy person and hung it on me." He laughed. "At times, having that as my name doesn't really make me happy."

"It's unique," I said, not knowing what to add.

Happy nodded toward his cat that was busy sniffing Pluto where animals appear to enjoy smelling other animals, and said, "The chunky feline is Raven Moon."

I bent and rubbed Raven Moon's head and received a glance as if she were saying, "Why do humans think that's what I want them to do?"

Charles, who by now was feeling left out, said, "Chris, can you believe Happy, and of course Raven Moon, are here for the fortune telling gathering?"

"Yes," I said, "a friend of mine, Roisin Stone, told me a little about you when she pointed out your Mini Cooper and camper the other day in the Tides parking lot."

Happy said, "Roisin is quite a fascinating young lady."

"I believe she said you were a tarot card reader. That's interesting."

Happy chuckled. "Yes, an IT support specialist by day, a tarot card reader by night. My friends call me schizophrenic because the two appear contradictory, or I think that's why they call me schizophrenic."

That left me at a loss of words, or words appropriate for his comment, so I said, "Are you going to or from the Bark Park?"

Dude said, "Met Hapster and Raven in the Bark Park. Cool, Raven be named Moon and Pluto be Pluto. They be celestial soulmates."

Charles, again feeling left out, said, "I was walking by and saw the four of them talking and, well, you know how I am about seeing Pluto and then Dude introduced me to his new friends. That's when I learned about Happy and Raven Moon being with the group visiting the island."

"Chris," Happy said, interrupting whatever Charles was going to add. No loss, I suspect. "Aren't you the guy who was near Wesley Thomas when he exited the confines of this earth."

"Unfortunately, I am."

"How'd you hear about it?" Charles said, sounding a lot like the beginning of one of his interrogations.

"Don't recall, for certain. It's the talk of all of us at the conference. If I had to guess, I'd say it was from Alice Clay. She'd another attendee. She was telling everyone she," He air quoted as he said, "'saw' it happen."

Charles said, "I heard she reads tarot cards, like you. That right?"

Happy glanced at the ground, then at Charles. "She claims to be a tarot card reader."

Charles said, "You don't sound certain."

"I'm not one to cast aspersions upon anyone's psychic gifts. Let's say, not everyone who practices the ancient art of tarot card reading is as confident of their ability as perhaps one should be."

That sounded like an aspersion to me, but before I could say anything, Dude said, "She be faker?"

Happy held up his hands like he was warding off Dude's words and said, "I'm not saying that. To be honest, I don't know. Let's simply say, some don't have as much faith in her gifts as they do in others' abilities." Raven Moon started pulling on the leash. Happy looked at his cat and added, "That's Raven's hint to move along. Gentlemen, and you too, Pluto, I've enjoyed our conversation, and Chris, I'm pleased you escaped danger when that townie killed Wesley."

Charles stepped between the tarot card reader and the direction he was planning to walk before saying, "Townie?"

"Yes, someone who lives here."

Charles said, "You think it was a local who shot Wesley?"

"Of course, it was. Everyone in the group knows it," he said and walked into the street and around Charles.

We watched Raven Moon leading Happy toward town.

Dude said, "Raven M be cool. Not sure about Hapster." He looked at his watch, tilted his head in Pluto's direction, and added, "Woe, gotta boogie to store. Pluto's union play and poop break be over."

Since Dude owned the successful surf shop, I suspect he could take as long as he wanted for Pluto's *play and poop break*, regardless which union the canine was a member of. But, as he might say, "Dude be Dude," and Charles and I nodded like we understood his need to "boogie to store."

"Good talking with you, Dude, you too, Pluto," Charles said, hesitated, then added, "Before you go, know any locals who would have it in for the fortune tellers?"

"Be knowin' bunches of townies, most surfers, but not hearin' bad vibes against future predictors."

"That's good," I said.

"Think townie killed visitor?"

"I have no idea but hope not."

Dude took a step toward town, stopped, faced me, and said, "Know what I hope?"

"What?"

"Hope future predictor be target and not be you." Dude pivoted and headed toward town and his surf shop, then raised his arm, and waved bye.

Charles watched him go and said, "Me hopin' Dude be right."

"Poor imitation, but I agree."

Charles smiled. "Me try." His smile faded and he continued, "At tonight's gathering, we need to find out as much as we can about the visitors. Need to learn if they are what they say they are, who are real, who are frauds, who might've killed Wesley Thomas." He scratched his chin, nodded, before adding, "Learn if someone tried to kill you and missed." Another chin scratch later, he said, "Anything else we need to learn?"

"Yes, how do you intend to get those answers?"

"Hell if I know."

20

————

Charles stared at three dogs playing in the Bark Park, seemingly unaware of our conversation or that I was beside him. Should I walk away or wait and see if my friend had anything else to add to the interrogation session he was going to perform at Shannon's gathering? It didn't take long for the answer.

He turned to me with a frown on his face, and said, "I had a dream—"

"Martin Luther King Jr's march on Washington in 1963," I said then smiled as Charles often does after he shares a quote.

He looked at me like I'd poked him with a stick, then said, "If you're going to attempt quotes be sure you know them. It was the 'I have a dream' speech, and not 'I had a dream.'"

It was futile arguing with a man who knows his quotes, so I said, "Was trying to lighten the mood. Tell me about your dream."

Charles leaned back on the wooden fence surrounding the playing canines, faced me, and in a voice barely above a whisper said, "It was so real it woke me up around three this morning. I almost called you."

I smiled and said, "Thanks for not calling."

My smile didn't change the look on my friend's face, who said, "I don't put much stock in dreams, but this one was disturbing."

"Tell me about it."

"You and me were walking to Woody's to get a pizza."

"So?"

"We didn't make it. We were walking up Center Street and talking about my deliveries for Dude, when you grabbed your chest and fell on the sidewalk."

I was about to make another smart aleck remark until I saw Charles's hand shaking. I said, "Heart attack?"

"I wish. You were shot."

"I'm not sure how to take the *I wish* comment, but it was simply a dream. Unless you've become psychic, there's nothing to worry about."

"You're right, but it was real. I even smelled gun power but never heard the shot."

"Is it possible you were thinking about Wesley's murder and subconsciously imagined the shooting?"

"That makes sense, but just in case, we'll skip trips to Woody's unless we drive."

I patted him on the shoulder and said, "Deal. Do you want to come to the house and we can go to Shannon's together?"

"Sure, but first, I need to get to the surf shop to see if Dude needs me to deliver anything."

I wondered why he hadn't asked Dude that twenty minutes ago when the surf shop owner was with us.

We followed the same route Dude and Pluto had taken. Halfway down the block, he stopped, turned to me, and said, "There are documented cases where a parent knew something was going to happen to their child, and they weren't psychics."

I knew the point he was making but didn't want him to obsess over it.

"I'm lucky you're not my parent."

He didn't offer a response before we went our separate ways.

~

AT FIVE-THIRTY I was stationed on my porch sipping a Diet Coke and watching two boat-tailed grackles fighting over part of a hotdog bun beside the drive. Shannon wouldn't be expecting us for another hour but that wouldn't stop Charles from arriving any minute.

The birds squawked then flew off leaving the bun. I looked towards Bert's and saw what had startled them. Charles was peddling his bike up the street and then turned into my drive. He leaned the bike against the side of the cottage. I was surprised to see he was no longer wearing the University of Michigan sweatshirt but had replaced it with a dark-gray polo shirt with a red Razorback hog logo over the left breast.

He joined me on the porch and pointed at my drink before saying, "Got one of those for an endurance cyclist?"

"If I see one, I'll tell him it's in the fridge."

Without defending his cycling habits, he went inside, then returned carrying not only a Coke but a couple of Oreos. He said, "I needed a snack, you ready to go?"

"I'm ready, but we're not expected for an hour. I've never seen that shirt," I added, hoping to distract him from wanting to get to the gathering long before it was to begin.

"It's new to the Fowler collection, representing the University of Arkansas. Did you know they have a course on witchcraft and the occult? It's part of the Honors College curriculum." He stared at the screen door and added, "Shannon might need our help getting ready, so we'd better get there early."

So much for my delaying tactic. "Is that going to be your ice breaker with the guests? Also, I doubt Shannon will need our help. Have a seat, finish your drink, then we'll go."

He took the seat across from me and took a sip. With our activity settled down, both grackles returned and picked up the debate where they'd left off. They were joined by three more of their friends.

Charles took another sip then said, "Plague."

"Huh?"

"That's a plague of grackles. It's like a murder of crows but some people call it a congress but why insult crows by accusing them of being members of Congress? I've also heard that a group of salamanders is called a congress."

"Who could've guessed?" I said while thinking who would've wanted to.

Charles was apparently finished with his *name a group of critters* lesson. He finished his drink and said, "Ready to go?"

We were still early, but instead of arguing, I nodded.

We were halfway down the driveway when he said, "Want to know what a group of baboons is called?"

Okay, he wasn't finished. I said, "Nope."

"I understand. We'd better put our detective caps on before we get to the gathering."

"Charles, tonight we're guests at an event where we'll be the minority. Let's not make Shannon regret inviting us."

"That hurt. I'd never insult friends of my friend. Shannon need not worry about something I might say."

I hoped that was true, and said, "Thank you."

The rest of the walk was in silence until I heard a golf cart speeding up behind us. I fully expected to turn and see a Mercedes-snouted cart with an angry Donald Braxton spewing hate in our direction. I felt relief when instead of Donald, the cart held an elderly couple who smiled and waved as they rode past.

I was still more nervous than I liked to admit, especially after learning about Charles's dream.

21

____

As we approached the Stones' cottage, its meticulously landscaped yard stood out among the others on the street. Colorful flowers, shrubbery, and herbs looking like a painting framed the light-blue house.

I didn't get a chance to study the scene since a booming bark drew my attention to the porch. Lugh, the pony-size Irish Wolfhound, was loping towards us. I stopped and let Charles greet the massive canine. Most people would worry if a hundred-fifty-pound pooch with teeth the size of salad plates bounded toward them, but Charles isn't most people.

Lugh skidded to a halt in front of my friend, stood on his hind legs, draped his front legs over Charles' shoulders, and stared him in the eyes. I patted Lugh on the head as I passed the duo and headed to the porch where Desmond Stone, dressed entirely in black with a studded collar around his neck, was standing with a scowl, his normal look.

"Thought Lugh would scare trespassers away," Desmond said as his face softened into a smile.

"You know there's not a dog alive Charles doesn't want to carry on a conversation with." I glanced at the studded collar and added, "Shouldn't Lugh be the one wearing that?"

"My turn today. He lets me borrow it."

I smiled and said, "How are you?"

"Flying high during the full moons, and you? I see you're still swift enough to avoid a bullet."

I ignored the sensitive topic of a bullet and said, "I wouldn't fly too high if I were you. Brooms aren't what they used to be."

"Told you before, I only use Eureka Mighty Mite vacuum cleaners for getting around." He laughed and walked down the steps to save Lugh from Charles.

I walked part of the way with him and said, "You're not staying for the gathering?"

"I'll be back. Lugh needs his evening walk. Usually the evil fairy takes him, but she's helping Mom."

"Roisin might not take kindly to you calling her an evil fairy."

"True, but as her older brother, I don't care," he said as he turned to Charles and Lugh. "Hey cane dude, can I borrow my dog?"

"Good to see you too, Desmond," Charles said. "Are we the first here?"

"Just the family and Stormy. She came early to help."

Charles gave me an *I told you so* look as he patted Lugh's head before the canine headed for his walk with Desmond. Charles squeezed around me on the stairs and knocked on the door.

Shannon appeared in the doorway with her long red hair tied back. She was wearing an ankle-length blue dress with embroidery down the front.

"Chris, Charles, sorry to keep you waiting. I thought Desmond was here." Shannon looked past us and shook her head.

"He was but left to take Lugh for a stroll."

"I'm sure that's how he put it," she said and chuckled. "Please come in and make yourself at home in the parlor. We're finishing in the kitchen and the others will be here any minute."

In most homes it would be called the living room, but the charm of the Stone's home made me think of parlors of old. The house was distinct with its beautiful garden and the interior décor including antique furniture and large tapestries on the walls. It wouldn't take much to convince someone they were sitting in an Irish cottage a century ago. Today the room had added seating. The coffee table was still in the middle of the room, two wingback chairs and a loveseat were flanked by two additional antique chairs and a handful of not-so-charming metal folding chairs filled out the seating options. The room was crowded but not uncomfortably so, that is unless Lugh wanted to join the party.

Charles chose a folding chair across the room next to the Wiccan altar. I wasn't ready to sit and moved around the room focusing on the tapestries. A knock on the door interrupted my gazing at the amazing woven works of art.

Shannon yelled from the kitchen asking if we could get the door.

Opening the door, I was greeted by a group of fortune tellers. No, I wasn't going to ask Charles what a group of fortune tellers was called. I never would've mistaken the visitors for Jehovah Witnesses.

Spencer Ford, looking like an old college student in his University of South Carolina Gamecocks' hoodie and jeans, was the first through the door.

"You're not Shannon," he said and laughed as we shook hands.

"The hair give it away?"

"Believe it was the lack of an Irish accent," Tori Bran said as she moved beside Spencer in the entry. She was dressed in a peasant blouse and long skirt. Her Norwich Terrier Otter sat at her heels.

"Nice to see you again, Tori, and of course, you too, Otter."

Spencer, Tori, and Otter moved into the parlor and Charles waved to them while pointing at his polo shirt. The guests smiled, not knowing how rare it was to see him in that style shirt. Heidi, looking as if she'd flown out of a vintage Halloween postcard, stepped into the house while looking at me from head to toe, nodded, then joined the others.

Standing a few feet from the door was an attractive African American woman with medium dark complexion, shoulder-length, black hair, and gray eyes. She was several inches shorter than I was but in far better shape. Her attire was exotic and included a dark-red head-scarf almost resembling a crown and a long, black dress with red abstract patterns.

She stepped closer to the entry, extended her hand to shake, and said, "Good afternoon, I'm Chloe Merriweather and you must be Chris."

"Pleased to meet you. How did you know who I was?"

"I have my ways."

"Shannon will be out soon; shall we join the others?"

Chloe walked past me, and I began to close the door when Preacher Burl, shouted, "Brother Chris, I was invited! There's no reason to slam the door in my face."

"Sorry, Preacher, didn't see you. Come in."

He glanced into the parlor, turned to me, and lowered his voice, before saying, "I have been meaning to reach out. How are you doing?"

"Everything is good." Not wanting to get into a discussion about the brush I had with death, I said, "How's your sermon coming?"

"Join us Sunday and you can find out."

Burl knew there was as good of a chance a jellyfish climbing the Alps as my attending his Sunday service, but he never tired of inviting me. Or as he puts it, "Shepherding my flock, even the little lost lambs."

I smiled, put my arm around his waist and escorted him into the parlor, now buzzing with multiple conversations. Everyone was seated and as could be predicted, Charles had Otter on his lap. I took a seat across the room from Charles and beside Tori.

"You'd better not let Lugh see you holding Otter, or he might be jealous," Shannon said as she entered the room carrying a platter of appetizers.

Before Charles could reply, Roisin and Stormy appeared carrying silver trays holding more appetizers. They placed the trays on the coffee table and returned to the kitchen.

Shannon set her tray down and said, "Brightest blessings. I'm glad nearly everyone accepted my invitation. I wasn't sure about what to serve, so I started with one recipe and kept going with so many until my little nymph asked what army was coming over."

Spencer furrowed his brow and said, "Happy and Alice send their regards, but they're unable to attend."

"It all looks lovely and smells so good," Heidi said then leaned closer to the table to get a better look.

Shannon curtsied then said, "We have Irish potato bites, shrimp and cucumber bites, sausage rolls, corned beef and Swiss on melba toast, and scones. The rest, common finger foods."

Preacher Burl said, "Sister Shannon, you have outdone yourself."

Roisin and Stormy returned pushing a vintage tea cart filled with a variety of drinks, napkins, and bone china appetizer plates. The next ten minutes passed with everyone filling their plates and choosing drinks. Shannon then asked if anyone needed anything to which they all responded negatively.

The hostess pulled a high stool into the room and sat with a cup of tea, and said, "Have each of you met all my guests?"

"Sister Shannon, you came in with this wonderful spread before I could meet everyone," Burl said then wiped a couple of crumbs out of his mustache.

"Very well, I will go around the room." She pointed to the lady to her left. "This is my friend Stormy Roserun who along with her husband Darrin own a shop in Charleston. This is a busy time of year at the shop, being close to All Hallows' Eve, so Darrin won't be joining us. Next is Roisin, my clone. The gentleman beside Roisin is Preacher Burl Costello, minister at Folly's First Light Church and a good friend of the family. Next, we have Heidi Strongmire a swamp tour guide from Waycross, Georgia. Spencer Ford has a shop in North Carolina. Then there's Tori Bran, a seamstress also from North Carolina. Which brings me to Charles Fowler, a lover of all canines, a friend, and longtime Folly resident. Otter is the adorable Norwich Terrier in Charles's lap and is in charge of Tori who has allowed Charles to bond with Otter. Next is Chloe Meriweather, a firefighter from Marion, South Carolina. Then we have Chris Landrum, a close family friend, who's also local. Finally, I'm Shannon Stone."

Burl looked around to see if anyone was about to speak. Seeing no indication of that happening, he said, "I would like to say I'm glad to have been invited and get to meet such as diverse group of people." He then reached for another scone.

Spencer stood and said, "Thank you, Shannon, for inviting us to your lovely home so we could get to know each other better in a setting that is more relaxing than the conference room at the hotel. All the conference attendees have talked and some of us are rooming together so it looks like the three who might have some questions are the local gentleman." He then waved his arm in the direction of Burl, Charles, and me.

Charles, to no surprise to Burl or me, was the first to speak. "What's the difference between a psychic and a medium?"

Junior had told me the difference, but I was anxious to hear if it lined up with someone who may practice one or both activities.

"Simply put, psychics predict the future, mediums talk to the dead," Stormy said then looked around the room to see if anyone was going to add anything.

No one did, and Charles said, "So why don't one of you ask Wesley who killed him?"

I glanced around the room trying to predict which witch was going to turn Charles into a dung beetle. No one did and I said, "I think what Charles is wanting to know is, anyone here a medium?"

Heidi, to my knowledge, the only self-proclaimed witch among the visitors, leaned forward to get a better look at Charles then said, "No, he said exactly what he wanted to say. There's only one medium present, but it's not my place to identify the individual."

Stormy said, "I'm a medium who also has psychic abilities. I don't tell that to outsiders because it creates issues. It's better most don't know." She spun the ring on her index finger as she smiled at Roisin.

Roisin returned the smile, then gazed around the room before saying, "Mr. Chris, Mr. Charles, and Preacher Burl will never judge or tell others. They are good, kind souls."

I said, "That's nice of you to say. Are people that judgmental? If they know someone professes to be a psychic or a medium, why would the ability to speak to those no longer among us or see into the future be such an issue?"

Shannon said, "Chris, did you hear what you said? If two years ago someone said they could predict the future and speak to the dead, what would you have thought? You know us, a Wiccan family, so we have eased you into our different beliefs." Shannon patted Stormy's knee and smiled at her.

Charles said, "Preacher, you have your thumb on the pulse of this community. Have you heard negative thoughts about our visitors?"

"Sadly, Brother Charles, I have heard whispers, but they have been simply that."

Tori said, "To answer your question, yes, people are horrible and judgmental. Earlier today on the way here ...." Tori bowed and slowly shook her head. Otter jumped off Charles's lap hopping onto Tori's.

Charles said, "What happened?"

Tori turned to Spencer and touched his arm before saying, "Spencer."

He took the hint and said, "Heidi and I walked from the hotel to the house Stormy and Darrin rented for some of us so we could get the rest of the gang. Heidi noticed a golf cart moving slowly behind us as we walked. When I turned to see the cart, it quickly turned down a side street. It seems we're all a little paranoid since Wesley's murder."

Roisin piped in with, "Just because you are paranoid doesn't mean you're wrong."

Heidi whispered, "You could not be more accurate."

I said, "That wasn't the end, was it?"

"No. We were early, and Chloe and Tori were still getting ready. We were there fifteen minutes or so."

Chloe added, "Once we were ready, the five of us headed this way. Tori, Otter and Spencer were in the lead, and Heidi and I walked behind them." She shook her head then continued, "I heard tires on the gravel behind me and glanced back where I saw this golf cart racing towards us. I couldn't do anything but yell for the rest of the group to get out of its path.

Tori leaned forward and squeezed Otter before saying, "That's when I looked back and saw this guy heading straight for Otter. I jerked his leash and Spencer scooped him up."

"Blessed be," said Shannon.

"Then what happened?" Charles asked, unable to stay out of the conversation.

Spencer said, "The man stopped about thirty feet in front of us and started hurling obscene comments in our direction. I handed Otter to Tori and started toward the man. Was going to adjust his way of thinking if you know what I mean."

Chloe shook her head, looked at Charles, Burl, and then me, and said, "I grabbed Spencer's arm and told him it wasn't worth it. You can't reason with ignorance."

Tori said, "The guy then sped towards us again saying something about knowing where we stayed."

I said, "You should call the police. It'd be good to file a report."

Spencer said, "This is nothing new. It's not usually that bold or vile but when you are different you invite problems. Sadly, it's what happens when we don't hide what we do." He walked over to get a Coke and asked if anyone else needed anything. Roisin said she'd love one, and Spencer graciously handed her a drink.

I pulled out my phone, and said, "I'm friends with Chief LaMond and know she wouldn't like this happening in her town."

"Please don't call," Spencer said. "We want to remain low-key. Attention only brings scorn."

I nodded but didn't say I wouldn't tell the Chief what'd happened.

"Do you think the guy on the golf cart killed Wesley?" Charles asked, having his fill of being quiet.

"Perhaps. I know none of us would've had reas ...." Heidi said as her voice trailed off.

Chloe said, "Were you going to say we had no reason to kill Wesley?"

"Yes," Heidi said. "He might have been a fake and trying too hard to convince us how good he was, but still, that's no reason for any of us to harm him. I mean, there are people attending who are not what they say they are." Heidi sat back and folded her arms.

"Who's the fake?" Charles said, sounding more like a thirteen-year-old rather than the great interrogator he claims to be.

Stormy entered the conversation with, "Darrin and I arranged this gathering, so I'll say what I know and have observed. Wesley was a nice man who didn't deserve to be killed. He was a charming gentleman who knew his crystals and stones." She lowered her head. "But from what I'd heard, some folks had doubts about his ability to predict the future."

Charles said, "That explains why he was walking on the street and didn't know he was going to get shot."

Burl glared at Charles and said, "Brother Charles."

"Sorry, didn't mean it the way it sounded. Don't suppose anyone could've predicted his death."

Tori went to the table holding the food, added a couple of sausage rolls to her plate, then turned toward me, and said, "Anyway, a couple of people who are still at the conference, but not in this room, have me concerned about what they say and do."

I said, "Then don't you think we should call Chief LaMond? You could tell her your suspicions about the other attendees and the man on the golf cart?"

"Not sure what good it would do," Tori said as she rubbed Otter's ear. "We don't know who the guy on the cart was, and it happened more than an hour ago."

Charles said, "Can you describe him?"

Spencer said, "Appeared shorter than me but that's hard to tell since he was seated. Had thinning brown hair. None of that will help much."

I said, "What about the golf cart?"

"Fancy. The front end looked like an imported car."

Charles glanced at me, I gave him a slight nod, then turned to Spencer, and said, "We might know who it was."

Heidi stood and walked around the room and stopped in front of the Stone's Wiccan altar and said, "If you want to report it, we will not stop you, but we would rather not get involved."

Most of the group members nodded, quickly ending any discussion of the incident. Over the next hour, the conversations went from how the 'locals' in the room ended up on Folly and about this year's great weather. Roisin brought up the Halloween party at Cal's, and in her charming style, invited the fortune tellers and told them how much fun they'd have celebrating the holiday in a local bar. Finally, Otter let out a long yawn and whimper.

Tori stood and Otter hopped to his feet. "Oh dear," Tori said, "I didn't realize it was getting so late. I must call it a night."

As if on cue, everyone stood and began saying their goodbyes. Soon, only Chloe and I remained in the parlor. I stayed to see if Shannon needed help cleaning up.

Chloe approached and said, "Can I speak to you?"

"Of course."

She reached into her pocket and pulled out a small leather pouch and handed it to me.

My puzzled look made her smile before she said, "I make gris-gris bags. It's one of my gifts."

"Why give it to me?"

Her smile faded. "Because you need it. It offers protection and I can see you need that in a big way."

"Thank you, but no offense, Chloe, I'm not sure I believe in magical things like gris-gris bags."

"You don't have to be a believer, but would you be willing to carry it with you?" She smiled and added, "Think of it as a good luck charm."

"Like a rabbit's foot?"

"There you go. And best of all, no rabbit was harmed in the making of this. The chamois tan leather contains seven items, and everything is anointed in sandalwood oil."

"Thank you, do I need to do anything with it?"

"Simply carry it with you," she said then headed out the door.

I looked around the room to see if there was anything needing rearranging when Charles stuck his head in the door and said, "You ready to leave or have you joined the Wiccan clan?"

"Was waiting to see if Shannon needed help."

Charles said, "I already asked, and she told me to be gone. Said that's the reason she has kids, or I should say kid since Desmond hasn't made it back."

Shannon met us before we were out the front door, gave each of us a hug, and said, "Glad you could share this evening with us. Be careful heading home; the sky looks angry."

Charles looked toward the sky and said, "How can you tell?"

Shannon laughed and pointed her thumb at her chest and said, "Me great witch."

"Mom," Roisin whined from the garden at the side of the house.

Shannon smiled at her daughter, turned to Charles and me, and said, "Okay, me great Wiccan, but that doesn't have the same ring to it."

Roisin rolled her eyes in the direction of her mother, then said, "Mr. Chris and Mr. Charles, please be careful and if you see Lugh send him home."

Charles said, "What about Desmond?"

"You can keep him."

22

Shannon was right last evening when she said the sky looked angry. A severe thunderstorm visited overnight, but by the time most residents and vacationers were greeting the day, the rain had moved offshore. The temperature was a comfortable seventy degrees so I figured a walk would give me some exercise and sooth my mind cluttered with thoughts of fortune telling, fake or real, and possible residents who may've wanted one, and possibly more of the visitors eliminated.

I grabbed coffee at Bert's, said hi to Lisa, one of the store's long-term employees, then walked a block to Center Street where I was faced with a dilemma I often encountered. Do I turn left and head toward the beach or go right, the direction of the bulk of on-island shopping opportunities? Barb's Books happened to be in that direction. So, right it was.

Barb's normal opening time wasn't for another half hour, but she may have arrived early. Unfortunately, the door was locked, and no interior lights were illuminated, so I continued up the street toward Pewter Hardware, where I knew the door would be open.

I reached for the door when it flew open and Brandon started to step outside when he saw me, took a step back, and said, "Sorry, Chris, didn't see you."

"Where're you off to in such a hurry?"

He glanced back toward the sales counter, before turning to me, and said, "Larry is sending me on a secret mission."

I stepped back into the parking lot and Brandon followed.

"Secret mission?"

Brandon chuckled, stepped closer to me, and said, "You know Donald Braxton?"

"Haven't formally met him but know who he is. Why?"

"He's always in here bitching about us not having something he needs. Thinks we should carry as much as those big box hardware stores. Guy's irritating as hell. Anyway, he called first thing this morning asking if we had Armor All Ultra Shine Tire Foam, something about the wheels on his fancy-dancy golf cart looking dull and he couldn't have that, now could he? I would've told him where to stick his dull wheels, but not my boss. Larry told him of course we had the Armor All product."

"Do you?"

"Nope. That's why I'm on my way to Lowe's to get some, so when *irritating as hell* Donald arrives this afternoon, he'll see how well stocked Pewter is."

"Isn't Larry losing money on that?"

"Yep, but he's tired of telling Donald we don't carry something. Guess that's why he owns the store and I'm a lowly salesperson." He glanced back at the door and added, "Don't tell Larry I told you."

"Your secret's good with me. You going to Cal's Halloween party tomorrow?"

"Hadn't planned to, but Stevie asked me to go with her and Albert. She's making efforts to get closer to me, so I said okay."

"Still have reservations about Albert?"

He sighed. "Yeah. Can't put my finger on it, but there's something there."

"Good luck figuring it out."

"Before I can do that, I've got to figure out where to find tire shine foam at Lowe's."

As I entered the store, Larry was talking with a man I didn't recognize. I didn't want to interrupt their conversation, so I wandered through the narrow aisle to see if there was something I needed for the house. Since I couldn't tell you much, if anything, about car tires other than they were round, and recently learned Larry didn't carry Armor All Ultra Shine Tire Foam, I skipped the automotive section.

I was ready to leave, when Larry said, "Chris, you trying to sneak out without saying hi?"

"Didn't want to interrupt," I said, smiled, and moved closer to the men standing beside the register.

Larry glanced at the stranger standing beside him, then turned to me, "You know Norman Colter?"

"Don't believe we've met," I said and stuck out my hand to shake Norman's hand.

Norman, who was roughly my age, thin, and a little over six feet tall, with collar-length salt and pepper hair, shook my hand, and said, "Pleased to meet you. Aren't you the guy who was with that fake fortune teller when he was killed?"

The way he said *fake fortune teller* reminded me why his name sounded familiar.

"I wasn't with Mr. Thomas but was walking near him when he was shot. I believe you know a friend of mine, William Hansel."

"Delightful gentleman. We're members of Preserve the Past."

"That's what he said. I've known William for thirteen years or so."

"Chris," Larry said, "Norman lives a few houses past here and is one of my regulars. He's a retired investment banker."

"That's interesting, Norman," I said, not meaning it. "Do you know any of the fortune tellers meeting at the Tides?"

He glared at me. "Why?"

"You'd mentioned the one who was shot, so I thought you might know some of them."

"No, and don't want to. I'm no expert on what they do, but there's no doubt they're evil, practicing witchcraft, claiming to predict the future, going around casting spells on people. Don't know whose idea it was for them to invade our peaceful, God-fearing island, but it never should've happened." He turned to Larry. "Don't you agree?"

Larry looked at the entry door like he hoped a customer would come in and give him a chance to change the subject. The door remained closed, and Larry turned back to Norman and me. "Don't think them meeting here is a good idea, but it's a free country."

"My friend, that's not what you said a little while ago."

Larry had already told me his theory about all fortune tellers being frauds and he didn't approve of them being here, so I didn't see any value for the conversation continuing down that path. I did want Norman's take on the killing.

I said, "There's no doubt some folks here are against the group meeting on Folly, but is it bad enough for someone to kill one of them?"

Norman jerked his head in my direction. "You think someone from here killed the fraud?"

"That's a possibility."

"Chris, that's your name, right?"

I nodded.

"One of those damned fakers killed the guy. You can mark my words."

"Why do you think that?"

"Why wouldn't it be? They're all frauds, liars, Devil worshipers." His voice rose and his face turned red. "My friend, they're evil. Killing their own would've been like nothing to one of them. I said it before and I'll say it again, mark my words, one of them did it."

Now I joined Larry and hoped a customer would come through the door. Larry started flipping through a stack of invoices on the counter and I was afraid Norman would have a stroke.

He didn't, so I said, "Anyway, I'm certain the police will get it sorted out." Now to change the subject before Norman passes out, I turned to Larry and said, "You and Cindy going to the Ghouls and Gals party tomorrow in Charleston?"

Larry smiled and said, "You bet. Where else can Frankenstein's monster hook up with a zombie and party the night away?"

"If I don't see you before then, have a fun Halloween. Guys, I'd better be going. Norman, it was good meeting you." I nodded then took a few quick steps to the door.

Before I was out of the store, I heard Norman say something to Larry about being sorry he got so riled.

Norman was convinced one of the fortune tellers was responsible for Wesley Thomas's death.

I was convinced Norman would be on the top of my suspect list.

23

I retraced my route after leaving the hardware store, hoping that Barb's Books was open so I could invite its owner to Cal's party and see if Stevie or Albert had been back. Before I reached Center Street, the blare of a siren disturbed the quite morning. I turned expecting to see Cindy laughing for startling me, but instead Officer Trula Bishop was behind the wheel of the patrol car. She was smiling.

I approached the passenger side window and said, "Good morning, Officer Bishop."

"Morning, Mr. Chris. I couldn't help myself. The Chief is always telling me how much fun it is harassing you."

I leaned close to the window and gave her my sternest look and said, "Was it fun?"

"More than I thought it'd be, but I was always taught to respect my elders so it's a one-time thing unless you go breaking the law," she said then laughed brightening the sour mood I'd been carrying since the conversation with Norman.

"Speaking of the chief jokester, I haven't seen her lately?"

"It seems Detective Adair keeps her going back and forth to Charleston."

"I'm surprised she's so accommodating."

"I believe her exact words were, 'Anything to keep that jerk off the island.' Whoops, I didn't say that did I?"

I smiled and said, "Didn't hear a thing, but if I had, it sounded like her. Why does Adair need her over there? Does it have to do with Wesley's murder?"

"How about everything to do with it? As usual, he's aggravated dealing with us 'Mayberry' cops." She'd air quoted *Mayberry* with a grimace on her face.

"His loss. Any new leads?"

"Seems with your track record, I should be asking you."

"Don't know why you think I'd know anything."

Trula lifted her right-hand palm facing me, "I know you, Mr. Chris. Please don't go getting yourself shot or worse."

"Worse than shot?"

The officer shook her head and said, "I see why the chief calls you a pain in her butt."

I smiled.

She returned my smile and said, "You going to Cal's party tomorrow?"

"Yes, are you?"

"Thinking about it. I'm scheduled off for a change, so I might as well have fun."

"Bring your husband."

"Mr. Chris, didn't you hear me say I wanted to have fun?"

"Got it. I hope to see you there."

Trula pulled back into the line of traffic and turned right on Center Street as I continued to Barb's Books. This time, the store was open and had drawn a crowd. I added myself to that number. Barb looked up from the customer she was helping and nodded toward her office. I took the hint, and headed to the office and fixed a cup of coffee, sat in one of the chairs near the desk, and waited for the proprietor to have a free moment.

I was halfway through the cup when she finally managed to break away from the browsing customers, gave me a kiss on the cheek, then reached for her empty mug on the desk.

Instead of coffee, she filled it with hot tea from her Keurig machine.

She took a sip and said, "Impressive."

"Me?"

"Ha, ha. I was talking about the number of people buying books." She glanced into the store to see if anyone needed help, then said, "How are you? I hope you're keeping out of trouble."

"I'm doing better than I was earlier in the week, Charles and I went over to Shannon's house last night. She was hosting a gathering for some of the fortune tellers and thought we would enjoy meeting them."

"Please tell me your buddy didn't receive a horrible curse for pestering the visitors and now we have to worry about getting warts from Toad Charles."

"No curse, no toad."

"Good, did you learn anything new about the murder of their colleague?"

"Not really, other than the group seems convinced a local was responsible."

"Why?"

"They claim none of them would've killed him, even if some of the participants had issues with Wesley."

"What kind of issues?"

"Apparently, they—"

"Hold that thought," she said and went to the cash register to check out a couple who appeared from my vantage point to be buying an armload of books. Barb stays busy, unlike when my photo gallery occupied the same space.

She returned with a smile and said, "Where were we?"

"How many books did they get?"

"A dozen."

"Seems if you're taking a vacation at the beach, you'd try to enjoy the scenery and what the venue has to offer rather than reading."

Barb chuckled. "I thought about telling them that, but decided I'd prefer the sale."

"That's the reason you're successful."

Barb reached around and patted herself on her back, or, more accurately, on her shoulder. She then sat in her ergonomic desk chair, reaching for her tea, and frowned. Her previous life as an attorney was written on her face as she waited for me to answer the question she had asked five minutes ago.

"A couple of them said Wesley was not all he professed to be. Said his fortune telling gifts were dubious but agreed it wouldn't have been a reason to kill him."

"It would've taken more than being a fake for me to kill someone."

"That's good to know."

"However, the man I'm dating failing to ask me to the biggest Halloween party on the island is another issue."

"That's the reason for my visit. Would you accompany me to Cal's party?"

"You don't give a girl much notice but thank you for the invitation."

"That mean yes?"

She nodded and said, "I'll meet you there. It'll be an early evening for me since I need to be in Columbia Monday morning."

"What's in Columbia?"

"Books Be Gone, a large used bookstore. I received an email from them yesterday announcing they're going out of business and are giving mom and pop stores the opportunity to purchase the rest of their inventory at ridiculously low prices."

"The name of the store was foretelling, wasn't it? Do you need a pop to help mom carry books?"

"Thanks, but I'm making a day of it and meeting college friends who moved there last year to work in state government."

"Hmm ...."

"Don't hmm me, Mr. Landrum, unless you'd like to sit around listening to three women converse about old times."

I smiled and said, "No thanks. I have enough old-time conversing with Charles. Speaking of Charles, since he's supposed to be *investigating* Stevie and Albert, have either of them been in since we talked about them?"

"Stevie was in yesterday. Said she was waiting for Albert so they could walk the beach. He was drooling over a surfboard at the surf shop."

"She mention anything bothering either of them?"

"Not to me, but she appeared distracted, wouldn't call it worrying, but she wasn't as friendly as she'd been on previous visits."

"She say when they were leaving?"

"No."

"At least I'll be able to report that to Detective Charles."

The bell over the front door jangled and a new round of customers walked in talking loud enough it made me think of being at a rock concert instead of a bookstore. Barb walked around the desk on her way to the salesroom, kissed me, before greeting the rowdy crowd. I left through the back door.

The morning's near-perfect weather had disappeared, and it looked as if a close relative of last night's storms was going to make an appearance, or to quote a Wiccan I know, "The sky looks angry."

Fortunately, the storm held off until I reached my driveway. I jogged the rest of the way to my porch before thunder and torrents of rain filled the air.

24

———

I rolled out of bed well before dawn Sunday morning, the Sunday known this year as Halloween. I dressed in my typical retirement attire of khakis, a polo shirt, and loafers. Instead of disturbing my aging Mr. Coffee machine, I headed to Bert's for coffee and a Danish. The rain had again moved elsewhere after drenching the island for most of the night. The only sound I heard on the way to the store came from an early-morning motorcyclist on Center Street. Most of the island was asleep.

As I stepped into the store, I was greeted by Lisa, who wasn't wearing her normal welcoming smile but a frown and a tall witch hat as she was sweeping in front of the counter and mumbling to herself.

I hoped to cheer her with my best smile and said, "Aren't you supposed to be riding the broom, not cleaning with it?"

I clearly failed when she said, "It's multifunctional. Can also whack unruly, smart aleck customers."

"Rough morning?"

"You could say that. I try to get along with everyone, but the witch in me comes out when people are rude simply to be rude. Guy came in, dropped a four-pound bag of sugar, and of course it split open."

"Big mess?"

"Duh. Most folks would apologize, accidents happen. However, this guy not only didn't apologize, he told me to get him another bag off the shelf. I suggested it would be quicker if he got it while I finished ringing up his items."

"How'd he take that?"

"Not well. He slammed his hands on the counter and glared at me."

"What happened?"

"It was going nowhere, so I rang up his items then grabbed him another bag of sugar. He paid but continued glaring."

"Sorry."

"As you can imagine, I've seen it all in here but what he said as he left was unnerving."

"What'd he say?"

"I told him to have a nice day as I handed him his change. He didn't move until Officer New walked in, then the guy grabbed the bags. Before he left, he told me I was lucky and mumbled something about me being evil."

"Did you tell Officer New?"

"No, some people are jerks, plain and simple. Suppose there's no law against that."

"True. Do you know who he was?"

"Seen him in here, but don't know his name and don't want to. He's creepy." She smiled and added, "I'm taking that as my trick for the day, everything else will be treats. Happy Halloween, Chris." She tipped her witch hat.

"Thanks, you too," I said and drew a cup of coffee from the urn near the counter, then grabbed two cheese Danishes to satisfy two of my Halloween meals. By the time I returned to the counter, Lisa had finished cleaning sugar off the floor.

She rang me up with the smile I was more accustomed to and said, "Don't let any low flying witches steal your food."

"Don't think that'll be a problem. It's the gulls I need to watch out for."

Instead of heading for the Pier to enjoy the ocean view or walking up Center Street to see if anyone else was out, I headed home. The chilly air was more than I wanted to deal with this early in the morning. I went into the kitchen, plopped down on one of the underused kitchen chairs, and ate breakfast. After killing an hour thinking about what Lisa had said about the rude customer and his comment about her being evil, whatever that'd meant, I thought back to how a handful of locals had such strong opinions about the visiting fortune tellers, and wondered if Lisa's customer was among that group or simply someone having a bad morning.

After not concluding anything, I decided to either clean the house or head to the Pier and enjoy the rest of the morning. If all decisions were that easy to make. I grabbed a jacket and headed to the Pier. The thousand-plus-foot-long structure was nearly deserted with only a few anglers either hoping for a fresh meal or avoiding a honey-do list at home. I walked to the far end and sat on the bench to savor nature around me. Gulls flew along the area searching for breakfast, while shore birds darted in and out of the waves pushing against the beach.

Near the end of the Pier, a group of dolphins played in the waves. If Charles had been here, he'd be telling me what a group of dolphins was called, but I'll somehow handle not knowing and enjoy the solitude.

I was jolted back to reality when one of the fishermen dropped his tackle box. It sounded like a gunshot. The image of Wesley smiling at me seconds before the shots that ended his life popped into my consciousness, bothering me more than I would admit. I tried to recall more of the incident. It'd been a week, so I hoped more of the details would be clearer now that the elevated adrenaline was gone. The killer's car remained a phantom as was the shooter, not unlike what Alice Clay had told Chief LaMond the day of the shooting. Not only did I not get a better view of the shooter or the vehicle, but I was no closer to learning the identity of the intended target.

The unmistakable sound of Preacher Burl Costello singing "Rock of Ages" arose from the beach east of the Pier. I saw the preacher leading his flock in First Light's preferred beach location for its Sunday services. Roughly thirty attendees were singing along with him but from the lack of volume, I'd guess most were lip-synching. I watched until the hymn finished, looked around at the breathtaking views and thought there's no better place to worship, then headed home.

My exciting afternoon consisted of housecleaning and a nap. Both took longer than I had anticipated when I realized it was time to head to Cal's. With no rain in the forecast, I left my car at home and walked to the party, surprised by how many houses had jack-o'-lanterns lighting the porches. As I approached the venue, I realized Cal and Junior weren't exaggerating the quantity of decorations for the event. A life-size horse skeleton and what was dressed to be a cowboy skeleton were guarding the entry. The cowboy leaned against a plastic hitching post where his bony equine was secured.

"Oh, to be that thin again, Brother Chris."

I turned to Preacher Burl standing a couple of feet behind me and wearing a black sweater with a glow-in-the-dark ghost on the front, and said, "Preacher, you startled me. I didn't hear you walk up."

"Sorry, Brother Chris. I forgot you might be jumpy after your near-death experience."

I smiled and changed the subject with, "Saw you leading your flock this morning."

"How was my sermon?"

"I'm certain it was as captivating as always. I was only around for the opening hymn."

"Every little step toward salvation counts."

Another subject to change. "I'm surprised you don't have a young lady on your arm tonight."

"Little Sister Roisin?"

"Thought you might bring her."

"I asked but Shannon, Roisin and Lugh are going to Charleston tonight to be with the Roseruns."

"Where's Desmond lurching about?"

"I got the impression he might stop by the party. Where's your date?"

"Barb's going to meet me. She'll be leaving early. Has big plans tomorrow."

"Yes, but I'm here now." Barb's voice pierced the quiet night air, causing both Burl and me to jump.

"You two are jumpy tonight, but I suppose that comes with the holiday." Barb walked beside me and kissed my cheek. Her form-fitting red dress appeared to glimmer in the light over the door and her long, black cardigan sweater added to the Halloween vibe.

"Sister Barb," Burl said, "you look lovely."

She curtsied and said, "Thank you, Burl, and I must say, what an interesting sweater."

"It is that. One of the female Hope House residents gave it to me as a Halloween treat."

"Sounds like someone's taken a fancy to you, Preacher," I said, laughed, put my arm around Barb, and walked to the entrance, followed by Preacher Burl.

If the horse and cowboy duo weren't spooky enough, there was an arch around the doorframe made from tree branches wound together forming an eerie sight dotted with flickering faux black candles. Above the arch, a weathered sign read *Creepy Cal's*.

Despite being impressed with the creativity exhibited and the overwhelming quantity of decorations Cal and Junior had put into the party, Halloween was still my least favorite holiday. Least favorite by a long shot.

The decorations in front of Cal's were borderline over-the-top, but paled in comparison to what greeted us inside. The first thing that caught my attention was a life-size animated Frankenstein's monster dominating the corner to the left of the door. Bolts of lightning were projected on the wall behind the monster with the rumble of thunder coming from a speaker near the ceiling. The second thing that caught my attention was a slightly less scary Charles behind the bar serving drinks.

Barb didn't appear as shocked as I was seeing my friend playing bartender. She looked across the room and saw a group of the local business owners, and said, "I need to speak with Eli and the others. Mind getting me a glass of red wine?"

"Of course, even Charles couldn't screw that up," or so I hoped.

I watched her weave through the crowd of a few people in costume, but most wore casual beach wear. I made my way to the bar when Charles saw me and held a finger up, indicating he'd be over.

A basketball-size animated crystal ball was sitting on each end of the bar adding to the spooky décor. The ball closest to me had fog and lights circulating inside the sphere. I didn't stare at it long enough to see what else might appear. As I waited for Charles to work his way over, I noticed the room was filled with smiling, laughing attendees. I recognized half of the group, and while I still wasn't a fan of the holiday, it was great seeing so many people having an enjoyable time.

Cal's vintage Wurlitzer jukebox, taking up a corner of the raised bandstand and normally stocked with classic country music, now appeared to be playing everything to do with spooky topics. Sheb Wooley's "The Purple People Eater," a novelty song popular in the late 1950s, could be heard over the laughter and chatter of the partygoers.

I looked down and shook my head while thinking Halloween is such a strange time. Staring up at me were two dogs. Dude's Pluto was wearing his rhinestone collar and a tiny shirt with a glow in the dark pumpkin. Next to him, Tori Bran's constant companion Otter was wearing a black vest with bat wings. I bent down to pet both dogs, then turned to see the two proud owners standing nearby.

"Great to see you both," I said, "I see the pups are dressed for trick-or-treating."

"No be trick-or-treatin'," said Dude. "Be Folly no-no. Pluto be showing off new duds."

Dude, not showing off any new attire, was wearing his usual tie-dye shirt with a peace sign on the front.

"Otter wears the same costume every year," Tori said and laughed. She tapped her leg and Otter ran back to his mistress who was dressed in a peasant skirt and embroidered blouse.

Dude looked at the jukebox, turned to me, and said, "Christer, ever see purple people?"

Dude was no stranger to asking odd questions, but I wasn't prepared for that one.

Before I could stumble through an answer, my best friend approached with Barb and my drinks, and said, "The creature is purple. Chris, take your drinks."

Dude said, "Be wrong trivia man. Creature be eatin' purple peeps."

Tori looked at me like I could run interference through this strange conversation. I smiled, shook my head, grabbed the drinks from Charles, and headed across the room to a table Barb had managed to seize. I left Tori to either referee or grab Otter and run for her sanity.

Barb took her drink and said, "Who's the lady with Dude?"

"Tori Bran and Otter, the canine standing next to Pluto. Tori's one of the fortune tellers and a seamstress from North Carolina."

"Interesting," she said and took a sip.

Cal delivered drinks to a group at the table beside ours, came over, tipped his trademark Stetson in our direction, and said, "Evening, Pard, and Miss Barb."

Barb smiled as she patted the septuagenarian's arm, and said, "Cal, the decorations are amazing."

"Finer than wine." Cal said, then spun and pointed to the back of his white rhinestone fringed jacket, where a huge orange rhinestone pumpkin now occupied the previously empty space.

"That's a new look," I said, probably not as enthusiastically as he'd hoped.

"You're telling me. Junior made it, was quite a surprise. Sticks on with VELCRO so I can take it off the rest of the year. I'll always be well dressed for this holiday."

"Yes, you will," I said and looked around before adding, "Where is Junior, and what blackmail material did Charles have on you to be working the bar?"

Cal laughed. "Your bud came in an hour ago and told me I looked too fancy for slinging beer. He chased me out. To be honest, he didn't have to strong arm me. His generosity lets me work the room and even dance a jig or two. Junior's busy in the kitchen." Cal looked towards the bar where Charles was waving to him. "Guess he's through playing bartender." He again tipped his Stetson in our direction then went to replace Charles.

As Cal walked away, I noticed two people sitting at the bar I hadn't noticed earlier. Norman Colter was closest to the kitchen and a couple of barstools past him was Donald Braxton, Mr. Mercedes Golf Cart.

Charles arrived at the table carrying a glass filled with a red liquid and said, "Evening, Barb, I see you're still hanging around with this geezer."

"I take pity on dapper looking older gentlemen," Barb said as she pointed to the glass in Charles's hand. "What's that?"

"That, dear bookstore owner, is a Bloody Bloody Mary."

"I'm almost afraid to ask, what's the extra bloody in it?"

"Makes it sounds more Halloweenish. Instead of regular tomato juice it's Spicy Hot V8 Juice."

"Okay," she said with little enthusiasm. "I'll let you two talk."

Bard stopped at the jukebox on her way to the restroom.

Charles glanced at the bar and said, "Did you see who was at the bar?"

"Norman Colter and Donald Braxton. How'd I do?"

"Shows you don't need glasses. Norman's been here longer than me." Charles looked at his naked wrist. "That's been over an hour."

"Has he said anything to you or any comments from Donald?"

"Norman asked for another beer, Donald keeps staring at me. He ordered a beer from Junior when he brought him a burger. Did Dude or Tori say anything interesting?"

"Neither of them mentioned who shot Wesley if that's what you're asking."

"Too bad. Let's go talk to Donald and Norman."

"What, and ask if they're both card-carrying members of the anti-fortune teller group? I spoke to Norman yesterday. It was an unpleasant conversation."

"That's why you need me. I can use my smooth, cool questioning skills."

"Smooth as a porcupine."

"Absolutely, you go with the quills, I avoid those sticky things. Detecting 101." Charles put his drink on the table and started toward Donald.

Before he reached the bar, Spencer Ford, Heidi Strongmire, and Alice Clay walked through the door with "Black Magic Woman" booming from the jukebox. I chuckled wondering if the fortune tellers waited outside for the appropriate music to be playing for their grand entrance.

Barb returned to our table, looked at me trying to stifle a laugh and said, "What'd I miss?"

"Not much other than a self-proclaimed witch and two fortune tellers entered the bar accompanied by 'Black Magic Woman' on the jukebox."

"My favorite Santana song."

"You're the reason its playing, not any paranormal timing?"

"Unless they influenced me to pick the song for when they walked in."

The expression on Barb's face was serious, which made me laugh louder.

I was pleased to see the visitors to the island approach. It had entered my mind what could've happened if they and the two anti-visitors had encountered each other at the bar.

Spencer reached to shake my hand and said, "Charles said we would have a better time at your table. With your cheery faces I can see why."

We shook and I turned to my date, "Barb, I'd like you to meet Spencer, Heidi and Alice."

She stood, smiled, and said, "Nice to meet you." She shook Spencer's hand and nodded to the ladies.

"Chris," Spencer said, "you've been keeping the loveliest local away from your visitors."

"No such thing," Charles said as he set four bottles of beer on the table. "Barb and I share Chris's time. You saw him on my day."

The visitors laughed or, in Heidi's case, smirked.

I said, "Before I relinquish my time to Charles, how much longer is the conference lasting?"

"Ended yesterday, but six of us decided to stay for the party," Heidi said, as she waved her arm around the room.

Spencer said, "Yesterday, Stormy told everyone she and Darrin rented the house for another week and if any of us wanted to stay we wouldn't be charged for a room." He nodded at Tori who was walking over carrying her canine.

"That's a great idea," Barb said, "Everyone can enjoy the area and not be stuck in meetings."

"Yesterday afternoon when we were packing up our tables, several people said they wanted to stay longer to see if we can use our gifts to answer who killed Wesley." Alice said shuffling a deck of cards as she spoke.

The other fortune tellers turned away from her, and Spencer said, "Barb, allow me to introduce Tori Bran and her constant companion Otter." Spencer put his arm around Tori's shoulder as she stepped closer to Barb.

"Nice to meet you," Tori said. "Dude was telling me about his rad sister and the Christer having been catching the same rays for years."

Tori's attempt at Dude speak must've been too much for Otter. He twisted out of her arms and moved close to Spencer's leg.

Barb smiled and said, "It's been nice meeting all of you, but I really must call it a night. I have to get up early and drive to Columbia in the morning."

"You sure we're not chasing you off?" Heidi said with hesitancy in her voice.

"Absolutely not. I'd prefer to stay but I'm afraid I can't change my plans."

"Be safe on your travels." Heidi said as she reached over and patted Barb's hand.

Tori shook Barb's hand, and said, "Blessed be on your journey."

"Watch out for large green trucks," Alice said then looked at me.

Spencer leaned out of Alice's line of sight and rolled his eyes.

"I'll walk you out," I said and pulled her chair back so she could get out.

As I led Barb to the exit, I was amazed how many people were dancing to some strange song, most likely titled "This is Halloween" since the phrase was repeated over and over. We left the music inside and moved to the sane, nearly silent exterior of the building. Sane, that is, considering the horse and rider skeletons on the sidewalk. Barb leaned over and gave me a kiss.

I put my arms around her and pulled her close as I said, "I'll walk you home."

"Not necessary. I won't suffer Charles's wrath for stealing you away."

"You sure? I could come back later."

"We both know you'd go home after you leave my condo. Besides, you haven't had one of Junior's burgers or heard Cal sing his world-famous rendition of 'Monster Mash.'" She kissed me again and added, "I'll text you when I get home. That is, unless a big green truck gets me first."

"That was weird."

"From what you've shared, weird is her forte."

I watched Barb walk down the street and disappear around the corner, before heading back into Cal's when I heard my name called from beside the building.

"You're not leaving, are you?" Trula Bishop said as she stepped out of the shadows. Her bright blue sweater and black skirt was a dramatic change from her police uniform.

"Happy Halloween, Trula. I see you're taking advantage of a night off by mingling with the common folk."

"Nothing common about residents of Folly Beach."

"Where's your husband?"

"He has a headache, or so he claims. He's not a fan of parties."

"Smart man. But that's good, it allows me to escort you into the scariest bar in town."

As we walked under the menacing arch, Trula whistled and mumbled something under her breath, but I couldn't make out what.

She stopped inside the doorway to survey the room before saying, "Never seen so much Halloween in one place in my life. Cal must've spent a fortune on it."

"It was Junior, but I agree. Want something from the bar?"

"Thanks, but I don't want to cramp your style by hanging out with a cop."

"I have no style to cramp."

"Then I'll take any beer they have."

She remained near the entry as I went to the bar where Cal handed me a beer and glass of wine. I asked how he knew what Officer Bishop wanted.

"I'm learning to be a psychic from our visitors."

I tilted my head and stared at Cal.

He smiled and said, "And, that's what she orders whenever she's in."

I also ordered two hamburgers when Junior had a chance. There was no reason to wait until Charles had a starving puppy dog face and hints about being hungry.

Trula was talking with Desmond Stone when I handed her the beer. For some reason, the teenager's face looked more respectful than his usual glare.

"Desmond," I said, "Preacher Burl said you might be here."

Trula said, "I was telling Mr. Stone how he's underage and if I see him with anything resembling an alcoholic drink—"

"She'd burn me at the stake," Desmond said and smirked.

Trula patted him on the back and said, "Nope, I said drawn and quartered. Mr. Chris, thank you for the beer, now I'll leave you two gentlemen."

"She's tough but funny." Desmond said as he gave Trula a salute as she walked away. "What else did the preacher tell you?"

"Told me the rest of your family was going to Charleston to spend the evening with the Roseruns."

"Preacher man knows all, or Roisin blabbed."

"Could be. Have you eaten? I ordered a couple of burgers for Charles and me if you want to join us?"

"I ate before coming. I'll get a beer, listen to the music, and watch old mummies dance."

"Beer?"

"Ok, root beer." He sighed. "Old people have no sense of humor."

Before I responded, he leaned in and gave me a half hug, then headed to Cal at the bar. Cal said something to him then pointed to the small, elevated stage, Desmond headed in that direction. Junior walked out of the kitchen with two plates, saw me standing near the door and made his way over.

"Here're your burgers, the last of the night."

"Thanks. Run out of meat?"

"Nearly, but no, Dad and I decided we'd keep the kitchen open the first part of the party then just a veggie tray or two until closing."

"That gives you time to enjoy your eerie creations."

"That's the plan. Want me to take these over to your table?"

"I'm good, but thanks."

Halfway across the room I was wishing I'd taken Junior up on his offer. With his height and wide girth, he could've easily parted the crowd dancing to Michael Jackson's "Thriller," with none other than Desmond Stone leading the dancers.

I managed to make it to the table and set Charles's burger in front of him and said, "Figured you could use some food, for your interrogation."

"Seriously?"

"Yes, no reason we shouldn't speak to Donald or Norman, but let's eat first."

26

We were almost done with our burgers when Charles pointed to the door where three new arrivals were standing. At first, I didn't recognize them.

"There's Dani," Charles said pointing to the lady standing apart from the other two, "Let's see if she goes and talks to Norman or Donald."

"You know anyone else in that group?"

"Don't know. It's too dark to tell."

Dani moved farther into the room where I could see her better. Her petite stature looked even smaller since she was dressed in black from head to toe. She looked around the bar with her arms crossed and a sour expression. Her eyes appeared to settle on Alice and Tori who were selecting songs on the jukebox. Instead of going to them, Dani's attention was drawn to the folks sitting at the bar. I lost sight of her when the other two people who'd entered around the same time as Dani, blocked my view.

I then recognized the others. Chloe Meriweather was wearing a floor-length yellow, and black dress. Happy Bishop was dressed in a green T-shirt, jeans, and bright neon-green tennis shoes. He turned to look at Frankenstein's monster and I noticed he was also wearing a multicolored backpack. Chloe and Happy were far from a subtle couple.

Chloe waved when she spotted Charles and me. She got Happy's attention and headed our direction. Before they got to the table, Spencer joined them.

Chloe said, "Evening, friends."

Before we could acknowledge the recent arrivals, Happy looked around as if he had never been in a crowded room, and said, "Nice to see such a turnout for such a small town. Do you know everyone here?"

I said, "About half. Charles knows nearly everyone."

Charles smiled, then nodded at Happy's backpack, and said, "What's with the backpack?"

"It's not only a backpack, it's Raven Moon's stealth mode of transportation." He then turned and we saw Raven Moon's head sticking out the top of the colorful carrier.

Charles walked around the table and rubbed the large cat's chin, mumbled something in cat speak, then said, "Nice but I thought she traveled on a leash."

"Most of the time she does. Figured this being such a dog-friendly town, there might be a few barkers in here that might not feel kindly to a cat in their midst."

"Wise decision," I said then added, "Spencer told us the house where some of you have been staying will be available for the next week. Are either of you staying?"

Chloe said, "I'd love to, but duty calls. I must be at the firehouse on Tuesday. Will be leaving tomorrow."

Charles turned to Happy. "You and Raven Moon staying, or need to get back to work?"

"I can do my job from anywhere with an Internet connection. Might as well stay and hang around with some of the people I've met at the conference."

"Sounds like a plan," Charles said. "Chris and I were getting ready to speak to some friends at the bar, so if you want to claim the table, it's yours. As you can see, tables are in short supply."

"Thanks," Chloe said. "Happy, why don't you stay here and guard the table while I see if the others want to join us?"

He smiled and echoed Charles's comment with, "Sounds like a plan."

Chloe then headed to the stage to talk to the three fortune tellers gathered around the jukebox.

Before Charles and I made it to the bar, Norman approached and said, "Strange seeing you here. I've been here for years and have never run into you. Now it's twice in as many days." Norman put his hands on his hips and stared at me as if I'd committed some sort of sin by allowing him to see me twice.

Charles moved beside me and said, "It's Norman, isn't it? Larry has spoken highly of you. I'm Charles Fowler."

His glare lessened and he said, "Nice meeting you." He pivoted and walked away without another word.

Charles turned to me and said, "You weren't lying when you said he was a pleasant chap."

"Pleasant as a rattlesnake."

"Let's see if we have better luck with Donald."

Fortunately, there was a vacant spot at the bar next to Donald's barstool. Charles ordered a beer from Cal, before turning toward Donald.

Charles said, "Excuse me, don't I know you?"

Donald looked at Charles and then past him at me. "Wouldn't think so."

"Yes, I do. Chris, this is the fellow yelling at us from his golf cart the other day."

The look on Donald's face made me wish we'd stayed at the table.

Instead of pulling out a handgun and shooting Charles and me, Donald said, "I'm Donald Braxton. You're Charles something or other, and I don't know who you are."

I smiled and said, "Chris Landrum."

"Why are you two bothering me when you're friends with the Satanists? Go back over there and leave us good citizens alone."

I said, "You have strong feelings towards the group of fortune tellers, but have you ever talked to them?"

"I don't need to talk to the Devil to know he's real. If you don't mind, I'd like to be left alone." He looked at his empty bottle and motioned to Cal for another.

"Sorry to disturb you. Have a good evening," I said and patted Charles on the shoulder as I turned toward the table.

Charles walked behind the bar and grabbed several bottles of beer and told Cal to put them on my tab. We then headed to the table of fortune tellers.

I had a feeling someone was coming up behind me. Worried it may be Norman or Donald, I quickly spun and came face to face with Desmond.

"Wanted to wish you a Happy All Hallows' Eve. I'm getting ready to fly around on this moonless night after I hear my jam."

"Your jam?"

"Took a long time to request it. You old folks have been hogging the music machine. You ready for 'Sympathy for the Devil' by my boys, the Rolling Stones?"

"Isn't that before your time?"

"Good music is good music, even if it was created in the dark ages." He smiled and added, "Watch out for crazy black cats or witches on your way home."

His words, about black cats and witches and not songs written in my younger days, were bouncing around my head as I continued towards a table occupied by a black cat, a witch, and who knows what else. Charles had cleared the empty bottles and glasses and had taken them behind the bar, then continued to clear the empties off the bar. I joined the fortune tellers crammed around the small table on the far side of the room.

Once I was settled, Spencer switched places with Tori and was standing next to me. He said, "That man you were talking to at the bar looks like the guy harassing us Friday night. I'm going to speak to him about his problems."

"That is the man you're talking about, but nothing good will come from confronting him, especially now that he's full of liquid courage. I understand your desire to set things right but at times doing nothing is the best option."

"I suppose, but how will he learn his actions are unacceptable?" He shook his head.

Heidi stared at the beer bottle. Her hands shook and she said, "If he has an issue with us doing what we do, what about this party? Halloween's not exactly a Christian holiday." She gazed around the room and continued, "Look at the décor. Nothing screams 'peace be with you.' One of these days, he'll learn not to cross certain people."

Tori said, "Chris is right. We should let it go. We're better than that."

Alice, who had been standing quietly a few feet away from the table said, "Not all of us," before turning and walked towards the fortune telling machine.

Happy mumbled something and followed Alice.

From the jukebox, Bobby Bare was singing about the famous Voodoo queen Marie Laveau and silence fell over the table. Charles waved to me from the bar. I assumed he didn't need me to serve as bartender, so I headed his way.

He sighed and said, "Did you see who walked in?"

"From the way you're acting, it must've been Ed McMahon carrying a Publisher's Clearing House check with your name on it."

"Not funny, besides we lost Ed more than a decade ago."

"Maybe it's Ed's ghost. After all, it is Halloween."

"Still not funny."

"Okay, Charles, who walked in?"

"Albert, as in Stevie and Albert, but he's by himself."

"Where is he?"

"Standing next to Frankenstein."

"Frankenstein's monster."

"Chris, so help me I'll—"

"Since you're working, I'll greet him."

I approached and he said, "Chris, right?"

"Yes. It's good seeing you made it. Where's Stevie?"

"She's with her dad. They'll be here in a few minutes."

"Let me buy you a drink."

"Thanks, but there's no need."

"I insist."

He followed me to the bar where Charles was waiting.

"What's your poison?" Charles said as if he'd spent the last thirty years behind a bar.

"Coke would be great."

"Need rum in it?"

"No thanks."

Charles turned and got a glass and was filling it when Cal appeared, took the glass, and shooed Charles out from behind the bar. Cal set the drink in front of Albert, smiled, and welcomed him to the party. Charles and I took the stool on either side of Albert.

Albert said, "It's nice walking into a bar in a city I'm visiting and see a couple of guys I know. Small town USA is nice. Ain't much like Atlanta. Stevie would love to move here, wants to be close to her dad and the beach."

As if Albert planned it, Brandon and Stevie were next through the door.

Charles waved them over and said, "Welcome to the party."

Brandon said, "Thanks, didn't realize you were the welcoming committee."

"We've been keeping Albert company."

Albert stood and motioned for Stevie to take his place on the barstool.

"Brandon, Stevie, let me buy your first round." Charles said and squeezed up to the bar.

Cal approached the newcomers, tipped his Stetson at them, and said, "What'll tickle your whistle?"

Stevie laughed and pointed to Albert's drink, "One of what he's having."

Brandon said, "I'll have a Bud, thanks."

Charles said, "Put that on my tab, Cal."

Cal glanced at me, and I nodded. He knew who'd be paying

Charles's tab. After a brief conversation with the new arrivals, I wanted Brandon to have more time with his daughter and Albert and motioned to Charles for us to return to the fortune tellers' table. I stepped back and bumped into someone and turned to apologize.

There was a handful of people I hadn't noticed earlier. Not knowing who I'd bumped, I addressed the group with, "Sorry, I wasn't looking where I was going."

A man in his late fifties, smiled and said, "No worry, I always get bumped in a bar."

A woman with the group said, "We thought if we came later, it wouldn't be crowded. Looks like we were wrong."

"It's been busy all evening," Charles said as he moved beside me. "It's the best Halloween gig in the county."

Brandon had been watching the interaction. He turned towards the group, a big smile came across his face, and said, "Karen, thought I recognized your voice. Glad you decided to give Cal's a chance."

Charles said, "Knew you looked familiar. I met you in Harris Teeter last week. Karen Johnson, right?"

"Yes," she said giving my friend a look like she'd never seen him before. I hoped his ego would survive. She turned back to Brandon and said, "We were going to Charleston but at the last-minute Rick reminded us of this party. And I remembered you told me about it the other day, so I met my friend here. Thought we'd check it out before heading to the other party."

One of the men in the group pointed to a table in the far corner of the room where a couple who had been there since I arrived was leaving. He rushed over to claim the table and the rest of the group followed.

Charles watched them go and turned to me. "Before you flatten anyone else, we should get back to the fortune tellers." Charles started leading the way but went off course and turned towards the jukebox.

Before I got to the table, there was yelling coming from near the door to the woman's restroom and I saw Norman inches from Chloe with his left hand on her shoulder and his right hand balled into a fist. Chloe was pulling away and yelled at him. I started across the room when out of the corner of my eye I saw Donald jump up, then stumble from his barstool towards Norman. On the other side of the room, Spencer handed Otter to Tori, hustled around the table, and headed for Chloe.

Preacher Burl Costello appeared between Norman and Chloe and in a tone he wouldn't use from the pulpit, growled, "Enough! Get your hand off that lady." He then grabbed Norman's wrist and twisted it enough to pull it off Chloe's shoulder.

Norman jerked his arm away from Burl and said, "How dare you interfere. It's none of your damned business."

I moved next to Chloe and grasped her above the elbow. She didn't strike me as someone who'd initiate a fight but suspected she'd finish one that'd already started. I didn't want this to become a bar brawl in my friend's establishment.

Donald had finally made his way to the conflict, was standing next to Norman, and said, "You're on the wrong side this time, Preacher. The Devil has you." Donald's words were slurred but the volume rose above "Werewolves of London" playing on the jukebox.

Spencer took a step closer to Donald, Burl stood in front of Chloe, and I was still at her side but felt she was calm enough to let go of her arm. With everyone watching, Cal and Junior made their way through the crowd, with Officer Bishop beside them.

Cal took a step closer to Norman and Donald and said, "I've been in bars longer than most of you've been alive. My friends, no one wins in a bar fight."

Norman looked around, lowered his hands, looked at Donald, shook his head, and then said, "Sorry, Cal, she just—"

Cal stretched his 6'3" frame to its full height and said, "I'm not the one you need to apologize to. It's the young lady you put your hands on, and everyone else in here after you stomped on their good time."

Norman glanced around the room and said, "Sorry to put a damper on your night." He then turned to Chloe and said, "Sorry," in a tone sounding like the combination of embarrassment and too many beers.

"You realize, you can be arrested for what you did?" Chloe said and shook her head, "I risk my life every day saving people. Today I'll save you. You're forgiven."

I glanced at Trula who'd inched closer to the action ready to put on her cop's hat if necessary. She looked at me and nodded.

Donald pointed to the fortune tellers and said, "You better tell the troublemakers they need to leave."

Cal turned to Donald and Junior took a step closer as did Burl and me.

"Mister, this is my place, and no one tells me who can or can't stay. If I were going to throw troublemakers out, it'd be you and your friend."

Donald turned and stormed out of the building. Norman hadn't moved as if he didn't know what to do. The rest of the crowd went back to dancing, talking, with others trying to sing "The Addams Family" theme song. I nodded to Spencer who encouraged the rest of the fortune tellers to return to their table.

Charles, who was near Norman, approached him and said, "How about I buy you a cup of coffee?"

Norman nodded and returned to his barstool with Charles following. I went back to the table where Spencer and Tori were finishing their drinks, Happy faced the other way as Chloe slid Raven Moon into the backpack. Heidi stared at Norman.

I said, "Looks like you're calling it a night. Where's Alice?"

Happy patted Chloe on the shoulder and said, "She left before the WWE."

Spencer picked up Otter and said, "Chloe, Happy, and Heidi are heading to the house., I'm going to take Otter for a walk then Tori and I are staying longer, since we're leaving tomorrow."

Spencer and Otter headed for the door following the others.

Several members of the groups who arrived later filtered out of the room, but there was still a good crowd, and finally, a peaceful crowd. Preacher Burl was leaning on the bar and talking with Cal. Charles was still talking to Norman. Trula had joined Brandon, Stevie, and Albert at a table. Brandon was trying a Bloody Bloody

Mary, but the others were sticking with Cokes. While Cal wouldn't admit it, he looked beat, so I grabbed some empty bottles and took them to the trash can next to the stage.

Lady Lilith in the fortune telling machine cackled at me daring me to ask my fortune. Instead of donating money to her, I reminded myself one more time how much I hated Halloween.

27

———————

Charles tapped my shoulder and pointed across the room. Officer Rodney New had stepped into the party and approached Officer Bishop who was still talking with Brandon, Stevie, and Albert. New whispered something to Trula who then accompanied the officer outside.

Charles watched them go, turned to me, and said, "Let's follow them."

"Why?" I asked, thinking it was a good and logical question, then reminded myself asking good and logical questions to Charles was like asking good and logical questions to a groundhog.

"To see where they're going," he said as if that explained why.

"Charles, what I meant was I don't see where it's our business and besides what are you going to say when they ask why we're following them?"

"You'll come up with something."

Our disjointed discussion was interrupted by Junior who approached and said, "You two look too serious to be at a party. Can I get you another drink?"

"No thanks," I said, "but you're right. This is a fantastic party. Your enthusiasm for Halloween has rubbed off on Cal. Good crowd, too."

Junior smiled, looked around at the packed bar, and said, "After the near battle between those two idiots and the fortune tellers, this party is what Folly needed after all the hubbub over the tragic death of the visitor. You sure I can't grab you something to drink?"

I declined and thanked him again for the offer before he headed to a group of regulars at a nearby table to see if they needed anything to improve their mood.

Trula Bishop appeared in the doorway, glanced in Charles and my direction, weaved her way around two groups of partygoers, and leaned close so we could hear her over the music.

"Mr. Chris, Mr. Charles, don't make it obvious, but follow me." She said before she headed to the exit.

Charles said, "Told you we should've followed."

By the time we'd made it outside, Trula was waiting for us by the far corner of the building.

I said, "Everything okay?"

"Not for one person."

Charles said, "What's going on? Who's the—"

Trula waved her hand in front of Charles's face to interrupt his questions. "Guys, I'll probably get reamed out by the boss when she finds out I'm doing this, so please don't make a big deal of it."

Charles said, "What—"

Trula interrupted with, "Let me finish."

Charles wisely closed his mouth.

"I know you two will be sticking your noses into this before the night's over, so I wanted you to know what's going on before you start hearing rumors and go off on a tangent. Think you can follow me behind Cal's without saying anything and stay out of the way?"

"Of course, Officer Bishop," Charles said, more confidently than he should have been about not saying anything.

As we rounded the corner to face the back of Cal's, it would've been impossible to miss the yellow crime scene tape attached to the corner of the building, wrapped around a palmetto tree twenty feet behind the building, and then attached to the far side of the bar. What was more difficult to see were the people inside the tape's perimeter since they were backlit by a high-powered security light attached to the building's soffit. I thought I recognized Officer New talking with another officer, and two of Folly's firefighters standing inside the tape surrounding the body of a dark clad male on the ground. The head of the unmoving man faced the other direction.

Trula pointed to the unlit corner of the building and said, "Stay there, don't say anything."

Since one of Charles's strengths is not following directions, he said, "Who's dead?"

Trula huffed, shook her head, and said, "Stay there." She lifted the tape, ducked under it, and moved to the first responders.

Charles stepped closer to the barrier, stood on tiptoes, and stared at the body. It was so dark where the people were gathered that I doubted he could tell anything, but that didn't stop the faux detective from trying.

I jumped when two more firefighters startled me as they rushed around the corner and headed to the taped off area. I hadn't seen emergency vehicles parked along the street, so I assumed the first responders had walked from the public safety building across the street from Cal's.

The bass sounds from whatever was playing on the jukebox inside the bar and the mumbling from the people near the body were the only sounds I heard. Charles had finally decided he couldn't learn anything by pushing against the tape and returned to my side.

He said, "Who do you think it is? What do you think happened? Think it's another fortune teller? Think the—"

"Charles," I interrupted. "I've been with you since Trula got us. How am I supposed to know any of that?"

"Hoped one of us knew something. Know I don't."

"That makes two of us."

"Think Trula will tell us?"

That I could answer. "Yes, if she can."

"Gee, that helps."

Our conversation was interrupted when a man in his mid-thirties, wearing a starched, white dress shirt, gray slacks, a navy blazer, and a frown came around the corner and made a beeline to the taped off area. The man, who could've been a model for Ben Silver, one of Charleston's upscale clothing stores, was known to me as Detective Kenneth Adair, not a member of my fan club.

Fortunately, he didn't notice Charles or me standing in the dark, so I grabbed Charles's arm and *suggested* we needed to either head into the party or around to the front of Cal's, in other words, anywhere but near the scene of whatever happened back here. We stealthily made our way to the front of the building and Charles suggested we remain outside so Trula could find us when she came to tell us what was going on.

Ten minutes later, a van from the Charleston County Coroner's Office arrived and backed into the lot beside Cal's before continuing around the back of the building. Charles asked if we should follow it. It took me a nanosecond to say, "No." For once he followed my *suggestion* and we continued waiting in front of the bar.

An eternity later, an exhausted looking Trula Bishop came around the corner, gave a weak smile when she saw us, and said, "Let's walk up the street."

Before we reached Center Street, she motioned us into a darkened driveway and started to speak.

Not quickly enough for Charles, who said, "Who is it? What happened? Why—"

"Mr. Charles, with all due respect, shut up."

He did and I smiled.

She looked at him as if she didn't believe he did what he was told, before taking a notebook out of her pocket, flipped through a couple of pages, and said, "Vic's name is Donald Braxton, lives on your street, Mr. Charles. You know him?"

"You sure it's Donald?"

"That's what his driver's license says."

"I know who he is, but that's about all," Charles said, hesitated, and added, "except, umm." He then described the encounter we had with the recently deceased Folly citizen a couple of days after Wesley Thomas's murder.

I reminded her how he'd been with Norman Colter at the party.

She turned to me. "Anything to add?"

I told her about what Albert, Stevie's fiancé, had said about being accosted by someone driving a golf cart like the one Braxton owned.

"Sounds like a peach of a man," Trula said, in an unprofessional voice. "Anything else?"

Charles said, "Nothing other than how he behaved tonight."

Trula grabbed the notebook she'd returned to her pocket and jotted down something.

Surprisingly, Charles waited for her to finish before saying, "What killed him?"

"He was stabbed."

I said, "Any connection to the death of the fortune teller?"

"Nothing obvious. Different cause of death. He clearly wasn't part of the group."

Charles said, "That doesn't mean it's not connected, does it?"

"I have no idea. You could ask one of your fortune teller friends, or psychics, still don't know the differences, but somebody who talks to dead people should be able to ask Donald or Wesley." She took a deep breath before continuing. "I need to get back. I called the chief, and she should be getting here soon. Tell you one thing, and I don't need to be a fortune telling psychic medium to know, she'll be one pissed lady getting dragged out of her party and having to face Detective Adair. Fellas, you didn't hear that from me."

With those parting words, Officer Bishop left us standing in the dark, deserted driveway.

28

C harles watched Trula head to the crime scene, then turned to me and said, "Think we ought to go back there and see what's happening?"

"Let's see, Detective Adair spots us, recognizes me, and arrests me for interfering in a police investigation. Or, how about Chief LaMond gets back from her party, sees us, and after being dragged from something she looks forward to all year, shoots one or both of us. No, I've got it. We go back there and learn absolutely nothing that would help us determine who killed Donald Braxton or know anything to help the police."

"You saying you don't think we should go back there?"

"Your detective insights never cease to amaze me."

"Making fun of me?"

"Yep, but seriously, I can't see anything good coming from being seen anywhere near the police tape, especially by Detective Adair."

"You're right. Let's go back to the party. Might as well enjoy the rest of Cal's big event."

I felt more like going home and trying to forget seeing what'd happened to Donald Braxton, but reluctantly agreed with Charles. There was nothing we could do about what'd happened and several of our friends were inside. Why not try to enjoy the rest of the evening instead of going home and worrying about who ended Donald's life?

As we reentered the festive event, "The Purple People Eater" was playing for what must've been the fifth time I'd heard it tonight, and no telling how often it'd been played while Charles and I were outside.

For some reason, the song reminded me of something I'd forgotten to tell Officer Bishop about the recently deceased Folly resident. We had told her about our encounter with Donald a couple of days after Wesley's death and I'd shared what Stevie's fiancé had told me about his interaction with the angry citizen. What we hadn't said was what the fortune tellers had shared during the social at the Stones's house about encountering someone fitting Donald's description while they were on their way to the gathering. Should I go outside and tell Trula about that confrontation?

Charles had gone to the bar to get us drinks, and I realized if I went outside now, there was a good chance I'd tell Officer Bishop, but she would insist I share the story with Detective Adair and or Chief LaMond. The fortune tellers had been adamant about not wanting to talk with the Chief about their encounter and I wanted to respect their wishes. On the other hand, what if one of them was responsible for Braxton's death? There was clearly no love lost between the group and the body out back.

Charles returned and handed me a glass of red wine, and I rationalized that what I'd learned from the fortune tellers could wait until tomorrow when I could call Chief LaMond without Adair being within hearing distance. Besides, by that time, she might not be as angry about being called away from her party in Charleston.

Charles interrupted my thoughts with, "Who do you think killed him?"

"I have no idea."

"Want to hear my theory? It came to me while I was waiting for our drinks."

"Sure."

Before I could hear his theory, Preacher Burl joined us. Charles offered to buy him a drink.

Burl declined and Charles said, "You did a good job preventing the battle between good and evil smack dab in the middle of a Halloween party."

The preacher shook his head and said, "I've played many a role in my lifetime, but tonight was the first time I put on my imaginary striped shirt and refereed a match between two angry men and a strong woman." He smiled. "Glad they didn't come to blows. I doubt my ample, but underutilized muscles could've done much to stop the fight."

I said, "Your words spoke loud enough."

Burl smiled again and said, "My words and Cal's use of skills he'd learned over decades in bars."

"Regardless," I said, "it worked, and everyone appreciated your efforts."

"Thank you, Brother Chris. I see Brother Brandon has rejoined his daughter and her beau. I think I'll spend some time getting to know the young lady better. Have fun during the rest of the party and please don't start any fights." He smiled as he patted each of us on the back and headed to Brandon's table.

Charles watched him go, turned to me, and said, "Well, you going to listen to my theory?"

"What's your theory?"

"Braxton hated the fortune tellers."

I nodded.

"They think he may've killed one of their own which would make them seriously pissed with him. You agree?"

"Yes."

"So, it's obvious. One of them stabbed Donald." He nodded like that solved the murder, then rubbed his chin with his finger. "Or it was pitch black out there and he was wearing dark clothes which could've made him look like one of the fortune tellers. We know there are several locals who've got their shorts in a knot about the group being here." He stared at me and added, "You agree?"

I nodded.

"So, one of the angry locals mistook Donald for a fortune teller and stabbed him."

I took a sip of wine, looked around to see if anyone else had heard Charles's theory, and seeing no one close enough to have heard, I said, "So, your theory is one of the fortune tellers or a local killed Donald?"

He nodded, glanced at the ceiling, then said, "If you put it that way, maybe it needs a tad more work before you tell Chief LaMond our theory."

"Your theory."

Junior interrupted our discussion about whose theory it was when he appeared and asked if we needed anything.

I said, "No thanks, but while you're here, I wanted to tell you this is the best Halloween party Cal's has ever hosted."

"Thanks, my friend. I'll be happier when I can say it was the best after it's over. My overweight body can't take more nights like this. I don't know how Dad does it at his age."

"It's his whole life; it's all he knows."

"Singing and hanging out in bars. And speaking of singing, he's about to officially put an end to the party with, or in his words, 'the grand finale.'"

The next sound I heard was Cal tapping on the oversized antique microphone on a stand in the center of the stage.

"Folks," Cal said, "I hope you've had as good a time as I've had tonight during this here Halloween party." He hesitated, stepped back, and waited for a response from the half-full bar of guests.

Charles yelled, "Great job, Cal!"

A few other patrons applauded, and Cal returned to the mic and said, "We're going to finish up tonight with a tradition at these gatherings. Join in if you want. Here's 'Monster Mash.' It goes something like this.

I was working in the lab late one night
when my eyes beheld an eerie sight.
If anyone joined in, I didn't hear them. I know I didn't. In addition

to Cal's country version of the Halloween song, all I heard was me telling myself how glad I was this nightmare of an evening was ending.

29

———

The next morning, with the thought, probably erroneous, that French toast would sooth my anxieties over viewing the body of the late Donald Braxton, I headed to the Lost Dog Cafe for breakfast. Of course, I was partially motivated by the knowledge there wasn't anything appropriate for the morning meal under my roof. The day started out cooler than normal, so my walk to the Dog could've been described as brisk. Even the jack-o'-lanterns on porches that were so festive last night appeared to shiver.

Both outdoor seating areas were empty although the parking area in front of the restaurant was full. Amber greeted me at the door and asked where I'd been hiding last week. Before I could answer, I saw Stevie and Albert at a table along the side of the room. Stevie saw me, smiled, waved, and pointed at the vacant chair across the table from the two visitors. I took the hint and approached them.

"Want to join us?" Stevie asked without involving her fiancé in the decision.

"I'd be honored, that is, if it's not a bother for the two of you," I said with an emphasis on *two*.

She glanced at Albert who nodded, and she said, "It'd be great getting to know you better. Dad has good things to say about you."

I wondered why Brandon would have said anything about me to his daughter but didn't ask. I took the seat and Amber arrived with a mug of coffee and said, "Albert was telling me about somebody getting killed behind Cal's last night during the Halloween party. He said he didn't know for sure but heard it from somebody outside the bar when they were leaving. Said the dead person was Donald Braxton. Did you hear anything about it?"

"It was Mr. Braxton. Officer Bishop shared that with Charles and me."

No, I didn't mention Charles and I were behind the building getting an up-close view of the activities surrounding the deceased retired attorney.

Albert looked around the room then leaned across the table, and said, "The guy telling me said Braxton drove a golf cart with the grille like a Mercedes. Chris, wouldn't that be the person I was telling you about who accused me of being one of those psychics?"

"Most likely it was."

Amber said, "I don't like talking bad about the dead, but from the few times he was in here and I had the privilege of waiting on him, he wasn't friendly. I don't know why he thought he could be a good bartender at Taco Boy or anywhere else. I heard they fired him. No surprise there." She turned to me. "Do the police have any idea who may've killed him or when it happened?"

"If they do, I haven't heard."

Albert said, "Bet it was one of those psychics, or whatever they call themselves. From the things Braxton said to me, I bet members of the group were pissed at him if he said his piece around any of them. I know I felt like sharing my fist with his nose when he confronted me."

Stevie patted Albert on the forearm and said, "Now, honey, we don't know anything about what he may have said to the psychics."

"I know. I'm going by what he said to me and the way he said it."

Amber glanced at a table of diners near the entry and said, "Suppose I need to get to work. Chris, French toast?"

I nodded.

"Shocking," she said, giggled then moved to the table near the door.

I said, "Did you enjoy last night's party?"

"It was good seeing so many people from here having a good time," Albert said. "Makes me feel good about Folly."

"Best thing about it to me," Stevie said, "was getting to spend time with Dad. It was great seeing him have fun and not stuck inside the hardware store." She tilted her head and added, "He really enjoys spending time with me. I was worried since I was nearly a stranger to him."

I said, "He told me how much he enjoyed you being here. Any idea when you're planning to head back to Atlanta?"

"Don't know," Albert said and took a bite of bacon.

Stevie said, "You know Karen Johnson?"

I wondered what that had to do with their plans to return to Atlanta, but said, "Not really. Met her a couple of times, and that included last night. Why?"

Stevie grinned. "Dad seemed, how shall I say it, alive when he was talking with her at the party."

"Stevie," Albert said, "believe you said he was smitten and not simply alive."

"Let's say he appeared to enjoy the time she and, what's his name?"

"Rick," said Albert.

"Yes, when Karen and Rick were talking with him."

"Albert said Karen said Rick was a friend, didn't say boyfriend. I didn't get the impression they were a thing. In fact, something your dad said gave me the impression he and Karen had gone out a few times."

I said, "Did they stay long at the party?"

Stevie laughed before saying, "You could ask Dad how long they were there. He kept checking on where she was and what she was doing. The poor man thought I didn't notice. From what he told me the other day, he hasn't dated much the last few years, but you could be right, Albert." She chuckled and added, "Maybe I'll ask him."

"Speaking of Brandon, have you made any progress on seeing if he'd lend you the money for the investment you'd mentioned when we were on the beach?"

Albert stared at me as if I'd asked if he'd robbed a bank.

Fortunately, the next words came from Stevie who said, "Dad told me last night he was still considering it, said something about having to cash CDs, but thought it may be possible."

"That's great news, isn't it, Albert? From what you told me, you have a great investment opportunity."

"Sure do. Best of all, it's great how Brandon is warming up to Stevie."

She smiled at Albert and said, "It's wonderful." She turned to me. "Did he say anything else to you about Albert or me?"

Amber set my French toast in front of me and said, "Sorry it took so long. The kitchen's backed up."

"That's fine," I said as she refilled my coffee mug then left to take checks to the table against the front wall.

I poured syrup on the toast then said, "I don't recall him saying more than how glad he was you were here." I hesitated then said, "Sure you don't know when you'll be leaving?"

"Not for a few days, isn't that right, Albert?"

He slowly nodded.

I figured that was as far as I would be getting with that line of questioning and asked how they liked tent camping. They weren't hesitant sharing how much they liked the campground, the people they'd met there, and especially how much they liked coming over here and walking on the beach.

A few benign comments later, they said how much they'd enjoyed sharing their table with me and how they were anxious to get to the beach so they could enjoy a walk on the perfect fall morning. Albert offered to pay for my breakfast, a rare happening in the Dog, but I declined, and he paid for their meal then they headed to the beach.

Amber watched them go as she stood behind the counter then returned to my table.

"Okay, let's have it, what else do you know about Donald Braxton's death?"

"Why, think I know more than I shared?"

"Chris, don't treat me like a feather-brained chick. After knowing you for a hundred years, I figure you know more about what happened than the cops, the FBI, the CIA, and all those other alphabet outfits. So, spill it."

"All I know is he was stabbed in the back. It was dark so I'm not sure the person who did it knew Donald or mistook him for someone else."

"Think it was the same person who killed the fortune teller?"

"No idea. One was shot, one stabbed, but that's all I know."

"But you and your buddy will find out, won't you?"

I shrugged.

She smiled and said, "That's your yes shrug."

I returned her smile and gave her a second shrug.

30

After leaving the Dog, I headed down Center Street and wondered if it was too early to call Chief LaMond and share what the fortune tellers had told me about their encounter with Donald Braxton.

That was one decision I didn't have to make. The chief's pickup truck was heading toward me. She stopped on the lightly traveled street and turned on her light bar in case someone missed seeing her large vehicle in the road.

She lowered her window and said, "Guess I missed my chance at a free breakfast."

I smiled and said, "Sorry. What're you—"

She interrupted with, "I don't have all day. Hop in."

I crossed the street and walked around to the passenger door of the truck. Before I slid into the seat, I had to move a small box of donuts to the console between the front seats.

"It looks like you already have breakfast. A breakfast of champions, or is that breakfast of cops?"

"I didn't invite you in for sarcastic comments."

"Chief, you knew what you were getting when you stopped for me. You do appear in a better mood than I would've expected."

She glanced in the rearview mirror to see if she was blocking traffic. Apparently, she wasn't, and said, "Why wouldn't I be in a fabulous mood? I spent my evening enjoying a party with hubby, the guy I never get to see enough of, while kicking up my heels as a member of the Walking Dead and not thinking one bit about my official duties." She snapped her fingers. "Oh, wait, could there be another reason you think I might not be in a good mood?"

I smiled. "I haven't lived as long as I have to be dumb enough to step in that mine field."

"Wise," she said and again, glanced in the rearview mirror, then made a U-turn, and headed toward the Tides. Instead of entering the hotel's lot, she turned left on East Arctic Avenue.

"Is everything okay?"

"Not really. I've got some questions," she said and continued to intently stare out the windshield.

"Questions?"

She glanced over at me; a small smile crossed her lips before she said, "I need to know what you know about the events last night and what might've led to Braxton's death."

"All I know is what I've already shared. What've you learned about it?"

Cindy sighed and said, "Did you forget, I was the one with questions?"

"Don't suppose you know who stabbed him, do you?"

"No. Now my turn," she said as she turned on 11th Street East then right on East Ashley Avenue.

I nodded.

"If you weren't such a loveable guy and good friend, I'd ... hell, I don't know what I'd do." She sighed and added, "From the looks of the wound, it appears Braxton was stabbed with a large hunting knife. I assume the stab was the cause of death, but that won't officially be determined until the autopsy is completed. Of course, with our luck, the weapon was nowhere to be found. From the amount of blood around the body, I'd say the murder took place where he was found. The time of death was no more than an hour before the body was discovered. So far, we haven't located anyone who witnessed it."

"I suppose having a witness would've helped."

"Not necessarily. As you recall, I had a witness to a murder last week. He proved to be worthless."

She got me there, I thought, and said, "True."

Cindy parallel parked along the Washout section of East Ashley Avenue, took a donut out of the box, took a bite, then mumbled, "I was told Braxton was at Cal's party. What, if anything happened while he was in there, or for that matter, anything prior to the party involving him?"

"I'm sure Officer Bishop told you about the confrontation between Norman Colter and some of the visiting fortune tellers."

"She shared what she witnessed. Can you add anything?"

"I was aware there was an issue when Norman grabbed Chloe Meriweather's arm and was yelling at her. She's one of the fortune tellers. Donald either heard or saw what was going on and went over to spew his hatred for the group. He even insisted Cal evict the visitors from the party."

"That lines up with what Trula said." She took another bite, looked in the rearview mirror, and said, "Between you and your friends, you somehow manage to know nearly everything bad happening here whether it's your business or not."

"Chief, that's not—"

"I'm not done. What else have you learned about Braxton and his attitude about the visitors?"

"I've heard of some interactions he'd had with them, and a couple of run-ins I've had with the guy."

"Now we're getting somewhere. Start with the ones you've had," she said as she moved the donut box and took a notepad out of the console then leaned against her door and faced me.

"Last week, Charles and I were walking along Center Street when Donald pulled up beside us. He started yelling about us keeping company with Devil worshipers, then at Cal's party, we tried to talk to him."

"I'm guessing that didn't go well."

"I'd never officially met Donald, so I wanted to introduce myself and see if we could have a calm conversation about his dislike, to put it mildly, for the visitors. Charles and I went to speak with him."

"No luck?"

"We had a brief, hostile conversation. That's all the interactions I've had with the man."

Cindy jotted something in her notebook then said, "Okay, how about the others?"

"Friday evening, Charles and I, along with a group of the fortune tellers were invited to Shannon Stone's house."

"A pre-Halloween party?"

"Not really. Shannon wanted to have an informal gathering of the group where we could get to know each other better."

"Okay, and?"

"A few members of the group told us about an encounter they had with a guy and described the golf cart he was in. I have no doubt it was Donald. He followed the group as they walked to Shannon's house. Donald sped up, yelled at the fortune tellers, and nearly hit Otter."

"They had an otter?"

I smiled and said, "Otter is a dog belonging to one of the fortune tellers."

Cindy shook her head. "Don't know about them being Devil worshipers, but having a dog named after a weasel-looking creature makes them weird."

"You done sharing your extensive knowledge of the animal kingdom?"

She smiled. "For now."

"In addition to Tori Bran, the group included Spencer Ford, Chloe Meriweather, and Heidi Strongmire."

She pointed her pen at me and said, "How do you spell Heidi's last name?"

"Heck if I know."

"There you go. Once again proving this old Tennessee mountain gal knows as much as you know, and you claim to be a college graduate."

"You're smarter and wiser than many college graduates I know."

She grinned and said, "Why didn't they report it?"

"I told them they should and even offered to call you, but they declined. I got the impression they wanted to forget the whole thing."

"Anything else?"

"Did you know Brandon's daughter and her fiancé are in town?"

"Larry mentioned it."

"Albert, the fiancé, was confronted on the street by Donald, simply because he thought Albert might be one of the Devil worshipers."

"Braxton's quite a guy. No wonder he ended up with a knife in the back. Anything else?"

"That's it."

"Do you think both guys were killed by the same person?"

"Don't know. Different murder weapons; one victim an outsider, the other a local. About the only thing that makes me believe they could've been was how close in time they were to each other. If we were in Chicago, New York, or LA, two murders a week apart wouldn't mean much, but on Folly?"

"Good point, but that doesn't necessarily mean they're related." She wrote something else in her notebook, looked out the windshield at the waves rolling ashore, and without looking at me, added, "Do you think Braxton was the intended victim?"

"Why wouldn't he have been?"

"Just a thought. You've been in proximity with two victims in a week. Perhaps the killer is inept."

"You still hinting I could've been the intended victim?"

She shrugged.

"Cindy, I look nothing like either victim and in case you forgot, I was at a Halloween party when Braxton was outside getting himself stabbed. I doubt the killer could be that inept."

She turned to me and said, "Granted, you don't look anything like

Wesley Thomas but were merely inches from him when he was shot. It was dark where Braxton was killed and you're about his size. Just a thought."

I shook my head and said, "No way."

Again, she shrugged.

"For sake of argument, is there any evidence I might've been the target?"

"Not that I'm aware of." She smiled. "Although, I think Detective Adair might be hoping you are. As you may've noticed, he hasn't questioned you."

"Who said prayers aren't answered?"

"I told him I'd take care of your interview. This is it."

"Thank you. Is he questioning everyone who was at Cal's? That'd be a lengthy list."

"Not everyone, we're talking with folks who were coming or going around the time of the murder. Do you recall anyone leaving immediately before or after Donald left?"

"People were coming and going all night, large groups would come in then others would leave. It was the most people I've seen in Cal's. Plus, it was dark, hard to tell who was there."

"That's what I understand. Let me narrow it down, did any of the fortune tellers leave right before or after Donald left the party?"

"I believe Alice Clay left before the confrontation between Norman Colter and Chloe, but I'm not sure how long before."

"Interesting. That would be the weirdo who claims to have seen Wesley getting shot while she was sitting in her hotel room. We tried to find her last night but failed. She checked out of the Tides yesterday afternoon."

"She might be at the house the Roseruns rented on East Arctic. She said she was going to stay there this week along with Heidi, Happy Bishop, Stormy and Darrin Roserun."

"We checked. She's not there and no one has heard from her. Did anyone leave right after Donald left?"

Cindy said it like she already knew the answer.

"I know Chloe, Heidi, Happy and his cat Raven Moon left, but there could've been others."

"We've interviewed all but the cat." Cindy smiled and added, "I'm not sure a cat would be considerate enough to stab someone in the back. They're more face-to-face killers."

I returned her smile and said, "Sounds reasonable."

"What about Spencer," she glanced at her notebook and said, "Ford?"

"He didn't leave when the others did but did take Otter for a walk."

"How long was he gone?"

"Not sure. I saw him leave but don't recall seeing him return. Do you really think the killer could be one of the fortune tellers?"

"We haven't closed the door on anyone. It's beginning to feel like one of those old gangster movies. They kill one of ours; we kill one of theirs. At least, that's Detective Adair's theory." She smiled and added, "That is, unless you're the target."

"Hope you're wrong."

"I don't want you taking unnecessary risks. After losing Allen Spencer last Halloween, I couldn't take losing a good friend."

Allen Spencer was one of Cindy's officers and a friend of mine who was killed last year, mere days before Halloween, while trying to apprehend a murderer.

"Cindy, I understand. I don't believe I've ever taken any unnecessary risks."

"Keep telling yourself that. Regardless, do this old Tennessee gal a favor and behave."

"Yes, sir," I said, giving her my best Gomer Pyle salute.

Cindy shook her head as she pulled back on the pavement, made a U-turn, and drove to my house.

She pulled into my driveway, turned towards me, and said, "I'm always giving you a hard time but please stay out of this. I have a bad feeling."

I could see concern in her eyes, so this wasn't the time to make a joke about her being a psychic, so I said, "Okay."

She waited for me to enter the house before leaving. An uneasy dread settled over me. Was it possible I was the target? I'm not the only one thinking it's a possibility, but why?

One thing I was certain of, if there was a possibility I was the target, there was no way I was going to sit back and not do everything I could to identify the killer. No way.

31

Doing everything I could to catch the killer was far easier said than done. Where to begin was the first question I needed to answer. I grabbed a Diet Coke and moved to the picnic table in my backyard.

Fifteen minutes later, I'd finished my drink but still failed to come up with a workable plan to identify the person who'd killed two people in the last eight days. I started back inside when I was surprised by Charles appearing at the corner of the house.

He glared at me and said, "There you are. I half thought someone had finally bumped you off."

In addition to being surprised by his sudden appearance, I was shocked to see him wearing a long-sleeve green T-shirt with the unmistakable yellow John Deere logo on the front.

"Planning on selling me a mower?"

He looked around the back yard which consisted of weeds interspersed with sad looking clumps of grass struggling to survive and said, "No, but you could use one. I got this shirt from a guy I knew long before I met you. He sold those big green mower thingies."

"So instead, you bought a shirt?"

"Nope, he said I was such a nice fellow he gave it to me even if I didn't have a yard or field or farm where I'd need one of his mowers."

I'd heard way more than I needed to hear about mowers, green or otherwise, and said, "Want something to drink?"

"How about a Bloody Bloody Mary?"

I stared at him.

"Okay, how about a Coke?" he said, grasping my silent rejection.

He followed me into the house where he pulled a Coke out of the refrigerator then spotted a bag of Doritos on the counter. He grabbed it and we headed into the living room.

Instead of asking why he was here, I said, "Are you between deliveries for Dude?"

"Had one earlier at the Regatta Inn for two 'old chaps.' Guess where they're from."

I smiled, figured when he'd air quoted *old chaps*, that was a hint, and said, "Mobile, Alabama."

"Crapola, Chris. Why do I even try to educate you? They're from London, England."

"So?"

"Never mind. Dude gave me the rest of the afternoon off. He figured I had a long night at Cal's and could use the rest."

"While you were pedaling towards the Regatta Inn and conversing with guys from Alabama, I had breakfast with Stevie and Albert."

"I said they were from ... never mind. Why didn't you invite me?"

"Didn't want to distract Dude's employee."

"Seriously?"

"I went to the Dog for breakfast and Stevie invited me to join them."

"Learn anything, like when they're leaving or if they got the money Albert wanted?"

"I asked about both. They really like Folly and aren't sure when they're leaving. Stevie said Brandon is still thinking about the loan but would have to cash CDs to get it."

"I wonder if that's true or he doesn't feel comfortable telling her no."

"Don't know."

"Anything else?"

"They asked if I knew Karen Johnson."

"Who?"

"The lady from Harris Teeter; the one we talked to at the party."

"The one who liked my fighting camel shirt."

"Yes."

"Why ask about her?"

"It appears Brandon may've gone on a few dates with the camel lover."

"Finally, some good news. A budding romance." He took a sip before saying, "Now can we get down to the reason we're gathered? We need to figure out this mess."

"I didn't realize that's why we were gathered, as you put it."

"Duh, why else?"

"Then I suppose I should tell you I saw Cindy today."

I waited for my friend to explode, since I'd buried the lead.

Instead of exploding, he took another sip of Coke, moved closer to the edge of his chair, and said, "Have they caught the killer?"

"No, it seems our law enforcement officials have no real leads except Alice Clay, the fortune teller, who is nowhere to be found."

"I bet she saw something, you know, like in her head and left town before she could be the next victim."

I said, "I think they're looking for her more as killer rather than victim."

"Good, she can be at the top of our list of suspects."

"That's a rather low bar for someone to make the list."

"Have to start somewhere. Did Cindy mention anything else?"

"Nothing related to the deaths."

Charles stared at his Coke can then at me. "Okay, so let's go over what we know. Mr. Congeniality is stabbed behind Cal's in the middle of the Halloween party."

"Shouldn't that be Donald was stabbed outside the bar, where inside, there were people celebrating?"

"Okay, someone from the party is the most likely suspect, but we need to narrow that down."

I didn't think that because there were people in the building near where Donald was stabbed meant the most likely suspect was among them. Let's see where Charles is going with his theory.

I said, "Cindy asked who left the party immediately before or after Donald departed. I could only think of a couple. Who do you remember leaving?"

"Donald left and I went to the bar with Norman. Some people left after that."

"Who?"

"Don't know. I was more concerned with Norman. What did you tell Cindy?"

"That Alice left before the confrontation and Chloe, Happy, and Heidi left after it. I also mentioned Spencer went out with them saying he wanted to take Otter for a walk."

"What about Raven Moon?"

"She was in Happy's backpack. Why is that important?"

"Don't know it is. I saw Spencer carrying Otter when he came back inside. I was a little surprised since I never saw him, umm, them leave."

"So, you have no idea how long he was gone."

"If the fortune tellers left soon after the blow up, I'd guess it was fifteen minutes or more before I saw Spencer come in. That would've been plenty of time for Spencer to give Donald a piece of his mind and a knife in the back."

"The police haven't found the knife," I said then added, "He wasn't conspicuously carrying one at the party."

"It could've been under the hoodie he had on. Did you talk to him when he came back?"

"No, but if he stabbed Donald, most likely, there would've been blood on his clothing or his hands."

"Neither of us talked to him after he returned, so we can't know if blood was on his outfit which was dark, if I remember right."

"So that wasn't helpful."

"My young apprentice, we added him to the suspect list," he sat back and smiled as if that solved the crime.

Instead of challenging his first three words: *my*, *young*, and *apprentice*, I said, "Do you really think it was one of the fortune tellers? They've been nothing but polite and open since they arrived. Granted, some of them are odd, but killers?"

"Good point."

"How about us getting out of here and get an early supper?"

"After finishing our Doritos, I'm not ready to eat."

"Our Doritos?" I said. "Then, how about a walk?"

We walked to Center Street and Charles said, "Which direction?"

"Let's head to the Post Office. I haven't checked my mail in a couple of days, and we'll pass several restaurants giving us an idea where we should eat."

"Like we don't know every restaurant in town and its menu."

"You have a better plan?"

"Chris, you should've eaten some chips. Sounds like you're on edge."

We passed Mr. John's Beach Store and I said, "I am, but not from lack of food. Several people besides you have speculated I might be the target while Wesley and Donald were simply in the wrong place at the wrong time."

He glanced at me while still walking. "If I thought you were a target, think I'd be walking this close to you?"

"True."

"But think about it, there's no way someone would get us confused. It's still daylight and you're much, much older than me."

"Slightly older."

We were in front of Our Lady of Good Counsel Catholic Church, when Charles stopped, faced me, and said, "How about a local?"

"What about a local?"

"Stabbing Donald?"

"Such as?"

"Off the cuff, anyone who ever met him. He was obnoxious."

"That'd be a lengthy list. Think we could narrow it down?"

"Yeah, but I'm not sure how."

Nothing more was said about the list of suspects or victims the rest of the way to the Post Office where I found a handful of junk mail in my box and Charles found nothing in his. We exited the small building and moved to the nearby trash container where I deposited the equivalent of a small tree of paper.

Then Charles said, "Isn't it time for that dinner you promised?"

"How about Planet Follywood?"

We turned and not a foot in front of us stood Norman Colter. I took a step back and so did Charles.

Norman said, "Didn't mean to startle you."

"Then you should've made a noise," Charles growled.

That was one of the few times I'd heard Charles short with someone. Norman must've startled him as well.

Norman bowed his head slightly and said, "Charles, thanks for talking to me after, you know, what happened at the party."

Charles said, "I'm glad things didn't get worse in there. It could've—"

"That's true, but I was thanking you for keeping me in the bar. Otherwise, I could've ended up like Donald."

"Oh." Charles said and glanced my way as if he wanted me to contribute to the conversation.

I wasn't quick enough and was uncertain what I would've said.

Norman said, "If you do-gooders didn't interfere and let Donald kick those Satanists out, he might still be alive."

"No one in the bar was a Satanist," I said. "The people you're talking about are like you and me. They simply have talents different from many of us."

Norman took a half a step in my direction, glared at me, and said, "They're not like me, period. One of them stabbed my friend, stabbed him in the back."

Charles finally reentered the conversation with, "If you have proof, you need to tell the police."

"The cops have plenty of proof. Now they need to do something about it." He held his hands in front of him. "I wanted to thank you and I did. Good day." He pivoted and stomped off toward Pewter Hardware.

Charles tapped his cane in the gravel beside the road, shook his head, and said, "Planet Follywood awaits."

32

―――――

Each day brought more questions than answers about the deaths. I realized little good could come from staring at my Mr. Coffee machine as it brewed a carafe of coffee and sitting at the kitchen table while getting excited about eating a three-day-old Danish looking up at me from the chipped plate upon which it rested. Heavy rain was forecast for later this morning, so while I had little insight into who'd committed the murders, I was certain walking to Bert's Market could ensure my breakfast would be fresher than the Danish that now had the consistency of a lawn ornament.

Two bites of a Bert's cinnamon roll and a sip of their complimentary coffee later, I remembered Barb had spent yesterday in Columbia purchasing books. She would've gotten back late so I doubt she'd unloaded last evening. I took my coffee and headed to Barb's Books to see if she was there and needed help.

The store wouldn't be open for another hour, but in the alley behind it there was a white cargo van with an Enterprise Truck Rental logo on the side and the back door to the bookstore was propped open.

I nearly ran into the store's owner as she was exiting the building. She looked at me, shook her head, and said, "You blew it."

"Blew what?"

"Bet you thought you'd show up after I hauled roughly thirty tons of books inside. Hate to break it, I've only been here ten minutes. So, thank you for offering to carry the books in."

"Thirty tons? Sounds like you had a productive day. When did you get back?"

"Little after midnight."

"That made a long day. What can I do to help?"

She smiled and pointed to the rental van. "See that big white thing parked there?"

I nodded.

"All you have to do is walk behind it, open the door, grab the boxes, and bring them into the store."

After looking in the van, two things became apparent. First, I saw why she'd rented the truck rather than trying to stuff the books into her Mercedes convertible. And second, if she had been exaggerating about the weight of her purchase, it wasn't by much.

She watched me lift the box closest to the door and I said, "How many books did you get?"

"Don't know. The owner stopped counting and charged me by the box. I ended up buying way more than I need, but the price was so good, I couldn't pass them up."

The next half-hour was consumed with me lugging boxes, Barb telling me where to put each one (none close to the door I was carrying them through) and telling me how weightlifting was good for my health. My back disagreed, but I wasn't about to complain.

The routine of me carrying the boxes in and Barb giving directions abruptly came to a screeching halt when I asked if she'd heard about what happened to Donald Braxton after she'd left Cal's party.

"What? He seemed like his obnoxious self the little I saw him there."

"Someone agreed with you and stuck a knife in his back. He was found behind Cal's."

"Dead?"

"Yes."

"Know who did it?"

"No. I was talking with Cindy yesterday and she said they didn't have any suspects. She, and of course, Detective Adair and his crew, are trying to talk with everyone who was at Cal's party, but doubts that'll help."

"Why does she think someone from the party would know anything about it?"

I told Barb about the altercation between Chloe Meriweather and Norman Colter, and how Donald tried to get in the middle of the conflict.

"Does she suspect one of the visitors?"

"That's a strong possibility since Donald had made it clear he didn't want any of them here."

"Sounds weak."

"I agree."

Barb started unpacking one of the boxes and said, "Does she think the same person killed both men?"

"That's their theory."

"That also sounds weak. Different weapons, one visitor, one local victim. If I were still a defense attorney and represented someone accused of killing both men, I wouldn't have to work too hard to create reasonable doubt. Do the police have anything else to tie the deaths to one suspect?"

"Don't think so."

"Were you at the party when it happened?"

"Yes. Why?"

"Couple of guys came in Halloween morning. They were mumbling something about the fortune tellers, although they weren't calling them anything that civil. I wasn't paying attention until one of them mentioned your name."

"Do I have to guess or are you going to tell me what he was saying?"

"Said he heard you were at the hotel getting all buddy-buddy with the group. Even said you were so close with them his friend figured you were one of them, whatever that meant."

"Who were they?"

"Never seen them before but had the impression they were from around here. They didn't buy anything, so I didn't see a credit card with a name on it."

"You sure they were talking about me?"

"You know other Chris Landrums?"

I shook my head, then remembered something she'd said earlier. "Why'd you ask if I was at the party when Braxton was killed?"

"It's a stretch, but is it possible the killer thought Braxton was you?"

"I don't see why," I said, although Cindy had said the same thing.

"Told you it was a stretch. It wouldn't have entered my mind if those guys hadn't been talking about you. It'd still be a good idea if you were extra careful until the police catch the person or persons who killed the fortune teller and Braxton."

I told her I would.

"Good," she said and smiled. "Know what we need to do?"

"Come up with a good suspect?"

"Dream on, Charles wannabe. The correct answer is for you to get out there and bring in the rest of the boxes."

"That may be easier than coming up with a suspect," I said, but wasn't sure I believed it. For the record, a box of books weighs about the same as a box of concrete blocks.

33

———————

Barb and I were still in the office behind the showroom, when I heard Charles say, "Yo, Barb, you here?"

She turned to me and said, "See, he knows when to show up. All the heavy lifting is finished." She then peeked around the door and said, "We're back here."

Charles appeared in the doorway wearing a dark blue sweatshirt with some sort of wild-looking cat and *Montana State* in gold on the front. Neither Barb nor I asked, but it didn't stop him from saying, "It's a bobcat."

"Interesting," Barb said, showing more enthusiasm than I could've mustered.

"Yes, it is," Charles said then looked around the office before continuing, "But what's more interesting is I saw a truck out back. Are you closing the store? Are you moving? Is Chris going with you? Well?"

She smiled at the distressed look on Charles face and said, "No, no, and no."

Before the conversation sank lower, I pointed to one of the stacks of boxes and said, "These are the books Barb bought yesterday in Columbia. We were unloading them from the van."

"I forgot you were doing that. Guess I didn't get here in time to help."

"That's better timing than your buddy managed," she said and nodded in my direction. "He got to carry in all the boxes, and I sure appreciate it. It would've taken me most of the day. When I get some of these unloaded, you need to stop by. I bet there're some you haven't read."

"I will. Now that I'm here, is there anything I can do to help?"

"Thanks, but I've got it under control. Chris used all his limited energy, so why don't you two go somewhere for lunch while I figure out what to do with the books?"

I said, "Sure you don't need help?"

"No, I'm fine, besides, you're too old to do much more manual labor."

"Okay, old man, want me to get a wheelchair so I can push you to a restaurant?" asked the man who was carrying a cane and only a year younger than I am.

Barb rolled her eyes and pointed to the door. "You two, out. I've work to do."

Charles and I left Barb to do whatever she planned to do with the books.

Charles looked up and down Center Street and said, "Where to?"

"How about the Crab Shack? That way you won't have to push the wheelchair far."

"I suppose I asked for that," Charles said as we headed to one of Folly's most popular restaurants, which happens to be fewer than thirty yards from Barb's Books. We were still a little early for lunch so there was no shortage of vacant tables. I let Charles select where he wanted to sit. I was certain he'd choose a table on the patio and close to the wall separating the restaurant from the sidewalk.

Charles proved predictable and the hostess took us to the table I'd anticipated being his first choice. She said Ellie would be with us shortly.

Her proclamation proved accurate when Ellie, who'd waited on me several times over the years, arrived at the table and asked what we wanted to drink. Charles said a Budweiser and I went with a glass of red wine.

She left to get our drinks and Charles said, "Well, who killed the guys?"

I would've preferred him asking about the books, or how my back felt after lifting a thousand boxes roughly the weight of a cruise ship, so I said, "Don't know."

"That's the same thing you concluded last night. You have a long way to go before you become a card-carrying detective."

"Yep. Who do you think did it?"

"Don't know."

Before I made the same observation about his having a long way to go, Ellie returned with our drinks and asked if we were ready to order. I said to give us a few minutes and she headed inside.

Charles stood, looked over my shoulder in the direction of the sidewalk, and said, "Hey, Stevie, Albert, had lunch?"

I glanced back and saw the young couple walking hand-in-hand. They stopped, gave Charles a blank look, then Stevie smiled as if she finally recognized who was talking to them.

"No."

That was all it took for Charles to say, "Come join us. Chris is buying."

Stevie glanced at Albert, then turned to Charles, and said, "We don't want to intrude."

"You wouldn't be," Charles said.

They headed toward the entry, and I said, "Charles, that's nice of you to let me buy their lunch."

He smiled.

Stevie and Albert arrived at the table and seconds later, Ellie appeared with our drinks and asked the newcomers what they wanted to drink.

Albert looked at our drinks and said, "Think we'll have iced tea, unsweet."

Ellie left to get their drinks and Albert turned to me, "Thank you for offering to get our lunch, but you don't have to."

I said, "We'll enjoy your company. Been walking on the beach?"

Stevie smiled. "I could do that forever."

Charles turned to Albert and said, "How's the international currency market doing?"

Albert tilted his head in Charles's direction. "It's booming. Why?"

"Think it's fascinating and since you were planning on investing in it, I knew you'd be the person to ask."

Charles, the man sitting with me who had no idea what the international currency market was, had now put on his private detective hat. I sat back to listen to the discussion.

"Oh, I see," Albert said. "I'm still in the process of bundling my funds and waiting to see if Brandon wants to participate. Anyway, thanks for asking." He then turned to Stevie. "Hon, tell them what you picked up on the beach."

His discussion about the market, currency or otherwise, had ended.

She pulled a two-inch-long shark tooth out of her pocket and held it up for Charles and me to see.

"That's a good one," I said. "Congratulations."

"I was shocked. We were walking along, and I looked down and there it was as if it had been waiting for me."

"It was meant to be," Charles said and smiled. "It can be your good luck charm."

Ellie returned with their drinks and asked if we were ready to order. Charles nodded at me, and I gave him a slight nod in return, before saying, "Stevie, Albert, you ready?"

They said yes, and we went with various seafood combinations and an extra order of fries to share.

The next few minutes were consumed by the kind of conversations people who're new to the beach have with locals. The weather was discussed and rediscussed, the price of housing was bemoaned, and the availability of jobs in the area hit upon lightly. Our food had arrived, and the discussion centered on how good lunch was.

Then Albert said, "Heard any more about who killed those men?"

I said, "No, have you?"

"Nothing since the Halloween party."

The way he said it made me think he may've heard something at or before the party.

"Albert, did you hear something about it at the party?"

He smiled. "Brandon was talking with Karen, you know, the lady he's sweet on?"

I nodded.

"She said some of her friends were certain one of the fortune tellers killed the man."

Charles said, "What'd she base that on?"

"Don't think she said, or if she did, I wasn't close enough to hear. How about you, sweetie?"

He was looking more in my direction when he said it, but I used my detective skills to figure he was talking to Stevie rather than me.

So did Stevie, who said, "Don't think Dad let her finish what she was saying. He tried to get her to talk about that guy she was with. Was Rick, wasn't it?"

Albert said, "I believe so, but you were standing closer to them, and the music was so loud, I couldn't hear much about what anyone was saying."

The conversation was interrupted by Ellie who appeared and asked if we needed anything else.

Charles finished his beer and said, "Albert, Stevie, I'm getting another beer, sure you don't want one?"

Stevie glanced at Albert before turning to Charles and said, "No, tea's fine, but thanks for asking."

Charles told Ellie about his desire for another beer, and the rest of us said we were okay with ours, and she left to get Charles's drink.

Charles leaned toward Albert and said, "Did Karen say who her friends were that were saying that?"

"Not that I heard."

"Then I don't suppose you heard which fortune teller they were talking about?"

"Didn't get the name, but think it was a guy because she said *he* a couple of times when talking about the killer."

Ellie returned with Charles's beer and our conversation again moved off the murders and centered around how much Stevie was enjoying spending time with Brandon. Albert expressed curiosity about Charles's sweatshirt, which, as could've been predicted, led to a lengthy discussion about what Charles knew about the state represented on his sweatshirt. While he knew next to nothing about Montana, it didn't stop him from discussing his extensive sweatshirt and long-sleeve T-shirt collection.

Stevie and Albert had finished their meals, and Stevie said, "It's supposed to rain later, so Albert, don't you think we should get in our second beach walk of the day before it starts?"

Neither Albert nor Stevie were as interested in Charles's outerwear as he was. They thanked me for lunch and said they hoped to see Charles and me again.

It's hard to believe, but they left before my friend shared how many states were represented on the front of his shirts.

Charles watched them go and said, "Don't know much about the international currency market, but I know a couple of alcoholics when I see them."

"Stevie and Albert?"

"Okay, I'm not certain about both, but one is. Probably Albert."

"Why, because they had tea rather than anything alcoholic?"

"Yeah, and at the Halloween party, the party where nearly everyone had an alcoholic beverage, they had Cokes. I even asked Albert if he wanted rum in his and he said no."

"You can't say someone is an alcoholic simply because he ordered non-alcoholic drinks on the two occasions where we saw them."

"Sure I can. Didn't you hear me?"

"Yes, but—"

"Mark my words, one or both of them are."

That, I couldn't argue with.

34

―――――

Not long after Stevie and Albert walked back to the beach, again hand-and-hand, Charles and I finished our meal, and I paid as Charles headed to the sidewalk. I joined him as he stared in the direction of the Tides.

Before I had time to ask what he was looking at, he said, "Did you see Dani walking Martha's pack of critters toward the beach?"

The hotel was three blocks away, so I said, "No, and didn't realize your eyesight was that good."

"I'm not certain it was Dani, but it was a short person walking a bunch of dogs."

"Since she's helping Martha with her wildlife, it could've been her."

"Chris, how many times do I have to tell you, dogs aren't wildlife? Davy Crockett, her raccoon, is her only wildlife critter, and I'm sure he doesn't go on beach walks."

"What about the snake?"

"Squeezy might enjoy the outing. The other day I read about a surfer in Australia that takes his pet snake surfing."

"Oh," I said realizing it was partially my fault that the conversation had run off the rails, or more accurately, fell off the surfboard.

"It's not like the snake paddles the board out to find the best waves. He, or I suppose she, although the article didn't say, rides around the owner's neck. Want to come see if Dani has Squeezy around her neck?"

"I'll skip that opportunity."

"Your loss. I'll let you know what I learn."

"Can hardly wait."

"Anyone tell you your sarcasm is getting worse?"

"Yep."

Charles headed towards the Tides, shaking his head as he went.

I passed the foul-weather sanctuary of First Light Church and noticed the interior lights were on. Preacher Burl probably wouldn't expect any manual labor from me, so I opened the door and saw the preacher and Roisin Stone seated on a pew in the front of the small sanctuary.

"Brother Chris, you're a few days early for our Sunday service," Burl said then laughed at his joke.

Roisin hopped up and gave me a hug then said, "Mr. Chris, I'm so happy to see you. Your house was next on my list."

I smiled and said, "Searching for leftover Halloween candy?"

"No, silly, I wanted to invite you to a gathering tonight at the beach house Stormy and Darrin are renting for the fortune tellers. Sorry for the short notice but they only decided to have it this morning." She rolled her eyes. "You know how grownups can be."

Burl moved beside Roisin and said, "Sister Roisin invited me, but I have a prior commitment. I hate to miss it. You won't disappoint her, will you?"

"The last thing I'd want to do is disappoint such a lovely young lady. What time and what's the address?"

She gave me the time and location, then added, "Do you know if Mr. Charles has plans for this evening?"

"Don't know. We had lunch and he left for the beach to look for someone. You should be able to catch him if you hurry."

She gave Burl and me quick hugs and rushed out the door in search of Charles.

Burl watched her go then turned to me and said, "How are you doing? I know this last week has been a roller coaster ride."

"Considering everything, I'm doing okay."

"I'm thankful. After the incident at Cal's party, I was on edge the rest of the evening."

I nodded and said, "That was a side of you I've never seen but was impressed with how you took control."

"I questioned myself since it flowed so easily."

"Preacher, occasionally good men need to be forceful."

He put his arm around my shoulder and said, "Then, we're birds of a feather. You were standing there with me." Burl stood and nodded toward the door. "I need a few things from Bert's. Care to walk with me? I'm trying to broaden my horizons and lessen my girth," he added as he patted his stomach.

The walk to the store was filled with talk about how crowded the streets were despite the heart of vacation season having ended.

A block from our destination, Burl stopped and turned toward me. "Brother Chris, I'm glad you agreed to attend tonight's gathering, but please be careful."

I wondered where that'd come from, but instead of asking, I said, "I will. Thanks for your concern."

I left Burl at the store and continued to my cottage where the rest of the afternoon passed slightly faster than a snail backing up.

I must've drifted off since I nearly fell out of my chair when the phone rang. Charles's name appeared on the screen.

"I'm surprised you're not here," I said mimicking the kind of comment I regularly received from my friend.

"That's why I'm calling. I'm not going."

That was the last thing I expected from Charles.

"Is something wrong?"

"It's hard to believe, but I'm not as young as I used to be. Roisin caught up with me before I got to the beach, and we had a nice talk. She said if I couldn't make it, she'd miss me but understood about me getting so old. I don't think she had to say *so old*, but I suppose to a teenager, it was accurate. Anyway, after she left, I kept looking for the dog walker. Finally found her."

"Was it Dani?"

"Yes, and five of Martha's pups, Dani and I walked and talked. Seemed like we walked a hundred miles. I'm tuckered out. You'll tell Roisin why I can't make it, won't you?"

I smiled. "Sure, I'll tell her you're tuckered out."

"You could leave out the tuckered-out part and say something came up and that's why I couldn't make it?"

"I'll see. Did you learn anything new from Dani?"

"Yep, she's back on the suspect list."

"What did—"

"I'll fill you in tomorrow."

I wasn't as tuckered out as Charles, so I started walking the few blocks to the house the Roseruns rented on East Arctic Avenue.

The large, elevated, two-story, sea green house was not unlike many others that had replaced small beachfront cottages demolished in recent years. It had a small front yard, but I was certain, like many other McMansions, there were large porches spanning the width of the rear of the house with panoramic views of the Atlantic. In the Halloween spirit, carved pumpkins illuminated by candles stared at me from the three upper-story windows, and two bookended the front landing.

Roisin was sitting on the steps. She saw me approach, stood, and smiled.

"Evening, Roisin, you look right at home with your pumpkin guards."

"Mom has been letting me stay with Stormy, so I'm pretending this is my home." She looked behind me and added, "Couldn't Mr. Charles make it?"

"He sends his regrets. I think today wore him out."

"Too much exercise can do that."

I chuckled and said, "Is everybody inside?"

"Stormy, Happy, Raven Moon, and Chloe, are. Darrin is on his way, but I'm not sure where Heidi or Spencer are. They should've been here by now. Want to go inside?"

"Sure."

Roisin stood and led me up the stairs. By the time we reached the entry, the door opened, and Chloe stepped outside. I barely recognized her since she wasn't wearing a headscarf, and her tan blouse and black slacks weren't as exotic as I remembered her previous attire.

She said, "Thought I heard voices. It's nice to see you again, Chris."

"I appreciate being invited."

"Why don't you two head in, and I'll wait for the others."

The doors from the family room to the deck were large, glass sliding doors. Roisin led me to the massive deck. Happy Bishop was leaning against the railing and wearing orange tennis shoes, gray shorts, and a black sweatshirt.

Stormy was sitting in an Adirondack chair, noticed me, and stood while making a slow turn. She was wearing a gray dress with ravens and tombstones on it.

She smiled and said, "Sometimes you need to dress like a graveyard."

"I'll keep that in mind," I said and smiled. "What a nice rental."

"It's been pleasant staying here. I'm treating it as a vacation and am going to enjoy every minute until I must return the keys."

Raven Moon walked over and gave me his best cat look of disdain, then jumped up on the railing. His all-black coat and gargoyle appearing ears would've been a welcome addition to Stormy's graveyard.

Happy slid chairs over for Roisin and me. "We thought since it's such a pleasant evening, the porch was the place to be."

I agreed and thanked him for getting the chairs.

"We all need a peaceful, quite gathering where no one dies," Happy said and sat near Roisin.

Chloe walked outside, followed by Heidi, again dressed in all black, and said, "Found our lost soul."

"Merry meet," Stormy said as she stood and offered her chair to the new arrival.

"I was not lost," Heidi said. "Was enjoying the weather, it's perfect for a ritual."

"Ritual?" I said as thoughts of a sacrificial lamb popped into my mind. After all, some of the folks here are witches.

"No rituals tonight," Stormy said as she smiled.

Heidi said, "Don't know if you were talking about it before I arrived, but have all of you been interviewed, or more accurately, interrogated by the police about the guy killed during that party?"

Happy glanced around the room and said, "Almost everyone has. Know I was, and, so was Chloe, Spencer, and Tori." He glanced at Heidi.

She said, "Yes."

"Me, too," Stormy said. "Told her I wasn't on the island when it happened. "Chris, you're friends with the Chief, do they have suspects?"

"Don't know for sure but they're looking at all angles."

"So, they're not determined to pin it on one of us, you know, the weird outsiders?" Happy said.

"No, they're—"

Chloe interrupted with, "What about Alice? I thought she'd be here. Have they talked with her?"

Happy said, "Alice told me she saw bad events going to befall several people and needed to ground herself." He then looked around as if waiting to see if anyone had anything to add.

No one spoke, so I put on my Charles hat and said, "What type of events and to whom?"

"There's no reason to believe what she claims to have seen," Chloe said. "Alice's visions are sporadic at best."

I noticed two or three nods among the group.

"Someone was killed, so her gifts might be better than you think," Happy said.

Heidi laughed and said, "Even a blind mouse gets the cheese sometimes."

On the word mouse, Raven Moon hopped off the railing and looked around the deck, apparently looking for the elusive, handicapped rodent.

The sun had disappeared behind the houses on the other side of the street and where we once could see up and down the beach, only shadows like phantoms moved along the sand. A phone ringing inside the house brought Stormy to her feet. She hurried inside to answer and end the irritating sound. Roisin, the young hostess, asked if someone could come inside and help her carry the appetizers and drinks to the lantern lit dining table at the far side of the deck.

Happy, who was closest to the door, led the procession as the rest of us followed. I'd made it to the door when what sounded like a large firecracker drew my attention toward the beach. The sharp sound was followed by a continuous volley. It took me no more than seconds to realize the noises weren't harmless fireworks.

The door's glass shattered, and projectiles slammed into the wall at the side of the room. I rushed through the shattered door, pushed Roisin to the floor, and covered her body with mine.

I looked to my right and saw Heidi on the floor no more than ten feet from the empty doorframe that'd been filled with glass seconds earlier. In the other direction, Chloe was kneeling behind the sofa. I couldn't see Stormy or Happy.

I closed my eyes and waited for the volley to end. It seemed like forever but in reality it was only seconds when the only sounds I heard came from remaining shards of glass falling and sobs and screams from the others in the house. I carefully pushed myself off Roisin and sat up. I looked towards the beach while wondering if someone was waiting for movement in the house to commence firing. I couldn't see anything.

Chloe shouted. "Get away from the windows and door. Stay low and shout out. Is everyone okay?"

Much closer to me and barely above a whisper, I heard, "Mr. Chris, I'm bleeding."

Roisin's face was ashen; tears welled up in her eyes.

I carefully slid her away from the area that exposed her to the shooter and gently moved her behind the kitchen island. There was a trail of blood behind us.

"Where are you hurt?"

"My arm," Roisin said, tried to lift her left arm, then gasped.

Remembering there was an experienced firefighter in the house, I yelled, "Chloe, we need you over here. Roisin's been shot."

Chloe, ignoring her own orders to stay low, ran to the kitchen. She gingerly examined Roisin's arm, told me to grab a dish towel off the island, then placed it on the wound and applied pressure. Roisin whimpered but amazingly didn't cry out.

Knowing she was well cared for, I looked around and saw Happy helping Heidi to her feet and slowly move as far away from the exposed doors as possible. I yelled for Stormy and received nothing but silence.

I walked towards the entry door and saw Stormy at the foot of the stairs leading to the upper floor. Blood was dripping from a gash on the side of her head.

I grabbed her arm to help her stand and said, "Were you hit?"

"I was upstairs when the windows exploded. Was running downstairs, slipped and fell."

I reached for my phone to call 911, but my pocket was empty. I yelled, "Someone call 911!"

Someone had beaten me to it. I heard the distant sound of the sirens from every occupied Folly Beach emergency vehicle headed our way.

35

I 'd helped Stormy onto a nearby chair in the great room when the first emergency vehicle arrived then went to the door to see Officer New jogging up the stairs.

"Hey, Chris," he said after he caught his breath. "What's going on?"

I gave him a capsule review of what I knew, and realized I wasn't telling him much. I said based on where I believed the sounds of the weapon had come from, the shooter was on the beach. Officer New turned his back to me and said something into his handheld radio before turning to me.

"Was anyone hit?"

I told him yes and led him into the kitchen where Chloe was still tending to Roisin's wound.

New said something else into his radio, then knelt in front of Roisin and softly said, "Young lady, an ambulance is on the way. They'll take good care of you."

"Thank you, sir," she said then looked up at me standing beside Officer New. "Mr. Chris, would you call Mom and tell her what happened?"

Officer Bishop was next to arrive. She immediately went to Stormy and asked if she was okay. Stormy removed the towel from her scalp and told Bishop she was fine and had slipped on the steps and hit her head. Bishop then looked toward the group of us in the kitchen and must've assumed everything was being taken care of since she went to Happy and Heidi standing in the corner of the room as far from the deck as they could get. I couldn't hear what they were telling Bishop but Happy was waving his arms toward the deck.

Two Folly Beach firefighters who doubled as EMTs entered next. One stopped in front of Stormy; the other joined Officer New and Chloe who were talking with Roisin.

I looked around the kitchen and found my phone near the island where it'd fallen out of my pocket then took a deep breath and called Shannon Stone.

She answered with, "Hi, Chris. How are you this blessed evening?"

"I'm fine, but something happened at the house where Roisin is staying with Stormy and her friends. Roisin's been injured. I think she'll be okay, but they'll want to take her to the hospital."

"What happened?"

I didn't want to alarm her more than I already had, so I didn't want to say her daughter had been shot.

"The ambulance isn't here yet, so could you come over and ride with her when it arrives?"

"Desmond, stay with Lugh. Chris, you still there?"

"Yes."

"I'm heading out the door. You sure she's okay?"

"I think she will be."

The phone went dead.

I barely had time to put the phone in my pocket when Chief LaMond stormed through the door, did a quick take of her surroundings, then came over to me.

"You good?" she said as she stared at the shattered doors.

"Yeah," I said then pointed to Roisin on the kitchen floor. "Roisin was shot in the arm, but according to Chloe Meriweather, one of the fortune tellers who's a firefighter, she doesn't appear to have serious damage to her arm. I'm certain when the ambulance arrives, they'll take her to the hospital. Shannon is on the way over." I nodded in the direction of Stormy seated near the front door. "Stormy Roserun is renting the house while the fortune tellers are in town. When the shooting started, she slipped on the stairs and hit her head. I think she'll be okay."

"Any idea how many shots were fired? Where the shooter was? And, oh yeah, anyone see who it was?"

"I don't know how many shots were fired, but it was a bunch. I'm no expert but guess they were from some kind of semi-automatic weapon based on the number and speed at which the rounds were fired. It sounded like it came from the beach or along the dunes. Finally, it was dark, and no one said they saw the shooter."

Over Cindy's shoulder, I saw Shannon Stone standing in the doorway. She immediately focused on her daughter on the kitchen floor and rushed to her. I excused myself from Cindy and went to meet Shannon.

Roisin's face was still covered with tears, but she managed to smile at her mother. Shannon cradled her daughter's head in her left arm and kissed her forehead.

Before Shannon said anything to me, two medics came into the room with a stretcher and a red medical bag. Officer Bishop motioned them into the kitchen. The EMTs approached Roisin and politely motioned for Shannon and Chloe to step back while they evaluated the injury. I moved beside Shannon and gave her a brief explanation about what had happened.

"Who did it? Who shot my daughter?"

"Shannon, I have no idea."

She gave me a tight hug and whispered, "First Mike shot dead in our driveway, now Roisin. Why, Chris, why?"

"Shannon, I don't know, but have confidence Roisin will be okay. She's a brave and strong young lady. You should be proud of her. If it's the last thing I do, I'll find the person who did this."

One of the ambulance crew came over and said they were ready to take Roisin to the hospital and asked if Shannon wanted to ride with them. She said yes, thanked me for calling, then followed the medic to her daughter who was now on the stretcher.

Cindy was on the deck and gazing toward the beach. I joined her and said, "Your guys find anything out there?"

She sighed and said, "Like a rifle covered in fingerprints or a note with a signed and notarized confession?"

"Either of those would be helpful."

"Dream on. Where was everyone when the shooting started?"

I gave her my best recollections but preceded them with I wasn't certain since several people were moving and going inside to help carry the food and drinks to the table when the firing started.

"Did it appear anyone specific had been targeted?"

"Not really. As you can see from the damage, the shooter was spraying the area rather than focused on any one person."

"I'm probably going to regret asking, but since you know as much about what's happened in the last week and a half than any of us in law enforcement, do you think the two killings and tonight's shooting were by the same person?"

"I can see Wesley Thomas's murder and tonight's, umm, event being by the same person. Donald Braxton's death doesn't appear like the others. He was a local and him being stabbed appears different than being shot or being shot at."

"Don't suppose you have any theories about who fired the shot, or shots?"

"If Donald Braxton hadn't been killed, I would've said it was a local who had a grudge against fortune tellers. Now, I don't know."

"Couldn't it be one of the fortune tellers who had something against Wesley Thomas and someone here tonight? And, after the way Donald Braxton treated members of the group, that could've pissed off the killer enough to add him to their naughty list."

"If that's the case, you can eliminate Heidi Strongmire, Happy Bishop, Chloe Meriweather, and Stormy Roserun. They were all here."

Cindy took out her notebook and jotted down those names.

"Okay," she said, "anyone not here who should've been?"

"Stormy's husband Darrin, your good buddy Alice Clay—"

"The nutzoid?"

"Yep."

"Anyone else?"

"Let's see, yeah, Spencer Ford. Roisin said he was coming, but she didn't know why he wasn't here." I hesitated then added, "That's it, I think."

Cindy started to say something, looked at the entry, and said, "Crap. Your best buddy is here."

I followed where she was looking and saw the *GQ* model, Sheriff's Office Detective, and my least favorite law enforcement person, Kenneth Adair. The deck was too far off the ground to jump, and I didn't know if any of the witches could make me disappear, or better yet, make him disappear. I exhaled and waited for the Detective to join Cindy and me.

He did with his typical arrogant demeaner, glare, and friendly, "Chief, why is Mr. Landrum here?"

"He was among the group who could've been killed in tonight's incident. Don't you think that's an appropriate reason he's being questioned?"

I was impressed by Cindy's snarky remark and remained silent.

Adair turned to me and said, "Okay, Mr. Landrum, what is your involvement in whatever occurred here."

"I'm a friend of the hosts and was invited. In fact, the young lady who invited me was wounded and is being transported to the hospital."

"Hmm," he said before turning his back on me and facing Cindy. "Chief, can we speak in private?"

"Of course."

I saw this as a perfect time to escape. "If there's nothing else, Chief, may I leave?"

"Yes," Cindy said.

Adair glanced at Cindy then faced me before saying, "Please don't leave the premises, Mr. Landrum. I'll have some questions."

His use of please sounded a lot like a nonnegotiable demand. I nodded and looked for anywhere in the house I could find where he wasn't.

36

I awoke the next morning thinking how yesterday had to be one of the worse days of my life. I didn't get home from the rental house until well after midnight.

Detective Adair interviewed everyone in the house, and, of course, left me for last. By the time he got to me his unpleasant self had morphed into an overbearing jerk. Soon as he finished interrogating, or more accurately berating me, Cindy escorted me to Officer Bishop's patrol car, and asked her to take me home. Not only did Trula give me a ride, she walked me to the door and cleared the house before letting me enter. She then told me to lock the door and get some rest. Neither suggestion was necessary since both were high on my to-do list although locking the door was easier than resting.

After the restless night, I padded into the kitchen, started the Mr. Coffee machine, and plopped down on a kitchen chair. My body was telling me there would be nothing wrong with going back to bed, but I knew the uneasiness that had accumulated over the last ten days, wasn't going to let me rest.

The smell of coffee brought me back to the present. I poured a cup and returned to the chair. Half a cup consumed later, a loud pounding at the front door dragged me from my *what if* thoughts, and paranoia made me wonder if I could escape through the back door before, umm, before what? Did I really believe someone wanted me dead and would be knocking?

I was relieved when the pounding was now accompanied by Charles Fowler yelling, "Chris, you in there?"

My friend nearly knocked me over as I opened the door.

He was carrying a bag of donuts. He grabbed my upper arm with his free hand, looked me up and down, and said, "When did our relationship dwindle to where you wouldn't call to tell me you almost had your ticket punched?"

"Charles, it was late, and besides, there was nothing you could've done."

"Fine excuse for a friend. How many times do I have to tell you to call immediately when something happens?"

"I will next time."

"That's what you said the last time, anyway, you okay?"

Not really, I thought, but said, "Yes."

Charles took a step back looking at me, shook his head, set the donuts on the coffee table, and said, "Yeah, right," and walked to the kitchen. "Want another cup of coffee?"

"Yes."

"Get comfortable in the living room. I'll be back."

At the sounds of clinking coffee mugs and Charles fussing at Mr. Coffee, I couldn't help but smile. Good friends are hard to find, and I had one of the best, although occasionally I needed to remind myself how good a friend he was as he was driving me crazy.

He returned to the living room carrying two mugs of coffee, handed me one, then grabbed the bag from the table, and pulled out a chocolate-covered donut.

He took a bite and held out the bag for me to take one.

I said, "Where did you get the donuts?"

"Bert's, I stopped to get snacks to bring over so we could talk about Dani and the gathering last night."

"How'd you learn about the shooting?"

"Sure wasn't from my best friend."

"Sorry."

"I understand but ... you know."

"Yes, so who told you?"

"Officer Bishop. She was in Bert's getting coffee. She saw me and asked how you were doing and if I'd heard anything about Roisin's condition."

"Again, sorry you had to hear it like that. Did Trula say anything else?"

"Nope, I didn't give her a chance. I left her standing there and charged over here as quick as a roadrunner."

"At least you got donuts before you left."

"Yes and no. I had the donuts in my hand when she told me. There was a line at the checkout counter, so I ran out of the store to get here. Roadrunner quick, remember?"

He held the bag open and motioned for me to grab another donut.

"Thanks, but don't think I want to be an accessory to your crime."

"They're pretty good. I don't think Lisa will call the cops, but we can stop by Bert's on our way out and pay for them."

Before I asked where he thought we were going, he took a sip and held up one finger. I sat silently.

He said, "Before we go to Martha's house, tell me about Roisin and what happened."

"Why are we going to Martha's?"

"Later. Tell me about last night."

"Roisin, Chloe, Happy, Raven Moon, and Stormy were there when I arrived. Darrin, Spencer, and Alice were supposed to be there but didn't show."

"Was anyone concerned about them not being there?"

"Yes, but they were more curious than concerned."

"So, you were there and?"

"We were on the deck overlooking the beach, Heidi was a little late arriving but when she showed, we were all on the deck."

"Didn't you see anyone on the beach or in the ocean?"

"It was after dark, so I didn't see anyone on the beach. The shooting started when everyone was going inside to help Roisin carry the appetizers and drinks to the dining table on the deck."

"Everyone got up at once and walked in?"

"Not sure what difference it makes, but the phone rang, and Stormy went inside to answer it. When she was gone, Roisin asked for help and the rest of us went inside to help her."

"So, everyone was inside when the shooting started?"

"Charles, don't interrogate me. I had enough of that last night from Detective Adair."

He huffed and said, "Okay, I'll sit here while you tell me everything that happened from the time you got up yesterday until now."

"Everyone was inside. I was a couple of feet from the glass door with the first shot was fired. At first, I thought it was fireworks, then more shots, and I rushed inside and pushed Roisin to the floor out of the line of fire and covered her body with mine." I paused and true to his word, Charles said nothing as he picked up another donut.

"Once the shooting stopped, I sat up and looked towards the deck but didn't see anyone. There was glass everywhere from the shattered doors. That's when Roisin said she was bleeding."

Charles started to interrupt, but instead took a bite of donut.

"She'd been shot in the arm. Chloe, as you know, is a firefighter with EMT training, so she tended to Roisin while I made sure everyone else was okay. Stormy had slipped and fallen down some of the stairs and received a large cut on her head, but said she was fine. I called Shannon to tell her about her daughter and she got there in time to ride in the ambulance with Roisin to the hospital. The medics suggested Stormy go to the hospital, but she refused. I waited for what seemed like hours to be interviewed by our favorite detective and then Trula brought me home. The end."

"Have you heard anything about Roisin's condition?"

"No, but Chloe said it wasn't as bad as it could have been. I was going to wait until later and call Shannon."

"I don't like this one iota. You're a target for some madman who's hellbent on killing you."

"There's nothing to say I'm the target."

"I disagree. Look at the facts. What, nine days ago, a man not a foot away from you was shot. It could've been you. Then at Cal's party a man your same build was stabbed in a dark lot. Now this. You said the shooting didn't start until you got up. Is Chief LaMond aware of all this? And, where's your protection detail?"

"Cindy and I discussed it, and she is concerned. Again, there's no proof."

"But what about protection? A madman could come to your front door, and you'd open it. Bang, you're dead."

"Charles, a madman carrying donuts came to my door a little while ago, and I'm still alive. Besides, there are no, as you call them, protection details for me."

"One more thing, did any of the three missing guests show up?"

"Darrin got there roughly twenty minutes after the shooting, Officer New came in the house to tell Stormy, but Darrin wasn't allowed in."

"That it? Doesn't it seem strange two people who were supposed to be there never showed?"

That had entered my mind sometime during the night, but that's as far as it got.

"Yes, that was odd. Now back to the shooting. I don't think whoever was firing was aiming at us. The shots were high and on either side of the group."

"Roisin was hit so they weren't far off."

"True, but out of everyone there, I would think Roisin would've been the least likely target."

"I agree, but the man behind her, you know, the one telling me this story, would fit that description. Anyhow, Spencer Ford, weird Alice Clay, and Darrin Roserun are on my suspect list then add Dani Crow, Norman Colter, and Tom."

"Who's Tom?"

"T O M, The Other Man, you know, the suspect we don't know yet."

"You learn that in private detective school?"

"Nope, saw it in a novel I was reading yesterday."

"Whatever. Speaking of Dani Crow, why is she on the list?"

"Once I caught up with her and Martha's pups, she seemed shocked I would remember her."

"Don't think that's suspect material."

Charles gave me a nasty look, and said, "Dani said it amazed her how someone so different than her and her beliefs would remember someone so insignificant to their way of life."

"Want to translate it for me?"

"I sort of asked her that. She said it was because I'd been associating with the fortune telling group, so much that I had drinks with them and gathered for some *satanic ritual*, someone like Dani would be of no concern to me and I wouldn't remember her name."

"That makes no sense. What ritual, satanic or otherwise, have you been to?"

"Again, that's what I asked. She referred to the evening I went to the gathering at the local witch's house."

"Sounds like she's keeping close tabs on the group. Did she say anything about Donald?"

"Yep, said he got what was coming to him for making such a spectacle at Cal's."

"So, if she thinks you're so horrible, why was she walking and talking to you?"

"Excellent question. I'm giving you a gold star for outstanding detective work. She told me everyone can be saved if they haven't gone completely to the dark side. Before you ask, I asked her how she knew I was still salvageable."

I smiled. "I've wondered that myself."

"Funny. She said dogs like me. She might be wrong about some of that other stuff, but she's not wrong about dogs. Everyone knows if a dog likes someone, at least part of that person is still good."

I wasn't about to argue with Charles's canine knowledge, so I said, "Remind me why we're going to Martha's?"

"We need to make sure the dear lady is okay. I haven't seen her since a couple of days after Wesley's death. If Dani's the deranged killer, no one knows if Martha might be sleeping with the fishes."

"From what I recall, Martha doesn't have fish."

"This is no joking matter. You know you'd feel bad if she was dead."

"True."

37

———

With our chat, coffee, and shoplifted donuts consumed, I was ready to visit Martha Wright to see if she happened to still be among the living and attempt to determine if Dani Crow could be the killer.

Instead of turning in the direction of Martha's house, Charles started toward Bert's, and said, "Going to pay for the donuts you ate. Wait here."

As Charles entered the store, I wasn't only amazed he didn't ask me to pay for the stolen loot, but also how quiet the street was. There were no cars or even golf carts whizzing by, a rare occurrence for one of the busiest streets on Folly.

Charles returned smiling and shaking his head.

"What's so funny, you already on the news as a wanted donut thief?"

"Nope, Lisa said she was about to report me to Officer Bishop but stopped because she was afraid what it would say about her."

"Do I have to guess what you're talking about?"

"You'd never get it. She was afraid Bishop would make fun of her because she couldn't stop an old guy who needed a cane to get around."

"Didn't you tell Lisa you were as quick as a roadrunner, and she couldn't have caught you?"

Charles laughed, patted my shoulder, and said, Nice to see you back to being your smart alack self."

My *back to being a smart aleck* mood didn't last long since on our way to Martha's we had to walk past the house where the shooting occurred. Whether real or imagined, I felt a cold chill come over me as we approached the house. I glanced at Charles who had no apparent reaction.

I looked at the yellow crime scene tape around the entry and said, "It's hard to believe such a horrible thing took place here."

"When we come back, we can walk along the beach and see how it looks from there."

"Maybe," I said and reached for my phone.

"If you're planning on calling me to tell me what happened, you're too late."

I rolled my eyes. "I'm calling Shannon to see about Roisin."

"Why call? Let's go to their house."

"First, we don't know if she's home from the hospital, and second, even if she is, the last thing Roisin needs now is people disturbing her or her mother."

Instead of waiting for his various arguments to the contrary, I made the call.

I didn't think Shannon was going to answer and had nearly touched *End call*, when she said in a voice barely above a whisper, "Hey, Chris."

"Shannon, I hate to disturb you, but wanted to check on Roisin."

"We're still at the hospital. That's why I'm whispering. She's doing okay, still a little dopey from the painkillers, but the doc says she'll heal quickly with no permanent damage."

"That's wonderful," I said as Charles pointed at the phone, his way of asking me to put the call on speaker. I did. "Charles is here with me."

"Hi, Charles. Roisin is doing fine, well, as fine as she can be."

"Can we come see her?"

"We're still at the hospital. Don't know when she'll be released. The doc has to come by and put in the order, or whatever. Think it'd be best to wait a day or two before she has visitors. Chris, want me to call when I know for sure?"

"That'd be great. Will you need a ride home?"

"No, Darrin is getting us, but thanks."

"Please tell her I'm thinking about her."

"Me, too," said Charles.

She thanked us for calling.

Charles turned to me and said, "Think you can remember to let me know when Shannon says it's okay to see Roisin? I don't want to hear it in Bert's."

I sighed and said, "Yes."

We'd walked past three houses when Martha's large beachfront house was visible on our right. I stopped and looked back in the direction of the house where the fortune tellers were staying.

Charles said, "What?"

"I hadn't realized how close Martha's house was to the rental."

Charles looked at Martha's then back at the house with the crime scene tape adorning the entry. "You're right. Wouldn't take much for someone to sneak out, walk down the beach, shoot up a house, and return home before anyone noticed." He started walking toward Martha's place and added, "Ready to do some detectin'?"

I wouldn't have put it that way but nodded.

A few paces later, Charles said, "Bet if you ask really nice, Martha will let you hold Squeezy."

I didn't respond and the rest of the walk was in silence. As usual, I wasn't sure what Charles was thinking, but my thoughts were about what we were going to say to Martha. *Sorry for the intrusion, wanted to make sure your boarder hasn't killed you. Or, Martha, has Dani confessed to any recent murders or attempted murders?*

I followed Charles up the steps to Martha's elevated front door and still had no idea what we were going to say when she answered. Charles rang the doorbell and tapped his knuckles on the door and received a disorganized chorus of barks announcing someone was at the door.

Charles turned to me and said, "Not sure if Martha could hear me knock over all that barking."

"Even if she didn't, she'll know someone's here from the racket."

He took a step back and said, "What are you going to say if Dani answers the door?"

"I have no clue. Remember, this was your idea."

He rolled his eyes. "Would have thought you'd be more prepared."

"Need I remind you again, this is your show. You're the detective."

You would've thought I'd crowned him Sherlock Holmes with that observation. He smiled, tilted his Tilley back on his head, and reached out to knock again, when I heard a female voice yelling at the dogs.

The barking seemed to move farther from the door and a familiar voice said, "Who's there?"

"Martha, it's Chris Landrum and Charles Fowler."

"Heavens to bees, let me unlock the door."

The door opened and the eighty-five-year-old, slightly overweight homeowner was leaning on her metal cane and cradled in her left arm a Chihuahua that looked old enough to need a cane. Martha straightened to her full height of 5'2", and was wearing a faded denim dress and yellow, rubber garden shoes with chicken decals on them. She could've easily been mistaken for a street person and not the wealthy widow I knew her to be. She took several steps back so we could come in and close the door.

"Who's this little guy?" Charles said. "I didn't see him the last time I was here." He raised his hand to pet the rat-looking canine.

"I'd watch it, young man. Major Fang is a highly trained guard dog."

Charles jerked his hand back before saying, "Major Fang is what, three pounds? A guard dog?"

"Young man, you ever seen a ticked-off Chihuahua?"

Our hostess didn't wait for Charles's response and led us into what she called a sitting room but looked more like an animal play-house with various toys and a three-foot-high, triple deck, carpeted cat tower. My seating options were a chair next to a large aquarium holding Squeezy, the boa that looked to have grown a mile longer since the last time I'd seen it, or near a killer dog the size of a squirrel. I chose to sit beside Major Fang, now quietly sitting in Martha's lap. Charles, with his inability to not talk to every dog he encountered, tried to start a dialog with the three-pound terror.

Martha ignored his dog talk and said, "Was I expecting you?"

"No," I said, "We wanted to stop by and see how you're doing. I saw your pack yesterday being walked by your new tenant and realized it's been months since I saw you."

Martha glanced at Charles who was still trying to communicate with Major Fang, then turned to me and said, "Did you think Dani killed me and stuck my body in the attic?"

"Of course not," I said, realizing she'd detected our real reason for visiting.

"That's okay, fellas, Dixie said I should be more careful, or I'd wake up dead one day letting any stray in here. She said strays come in all shapes and sizes including people."

Dixie Thompson was Martha's across-the-street neighbor and longtime friend.

I said, "Does Dixie know Dani?"

"They hadn't met until Dani took a room here. Dixie always needs something to worry about. Dani met that need. Now Dani is a bit strange but has been nothing but helpful since she moved in." She smiled. "Sometimes she goes on a tangent about this or that, but I was married to my dearly departed Tommy enough years to let things like that go in one ear and out the other."

"I'm sure Dixie is simply concerned for your safety," I said. "That's even if you have a trained guard dog." I looked at Major Fang who returned the look and snarled. I didn't have Charles's way with animals.

"You're right. Dixie gave me these shoes; said they'd help me garden with her. You know how obsessed she is with her danged garden. I'd rather sit around with her drinking bourbon and me sipping on a hot toddy." She raised her hand and added, "I know, I know, that stuff ain't good for my health." She chuckled and added, "Neither is danged gardening."

Charles said, "Speaking of safety, did you hear all the shooting down the street last night?"

"Why do you think I answered the door holding my guard dog? I spent yesterday in Charleston with Dixie, so I went to bed early. Then bam, bam, bam. It sounded like a war going on. Fellas, I hope no one was hurt." She shook her head. "What's the world coming to?"

Charles said, "I'm guessing your dogs didn't like that racket?"

"That's one Great Dane size understatement, young man. It wasn't only the dogs. The cats all hid under the couch or my bed. Davy missed his nightly meal and Paul wouldn't stop screaming."

Davy, full name Davy Crockett, is her pet raccoon and Paul's a parrot she keeps upstairs because of the cats and what Martha claims, accurately, I might add, is his sailor's salty language she doesn't want him sharing with visitors.

"Sounds like it upset everyone living here," Charles said.

"Not much rest was had in this house with all the shooting and the emergency sirens. The only one getting sleep was Dani. She never came out of her room."

Charles leaned closer to Martha before saying, "I thought Dani would've been out here helping with the upset critters."

"I asked her at breakfast if she heard the commotion. She told me she's always been a sound sleeper. Perhaps being in the back bedroom doesn't get as noisy as the rest of the house."

Charles looked around the room and asked Martha if she needed anything or if he could help get the dogs out of their temporary confinement.

"Thank you, but Dani should be home soon. She left after breakfast saying she was going grocery shopping. Thought it a little strange, but whatever."

I said, "Why strange? I thought she would be helping so you don't have to go out unless you wanted to."

"She is a big help. Was strange because she went grocery shopping the other day before she went to that Halloween party at, umm—"

"Cal's?"

"Yeah, Cal's. Anyway, you know how today's youth are always on the go."

Martha stood and put Major Fang under her arm and patted my hand and Charles's arm then said, "You young men are nice to check on me. As you can see, I'm healthy as a horse and sharp as a spoon."

I assumed she was being humorous with the spoon comment, so I smiled as she led us to the door. She opened it and Charles leaned over and kissed her on the cheek cautiously avoiding the bared teeth of the terror in her arms. I nodded and thanked her for meeting with us.

Charles had forgotten about walking on the beach behind the fortune tellers' house and I wasn't about to remind him. We were in front of my cottage before he said anything.

He watched a pickup truck drive past carrying three surfboards, then turned to me. "You were there last night, were the shots muted? Seems like they'd have been loud."

"You wondering if Dani was in Martha's house how she could've slept through everything going on?"

He nodded. "Let's say Dani did sleep through the gunshots. How could she have slept through a dozen dogs, a bunch of cats, and a cussing parrot making more noise than a freight train going through a tunnel?"

"Excellent question."

38

———————

The sun was shining bright, but my mood was dark, and I felt a cloud of dread hanging over me. Over the last few days, I'd heard some of the local cynics talking about how the fortune telling visitors had put a curse on Folly. I didn't put credence in the naysayers' comments, but the thought had entered my mind. On the other hand, after what'd happened to Wesley Thomas and at the house on East Arctic Avenue, I could argue that one of Folly's residents had put a curse on the fortune tellers. After what Charles and I learned from Martha Wright about Dani Crow allegedly sleeping through the shooting, I moved her ahead of any fortune teller as the most likely suspect in the shooting and the killings.

I was trying to recall everything Martha had said about Dani's answer when questioned whether she'd heard the shooting, when the phone rang.

I answered and heard a vaguely familiar voice say, "Chris, this is Stevie, Brandon Tigert's daughter. Did I catch you at an inconvenient time?"

"Hi, Stevie. No, that's fine. What's up?"

"Do you think you could join Albert and me for an early lunch?"

That wasn't a question I anticipated, but said, "Sure. Where and when?"

"We're getting ready to leave the campground, so how about in a half hour at the Lost Dog Cafe?"

"Great. I'll see you there," I said and caught myself before asking why they wanted to meet.

As I reached the small parking area in front of the Dog, Amber saw me approaching and rushed to meet me.

She hugged me and said, "Are you okay?"

"Yes, why?"

"I was off the last couple of days and just heard from Marc about what happened at that house out East Arctic. He said you were there during the shooting."

Marc Salmon was one of Folly's city council members I'd known since I moved to the barrier island. He's also one of the city's most prolific gossips.

"I'd be lying if I said it wasn't scary, but I'm fine. Thanks for asking."

"Am I going to have to put some sort of tracker around your neck so I can see where you are and keep you out of trouble?"

Before I asked how a tracking device could keep me out of trouble, Stevie and Albert arrived. I turned back to Amber. "Think you can find a table for three somewhere inside?"

"Sure, and I'll start looking for that tracker," she said, smiled at the new arrivals, then led us inside to a table along the wall.

We each said we wanted water so Amber left to find three glasses, and Albert said, "Thank you for agreeing to meet. I know it was short notice."

"It wasn't a problem."

Albert turned to Stevie who said, "I suppose you're wondering why we wanted to meet."

I smiled and said, "It'd crossed my mind."

"Dad said you were good at keeping secrets." She chuckled and added, "Sometimes too good at keeping them, he said."

Amber arrived with our water and asked if we were ready to

order. Stevie and Albert hadn't touched their menus, so I asked her to give us a few minutes. She said to wave when we were ready and headed to the kitchen.

Stevie took a sip, glanced at Albert, then turned to me. "We don't know many people here, and to be honest, don't even know Dad that good. That's why we wanted to talk to you since you've known him for years."

"I don't know him well, but yes, we've known each other a long time."

"Albert and I were talking and wanted to share something and see how you think Dad would take it if we told him." She was twisting her napkin and glancing at the table as she spoke. "This is sort of hard to talk about."

I gave her my best effort at a kind smile and said, "That's okay, Stevie. Take your time."

Albert leaned forward and said, "Stevie and I are drunks, umm, alcoholics."

"But we've been sober five months."

"Five months, six days," Albert said.

Private Detective Charles finally got one right.

"That's great," I said. "Staying sober is a rough process to go through."

"Never could've done it if it wasn't for Stevie. She's been so supportive. More than I deserve, to tell the truth."

She leaned over and patted him on the arm. "That's not true."

"Congratulations. I'm no expert but know it's important you have a dedicated support system. Have you found somewhere to go to meetings while you've been visiting?"

Stevie said, "There's a church near the campground that holds AA meetings. We've been going there. Didn't want to go close to Folly where Dad could've found out."

"He doesn't know?"

"No, that's one of the reasons we wanted to talk with you. I'm afraid to tell him, you know, not knowing what he might say. What do you think?"

"Like I said, he and I aren't close friends, but I'd tell him. I think he'd be proud of you, of both of you, for addressing the problem. That took dedication and a lot of courage."

Amber returned and asked if we needed more water. We each said yes, and I asked my tablemates if they were ready to order.

"Guess we better," Stevie said and glanced at the menu.

They each ordered chicken salad croissants, and I said, "French toast."

Amber said, "I'm shocked," then turned to Stevie, "That's what he orders every time he's here." She shook her head before leaving to put in our orders.

Stevie turned to me and said, "Are there FTAA meetings here you could go to?"

It took me a couple of seconds to figure out FTAA stood for French Toast Addicts Anonymous.

I laughed. "No, but there should be."

Stevie said, "Albert's been telling me I should tell Dad about our problem, but it's good hearing it from someone who's known him as long as you have."

Albert said, "Can we ask something else?"

"Sure."

"I know you asked us how long we planned to be here. I don't remember what we said, but know it was vague." He glanced at Stevie then back at me. "We're thinking about moving to Folly, or somewhere close to here."

Stevie said, "We want to get away from Atlanta and some people who're friends, or maybe they're people we know and not real friends. I don't think good friends would keep pushing us to go out drinking with them. What do you think, Chris?"

"Real friends would respect your wishes, and I think it would be great if you lived closer to Brandon. I bet he'd be thrilled."

"See, Stevie, that's what I keep saying."

Amber returned carrying our food. We thanked her and she said to wave if we needed anything else.

We each took a bite before Stevie said, "Albert, want to tell him about the other thing?"

"Might as well. See, when I met Brandon, I asked if I could borrow some money. I told him it was because I had a source that'd help me make a large amount of money in the international currency market but needed money to invest."

I waited, but he didn't continue. I didn't want to tell him I'd learned that from Brandon when he asked Charles to see what he could find out about the plan.

"Albert," Stevie said, "tell him."

He sighed and said, "Chris, that was BS. You saw that heap of junk we rode in on. It came from a sort of shady *buy here, pay here* car lot in Atlanta. Stevie told me not to do it, but, well, stupid me didn't listen. I needed a way to get around and couldn't borrow from a bank or anywhere legitimate. Who'd lend anything to a part-time bartender? Anyway, I did it and still owe a little under five-grand. I want to have those crooks paid off before we leave Atlanta, and that's where the money would go if Brandon lent it to me."

"First, Albert," I said, "it's admirable you don't want to default on the loan, but, if you don't mind me asking, is it right lying to Brandon to get the money?"

He looked at Stevie then turned to me. "Stevie tell you to say that?"

I smiled and said, "No, why?"

"Because that's her opinion."

I said, "Could be because she's right."

"Told you so," Stevie said and took a bite of her croissant.

"Yes, you did. Chris, you really think it'd be best to tell him about our, recovery efforts and the real reason I wanted the money?"

"I think he'll respect you even more for wanting to stay sober and for wanting to pay off your debt. It's still your decision. I won't share any of this with him, so you don't have to worry about him finding out from me."

Stevie said, "Thank you," then looked at Albert and said, "How about us telling him today after he gets off work?"

"If he's going to be around. Didn't he say something about having a date tonight?"

Stevie chuckled and said, "Think that's what he meant, although he seems to be as reluctant to tell us about his love life as we are about our issues."

"So, he is dating Karen Johnson, the lady you mentioned at the Halloween party?"

"Yes," Albert said. "Speaking of the Halloween party, we heard you were visiting some of those fortune tellers when that house they're staying in got shot up. You all right?"

"Yes, thanks for asking. How'd you hear about it?"

"Dad and Karen were talking about it last night."

"I suppose they were saying bad things about the fortune tellers. I know Brandon isn't a fan of them being here."

Stevie said, "He doesn't believe in all their hocus-pocus but isn't hostile to them like Brandon's boss. Karen was defending them, saying they have as much right to their opinions as the angry locals. I know next to nothing about what they do or believe, so any opinion I have is worthless."

Albert leaned close to Stevie and put his arm around her and said, "I figure Stevie and I have enough problems without taking sides on something we don't know anything about. We are glad you're safe. That had to be scary being in that house with bullets flying."

Stevie smiled and said, "Almost as scary as talking to Dad about our issues. Want to go with us?"

"No thanks, but to be honest, if you're as candid with him as you've been with me this morning, everything will be okay."

Albert glanced at me then at Stevie and said, "Think we ought to tell Chris about the other thing?"

"Why not. He already knows more about us than anyone here."

Albert returned putting his arm around Stevie and said, "We're thinking about getting married. Maybe doing it soon and on the beach."

"Congratulations."

39

———————

The phone rang as I returned home after having an early lunch with Stevie and Albert. I was surprised to see Shannon Stone's name on the screen.

"Good morning, Shannon."

"Chris, is it okay to be calling?"

"Of course, it is. I'm glad you did. How's Roisin?"

"She's still in some pain but we're home. That helps a lot." She chuckled and said, "Hospitals are no place for sick people. I'm feeling bad and all I did was sit there with Roisin."

"I know what you mean," I said and waited for the reason for her call.

"I didn't call about my health. I'm acting as my daughter's appointment secretary. The first thing she said when we got home was wanting you and Charles to visit. And before you say it, yes, I did ask if she thought she needed a couple more days to recuperate before having visitors." Shannon hesitated and laughed. "My little angel said, 'Mother, I'm not sick. All I have is a hole in my arm.' It would've been a waste of time arguing with her. So, I'm officially asking if you and Charles could visit the young lady with a hole in her arm?"

"Shannon, if you're certain it'd be okay, I'll call Charles and see if he's available. If he is, we'll be there soon."

"Great. Make it as quick as possible, otherwise, she'll mope around until you show up."

I was expecting too much for Charles to answer his phone. He gripes when I don't tell him everything I learn immediately but doesn't think it's his fault when I can't get him to answer. So, without Charles, I drove to the Stone's cottage and was met by Desmond wearing all black and sitting on the small front porch with Lugh beside him posing like one of those regal concrete dog statues adorning many upscale homes.

"Bet if I got shot you wouldn't come running as fast as you did for Sis," Desmond said as he stood.

Lugh barked a greeting.

"Don't underestimate yourself, Desmond," I said and cautiously approached Lugh who hadn't moved.

"Whatever. Where's Charles? He was invited."

"He didn't answer his phone when I called to invite him."

"Too bad, Lugh will miss him. Anyway, you didn't come to see me, so come on in. The queen awaits your arrival."

Shannon appeared in the doorway wearing an ankle-length light green dress. She smiled, and said, "These guys blocking your way?"

"No, your wonderful son was welcoming me and inviting me into the house."

Desmond smiled, Lugh tilted his head, and Shannon said, "I'm sure that's the case. Was Charles unable to make it?"

I repeated what I'd told Desmond about my missing friend. Shannon said she hoped he could visit soon. I assured her he would. And she led me into the parlor where Roisin was half-sitting, half-leaning in the loveseat. She wore a colorful multilayered gown. Her injured left arm was wrapped in gauze from her shoulder to her elbow and was resting on her stomach. A black sling was hanging over the back of the loveseat.

In a voice softer than I was used to, the *queen* said, "Mr. Chris, thank you for coming. Was Mr. Charles not able to visit?"

I told her the same thing I'd told Shannon and Desmond about Charles then added, "How are you feeling?"

"My arm's, I think the right word is throbbing." She grimaced as if giving me a visual of a throbbing arm. "Anyway, it hurts."

I patted her on the head and said, "I'm terribly sorry about what happened."

She looked past me before I realized Desmond, Lugh, and Shannon were standing in the corner of the room listening to the exchange. "Mom, Desmond, and you can bring Lugh, come over where Mr. Chris can see you. I want to tell all of you something."

The rest of Roisin's family obeyed her directive and moved closer to the loveseat.

Roisin waited for them to stop moving and said, "I wanted you to hear it from me, cause it's important. You listening?"

Shannon and Desmond nodded. Lugh stared at her.

Roisin said, "Mr. Chris saved my life."

I started to deny it when the teenager raised her uninjured arm and said, "You were going to say you didn't save me, but you're wrong. You heard that awful person shooting at us and pushed me to the floor and threw your body over me." She smiled. "Sort of squished me a little, but if you didn't, I would've been shot more than once in the arm. Mr. Chris, I owe you my life, so don't try to argue about it. That's why I wanted Mom, Desmond, and even Lugh to hear it from me." She took a deep breath and lowered her right arm that was still above her head.

Shannon looked at Roisin then leaned and put her hand on her daughter's forehead. "I wasn't there, so don't know what happened, but if you say Chris saved you, he must have. Now why don't you close your eyes and try to get a little sleep?"

"You need sleep more than I do. You were in that hospital chair all night while I was in that comfy bed. Mom, if it's okay with you, I'd like to talk with Mr. Chris a little while, then I promise, I'll take a nap."

"Don't take too long, you know that nice doctor said you needed to get plenty of rest."

She sighed. "Yes, Mom."

"Chris," Shannon said, "I'll be in the kitchen if you need anything or if you need me to give the patient a whack on the bottom, so she takes a nap. Desmond, Lugh, come with me."

After everyone left except Roisin and me, the teenager said, "Mom's a great nurse, but she worries too much. I know my arm will get better and the hurting, the throbbing, will end soon."

"She simply cares about you and doesn't want you to hurt more than you already are."

"I know. Mr. Chris, I was wondering what happened after they took me to the hospital. I knew if I asked with the rest of the family here, they'd make us stop talking and want me to take a nap."

"First, how's your arm really feel?"

She grinned and said, "As Desmond would put it, 'It hurts like hades.'"

"Don't you think you ought to tell your mom?"

"Nope. She'll make me take more of those pain pills and get in bed. I'm already taking enough of those pills. They make me loopy."

"Okay, but promise me, if it gets feeling worse, you'll do what your mom wants you to do."

"I promise, now what happened?"

I gave her a brief, or brief by Charles's standards, overview of what occurred after she'd left for the hospital. I asked if anyone from the Sheriff's Office or the Folly Beach Department of Public Safety had interviewed her and she said no and added, "They probably think I'm a little kid and wouldn't know anything."

"Do you know something?"

She twisted around on the loveseat and moved her injured arm to a pillow in front of her before saying, "I don't know."

"What's that mean?"

"Remember, when the shooting started it was dark, dark and foggy on the beach. Before I went inside to help carry stuff to the table, I was looking down at the beach. The moon was out, so I could see shadows and stuff, but not much else. Then I saw something."

She twisted again and I waited for her to continue. When she didn't, I said, "What do you think you saw?"

"Mr. Chris, you're going to think I'm as loony as Desmond."

I smiled. "Don't think that's possible."

She returned my smile and said in a voice softer than it already was, "I thought it was a phantom."

"Why'd you think that?"

"I sort of think it was because I'd been listening to some of the group telling stories about talking to dead people, or seeing the auras of people who'd already passed, and stuff like that."

"Describe what you saw."

"I will try if you promise not to laugh."

I patted her on the good arm and promised.

"It was someone, or looked like someone, walking slow in the sand and carrying something, thought maybe it was a long stick or a board."

"Could it have been a rifle?"

She closed her eyes as if she were recreating the scene in her head. "Maybe," she said and grimaced.

I leaned closer and said, "Remember anything else about the person?"

"Remember, I'm guessing, but I think it was a girl."

"Why do you say that?"

"I said I'm guessing, but it seemed like it walked like a girl. That's the best I can do."

"Do you mean someone your age or younger?"

She slowly shook her head, "No, guess I should've said like a woman and not a girl."

"Anything else?"

She grimaced again and closed her eyes.

"Hurting worse?"

She whispered, "Yes."

"Roisin, you've been a big help. I'm going to leave now so you can do what your mom said. You promise you'll take a nap, and if it's time, take another pill?"

"I promise."

"Good," I said as I leaned down and kissed her on the forehead.

Her eyes remained closed, and I slowly stood, walked into the kitchen, and said bye to Shannon, Desmond, and Lugh. They thanked me for coming and I told them if they needed anything to call. Shannon said she would. Desmond said, "Whatever."

40

The next morning, I thought about what Roisin had said about seeing a female on the beach. Her description couldn't have been vaguer, but if it happened to be a female carrying a rifle, Tori Bran and Alice Clay came to mind. Both had reportedly left Folly, but had they? Then, of course, there was Dani Crow, the most likely suspect, the person who wasn't a fan of the fortune tellers, and someone staying a handful of houses away from the bullet-riddled house.

If Charles had been with me when I was talking with Roisin, he would've been on me to call Chief LaMond and tell her the killer was, umm, Tori, or Alice, or Dani. Something else I was certain about was the first thing Chief LaMond would ask was what was the motive for one of the three to be shooting into a house filled with fortune tellers, witches, and one old local who had no extraordinary powers other than constantly pestering a chief of police. So, regardless of what Charles's wishes would have been, contacting Chief LaMond would be a bad idea.

The second phone call in two days from Shannon Stone interrupted my two-course breakfast consisting of two slices of toast and a handful of peanuts.

"Shannon, is everything okay?"

"Yes, I know it's strange calling again."

"No, that's fine, just worried about your daughter. I know she was hurting when I left yesterday."

"She still is, but as you are aware, she has a well-developed stubborn streak. Got it from her father."

"She is persistent."

"Anyway, she awakened this morning and insisted I call. She remembered something she claims might help you and Charles catch the person responsible for the shooting at the rental house and insists you return so she can tell you in person."

"She couldn't tell me over the phone?"

"That was my preference, but she said it would be better if you came back. Would that be possible?"

"Of course. Now?"

"Please."

Knowing how much pain Roisin was in yesterday, I didn't think she needed two visitors, so I didn't call Charles.

This time, there wasn't a greeting committee on the porch. Shannon rolled her eyes when she answered the door and apologized for having me return. She took me into the parlor and said Roisin would be out in a couple of minutes, then whispered, "She didn't want you to see her in her gown. Said she wanted to be dressed so she'd look like she felt better than she had during your previous visit."

"Mother," Roisin said as she entered the room. "You weren't supposed to tell Mr. Chris that."

She had on navy shorts and a yellow short-sleeve blouse. This time she was wearing the sling and slowly lowered herself onto the loveseat.

Shannon waited until Roisin appeared settled and said, "I'll leave you two to talk. Roisin, please don't overdo it. You can always talk to Mr. Landrum later."

After Shannon left for the kitchen, Roisin said, "Thank you for coming back. I know it's a lot of trouble."

I smiled and said, "Yes, I had to take time out of my busy retirement and drive a whopping three blocks."

She chuckled. "Well, I'm glad you did."

"Your mom said you remembered something that may help the police catch the person who shot into the house."

"I don't know if it will help or if it means anything. In the middle of the night, I woke up and thought about something else that happened that afternoon. An hour before the shooting, it was still light outside. I was taking a walk." She whispered. "I was getting tired of listening to spooky stories. Thought a walk would be good. I saw a woman walking toward the beach from the road. She looked sort of familiar, but I didn't know why when I first saw her."

"Was she carrying anything?"

Roisin grimaced and said, "You mean like a gun?"

I nodded.

"No."

"Could you describe her?"

"Older than mom but not as old as you, umm, sorry."

"That's okay. I know I'm old."

"Anyway, she was thin and sort of tall, almost as tall as you, I think."

"Hair color?"

"Dark, didn't notice if it was black or brown, again, sorry."

"That's okay, you're doing great. I know this is hard to answer, but did she appear suspicious for any reason, or say anything to you?"

"No, like I said, it may not have anything to do with what happened. She could have been going for a walk on the beach. I didn't see where she went since I was going the other direction."

"You said you didn't remember why she looked familiar when you first saw her. Does that mean you know now?"

"Mr. Chris, you listen good. I wish Desmond, and some other people I know could learn how to do that. Anyway, right when I woke up, it came to me. She was wearing a sweater with bright red and white stripes going up and down. I think it was the same sweater she was wearing when I saw her the first time. I remembered it because I thought it looked like a sweater she should wear to a Christmas party and not a Halloween party."

"She was at Cal's Halloween party?"

"Yeah, but I didn't see her go in. Mom and me dropped Desmond off before we went to Charleston and spent the evening with Stormy and Darrin. I saw her beside the building. She was looking around like she was waiting for somebody."

"And you remembered her because of the sweater?"

"Yes."

"You're certain it was the same woman?"

"Think so. Mr. Chris, you were at the party, so did you see a woman in a red and white sweater? The stripes went up and down."

"I don't recall seeing anyone like that, but she could have been there. It was crowded and dark. Do you know who Donald Braxton is?"

"The man that got stabbed Halloween?"

"Yes. Would you recognize him if you'd seen him near Cal's that night?"

"I don't think I've ever seen him."

She touched her injured arm and grimaced.

"Hurting more?"

She looked toward the kitchen door then turned to me and said, "Yes. I need to climb back in bed before Mom gets mad."

I agreed with her and thanked her for the information on the mysterious woman.

"Like I said, I don't know if she had anything to do with what happened, but isn't it strange that she was near Cal's when that Braxton man was stabbed and near the house that got all shot up?"

"Yes, you've been extremely helpful."

"Okay, you two," Shannon said as she reentered the room. "Think you've gabbed long enough."

"Yes, Mom," she said and winked at me, knowing we'd already come to that conclusion.

I gave Roisin a hug, careful not to touch her wounded arm, then she headed to her bedroom.

Shannon walked me to the door, thanked me for coming, and said, "I'll try not to call you again."

"Call anytime, and by the way, she was a big help."

507

41

"Did you try to call earlier to invite me to lunch at The Washout?" Charles asked after I answered the phone with his name on the screen.

"No and no."

"What're you talking about?"

"No, I called yesterday and no, it had nothing to do with an invitation to lunch at The Washout."

"Are you going to meet me there or not?"

I smiled and said, "Yes."

"Good, you're late."

Meaning he was already there. I touched *End call*, utilizing another of Charles's favorite moves, and headed toward Center Street and another of Folly's popular restaurants.

Charles was sitting inside at a booth near the back of the room and talking with Danielle, a college-age server. He nodded when he saw me headed his way and the server asked what I wanted to drink. I told her a diet soft drink and she went in search of one.

Instead of saying anything civil, Charles said, "Well, why'd you call yesterday if it wasn't to offer to buy me lunch today?"

"If you'd answered your phone, you'd know."

"Sorry," he said, a word as close to a full-throated apology as I'd heard him offer. "Had to make an early delivery for Dude and forgot to take my phone. Then its battery was dead, and I didn't charge it until a little while ago, and then ... oh, never mind, why'd you call?"

I shared Roisin's condition and was interrupted twice by Charles asking why I hadn't taken him to see her. Yes, he'd admitted he didn't have his phone with him and then it wasn't charged, but somehow still managed to make it my fault for not inviting him.

"Is she going to be okay?"

"Think so. She's in some pain but she should have a full recovery."

"Great."

My drink arrived and Danielle asked if we were ready to order. I looked at Charles who said, "Flounder sandwich," and I added, "The same." We each declined an order of fries with Charles saying, "That's part of my new diet. Got to maintain this trim, fine-tuned body."

Danielle did what good servers should do, she didn't laugh.

"Where were we?" Charles said after the server had left.

"I was telling you about Roisin."

"You learn anything that'd help us catch the person that committed the dastardly deed of shooting that young lady?"

I told him about what Roisin thought she saw on the beach immediately preceding the shooting.

"You sure she said a phantom?"

"That's what came to mind. Remember, it was dark and foggy so I'm sure someone walking on the beach could appear to be a phantom to a thirteen-year-old."

"And she thought the person was carrying a stick or board? What about a rifle?"

"When she saw the person or whatever, it was before the shooting, so I doubt a rifle would've been something that would've entered her mind."

"And it was a female?"

"That was her impression."

"She didn't remember anything else about the phantom-like image?"

Our sandwiches arrived and Danielle refilled our drinks before bussing the booth behind us.

I took a bite then said, "Now, I have a question. Do you remember a woman at Cal's Halloween party wearing a red and white vertically striped sweater?"

He pointed his sandwich at me and said, "What's that have to do with Roisin seeing a ghost, phantom, or whatever on the beach? I'm no expert on ghostly attire but doubt a red and white sweater is a haint's go-to outfit."

I explained about the woman Roisin saw near the house where the fortune tellers were staying an hour or so before the shooting and how she saw her wearing the same sweater outside Cal's when she and Shannon were dropping Desmond off.

Charles started to point his sandwich at me a second time, but instead, took a bite, returned it to the plate, and said, "Karen Johnson."

I didn't think anything of it at the time and didn't remember it until now, but Karen Johnson was wearing a colorful sweater, but I couldn't recall what colors.

"The woman dating Brandon and who we met at Harris Teeter?"

"There you go. She's the person that shot Roisin and Wesley, and stabbed Donald. Ready to call Chief LaMond?"

"What's her motive?"

"Heck if I know. Do we have to do everything for the cops?"

"Okay, let's for a moment agree we don't know why she did it. What do we know that implicates her other than she was walking near the house where Roisin was shot and that was well before the shooting occurred?"

Charles said, "I need more food to figure all that out. Why didn't you order fries?"

"Because you said they weren't part of your new diet, you know, the one so you can maintain your trim, fine-tuned body."

He shook his head, and said, "When are you going to stop

listening to everything I say? I occasionally don't know what I'm talking about."

If occasionally meant often, I'd agree, but instead of sharing that observation, I said, "Take another bite of your sandwich and I'll start. When we met Karen Johnson, she said she lived several miles from Folly, so why would she have been walking to the beach when Roisin saw her? On the other hand, she could've done what folks do every day and drove here to walk on the beach."

"That's good," Charles said. "Closeness to where the shooting occurred."

"Proximity."

"Whatever." He hesitated, snapped his fingers, and said, "When we met her, didn't she say a friend and the friend's boyfriend saw the emergency vehicles at the shooting and asked what'd happened?"

"Yes, I'd forgotten about that. So, how does that say Karen was there?"

"Good question. What if she made up the story about a friend being there so we wouldn't think she was near Folly when it happened so she couldn't have been the killer?"

"It's possible, I suppose, but it's a pretty big leap."

"Yes, but if true, it means she was near both shootings and the stabbing. She was at Cal's when Donald was murdered. But wasn't she there with some guy. What was his name?"

"Rick. Didn't hear his last name."

Charles said, "If she was with this Rick guy, when would she have had time to go behind the building and stab Donald?"

"Roisin said Karen was by herself when she saw her outside Cal's, and I think when we were talking with her at the party, she said she'd met Rick there, so they would've driven separately and left the same way. Roisin could've seen her before she met Rick, and remember, didn't she tell us she was stopping by Cal's before heading to the other party? Did you notice when she and Rick left?"

"No. You saying she could've dumped Rick and gone out back to stab Donald?

"Yes, or Rick could be an accomplice."

"So, are you calling Cindy?"

"Before that, I think we need to come up with a possible motive, regardless of how farfetched it may be."

"Okay, farfetched is one of my specialties."

He could say that again, I thought.

"As you know, the general feeling among the fortune tellers is Wesley's murder and the shooting at the rental house were by someone who had a problem with the group being here. But Stevie told me she'd heard Karen Johnson defending the fortune tellers when discussing them with Brandon."

"Are you saying she didn't kill Wesley and shoot up the house because she'd defended the visitors?"

"That'd be an argument against her being the killer unless she had something specific against Wesley and someone she was targeting at the house and not simply because they were fortune tellers."

"Okay," Charles said, "I have no idea what that means, but Donald was one of the people who hated the visitors. Why would she have killed him?"

"I don't know, and don't look forward to telling Cindy that when she asks, and you know she will."

The god of bad timing must've been watching over us. I glanced toward the entrance and saw Chief Cindy LaMond heading toward our booth.

"Hey, Chief," Charles said, "we were talking about you."

"Were you offering to buy me lunch?"

"Sure, Chris will."

I smiled as if I had a choice. Cindy had me scoot over and sat beside me.

Danielle was quick to the table and Cindy said she'd have a diet drink. Charles generously told her to order anything she wanted to eat and before Danielle left, Cindy added blackened mahi tacos to go with her drink.

"So, guys, what were you saying about me other than I'm a wonderful person?"

Charles said, "That goes without saying. Chris wants to tell you who killed those two guys and shot up the house where the fortune tellers are staying."

I glared at Charles then turned to Cindy who was staring at me. "Chief, we have a theory."

"You going to tell me what it is, or do I have to guess?"

She wouldn't have to guess. I started with what Roisin had told me and added everything I knew about Karen Johnson. During my monologue, Cindy did something I'm not accustomed to from my friends. She listened and jotted notes.

I finished, she looked through her notes, and said, "Do you know how farfetched that sounds?"

I nodded and hoped Charles would say something, especially since he'd admitted *farfetched* was one of his specialties.

He and I remained silent, and Cindy said, "You realize much of your theory came from a thirteen-year-old who'd been shot, and first thought what she saw was a phantom?"

"Yes, but she saw the lady in the red and white sweater long before she'd been shot and remembered seeing her outside Cal's the night Donald Braxton was killed. I'd trust Roisin's memory more than the memory of many adults I know."

"Charles, do you agree?"

"Absolutely."

Cindy closed her notebook and said, "Okay, let's say I don't disagree, but do you have any thoughts on why Ms. Johnson would've done it?"

"Nope," Charles said.

I shook my head.

"Chris, I hate to keep bringing this up, but what if you were the target?"

Cindy's food arrived and she took two bites of taco while I pondered her theory. I didn't like the possibility of being the intended victim, but not liking it didn't mean it wasn't true. And, if true, there's no way the killer is Karen Johnson. I'd never met her until a casual meeting in Harris Teeter, and the only other time I'd spoken to her was briefly at the Halloween party. I shared that with Cindy while she continued devouring her food.

She wiped *pico de gallo* sauce off her upper lip and said, "Guys, unless someone can come up with a motive for Johnson, your theory is weak."

Charles leaned his elbows on the table and said, "Chief, Karen Johnson is the killer. It all fits. I hope you—"

Cindy waved her hand in Charles's face. "After I finish my free lunch, I'm going to go to the office, call Detective Adair, and share everything you said. He's going to ask if I think you're right. I'm going to stretch the truth and say, 'Yes, it came from impeccable sources.'"

Charles smiled and said, "You'll let us know when he arrests Karen Johnson?"

"Nope, one of your crystal-gazing buddies can tell you before it happens."

Although I'm no fortune teller, I predict that won't happen.

Charles had more deliveries to make for Dude, so I spent the remainder of the afternoon wandering around Folly while going over in my mind the two deadly and one nearly deadly incidents. Yes, a good argument was made that Karen Johnson was responsible and there was evidence she was nearby when the shooting of Wesley Thomas and the stabbing of Donald Braxton occurred. There was a better than average chance she was near the rental house when Roisin was shot. But, if she happened to be the person committing the crimes, why were the victims chosen? If the same person committed each crime, why use different weapons?

Could the variety of weapons used indicate more than one person was responsible? While it seems unlikely, it was possible. That could explain why one killer wanted a fortune teller dead, and a second killer could've wanted Donald, for lack of a better term, an anti-fortune teller killed. It was beyond my imagination to think there could be a third person wanting to kill someone with the attack on the rental house.

I walked to the far end of the Folly Pier, sat on one of the colorful blue tables, stared out to sea, and began thinking about the killings. I looked to the sky for inspiration, but instead of inspiration, large drops of rain began pelting my face. I moved under the Pier's roof to wait out the storm that'd taken me by surprise, but after fifteen minutes, decided Mother Nature was going to win the battle and walked home, getting soaked along the way.

I spent the evening wondering if Cindy would call to let me know how her conversation with Detective Adair had gone. She didn't, so I managed to fall asleep without spending more time trying to figure out the who, what, and especially why about the killings and attempted murder.

42

____

Having used most of my chef skills last evening when I unwrapped the half-sandwich and opened a package of Oreos, I headed to Bert's to grab something for breakfast. The rain had left the area, and the sky was empty except for a few clouds hugging the coastline. The pastry cabinet was my usual destination for breakfast items, and I didn't see any reason, except for my expanding waistline, to deviate from that plan after I'd drawn a cup of coffee from the urn near the front of the store.

I was in line to pay for a cheese Danish, when someone behind me said, "Hey, Chris."

I turned and saw a smiling Albert McGrady with his arm around Stevie Tigert. They each held a small package of mini donuts.

"Morning, guys. You're here early. Heading to the beach?"

"Sure are," Stevie said and smiled. "It's a lovely day."

I paid and stepped aside so the person behind me could get to the counter, then waited for Stevie and Albert to finish paying.

Stevie whispered something to Albert then turned to me. "Want to join us while we eat our healthy meals?" She asked then laughed.

"Sure."

We exited the building and Albert looked around as if he was trying to find somewhere for us to dine.

I said, "Let's walk over to Chico Feo. They aren't open and they have picnic tables. I don't think they'd mind us eating breakfast there."

They followed me across the street at the side of Bert's to one of the long tables close to Chico Feo's bar. The outdoor seating area was vacant except for a middle-aged man fiddling with his cell phone while his black and white border collie gnawed on a bone. Since Charles wasn't here, we didn't learn the dog's name, its pedigree, or its astrological sign.

Stevie and Albert sat with their shoulders touching on one side of the table and I on the other side, as we opened our meals.

A couple of bites in, Stevie said, "Glad we ran into you, got a lot to share."

Albert gently touched Stevie's hand and said, "Perhaps Chris wants to eat in peace."

"No, that's fine. What's new?"

"Like you suggested, we had a long talk with Dad. Was scary going into it, but amazing how it turned out."

"Fantastic."

Albert said, "We told him about us being alcoholics and the truth about the stupid debt I have. Know what he said?"

Of course, I didn't, and shook my head.

"Said he didn't care about the past. The past is past, or something like that. Anyway, he said Stevie is his daughter and that's all that matters."

"On top of that," Stevie said, "he loaned us the five grand."

"That's wonderful. I know you must be thrilled with his reaction."

"There's more, a lot more," Stevie said. "You tell him, Albert."

"When we told him we were getting married, I thought he was going to jump out of his Pewter Hardware shirt. He grabbed Stevie and hugged her so hard I was afraid she was going to break, then he hugged me. Wow, were we surprised."

"Did you tell him you were thinking about moving here?"

Stevie said, "Yes, and know what he did?"

"What?"

"Said he was going to find us an apartment or house where we could live on Folly. He knows people who have places to rent who owed him a favor or two. Thought he could get us a good deal. On top of that, he said he had contacts and could get us jobs if we wanted them."

"Did we ever want them," Albert said.

"That's great news all around. Have you decided when you'll get married?"

Stevie kissed Albert on the cheek then turned to me. "Tomorrow."

"You're kidding."

"Nope," she said. "Didn't figure we needed to wait. There's nobody in Georgia we want to invite, and Dad said he's off, and it's fine with him. Remember the preacher from the Halloween party named Burl, I believe it's Costeller?"

"Burl Costello," I said. "Yes, he's a good friend of mine. Why?"

"Dad called him while we were there to ask if he could officiate the ceremony. Mr. Costello said he remembered talking with us at the party and would be glad to officiate. After today's walk, we have to get our marriage license since we must get it twenty-four hours before the wedding. The preacher also said since the wedding will be on the beach, there wasn't any problem with scheduling. He even knows a man named William that has a great voice and would see if he could sing a couple of songs."

I suspected Burl was talking about William Hansel who in addition to being a wonderful person, had a fantastic singing voice that would be welcomed at anyone's event.

"Sounds like it's all planned. Congratulations."

Albert said, "Think you could come? You encouraging us to talk with Stevie's dad made it all possible."

"I wouldn't miss it for anything."

"Great. It'll be an hour before sunset. You can invite any of your friends you want. It won't be too crowded. The preacher said it'll be close to the Pier near where he has his Sunday services."

My phone rang with Cindy's name on the screen.

"Hi, Cindy."

"What's wrong, you're usually not that nice when you answer?"

"Nothing's wrong. I'm having breakfast with Stevie, Brandon's daughter, and Albert, her fiancé."

"Call me when you get a chance. I've got something interesting to tell you about your number one suspect."

"You can tell me now."

"It'll wait. Later." The phone went dead.

"Sorry for the interruption." The call reminded me of my previous conversation with Cindy, so I added, "Will Karen be coming with Brandon?"

"Doubt it. Think they've broken up."

"What happened?"

Stevie smiled. "Dad's an old hippie. He thinks Karen is too opinionated and set in her ways for him."

"In what ways?"

"The example he gave was about her being fond of those fortune tellers meeting over here. He isn't a fan of them. Said she wouldn't listen to his problems with the group. He also said she was pissed, excuse my language, at that guy who was killed."

"Wesley Thomas?"

"No, the other guy. The one who lived on Folly."

"Donald Braxton?"

"Yeah. She told Dad she was glad he was dead. Dad didn't know him well other than he was a pain to deal with in the store, but he still didn't like someone cutting him down like she was." She smiled. "He said he was too old for all that drama."

"I'm sorry to hear it."

Albert said, "I didn't know her much at all, but something about her bothered me. Can't put my finger on what."

"Albert," Stevie said, "that's not fair. You had what, two conversations with the woman?"

"You're right, sweetie. Chris, I'm glad you'll come to the wedding."

They'd finished their donuts and were looking around as if they were ready to get on with their day.

"I'd better let you get to the beach. Thanks for inviting me to the wedding."

Albert hopped up quickly, reinforcing my thought about them wanting to be somewhere other than on a picnic table at Chico Feo.

Stevie followed and said, "See you at the wedding."

The person who'd been nearby with his dog had walked up the street, so I remained at the table and called Cindy.

The chief answered with, "How was breakfast?"

"Best Danish I've had all day."

"Rub it in. I haven't had anything to eat since an ice cream sandwich last night."

"Sorry," I said and waited for the reason for her call.

"Enough about my exciting eating habits. I called Adair yesterday, shared the information you'd given me, and then was privileged, that's me being facetious, to hear him rant and rave about how stupid Charles's and your theory was. After all that ranting, he agreed to interview her."

I waited for more, but hearing nothing except a car on the street behind me gunning its engine as it turned on East Ashley Avenue, I said, "Well, did he interview her? What did she say?"

"No and nothing."

"He hasn't interviewed her?"

"Very good, Mr. Detective."

"That's Charles."

"Would you prefer I call you Mr. Old Geezer?"

"Chris will do."

"That's no fun. Anyway, no, Adair hasn't interviewed her, but that's not the most interesting news."

"It wouldn't take much to be more interesting than that."

"Smartass."

Maybe Mr. Detective wouldn't be that bad after all, I thought.

"Cindy, what's the most interesting part?"

"Adair went to her apartment early this morning. No one

answered the door, so he went to the office to see if he could talk whoever was on duty into opening her door. He failed, but that's still not the most interesting news."

"Do I need to beg you for what it is?"

"That'd be nice, but no, the manager said Karen Johnson left a couple of hours earlier. Packed up her things, shoved them into a U-Haul truck that was pulling her car and skedaddled, that's my word, not his."

"Did she say where she was going?"

"Something about heading to New York. The manager didn't get a forwarding address, nor did he know if she meant New York State or New York City."

"I don't suppose he learned why she was leaving?"

"Correct, he checked her apartment before she left, and everything appeared okay. She'd paid her rent through November, so he didn't care since she didn't owe anything."

"So, what now?"

"Shocking as it may seem, Adair is taking your suspicions seriously. He and his folks are tracking down where she got the U-Haul and will be getting the information on the unit, then they'll put out an APB. I could be oversimplifying this, but it appears the person who killed two people, shot little Miss Roisin, and killed the people she intended to kill, or was trying to kill you and missed three times, is headed north and out of our hair. Good riddance and *adios*."

"I hope you're right."

"That makes two of us."

43

It'd been a week since the Halloween phantoms haunted the streets, not to mention the murder of a man walking beside me two weeks ago, but by late afternoon the cloudless morning had disappeared and ominous dark clouds, streaks of lightning, and the rumbles of the accompanying thunder, felt like a horrifying repeat of Halloween. This was turning out to be an evening to stay home while hoping the weather improved for tomorrow's beach wedding.

The phone interrupted my thinking about Stevie and Albert's big day. I was tempted to not answer since there was no number or name on the screen, but I did anyway.

"Chris, this is Brandon. Have time to talk?"

"Sure, and by the way, congratulations on tomorrow's big event."

"I tell you, my friend, that came as a surprise, but it seems they're both happy, so I'm happy for them, but that's not why I called. It may not have anything to do with anything, but it's turning knots in my stomach. I know how good you are at figuring out stuff, especially when it comes to catching bad guys, so I wanted to bounce it off you."

"I don't know about that, but why don't you tell me what it is?"

"It's about the Stone family, you know, Shannon, Desmond, and Roisin?"

"What about them?"

"Shannon and Desmond were in the store a little while ago buying stronger locks for their house. Shannon didn't say it, but I think after what happened to Roisin, she must be concerned about their security. Anyway, Shannon said Roisin was outside with Lugh. I had to grab the store's mail, so on the way to the post office, I stopped to talk to the young lady and their monster dog. Roisin looked so pitiful sitting on the ground with her arm wrapped up and in a sling. She started talking about what'd happened at the fortune tellers' house where she was shot, and asked if I knew anything about who might've shot her. I told her no, and she mentioned the lady she had seen that day and then again near Cal's party."

He hesitated. Was he still on the phone?

"Brandon, you there?"

"Yes, sorry, was thinking about something else you need to know for this to make sense, that is, if it does make sense. Do you know I've had some dates with Karen Johnson?"

"I'd heard that. Stevie told me she thinks you and Karen broke up."

"Stevie's right. But here's where I think I may've said something that, to be honest, I shouldn't have. When the Stones were getting in their car and getting ready to pull out of the lot, Karen pulled up in a big U-Haul with a tow dolly holding her car, and said she wanted to tell me she was leaving the state. She also said she saw me talking to a teenager and wondered who it was. Chris, I didn't think anything of it at the time, but we talked for a little while and since it was on my mind, I told her Roisin had mentioned seeing a woman the night she was shot and may've seen the same person near the Halloween party at Cal's. Karen asked if Roisin knew the woman. I said she didn't."

Oh great, Brandon, I thought. "Did you tell Karen who Roisin was?"

Again, there was a long hesitation, before he said, "Umm, yeah. I thought she would be interested in knowing Roisin and the rest of the Stone family were Wiccans since Karen had told me she had experience with Wiccans when she was in the military. Karen and I'd also talked about the Stones a few nights ago when we were talking about the fortune tellers visiting the island. We even drove by the Stones' house one afternoon. Karen said it looked like something out of a fairy tale."

"Did Karen say anything about Roisin?"

"No, she said she'd better be going and was sorry it didn't work out between us. To be honest, I don't know why she even came by. She could've called to tell me she was moving. Anyway, that's about it."

"Did you see where she went after leaving you?"

"No, I headed to the post office before she pulled out."

"Why do you think what you told her may get Roisin in trouble?"

"Chris, it never entered my mind until after Karen left, and I hate to think it, but is it possible she's the person who killed those two guys and shot up the house where the fortune tellers are staying?"

"The police have her on their list of suspects."

"They do?" he hesitated again, and finally said, "Crap. What should I do?"

"Tell you what. I'll call Chief LaMond and share our conversation. Then I'll go to the Stones' house to make sure Roisin is okay."

"Want me to go with you?"

"No, I'll be fine. You do whatever you have to for tomorrow's big wedding. One more thing, how long ago did Karen leave?"

"Half hour, maybe."

"Okay, see you at the wedding."

I ended the call and echoed Brandon's sentiment: Crap.

Claps of thunder had intensified, and lightning lit the sky. Adding to the sound and light show, heavy rain pelted my metal roof. None of that was going to stop me from checking on Roisin. I sloshed to the car then drove to her cottage. I knocked on the door as hard as I could and wondered if anyone inside could hear me over the thunder and rain.

My wondering ended when Lugh's window-shaking bark drowned out Mother Nature's tantrum. Shannon inched the door open, saw me dripping wet on the porch, opened the door the rest of the way and said, "Poor, dear man, get in out of the storm."

I stepped inside the entry where Lugh sat in guard-dog mode at Shannon's side. I slowly rubbed the Irish Wolfhound's chin and said to Shannon, "Is Roisin here?"

"No, Happy, his cat, and Chloe are leaving tomorrow, and my stubborn daughter begged me to let her go with Stormy to the beach house so she could say goodbye." She smiled and added, "Yes, I know, it's a horrible night for her to be out in this weather, but as you know, she can be quite convincing."

"Couldn't they have come here to say their farewells?"

"Roisin said she needed to go back to where she was injured, so she could move past that horrible evening. I offered to go with her, but she insisted she needed to do it without me." Shannon shrugged as if to say, "What could I say to that?"

I smiled hoping to mask my fear for her daughter's safety and said, "That sounds like her. I'll go over there so I can say bye to some of the folks. I'll encourage Roisin not to stay long."

"Thank you."

I patted Lugh's chin one more time before heading to the car, leaving without telling Shannon why I'd come by.

A block before the rental house, a U-Haul truck pulling a tan Toyota Corolla was parked on the side of the road. How big a coincidence would it be for the truck not be the one Karen had rented?

I parked in front of the large vehicle and tried to look in the windshield to see if the truck was occupied. The heavy rain made that impossible. Instead of walking back to the truck, I called Cindy and told her what Brandon had said and where Roisin was. She said she was approaching downtown Charleston but would turn around and head my way, and for me to wait for her to get here before doing anything.

She'd ended the call before I agreed to stay put, so I didn't feel guilty when I drove the additional block and parked in front of the rental house.

44

Instead of climbing the steps and knocking on the windowless front door where there was no way to see into the house, I walked around back where I had a view of the deck and into the back of the rental. There was no letup in the rain, so I'd have to move closer to have a chance of seeing anything. I slowly walked up three steps to where I could see the entire porch and the great room.

A body was on the floor near the door to the kitchen. I couldn't tell who it was, but it was a female, a female with a different color hair than Roisin's, thank goodness. I'd reached the porch when the lights in the kitchen went out. Lamps in the great room were still on so there wasn't a power failure caused by the storm. Had someone seen me and turned the lights off so I couldn't see who was there?

I inched my way across the deck and slowly opened the door next to the damaged one that had been boarded up. The body on the floor hadn't moved. What looked like a small pool of blood was beside the head but the shadows from the body made it impossible to tell for sure.

Other than the sound of thunder, I didn't hear anything or anybody. Now what?

The sound of gunfire and the light from the muzzle flash coming from the dark kitchen answered my question. At the same time, the doorframe six inches from my head exploded into shards of wood.

I dove behind the chair closest to the door. I knew the cushioned chair wouldn't stop a bullet but might give me a degree of cover so the shooter might not know exactly where I was.

A second shot told me my hiding spot wouldn't work for long. The bullet struck the side of the chair, not more than a few inches from my arm. Staying where I was wasn't an option but moving from behind the chair would make me an easy target for the person wielding the gun. I peeked around the corner of the chair to try to see where the shooter was.

Karen Johnson stepped out of the darkness of the kitchen and was slowly shuffling in my direction. She was no more than eight feet from my inadequate hiding place. If I tried to get to her, the next bullet would easily end my attempt at catching the shooter. Running the other direction would have the same result.

A loud thud coming from near the front door some thirty feet behind Karen startled her. She pivoted and fired two quick shots in the direction of the sound before ducking behind the sofa.

If I had any chance of surviving, I had to act. I pushed myself into a standing position and took long strides toward the killer who was still facing the front door. Before I reached her, she glanced over her shoulder then turned facing me. Her firearm was no more than a second from pointing at me when I reached for it. I grabbed her wrist and twisted it as she pulled the trigger. The exploding round was deafening but the barrel was pointed away from my body.

I'd avoided being shot, but she still held the firearm and was at least fifteen years younger than I was, nearly my height, military trained, and in better shape. The last thing I wanted to do was to let go of her wrist, but she still controlled the gun.

Instead of trying to wrangle the weapon from her hand, I shoved her backwards, while still grasping her gun hand. She moved back a step and swung her other hand at my face. I ducked as her hand bounced off the top of my head. I pushed her again. Her left leg hit the side of one of the chairs and she tripped. She reached back with her free hand to grab the chair, missed, and fell over the heavy, wood coffee table.

I still held a death grip on her wrist and was pulled with her over the table. Her head smacked the tile floor as I landed on her cushioning the blow. The gun slipped out of her hand. Her eyes rolled back in her head. She didn't move.

I rolled off her body, stood, and looked to see what I could use to secure her hands. As I looked around, I saw a smashed pumpkin near the front door and realized it's what made the sound that distracted the killer. I also realized it hadn't fallen from the upper floor by itself.

I yelled, "Roisin, are you here?"

"Is that you, Mr. Chris?"

"Yes, are you okay?"

"I'm upstairs. Is it safe to come down?"

"Yes. I need your help."

I heard the teenager scampering down the stairs and saw her wide-open eyes as she looked at Karen Johnson near me on the floor.

I said, "See if you can find something I can use to tie her hands."

Without saying anything, she ran into the kitchen where I heard her fishing through drawers and then opening the pantry before she returned with a roll of twine.

She handed it to me and said, "Mom uses this stuff to tie up the turkey every Thanksgiving. It's the best I could find."

I took the twine and began wrapping it tightly around Karen's wrists, and said, "It's perfect."

Karen began moving and tried to sit. I pushed her down and told her to stay put. Roisin went over to Stormy and began talking to her in a muffled voice. Stormy's arm moved and I turned my attention back to Karen.

"Why kill Wesley Thomas, Donald Braxton, and try to kill the other fortune tellers? What'd they have in common?"

"It's none of your damned business," she said and tried again to sit using her shoulders to push herself up.

"It is my business. You shot that young lady over there and came back after her tonight. She's my friend."

Karen glanced over toward Roisin and Stormy and said, "You think I wanted to kill a kid?"

"Looks like it."

She sighed and lowered her head to the floor. "If it wasn't for Donald, none of this would've happened."

"What'd Donald do?"

"Caused this whole mess, that's what."

"Was he who you wanted to kill?"

She nodded but didn't say anything.

I looked over at Roisin holding Stormy's head in her lap and said, "Roisin, is she okay?"

"Says she is, but her head's still bleeding a little."

"Why don't you grab a towel from the kitchen and press it on her head?"

Instead of answering, Roisin gently laid Stormy's head on the floor and rushed to the kitchen for a towel.

I turned my attention back to the captive.

"Karen, are you saying you didn't have anything against the fortune tellers?"

"Yeah."

"Yet you killed Thomas, shot up this house, and tonight wanted to kill Roisin?"

She mumbled something I didn't understand and asked her to repeat it.

"If I didn't do something to deflect suspicion, the past would've caught up with me. I would've been caught."

"This way it appeared the fortune tellers were the targets and Donald got shot, umm, why, so the police would think it was a mistake, that he was one of the visitors?"

She slowly nodded then closed her eyes.

"Why come after Roisin? You'd already killed one of the fortune tellers and shot up this house looking like they were your intended victims."

"Didn't want to hurt her, but after Brandon said she saw me near here and at the bar where that Halloween party was going on, she had to go. Sorry, but she did. I knew where she lived and headed there. Saw her leave the house with that other woman and followed them here."

"Again, why kill Donald? What'd he do to you?"

Before she could respond, the front door was smashed open and Chief LaMond burst in, handgun raised."

"Everything's under control, Chief," I said to lower her stress level and move her finger off the trigger, then gave her a thirty-second summary of what was going on.

She took handcuffs off her duty belt, cuffed Karen, yanked her off the floor, and escorted her to the sofa.

Two EMTs were next through the door. Cindy pointed them in the direction of Stormy who was holding the towel against her head and talking with Roisin.

Officer Bishop followed the firefighters into the house. Cindy told her to take care of Karen and waved for Roisin and me to join her on the deck while the EMTs worked on Stormy.

I put my arm around Roisin as we followed the chief to a grouping of chairs. After we were seated, Cindy said, "Other than Chris ignoring a direct order to wait for me outside, would either of you like to tell me what happened?"

Roisin glanced at me, so I said, "Chief, as I told you on the phone, I was talking to Brandon when he told me about a discussion he'd had with Karen Johnson. He'd mentioned Roisin saying she'd seen someone wearing a red and white sweater outside Cal's."

Cindy held up her hand. "You hung up before I could ask you, why in hell, excuse me, Roisin, was Brandon telling Karen about what Roisin saw?"

"I have no idea."

"I'll be asking him later."

"After I heard that, I went to the Stone's house to make sure Roisin was safe and Shannon said she'd come here with Stormy Roserun to say bye to some of the fortune tellers who are leaving tomorrow. That's when I saw the rental truck and called you."

"And didn't follow my orders to stay outside until I got here."

"Got it. I couldn't see anything from the front of the house, so I came around back and saw someone on the floor. It was Stormy but I didn't know it at the time. That's when Karen started shooting at me."

"Where are the rest of the fortune tellers?"

Roisin raised her hand, her good one. Cindy told her she didn't need to do that, and to tell her where everyone was.

"When me and Stormy got here, there was a note saying Happy and Chloe went shopping for Folly Beach sweatshirts and snacks for the road. They're leaving tomorrow, you know." She looked toward the kitchen and continued, "Stormy went in the kitchen to pack some things she and Darrin brought over for the group to use while they were staying here. I was in the other room and saw Raven Moon, that's Happy Bishop's cat. It ran up the stairs. I figured she knew someone from the group was up there, so I followed. Glad I did."

Cindy said, "Why?"

"Cause Stormy was in the big room, and I heard a loud noise and she moaned. I turned and saw her fall and that Karen Johnson woman was standing over her holding something heavy, couldn't tell what. I ran upstairs and hid under a bed. I heard her coming up looking for me, but she didn't look under the bed. She went downstairs, and I heard a gun go off. That's when she shot at Mr. Chris." She turned to me. "Glad she missed."

"Me too, Roisin. Cindy, that's when Roisin's quick thinking saved my life."

Cindy turned to Roisin. "What did you do?"

"Mrs. Chief, after I heard the gun go off, I got out from under the bed and went to the stairs and peeked down here. I saw the woman with the gun pointing it where Mr. Chris was hiding. I saw the top of his head over the chair. I took one of the carved pumpkins out of the front window and threw it downstairs, so it'd land near the front door. It was heavy, hurt my bad arm a little throwing it. Anyway, I hoped the woman would think it was somebody coming in and get confused so Mr. Chris could do something to catch her." She smiled and added, "And he did."

I smiled and said, "Karen fired twice in the direction of the crash thinking it was someone at the front door."

Cindy looked at me and said, "Those two bullet holes in the door are why I kicked it in." She then turned to Roisin. "That took a lot of courage, young lady."

She smiled at Cindy and said, "Then Mr. Chis asked me to get something to tie her up. Found the string stuff in the pantry and he used it to hold her hands together." She chuckled and added, "that string stuff always held the Thanksgiving turkey together when Mom used it."

"Cindy," I said. "Roisin saved my life."

"She sure—"

"Yeah," Roisin said, "but he already saved mine twice."

"Roisin," Cindy said, "Do you know why she came here?"

She shook her head and said, "I didn't hear her say anything."

I said, "Karen told me it was to silence Roisin since she's the one who saw Karen near Cal's during the Halloween party and then near here the day she shot up the house and wounded Roisin."

"But Mr. Chris, I didn't see her shoot me or stab poor Mr. Braxton."

"She didn't know that. I think she was trying to eliminate loose ends before she left town."

"Roisin," Cindy said and handed her the phone, "why don't you call your mom and tell her you're okay but you'll need to stay here a little longer to talk with the detective from the Sheriff's Office."

"Mr. Chris, will you talk to Mom to let her know I'm fine."

"Absolutely."

One of the EMTs came over and told Cindy they were taking Stormy to the hospital.

Roisin said, "Will she be okay?"

"I think so. She took a blow to the back of her head, so she probably has a concussion. The docs will check her over to make sure there's nothing to be concerned about."

The EMT left and Rosin turned to me. "Will you stay here and take me home when the detective lets me leave?"

I repeated, "Absolutely."

<h1 style="text-align:center">45</h1>

Stevie and Albert's wedding was scheduled for 4:30, an hour before sunset, and Charles said he'd be at the house a half hour before so we could walk to the beach together. Knowing his penchant for time-shifting, I expected him to arrive no later than 3:30, but wasn't ready when I heard a rapping on the front door a little after 2:00.

I opened it to see my friend wearing a light gray sweatshirt with UNLV in inch-high, scarlet letters on the sleeve.

"Know why I wore this?" He said as he pushed past me and headed to the kitchen.

"To stay warm," I said as he rummaged through the refrigerator and grabbed a Coke.

"And you call yourself a detective," he said and held the Coke out as if he was making a commercial.

"No thanks," I said to his generous offer. "Why?"

"Why what?"

"Why did you wear that sweatshirt?"

"Wanted to wear something subtle so I wouldn't draw attention away from the bride and groom, besides, the University of Nevada,

Las Vegas has a hospitality management program and teaches students how to plan weddings. Perfect, right?"

I didn't respond but joined him at the kitchen table and waited to hear why he was early, even for Charles. I didn't have to wait long.

"Okay, got the Joe Friday version of 'Just the facts, ma'am' stuff when you called. I didn't pester you for more since Karen wasted bullets shooting at you. Incidentally, you know I'm a fortune teller."

"How could I have missed that? Why are you a fortune teller?"

"Did you forget I had a dream about you getting shot at?"

"You did say that."

"See, I'm a fortune teller."

I sighed. "Whatever."

"Now that you understand my amazing talent, I knew you were traumatized then, so I waited until now for you to spill everything."

"Some of this may be a repeat, so—"

"You sure Roisin is okay?"

"Yes, now after—"

"She was really hiding under the bed?"

"Yes, once she saw Karen in—"

"You could learn a lot from her. Instead of barging in and getting yourself shot at, you could've hidden and sneaked up on Karen."

Thirty minutes and a zillion interruptions later, I'd shared everything I remembered about going to Roisin's house, the drive to the rental house, seeing the U-Haul, calling Chief LaMond, ignoring her directive to stay put, getting shot at, catching the killer, and ending with a long hug from the relieved teenager.

"Interesting take on the events but left out why you are uninjured. Since you really didn't take my advice of being careful."

"Karen was distracted, and dumb luck was all that saved me."

"Wrong. You forget the gift Chloe gave you? The gris-gris bag for your protection. You might want to thank her today."

I reached into my pocket to feel if it was still there. It was.

"I doubt she's still on the island. With Karen under arrest there's no reason for her to still be here."

"Just proves you're not a top dog detective yet."

"Does the self-proclaimed top dog care to enlighten this mere mortal?"

Charles patted himself on the shoulder, and said, "I was checking with Dude this morning to see if he needed me to make any deliveries."

"What does that have to do with Chloe?"

"Patience my friend, Dude wasn't there."

I was beginning to wonder if Charles had arrived so early to add more than a bit of craziness to my afternoon or if it was punishment for not picking him up before nearly getting shot.

"Charles what—"

"Enough lollygagging. Raven Moon was escorting Happy past the surf shop when I was leaving. We had a nice talk. That's how I know you'll see Chloe at the wedding."

"How did that come about?"

"Glad you asked, Happy and Chloe had already packed to leave, and she'd gone for a walk on the beach with Spencer. He was walking Raven Moon so the giant feline would sleep during their trip."

"Is Spencer still in town?"

"Nope, Chloe was saying bye to him when Happy called to add folks to my invitation to the wedding."

"You invited people who don't know the couple to a wedding you have no say in?"

"Exactly."

"Are they coming?"

"Chloe will. Spencer couldn't postpone getting back to Charlotte, something about his business partner needing him there."

"Heidi?"

"Left town after Detective Adair finished the interviews. Happy said Heidi didn't care that they were told not to leave town. Told Happy they could find her in the Okefenokee swamp giving tours. Heidi added that 'Gators are safer than some people.'"

"That would leave the two and Raven Moon."

"Only Happy and Chloe. Raven Moon has better things to do, like ignore everyone."

"Anyone hear from Alice since her disappearing act?"

"Not that Happy mentioned. I did learn something about Dani."

"From Happy?"

"Why would Happy know anything?"

"He's a fortune teller?"

Charles rolled his eyes and said, "Yesterday afternoon before you were running around getting shot at, I saw Dani."

"Tell me you didn't accuse her of the murders."

"Was about to, but she stopped me before I could," Charles said then took a long sip of his drink then stared at me.

I returned the stare and won the contest when he broke the silence.

"Dani was heading to Martha's carrying a bag from Coconut Joe's. She saw me across the street and walked over. Before I could say anything, she said Martha told her about our visit. She said it was nice we cared so much for Martha, then told me she had been having trouble sleeping, and was awake for hours every night."

"That's not what Martha told us Dani was doing the night of the shooting."

"That's what I told Dani. She laughed and said she finally went to the doctor last week and got a prescription for sleeping pills. The night of the shooting was the first night she'd taken them. Said they worked but she's now worried she wouldn't wake up during a volley of gunfire and barking dogs." He shrugged and added, "Oh, by the way, are you good?"

"I was wondering if you were going to ever ask, but yes, I am now."

"One more question."

"What?"

"All the visitors were fortune tellers, psychics, mediums, whatever, right?"

I said, "Yes."

"Then why didn't one or more of them know all the trouble they'd be getting in and hightail it out of town the first day?" He then looked at the clock on my stove, hopped out of his chair, and said, "Let's go, we're going to be late."

Since I didn't have a good answer for his question, I said, "You're right, we only have forty-five minutes to walk two blocks."

"Smartass."

I smiled and said, "Yep."

46

The weather gods had put the stereotypical, ominous, Halloween weather in the rear-view mirror, or in a haunted mirror. The temperature was in the low seventies, white Cumulus clouds were beginning to reflect the sun beginning its descent over the marsh.

What a difference a day makes, I thought as I saw a group gathering around white, folding chairs fifty yards east of the Fishing Pier. Preacher Burl Costello was huddled with William Hansel, Stevie Tigert, soon to be Stevie McGrady, and her future husband, Albert. Most likely, they were finalizing details of the ceremony. On the opposite side of the chairs, Roisin and her mother were looking at the waves rolling ashore. Roisin saw me and started running my way. Her light-blue dress billowed behind her; her smile brightened the already radiant late afternoon atmosphere. Shannon smiled and followed her daughter.

"Mr. Chris," the effervescent teen said as she reached me, "I want to wrap my arms around you and squeeze, but my injured wing is telling me that would be painful."

"Then we'll save the hug for when it's better."

Shannon moved beside her daughter. She was wearing an ankle-length dark blue dress and looked more like Roisin's older sister than her mother. "Chris, thank you for helping save Roisin from that evil woman."

"Mom, he didn't help save me, he did save me. He saved me two times."

I put my hand on her good arm and said, "Young lady, not true. You saved yourself by hiding under the bed, then saved me by throwing the pumpkin to distract the killer."

"I'm glad you're safe," Charles said, feeling left out of the conversation. "Where're Desmond and Lugh?"

Shannon looked at her watch and said, "Lugh is at the house, but Desmond will be coming with Stormy and Darrin. I hope the couple to be wed doesn't mind them attending. They wanted to thank Brandon Tigert for providing a key clue to solving the, umm, unfortunate deaths."

I didn't mention how Brandon could've inadvertently added Stormy and Roisin to the list of victims, but instead said, "Is Stormy okay?"

"Yes, she has a minor concussion and a few stitches but wouldn't let them keep her in the hospital."

I said, "I'm glad to hear that, and certain they'll be more than welcome."

Barb, Larry and Cindy LaMond were next to arrive. The father of the bride accompanied them, or I assumed it was Brandon since I'd never seen him in a white shirt, tie, and black, leather dress shoes. He looked as out of place as a camel at a tortoise family reunion.

Burl looked at those gathering and said, "If you're attending the wedding, shall we begin taking our seats?"

We started moving in that direction, when I noticed Happy and Chloe inching their way closer to the gathering. There were plenty of vacant seats, so I motioned for them to join us.

I whispered to Happy, "I'm glad you're still here."

"We'd planned to leave this morning, but after hearing what'd happened to Stormy and what Roisin went through last night, we wanted to make sure they were okay before heading out." He chuckled and added, "Besides, who could pass up attending a beach wedding?"

I repeated I was glad they were here as Preacher Burl moved behind the repurposed high school gymnasium lectern he'd lugged from his foul weather sanctuary. William Hansel stood six feet to the side and Albert stood close to the preacher.

Brandon took Stevie's arm and moved behind the seated attendees.

Burl gave a nasty look to a little boy yelling for his parents to watch him as he buried his legs in the sand. His dad saw Burl, shrugged, and grabbed his son before distancing them from the wedding.

Burl then said, "Please silence thy portable communication devices."

I smiled knowing that was how he started all his worship services, and apparently, weddings.

Barb was seated to my left and Charles to my right.

He leaned over and whispered, "Lyndon Johnson said, 'I have learned that only two things are necessary to keep one's wife happy. First, let her think she's having her way. And second, let her have it.'"

"You need to tell Albert."

"I did."

"What'd he say."

"Said for me not to tell Stevie."

Our conversation was interrupted by William singing:

I see trees of green

red roses too

I see them bloom

For me and you.

Brandon slowly walked arm and arm with his daughter toward Preacher Burl and Albert.

Casual beach goers stopped talking and stood in silence as William finished his touching version of the Louie Armstrong classic.

Albert joined Stevie in front of Burl who began his role in the ceremony.

Instead of taking in each of the preacher's words, I caught myself focused on the young lady in the light-blue dress in the row in front of me. After nearly being killed four days earlier, and hunted by the killer who was determined to end her life yesterday, Roisin was laughing at the humorous remarks Burl interspersed into his ceremony and had a wide smile on her face throughout the rest of the event. It made me think how much better off we all would be following the example of the thirteen-year-old.

Preacher Burl was telling Albert he could kiss the bride before I returned my focus to the ceremony.

William began singing "All You Need Is Love," then asked the rest of us to join in as he—we—accompanied the newlyweds as they walked down the sand covered aisle as husband and wife to the back of the informal open air wedding chapel where they were quickly surrounded by well-wishers. None of the nonparticipants who were watching from the beach mistook those singing for The Beatles.

Barb joined me and said, "Considering everything that's happened, that combination of joy and celebration couldn't have come at a better time."

"I agree."

"Is Roisin okay?"

"I think so. She's a strong young lady. I'm also fine in case you were wondering."

She smiled and said, "I knew that. That's why I didn't ask."

Chloe and Happy moved beside Barb and me and Chloe said, "May I interrupt?"

I thought that's what she'd already done, but said, "Sure."

"It's fortuitous we weren't at the house when that crazed woman got there, so I'm asking for the rest of the group. Why us? Why kill Wesley? Why try to kill all of us that night in the house? Why break in last night and try to, umm, whatever she wanted to do? Chris, we've done no harm to anyone." She shook her head and repeated, "Why us?"

Chief LaMond approached with her phone to her ear. She took a couple of steps back from the group, took the phone from the side of her head, stared at the screen, and shook her head.

I moved closer to her and said, "You okay?"

She continued shaking her head and said, "Better than that nutcase."

"Who was it?"

"Alice Clay."

"What'd she want?"

"To tell me she saw the killer."

"The person who shot Wesley Thomas or stabbed Donald Braxton?"

"Both and add shooting Roisin in the arm."

I smiled and said, "Did she see the person from somewhere here?"

"Of course not. She was sitting on her sofa in Kure Beach, North Carolina."

I chuckled and said, "Did she say who it was?"

"Sure did. It was a woman who loved Christmas."

"What'd you say to that?"

"Should've said Ho, Ho, Ho, but thanked her and hung up."

"Wise."

She patted my shoulder and said, "That's why I'm chief."

I looked toward the group I'd been talking with. They were in deep conversation about something, so I turned back to Cindy and said, "Last night I asked Karen Johnson what she had against Donald, but she wouldn't say. Did she tell Detective Adair why she wanted him dead?"

"How come you didn't ask if she loved Christmas?"

"Ho, Ho, Ho."

"Okay, okay, yes, she told Adair she and Donald lived in New York and were engaged a few years back. Her parents and grandparents were killed in a plane crash, and she inherited a bundle of money. Donald, being an attorney, convinced her the best thing to do with her inheritance was to set up a trust where he could handle all the investments and she'd never have to worry about it again. She said all she knew when it happened was life in the military and had no idea what she was signing over to Donald."

"And Donald stole all of it and disappeared?"

"Excellent summary."

"Then how'd she know he was here?"

"Luck. Turned out to be bad luck for both. When she retired from the military, she'd saved enough to spend much of that time traveling through the South. She finally settled on James Island last year, the stars aligned, and she happened to see Donald in Harris Teeter and followed him over here."

"Then concocted her scheme to kill him?"

"Another excellent summary. Not only how to kill him, but after learning about the fortune tellers' meeting, she came up with the creative way to confuse the hell out of the cops by killing Wesley first, killing Donald, then shooting up the house with the fortune tellers. She figured we'd tie Donald's death with the fortune tellers and not dig deep into his past and discover their relationship. I hate to say it, but she was probably right."

"Did she know Wesley?"

"Claims she never saw him before the night she shot him. Didn't even know he was one of the group, but assumed from his clothes he was."

"Cindy, that's horrible."

"That's an understatement," she said then looked over my shoulder toward the group I'd been talking with. "You'd better get back to those folks."

"Come with me. One of them asked a question you'd be the best person to answer."

"Wasn't about Christmas, was it?"

I rolled my eyes and led Cindy over to the group and said, "Chloe, you know Chief LaMond, don't you?"

"Under horrible circumstances, but yes."

"A few minutes ago, you asked a question I believe Chief LaMond can answer."

I repeated the question for Cindy's benefit.

Cindy turned to Chloe and said, "Sadly, it had nothing, and I mean nothing to do with you or any of your group. Karen Johnson told Detective Adair her attacks on you all were to make us believe the fortune tellers were the intended victims. You were simply a diversion to keep us from knowing her real target was Donald Braxton."

Happy said, "And to think, some of you locals thought we were evil."

I couldn't argue with that, and it appeared neither could Barb or the Chief.

CROSSFIRE

BILL NOEL

1

My second cup of morning coffee was interrupted by the shrill sound of my phone. A glance at the screen told me the call was from my friend Charles Fowler.

"Good morning, Charles."

"Called the chief yet?"

One of several things I could predict about my best friend was his inability to begin a phone conversation like a normal person; not surprising since he was far from normal.

"I must've forgotten. Why would I be calling Cindy?"

Cindy LaMond is police chief on Folly Beach, the barrier island I've called home for the last fifteen years. She's also a good friend.

"The dead guy, duh."

"Who?"

"The dead guy. Didn't you hear me?"

I told you he wasn't normal.

"I know that, who's the dead guy?"

"Matthew Seward the thirty-seventh, or something like that."

I didn't know about the deceased man being the thirty-seventh of anything, but I was vaguely familiar with Matthew Seward III since I'd met him in Bert's Market, the small grocery next to my cottage. I also knew Matthew was the third since that's how he introduced himself. I'd told him I was Chris Landrum without any Roman numerals behind my name. No, I didn't say that to the man. Since then, I'd run into him at Bert's a half-dozen times and shared brief conversations. Other than his desire to tell me which Matthew he was, I'd learned he was an accountant in his family's business, and he, or more accurately his family, had a second home on Folly.

"What happened?"

"Told you, he's dead."

Okay, let's try this another way. "How'd you hear about his death?"

"That's why you've got to call Chief LaMond. All I heard was he was found yesterday at his house out East Arctic Avenue."

"Who told you?"

"Loretta Thompson, saw her in Mr. John's."

"She tell you anything else?"

"She thought he was a stuck-up prick."

"Anything about his death. He's young, I'd guess in his mid-twenties. You're sure she didn't know anything else about it?"

"Loretta is a waitress, not a medical examiner."

I assumed that meant no, and most likely Charles had shared everything he knew about the death.

"Tell you what, why don't I call Chief LaMond and see if she can add anything to the countless details you gave me."

"Great idea," he said before hanging up.

I'd met Cindy LaMond a dozen years ago after she'd moved from Tennessee to take a job as one of Folly's Public Safety Officers, more commonly called cops. She was promoted to Chief six years later. Since Cindy arrived on the small island, she married Larry LaMond, owner of Folly's tiny hardware store.

After her phone rang several times, I was afraid I was going to be rewarded with her voicemail. Instead, she answered with, "What are you going to do to ruin my fifth, no sixth cup of coffee, while digging through a seven-foot-high pile of police reports that look like my officers filled out in hieroglyphics?"

I didn't think anything I'd say could be worse than what she was enduring, so I said, "Just a question. Sorry to interrupt your fun-filled, beautiful spring morning."

"I'll regret asking, but what's the question?"

"I heard that Matthew Seward was found dead in his house yesterday. What happened?"

"You're asking because you're a reporter, no, a funeral director, no, I got it, you want to buy his house. How am I doing?"

"I'm curious. I'd talked to him a few times and knew he was young, so I wondered what happened."

She sighed before saying, "Curious, right. I believe that like I believe the guy in an email who told me I had a relative in Somestan or some other exotic country who left me seventy-three million dollars. You and your buddy Charles want to stick your noses into whatever happened and help us helpless cops catch the person who bumped off Matthew."

Over the years, Charles and I, along with the assistance of some of our friends, had helped the police catch a few bad guys. Charles had even proclaimed that he was a private detective.

"I have complete confidence that you, your officers, and the folks from the County Sheriff's Office will get to the bottom of whatever happened."

The Charleston County Sheriff's Office investigates suspicious deaths on Folly.

"You finally got something right. We thought we'd already figured out who was responsible for the death of Mr. Seward the whatever number."

"Who?"

"Matthew Seward III."

"Suicide?"

"Drug overdose was our first thought. Figured he'd killed himself."

"Now I'm confused. Was it a drug overdose or not?"

"Not. The ME will need to come up with the final determination."

"I'm confused."

"About time you admitted it."

"What killed him?"

"He was found in his bedroom. Cocaine was all over the dresser and beside the body, so we assumed it must've been an overdose."

"What made you change your mind?"

"I suppose it was the hole in the back of his head. If you tell anybody what I'm going to share, I'll put another hole in your head."

"Okay."

"My guys didn't notice the gunshot wound before the coroner hauled the body away."

"How could they miss something that obvious?"

"Mainly because it wasn't obvious. Seward was on his back. My guys couldn't see any blood, but saw cocaine on the dresser, and on the floor around the vic. The gun that shot him was a small caliber, most likely a twenty-two, so the bullet lodged in his brain with little blood under the body."

"Any idea who may've shot him?"

"No."

I started to ask her more, but I would've been asking a dead phone.

Patience was a virtue God had not gifted Charles, so I called him as soon as Cindy hung up on me. Remembering to take his phone when he left his tiny apartment was another shortcoming. The phone finally rolled over to voicemail and I left a message for him to call when he had a chance.

THE PHONE DIDN'T RING AGAIN until a little after eight p.m. Assuming it was Charles, I answered with, "It's about time."

"About time for what?" asked a familiar female voice.

"Sorry, Noelle. I thought you were someone else."

I'd met Noelle Ward, the rightly confused person on the other end of the call, a little over three years ago. She works in an advertising agency in downtown Charleston, a fifteen-minute drive from Folly, and is in the process of writing a novel.

"Umm, no. I'm fairly certain I'm me." She laughed before continuing, "Could you, umm, we meet for breakfast in the m... morning, the morning. Got something to tell you. Umm, could you?"

"What is it?"

"I'd rather wait until tom...tomorrow to get into it."

She sounded like she'd been drinking, so I doubted I could get more out of her now, so I said, "Where and when?"

"The Last, umm, Lost Dog Cafe, maybe eight."

"That'll work. See you there."

"Okey-dokey," she said and was gone.

2

———————

I still hadn't heard from Charles as I left home for the short walk to Folly's most-popular breakfast restaurant. The temperature was already in the low seventies, well above average for this time of day in late March, so I took my time to enjoy the warm weather and the smiles on faces of a few people I encountered along Center Street on the six-block walk to the restaurant.

I wasn't the only person taking advantage of the weather. Half of the tables on the Dog's front patio were occupied and I stepped inside the unique, quaint restaurant, looked around to see if Noelle had arrived. Not seeing her, I told the hostess there would be two of us and preferred an outdoor table. I followed her to a table where I was told a server would be with me shortly.

Autumn, one of the friendly servers, arrived at the table, set a red mug of coffee in front of me, and asked if I was ready to order French toast, the menu item I selected most every visit. I told her yes, but not yet, since I was waiting for someone.

The wait was short. Noelle was walking up the street toward the restaurant. My breakfast mate is in her early thirties, African American, thin, and short at five-foot-two. She was wearing a dark brown T-shirt and jeans.

She saw me, smiled, then headed to the patio's side entry. A couple was seated near the entry and had a large collie on a leash standing near their table. Noelle patted the dog then headed to the chair across from me.

"Thanks for agreeing to meet. I wasn't at my best when I called. Hope I made sense." She smiled. "Must've made some sense since you're here."

Autumn returned before I could respond, asked if Noelle wanted anything to drink, then headed inside to get coffee for my tablemate.

"Again," Noelle said, "sorry for calling after I had, umm, several beers at Planet Follywood." She stared at the menu then said, "What do you recommend?"

I told her what I nearly always ordered then added that everything was good.

Autumn set Noelle's mug in front of her and asked if we were ready to order. Noelle said an order of French toast. The server smiled at her and asked if I'd talked her into it.

Noelle said, "Yes, ma'am. My arm's still sore from Chris twisting it until I said I'd order his favorite."

Autumn didn't wait for me to respond and headed inside.

Noelle, played with her napkin, looked around at the other tables, then stared in her coffee mug.

I took the fidgeting to mean she either wasn't ready or able to say what was bothering her. I took a lesson from my nosy friend and said, "Last evening you said there was something you wanted to tell me."

"To be honest, it seemed more important last night then it does now." She shook her head, then continued, "When I was in Planet Follywood, I heard two guys talking about a body found in his house the day before. I was shocked when I heard one of them say it was Matthew Seward and he'd died of an overdose." She continued to stare in her mug.

"Did you know him?"

She nodded.

"Tell me about him."

"Met him at a New Year's Eve party at Austin Middleton's house.

Austin's dad is a client of the agency where I work. Austin's place is a couple of houses up the street from Matthew's. Austin introduced us; saying Matthew was his best friend and they often played cards, poker, I think. Later that night, Matthew asked if I'd have supper with him a couple of days after the party. I didn't see any harm in it, so I said I would."

Our food arrived and for the next few minutes eating took priority over Matthew or Austin. I still had no clue why Noelle wanted to meet.

Noelle said it was the first time she'd had the Dog's French toast, but it wouldn't be the last. She then said, "Suppose you're wondering why I wanted to meet."

"It'd entered my mind."

"On our first date we went to Rita's for supper. We went out a couple more times after that. He was nice, but to be honest, I didn't see a long-term relationship with him."

I nodded and remained silent, hoping she'd speed up her reason for meeting before we'd have to order lunch.

"You know Rachel Little?"

"Don't believe so. Who's she?"

"Woman Matthew dated. They broke up, actually, he said he broke up with her, three days before Christmas. On our dates, he brought her up more times than I thought he should've since he was out with me. He didn't say it, of course, but I had the feeling he wasn't over her." She smiled and pointed her fork at me. "Anyway, that has nothing to do with why I asked you to meet me."

"Maybe not, but it's interesting."

"Two days before he, umm, died, he called and asked me to supper the next night. I already had plans and said I couldn't make it. He would've been more fun than the grin-and-bear-it dinner I was required to have with a client. Matthew then asked if I was available." She glanced at her iPhone and continued, "It would've been tonight. Told him that'd work. He brought up about me writing a murder mystery. I thought that was a little strange. He said he'd learned about a crime; a major crime was how he put it. He added since I was writing a mystery, I might be able to use some of it, at least some of the details, in the novel I'm working on, or the next one I write."

"What'd you say?"

"That'd piqued my interest. I asked him to tell me something about it. He said he'd tell me when we met."

"He didn't share anything else about what it was?"

"No. I don't know what the police are saying, but I'd put money on it being the reason he was murdered."

"The police first thought he'd overdosed then the coroner found a gunshot wound in the back of his head."

"They're wrong."

"Wrong about the gunshot wound?"

"No, about drugs."

"Noelle, since I met you, you've been working hard on your book. You haven't shared much of what's in it, but you've told me there was one or more murders in your imaginary town in Georgia and the murders were drug related."

Noelle earned a good salary in advertising but had moved to what she called a "dump" on Folly to get into the character of her protagonist, a private detective who, in the book lived in a barely habitable apartment. She'd even bought an older, black Dodge Ram pickup truck because that's what she pictured her main character driving.

"Yes, so?"

"Could it be because it was similar to something in your novel?"

"The guys I was snooping on in Planet Follywood kept saying Matthew died of an overdose, but I knew they were wrong."

"It turns out you were right."

"I'm also right about the drugs. Matthew wouldn't have had anything to do with them now."

"What makes you so certain?"

"Going on three dates didn't make us best buds, but Matthew was a talker, which was fine with me. He shared that when he was in college, he got into drugs big time. Took a year off school and spent some of it in rehab, in rehab twice actually. The reason he told me was because he was proud of what he'd done, more accurately what he hadn't done. Chris, he swore he hadn't taken an illegal substance since his second time in rehab five years ago. He told me that three days before he was found, found murdered."

Autumn returned to take our empty plates and asked if we needed more coffee. Noelle said, "Yes," and I nodded.

Autumn left to get our coffee, and Noelle said, "I believed him."

"I understand, but occasionally someone will think he or she had kicked the habit for years yet backslides."

"I know people like that, but you didn't hear Matthew talk. He couldn't have been happier if I'd given him a million dollars."

"Okay, let's say you're right, shouldn't you be telling the police?"

"In a perfect world, yes, but we're not in a perfect world."

"Why tell me?"

"Remember how a couple of years ago, you saw me in the Folly River Park and asked what I was doing?"

"You said you were observing people going in and out of the post office to help you create characters for your book."

"Wow, how'd you remember that?"

"You're the only novelist I've met in my seventy plus years. I was impressed and remembered a lot of what you'd said."

She laughed and said, "Don't think you can call me a novelist until I've finished a novel."

"You're almost there, aren't you?"

"Closer by the day, now back to my point. The police wouldn't take me seriously. Why would they? They'd smile and humor me if I said I thought Matthew was murdered because he told me he had something to tell me about a crime."

"I think you're underestimating yourself."

"Maybe, but to my point about watching people. I've seen you and some of your friends find ways to catch murderers in cases where the police were stumped."

"Noelle, I don't think—"

She waved a hand in front of my face and said, "The drugs were planted after Matthew was shot. Probably planted to make the crime appear drug related. I know it was because of something he'd learned, something he was going to tell me tonight. I trust you. I don't trust the police. Period."

Our coffee refills arrived and interrupted Noelle's argument.

I took a sip, set the mug down, and said, "What do you want me to do?"

"Do what you've done before. Keep your eyes and ears open. Talk to people who might've known Matthew." She reached across the table and patted my hand. "I have faith you'll get to the bottom of it."

I could give her fifty good reasons why that'd be a foolish idea. Instead of sharing any of them, I said, "I'll try."

3

———

Before leaving the Dog, Noelle said she had to get to her office in Charleston and I had to get to, umm, nowhere. I told her I enjoyed sharing breakfast and wished her well at the office. Times like this reminded me how fortunate I was to have retired from a high-pressure job at a large healthcare company in Kentucky and had been able to move to a small cottage a block from the Atlantic Ocean.

With that in mind, I decided to take advantage of the fantastic weather and walk on the Folly Beach Fishing Pier, six blocks from the Dog. Vacation season was rapidly approaching and the sidewalks along Center Street, the figurative center of the six-mile-long, half-mile-wide island and the literal center of Folly's retail establishments, were already showing increased pedestrian traffic.

I was crossing East Arctic Avenue and about to enter the Pier's parking lot, when I heard a horn behind me, and turned to see Chief LaMond's Ford F-150 pickup truck pulling into a parallel parking slot along the street.

I walked back to the driver's door where Cindy lowered her window, and said, "You planning on jumping off the Pier?"

"Not now that you're here."

"Then my trip here was worth it. Saved the life of one of Folly's geezers."

I ignored her insult and said, "I thought you'd be stuck in your office trying to whittle down that seven-foot-high pile of reports you were working on yesterday."

"I was doing that a half hour ago when I started thinking about the convicts stuck in jail cells over in Charleston, and thought I'd rather be where they are than going blind staring at those reports. So, like a conscientious police chief, I left the reports to gather dust and hopped on my trusty steed and headed out to do real police work."

She tapped the dashboard on her *trusty steed*.

"And now you've saved a geezer from drowning. Excellent police work."

"Smartass."

"Yes, ma'am. Don't forget to write a report about your heroic deed."

"I repeat, smart ass."

I smiled and said, "Speaking of police work, is there an update on Matthew Seward?"

"If you're referring to Matthew Seward III, he's still dead. Why?"

"I had breakfast with Noelle Ward."

"The lady writing a mystery?"

"Yes. She had gone out with Mr. Seward three times."

"And?"

"He asked her out a few days ago and she said she wouldn't be available until today."

"A date I doubt he'll keep."

"She is aware of his death."

"I suspect there is a point to this story. You close to sharing it?"

"Mr. Seward told her he wanted to tell her about a crime he'd become aware of."

"Why would Seward tell Ms. Ward rather than the police?"

"He told her she might be able to use it in her book. She didn't know anything more about it than that."

"Let me go out on a limb and say Noelle took that tiny bit of information and since he died before he could tell her, figured he was murdered before he could tell her the deep dark secret. How am I doing?"

"Clearly, your skill at coming up with that astute analysis is why you're Folly's top cop. Yes, that was her point."

"Did she say anything about him using drugs?"

"Yes, he told her he'd been addicted while in college; had to stay out of school a year and was in rehab twice during that period. He also told her he hasn't used any illegal drugs since then."

"After three dates, she knew that was true?"

"Yes."

"Everything you told me has the makings of a made for TV movie, or a Noelle Ward novel, not the real world."

"I'm simply sharing what she told me."

"Here's what I'm telling you. Mr. Seward III died of a gunshot wound, and there was cocaine all over his bedroom."

"But, Cindy—"

"The ME will determine if any drugs were in his system, but there's no doubt they were in the room."

"Noelle is convinced he was clean and had been for several years."

"If I had a dollar for every time I've heard someone say they'd stayed clean after getting out of rehab then regressed into drugs, I'd be rich, or if not rich, have enough dollars to quit this job and interfere with everything the real police do. I'd be like someone I know, someone standing in front of me."

"I'm sharing what Noelle told me. From my limited experience with her, she's not prone to exaggerate or go off on tangents."

She looked at her watch and said, "I need to be heading back to the office, but I'll tell you what. I'll keep an open mind in Seward's case, but to be honest, I don't see anything other than a man getting killed with a room full of dope."

"I appreciate you keeping an open mind."

"And now I'm off to the office to file an incident report on how I heroically saved a fossil from jumping off the Pier and cluttering up the beautiful Folly shoreline."

"And I thought Noelle Ward was the only fiction writer I knew."

4

———

I hadn't given much thought to Noelle's belief about Matthew Seward's death since talking to Chief LaMond yesterday. From my limited experience with addicts who'd gone to rehab, I could see how the late Mr. Seward could easily have reverted to his addiction. Whether he had or hadn't, a bullet in the brain was the cause of death. While Noelle was convinced he wouldn't have had drugs in his house, I hadn't heard enough to join her in that belief.

The phone's ringtone interrupted my thoughts about Matthew.

"Good morning, Charles."

"What time are you picking me up?"

"Why would I be picking you up?"

"So we could ride together. Duh."

"Perhaps I should've started with where are we going? Why are we going? When do we have to be there?"

"The funeral home, of course. To talk to folks about Matthew Seward the twenty-fifth murder. Visitation begins tomorrow at five. I think that covers your questions, so I repeat, when are you picking me up?"

"Four-thirty," I said then tapped *end call*.

It still felt good hanging up on the person who habitually hangs up on me.

Most people attend a visitation for a friend or relative to express sympathy and offer condolences to friends and family members of the decedent. Charles was convinced visitations were created to be fact-finding events to learn what happened to the decedent and talk to people who could help him determine who killed the person resting in the coffin or urn. Sadly, I admit I'd been part of these outings on more than one occasion.

I went to my computer in the spare bedroom I'd converted into an office and began searching for Matthew Seward's obituary.

I learned the visitation would be held tomorrow between five and seven at the J. Henry Stuhr Funeral Home on Calhoun Street in Charleston. The obit further revealed Mr. Seward was twenty-six-years-old and had been an employee of Seward Wealth Management where he'd held various positions. He was survived by his parents Matthew Seward II and Lois Wentworth Seward, two sisters, Katherine Seward and Samantha Seward Riley. There was no mention of cause of death.

I printed a copy of the obituary, put it aside, and Googled Seward Wealth Management. According to its website, Matthew Seward founded Seward Accounting in 1951. The name was changed to Seward Wealth Management when Matthew II took over the reins in 1986. The site featured photos of a smiling couple toasting with champaign flutes with the Eiffel Tower in the background, a family lounging on a yacht, and a middle-aged man golfing with the ocean in the background. The photos weren't captioned, but I suppose represented happy, successful clients.

One thing I found interesting was the list of officers which, of course, had Matthew Seward II as president, but someone named Francis Goss as executive vice president. Matthew Seward III wasn't mentioned. I printed a couple of pages from the website and stapled them to the obituary.

The closest I ever got to meeting a wealth manager was when I received a mailing inviting me to a "free" supper at one of Charleston's finer restaurants. All I would have to do was eat steak and then listen to a sales presentation about how the person paying for the meal could ensure me amazing wealth for the rest of my life. I declined the invitation. With me missing the "incredible wealth management opportunity," I wondered how I could learn more about Seward Wealth Management.

The answer was so obvious I almost missed it. Two words: Virgil Debonnet. I'd met Virgil a couple of years ago. He'd been a successful stock market analyst before losing everything, and by everything, I mean everything. He'd been married, owned a mansion overlooking the bay and Charleston's historic Battery, and a yacht. Poor choices, including massive gambling debts, illegal substance abuse, and losing battles with the Internal Revenue Service, took him from living large in Charleston to living in a tiny apartment in a deteriorating apartment building on Folly.

Despite his fall from wealth, Virgil was one of the most optimistic people I'd ever met. I also consider him a friend.

I dialed his number and heard, "Christopher, is that you?"

Virgil was one person, perhaps the only one, who calls me by my given name.

"It is," I said. "How are you?"

"Better than I was an hour ago when I was plunging sewage out of Mr. Arnold's toilet in apartment 201."

Virgil earned his rent by doing plumbing and other menial tasks for his landlord.

"I suspect it wouldn't take much for you to be doing better than that."

"True, oh so true, Christopher. I don't suppose you called to learn about Mr. Arnold's toilet."

"You suppose correctly. Think you could meet me this morning?"

"I'll clear my calendar for whatever time you wish to gather. The reason must be more exciting than what I'm doing now."

"Where are you?"

"Pewter Hardware, purchasing a toilet flange for dear, sweet Judy Davis in apartment 104."

"I wouldn't want to take you away from that important task."

"I'm in no hurry. She works until six-thirty, so I'll have plenty of time to fix her toilet. Why don't you meet me at the Folly River Park?"

The Folly River Park is a small park bounded by Center Street, East Indian Avenue, the Folly River, and a private residence. It's also catty-corner from Pewter Hardware.

"I can be there in ten minutes."

Virgil was standing by a picnic table in front of the park's small pavilion. He's in his early-forties, my height at five-foot-ten, but unlike me, he's thin, wearing a long-sleeve, button-down, white dress shirt with frayed cuffs and navy chinos. It was cloudy but he was wearing his ubiquitous sunglasses as well as resoled Guccis. A man walking his pug was the only other person in the park.

"Thanks for meeting me," I said as we shook.

"No, thank you. You kept me from having to perform one of my least favorite tasks. Judy's toilet can wait."

We sat on the top of the table, and I said, "What, if anything do you know about Seward Wealth Management?"

Virgil smiled. "That question wouldn't have anything to do with the untimely death of Master Seward III, would it?"

I nodded and said, "Yes."

"Are you and Charles playing private detectives again?"

Virgil was familiar with the last couple of police investigations Charles and I had stumbled upon. In fact, Virgil played a major role in one of the incidents and proclaimed that he was included in Charles's imaginary detective agency and even called us the crime fighting trio. Only he felt that way.

"No. I learned about his death and was talking to Noelle Ward who had dated Matthew."

Virgil said, "I'll assume there's more to that story, so until you feel comfortable sharing, let me say, I'm vaguely familiar with Seward Wealth Management."

"What do you know about them?"

"They've been around a long time, since the 1950s if I'm not mistaken. When I was wealthy, I attended a Christmas reception at

Seward II's house, a mansion on Lamboll Street. Was quite an affair. Food galore, three fully stocked bars, a trio playing holiday music."

"That sounds lavish. Know anything about Seward II or III?"

"Matthew II's reputation was a bit shady."

"What's that mean?"

"I have no firsthand knowledge you understand, but stories going around at the time were that the firm focused on wealthy widows and somehow managed to syphon huge amounts of money from their investments."

"Did anyone bring charges?"

"I'm not aware of any, but as you might imagine, I no longer have contacts in that circle. Matthew II did, and I suppose still does since he gives generously to several causes and Charleston groups. If I were the suspicious type, I'd say that insulated him and the company from tighter scrutiny."

"Do you know anything about Matthew III?"

"Other than he's dead?"

I nodded.

"Met him a few times over here. The family owns the big house in Charleston and the oceanfront one on Folly, somewhere out East Arctic Avenue. Matthew III spends most of his time here. I've run into him a couple of times in Bert's. Seems, umm, seemed like a nice fellow."

"Charles and I are going to his visitation tomorrow afternoon. Want to go?"

"And miss out on sticking my hands in raw sewage? I suppose I can make that sacrifice."

5

———————

Virgil was waiting for me in front of his eight-unit apartment building. Or, I assumed it was Virgil since I'd never seen him wearing a blazer, gray slacks, and a red and white striped tie.

Before he got in the car, he pirouetted like a model showing off a stylish outfit. He finished his twirl and said, "Well, what do you think?"

"I think you're making me look like a bum in my short-sleeve gray polo shirt and navy slacks. I didn't think you had a tie."

"I didn't, that is until yesterday when I convinced one of our tenants to take me out to that fine, men's clothier, *le Goodwill*. Got the entire outfit, except for my Guccis, of course, for thirty-five bucks, that's one unstopped toilet in work lingo."

"It looks good."

He smiled. "Haven't had a tie on since, well, since I had a job, not the plumbing job, but the hoity-toity one. I met Matthew number two when I had money, so I didn't want him to think I was a bum." He shrugged. "I am a bum, but number two doesn't need to know it."

Virgil had opened the back door and climbed in while telling me his anti-bum rationale, then added, "I know Charles has ownership of the front seat, so I'll sit back here and let you chauffeur me to the funeral home."

"That will make the drive more pleasant."

As could be predicted, Charles was waiting for us in front of his apartment. His attire was more in line with mine rather than Virgil's. Charles's idea of dressing up was wearing a long-sleeve T-shirt without a college logo on the front. Today he had on a dark-gray long-sleeve T-shirt and black chinos. He glanced at his wrist where normal people wore a watch. His wrist was bare, but the motion signaled he thought we were late. We weren't.

He slid into his reserved seat, turned and stared at Virgil, and said, "What'd you do with Virgil?"

Virgil smiled. "Wanted to dress like the guy in the coffin will be attired."

I ignored their conversation and navigated my way off Folly and headed toward the funeral home. To my relief, Charles and Virgil settled into silence until we crossed the Ashley River on the road that became Calhoun Street. The Stuhr Funeral Home was a couple of blocks past Charleston's hospital complexes. The exterior of the building was what I would've expected for someone from one of the cities wealthy families. The brick structure featured a curved portico with colonial columns. We parked in the lot beside the building after I had to drive through it twice to find a vacant spot.

"See what happens when you're late?" Charles said although it was still five minutes until the posted time for the visitation.

I ignored him and Virgil said, "Wonder who all these people are?"

I didn't know who they were, but noting how many Mercedes, Lexuses, and Jaguars were in the lot, suspected they weren't among Charleston's poor.

We were greeted at the door by a dour looking gray-haired gentleman dressed in a black suit with a matching black tie. He asked who we were "visiting," and Virgil, the best dressed among us said Matthew Seward III. We were directed to a room at the end of the corridor.

The large room looked like it could be in one of the mansions south of Broad. While the room was sparsely furnished, I assumed so there was plenty of standing room for mourners, the furniture was either antiques or antique replicas. A large sofa was at one end of the room, a mahogany coffin at the other. Between the two, there had to be fifty people with the starting time still minutes away.

As we signed in, I noticed roughly half of those assembled were in their sixties or older. White hair topped many, along with stylish dresses in muted colors on the women and dark suits on the men.

The other half of the mourners were mostly in their twenties or thirties, with a few between forty and the older group. Only a couple of the younger mourners were professionally dressed. I didn't feel so out of place.

A group of younger attendees was gathered in front of the coffin. Once they moved, I nudged Charles and Virgil in that direction.

A heavyset, white-haired gentleman, whom I would guess to be in his late-seventies, stood at the side of the coffin in front of a large flower arrangement. There had to be at least forty arrangements bookending the bier holding the coffin.

Virgil leaned toward me and said, "That's the father."

We were still ten feet from the coffin, and I said, "You see his mother?"

"Think that was her on the sofa when we entered the room, but I'm not certain. I only saw her once, and that was years ago."

Charles whispered, "I'll ask where his wife is."

I could imagine Charles saying something like, "Hey, Pop, where's the Mrs.?"

I said, "Why don't you let Virgil ask? He's met Mr. Seward."

The three of us moved near the closed coffin and with our heads bowed looked at it for an appropriate amount of time, and Virgil turned to move closer to Mr. Seward and expressed sympathy for his loss. Charles and I mumbled similar sentiments.

Mr. Seward glanced at each of us and said, "I must apologize. I don't believe we've met."

Virgil took the lead and told Mr. Seward he'd attended a Christmas party at their house a few years ago, and that we live on

Folly. I said I'd talked with his son on a few occasions, but we weren't close.

Mr. Seward narrowed his focus on the three of us, and said, "Were any of you poker buddies of his?"

"No," I said.

Virgil said, "I don't believe I've seen your wife. Is she here?"

Seward glanced around the room, sighed, and said, "She was back on that sofa earlier. She probably stepped out for a moment. I'm sure she would like to see you."

I noticed others gathered behind us waiting to speak with Mr. Seward, so I said, "Again, we wanted offer our deepest condolences for your loss."

He graciously shook our hands as we stepped aside so others could talk with him.

I thought the room was full when we arrived, but there must've been thirty or more who had arrived since we were at the coffin and talking with Mr. Seward. I suggested we move to the side of the room.

"Good idea," Charles said, "That way we can see who we want to talk to next about the murder."

I was glad to see no one was close enough to hear his comment other than Virgil and me.

"That's interesting," Virgil said as he focused on a couple of people who'd just entered the room.

I said, "What is?"

"The woman by the door in the burgundy dress."

The woman he was referring to appeared to be in her mid-twenties, tall, thin, with long blonde hair.

Charles said, "What about her?"

"That's Rachel Little."

I said, "The woman Matthew broke up with before Christmas?"

Virgil nodded.

Charles didn't make any head motions. Instead, he made a beeline in Ms. Little's direction. I turned away, hoping no one would associate me with the man currently in search of answers about Matthew's death.

Virgil tapped me on the shoulder. "Charles motioned for us to join him and Ms. Little."

I took a deep breath, smiled in Charles's direction, and along with Virgil headed his way.

Virgil said, "Charles, I see you've met Rachel."

She looked at Virgil like she was trying to figure out who he was.

"Yes," Charles said. "She was telling me she was dating Matthew. I was expressing my sadness for her loss."

Dating, I thought, but didn't pursue it.

Virgil said, "You may not remember me. I met you one night a few months ago when you and Matthew were at Loggerhead's outdoor bar."

"Umm, yes, I believe I recall. Aren't you one of his poker buddies?"

"We talked about poker a couple of times, but I never played with him."

"Oh, I guess I heard you talking about it."

She kept glancing around the room like she'd rather be talking with someone else, anyone else. She said, "I'd better get over to speak with Lois. Nice seeing you."

She turned and headed to the sofa where a lady I assumed to be Mrs. Seward, Lois, had returned to the room and was seated by herself.

Charles watched her go, pulled Virgil and me closer and whispered, "She said she was dating Matthew? I thought they broke up months ago."

Virgil said, "Perhaps she misspoke in her time of grief."

"Bull hockey," Charles articulately said. "Said she was going to talk with Lois. If that's Matthew's mother, isn't that awfully friendly to be calling her by her first name."

"Some people prefer it that way," Virgil said.

"Bull hockey."

I'd had enough bull for now and pointed to a distinguished looking man with graying hair and the posture of a Buckingham

Palace Guard. "I believe that's Francis Goss, the executive vice president of Seward Wealth Management."

"Christopher," Virgil said, "I'm impressed. Yes, that's Fritz Goss."

Charles said, "As in Fritz the cat?"

Virgil smiled. "If your first name was Francis, wouldn't you want to go by anything other than Francis?"

"Think I'd go for Frank before Fritz."

"Virgil, what do you know about him?"

"Not much. He was at the Christmas party I attended. He spent most of the time glad-handing clients and schmoozing with others he wanted to recruit as clients. He won't remember me, but I think I'll go say hi."

We'll wait here," I said.

Charles said, "Speak for yourself. I'm going with Virgil."

I was watching them begin a conversation with Francis/Fritz/Frank when a man in his twenties moved beside me.

He said, "You're from Folly, aren't you?"

"Yes."

"Thought so. I've seen you in Bert's Market a time or two."

I smiled. "That's one of my hangouts. I'm Chris Landrum, and you're?"

"Austin Middleton, Matthew's best friend."

"Sorry for your loss. I was shocked to hear about his death, so young."

"Some things can't be explained. It's ridiculous how many people my and Matthew's age are dying from drug overdoses."

"Is that what happened?" I asked, then lied. "I hadn't heard."

"I assume that's what happened. He'd had issues with drugs when he was in college but had been clean until a few months ago. So sad."

"He was using again?"

Austin slowly shook his head. "Afraid so. I warned him about what could happen, especially with so much Fentanyl floating around." He shook his head a second time. "I told him today's drugs aren't what they used to be when he was in college." He looked toward the coffin. "I'd better go see Mr. Seward. Nice chatting with you."

"You, too."

Charles and Virgil returned from talking with Fritz.

"Boring, boring," Charles said.

Virgil added, "He does tend to be a bit stiff."

"Like a piece of rebar," Charles said. "Who was the guy with you?"

"Austin Middleton, Matthew's best friend, according to Austin."

Charles said, "Learn anything?"

"Not really. You two ready to head out?"

Virgil said, "Yes."

I was surprised when Charles agreed with him.

6

After we pulled out of the funeral home's lot, I said, "Okay, guys. What'd we learn?"

Charles said, "Rich people have lots of friends."

"Wrong," Virgil said. "They have many people who want to be around them in hopes some of the wealth rubs off."

"Good," Charles said, "I could use some of that wealth."

Virgil laughed and said, "From my experience, it seldom works. Another reason they're there is the wealthy are always looking for ways to increase their wealth. Boy, could I tell you stories about back when I had money."

Charles said, "Like what?"

"The wealthy make money several ways. Many get it the old-fashioned way. They inherit their fortune. The only thing they managed to do was being born to rich parents."

Charles looked out the window, then returned to looking at Virgil. "What's that got to do with them looking for ways to increase their wealth?"

"Nothing. That was one way they get wealthy. Others earn it, either through legal ways or, well, not so legal ones. They make contacts, they network, they pretend to like people they can't stand in hopes of cashing in on the contacts."

"You mean some of the people at the viewing were there to be seen and not to offer sincere condolences to Matthew's family?"

Virgil smiled and said, "That's why they call it a *viewing*. They want to be viewed. Some were there to offer condolences, but I guarantee, some were there to be seen."

"That's sad," I said.

"Okay," Charles said, "now that you shot down my theory of rich folks having a herd of friends, what else did we learn?"

"I was talking with Austin Middleton," I said. "He said he was Matthew's best friend and was under the assumption Matthew died of a drug overdose."

Charles said, "Why'd he think that?"

"He said Matthew was back on drugs and figured that's what killed him."

"Hasn't the cause of death been released?" Virgil said.

"I saw it on Live 5 News' web site last evening," I said, "so he could've known it if he'd been paying attention to the news."

Virgil said, "He's still in his twenties, right?"

"Yes," I said.

"One of the units in my apartment building is rented to two gals that're under thirty. They don't get the newspaper, don't have local stations on their TV, and appear oblivious to whatever is going on in the news." He chuckled. "They get their news from social media. You can imagine how objective and complete that news is. Austin could be like that."

"You might be right," I said. "Wouldn't you think if your best friend were killed you would do whatever you could to learn what killed him?"

"Yes, but I'm not in my twenties," Virgil said.

"Okay," Charles said, "we learned that Austin not only doesn't listen to the news, but he assumed his best friend killed himself simply because he was using drugs."

"Weak," Virgil said.

I agreed.

Charles said, "We learn anything else?"

"Yes," I said. "Rachel Little either is delusional or wanted us to believe something she told us that wasn't true." I hesitated and then reluctantly added, "Or, Noelle Ward was mistaken."

Virgil beat Charles to a response. "When she said she was dating Matthew?"

"Correct," I said. "Noelle told me Matthew had broken up with Rachel before Christmas."

Virgil said, "You believe Noelle?"

"She had no reason to lie about it."

"Rachel seemed uber-friendly with Matthew's mother, calling her by her first name, and rushing over to talk with her," Virgil said. "Think she'd be that buddy buddy with Mrs. Seward if he'd broken up with her months ago?"

Charles said, "Maybe she's one of those people you were talking about who're trying to get ahead through contacts. Mrs. Seward would probably be a good person to help her."

We'd crossed the Folly River, and I asked Charles if he wanted me to drop him at his apartment before taking Virgil home.

"Yeah, I've got to get out of this formal wear and make a delivery for Dude."

I didn't think he could go much longer without a college mascot on his chest.

Charles's main source of income was from making deliveries to local customers for our friend Dude Sloan who owned the surf shop. The deliveries were limited to local customers since Charles made them on his classic Schwinn bicycle.

I pulled in his parking lot where he hopped out of the car before saying, "We'll get together tomorrow to figure out who snuffed young Master Seward."

He didn't wait for me to say whatever happened to Matthew was none of our business.

On the way to Virgil's apartment, he said, "That reminded me of attending gatherings back when I was rich."

"You miss it?"

"I miss it a little more than I'd miss typhoid fever."

Before he got out of the car in front of his building, he said, "You think it's up to the famous private detective trio to solve the mystery of who put Matthew in that coffin?"

There were so many things wrong with that sentence that I wouldn't have known where to start correcting him, so I said, "It's in the capable hands of the police."

Virgil smiled and said, "Sure it is."

He was walking to his door before I could respond.

7

———

Morning began with a phone call from Virgil. "Christopher, did I interrupt anything important?"

I wasn't accustomed to polite salutations, so it threw me for a second before I said, "Sure did. I was fixing another cup of coffee to go with a stale apple Danish."

"I apologize, although that sounds like one of the saddest breakfasts I've heard about, and that's going some since sad breakfasts are what I start my days with."

"I can eat and talk at the same time. What did I do to deserve hearing your cheerful voice?"

"On the way home from the funeral home I kept thinking I recognized someone at the viewing but at the time couldn't put a name to the face. It came to me in the middle of the night. You know Foster Rodman?"

"The name's not familiar. Describe him."

"Mid-thirties, short, about five-foot-two or so, premature balding. At the viewing he was one of the few youngsters wearing a coat and tie."

"Doesn't sound familiar, sorry."

"Wish I'd thought of his name when we were there. I would've talked with him."

"How do you know him?"

"Ran into him a few times in our local drinking establishments. Like people running into strangers a few times, we started talking. Nothing important, shared names, shared where we lived, yada yada yada."

"That's interesting, but was there something about him you think is important?"

In other words, why interrupt my nutritious breakfast to ask if I knew him.

"Interesting, perhaps not, but curious."

"Meaning?"

"You probably have noticed that I'm an open book about my life, my past, my foibles."

He could say that again. The first time I'd met him, he shared how he'd been wealthy, how and why he'd lost it all, and a few things I can't recall.

"True. What's that have to do with Foster?"

"As part of me getting to know strangers in a bar I ask where they live and what they do for a living. Foster hemmed and hawed about where he lived. Started telling me about the inside of his apartment. Don't know why he thought I'd care about the color of the refrigerator. It's black in case you were interested. Anyway, the first time I asked him what he did for a living, he said something like *have a business*."

"What kind of business?"

"That's the same thing I asked."

"What'd he say?"

"He looked at me and said, 'Want another beer? I'm buying.'"

"What'd you say?"

"Christopher, you ever know me to turn down a beer?"

I sighed and said, "Did he answer your question about his business?"

"Nope. And that was the first time I asked him. I tried again a few days later in The Bounty Bar and received, well, received nothing. He changed the subject, and hell, didn't even offer to buy me a beer."

"Why do you think he avoided answering your questions?"

"I'm no psychiatrist, so the best I can come up with is he didn't want to."

I said, "Or he simply didn't want to tell you where he lives and didn't answer your question about what business because he doesn't have a business, or—"

"Or his business is selling drugs."

"Like the cocaine in Matthew's house?"

"The thought entered my mind. Think we ought to tell the police?"

"Tell them what? Foster said he has a business but didn't tell you what it was."

"Sounds weak, doesn't it?"

"Afraid so."

"Suppose I need to saunter around the local drinking establishments and see if Foster happens to be in one of them. Then I could do my Charles imitation and say 'Hey Foster, nice night. Did you sell cocaine to Matthew?' What do you think?"

I coughed back a chuckle and said, "Don't think that's a good idea."

"I'm getting better at the private detective stuff because that was my thought before I got it all out. What do you think I should do?"

"Keep your ears open, but don't start quizzing anyone. Matthew was murdered. Whoever shot him, probably wouldn't hesitate to pull the trigger again if he or she thought someone was getting close to exposing him or her."

"Ears open, got it. Thanks, now I have to see what's wrong with Mrs. Allister's sink. No matter how dangerous it may be, private detecting is way more fun than plumbing detecting."

"I don't see anything fun about fixing plumbing problems."

"One more thing before I go, you were talking about Noelle Ward on the way to the funeral."

"Yes."

"I've talked with her a couple of times when I've been out and about. Seems pleasant. What do you know about her?"

"I've always had pleasant conversations with her. She's interesting in that she makes a good living working in an advertising agency yet chooses to live in a tiny apartment so she can get in character with the private detective in the novel she's writing."

"That's what she told me. Know anything else about her?"

"Why are you asking?"

"Now don't take this as gospel. I might not do it. Anyway, I'm thinking about asking her out."

"When was the last time you talked with her?"

"Couple of weeks ago. Why?"

"I was curious if you knew before I mentioned it on the way to the funeral home she'd had a few dates with Matthew Seward?"

"She hadn't mentioned it. So, what do you think I should do?"

I took a deep breath and said, "I'm no expert on dating, but I don't see any reason for you not to ask her. I think she only had two or three dates with Matthew." I chose not to mention the obvious how Matthew was no longer in the picture.

"That settles it. What about her having a good job and me not having a job? If I count the money in my pocket, I have, let's see." His phone clunked on something, probably when he set it down. He finally returned and said, "$2.53. See my problem? Where do you think I could take her and not deplete my net worth?"

Virgil sounded like he was serious, so I resisted the temptation to laugh. Instead, I said, "People from all over the country spend thousands of dollars coming here to walk on the beach and enjoy the ocean. You could ask her if she wanted to take a sunset walk on the beach with you. That wouldn't take any of your net worth, and you could learn if you wanted to spend more time with her or her with you."

"Christopher, that's an exceptional idea. I knew I could count on you. Now I suppose I'd better get to fixin' Mrs. Allister's sink. Thanks."

I reheated my coffee in the microwave and got back to eating my stale Danish, when the phone rang again.

This time the name Bob appeared on the screen.

"Good morning, Mr. Howard."

Bob had been my realtor when I bought the cottage I now call home and when I rented a storefront on Center Street and opened Landrum Gallery selling my photos. He retired a couple of years ago and bought a dilapidated bar from a longtime friend who'd been having serious health issues. Bob knew as much about running a bar as I do about conjugating *to fly* in Hindi. Bob had recently turned eighty, was six-foot-tall, obese, with a personality that could generously be labelled gruff. Regardless, we'd been friends since I arrived on Folly.

"Tell me one damn thing that's good about it," he said then coughed.

"You're talking to me."

"If that's the best you can up with, the day's worse than I thought."

"What's on your mind?" I asked to move the call into a kinder direction.

"Saw on TV where there was another damn murder on your island. Your citizens are getting whacked faster than in Chicago."

"Did you know the victim?"

"What makes you think I'd know a damned drug addict young enough to be my grandson?"

"Because you called?"

"Wrong again. I don't know anything about the stiff but am familiar with his family's wealth management company."

"What do you know about it?"

"A few years ago, I contacted them to see if they could double my money in a couple of weeks."

By most standards, Bob and his wife Betty were wealthy. He'd been a successful commercial real estate broker before switching to residential real estate. Although it took him several years before he admitted it to me, he has a degree in economics from Duke University and lives in a large, two story, Georgian style home on one of Charleston's high-status streets.

"Could they?"

"Hell, no. They said the same thing my current financial advisor had told me. There was no way to continually outguess the market, on and on."

"Did you meet with Matthew Seward II?"

"No, my contacts were with Fritz Goss, the executive vice president. Stuck-up fellow, thought he was the god of wealth management."

"Did you ever meet Matthew III, the man who was killed?"

"No."

"Did anything Francis, umm, Fritz tell you throw up red flags?"

"No, why?"

"I'd heard it was rumored a few years ago that Matthew II or someone else with the firm had been involved in some questionable practices regarding his dealings with elderly widows."

"I knew it, yep, I knew it."

"Knew what?"

"You and your posse of pals are sticking your noses where they don't belong."

"Not really. It was something someone who knew Matthew II shared. I don't see how it could have anything to do with the death of his son."

"This is old Bob you're talking to. If my memory is correct, and by the way, it often is, you've said something similar on more than one occasion, and low and behold, you went and caught yourself a killer or two, or three, or—"

"Okay, I get your point."

"It's about time. Tell you what, if you run into anything while you're not getting involved that I can help with, give me a call. Better yet, get your scrawny ass over to Al's and let us fix you one of the best cheeseburgers in the US of A."

I said I would.

He said, "You'd better," before he hung up.

I wasn't off the phone with Bob more than ten minutes when it rang again.

This time, Noelle's name appeared on the screen.

"Good morning, Noelle."

"Did I catch you at a bad time?"

Two out of three civil call openings in one morning had to be a record, at least for my phone.

"You caught me at a good time. I'm goofing off while drinking coffee."

"Good. I hate to bother you but was wondering if you could meet me after I get off work."

"Sure. Where and when?"

"I should be back over there by five-thirty. How about at The Washout?"

"I'll be there."

8

The Washout is one of Folly's larger restaurants and features good food and an outdoor, covered bar. I arrived twenty minutes before the time I was to meet Noelle. I was glad I did, since the bar was nearly full, and I was fortunate to corral two barstools.

I was sipping on a glass of chardonnay while trying to avoid the glares from customers who were expressing displeasure with me hoarding the empty stool when Noelle entered, smiled, and headed my way. She was wearing a white blouse, dress slacks, and black dress shoes. This was the first time I'd seen her in work attire as opposed to jeans and a dark-colored top.

"Hope you haven't been waiting long," she said as she sat on the stool that'd been coveted by irritated customers.

"Not really," I said as the bartender slipped a coaster in front of Noelle.

She looked at my drink and told the employee she'd have the same.

The bartender was quick to bring Noelle's drink. She took a sip, a deep breath, then said, "Thanks for meeting me. This has been one busy day."

"Busier than usual?"

"We had to finish a presentation my boss is giving tonight to a potential client. We didn't decide on a focus for the presentation and what we had to offer the client until noon. Four hours later, we'd put together a thirty-five-page PowerPoint presentation. With luck it will get us the account."

"Congratulations, I guess."

She smiled and said, "Thanks, I guess."

She spent the next few minutes giving me the highlights of the presentation. My experience in the world of work had ended fifteen years ago, but I thought the approach her firm was taking sounded solid and told her so.

"I hope so," she said, took another sip of wine, and added, "Guess you're wondering why I wanted to meet?"

Before I answered, the bartender asked if we wanted to order something to eat at the bar or were we waiting for a table. A quick look at the entry revealed several groups waiting for tables. I asked Noelle if eating at the bar was okay.

"As long as it's food, I could eat anywhere. I'm starved. We didn't get lunch today because of the presentation."

We each ordered a flounder sandwich and agreed to share an order of fries.

The bartender left to put in our order, and I turned to Noelle to wait for her answer to the question about why she wanted to meet.

"Did you go to Matthew's viewing?"

"Yes, Charles Fowler, Virgil Debonnet and I attended. In fact, I thought I might see you there."

"I didn't go," she said and took another sip.

I waited for her to say more.

When she didn't, I said, "There was a crowd. Charles and I didn't know anyone; Virgil knew Matthew's parents and a couple of the others."

"How did Virgil know the parents?"

"He'd met them a few years ago when he was a financial analyst in Charleston."

The noise in the bar had increased dramatically since I'd arrived so I had to lean closer to hear what Noelle was saying.

"How well do you know Virgil?"

"He's a friend. We shared some frightening moments three years ago and I occasionally run into him. He's a good person."

"I remember how the two of you were nearly killed by the person who killed the men in the airplane. Bet you're wondering why I'm asking?"

"To be honest, yes."

"He and I've had a few conversations over the last three weeks. I could be wrong but get the impression he wants to ask me out but can't manage to get the question past his lips."

"That's interesting."

No, I'm not going to tell her what Virgil told me this morning, but that won't keep me from bragging about my friend.

"He's a great guy. You could do a lot worse."

She laughed. "And I have. Know why I think he's reluctant to ask?"

"Why?"

"He's shared his story about how he'd been wealthy before running into hard times. I know where he lives and am certain he doesn't have a car. I think he's hesitant because he doesn't have much money."

I didn't share his net worth was $2.53.

"Would that be an issue?"

"Absolutely not. I haven't dated much in the last few years, but the few dates I've been on have been with a professional in the advertising world, a couple of attorneys, and one guy who never told me what he did but didn't hesitate to tell me about his yacht and house in the Bahamas."

"And Matthew."

"And Matthew. Virgil seems much nicer than any of those guys, and I know he has a great sense of humor. That's important to me. I'd take him over any of those others."

"So, you'd go out with him if he asked?"

She nodded. "Yes."

"Good. Talking about Virgil, he saw someone at the visitation he didn't talk to since he couldn't remember his name. Later, he told me the man was Foster Rodman and that he lives on Folly. Do you know him?"

Our food arrived and Noelle grabbed a fry as soon as the plate hit the table. Yes, she was starved.

She swallowed and took another sip of wine, before saying, "I haven't met Foster, but Matthew mentioned him a few times. Apparently, Foster was one of Matthew's poker buddies."

"That's the second man who has been described as one of Matthew's poker-playing buddies. How often did he, did they, play?"

"Too often, if you ask me. They got together a couple times a week."

"Where?"

"No one place. Matthew said they moved the game from one member's house to another. The host had to furnish snacks and drinks. The host also got to call what games they'd be playing. I don't know enough about poker to know what that meant."

"Did Matthew share anything that gave you the impression one of those guys could've been the person who killed him?"

"Not really, and I've been thinking the same thing the last two days. If it was one of them, Matthew didn't say anything that'd point to which one."

She took a bite of her sandwich and I said, "It's none of my business, but you didn't appear to want to say more when I asked if you'd attended the viewing."

She looked at me then down at her plate. Without looking up, she said, "I didn't go because of his parents."

"What about them?"

"I never met them, but Matthew said he told them about me. When he told me, he laughed and said his parents weren't very happy with their son's choice in lady friends."

"Why?"

"Two reasons I suspect although Matthew didn't say it." She took another sip, hesitated, then said, "In Charleston, a person's name is important, not necessarily about snobbery or wealth. It's more important because it shows the person is, or isn't, tied to the town's past, about having roots, and about feeling connected to the city and its way of life. Ward doesn't meet any of those lofty expectations." She shrugged and held out her hands.

"You said two reasons."

She frowned, slowly shook her head, and said, "Chris, look at me."

I did.

"See anything different about me?"

"You look smarter than many people I know."

She laughed then said, "Anything else?"

"You're Black?"

"Bingo."

"That was the problem they had with you?"

She nodded. "Matthew didn't put it quite like that. He said his parents were wonderful people, but they, especially his mother, aren't very tolerant."

"And that's why you didn't go to the visitation?"

"Yes."

"I'm sorry."

"Me, too."

9

I rolled out of bed the next morning with a headache and thoughts about Matthew Seward's death bouncing around in my aching head. After awakening my Mr. Coffee machine and taking a few sips of caffeine, my thoughts switched from thinking about Seward's death, to why I was thinking about it. I didn't know Matthew more than I knew anyone I'd shared casual and benign greetings with after seeing them around town. Noelle had gone on a few dates with him and was convinced he hadn't regressed into the world of drugs, but even then, she said the dates were casual and didn't think she was getting more serious. Bob Howard had met with someone from the wealth management firm years ago but didn't know either Matthew II or Matthew III. Finally, Virgil had attended a Christmas party at the deceased man's parents' house. None of these things were enough for me to get involved nosing into the death.

So, why was I waking up thinking about it? Probably because I'd been talking with Virgil and Noelle yesterday. That's what I told myself as I walked next door to Bert's to grab breakfast. It was before 7:30 and a handful of construction workers were congregating around the coffee urn and two more were selecting items out of my destination, the pastry cabinet.

Someone tapped me on the shoulder. I turned to see Chief LaMond's smiling face and got to listen to her say, "I see you're too old and lazy to walk to the Dog for your heart-unhealthy French toast so you're getting ready to grab a heart-unhealthy clump of dough for breakfast."

"Good morning, Chief. And what might you be doing standing behind me at the pastry cabinet?"

"Waiting to get a healthy Danish to fuel this well-toned chiefly body."

The construction workers in front of me made their selections and headed to the register and I grabbed one of the two remaining cinnamon Danishes and stepped aside for Cindy.

She took the remaining Danish, the one that looked as unhealthy as did my choice, and said, "Why haven't you called?"

"Why would I?"

"To talk to lovely, vivacious, charming me, of course."

"You left out modest."

"That goes without saying. Anyway, the other reason I've been waiting for your call is it's been, what, two days since you've asked what I'd learned about Mr. Seward's death. You're slipping, nosy one."

We stepped away from the pastry cabinet and I said, "What have you learned about Mr. Seward's death."

"That's more like the nosy senior civilian I'm familiar with."

"Well?"

"It's none of your business."

"Then why ask?"

"Being none of your business has never stopped you before."

"Have you learned anything you're able to share?"

"There you go, begging me again." She looked around and lowered her voice. "Remember the cocaine we found near the body?"

I nodded.

"According to the medical examiner, he didn't have any in his system."

"Noelle could be correct when she said he hadn't relapsed."

"That's possible, but if he hadn't, it looked like he was getting ready to. Otherwise, why was it there?"

"Good question. He had a relatively new and expensive house. Were there security cameras?"

"Excellent question. There were three. One facing the front yard, one overlooking the back yard, and even one inside the front hall facing the entry door."

"Well?"

"What you didn't ask was if any of them were operational at the time of his death."

"From that, I assume they weren't."

"Excellent assumption. They weren't turned on. Neither house on each side or the ones across the street have cameras. In other words, there's no recording of the killer."

"Who found the body?"

"A lady from his office. He'd missed an important meeting with a client and didn't answer his phone. His father sent the poor lady to his house. The door was unlocked, and you know the rest."

"That had to be traumatic. Do you know Austin Middleton?"

"No, who's he?"

"From what I hear, he's a poker buddy of the deceased."

"You know that how?"

"Charles, Virgil, and I attended Matthew's viewing."

"Why doesn't that surprise me?"

"A few years ago, Virgil attended a Christmas party at Matthew's parents' house, and he wanted to attend the visitation to extend his condolences. As you know, he's vehicle challenged, so I took him."

"That was kind of you to take Virgil to the event so he could see the parents. I suppose you're now going to tell me that was the only reason you went."

"As I told you before, I'd run into Matthew in here a few times. That's why I was there."

"So tell me, why was your friend who claims to be a private detective there?"

"He heard I was going and wanted to tag along."

"And I'm supposed to believe that?"

"It's true."

"While you were innocently expressing sympathy to Matthew's family, did you happen to learn anything that would help the police learn the identity of his killer?"

"Not directly, but it was interesting to hear Rachel Little, the person who'd dated Matthew until right before Christmas according to Noelle Ward, say she was dating Matthew."

"Still dating him?"

"That's how she said it."

"Anything else?"

"She also seemed overly friendly to Matthew's mother. Especially if she hadn't dated him since before Christmas."

Cindy sighed then said, "What did you learn about Austin Middleton? You brought him up."

"Thanks for reminding me. He said one thing I found interesting. He was under the assumption, or wanted me to believe he was, that Matthew died of a drug overdose."

"Has he been under a rock the last few days?"

"If he was, he didn't mention it."

"Stop being so obtuse. You know what I mean."

I smiled. "Still working on improving your vocabulary?"

"Mayor's orders. He said if I kept learning new words, I might be able to carry on a conversation with an educated citizen." She rolled her eyes. "As if that'll ever happen. Stop changing the subject. You know the murder's been all over the media the last three days."

"I agree. He should've known it wasn't an overdose. I don't know if he truly didn't know, or assumed I was so obtuse he could fool me."

"Smartass."

"Yes, ma'am."

"Regardless, I'll share those tiny-tiny bits of most-likely worthless information with Detective Adair." She looked at her watch. "I need to get to a meeting with the mayor. That's what I live for, you know."

Kenneth Adair was a detective with the County Sheriff's Office. I'd had dealings with him during his previous investigations of deaths on

Folly. He considered me a nosy busybody, but reluctantly admitted I had helped solve a couple of the crimes he'd been investigating.

I followed Cindy to pay and then to her vehicle.

She got in, lowered the window, and said, "You sure there's nothing else you learned while you were not butting into another police investigation?"

I assured her there wasn't and if I did happen across anything she should know, I'd tell her immediately. At the time, I meant it.

10

————

I managed not to think about Matthew's death the rest of the morning and until mid-afternoon when someone knocked on the front door.

That someone happened to be Virgil. He looked at me than glanced over my shoulder into the living room and said, "You busy?"

"No. Want to come in?"

"Don't mind if I do. Sure you're not busy?"

"I'm sure," I said and pointed for him to have a seat on the sofa. "Want something to drink?"

"I'm fine, but thanks for the offer. Don't know if I'd be as hospitable if someone arrived at my door without an invitation."

I sat in the chair facing the sofa and said, "What's on your mind?"

"Can't get Matthew, the dead one, out of my head."

I waited for him to continue. When he didn't, I said, "What's bothering you about it?"

He rubbed his chin, removed his sunglasses then put them back on, before saying, "What's bothering me about it? Good question. Let me try to throw some of them out. Was he or wasn't he back on drugs? Umm, guess other than who killed him, that's my big question. What do you think?"

I didn't know if he wanted me to give my thoughts on the drugs question or if he had other questions to add.

"I have several questions but can partially answer your first one. I talked with Chief LaMond this morning. She shared that the medical examiner didn't find any trace of illegal drugs in Matthew's system. That's consistent with what Noelle said Matthew had told her about being off drugs since college."

"Then what's with the cocaine in the room where he'd been murdered?"

"Either Matthew was about to start using again and it was his cocaine, or whoever killed him brought it with him."

"Makes sense. I learned a bunch of things, most I never wanted to learn, back when I was into drugs big time. We've all heard the saying misery loves company."

I nodded.

"I learned being high loves company, too."

"Explain."

"When I was high on, let's say inappropriate substances, I wanted to have people around me doing the same thing. Suppose it made me feel I was in good company and whatever I was doing was okay. I was also sharing a good, no, great feeling with others. That way I belonged and felt important."

"I don't think—"

"I know," Virgil interrupted. "I know that's stupid, but the point is that's how I felt."

"Are you saying Matthew wanted to be with someone if he was going to use the cocaine?"

"Wouldn't that explain why someone was there?"

"Maybe, but it doesn't explain who the drugs belonged to, who was with him, or if anyone else was invited. If he was, it was a friend of Matthew's and not an intruder who shot him."

"See why I can't get it out of my head? Before you answer, is the offer of something to drink still good?"

"Water, Diet Pepsi, Pepsi, possibly a Coke, wine, beer?"

"Better stick with a Pepsi. My mind's already discombobulated, better not add to it."

Virgil followed me into the kitchen and pulled out a chair at the table as if he thought I'd be serving appetizers along with his Pepsi. I set his drink in front of him and grabbed a Diet Pepsi for myself.

Virgil took a sip before saying, "I'm nowhere near as great a private detective as you and Charles, but it seems logical the person who shot him was a friend, or at least Matthew thought he was a friend. A bullet in the back of the head, would seem to dispel that characterization."

I didn't remind Virgil for roughly the thousandth time I was not a private detective. Instead, I said, "That's probably a safe assumption."

Virgil nodded. "If we assume it was one of his friends, would it be safe to rule out Austin Middleton?"

"Because he told me at the visitation he thought Matthew had died from a drug overdose?"

"Yes."

"It would if Austin were being truthful."

Virgil nodded again. "Got it. He could've said it so you, and whomever he told that to, wouldn't think he was a potential suspect because he didn't know what killed his friend?"

"Yes. Who were some of his other friends?"

"Foster Rodman was one of his poker buddies. Rachel Little, his ex-girlfriend, or if she could be believed, his current girlfriend. Umm, who else?"

"The only other people I've heard about who knew him are Noelle and you."

"Christopher, I'm taking myself off the list of suspects. I occasionally tend to take a sip too many but I'm fairly certain I would've remembered shooting him."

"I'm not saying you did, but if the police were putting together a list of everyone who knew him, you'd be on it."

"I suppose. Anyway, I'd also eliminate Noelle."

"I would too, but again, she knew him, actually went on a few dates with him, so she'd have to be a suspect."

"Let's see, my list has three names on it; your list has five. Now where do we go, Mr. Detective?"

"We know two of the three names on your list were Matthew's poker buddies. Do you know anyone else who would be in that group?"

"No. Do you know if the police know about our three suspects?"

I'd told Cindy about Austin but not Foster. She also knew about Rachel. I shared that with Virgil.

"Think we ought to call the chief and tell her?"

I translated that as I should call her. Instead of asking why he couldn't do it, I punched her number on my phone. My effort was rewarded by receiving her voicemail. I told her what I knew about Foster, tried to sound like I wasn't telling her what to do by couching it with, "You probably already know about him, but in case you don't, I wanted you to know so you could share it with Detective Adair. Have a good day."

"Virgil, speaking about his two poker buddies, what do you know about poker being played on Folly?"

"Like what?"

"Since we know of three people who played, are there regular locations where it's played?"

"I haven't heard of any. Most likely, there's a group like Matthew and his buddies who play in their houses. Gambling is still illegal, so you won't find it in any of the reputable businesses, although I suspect there are more than a few people here who'd play if they got a chance. Heck, if that Indian tribe was still around, you know the one that was on Folly before we white folks ran them off."

"Bohicket Indians."

"Yeah, that's them. If they were still around, I'd bet they'd have already opened a casino here."

"Maybe."

He tapped his empty Pepsi can on the table and said, "So what do we do now?"

"We've told the police everything we know about Matthew and the possible suspects we're aware of. I'm certain Detective Adair will be identifying others. To answer your question, it's in the capable hands of the police."

"Is this where you tell me it's their job to catch the killer and for us to stay out of their way?"

I smiled and said, "Something like that."

He shook his head, sighed, and said, "I'll try."

11

____

Late that afternoon, I took a walk around several blocks near the center of town and along the beach. I'd told Virgil we'd done all we could regarding Matthew's death, but I was catching Virgil's inquisitiveness about what might've happened to Mr. Seward III and thought I could put it out of my mind if I'd focus on something else, in this case, going to the beach and watching laughing children running into the water, screaming, scurrying to shore, then returning to the water. I'd never been to the ocean when I was growing up and wondered if I would have acted like today's youngsters, many seeing the ocean for the first time, if I'd dipped my toes in the Atlantic. Of course, I couldn't answer that question but at least for an hour or so, it kept my mind off Seward's murder.

After the walk, I ended up on Loggerhead's large, elevated deck speaking with Ed, the restaurant's owner. He was sharing how busy the restaurant had been, especially for late March. I didn't catch the last thing he said since I was distracted by a woman reaching the top of the stairs and looking around. She was probably in her mid-20s, tall, thin, with long blonde hair pulled into a ponytail. She was wearing tan shorts and a maroon T-shirt with a College of Charleston on the front. She looked familiar but I couldn't recall where I'd seen her.

"Ed, do you know who the young lady is standing by the stairs?"

He looked toward the entry to the deck and said, "Name's Rachel something. That's about all I know. She and her boyfriend were regulars last summer. Haven't seen her much since then. Why?"

"Rachel Little, it's coming back to me. I met her at Matthew Seward's visitation the other day."

Ed smiled. "You getting senile in your old age? Met her, what, two, three days ago and forgot who she was."

"Senile? Maybe, but when I met her she was wearing a dress, and her hair was fixed differently. I don't know if I would have recognized her if you hadn't said her name."

"I'll stick with senile," he said and laughed.

"When she was here last summer, was she with Matthew Seward?"

He glanced over at her, then turned to me. "Yes, the same Matthew Seward who was killed the other day. Don't tell me you're trying to find the person who shot him."

"You know Virgil Debonnet, don't you?"

"Sure. I suspect most everyone on Folly knows him. He's an interesting fellow. Why?"

"He's the reason we were at the visitation. He'd met Matthew's parents a few years ago and wanted to express condolences."

"Um hum. I'm sure that's why you were there," he said, sarcastically, I assumed.

Rachel had now moved to the bar and was talking to two women I didn't recognize.

"Ed, good talking with you. I'm going to say hi to Rachel."

A couple who'd been seated on the barstools beside Rachel were leaving the bar to follow the hostess to a table near the railing overlooking the Charleston Oceanfront Villas. I moved to the stool closest to Rachel who was sipping on what appeared to be a margarita and still talking to the lady on the other side of her. I ordered a glass of white wine and turned to listen to Mac Calhoun playing guitar and singing from the small bandstand close to where I was seated.

The women who Rachel had been talking with stood, hugged Rachel, and headed to the stairs leading off the deck. Rachel turned to the bartender and ordered a second drink. She then glanced my direction before turning back to the bar.

I said, "Aren't you Rachel Little?"

Her gaze narrowed and she said, "Yes." Her tone was what I'd expect from a young lady thinking she was being hit on by an older guy. Okay, a much older guy.

"You probably don't remember, but I met you the other afternoon at Matthew Seward's visitation."

Her cold stare became friendlier. She came close to smiling, before saying, "Sure, you were there with Virgil and another guy."

"Yes, I'm Chris Landrum, and the guy with me was Charles Fowler."

"Did you know Matthew?"

Mac began "Sweet Caroline," and I leaned closer to Rachel to hear her better.

"Not well, but I ran into him a few times in Bert's. Seemed like a nice guy."

The bartender set as second margarita in front of Rachel and asked if I needed anything else. I told him I didn't.

"We were dating; had been for a couple of years."

"You mentioned that the other night. I'm terribly sorry about your loss. How'd you meet?"

"I'm an accountant at a small firm on James Island. Matthew crunches numbers and works in client relations in his family business. We were attending a meeting of local accountants and started talking." She smiled and added, "We hit it off right away."

"I believe after I met you at the visitation, I noticed you talking with Matthew's mother. Had you spent much time with his parents?"

"Mrs. Seward, Lois, and I are friends. She welcomed me into the family; the family I expected to be part of later this year. I didn't know his dad that well."

"Oh, you and Matthew were engaged?"

"Yes. We'd even started planning a Thanksgiving destination wedding in the Bahamas." She shook her head. "Won't be happening now."

"Again, I'm terribly sorry. I hate to ask, but do you have any idea who might've been responsible for his death?"

"Everybody loved Matthew. It doesn't make sense that anyone would've had a reason to, well, you know."

"My friend Virgil knew Matthew way more than I knew him. He even attended a Christmas party Matthew's parents held a few years ago. I think Virgil and Matthew talked a lot."

"That must've been before Matthew and I met."

"I suspect it was. Virgil admired Matthew because both had difficulties with drugs years ago and both had beaten the habit."

Rachel took a sip of her drink, and looked at her watch, either because she had somewhere to be or was looking for an excuse to end our conversation.

"That was before my time," she said. "I don't know anything about drugs."

"Oh, I'm not saying you did, I was just letting you know how much Virgil admired him for what he'd accomplished."

She looked down in her drink and barely above a whisper said, "The police said there was cocaine in his room when they got there. I don't understand it; I really don't." She took another sip, reached for her purse, and pulled out a credit card, and placed it on the bar. "Chris, umm, it is Chris, isn't it?"

I nodded.

"I need to be going. Thank you for going to Matthew's visitation. I'm sure he would've appreciated it."

"It was nice talking with you. Again, I'm sorry for your loss."

She gave me a forced smile and whispered, "Guess we won't be getting married in November."

There was nothing I could say to that. Fortunately, I didn't have to since she'd already grabbed her credit card, turned, and headed to the stairs.

12

I was passing Rita's Seaside Grille while on my way home from talking with Rachel when a man leaving the restaurant nearly collided with me. He appeared to be in his mid-30s, five-foot-ten, rotund, and wearing jeans and a polo shirt with *Dillon Plumbing* on the breast pocket.

He said, "Sorry. Didn't see you."

"That's okay."

He snapped his fingers, stared at me, and said, "You were at Matthew Seward's visitation."

"Yes."

"Thought I saw you there." He stuck out his hand. "I'm Ron Dillon."

We shook, I introduced myself and added, "Were you friends with Matthew?"

"Known him for years. Met him when I was doing plumbing on his family's house out East Arctic. Got invited to play cards with him."

"I heard his family owned a house on Arctic, but never knew the address. Do you remember what it is?"

"Don't recall the number, but it's in the five-hundred block. Big, two-story house painted light blue with white trim. You should be able to find it. It's the only one that color in that block."

"Thanks. You all been playing poker a long time?"

"Since forever."

"I met another of his poker playing friends at the viewing."

He nodded. "Must've been Austin Middleton. He was the only other one of us there."

"Yes. Seemed like a nice guy. Someone told me another poker friend was Foster something."

"Foster Rodman."

"Yes, that's it. Anyone else in the group?"

"Not really. Occasionally, if one of us couldn't make one of the games, Matthew would grab another friend to sit in. That hasn't happened for a while, though."

I ushered Ron around the corner of the building and stopped in front of a large painting featuring a woman on the beach holding a drink. We were now out of the line of heavy foot traffic along Center Street. "Where'd you play?"

"We alternated houses. The host chooses games, furnishes snacks and drinks, that kind of stuff. Guess I should say, three of us hosted the group. Foster always managed to find an excuse not to. No problem, hosting wasn't a big deal and he brought food and drink when it would've been his turn."

"Where do you live?"

"East Huron, couple of blocks off Center Street."

"What about Foster?"

"What about him?"

"Where's his house?"

"Good question. When we asked, he never gave us any more than on Folly." He shook his head. "We stopped asking months ago. Doesn't matter, anyway. He shows up, has cash, loses most of the time." He smiled. "None of us wanted to discourage him from playing."

"That makes sense."

"You sound like you're hinting for an invite."

"No way. I've never played poker, at least, not for money. Don't know much about it. Just curious since I'd already met Austin." I hesitated then said, "I heard Matthew was shot?"

"That's what the police said when they interviewed me."

"Why'd they interview you?"

"The guy, Detective Adler or something like that, said they were talking to all of Matthew's friends to get a better handle on him. If you ask me, they're trying to figure out who shot him rather than learning more about Matthew."

"When I was talking with Austin at the funeral home, he told me he thought Matthew died of a drug overdose."

Ron glared at me before saying, "Don't know why he thought that. Seems like it was the day after the death that the media was saying he'd been murdered."

I'm probably pushing my luck by talking about murder.

"Ron, it sounds like you were good friends with Matthew, so I'm terribly sorry about your loss."

His glare turned into a smile. "Yeah, we were good friends until I was sitting across from him at the poker table."

"I would think it would've been highly competitive."

"You can say that again, competitive and most of the time fun."

"Why only most of the time?"

"If I was losing, it wasn't much fun. Plus, when Matthew hosted, he was big into crossfire. Irritated the hell out of me."

"Remember, I don't know much about poker, what's crossfire? It sounds like you sit around shooting at each other."

He laughed. "Not that kind of crossfire. It's when the dealer talks too much about things other than poker. Matthew was always talking about surfing, chicks, drinking, hell, even his work schmoozing clients." He shook his head again. "Boring, boring, boring, and distracting as hell."

"I see how that could be irritating."

"The good news is he only did it when we were at his house. Think it was because he was nervous about everything being okay. He was more worried about it than we were. All we needed was cold beer, junk food, and, of course, beating the other three guys at the table."

"It sounds like you were pretty close. Any idea who may've killed him?"

He smiled. "You're beginning to sound like that detective. Most everything I knew about Matthew I learned at poker. I didn't really know about his friends other than what he said about the girls he was dating. I knew nothing about the people at his work. Like I said, he talked some about work, but not about the people there other than that guy who runs the place, some guy with a German sounding name."

"Fritz Goss?"

"Sounds right."

"What'd he say about Fritz?"

"Let's just say they weren't bosom buddies."

"What's that mean?"

"Matthew's dad was the real boss; he owned the business. Fritz was second in charge. Matthew thought he should be in that position. I figured Matthew's dad knew what he was doing. Besides, if I remember correctly, Fritz was a lot older than Matthew, maybe in his late fifties, or something like that. Matthew's only twenty-five, twenty-six, in that range. I figured Matthew would get his turn when he got older. That wasn't what he thought." He chuckled. "Think I got off track. To your question, I have no idea who may've wanted Matthew dead."

"You mentioned he talked about girls he was dating. Do you know who he was dating recently?"

His gaze narrowed again, and he said, "You planning on writing a book about Matthew?"

"No, sorry. Somebody mentioned that he was still dating Rachel Little but someone else said it was another woman. I'm simply curious."

"Funny you should ask. Rachel came up to me at the funeral home. Said something that made me think she and Matthew were still dating. Struck me as strange."

"Why?"

"At our last game, three, four weeks ago, he kept talking about someone he'd met over here. How they'd been on a few dates and how happy he was. How much nicer she was than Rachel."

"Did he say who it was?"

"Don't remember her name, but he said she worked at an advertising agency in Charleston."

"Did he say if he was still going out with Rachel in addition to the new person?"

"To be honest, I wasn't paying much attention to his crossfire. I was focused on poker, but if I'm remembering right, he said something about breaking up with Rachel around Christmas."

"Did he say anything else about Rachel?"

"If he did, I wasn't paying attention." He looked at his watch and added, "It's getting late. I've got to be at work by seven in the morning. Nice talking to you, Chris."

I shared that sentiment and watched him walk behind the restaurant to his vehicle.

13

Sunshine bathed the front of my house as I fixed my first cup of coffee and moved to the screened-in porch to watch the stream of vehicles transporting sleepy workers to their jobs. I leaned back in the chair and thought how fortunate I was to have been able to retire from being a sleepy worker driving to work.

My mind then drifted back to yesterday's conversations with Rachel Little and Ron Dillon. I couldn't recall anything being said leading to the identity of the person who took Matthew's life but was once again struck by the differing version of when Matthew and Rachel had stopped dating. She told me they were not only still dating but were engaged and planning Thanksgiving nuptials.

Ron's version of Rachel and Matthew's relationship was consistent with what Noelle had shared. Their relationship had ended before Christmas, four months ago. Could both versions be true? I didn't see how.

Chief LaMond once told me that contradictions are one of the most significant clues to solving a crime. I didn't know about that, but there was a large contradiction staring me in the face.

The temperature was predicted to reach the mid-70s under full sun, perfect for a walk; a walk to distract me from sitting here thinking about Matthew, a man I barely knew. I grabbed my camera, Tilley hat, and walked the short block to East Arctic Avenue. Standing fifty yards from the ocean, a couple hundred yards from the iconic Folly Beach Fishing Pier, and roughly the same distance from the town's center of commerce, I had to decide which direction to go. I then remembered what Ron Dillon had said about the location of Matthew's house. I turned and headed out East Arctic Avenue. I didn't anticipate learning anything, but I'd at least be able to see the Seward's house located three long blocks from where I was standing.

It was easy to find the house Ron had described. The third house in the five-hundred block of East Arctic fit that description. It wasn't the largest or most elaborate house on the street, but as a second home, it was far from shabby. A concrete driveway on each side of the property led to white garage doors. Between the two drives there was a well-manicured landscape area with a five-foot-high statue of an eagle surrounded by small shrubs. There was no evidence of anything horrific having happened at the residence, no crime scene tape, no sign of emergency vehicles having disturbed the land-scaping.

A white Lexus was in the driveway. At the top of the long stair-case, the front door opened, and Matthew Seward II exited, carrying an accordion file folder holding at least four inches of paperwork. He saw me in front of the house, set the folder on the landing then slowly walked down the stairs, carefully holding the handrail as he navigated the path down.

He reached the drive and continued staring at me. He looked as if he'd aged a dozen years since I'd seen him at his son's visitation."

"Hello, Mr. Seward."

"Hi, umm."

"Chris Landrum. We met at your son's visitation."

"I'm sure we did, but that whole evening is a blur. You'll have to excuse me for not remembering. Do you live near here?"

"A few blocks away. I try to get out and walk whenever I can. Is this your beach house where your son stayed?"

He glanced back at the house as if he checking to see which

house I was talking about. "Yes, this is where Matthew lived. This is the first time I've been here since, you know."

"This must be traumatic."

"Yes, I couldn't bring myself to see it, see where he, umm, died. I had a man from my office meet the crime scene cleanup crew the day before yesterday. I had to force myself to come today to get some items I needed."

"Is there anything I can do to help?"

"Tell me again how you knew Matthew?"

"I didn't know him well. I ran into him a few times in Bert's, and we talked about the weather, vacationers, nothing important."

"You're not one of his poker buddies?"

"No."

"Thought you were too old to be one of them."

"Anything I can do to help you move whatever you need out of the house?"

"Lois, my wife, is so shook I doubt she'll ever step foot in there again." He pointed over his shoulder at the house. "Suppose I'll sell it. What was your question again?"

"I wondered if there was anything I could do to help you move whatever you need out of the house?"

"Thank you, but no. There are only a few things I wanted to get. That police detective is coming to the house in the city later this morning. I don't want him to get there and find only Lois. Don't know what that'd do to her."

"Have the police said anything to you about who might've killed Matthew?"

"Don't know how much you know about the police, but they ask questions, questions, and then more questions. They don't answer any. That was a long way to say no, they haven't told me anything."

"Do you know if your son had enemies?"

"Enough to shoot him, you mean?"

"Yes, or anyone else who had issues with him?"

"Matthew and I were never close. He was a mommy's boy."

"Didn't he work at your firm?"

"Yes, at his mother's insistence. He never wanted to be an accountant or do any marketing, never wanted to join the firm. Think if he was left on his own, he'd have moved to LA or Vegas and become a professional gambler or anything but what he did at work."

"It's a shame he didn't want to be part of the family business."

"The only time he expressed interest was when I made Fritz Goss executive vice president, next in line to be president. My son had a grand total of two years' experience with the company and thought he should run it when I retire. Fritz had been with me seventeen years."

I didn't hear an answer to my question in there, so I'll try again.

"Matthew have any enemies?"

"Don't know. The only friends of his I ever met were the card-playing guys. Three of them. One was a damned plumber and the other two never said what they were, probably menial jobs they were ashamed to tell me about. I didn't particularly care about any of them." He hesitated, looked back at the house, then continued, "I wouldn't call them bums, but none of them seemed to have a bright future if you know what I mean. Don't know enough to accuse one of them but wouldn't put it past one of them to want Matthew dead."

"Any one in particular?"

"No." He looked at his watch, then glanced up at the door.

"I heard he was engaged."

"Did that woman tell you that?"

"Who?"

"Rachel, his alleged fiancé."

"Yes. What do you mean alleged?"

"Matthew never told my wife or me anything about being engaged. Lois heard it from Rachel."

"When did she tell your wife?"

He sighed and twisted his foot on the concrete drive as if he was putting out a cigarette butt. "At the funeral home. Can you believe that?"

"That seems strange."

"Strange? More like opportunistic. She waited until my son couldn't deny it to brag about being engaged."

"Do you think she was lying?"

"No doubt about it." He looked at his watch again, and added, "Good seeing you. Would talk longer, but I need to get home. It wouldn't turn out good if that detective got there and only Lois was there to meet him."

14

After I left Matthew's father, I headed toward town and had passed two houses when I remembered something that seemed unusual when I first saw him coming out of the house. I hadn't given it more thought at the time since I was distracted by my encounter with Mr. Seward. Why did he leave the accordion file on the landing instead of bringing it down to his car since he was coming down anyway? It would've made more sense if he'd put it in the car before speaking to me. So again, why leave it on the landing?

I slowed my walk in case he was looking in my direction, then glanced over my shoulder at the house to see if he was still outside. If he wasn't, I could veer off the road and hide behind a vehicle or another house to see what else he may be removing.

I didn't have long to wait. He was already heading down the stairs carrying the stuffed accordion file. I waited to see if he was going back inside to get more items. That wait also wasn't long. He threw the file in the backseat, climbed in the vehicle, and backed out of the drive. I remained out of sight until he'd gone a block before turning off Arctic Avenue, and I assumed on his way home to wait for Detective Adair. Was the file the only thing he needed to get from the house, or did the rush to get home cut his mission short?

The phone ringing ended my speculating. Charles's name appeared on the screen.

"Morning, Charles."

"Yeah, yeah. Are you on your way to the Crab Shack?"

"Why would I be?"

"Because I'm buying lunch."

A pickup truck passed me, and I had a hard time hearing all Charles had said, and what I thought I heard, I didn't believe.

"You're doing what?"

"You going deaf in your old age? I'm buying lunch, that is if you stop gabbing on the phone and get over here."

That was twice that I must've misheard him, but regardless of who got the check, I figured he was at the popular restaurant.

"On my way."

The Crab Shack was on Center Street, and was, in fact, where I'd first met Charles many years ago. He was now sitting on the patio in an intense conversation with Virgil, who was sitting across from him. I entered the building then walked through the door leading to the patio.

Virgil was seated facing me, and said, "Hey, Christopher. Glad you could make it."

Charles turned facing me and chimed in with one of his often-used phrases, "About time you got here."

"Good morning, gentlemen," I said ignoring Charles's remark.

I took the empty chair beside Virgil and waited to see why Charles had wanted me to be there. Before he had a chance to share whatever it was, Kimberly, one of the Crab Shack's long-term servers approached and asked what I wanted to drink. I said, "A diet whatever." She nodded and headed inside.

Charles watched her go, then said, "Know what Virgil told me that threw me for a triple loop?"

I wanted to ask what a triple loop was, but instead said, "What?"

"Said you two had a meeting, a meeting I wasn't invited to, a meeting that wasn't held this morning, but way back yesterday, a meeting I'm only learning about from Virgil. Can you believe my best friend didn't think it was important enough to tell me?"

I sighed, and said, "It wasn't even a day ago, and here you are learning about it from Virgil, and here I am, to fill in anything he doesn't mention."

Charles said, "You know—"

I interrupted, "In addition to my grievous error of not calling you late last night to share what Virgil and I talked about, you might be interested in who I was meeting with before you called."

"Grievous error, I like the sound of that. Apology accepted."

Whatever, I thought.

Virgil said, "Who'd you meet with this morning?"

"I'm glad you asked," I said and stared at Charles, "Mr. Matthew Seward II."

Virgil said, "And you didn't invite your *chuckaboo*. There, I said it before he did."

Charles said, "I wouldn't have said that. Don't know what a chicken poo is."

"*Chuckaboo*. It's a Victorian phrase meaning close friend."

Virgil's ex-wife majored in English with an emphasis on Victorian culture, literature, and unfortunately, language. Occasionally, my friend, my *chuckaboo*, throws one of her phrases into the conversation.

Charles said, "Why didn't you say close friend?"

Charles wasn't the only person at the table wondering that.

"Christopher, you didn't invite your close friend, I repeat, close friend, Charles."

"Afraid not. I was taking a peaceful walk to enjoy the beautiful day."

Charles said, "And ran into Mr. Seward, that guy that lives and works in Charleston?"

Virgil said, "I'm not a great detective like you, but I have a hunch if you let Christopher finish, he'll tell us the how, who, why, where, and what we need to know about him meeting Mr. Seward."

Go Virgil, go, I thought, smiled, and turned to Charles. "As I said before being interrupted, I was walking, walking out East Arctic Avenue and saw Mr. Seward coming out of the house where Matthew's body was found."

"How'd you know it was that house?"

Virgil said, "Charles," and put his forefinger in front of his closed mouth.

I didn't tell Charles who'd described the Seward's house since that would've ambushed my story more than the Victorians and Charles already had. I said, "I figured it was the Seward house and Mr. Seward confirmed it when he stopped to talk with me."

"Did he know who killed his son? Did he tell you why he was there? Wow, maybe he killed his son. Did he confess?" He looked at the ceiling, then back at me, before adding, "Stop stalling, what'd he tell you?"

"Not much—"

"See," Charles interrupted, again, "if you had me with you, I would've known what to ask so he'd tell you who bumped off his kid."

Kimberly slid my soft drink in front of me and asked if we were ready to order. I was as were my tablemates. We each ordered a version of fish and chips, and she headed to the kitchen.

Virgil had patiently waited to ask a question, and said, "What'd he tell you?"

"He claimed he didn't know who killed his son, but he didn't have anything good to say about Matthew's poker buddies."

Charles said, "He thought one of them killed him?"

"He didn't say that. He didn't use those words, but I got the impression that he thought the three guys we know were regulars in the poker games, were beneath his son, beneath in status, wealth, and I suppose, character."

"Good," Charles said, "we now have three leading suspects in Matthew's murder."

I ignored the list Charles had created, and said, "He also said Matthew didn't want anything to do with the wealth management company until his dad made Fritz Goss executive vice president over Matthew who thought the position should've gone to him."

"Aha," Charles said, "Fritz killed Matthew so he wouldn't have to worry about him taking his place as head of the company."

Virgil leaned closer to Charles. "Seems to my little brain, that would've been a good reason for Matthew to kill Fritz rather than the other way around."

Charles ignored what I thought was Virgil's astute observation, and said, "Okay, let's add Fritz to the suspect list."

Virgil turned to me and said, "Did he tell you anything else that could help us, I mean help the police catch the killer?"

"I don't know if it had anything to do with his murder, but he said Rachel Little told Lois, his wife, that she and Matthew were engaged and had been planning a Thanksgiving wedding."

Charles said, "Didn't Matthew tell Noelle Ward that he and Rachel split months ago."

I said, "Yes, and I found it interesting that Matthew's parents didn't know anything about the engagement until his viewing at the funeral home."

"He would've had a hard time disputing it from inside the coffin," Charles said.

"That's precisely what his father said."

Charles turned to me, rolled his eyes, then said, "Why didn't you lead with that? That's clearly the reason she would've killed him. There, we've done solved the murder. You going to call Cindy and make her day?"

Kimberly arrived with our lunch to make my day before I could tell Charles calling the chief was a horrible idea. We each took a bite before Charles repeated the question.

I said, "Mr. Seward didn't tell me anything he probably hadn't told Detective Adair, and even if he hadn't told the detective, he didn't say anything that pointed to anyone as being the killer."

Charles took another bite of his sandwich and mumbled, "That means it's up to us to catch the killer."

Virgil said, "How do you figure that?"

"Chris said the police already know what Mr. Seward told him, right?"

"I suppose so."

"And the cops haven't arrested anyone, right?"

"I haven't heard if they have or haven't."

Charles said, "If they've arrested the killer, don't you think they would've told the parents of the dead guy?"

"Probably," Virgil said. "Or if they haven't, maybe that's what the detective is going to see the parents about."

"Good point, that's why Chris needs to call Cindy. She can tell him if an arrest has been made."

Virgil looked at me, probably to see if I was going to tell Charles how his reason for me to call the chief made little sense. I didn't say anything, so he said, "Charles, in case I missed someone, why don't you tell us who the suspects are."

"His poker playing buddies are Austin, Foster, and, umm, Chris, what's the name of the third one?"

"Ron Dillon."

"Yeah, Austin, Foster, and Ron."

Virgil nodded and said, "So, let's see if I have this right. One of them killed Matthew because his father thought whoever it is didn't have enough social status to be hanging with his son?"

Charles sighed, then said, "Not if you put it like that."

"How would you put it?"

"Let's come back to that. The next suspect is Fritz Goss."

Virgil said, "Because he's top dog in the firm and not Matthew III?"

"Yes, I guess."

"Okay," Virgil said. "Then the last suspect is?"

"Rachel Little."

"Because she lied to Matthew's mother and said she and Matthew were engaged and getting married on Thanksgiving?"

"Yes."

"Charles, like I told you a few minutes ago, I'm nowhere near as good a detective as you, so who should we tell Chief LaMond the killer is?"

I smiled to myself and turned to Charles for his answer.

He took a bite of fry, looked at the catsup bottle on the corner of the table, then mumbled, "One of them."

Virgil said, "Don't you think we need to do a fraction more detective work before helping the police catch the person who killed Matthew?"

Charles said, "Suppose so. Chris, who do you think did it?"

I pointed a fry at Charles. "Could be one of the people you mentioned or—"

Charles interrupted, "See, we've narrowed it down."

I sighed before saying, "Or, as I was about to say, it could've been a thousand other people, friends or enemies of Matthew we've never heard of."

Charles said, "I like my number better."

The only thing I liked better was the sight of Charles paying for lunch. That was a historic moment to end lunch with.

15

——————

On the way home from the Crab Shack, I reviewed what I'd learned from meeting Mr. Seward, Charles, and Virgil other than *chuckaboo* is Victorian for a close friend. Mr. Seward thought poorly of his son's friends, at least his poker buddies. The senior Seward didn't believe Rachel's story about still dating his son or that they were planning to wed. Another thought was ready to pop into my consciousness, when the phone rang

Noelle's name appeared on the screen. "Hi, Noelle."

"Bet you're beginning to think I'm stalking you."

"If that's what you're doing, keep it up. I've never had a more pleasant stalker."

"For an old guy, you're pretty cool."

"Now calling me an old guy is something a bad stalker would say."

"Just teasing. Got a question, are you going to be around today about 3:30?"

"As far as I know. Why?"

"I've got a couple of things I'd like to bounce off you."

"As long as they're not rocks, I'm available."

"Cool and funny for an old guy."

"Multi-talented. Want to meet me somewhere?"

"Tell you what. Let me park at your place and we can walk on the beach. That okay?"

"Excellent plan."

"Cool, funny, and accommodating," she said then hung up.

I smiled at the dead phone then continued walking home and wondering what I was about to remember when Noelle called. Cool, funny, accommodating, and forgetful.

Five minutes before the time she said she'd be here, Noelle's black pickup truck pulled in the drive. She stepped out, opened the back door and grabbed a pair of tennis shoes.

I met her in the drive and said, "Ready to walk?"

"Let me change out of my work shoes then I will be."

She wore dark-gray slacks, a yellow blouse, and black leather dress shoes.

I held the porch door open for her. Instead of entering, she sat on the steps and quickly changed into the more comfortable shoes.

"Lead the way," she said then headed to the road.

After she put her dress shoes in her vehicle, I moved beside her, and we crossed East Ashley Avenue to begin the short walk to the beach entry point.

"Did you get off early today?"

"Yes. The boss felt guilty about having me work a few twelve-hour-days lately. Said I could leave at three unless I was going to a job interview." She laughed, then continued, "Told him I was thinking about becoming a sea captain and was heading to the beach to get a feel for the ocean."

"Did he shake in his boots at the thought of losing you?"

"More like he shook with laughter."

We reached the beach, and I asked which way she wanted to go.

"Lead the way," she repeated.

I turned left and away from the most crowded part of the beach near the Pier and the Tides Hotel.

"How's the book coming?"

"I'm about seven chapters from finishing the draft."

"That sounds great."

"I thought so, too. Except I read that's when the real work begins. Editing, reviewing, changing, adding and cutting, on and on. You want to do all that for me?"

"Sorry. You'll never be able to add editor to cool, funny, and accommodating."

"Don't forget old."

"How could I? I think about it every morning when I stumble out of bed with an aching back and arthritis."

We passed two couples watching three kids no older than seven splashing in water up to their waists. The shoulders of two of the men watching the kids were slightly less red than a stoplight. The women, reinforcing that they were the wiser gender, had white sunscreen globed on their arms.

Noelle leaned toward me and said, "I never got into this sunbathing thing. Think I'm dark enough."

I smiled as we continued a hundred more yards along the beach.

She didn't stop walking, but moved a few inches closer to me and said, "Suppose you're wondering why I wanted to meet?"

"It'd crossed my mind."

"Been thinking about Matthew, actually more about his death. When I was with you at The Washout the other day, I think I said Matthew hadn't said much to me about his poker playing and the guys he played with."

"That's true."

"After we talked, I remembered something I thought may be important or not. Don't know either way."

"What was it?"

"I mentioned that he played a couple of times a week."

I nodded.

"When I asked where they played, he said they alternated among the players' homes. That made sense, but he also said one of the guys, Foster Rodman, never hosted the group. Said he always had an excuse to get out of it."

That was similar to what Ron Dillon had shared.

"Did he say why Foster didn't want to host?"

"Not really. Add to that, Matthew said Foster never told the group where he worked, what he did for a living."

"That's strange since they were together twice a week."

"I thought so. Here's where I wanted to bounce something off you —not a rock, so don't worry."

I smiled.

"I may be so caught up in the murder mystery I'm writing I can't tell reality from fiction, but I'll throw it out anyway. Let's say Foster makes his money selling drugs and that's the reason he never told any of the others what he did for a living. That could also be the reason he never told them where he lived."

"You think he was selling drugs because of the cocaine the police found at Matthew's house?"

"Makes sense, doesn't it?"

"Yes. Now don't get me wrong. That makes sense, but don't you have drug dealers and murder in your novel?"

"Yes. That's my point. Am I conflating the two?"

I smiled and said, "I might've thought that if I hadn't been thinking the same thing."

"You were? Good. Now I'm not going crazy."

We'd reached the point where the first exposed concrete groin ran perpendicular to our path.

I said, "Now that you've called me old, I need to sit a few minutes."

"That's why the Corp of Engineers placed that groin over there. It's seating for old men."

I sat on the structure without disagreeing with her.

She joined me on the groin proving it wasn't only seating for old people, and said, "Let's say Foster Rodman is the killer. How do we prove it?"

"Noelle, we don't. What we can do is tell Chief LaMond our theory. She, along with the County Sheriff's Office, have the resources to investigate, surveil, and do whatever trained investigators do to determine if Foster was involved."

"You sure can throw a wet blanket over my enthusiasm."

"Before I drown all your enthusiasm, want to call Chief LaMond?"

"Now, from here?"

"Why not?"

"Well, there're several reasons...umm..." She sighed and said, "Have at it."

The chief answered on the second ring. "You calling to ruin my day?"

"Don't think so."

"Okay, let's have it."

"Noelle Ward and I are at the beach and were thinking—"

"Thinking about inviting me to come play in the sand with you?"

"Sorry, no."

"Then to rub it in that you're gallivanting along the beach while I'm slavin' away at the office?"

"Nope."

"Okay, why are you calling?"

I shared what Noelle and I were thinking about Foster Rodman; shared with a minimal number of interruptions from Cindy. I finished and waited to be chastised for butting into something that was none of my business. To my surprise, Cindy asked me to repeat a couple of things, then said, "Thanks for sharing. I'll contact Detective Adair and let him know."

"Good," I said. "Noelle and I appreciate it."

"You'd better. When Adair starts screaming at me about how ridiculous the theory is, I'm giving him your number before hanging up on him."

"What more could I ask?"

I didn't know if Cindy had heard my comment since she'd practiced her hanging up skill on me.

Noelle looked at me and said, "Suppose that's all we can do."

"Yes."

I wasn't ready to leave it at that, but wanted to discourage her from pursuing it, possibly putting her in danger.

She said, "Ready to head back?"

"If you are."

She nodded and hopped off the concrete structure.

A hundred yards or so later, I said, "Seen Virgil since we talked?"

"Once. I was pulling in my apartment's parking lot, and he was riding by on that old scooter that he calls his imported luxury convertible. He pulled over and chatted a few minutes."

"He ask you out?"

"No."

"You ask him out?"

"Almost, but before I got up enough courage, he said he had to get to his apartment building and fix someone's toilet." She chuckled. "That's one hell of a demotivation for asking someone out."

I agreed as we continued our walk to my cottage and her vehicle.

16

"Think we need a shot of country music," Charles said after I answered the phone. "How about meeting me at Cal's tonight?"

"Seven o'clock," I said and hung up.

While it felt good to hang up on Charles, he was still roughly 13,000 times ahead of me at making that rude move.

I entered Cal's Country Bar and Burgers, known to everyone simply as Cal's, a half-hour before the time I said I'd be there, knowing Charles would already be in attendance. George Jones was crooning "The Race is On" from the classic jukebox and Cal was singing backup to the recorded music while cleaning two tables with a red, white, and blue bar towel.

Cal saw me at the entry and tilted his head toward a table in the back of the room where Charles was sipping a beer. I nodded thanks, although I suspect I would've found my friend without Cal's clue since there were only a dozen tables in the building.

Charles gave me his oft-repeated glance at his bare wrist reminding me that I was late. I sat catty-corner to him at the four top so each of us could have a view of the room.

Without a glimmer of irony, "The Race is On" ended and Jones's ex Tammy Wynette followed with "Good Lovin'." Cal switched from backup singer to server as he brought a glass of white wine to me, pulled out the third chair at the table, and sat.

"These old legs are running short on stand-up strength," he said as he removed his ever-present Stetson that had been a constant part of his life for the last forty-five years and set it on the table.

Cal had been around for more than three-fourths of a century and had spent most of those years traveling the south sharing his brand of traditional country music wherever he could find an audience. He'd fallen into ownership of the bar a decade ago when the previous owner committed a serious breach of etiquette by killing a local attorney and was now regretting the error in prison.

The bar's owner leaned forward and said, "Hear you boys are nosin' into another murder."

I said, "Where'd you hear that?"

"Pard," Cal said, "I'm in here thirty hours a day. Where do you think I heard it?"

I smiled at his mathematical acumen. "I should've said who told you?"

"Junior, Amber, and let's see," He ran his hand through his long, white head of hair and added, "two young fellas were drinking, talking, drinking more, then talking louder, nearly soused—"

"Who were they?" I interrupted before he could tell us more about their drinking habits.

"Hell if I know," he said as his son Junior called to him from the kitchen.

"Boss is a'callin'," Cal said, replaced the Stetson on his head, and headed to the kitchen on legs that're short on stand-up strength.

I assumed when he mentioned Junior he was referring to his son and when he said Amber he meant Amber Lewis my favorite server at the Lost Dog Cafe. I was in the dark as much as Cal indicated he was when it came to identifying "two young fellas" who apparently had over-consumed adult beverages.

Charles tapped his beer bottle on the table, smiled, and said,

"Looks like you're the only person over here who doesn't know you're helping me catch Matthew's killer."

"Charles, if you believed every rumor that's spread in here, you'd already have the tinfoil cap on your head instead of your Tilley so the Martians couldn't suck your brain out."

Patsy Cline was singing "I Fall to Pieces" as Charles said, "Don't think the Martian story is true, although I knew a few guys over here who're missing a brain. Just sayin'."

I took a sip of wine, leaned back in the chair, and soaked in the music. As I should've anticipated, relaxing wasn't in the cards. Charles hadn't called and invited me simply to spend time enjoying the music and each other's company.

"Glad Cal brought it up," he said, "how're we going to figure out who snuffed Matthew three?"

Silly me, I thought we'd covered all that yesterday when we were with Virgil.

"Don't know. You have any thoughts?"

"Yeah, you're the college graduate in the group. It's up to you to outline a foolproof plan to solve it, then it's my job to stumble into what really happened, then you nearly get yourself killed catching the bad guy, then I come in and save the day." He paused, nodded, then added, "Think that covers it."

I wanted to ask if he had any aluminum foil at his apartment but knew questioning him wouldn't lead to a good spot. I figured my next comment would rearrange his questioning.

"Know what Noelle told me this afternoon?"

His hands flew over his head. "Whoa, where'd you see Noelle? What'd she tell you? When were you going to tell me about it?"

Before I could begin answering his questions, assuming I could remember them, Calvin Richardson, aka Junior or Cal's son, appeared at the table carrying a beer and glass of wine.

"Dad said you'd probably need these by now."

Cal didn't know he had a son, now in his mid-50s, until a couple of years ago when Junior appeared one night in the bar.

Charles pointed to the chair that Cal had relinquished a few minutes earlier, and said, "Sit a spell."

Junior looked back toward the bar and the kitchen and said, "Don't mind if I do."

Knowing Charles like I do, Junior might regret that decision.

Charles said, "Your dad was telling us someone told you Chris and I were investigating the Seward guy's murder. Who was it?"

"Don't know."

That wouldn't fly with Charles.

"What do you mean you don't know? How's that possible?"

Yes, Charles was often predictable.

"Heard it in Bert's yesterday afternoon. Some kid was in the back of the store talking to another guy. I didn't catch everything, but did hear him say Chris Landrum and Charles Farnsley—"

Charles interrupted, "Farnsley? You correct him?"

"No. I wasn't supposed to be eavesdropping so how was I going to correct him?"

I glared at Charles and turned to Junior. "What else did they say?"

Jim Reeves interrupted our conversation singing "He'll Have to Go."

"I could've got it wrong, but it sounded like he was telling the guy with him he'd better be careful."

Charles said, "You sure?"

"No. Didn't I say I could've got it wrong?"

"Yes," I said. "Did you catch anything else they were saying?"

"No. One of them saw me and nudged his buddy around the corner. I figured my eavesdropping was over, got the food I came for and headed out."

I said, "You didn't know who they were?"

He shook his head.

"How old would you guess them to be?"

"Late 20s, early 30s."

I said, "Do you know Ron Dillon, Foster Rodman, or Austin Middleton?"

"Names don't ring a bell. Who're they?"

"Poker buddies with the man who was killed."

"If you want, write those names down, and I'll ask around to see if any of our regulars know them."

Charles smiled at Junior. "We'll make a detective out of you yet."

"No way. I'm happy being Cal's executive chef. Fixing burgers is something I'm pretty good at."

Cal had named Junior executive chef, saying it was cheaper than giving him a decent salary. I suspected Junior would work for his dad for nothing, but didn't tell Cal.

During a break in the music, Cal yelled for Junior to get back in the kitchen. He added. "Those two skinny guys at the bar are starving. Need burgers."

Junior smiled. "That's a subtle cue for me to return to my place in front of the grille."

Charles watched him go, and said, "What'd Noelle tell you?"

I shared Noelle's theory that Foster Rodman was a drug dealer and had either sold or gave Matthew the drugs that were found in his apartment.

"Not bad," Charles said. "That'd explain why they were there. It'd make Foster the killer. You need to call Cindy and tell her."

"First, even if Foster was a dealer, it doesn't mean he killed Matthew. And I've already told Cindy what I just shared with you."

"When?"

"This afternoon."

"Then she's had time to arrest him. Call to let her thank you for solving another murder."

"If anyone arrests Foster, it'd be Detective Adair with the Sheriff's Office. I'm also certain if that has occurred, Cindy would've let me know."

"So, you're saying he hasn't been arrested?"

"That's my guess."

"Hmm, now that you're guessing things, who do you guess Junior heard talking about us?"

"I have no idea."

"They were about the same age as Matthew's poker pals."

"Yes, and so are hundreds of others in the area."

"Know what I think we need to do now?"

"Sit back and enjoy our drinks and the music," I said, knowing there would be a near zero percent chance of that being what Charles had in mind.

"I think that's a good plan."

I nearly fell off the chair.

After regaining my composure, I sat back and listened to Donna Fargo sing "Funny Face."

Charles was right. I needed a shot of country music.

17

———————

It'd been nearly a week since I talked to Barb Deanelli, owner of Barb's Books, a used bookstore on Center Street, and the lady I'd been dating the last few years. It was time to rectify that oversight.

"Hello, stranger," Barb said as I entered the store. "Where've you been hiding?"

She was a couple of years younger than me, my height, and thin.

"Guess I've been busy."

She looked at me with her hazel eyes, gave me a captivating smile, and said, "Must be awfully busy being retired. I don't see how you keep up with all the nothing you have to do."

I deserved that. "Got coffee?"

I knew she did but didn't want to spend more time hearing about the nothing I had to do.

"You do know this is a bookstore and not Starbucks?"

I smiled and was pleased when she gave me one in return and pointed to the small office in the back of the store. Barb's Books was located in the retail space that'd housed Landrum Gallery, my former business. She followed me back and waited while I inserted a pod in the Keurig coffeemaker. After it finished brewing, Barb followed the same procedure. When I occupied the space, the office served more of a storage room, and area for some of my friends to gather to talk about whatever was on their mind. I was glad to have company during those years since the Gallery was seldom busy.

Barb rolled her office chair near the opening into the store so she could see if potential customers entered. I sat in a chair beside her professional appearing desk, appropriate since she'd been a successful defense attorney prior to moving to Folly.

"Know what I heard yesterday?"

"What?"

Her smile had disappeared, and a glimmer of disappointment crossed her face as she said, "Heard that a retired gallery owner has been playing cop again. Seems he's trying to catch the person who shot one Matthew Seward III."

"Who said that?"

"Who do you know who comes in here two or three times a week but never buys anything?"

"Virgil?"

She nodded.

"I'm afraid he's exaggerating my involvement. Virgil wanted to go to the visitation for young Mr. Seward because a few years ago he'd attended a Christmas party at Matthew's parents' house. I'd talked with Matthew a few times in Bert's but didn't know much about him."

"So, all you did was take Virgil to the funeral home?"

"That's about it."

"*About*. That's an interesting word choice. If I were the suspicious type, it'd make me wonder why you didn't leave it out of the sentence. You know, saying 'That's it,' instead of 'That's *about* it.'"

Barb never failed to show why she'd been a highly regarded attorney. I know I'd hate to have her interrogating me in a trial, that is, if I were on the opposite side.

"I have learned a few things about the death, more accurately, learned some things about Matthew's friends, but not his death."

"Have you shared what you've learned with the police?"

"Yes."

"And they're taking it from there?"

I nodded.

"So, you're no longer pursuing learning more?"

"Correct."

She rolled her chair over to where I was, smiled, leaned over and kissed my cheek, then said, "Do me a favor, be careful."

"About what?"

"About what you know you're doing, and what I know you're doing."

"What's that?"

"Trying to learn who shot the person you ran into a few times in Bert's."

I know when I'm defeated.

"I'll be careful. Talk to Dude lately?"

Dude Sloan was Barb's half-brother and was the reason she ended up on Folly after a contentious divorce in Pennsylvania. She was also about as opposite from Dude as a snail was to a box of Cracker Jacks. She was attractive, articulate, and perceptive while Dude was, let's just say, inarticulate, which was giving him more credit than he deserved.

Barb said, "If that was your idea of changing the subject, you need to work on transitions. Anyway, Dude's been in a couple of times in the last week. This is the beginning of his busy season, so he can't escape his shop as much as he did over the winter."

Dude owns the surf shop, all letters in lower case, reason known only to the owner.

"Seen Noelle lately?"

After Noelle Ward's apartment building burned, Barb graciously let her stay in her condo until she found suitable housing.

"A few days ago."

I said, "She say anything about Matthew?"

"She was shaken because of his death, but you already knew that didn't you?"

I smiled. "She told me about going out with him a couple of times but didn't see it getting serious. That's about all."

"There's that word *about* again," she said and shook her head. "Did she tell you who she thought shot him?"

"Not directly but said she wouldn't be surprised if it was his former girlfriend, Rachel Little. I'm sure I'm not telling you anything you don't already know, but Virgil thinks it's Foster Rodman."

"Yes," Barb said, "Virgil shared that."

"You have any thoughts about it?"

"I never met any of them, but if I had to defend Rachel Little, I'd cast Rodman as the murderer."

"And if you were defending Rodman?"

"Rachel Little would be the person I'd try to implicate. What do you think?"

"I have no idea but wouldn't be surprised if it were either of them, plus a couple of other likely suspects."

"His poker playing friends?"

"Yes."

"That's what Virgil said."

The bell over the front door rang announcing a potential customer and Barb said she'd better see if she could help.

I said I'd let her get back to work.

She said, "And you better get back to being retired."

18

───────

After leaving Barb's Books, I remembered my New Year's resolution to get more exercise. I also remembered how much aversion I had to jogging, using gym equipment, or any of the other socially acceptable means to torture my body. Walking was the only form of exercise I could tolerate, that is if taken in small quantities. Walking up and down Center Street which measured a whopping third of a mile in length met that need. So, I was ready to feel the pounds fall off as I headed down Center Street toward the Tides Hotel.

I was in front of Rita's Seaside Grille on the corner of Center Street and East Arctic Avenue when I spotted Charles on the patio seated at one of the bar height chairs at the small outside bar. He saw me at the same time and motioned for me to join him, ending my exercise regimen after roughly four-hundred feet. Deciding that I couldn't walk off all the extra pounds I'd gained over the winter all at once, I entered the patio at the gate facing the sidewalk and joined my friend at the bar.

Charles held up his glass of beer and said, "Want one? I'm buying."

He knew I'd say yes to beer as often as I'd accept a glass of sawdust. I declined then turned to the bartender who was waiting for my selection and ordered white wine.

Charles smiled. "There went your chance for me to pick up the tab."

I ignored his comment and since he seldom visited Rita's, one the island's better restaurants, on his own, I said, "What are you doing here?"

"Detectin'."

"And what might you be detecting?"

"Not what, who."

I sighed before saying, "Okay, who are you detecting?"

He swiveled in his chair and faced the tables on the patio, turned back my direction, and said, "See the guy in the corner talking with some other guy?"

There were two tables with two men seated at each.

"Which guy?"

"Red polo shirt, in his 20s, losing his hair."

I glanced back at the two occupied tables, and then turned to Charles. "What about him?"

"It's Foster Rodman, the guy that killed Matthew the third."

"How do you know it's Rodman?"

"Did you forget I'm a detective?"

No, because he tells me nearly every time we talk.

"Okay, how did you use your detective skills to determine that's Rodman?"

"I came here to say hi to Carrie, one of the servers, when the other guy with Rodman was already at that table. Rodman was walking by like you were a minute ago and the other guy yelled, "Hey, Foster. Foster Rodman!" Rodman looked over, smiled, then came onto the patio like you did. He joined the other guy. And there they are."

"Excellent detective work."

"You making fun of me?"

"A little."

"That's what I thought."

I refrained from saying *don't you mean, that's what you detected?*

"Now what's your plan? You can't hear what they're saying, can you?"

Only half of the outside tables were occupied, and Charles and I were the only two people seated at the bar, so it was relatively quiet, but not quiet enough to hear their conversation.

Charles took a sip of beer as the bartender set my drink in front of me.

"You're right. I haven't got it all figured out so I'm glad you showed up. We can work out a plan together."

My plan was to take a sip of wine. Charles tapped me on the arm as I was implementing my plan, and said, "You hear that?"

"What?"

"The guy with Foster said something about needing to get four more and Foster said he could take care of it."

"Four more what?"

"Couldn't catch the last of it. Probably drugs, don't you think?"

That wouldn't have been my first guess, but I didn't want to discourage Charles.

"Could be."

"How're we going to find out?"

"Charles, I don't think—"

He smacked my arm and said, "The other guy's leaving. Here's our chance."

Charles hopped off the chair and headed toward the table where Foster had remained seated before I could ask what our chance happened to be.

I didn't have to ask. Foster had finished his drink and stood when Charles said something to him. They shook hands, exchanged a few more words, before Charles put his arm around Foster and ushered him over to where I was seated.

"Chris," Charles said, "you wouldn't believe who I just met."

Actually, I would since the man he *just met* had been the subject of our conversation before Charles headed his way like a laser beam.

I smiled at the man standing beside Charles and said, "Hi, I'm Chris Landrum."

He returned my smile although nowhere near the same wattage and said, "Pleased to meet you. I'm Foster Rodman."

Charles turned to me and said, "Foster was one of Matthew Seward's poker buddies. I heard the guy who'd been with him a minute ago call him Foster before he left. I took a chance that he was the Foster who knew Matthew. And he was." Charles then pointed to the empty seat beside his chair. "Join us for a drink."

Foster looked at his watch before saying. "I have to be somewhere in a little while. Maybe next time."

"Just a quick drink," Charles said, then added the magic words, "It's on me."

Foster smiled. "Maybe I've got time for one," he said and pulled out the empty seat.

Charles waved for the bartender, who was quick to ask what Foster wanted.

"Corona," he said, then turned to Charles, "How'd you know Matthew?"

"Ran into him a few times, mostly at Bert's since he lived nearby. Where do you live?"

Charles was *detectin'*.

"Not far from here. How'd you know I was one of his friends?"

"Chris, and I, along with another friend went to his viewing. So tragic the loss of such a wonderful guy."

"Yes, his death is hard to comprehend. Did someone at the funeral home say we were friends?"

Good question, I thought.

Charles said, "Yes, think it was Matthew's dad. He was talking about how close his son was to a few friends. If I remember, he mentioned you and, umm, Ron someone, and one other guy."

"Ron Dillon, and probably Austin Middleton," he said and took a draw off his beer the bartender had set in front if him. "We played a couple times a week."

"Think you're right," Charles said and slowly shook his head. "Someone also said Matthew may've gotten back into drugs. I didn't know it, but apparently, he'd had trouble with them back when he was in college. Did you know that?"

Foster took another sip, then looked at his watch. "Don't know anything about him and drugs." He looked at his watch a second time like he didn't know how much time had passed in the last thirty seconds. "Gotta be going, guys." He slid off the chair, set his half-full beer bottle on the counter, and added, "Nice talking to you. Thanks for the drink."

It wasn't my impression it was nice talking to us.

Without another word, he headed to the exit.

Charles watched him go, nodded twice, and said, "Plum near confessed to killing Matthew, didn't he?"

"How do you figure?"

"He wouldn't tell us where he lived, and that was after I directly asked him. Then look what happened when I mentioned Matthew being back on drugs."

"What, because he said he didn't know anything about Matthew and drugs, you figured that was a confession?"

"No, because as the topic came up, he rushed out of here like a pack of zombies was chasing him. He did it, no doubt."

"You do understand nothing he said could be used by the police to make an arrest, don't you?"

"Sure, if you're going to be picky."

I leaned back in the chair and took another sip of my drink hoping Charles would follow my lead and drop the subject, at least for now.

Instead, he leaned toward me and said, "You going to call Cindy now or later with the humongous clues Foster gave us?"

"Why don't you call her?"

"She'd believe you. You won't believe this, but she thinks I leap to too many conclusions, leap too fast."

She was right, of course.

"I'll call her later."

"Great, and you'll let me know if she's going to arrest him?"

I knew the answer to that question now, but for obvious reasons, kept it to myself. Instead, I said, "Absolutely."

19

——————

The first thing I noticed the next morning was heavy rain pelting the roof. The first thing that struck me as being unusual, no, extremely unusual was that Charles hadn't called me after I got home from Rita's demanding I tell him everything Cindy had said when I called her. I was relieved since I hadn't called her to share our, aka Charles's, theory that Foster Rodman was the person who killed Matthew Seward.

I also knew my friend enough to know my luck would soon end. I have no doubt he'll be calling before I finish my second cup of coffee. I fired up the Mr. Coffee machine, got dressed, poured a cup of caffeine, then headed to the front porch to call the chief.

She answered with, "If you're trapped in your car on one of our flooded streets and need someone to haul you out, hang up and call —call anyone, anyone but me."

"Having a bad morning?"

"How is it that we have residents who've lived here since Lincoln was president and still don't know which streets not to drive on in this much rain?"

I didn't have much of an answer, so instead, said, "I'm safe and dry on my front porch and sipping on a cup of coffee. You don't have to worry about me."

"Any coffee left?"

"Sure."

"Are boats floating past your front yard?"

"No."

"Good. You're about to have company."

She must've been nearby since her pickup pulled into my non-flooded drive seconds after ending our conversation.

"Thanks for the invitation," she said as she flung water off her hat and raincoat. "Got any bacon, eggs, toast, hell, I'd settle for pancakes."

"Sorry, no to everything you mentioned."

"My fault for asking. I knew there was a better chance you'd have a camel in here than you'd have anything resembling real food."

"With that out of the way, have a seat and I'll get your coffee."

"Talked me into it," she said and flopped down in one of the three porch chairs.

I returned with her coffee and a refill in mine, and she said, "Know how many vehicles my guys and I've been working with the last two hours to haul them to safety, or at least, to a part of the road they could drive on rather than float on?"

"How many?"

"Five, and one of them belonged to an elderly gentleman who lived in the house a half-block from where his 1980-something Cadillac land yacht learned it couldn't float. Chris, he's lived there thirty-seven years. That road's flooded roughly 7,000 times since he moved in. Did it enter his mind that today's downpour would be number 7,001?"

"Sorry, that had to be a rough morning."

"Don't suppose you called to get a flooded-street update."

No, but I suspect she'll think the owner of the flooded land yacht is a genius once I tell her Charles's theory.

"Charles and I met Foster Rodman yesterday at Rita's. Charles, as you can imagine, introduced himself to Rodman and bought him a beer so he'd talk with us."

"I can imagine Charles introducing himself to the man, but there's no way my imagination can fathom him buying a beer for anybody."

"That was shocking."

She took a sip, set her mug on the small table beside her chair, then stared at me, before saying, "Is it safe to say Mr. Rodman is the Foster Rodman who was one of Matthew Seward's poker-playing *amigos*?"

"You're safe to say that."

"The same Mr. Rodman who some of your buddies are convinced killed Mr. Seward?"

"Yes."

"Tell you what, I'll skip over yelling at you for butting into police—"

"Cindy," I interrupted, "I'm not—"

She waved a hand in my face and said, "Chill. I'm skipping the lecture. What did you and Charles learn that would either convince me that Rodman is the killer or that you and Charles are complete idiots."

"I wouldn't rule out the *complete idiots* analysis, but I'll tell you what was said and let you judge if it has merit."

"Regardless of what you tell me, it beats me pushing cars out of flooded streets."

"That's a low bar to leap."

She smiled.

I sighed. "Charles asked Foster where he lived, and all that Foster revealed was he lived nearby. That made Charles think Rodman was hiding where he lived."

"Why?"

"Why did he think that or why was Rodman hiding it?"

"I'll never ask you why Charles thinks anything."

"Charles thinks Rodman is hiding where he lives because he's a drug dealer and didn't want us to know the location. Plus, he killed Matthew over a drug deal."

"All that because he didn't tell Charles where he lived?"

I nodded and added, "Also because Charles heard the man who was meeting with Foster say something about needing four. He figured that was him wanting to buy drugs from Foster."

"Where were you when Charles heard the guy say that?"

"Sitting at the outside bar."

"Where was Foster and the other guy?"

"At a table across the patio from us."

"What, twenty-five, thirty feet away?"

"I guess."

"And you and Charles think the guys were so stupid they'd be talking about a drug deal in a public restaurant loud enough for Charles to hear?"

"That's Charles's theory."

"Do you agree?"

"I think he may be a dealer, may even have killed Matthew, but I don't think he was talking a drug deal with the guy at the table with him."

"I agree."

Cindy's radio came alive with the dispatcher telling her some code and that her presence was needed.

She uttered a profanity, thanked me for the coffee, and added, "Tell you what, I'll contact Detective Adair and encourage him to take a closer look at Foster Rodman. I won't tell him why Charles thinks he's the murderer."

"I appreciate it."

"One more thing before I leave, you sure Charles bought Foster a beer?"

"Yep."

She glanced at my phone. "Did you video it?"

"Nope."

"Crap."

20

Yesterday's rain had moved out of the area, and it looked like it was going to be a beautiful, warm spring day. I was thinking about walking to the Fishing Pier to watch surfers doing what surfers do, when the phone rang, and Cindy's name appeared on the screen.

"Morning, Cindy."

"Yes, it is for most of us." She hesitated and I heard her sigh before she continued, "Want the good news or the bad news first?"

"Let's start with the good. It's too nice a day to begin with bad news."

"I know where Foster Rodman lives."

"Great."

"You say that because you haven't heard the bad news. Want to guess?"

No, I screamed to myself, and said, "Why don't you tell me?"

"He's dead."

I almost asked her to repeat it since I couldn't grasp what she'd said.

"You're kidding."

"Police chiefs don't kid about things like that."

"What happened?"

"We're still trying to piece it together, but the woman who lives in the apartment next to his, heard a loud noise around 9:30 this morning. She thought it was a door slam or someone dropping something on the floor, anyway, she didn't think it was a gun shot. That was until she left her apartment around ten and noticed the door to Mr. Rodman's unit partially open. At first, she didn't think anything of it; thought he must've gone to get something out of his car and left it open. Her car was parked next to his, and when she got to her vehicle, she didn't see Rodman and worried that something may've happened to him, and he might need help. She was partially right. She went back to his apartment and pushed the door the rest of the way open and called his name. As you can guess, he didn't answer. She, being somewhat a busybody, went in and found Mr. Rodman on the bedroom floor."

"You said she was partially right. What wasn't she right about?"

"Good grief. Of all the things I've said, you're asking about that?"

"Wanted you to know I was paying attention."

"So noted. She was wrong about him needing help. He was beyond it."

"What'd she do then?"

"Scream."

I sighed. "Then what?"

"She wisely didn't touch anything in his apartment except her shoes on his floor, then backed out and called us."

"Cause of death?"

"Most likely the bullet that's lodged in his skull."

"Anything else you can share?"

"I can answer the question that you and your faux detective pal have been obsessing over."

"That being?"

"Where Foster Rodman lives, correction, lived."

"Okay, where?"

"In one of those apartments over the beach store on Center Street. Unit 3 if you're anal about the exact location."

"Amber lives in one of those apartments."

"I know. I didn't see her, so she was probably at work when he was shot."

"I hope so. Anything else?"

"I think that's way more than I should've shared with a nosy senior citizen. Besides, I need to get back to the scene and pretend I'm in charge. That'll last until Detective Adair gets there."

"Thanks for letting me know."

If I valued my life, the next thing I had to do was call Charles.

When he answered I could hardly hear him for the background noise.

I said, "Where are you?"

"Harris Teeter doing my annual grocery shopping. Why, you conducting a survey?"

"Just got off the phone with Cindy," I said, with an emphasis on *just*.

"So?" he asked, or I thought that's what he said, since the background noise was bleeding into the foreground.

"So, she called to tell me Foster Rodman is dead, shot this morning."

"You're kidding."

"Afraid not."

"What happened?"

"She didn't know much. His neighbor found him in his apartment."

"Did she tell you where he lived?"

"Yes, but I doubt it means much now."

"Who did it?"

"Too soon to know. She's waiting for Detective Adair to get there."

"You know what that means?"

I was afraid to ask, but I was going to anyway. "What?"

"We now have two murders to solve." He hesitated and mumbled something I couldn't understand.

"What?"

"Wasn't talking to you. Some guy asked where the Lysol was."

"Don't suppose you knew."

"Nary a clue. I'm blocking the aisle, so I'd better get a move on and get finished. Have I told you how much I hate grocery shopping?"

"Not since you did it a year ago."

"Let me know when you have a plan for catching, umm, I suppose the poker player killer."

If he hadn't already hung up on me, I would've told him, it was a job for the police and not two aging citizens. It wouldn't have mattered. He wouldn't have paid attention. And, truth be known, I wanted to find out who killed the two men as much as he did. Yes, I'm becoming another Charles.

21

———————

I hadn't been off the phone more than five minutes when it rang again. This time with Virgil's name appearing on the screen.

"Christopher, up for a walk?"

That reminded me what I had initially planned to do this morning.

"Good morning. A walk where?"

"Oh, we could mosey up Center Street."

It was beginning to make sense, coming from the alleged private detective in training.

"Sure. Where are you?"

"Standing in front of your house. Ready to go?"

"Sure," I said and tapped *end call.*

Thirty seconds later, Virgil and I were in front of Bert's Market, when he said, "Did you hear all the police and fire sirens this morning?" Virgil asked. "Sounded like every building on Center Street was either burning down or a band of marauding bandits was on the loose."

I hadn't heard any of that but had an educated guess where they were headed.

"Didn't hear anything."

"I understand," Virgil said and tapped me on the shoulder. "Know how hearing starts to go as we age."

I'm sure he wasn't referring to me, so I didn't respond to the comment but instead said, "If that was on Center Street, where were you so you could hear it?"

His apartment was a couple of blocks farther from the center of town than my cottage.

"Last night, a nice man visiting from Michigan bought me a couple of beers at Planet Follywood. It always amazes me how generous strangers are when you say something nice to them. I told the guy, Frank's his name, anyway, I told him how much I liked his socks. They had cute kittens on them. I didn't get out of there until, don't know for certain what time it was, but think the little hand on the clock had already crossed into today. Sometime this morning, I got up to, well, let's say to use the facilities."

He stopped talking before we reached Taco Boy. I waited for more of his story. With nothing forthcoming, I said, "And?"

"Before going to bed, I remembered how nice it was outside, so after I used the facilities, I want outside to welcome the morning."

"That's when you heard the sirens?"

"Christopher, I was about to say that."

"And we're taking this walk to see if we can learn what was going on?"

"I was about to say that too."

Why couldn't I have asked why Virgil wanted to walk to Center Street? It would've saved me from having to learn about his new friend from Michigan, his friend's cute socks, and whatever else he said that I'd already forgotten.

I looked down the alley behind Center Street's stores. Two Folly Beach patrol vehicles and a dark blue Crown Vic, I assumed that'd transported Detective Adair from Charleston, blocked the alley.

Virgil followed my gaze, and said, "What's going on back there?"

Instead of answering him directly, I said, "Chief LaMond called me a little before you called."

"She tell you what the ruckus was about?"

"Yes," I said then proceeded to share everything Cindy had told me.

Virgil smacked his forehead with the palm of his right hand, and said, "Holy moly, Christopher. We're having a hard time solving one murder. How are we supposed to solve two?"

I knew it would be futile to point out that the folks driving the vehicles in the alley were responsible for solving the murders.

We finally reached Center Street and I assumed nothing good could come from Virgil bothering the police as they investigated the murder, so I said, "Let's head over to the Pier and talk about it."

"Should we call Charles and have him meet us?"

"He's busy this morning. We can talk with him later."

At the top of the stairs leading to the Pier, Virgil said, "Think I'm going to need something to drink if we're going to figure out who killed the guys."

I assumed that was a hint to offer to buy him a drink. "Let's grab something in Pier 101 then head to those tables on the other side of the deck."

Pier 101 Restaurant & Bar was on the deck overlooking the Pier.

I was surprised when he ordered a soft drink, but it made sense after he finally told me his new buddy from Michigan had treated him to "four, maybe more," beers. I went with a diet soft drink, paid, and we headed to one of the vacant tables.

"Christopher, that means half of the poker guys have been killed. Think the other two are in danger?"

"Could be, although I can't see a motive. Can you?"

He removed his ever-present sunglasses, swiped his hand across his forehead, returned the sunglasses to his face, and said, "I had it all figured out until my number one suspect Foster screwed it up by getting himself shot. Still think it may have to do with drugs. Foster selling them; Matthew using them. And who knows about the other poker pals?"

"If drugs had to do with both guys getting killed, who do you consider to be the suspects?"

He pointed to his watch and said, "Right this minute, unless one of the other poker guys gets killed, Ron Dillon and Austin Middleton would be near the top of my list."

"What about Rachel Little?"

"Okay, I'd stick her on it, so no one accuses me of sexism."

"You said Ron and Austin would be near the top of your list. Does that mean someone else is at the top?"

"Yes," he said and nodded like that said it all.

"Who?"

"Fritz Goss."

"Why?"

"We've already said that Matthew thought he should be president of Seward Wealth Management. Fritz would've felt threatened and wanted to eliminate the threat. A bullet would do it."

"Do you think he would've killed just to keep his job?"

"Absolutely. Back when I was rich and with my job as a stock market analyst, I had to hobnob with all sorts of rich jackasses. The worst were the ones charged with handling money for the wealthy, people like Fritz, who would do anything to help their clients. By helping their clients, that meant helping themselves. The richer the clients became so did their Fritzes, the people helping them get there. Would one of them kill to stay at the top? You bet."

"Then why kill Foster?"

"He must've learned about Fritz bumping off Matthew. Then Fritz learned what Foster learned, and then killed him." He hesitated then added," Or something like that. Basically, Foster got caught in the crossfire between Fritz and Matthew. Figurative crossfire, not between them shooting real bullets at each other."

I hadn't been part of that world, but it seemed unlikely Fritz would've killed both men to retain his position with Seward Wealth Management. From what I heard, Matthew's father was high on Fritz, and it seems unlikely he would've fired or demoted him to insert his son into the company's top position. I still came back to drugs being the connection between the killer and the victims.

Before I responded to Virgil, I saw Officer Rodney New at the top of the steps. He also saw Virgil and me and headed our way.

Virgil stood, smiled at the officer, and said, "Officer New, it's a pleasure and honor to see you this lovely day. Would you care to join us and allow Chris to buy you a drink?"

He glanced over at me, rolled his eyes, then turned his gaze to Virgil, "That's kind of you, Virgil, but I'll decline. I'm grabbing something and heading back to work."

I said, "Hi, Rodney."

"Chris."

"Officer," Virgil interrupted, "while you're here, is there anything you can share about this morning's tragic death of Foster Rodman?"

He smiled and nodded at me. "I know Chief LaMond had a conversation with your tablemate a little while ago and told him some things about what happened."

I didn't ask how he knew about the call. Instead, I said, "Do you know if drugs were found in Mr. Rodman's apartment?"

"A couple over-the-counter drugs, nothing illegal. Why?"

"There's been speculation that Matthew Seward's death was drug related, so I was wondering since Rodman played poker with Matthew."

"How about cameras?" Virgil asked as he jumped back into the conversation.

I thought that was an excellent question. Maybe he was learning from Charles.

"I did the canvas of the area to see if anyone saw anything and to determine if there were cameras that could've caught the killer either entering or leaving Foster's apartment. The answer is no cameras, no witnesses." He looked at his watch. "Guys, I'd love to stay out here but I've got to get back to work."

I thanked him for taking time to share what he'd learned. Virgil stood, shook Rodney's hand before he managed to pull it away and quickly leave our table.

"There you go," Virgil said, "more proof that Fritz is the killer."

"Remind me, what was the proof?"

"The other three suspects we were talking about killed Matthew and then Foster because of drugs. There were no drugs in Foster's apartment, so that eliminates the three other suspects."

"Maybe," I said, rather than trying to argue with him about how the lack of drugs in Foster's place didn't eliminate them from being the reason for the deaths.

Our conversation turned to more pleasant topics before Virgil said he probably should get back to his building and unclog a sink for his neighbor.

He left to put on his plumber's hat, and I walked to the far end of the pier to watch the handful of surfers enjoying the beautiful morning and share my views on the morning with several anglers I'd seen on the pier numerous times. After all, that had been my original plan.

22

———————

Instead of heading home after talking with Virgil, sharing greetings with a few fishermen, and watching surfers, I headed to the Dog for an early lunch and to see if Amber had heard about Foster Rodman. If I remembered correctly, his apartment would have been two doors down from hers.

The breakfast crowd had already finished and headed to wherever it was headed. The lunch crowd was trickling in, and there were three vacant tables on the front patio.

Heather, one of the Dog's longtime personable employees, was handling the hostess duties inside the front door. I asked if Amber was working.

"Isn't she always?"

"Seems like it. Are her tables inside or outside?"

"Front patio and a couple in here."

I said I'd take one of the tables on the patio. Instead of escorting me to the table, she pointed to the door leading to the patio and told me to grab whatever table I wanted.

"Well, if it isn't my favorite customer?" the smiling Amber said when she spotted me at a table against the railing separating the patio from the small parking lot.

"Bet you say that to all your customers."

"Not all," she said and added, "let me grab your coffee."

No more than a minute later, she'd returned with coffee, water, and using her incredible psychic power, said, "French toast?"

I smiled and said, "Not today. Think I'll have a chicken salad croissant."

"Whoa! What did you do with Chris?"

I smiled. "Considering the time, thought I should get lunch instead of breakfast." Enough about food, I thought, and said, "You hear what happened in one of the apartments in your building?"

"What?"

"What time did you get here this morning?"

"Six-thirty."

"After you got here, someone shot the man who lives a couple of doors down from you."

"You're kidding."

"Afraid not."

"That explains the sirens."

I nodded.

"Who was shot? Is he dead?"

"Foster Rodman, and yes, he didn't survive. Did you know him?"

"Barely. If you hadn't just said it, I doubt I would've remembered his name if you'd asked who he was. The only time I saw him was when we were outside our apartments and ran into each other. Who did it?"

"Don't know. You have any idea what he did for a living?"

"Worked at that tire store up Folly Road, the one near the intersection with Ft. Johnson Road."

"If you hardly knew him, how do you know where he worked?"

"The only extended conversation I had with him was when he saw me leaving my apartment a couple of months ago, he told me if I ever needed tires, to let him know. He could get me a good deal."

"That was all he said?"

She nodded and said she'd better get my order in then headed inside.

Heather escorted two couples to the large table across from me as I took a sip of coffee and wondered why Foster was reluctant to tell his poker buddies or Virgil where he worked. Charles had speculated it was because he was a drug dealer, which made less sense now that I knew where he worked. Could his reluctance to share be because his poker friends had successful, aka high-paying jobs and he didn't?

Amber returned to the patio and greeted the recent arrivers and took their orders, turned to me, and said she'd be back with my food.

Good to her word, she set my croissant in front of me, looked at the group at the nearby table, leaned closer to me, and whispered, "The police have any suspects?"

"Don't know for sure, but think they probably have a couple. Did you notice if many people visited his apartment?"

"Not really. Why?"

"There're rumors that he was dealing drugs, so I figured if that were true, he might have been selling them out of the apartment."

"As you know, my apartment is on the end of the row. His was in the middle near the stairs, so if people went to his place, they wouldn't walk past mine. There's no reason I would've noticed."

"True." I said before she went back inside to get food for the table of four.

She returned with their orders and returned to my table.

"Was thinking about poor Foster and remembered one time I was getting home from work and nearly ran into him. He and another guy were leaving his apartment. I thought it was unusual because it was in the middle of the afternoon on a workday. Seems like he would've been at work. Anyway, the other guy walked past me like I didn't exist. At least Foster always acknowledged me when I saw him."

"Do you recall seeing the other guy before, either by your building or anywhere else?"

"Not really."

"Can you describe him?"

"Chris, that was weeks ago, and I saw him for five seconds. Seems he was average height, maybe in his late-twenties."

"That's good. Anything else?"

"He was better dressed than most guys around here. I don't mean he wore a coat and tie, but his slacks were gray or black, and he had on a white dress shirt." She rubbed her chin. "That's all I remember."

"That's great, Amber."

"Think it could've been the killer?"

"No idea. Think you'd recognize the guy if you saw him again?"

"I'm fairly good with faces, but again, I only saw him a few seconds, so I don't know." She looked over at the table of four. "Better get back to work. I'll let you know if I remember anything else."

Amber's description sounded a lot like Austin Middleton, but it also could've described a zillion other young guys. And, even if it was Austin, it didn't mean he was responsible for Foster's death. I took another couple of bites of lunch and remembered how the other poker players had said Foster never told them where he lived. That means either the person Amber saw wasn't Austin, or Austin had lied about not knowing where Foster lived.

Regardless, whether it was Austin or not, two members of the group have been murdered. The odds on that simply being a coincidence seemed beyond believable.

23

―――――――

I was in front of City Hall on my way home from the Dog when an older, gray, Dodge Grand Caravan pulled into a parallel parking space beside me. I wasn't paying much attention to it until I heard, "Brother Chris."

That salutation told me the speaker was Preacher Burl Costello, minister of First Light, the newest church on the island.

He exited his van and approached me. Burl was in his mid-50s, five-foot-five inches tall, portly in polite terms, with a milk-chocolate-colored mustache.

His blue eyes sparkled as he said, "How are you, my friend?"

I first met Preacher Burl when he arrived on Folly seven years ago, when he started holding services on the beach, and immediately became the leading suspect in a murder. That wasn't the best introduction into the Folly Beach community. Through luck, being at the right place at the right, or wrong, time, and according to Burl, prayers being answered, we managed to identify the killer, who, if not obvious, wasn't Burl Costello.

"I'm doing well," I said, "And you?"

"The same."

I looked over my shoulder at City Hall, and said, "Going to City Hall?"

"Off to pay the water bill for Hope House."

Hope House is a large residence one of Burl's flock, as he calls members of his church, donated a few years ago. Burl uses it to rent rooms on a sliding scale depending upon their ability to pay for people who couldn't afford to live anywhere else. It has some semi-regular residents and occasionally one or two who needed only a few days in which to find other accommodations. Burl also lives in the house.

I smiled. "That sounds exciting."

Burl chuckled, then slowly shook his head. "Exciting, no, but necessary. Got a question."

"Okay,"

"Are you in a hurry?"

I suspected that wasn't the question.

"No."

He looked at the door to the building. "Let me run in and pay, then we can talk."

Fewer than three minutes later, he was back on the sidewalk. He patted his ample stomach, and said, "Brother Chris, I'm tired of carrying this extra weight around. I'm trying to walk more, which wouldn't take much, since I seldom walk anywhere. All of that said, would you like to walk with me?"

"Sure."

"Any preference where we go?"

"It's your walk. I'll go wherever."

He nodded then turned right at the corner of Center Street and West Cooper Avenue.

We passed the entrance to the Folly Beach Department of Public Safety. Burl nodded toward the entrance and said, "Are you aware that one of our citizens lost his life this morning?"

I assumed he was referring to Foster Rodman, and said, "Yes, Foster Rodman."

Burl nodded.

I said, "Did you know him?"

"Sort of."

"Meaning?"

"He attended one of First Light's services a few months ago, but that was my only contact with him."

"You remembered him from that one time?"

"One of my friends growing up was Foster Oldham. Not many Fosters around, so I associated it with my friend's name."

"Remember anything else about Foster Rodman, not your childhood friend?"

"The time he attended, he was accompanied by a young lady."

"Do you recall her name?"

"Can't say I do. She told me, but apparently, she didn't remind me of anyone from my youth. Sorry."

We'd gone a block west of Center Street and Burl was slowing considerably.

"Preacher, you okay?"

"I'm not accustomed to this much exercise."

"Want to head back?"

"I believe the Lord would want me to continue. My extra weight won't disappear if all I do is walk this short a distance."

From the way he was having trouble catching his breath, I hoped the Lord wouldn't get to tell him in person that he should've stopped walking.

We walked a few more yards and I said, "By any chance, did you know Matthew Seward?"

"The gentleman who lost his life a few days ago?"

"Yes."

"Why ask if I knew him?"

"He and Foster Rodman were friends."

He gave me a sideways glance and said, "Would I be safe saying you and Brother Charles are taking it upon yourselves to insert yourselves into the investigation of their deaths?"

"Not really. I'm curious since both men lived over here, and Virgil

Debonnet knew Matthew Seward's father. We attended the visitation at a funeral home in Charleston."

"Brother Chris, please don't take this wrong, but if you truly believe you're not getting involved, history tells me you're fooling yourself."

I smiled. "You may be right."

He returned my smile and said, "This out of shape body needs to be heading back."

And we did.

24

———

The next two days passed quietly, meaning I had no conversations with Charles, any of my other friends, or the police. I had been pushing my luck avoiding discussing murder when my phone rang and proved my point.

"Morning," Chief LaMond said.

"Good morning. What did I do to have the pleasure of hearing your pleasant voice this sunny morning?"

"Absolutely nothing."

"I don't suppose you called to tell me that."

"No, wanted to make sure my call didn't give you any pleasure. My peaceful morning consisted of sipping coffee while reading a fascinating report about a guy's paddle board flying off the back of his thirty-five-year-old pickup truck speeding out East Ashley Avenue. The flying board then smashed the grille of a new Audi following the now board-less pickup. Can you believe the Audi's vacationing owner saw no humor in the accident? Anyway, that was interrupted by a call from Detective Adair screwing up my peace and quiet."

I waited for her to continue, but when she didn't, I said, "Thanks for sharing that glimpse into the life of a police chief."

I heard her laugh then say, "I knew you'd be interested, and, oh yeah, while I have you on the phone, you might be interested in why he called other than to ruin my peaceful morning."

"I would."

"I'm certain you haven't been playing detective and trying to figure out who killed the poker pals." She laughed for a second time. "Why didn't you laugh? That was a joke."

"You mean you don't believe I'm not meddling?"

"Absolutely. Now with that lie, umm, joke out of the way, you've probably decided both men were killed by the same person. Right?"

"I agree. If I were playing detective, which, of course, I'm not, that would've been my belief."

"Even your city's Director of Public Safety, *moi*, figured that was the case."

"Can I assume, you and I are wrong?"

"Absolutely."

"Is that your word of the day?"

"Absolutely," she said then chuckled.

Time to move by her word of the day. "Cindy, what did Detective tell you that blew your theory?"

"Our theory."

"Our theory."

"That's better. According to the folks who knew that kind of stuff said Matthew was shot with a .22, Foster killed with a .38."

"Two guns?"

"Absolutely, Mr. Amateur Detective."

"Correct me if I'm wrong, but that doesn't mean they were killed by different people."

"You're right, but Adair said, and I agree, it's unlikely one person used two guns."

"Did he say anything else?"

"Oh yeah, I nearly forgot, you need to thank me."

"Thank you."

"You're welcome. You going to ask why?"

"No, figure you'll tell me."

"Amateur detective and psychic. I'm impressed. I didn't get a chance to tell Adair your theory that Foster killed Matthew. In other words, that kept him from either laughing about your harebrained theory, of threatening to arrest you for imitating a cop."

"It's Charles's theory, not mine. Anyway, he still could've killed Matthew, couldn't he?"

"Anything's possible, but unlikely. Adair isn't a big fan of unlikelies."

"Unlikelies?"

"You know what I mean."

I didn't get a chance to either agree or disagree. She'd hung up.

Before I poured another cup of coffee, the phone rang.

"Cindy, what's Adair theory?"

"Christopher, you've called me several names, but never Cindy. Do you know something I don't know?"

"Sorry, Virgil. Thought you were someone else."

"Apology accepted. Know what I was thinking?"

"Afraid not."

"Thinking how pleasant it'd be sitting on the end of the Pier sharing a conversation with you."

"Is that an invitation?"

"Yes."

"When?"

"How about now?"

"Works for me."

"Good, you at home?"

"Yes, want to meet me at the pier?"

"We could, but it might be better if we headed out there together."

"Why?"

"Because I'm sitting on your front step."

I sighed, said, "Bye," and opened the front door to greet Virgil in person.

On the walk to the Pier, Virgil made a couple of comments about the weather, how crowded town was becoming as we approached vacation season, and how unstopping toilets wasn't nearly as exciting as I may think it was. Yes, I reminded him I'd never said, nor would ever say, unstopping toilets was exciting.

We sat on a colorful bench at the Atlantic end of the Pier and faced the shore, the Tides Hotel, and the small condo buildings on the other side of the Pier.

"Christopher, I've been thinking about the murders. Remember I had Fritz Goss at the top of my suspect list?"

"Yes."

"Here're my latest thoughts. People like Fritz don't go around shooting people. He's probably not a billionaire but you can bet he's got a few million bucks more than I have, maybe even more than you have."

"Virgil, if he has one million bucks, that's more than I have. What's your point?"

"Rich people like Fritz don't soil their hands by shooting people. It's beneath them."

"So, you're now saying he didn't kill the two men?"

"Yes and no."

"Meaning?"

"He didn't pull the trigger. He hired someone to pull it for him."

"You think he hired a hitman?"

"You got it. The problem as I see it isn't figuring that out, it's how to prove it."

I said, "To compound it, Chief LaMond called right before you did and told me different guns were used to kill the men."

Virgil looked down at the deck, at three surfers off to our left, then back at me, before saying, "That means he could've hired two hitmen. I'm no expert like you and Charles, but that doesn't make a lot of sense. If one guy or gal was good enough to kill Matthew, why would Fritz hire a second person to bump off Foster? I doubt there's a hitman union limiting the number of hits an assassin can carry out in a certain period of time." He pointed a finger at me, and said, "Or, if the same person shot both guys, why did he change guns?" He took a deep breath, and added, "Let me ask another question that's been rolling around in my amateur detective brain, do you think the other two poker buddies are next in line to be shot?"

I didn't know how much of Virgil's hitman theory I thought was possible but didn't see any benefit in challenging him. Instead, I said, "Those are good questions."

"You have any good answers?"

"Not really. What do you think we ought to do now?"

Virgil once again looked toward shore, at the surfers, then back at me, before saying, "*Damfino.*"

"Victorian word?"

"Yep."

"Meaning?"

"Damned if I know."

"You don't know what it means, or it means *damned if I know*?"

He smiled and said, "Yes."

For the first time in my life, I wondered where I could find a hitman.

25

I answered the phone to hear Charles whisper, "Ready to do some detecting?"

"First, why are you whispering. Second, what are you talking about?"

"Didn't want them to overhear and if you get to Taco Boy, we're on the patio."

Knowing little more than I did when I answered the phone, I ended the call and made the short walk to Taco Boy to meet them and do some *detecting*.

For years, Taco Boy had been on Center Street but had moved to its current location in a large, multi-level facility that'd previously been home to Wiki Wiki Sandbar. It was also a block from my cottage.

The *them* part of Charles's brief invitation was answered as soon as I reached the top of the stairs and saw Charles at one of the multi-colored picnic tables. Virgil was seated beside Charles, across from them Ron Dillon and Austin Middleton were sipping margaritas.

"Well look who's here," Charles said when he saw me. "Want to join us?"

"Sure, why not?" I said, figuring it was the correct answer.

Virgil moved his drink closer to the center of the table and patted the green seat beside him.

I joined him. "Thanks, Virgil," I said then looked across the table. "Ron, Austin, good to see you."

They nodded and didn't say anything as they were probably trying to recall my name.

Virgil, as usual, didn't hesitate speaking. "Christopher, what brings you over to this fine ethnically-oriented restaurant?"

I didn't think answering that Charles had called and invited me was the best response, so I said, "Dropped by for a glass of wine. Did I interrupt a party?"

Virgil pointed to the stairs leading to the rooftop bar. "I was up there getting ready to order a drink, when I saw Ron and Austin walking in. I couldn't help but notice how great their shirts looked and went over to tell them. They asked if I wanted to join them, and I said it sounded great. The bar up there was packed so I suggested we move down here where there were vacant tables."

I smiled thinking how Virgil had nearly perfected the strategy of telling someone how great their clothing looked, how great their haircut looked, or some other how great something looked. Most of the time, it resulted in the great-looking person buying Virgil's drinks. I suspect tonight won't be the exception.

"Thanks for letting me join you. Charles, did Virgil pick you up as a stray?"

"Ha, ha. I saw the three of them and came to say hi. Virgil invited me to join them. And here I am."

A server appeared at the end of the table, told me she was Lauren, and asked if I wanted something to drink.

I told her a glass of white wine and Virgil chimed in saying, "Another Dos Equis Amber for me." Everyone else said they were okay.

Lauren left and Charles said, "Ron and Austin were telling us how scared they were about a killer being on the loose."

"Not just a killer," Ron said, "someone who has already murdered two of our poker group."

Charles said, "Chris, before you got here, Austin was saying he was terrified that the killer would be targeting him and Ron next."

Ron leaned his arms on the table and said, "Don't believe Austin said he was terrified. I think he meant we were worried since the two guys killed were part of our foursome."

Lauren returned with my wine and Virgil's beer and asked if we wanted anything to eat.

Virgil said, "Dear sweet Lauren, what's in the appetizer trio you have?"

She said, "Salsa roja, guacamole, and queso."

Virgil said, "Anyone want to share one?"

Ron nodded. Apparently, that was enough for Virgil who told Lauren that's what we wanted.

"We weren't best friends," Austin said. "About the only thing we had in common was an interest in cards. That's what's so frightening. I don't think Matthew and Foster knew each other outside our games."

Charles said, "I apologize if I misquoted you, Austin. All I was trying to say was the two of you were worried. I would be if two of my friends were killed."

"Austin," Virgil said, "have any idea who might've been angry at your card-playing buddies enough to shoot them?"

"Not really. That's about all Ron and I've been talking about since we learned of Foster's death."

Charles said, "Had either guy said anything about problems he was having with anyone?"

Austin shook his head and Ron said, "Not really."

Virgil said, "What about the chick Matthew was dating?"

"Rachel Little?" Austin said.

"Yes."

Ron said, "Never heard Matthew say anything about her being really mad at him, but if you ask me, she's got a screw loose."

Virgil said, "What's that mean?"

Austin glanced at Ron, then turned back to Virgil, "Saying she's got a screw loose may be making her seem worse than she is. All I know is she has a problem with the truth."

Ron said, "Austin means she's no stranger to lies."

"At Matthew's viewing, she said they were still together," Charles said. "Was that true?"

"Not by a long shot," Ron said. "That's what I mean about her lying. Don't know the exact date, but Matthew told us he'd broken up with her before Christmas."

"Matthew was excited about a lady he was dating," Austin said.

I said, "Noelle Ward?"

"Yes," Ron said as Austin nodded.

Charles took a sip of beer then looked at Ron. "Think Rachel could've killed them?"

"I can see her shooting Matthew," Ron said. "The last couple of times I talked with her she said Matthew was putting her in his will. She said she'd be rich if anything happened to him. Don't know if that's true."

Charles said, "Think she could've killed Foster?"

Ron shook his head and said, "Don't see any reason she would've. Do you, Austin?"

"No. She had a temper but killing someone takes more than a short fuse, doesn't it?"

Virgil removed his sunglasses and pointed them at Ron and then Austin. "Can either of you think of anyone other than Rachel who had conflicts, regardless of how minor, with Matthew or Foster?"

"Not really," Austin said. "That's the reason I'm worried about someone coming after us next."

"I agree with Austin," Ron said as Lauren set our appetizer platter in the center of the table and a small plate in front of each of us. Ron watched her leave, tapped his fingers on the table, and continued, "This probably won't mean anything, but Matthew talked to me a few times when we first started playing, saying things like he'd lost a ton of money in Orange Park. It's possible he owed someone down there money and that person came after him."

Charles said, "What's Orange Park?"

"Probably the casino in Orange Park, Florida," Virgil said. "They're big on poker options for their customers: Texas Hold'em, 7 Card Stud, Omaha, and a bunch of other games with weird names.

I wondered how Virgil knew about it, but instead of asking, said, "Austin, did he say anything to you about the casino?"

He smiled, took a sip of his drink, and said, "Don't recall, but he could've. He was a big talker. When we played at his house, he'd crossfire all night. After a while, you had to tune him out or go crazy."

"Know what the scariest thing is?" Ron asked.

Virgil said, "What?"

"We, honest to God, have no idea why our friends were killed. And because of that, the only conclusion we can draw is they were killed because of the poker games. Now there are two of us left. That's scary as hell."

"Ron's right," Austin said as he patted Ron on his back. "I wasn't worried when I thought Matthew's death was because of an overdose. Don't get me wrong, it was tragic, but didn't threaten us, you know."

"Austin," I said, "did you hear the coroner said there were no illegal drugs in Matthew's system?"

"Yes."

I said, "Don't recall where I heard it, but I had the impression that Matthew was back on drugs."

Yes, Austin was the person I heard it from, but I didn't want to put him on the spot.

Austin shook his head. "I thought he was. He'd told us he kicked them back when he was in college, but I knew or only thought I knew he was back on them."

Charles said, "Ron, what about you?"

"What about me?"

"Was Matthew back on drugs?"

"If he was, I never saw any indication."

Lauren returned to ask if the appetizer was okay and if we wanted more drinks.

Charles, Virgil, and I said we were okay. Austin and Ron each ordered another margarita.

She said she'd put the drink order in then went to the table beside ours to see if the family of five was ready to order.

Charles said, "Did either of you have any contact with Fritz Goss?"

"Who?" Austin asked.

Ron said, "He was Matthew's boss."

"Don't know if I ever met him," Austin said. "The most time I ever spent with Matthew was at the poker table. Now that you mention him, I remember Matthew talking trash about him a couple of times."

Charles said, "What'd he say?"

"He was pissed that guy was in charge of the place rather than Matthew."

"How about you, Ron?" Virgil said.

"I didn't pay much attention to what Matthew said. I figured Matthew's dad knew what he was doing when he put Fritz in charge. After all, Fritz was much older than Matthew, and if I'm not mistaken, had been with the company years longer than Matthew even though it was owned by Matthew's dad."

Charles said, "Think Fritz could've killed the guys?"

Austin said, "Why would he? He was already Matthew's boss, and did he even know Foster?"

"I agree with Austin," Ron said. "That wouldn't make sense."

"Not saying I disagree," Charles said. "I'm looking for suspects."

"Why are you looking for suspects?"

"Guys, you probably don't know this, but I'm a private detective. Not to brag, but I have a good record helping the police catch bad guys."

Austin said, "Are you saying you're trying to catch the person who killed the guys?"

Charles gave our tablemates his most serious head nod, and said, "Yes."

Ron said, "If you're a private detective, do you think the killer will come for one of us next?"

"I don't know. What I do know is if I were you, I'd keep my eyes on a swivel until the killer is behind bars."

"I agree," Ron said and shook his head. "I don't know anything about your detective skills, but if you can catch the killer," He pointed to Austin, and added, "I hope you do it before one of us becomes his next victim." He then looked at his watch. "Fellas, I don't know about you, but I've got an early morning tomorrow." He smiled and signed, "A plumber's life, you know."

"Boy, do I ever," Virgil said.

Apparently, Charles, Austin, and I didn't know about a plumber's life. We remained silent other than saying it was nice spending time with Ron.

Small talk dominated the next ten minutes until Austin said he had to be going, stood, shook our hands, and headed down the stairs. Lauren returned and asked if we needed anything else.

I said, "No." Virgil and Charles agreed with me, and Lauren said she'd bring the check.

The check arrived with the drinks for all four of us. At least, Austin paid for his on the way out.

Virgil said, "Christopher, think you could lend me—"

Although Virgil hadn't complimented my clothes, I said, "I'll get it."

26

––––––––––

A white cargo van with Dillon Plumbing in dark blue inside a wide yellow stripe along its side was parked in front of Bert's Market as I walked to the store to grab something for breakfast. I didn't know how large an outfit Ron's company was, so I wasn't sure if it was his vehicle.

My curiosity was answered when I saw Ron in front of the coffee urn. He finished pouring a cup, turned, and saw me standing behind him.

He smiled and said, "You caught me goofing off."

"It's your company, so I suppose you can goof off whenever you want."

He moved to the side of the table holding the coffee. I got a cup and joined him out of the landing pattern for people desperate for coffee. This time of the morning, it was a serious *faux pas* to block the coffee, especially from workers getting their fill of caffeine before heading to work.

Ron took a sip, sighed, then said, "I'm glad I ran into you this morning."

"Why?"

"Last night your friend Charles shared that he was a private detective. I'd heard you were his assistant and the two of you had caught a couple of murderers."

"Who told you that?"

"Not certain, but it could've been Austin."

I smiled. "I wouldn't go as far as saying we were detectives, but we've been fortunate to help the police a few times."

I still hadn't heard why he was glad to have run into me. Do I wait for him to share the reason, or do I ask? Oh well, why not?

"You said you were glad you ran into me."

He took another sip, looked at the line of men waiting to grab a coffee, then said, "I didn't want to mention it last night in front of Austin. I think he has a crush for lack of a better term on Rachel."

"But she was Matthew's girlfriend, or fiancé according to her, right?"

"Until he dumped her months ago. I know Austin called her a few times since then."

"How do you know?"

"He told me at one of our games."

"What did Matthew say?"

"What I should've said was, he told me during a break. The games went several hours, and we all needed to go, you know."

I nodded.

"He waited until Matthew wasn't nearby to tell me. Don't think Matthew knew."

"Did Rachel ever go out with Austin?"

"He never mentioned it when we were at the games, and I've had little contact with him since Matthew was killed. In other words, I don't know."

Unless I missed it, he still hadn't told me why he was glad to see me.

"Ron, are you saying that Austin may've killed Matthew so he wouldn't be able to stand in the way of Austin dating her?"

"I suppose it's possible, but that wasn't what I wanted to share. It's more about Rachel."

"What about her?"

He glanced around and said, "Let's move more to the back where it's not as crowded."

I followed him to the corner near the cooler and repeated, "What about her?"

"When they were dating, Matthew told me, I suppose the other two poker players as well, that Rachel was an accountant and made a good income at an accounting firm on James Island. If that was the case, why would she have approached me asking to borrow $3,500."

"That seems odd. What'd she say the money was for?"

"She didn't say, and believe me, I asked. I finally told her I had a small business and often had difficulties meeting my financial obligations, so there was no way I'd be able to come up with the money to lend her."

"What'd she say to that?"

"I could tell she was pissed, but she acted all sweet and said she understood. To be honest, even if she gave a reason, I wouldn't have believed her. Remember how we told you she was prone to lying?"

"You think she killed Matthew?"

"If I had to guess, I'd say yes."

"Why?"

He looked around then said, "One night during one of our games, Matthew said something about adding her to his will."

He'd briefly mentioned that when we were at Taco Boy, but hadn't elaborated, so I said, "Adding or added?"

"Think he said adding, like he hadn't done it yet."

"Are you thinking she may've killed Matthew because she thought she was in his will?"

"I don't know. That's why I wanted to tell you or Charles. I'm no detective."

"What reason would she have had to kill Foster?"

"You've got me there. That's why I wanted to tell you."

"I'll share this with Charles. It may be important if we or the police are getting closer to learning who killed Matthew or Foster."

He looked at the floor than back at me. "Last night we said that we were worried since we were the last two members of the poker group."

"Yes, and Charles said you needed to be careful until the killer was caught."

"That's easier said than done. I wouldn't say this in front of Austin, but I'm really scared." He took a deep breath before continuing, "What does be careful mean in this kind of situation? I can be careful by looking both ways before crossing the street; I can be careful by not speeding when I'm driving around dangerous curves. How in hell can I be careful to not get shot by someone who wants me dead?"

Good question, I thought.

"I could be wrong, of course, but if someone wants to injure you or Austin, it's probably someone you know. Being careful could simply mean trying to avoid being in one-on-one situations with people you know. Try to stay in public places, and hope the police figure out who's guilty sooner rather than later."

He nodded, looked in his coffee cup, and said, "Thanks, I guess that helps. I need to refill my coffee and get back to work. It was great talking with you."

"You, too."

"One more thing. Would you and Charles hurry up and catch the person doing this?

I nodded.

27

Barb wanted to meet for supper, saying she had exciting news. I'm always all in for exciting news, so I agreed to meet her at Jack of Cups.

When I arrived at the popular Center Street restaurant known for its eclectic menu, Barb was already seated at a table along the sidewalk in front of the restaurant. I smiled and said, "In a hurry to eat?"

She stood, pecked me on the cheek and said, "Always?"

I was impressed and often irritated by her robust appetite without ever gaining an ounce.

I sat opposite her and said, "I hate to admit it, but this is my first time here."

"That's hard to believe. You've lived here a thousand years longer than I have, and even I've eaten here."

A server appeared at the table, smiled, told us she was Fredrica, and asked what we wanted to drink. Barb looked up from the menu and said, "Think I'll go with a Deluxe Pickle Martini."

That almost made me forget what I was going to say. Fortunately, it came back to me, and I said, "A glass of chardonnay."

Fredrica headed inside to get our drinks and I said, "What's a Deluxe Pickle Martini."

Barb shrugged. "I don't know but suspect it's a deluxe martini with a pickle in it. It sounded interesting and I'm celebrating."

"What could you be celebrating that's rewarding you with a pickle martini?"

"As you know, since the day the store opened, I've been the sole employee. Most of the time that hasn't been a problem, but I'm not young enough to keep up that pace. I finally bit the bullet and hired a part-time employee."

"Congratulations. I wondered when you'd hire someone. When does the employee start?"

"Today. That's why I'm sitting here with you while the store is open. That's why I'm treating myself to a pickled martini, whatever it is."

As if on cue, Fredrica appeared and set Barb's drink in front of her, and in front of me, my mundane, boring-looking when compared to Barb's drink, glass of chardonnay. She then asked if we were ready to order.

I glanced at Barb who mouthed "No," so I told Fredrica to give us a few minutes.

Barb sipped her martini which came as advertised with a slice of pickle then said, "It's nice being able to sit out here and enjoy a drink without worrying about having to rush back to the store."

"I'm glad you can do it. Tell me about your employee."

"Name's Samantha Law, goes by Sam. She's in her late twenties with a recently acquired degree in English from the College of Charleston."

"How'd you find her?"

"It's more like she found me. She came in last week, said she'd graduated a couple of weeks earlier with a degree in English, and joked that she had a minor in surfing, and asked if I was hiring. She and two other gals rent an apartment here so she can be close to the ocean where she can work on a graduate degree in her minor."

"That's great."

"Is for now. I don't know how long I can keep her. At some point she's going to want to do something using her major."

I smiled. "I hope she didn't specialize in literature like Virgil's ex-wife. I already hear more Victorian phrases than any kid from Kentucky needs being exposed to."

"I think you're safe." She took another sip of her martini, and said, "Anything new on the murders that you claim you're not nosing into?"

"I ran into Ron Dillon this morning in Bert's. He's one of the poker pals of the victims."

"So?"

Fredrica returned before I could answer Barb's question. She asked if we were ready to order.

Barb said she was ready and said that the Bombolini Butterbean Burger sounded good. I didn't recognize half the ingredients in it, so I want with the Buffalo Mac and Cheese.

After she headed inside, Barb, said, "Back to my question, you ran into Ron Dillon and?"

"He told me he and Austin Middleton, the other surviving player, are worried one of them may be the next victim."

"Why?"

"He wasn't clear, but his perception is the poker games were the only thing the two victims had in common, and since he and Austin were in the group, they may be in danger."

"Do you agree?"

"It makes as much sense as anything. The only other thing he said that could possibly be connected was he had the impression Austin had a crush on either Matthew's girlfriend or ex-girlfriend depending upon the person you ask and thought Austin may've killed Matthew, so it would've given him a chance to court, for lack of a better term, Rachel."

"That's the closest thing you've said that could be an actual motive. The fear they were in danger simply because they played poker with the dead gentlemen makes little sense. So, why wouldn't that be the best motive?"

"Apparently Matthew made it clear to the group he'd broken up with Rachel before Christmas, so he would've been out of the picture and not standing in Austin's way."

Our food arrived and Barb chose to quench her hunger rather than continuing our conversation, at least temporarily.

After saying the burger was scrumptious, and taking two more bites, she returned to the previous topic. "Have you had much discussion with Austin Middleton?"

I realized I hadn't told her about Charles and my visit with both Austin and Ron at Taco Boy. Instead of mentioning it and then being accused of sticking my nose in police business, I said, "Not much. But the first time I talked with him we were at Matthew's viewing, and he was convinced Matthew had died from an overdose. The other time we talked he had finally been convinced the death wasn't drug related."

"From what you're saying, it doesn't sound like Austin or Ron had strong suspects."

"That about sums it up. Their main concern was whether they were now in the killer's crosshairs." I took a bite of food and another sip of wine, then added, "Why don't you put on your attorney hat and let me ask you something?"

She smiled. "That's easier to do now there's someone wearing the bookseller's hat. What's the question?"

"I think I know the answer, but since you're the expert I'll ask. Can a person leave something in his will to anyone he chooses?"

"Yes, there're only two prohibitions. The recipient must be alive and cannot be one of the witnesses to the signing of the will. Why?"

"Apparently Rachel Little told one or both living poker-playing gentlemen Matthew was leaving her something in his will. She had the impression it'd be a substantial amount of money."

"Did he?"

"They don't know but didn't think so since Matthew ended their relationship months ago."

Barb looked at her watch, took the final bite of her *scrumptious* burger and said, "I've been away long enough, especially on Sam's first day."

I told her I'd take care of the check if she wanted to leave.

She thanked me, and added, "Of all the things you said about motive to kill Matthew, Rachel clearly had the most to gain from his death, that is, assuming she's in his will. I might add, that's how the police will see it."

She headed back to the bookstore before I could agree or disagree.

28

———

The phone rang as I was fixing coffee, and Charles's name appeared on the screen. "Morning, Charles."

"Know what I've got a hankering for?"

"Peace on Earth, good will toward men," I said suspecting I may not be right.

"That, too. That your only guess?"

"Yes."

"You're no fun. How about coffee and something gooey from Bert's and an early-morning walk on the Pier?"

"Is that what you're hankering for, or did you change the subject?"

"I'll meet you there in fifteen minutes and answer your question."

Ten minutes later, I was moving behind Charles at Bert's coffee urn as he drew a cup, turned, looked at me, and rolled his eyes while shaking his head, another of his countless ways of showing displeasure.

"About time you got here," he said as I fixed my coffee. "You live three feet from Bert's, I live a thousand miles away, and still beat you."

Measuring distance wasn't one of his talents. Ignoring me if I tried to tell him that, was in his talent pool, so I didn't waste my breath. He followed me to the pastry case, grabbed a cheese Danish after I chose the apple version, then to the register. I was surprised, correction, shocked when he paid for both "breakfasts," and said, "The Pier?"

I told him it was his trip and I'd follow wherever he chose to lead.

Our walk ended on the Atlantic end of the Folly Beach Fishing Pier, aka the Atlantic Office of Charles's private detective agency.

We sat facing the Tides Hotel, as each of us took a bite of Danish. Charles had a purpose for us being here, but I knew it'd be futile asking what it was. I would find out when he was ready to share.

He took a sip then glanced over at me. "How many times have we managed to put ourselves in situations that should be jobs for the police?"

"A bunch."

"How did we manage to do that?"

"Good question. I can't remember every time, but mostly it was because you, I, or both of us knew the victim and we took their death or loss personally."

Charles nodded. "Or somehow stumbled across a dead body and figured it was up to us to catch the killer."

"True."

"Andrew Jackson said, 'One man with courage makes a majority.'"

"Are you saying we have the courage to get involved?" I smiled. "It's more like we're too dense to know we shouldn't get involved."

"Because we have the courage to get involved, we have a good chance at doing what the police, who do it because it's their job, are unable to do."

"Could be."

He nodded as if what I said was both profound and enlightening, rather than my perception that it was simply confusing. He then said, "Ready to hear why I called this meeting?"

"Yes."

"Matthew Seward the nineteenth and Foster Rodman have been murdered. Agree?"

I didn't agree that Matthew was the nineteenth Seward, but wisely overlooked that error in genealogy and said, "Yes."

"Your extensive contact with Matthew was seeing him a few times in Bert's. My contact with him was, well, never."

I nodded.

"Other than a brief meeting at Rita's, neither of us had much dealings with Foster Rodman, much less were buddies. Right?"

"Yes."

"Then why are we in the oft-repeated words of Chief LaMond, *butting into police business*? Neither of us knew either guy more than to say hi in a grocery store. We didn't even stumble across their bodies."

"Are you saying we should let it go and leave it up to the police to catch the murderer?"

"Yes, umm, no. Maybe."

Now why hadn't I figured that out?

"I'm not saying we should or shouldn't pursue it, but Virgil had some familiarity with Matthew's family, and since Matthew's death, we've met and talked with each member of the poker group, plus Rachel, Matthew's girlfriend or former girlfriend depending upon who you ask. Add to that, my friend Noelle dated Matthew up until his death."

"Now I'm confused. You saying we should drop it, or not?"

"Whether we did or didn't have a solid connection to the first victim, we know most of the key players, although we have no reason to believe that someone we know may be the murderer, or even a potential victim."

"I'm still confused. Drop or not?"

"Not."

Charles jerked back like he'd been hit in the face. "Whoa, you're the one always preaching it's none of our business getting involved. Make sure I understand, you think we should stick our necks out and butt into police business?"

"Charles, I'm not saying we should run around trying to catch the person, or persons who killed the men, but history tells me, for whatever reason, we're fairly good at listening and drawing conclusions that have solved some horrible crimes. If we learn anything to help the police, we should tell them and let them do the dangerous work."

Charles pounded the seat with his fist, faced me, and said, "Well, what're we waiting for? Let's catch a killer."

Not exactly what I said, although not far off.

We'd finished our food and were on the last sip of our drinks.

I held up my coffee cup and said, "Let's head back to Bert's for a refill."

"Good plan. That'll give us enough energy to get this murder stuff figured out."

I wasn't that optimistic but needed more coffee.

With our cups refilled, Charles headed toward Center Street with a renewed energy in his step, his strides longer than earlier, and his cane tapped forcefully on the berm as we headed to the center of town.

We reached the traffic light, Folly's only traffic light, and Charles pointed his cane at the green-painted brick Sand Dollar Social Club on the other side of Center Street. "Let's go to the bench in front of the Sand Dollar. We can hold the rest of our private detective meeting there."

It was still early, so the iconic private club hadn't opened and the motorcycle parking spaces in front of the building were unoccupied. Charles plopped down on the bench, set his cane beside him, and said, "Okay, since you insist that we stick our noses where they don't belong, what do we know about the deaths?"

Instead of rehashing everything both of us knew, I mentally prepared myself for a scolding and said, "I was talking with Ron Dillon yesterday in Bert's. He said—"

Charles waved his hand in front of my face and interrupted with, "You what? Why didn't you call me as soon as you were done? No, why didn't you call me when you saw him so I could help you interrogate him? No, why didn't—"

This time, I interrupted, "Enough. You want to hear what he said, or waste time complaining?"

He sighed, looked at the sky, shook his head, then mumbled, "What'd he say?"

"He thinks Rachel killed Matthew."

"Why didn't he say that when we were talking with him and Austin at Taco Boy?"

"He thinks Austin has a thing for Rachel. He didn't want to tell us because Austin was there?"

"Why does he think she did it?"

"Rachel thinks Matthew left her money, a good amount of money, in his will. Since they broke up, she's afraid he'd change the will and cut her out."

"So, she killed him before he had time to change it?"

"That's what Ron thinks."

"What does Chris think?"

"That makes sense, but it's only a theory."

"That's right, and I don't think she did it."

"Why not?"

"Because Fritz Goss did."

"That's a possibility," I said, while thinking it wasn't much of one.

"Charles snapped his fingers and said, "Got it. Wasn't each guy shot with a different gun?"

"Yes."

"So, Fritz killed Matthew and Rachel killed Foster. Case closed."

"That's a possibility."

"So, assistant private detective, all we have to do is prove it."

If only it was that easy, I thought. "How're we going to do that?"

"Hell if I know."

Guess that's why he was the private detective, and I was only an assistant.

29

It's my next-door neighbor, so I did most of my grocery shopping, what little there was of it, at Bert's. Occasionally, I ventured to the nearest Harris Teeter to grab something not available next door. Harris Teeter was a mere two and a half miles from my driveway, but I treated it like it was a major trip, further proof I was spoiled by living on Folly where most everything was within walking distance of my cottage.

Today was one of those adventurous days. I needed gas and figured I could kill two birds with one stone, or in this case, two unpleasant tasks from one parking lot, and made the short trip to the Harris Teeter gas station located adjacent to the store. With my car fueled, I drove an additional hundred yards and entered the grocery to purchase fuel for my body.

I was studying the 3,159 choices of cereal when someone tapped me on the shoulder. I turned and found a young lady, probably in her mid-20s with long blonde hair, smiling at me. She looked familiar, but I couldn't recall where I'd seen her.

Being my articulate self, I said, "Hi."

"Sorry to bother you, but didn't we talk at Loggerhead's a while back?"

Then it struck me. "Yes, it's good seeing you again, Rachel."

"Chris, right?"

I nodded.

She pulled her shopping cart off to the side of the aisle and said, "If I remember right, we also spoke briefly at Matthew's visitation. Weren't you there with a couple of guys?"

"Yes, I knew Matthew from a few conversations we had in Bert's, and Virgil Debonnet knew both Matthew and his father." I chose not to add Charles, the other person with me, was there to play detective.

She smiled, "Yes, I recall Matthew speaking of you a couple of times. He and I were engaged and planning a wedding for later this year." Her smile faded and she bowed her head.

She'd made a point of telling me about their alleged engagement when we met at Loggerhead's. Her grief would've been believable if I didn't know that their relationship had ended months ago.

Instead of asking her if she killed Matthew so she'd stay in his will, I said, "I'm sorry for your loss."

"Thank you."

To channel Charles, and while already knowing the answer, I asked, "Were you in his poker group?"

"No, thank God."

"Why's that?"

"Don't get me wrong, Matthew really liked those guys. I suppose they had fun while wasting nights playing games, taking money from each other then losing it back the next time they played. I simply saw no use for his hobby, or more accurately, his obsession."

"Obsession?"

"Suppose you could say gambling was."

"You think because he played a couple of times a week, he was obsessed?"

"Not just that. I went with him a few times down to the casino in Florida. He'd play everything there until he lost an ungodly amount of money, then he'd play more if they let him."

That was the second time someone had mentioned the casino in Florida. That also reinforced what Virgil had suspected when he was talking about Matthew's gambling, and possibly getting in deep with someone down there, deep enough to kill him if he didn't pay up.

"That's too bad. I hate to ask, but do you have any idea who may've killed him?"

"Not really. I suppose he had enemies, who doesn't? If I had to point my finger at anyone, I wouldn't know where to begin." She looked at her shopping cart then her watch, and said, "I shouldn't be saying this, but it doesn't matter now that he's gone. You know where he worked, don't you?"

"Seward Wealth Management."

She nodded.

"What about it?"

"I really shouldn't say anything." She again looked in her cart.

"It's okay, Rachel," I said and gave her my best sympathetic look. "What is it?"

She sighed before saying, "Matthew lived large. Always wanted the biggest, best, and most expensive everything." She again hesitated.

"Was that a problem?"

"I'm an accountant in a small firm near here. I make an okay salary but struggle to meet my rent and car payment."

I wondered what that had to do with Matthew but assumed she had a point to make. I couldn't tell what she was thinking but the vacant look in her eyes told me it'd taken her far from Harris Teeter.

She shook her head like she was trying to return to standing in front of me, then said, "Matthew didn't make as much as I do. He had a nice title at work, but his dad said he had to prove he could earn a better salary. Said just because he was a Seward, didn't put him above everyone else."

"That had to be rough on him."

"Yes and no. It didn't cost him anything to live in that large house on the ocean. His parents paid all the expenses for the house. His BMW was leased, and he was behind a couple of months on it. Yet he always wanted to head to the casino and gamble money he didn't have."

"Did he often win?"

"The funny thing about that is he wouldn't tell me how he did. It wasn't for me not asking."

"What'd he say?"

"He wouldn't talk about it, but I could tell. He wasn't good at hiding his feelings. The look on his face told me everything, and most of the times when he got back, the look could kill."

"Think it could've been someone from down there who killed him?"

"It's possible."

"Did he mention anyone who might've wanted harm to come to him?"

"No, but if he owed someone money, why would they want him dead where he couldn't pay them back?"

"Rachel, that's a good question, and like you said, it wouldn't make sense."

"It's still possible, isn't it?"

I nodded.

"Why are you asking all these questions? The police didn't ask this much."

"I didn't know Matthew well, but he seemed like a nice person. I hate to see whoever did it get away with it. I figure if I learned anything that could help the police get closer to catching his killer, I'd tell them."

"Makes sense."

"How well did you know Foster Rodman?"

"Better than I knew Matthew's other two regular poker buds. He had supper with Matthew and me a couple of times. Seemed like a nice guy. A little standoffish, but okay."

"How was he standoffish?"

"Funny ways. I remember asking where he lived, just making conversation, you know. He said on Folly, that's all. Another time I asked what he did for a living. Know what he said?"

I shook my head.

"He made some comment about our food. He never answered."

"Did you ask him again?"

"No. To be honest, I didn't care, was only making conversation like when I asked where he lived."

"Any idea who may've killed Foster?"

"Didn't you already ask that? You ask a lot of questions, don't you?"

I smiled. "Sorry. Yes, I guess I already asked if you had any idea about who killed him. I didn't mean to sound like I was interrogating you. I hated that your fiancée was killed and it's possible the two deaths are connected."

"How's that possible? I thought they were killed by different people."

"Why do you think that?"

She rolled her eyes. "Another question."

"Again, sorry."

She smiled. "Teasing. I heard Matthew was shot with a different gun than the one that killed Foster. That sounds like it must've been by someone else."

"I don't think the police know for certain."

"I haven't forgotten your first question."

That's good, because I had. "That was?"

"If I knew who may've killed Foster."

"Do you?"

"Not really."

That was the same answer she gave the first time I asked.

"You sure you don't have any idea, not even a guess?"

"Umm, I don't want to get anyone in trouble if they had nothing to do with his death."

"Rachel, no one will get in trouble if they didn't do it."

"I know, it's that, umm, never mind. I'll tell you what I do know."

"What?'

"I need to get home."

"Sorry, I didn't mean to slow down your grocery shopping."

"Don't be. It's good talking about Matthew with someone other than my friends. They get all mopey about it."

"Do you live near here?"

"Not far. In the Turn of River condos."

"Isn't that just before the bridge to Folly?"

"Yes, I like it there. It's close enough to walk to the restaurants on Folly and the ocean, yet outside the hectic pace on-island." She glanced again at her watch. "Nice talking with you, Chris. Maybe I'll see you again on Folly."

30

———

After putting the groceries away, I moved to the recliner in the living room and tried to recall if Rachel had said anything that'd move me closer to learning who killed Matthew. While it didn't point me to the killer, her comments about her ex-boyfriend's finances differed greatly from the perceptions of his two poker friends. They thought Rachel's motive for killing Matthew assumed he had left her a substantial amount of money in his will, and she may have killed him to make sure he didn't cut her out since they were no longer dating. Yet according to Rachel, Matthew hardly had any money and was having difficulty keeping up with his fiscal obligations. If true, he wouldn't have had much to leave her, so that wouldn't be a reason to take his life. Even if he had money, why would she have waited months to kill him since he could've updated his will at any time?

It didn't eliminate her from being the murderer, but it eliminated the motive his friends had mentioned. Of course, that assumption hinged on her telling me the truth about his wealth, or lack of wealth, which led me to thinking about her saying they were still dating, and even planning a wedding. If she was lying about that, she could as easily have been lying about him not having much money. She also said she didn't know who killed Foster Rodman but was holding something back. I failed my Charles imitation by not pushing her.

Surely, my deductive reasoning and august status as an assistant private detective allowed me to identify Matthew's killer. It's too bad I couldn't recall who it was since I fell asleep in the chair and probably snored through the brilliant revelation.

It was a near-perfect Spring afternoon with the temperature in the low-70s and a cloudless sky which reminded me of my resolution to walk more. I tried to come up with a viable reason not to add to my walking mileage but failed. I pushed out of the chair, grabbed my Tilley to block the sun from my balding head, and my camera to digitally capture anything I found photo worthy.

Five minutes later, I was on Center Street headed toward the Tides Hotel when I passed Dude's surf shop. I noticed a familiar face leaning against the side of the building.

"Hi, Noelle."

"You caught me."

"Caught you doing what, or shouldn't I ask?"

She smiled. "Research."

"You're researching if the surf shop's wall will take your weight leaning against it before falling?"

She laughed. "I may've been doing that if I were writing a physics book."

"But you're writing a mystery, so you're researching, umm, I give up, what?"

"There are a lot of surfers in my book, and to be honest, I've never surfed, so—"

"Noelle," I interrupted, "I'm no expert, but I don't think you'll see many people surfing past you on Center Street."

She smiled. "Wow! I never would've thought of that."

I returned her smile and said, "Sarcasm, right?"

"I call it smartassery in the book."

"I'm impressed, you're writing a mystery and a dictionary."

This time, she said, "Sarcasm, right?"

"Absolutely. What are you observing?"

"Watching guys and gals head up the steps to Dude's shop. I figure most are surfers and I wanted to make sure I captured any quirks in their behavior or speech pattern as compared to people, well, people like you and me."

"Brilliant, good looking, and wise people?"

"Yes."

Enough sarcasm or *smartassery*.

"Speaking of your book, how's it coming?"

She either sighed or growled before saying, "It's frustrating."

"In what way?"

"Let's change the topic."

"Okay, I'm taking a walk. Want to tag along?"

"Sure. From my extensive research of observing three potential surfers heading into the surf shop, I'm going to conclude that there's nothing different in the way they walk or talk from us *brilliant, good looking and wise people*."

We headed to where Center Street ends at Arctic Avenue and turned left and passed the Pier's parking lot that'd already reached its capacity and had a *Full* sign at the entry. This time of year, it was practically impossible to find free parking near this spot and I was always grateful that my cottage was within walking distance of the island's businesses and restaurants.

As we walked, I said, "I had an interesting conversation this morning with Rachel Little."

She turned her head facing me but continued walking and said, "How'd that happen?"

"We were in Harris Teeter when she saw me and started talking."

"Did you recognize her?"

"Not at first."

"What'd she have to say?"

"She still claimed Matthew was going to marry her in the Fall."

"No offense to your new grocery-store friend, but she's either lying or delusional."

"I agree. I'd put money on her lying."

"She say anything else?"

We'd walked a block and were standing beside the sandy parking area filled with vehicles.

I said, "Want to go to the beach walkover where we can see how crowded it is?"

She smiled. "Is that part of your walking?"

"No, but it's easier to talk while standing still."

She followed me past the vehicles to the path across the dunes where we had a good view of the Pier and could see the beach for a good distance in each direction. Colorful beach umbrellas and chairs stretched a couple of hundred yards on either side of the Pier with most occupied and the surf full of the remaining chair renters plus others who were enjoying the beautiful day.

Noelle looked left and right before staring at me. "Okay, I repeat, did Rachel say anything else of interest?"

"Yes, but first let me ask you, did Matthew ever share information about his financial status?"

She looked at me like I'd asked a trick question and said, "He never shared his financial statements, checkbook, or investment portfolio. I figured it'd take more than three dates before he gave me copies of that stuff."

"Noelle, that's not what I meant."

"Okay, what'd you mean?"

"He ever say anything about having money problems?"

"No. When we went out, he didn't cut corners at the restaurants. He drove a two-year-old BMW 5 Series, not the least expensive BMW, lived in a multimillion-dollar house on the beach, and was a VP at, from what I heard, a successful wealth management firm. He tipped well. That said, he never bragged on being wealthy, but I never saw anything leading me to believe he wasn't."

"So, no mention of either having a lot of money or money problems?"

"The only thing I recall him saying about money was he told me someone owed him nearly $50,000."

"What brought that up?"

"Something about an investment he wanted to make but couldn't until he got the money he was owed."

"He say who owed it?"

"No, it was said in passing. He didn't mention it again; I didn't bring it up. Your turn, why the questions about his wealth?"

I shared what Rachel had said about his salary and being behind on his vehicle's lease payments.

"We weren't close enough for him to share any of that. If anything, he never appeared worried about money. You think Rachel was telling the truth? Her track record when it comes to honesty leaves something to be desired."

"Good question. You're right, she'd already lied about dating Matthew, so it'd be easy to believe she lied about his money. In other words, I don't know?"

"You and your friends are determined to figure out what happened, who killed the two men. Right?"

"Yes. Ready to start walking?"

"It's your plan. I'm just tagging along."

We returned to East Arctic Avenue, turned away from the center of town, and didn't say anything for a block.

Noelle finally broke the silence. "Want to know why I'm frustrated with my novel?"

"Sure."

"I think I told you before that I was approaching the finish."

"Yes."

"I sort of know who the killer is. Of course, I know who he killed since that happened early in the book. I know mostly everything I need to know about the other characters. Now I'm stuck."

"Stuck how?"

"How in hell does my private detective catch the killer?"

"I don't know a thing about writing a novel but would've thought that would be something you figured out long before getting near the end of the book."

She smiled. "Yes, one would think that, wouldn't one?" She pointed to the side of her head. "That's not true with this one."

"I know the feeling."

"How?"

"Well, if you switched from your novel to real life, that's exactly where I am regarding the two deaths here. I know who's dead and much about the other cast of characters, but when it comes to the murderer or murderers." I shrugged.

"Hadn't thought of it that way." She chuckled. "Maybe I should give you my manuscript and you can help me figure out the killer and how to catch him."

"You really don't know who the killer is?"

She shook her head. "I've planned to have three characters who may be the bad guy."

"Three?"

"Yes, I want the readers to think it could be any of the three. It should be a mystery for the readers as much as for my detective."

"That makes sense."

She stopped, looked between two houses on our right like she was looking toward the beach, and said, "In most mystery novels, there's one person who's the obvious suspect, and then a few others. Almost every time, the obvious suspect isn't the killer. That way the writer can surprise the readers or try to."

I smiled. "There you go. You've narrowed it down to your two other suspects."

"Maybe, but what if I make the obvious suspect the killer?"

"You'd have your surprise ending."

"True, but then some readers and critics could say it wasn't a very good book since the obvious suspect was the killer."

"So, what're you going to do?"

"Remember back at the surf shop when you asked how the novel was coming?"

I nodded.

"That's why I'm frustrated. If I knew the answer to whodunit, I'd almost be done."

"Almost?"

"I still don't know how my protagonist will catch the killer regardless of if it's the obvious one or one of the others."

"Wow. I'm afraid I can't help you there, but I have faith you'll figure it out. I'd better stay focused on the poker-player killer. There's a chance he or she may kill again."

"You drive a hard bargain. You figure out your mystery, and somehow, I'll muddle through mine. One more thing, be careful, your killer could kill you. Mine can only kill somebody I've made up."

"Deal."

"Good, because if you get killed, who will I stalk?"

31

By the time Noelle and I returned to the center of town, we'd discussed many things and solved a couple of mysteries. Unfortunately, learning the identity of her fictional killer and the real-life murderer of Matthew Seward and Foster Rodman were not among the mysteries solved. I wished her well with her dilemma. She wished me a safe journey toward solving the two murders. I prayed her wish would come true.

When I got home, I poured a glass of chardonnay, headed to the back yard, and sat on my picnic table under a sturdy live oak that had shaded the table since I'd moved into the house fourteen years ago. Music from someone playing guitar and singing on the outdoor stage at Chico Fio located on the other side of Bert's Market could be heard over the occasional sound of a vehicle on the street behind me.

Ever since Matthew was killed followed by the death of Foster, several names had been mentioned as suspects. Then I thought about what Noelle had shared about identifying the most likely to least likely suspects in mystery novels. Would taking the same approach work for me? It was worth a try. I went in the house and grabbed a legal pad and pen from my office then returned to the picnic table. Now to begin a list.

If I left it to Charles to name the top suspect, and in his mind, only suspect, for the murder of Matthew, it'd be Fritz Goss. Most likely Virgil would concur. They could be right, but the motive appears weak. Charles has said and Virgil agreed that Fritz was worried that Matthew was trying to sabotage Fritz's hold on the top position at Seward Wealth Management so he could take over. No matter how often Charles said it, I couldn't picture the top executive sullying his hands by shooting Matthew, and even if he had, what reason would he have for killing Foster Rodman? Virgil had countered that argument by suggesting that Fritz could've hired a hitman or possibly two hitmen to kill the men. Possible? Yes. Probable? Unlikely. Or was it?

Fritz may be at the top of Charles's and Virgil's list, but I wasn't ready to make that leap, which brings me to Rachel. I took a sip of wine and looked toward Bert's Market as if that'd clarify my thinking. It failed but gave me time to think about what had been said about Rachel being the killer. Ron and Austin suspected her, but their reason was that she'd killed him because he'd left her a substantial amount of money in his will and since they had stopped dating months ago, she killed him so he wouldn't be able to remove her from the will. That argument had collapsed when she told me that Matthew was having serious money problems. That is assuming she was telling the truth about his financial status. Was she, and even if she was, could there be other reasons Rachel wanted Matthew dead?

The best suspect had been Foster Rodman. He was thought to be a drug dealer, cloaked in mystery because he'd avoided telling anyone where he lived and what he did for a living. Of course, he dropped off most of our lists when he became the second victim. But that would only be true if there was one killer. If two killers, Foster could've killed Matthew and someone else killed Foster. Different weapons would've supported that theory. It made sense, but it seems unlikely that there were two killers. If I'm right, Foster would've been off the list.

Closer to the bottom of the list rather than the top, I'd add Ron Dillon and Austin Middleton. The only reason I'd put them on it would be their proximity to Matthew and Foster since they were the only names mentioned as being poker-playing buddies with the dead gentlemen. Beyond proximity, a reason for either killing the men was elusive with Austin having the closest thing to a motive. Ron had hinted that Austin "had a thing" for Rachel and could possibly have killed Matthew so he'd have a chance at getting closer to her. But wouldn't that only be true if Rachel had been telling the truth about still dating Matthew? If they'd broken up before Christmas, Matthew would've already been out of the way months before the murders occurred.

At the bottom of the list, I'd add the person who Noelle said Matthew had told her about, the person who owed him around $50,000. Unfortunately, he hadn't shared who it was, where he or she lived, or if the debt had been paid. If it hadn't been settled, that person would have a motive for wanting Matthew dead. I'd also add to the bottom of the list, a person from Florida or the casino there to whom Matthew was indebted. I knew as much about the bottom of the list suspects as I did about who killed Noelle's fictional victim.

I took another sip of wine before realizing I had listed several potential killers; killers others had named as their choice. The question is who did I think was responsible for the untimely deaths?

The more I thought about the names, the more I focused on Rachel. The original reason for suspicion may be discounted, but her lack of truthfulness bothered me. Add to that, if what Matthew shared with Noelle was true, he broke off their dating and possible engagement months before Rachel claimed they were still dating. She must've been angry with him; angry enough to kill? Possibly. I had no idea why she would've killed Foster, but no one appeared to have a good theory about what precipitated his death. Until I was proven wrong, Rachel was at the top of my list.

On the other hand, she'd hinted she knew something about the killer. Now all I have do is figure out how to convince her to tell me what it is.

Being from Kentucky, I can't help comparing things to horse racing. With Rachel at the top of my list, leading the race, I see most of the rest of the field bunched up far off the lead including Fritz with his possible hitmen, Ron, Austin, someone from Florida Matthew owed money to, and someone who owed Matthew money. Lagging far behind everyone else, I would have Foster, mainly because he'd been murdered.

I finished my wine, thought about getting a refill, but rejected it knowing it would cloud my thinking more than it already was. For a fleeing moment, I thought possibly I could write a murder mystery. If I could create a scenario with only three murder suspects, it'd be easy to figure out. I also reminded myself not to share that thought with Noelle.

My ringing phone refocused my attention, fortunately because I didn't feel I was getting anywhere identifying the killer.

Virgil's name appeared on the screen.

"Good afternoon, Virgil."

"It's a dandy, I must say."

I didn't figure he called to tell me how dandy the day was, so I said, "What's happening?"

"Glad you asked. How would you like to have supper with me this evening at The Washout?"

"Sure."

"Good. Would you mind inviting Barb to join us?"

That was a strange request, but strange often described Virgil's words and actions.

"I could invite her. What's the occasion?"

"Did I mention that Noelle Ward will be there?"

"Did you finally ask her out?"

"I did, and to my amazement, she said yes."

"Is tonight your first date?"

"It is."

"Why do you want Barb and me crashing your first date?"

"Technically speaking, I invited you, so you won't be crashing."

"Are you nervous about it?"

"Nervous, nah, I'm terrified."

"Why?"

"Like I told you before, Noelle has a nice job, most likely, a nice income, and I'm, umm, I'm broke as a pinecone and the closest thing I currently have to a career is unstopping toilets. I fail to see the appeal I may have for her."

"Virgil, unless I misunderstood what you said a moment ago, you asked Noelle out and she said yes."

"Correct."

"And she knows about your work status?"

"Yes."

"Yet she said yes?"

"True."

"Doesn't that tell you something?"

"Yes, it tells me I'll be so nervous I won't be able to string together three words, much less a coherent conversation. It would be quite advantageous having you and Barb there to, well, to keep me from making a fool of myself."

"You underestimate yourself. You're a wonderful, humorous, articulate gentleman, and from what I know about Noelle, she wouldn't have said yes if she didn't want to go."

"See, comments like that are why I'd like you there. I'll need all the help I can get."

"I don't think it'll be necessary, but if you want us there, let me call Barb and see if she's available."

"Christopher, you're a fine friend."

"One more time, are you certain you want us there?"

"Affirmative."

"What's Noelle going to think of two more people being there than she knew about?"

"That's where I'd like to ask another favor."

"What?"

"I wouldn't want Noelle to think we're ganging up on her, so would you mind arriving a little after we get there? I could see you enter and ask if you wanted to join us. Noelle knows you and Barb and I'm certain she wouldn't mind. Would you? Please."

"If you're sure that's what you want, we will, that is if Barb's available."

"Then I suppose I should end this call so you can check."

He did. I called Barb, shared the plan, and she agreed, saying, "At least I'll get a good meal out of it."

I called Virgil, gave him the good news, and we agreed on a time.

Chris Landrum, matchmaker. What have I got myself into now?

32

I met Barb at her store a little before we were to be surprised seeing Virgil and Noelle at The Washout restaurant. She introduced me to Samantha, then told her new employee to call if she had any problems. Barb then put her arm through mine and said, "Shall we begin playing our role in the Virgil and Noelle budding romance?"

I wouldn't have put it like that, but said, "Yes," as we began our short walk to our rendezvous spot with Virgil and his unsuspecting date.

We reached the front of the restaurant where I spotted Virgil and Noelle at a table butting up to the half-wall separating the large patio from the sidewalk. It was a good sign seeing them laughing.

Virgil saw me, waved, and said to the lady sitting across from him, "Noelle, look who it is, Christopher and the lovely Barb."

Noelle smiled and started to say something, when Virgil interrupted and said, "Where are you two going this evening?"

As if he didn't know. I said, "Here, for supper."

"Why don't you join us?" he said, then turned to Noelle and continued, "That's okay, isn't it?"

"Of course," she said with a smile, as if she could say no in front of us.

I looked at Barb, she nodded, and I said, "That'd be nice. Thank you."

Before we'd walked around the patio to the entrance and were headed to their table, Virgil had moved to the bench seat next to Noelle and motioned for us to take the seats across from them. Virgil was wearing a white, long-sleeve dress shirt, gray slacks, and even though the patio was shaded, sunglasses. Noelle had left her black, stealth-appearing clothes at home and was wearing a bright yellow blouse and navy slacks.

"Thanks for the invitation, Virgil," I said. "I hope we're not interrupting something."

"Nonsense," Virgil said, "we're honored that you agreed to join us. Isn't that right, Noelle?"

She smiled and said, "Yes."

Virgil and Noelle already had drinks and Caroline, a longtime server at the restaurant, appeared at the table and asked Barb and me what we wanted."

We placed our order and for no reason other than to get the conversation going, I asked if they'd been here long.

Noelle, in her longest statement tonight, said, "We got here no more than ten minutes ago."

I wanted to ask how they got here since Virgil's only means of transportation is an old scooter he bought used and Noelle lives several long blocks away. I wanted to ask but didn't.

Virgil said, "Christopher, hear anything new on the two deaths?"

Great, Virgil, I thought, the perfect topic for your first date.

"I haven't—"

"What sounds good?" Barb said as she reviewed the laminated menu in front of her.

Thanks, Barb, I thought as she changed the direction of the conversation away from murder.

"I was thinking the flounder sandwich," Noelle said. "How about you, Virgil?"

"That sounds delightful. You have excellent taste."

She smiled and turned to Barb and me. "What're you having?"

Barb said, "Probably the Buffalo Caesar Wrap."

I added, "Think I'll go with the burger."

Virgil didn't tell us our selections were delightful.

Caroline returned with drinks for Barb and me and asked if we were ready to order.

I looked at Virgil who looked at Noelle who nodded. I told Caroline yes and we shared the items we'd discussed.

"Barb," Virgil said, "did you know I knew Matthew Seward II from several years ago? He's the father of the man who was killed over here."

"I believe Chris mentioned that. Noelle, how's the world of advertising?"

"About the same as always. I'm staying busy. How about the bookstore?"

Barb told them about her new employee and how happy she's been with how well the lady was picking up the business. She also shared that with the new employee she was able to go to supper with me tonight.

Virgil didn't ask me how retirement was progressing, and I didn't ask him how unstopping toilets was going.

Barb and Noelle began a comfortable conversation about the bookstore and advertising. A couple of years ago, Noelle had spent several weeks as a guest of Barb in her condo after Noelle's apartment building burned, so they found no shortage of things to talk about, and no problem cutting Virgil off when he tried to move the conversation to the murders. Noelle also did a good job including Virgil in whatever the ladies were discussing.

The longer we sat, the more comfortable Virgil appeared with Noelle. He wasn't forcing the conversation and at one point told a humorous story about when he was unclogging the sink for one of the tenants in his building. Noelle didn't appear put off by Virgil's "career," and seemed sincerely interested in whatever he chose to talk about.

For Virgil's part, he asked Noelle several questions about the book she was writing and added some good follow-up questions which indicated he was listening to what she'd shared. He'd been a quick study since when she was talking about what had her stumped in completing her novel, he didn't bring the true-live murders into the conversation. He'd also thrown in only one Victorian phrase the entire evening.

I was feeling good about the way dining together was going and glad that Virgil had invited us. I could be wrong, but it appeared that Noelle was having a good time and I hoped only the two of them were together on their next date.

I started to say something about how many restaurants had been at The Washout's location since I'd moved to Folly when a high-pitched siren from one of Folly's patrol cars interrupted my question as it sped past us headed off the island. It was quickly followed by a second patrol car.

Virgil turned and watched the second vehicle speed off island and said, "Wonder what's going on?"

"Probably an accident on Folly Road," Barb said. "Seems like that happens several times a week."

"You can say that again," Noelle said. "Last week I got stuck in the traffic from a wreck for nearly an hour. That's the only thing I don't like about living here and working in downtown Charleston."

Barb smiled. "You're right. The rest of us don't have to make that daily trek."

One of Folly's fire engines provided our next disturbance as it followed the patrol cars' path.

While we were watching the fire apparatus heading off island, Caroline returned to ask if we wanted dessert. Virgil looked at Noelle, who looked at Barb, who slowly shook her head before looking at me.

I figured it was my turn to talk. While everything on the dessert menu, or as the menu called them *Beach Treats*, sounded good, I said I didn't think we wanted anything. Noelle echoed my comment. Caroline then brought our checks. I watched Virgil carefully count out the money to pay for their meals.

As I was paying for Barb and me, I heard an ambulance heading our way from somewhere in Charleston. Its siren stopped before it crossed the bridge to Folly. From the numerous sirens, I guessed the wreck was serious and near the bridge.

We were standing in front of the restaurant's entry. Virgil said he was walking Noelle home, which answered my unasked question from earlier. Barb said she had to return to the store, and I told her I'd walk her there. We exchanged hugs and handshakes and headed to our destinations.

All and all, I thought it was a pleasant evening, made even more pleasant when Virgil relaxed and became more comfortable on his first date with Noelle. Nothing was said, but I suspected it wouldn't be their last.

On the walk home from Barb's Books, I understood how fortunate I was to have such good friends as Virgil and Noelle. I also realized how fortunate Virgil was to have someone who wasn't judging him, judging him for his lack of finances, a job, and whether he let it show or not, his insecurities.

33

The next morning, I was awakened by rain pelting my roof. This was the first significant rain in several days, and I was almost looking forward to it so I wouldn't have to leave the house and could enjoy a peaceful, stress-free day doing little.

My stress-free, doing little day was first interrupted by the phone. Cindy's name appeared on the screen.

I answered with a simple "Hello, Cindy."

She responded with a more complex, "You home?"

"Yes. Why?"

I'm thinking she probably didn't hear my second word since the phone went dead.

Less than a minute later, there was a knock on the front door, with a soaked police chief on the other side when I opened it.

"You been pushing cars out of flooded roads again?" I said as I waved her in.

She removed her raincoat and shook the excess water out of it onto the porch before she left it on a chair and moved into the living room.

She pointed to the kitchen and said, "Any coffee back there?"

"It's brewing."

"Then why are you standing there looking like a statue of an old man?"

"You certainly know how to charm me out of a cup of coffee," I said and headed to the kitchen with Cindy following.

"Charm's my middle name," she said as I got two mugs out of the cabinet and began filling them for my guest, uninvited visitor, or whoever, and me.

She plopped down in one of the chairs at my kitchen table, took a sip, then said, "Know where I've been for the last two hours?"

"From the looks of you, I'd say either swimming or surfing."

"I wish. Unfortunately, I've been over at the Turn of River condos doing a grid search with a couple of my guys and three techs from the Charleston County's Forensic Services Division."

"I don't like the sound of that. What happened?"

"A little after seven last night, we got a call saying someone had been shot at the complex. When we got there, we found Rachel Little beside her Honda Accord. She'd been shot in the head."

I was afraid I knew the answer, but asked anyway, "Dead?"

Cindy nodded.

I shook my head. "That's terrible."

"I'm surprised you didn't already know."

"I was with Barb, Virgil, and Noelle at The Washout when your emergency vehicles responded. We figured it was because of a wreck. Anyone see it happen?"

"Not that we've found. Her car was parked in front of the building, and there were only a few people in condos with most of them being vacationers. The closest we came to a witness was a lady from New Hampshire staying at the condo while waiting for her husband to get back from golfing. She was in the unit and heard a noise but thought it was a car backfiring." She rolled her eyes. "When was the last time you heard a car backfire? Ages, I bet."

"She didn't look or go outside?"

"Of course not. That could've made our job easier, so you know that wasn't going to happen."

"Think it was a robbery gone bad?"

She shook her head. "No, her purse was still in the car, wallet with thirty-five bucks in it untouched."

"Could you tell what kind of gun?"

"I'd guess a small caliber handgun. Won't know for sure until the coroner does his thing."

"I assume Detective Adair made an appearance."

She sighed and said, "Yes. He pulled in the lot looking like a GQ model, looked around, then asked me what I knew of the situation. I told him about Ms. Little's history with Matthew Seward."

"What'd he say?"

"He uttered a profanity, made me proud by the way. Sounded like something I'd say and I'm not even a detective. Anyway, he asked if I thought it was connected to the other two deaths. I told him that's where I'd put my money."

"Did he agree?"

"He said that's where he'd start." She held up her near-empty mug.

I took the hint and refilled it then said, "I ran into Rachel at Harris Teeter a couple of days ago."

"Why am I not surprised?"

"She saw me and came over to speak. I didn't initiate it."

"Okay Mr. Butting In Police Business, did she happen to mention anything about being afraid or threatened?"

"No. The main thing I remember is how she once again said she and Matthew Seward were still dating and planning a Thanksgiving wedding."

"Which means she either was hallucinating, out-and-out lying, or was telling the truth and Matthew was the hallucinator or liar."

"I'd think she was the liar since Matthew's poker buddies said he'd broken up with her which is consistent with what Noelle told me."

"If all we have is what Matthew told them, that still leaves the possibility open that Rachel was telling the truth."

"True," I said, although I doubted it.

"Don't suppose you're going to pull some donuts or a turnover or two out of the cabinet to go with my coffee?"

"Haven't you learned by now if you want something to eat, you pulled into the wrong drive?"

"Yes, I knew it was a longshot to expect a miracle, but thought I'd ask."

"It's not I don't appreciate it, but why did you stop by to tell me about Rachel. Usually, you go out of your way to tell me it's none of my business when something bad happens."

"If you share one word of this with Detective Adair, I'll be attending your funeral."

I smiled. "That almost sounds like a threat."

"If the shoe fits, cram it up your, umm, never mind. The first reason I'm telling you is to keep you from pestering me later today after you learn about the murder from someone else. The second reason is so I could get dry. The third reason is because you, and yes, your buddy Charles, have a better killer catching rate than Detective Adair. Are those enough reasons?"

I smiled and said, "Yes."

"Good, cause that's all I have. I know you're probably going to tell me you're not going to get involved, and if you learn anything that could help the police catch the killer or killers, you'll let us know. I know even if you think you mean that, you don't, so, with that said, like I've told you before, please be careful and try not to get yourself killed nosing where your nose don't belong."

"I'll try."

34

———

After Cindy decided the rain had eased enough to venture out, thanked me for the coffee, and suggested I stock food in the house, she left to fight crime or to find something to eat.

The phone rang before the chief had enough time to get to wherever. This time, Bob Howard's name appeared on the screen.

Again, I tried the civil although boring greeting of, "Hello, Bob."

He replied with, "You getting hungry for one of the best burgers in the free world?"

"Subtle."

"Well, are you?"

"Absolutely."

"A simple yes would've sufficed. What time will you be here?"

Safely assuming he meant at Al's Bar and Gourmet Grill, I said, "Noon."

"Don't be late. No telling how long the line out the door will be waiting for tables."

"I'll risk it."

The next thing I did was call Charles to tell him about Rachel Little and see if he was in the mood for one of the best burgers in the free world. I was afraid I was going to get his voicemail, but after five rings, he answered. Instead of telling him about the recent death over the phone, I asked if he wanted to go to Al's for lunch. He said yes without asking any questions except when I was picking him up. After agreeing on the logistics, his telling me he was reading a biography on Millard Fillmore, and my faking excitement about his reading material, we ended the call.

I spent the next hour trying to remember everything I knew about what now was three deaths. The only connection between Matthew and Foster that I knew about was their poker playing. Beyond that, nothing. According to everything I heard, beyond Matthew who'd dated Rachel, the other players had little contact with her.

The thing I kept coming back to was my top suspect was the latest victim. Plus, when I talked with her in Harris Teeter, I had the feeling she was suspicious of someone regarding Foster Rodman's death. Now I'll never know who.

I pulled into Charles' parking area at eleven since I told him I'd be there at eleven-thirty. The rain had stopped and as I could've predicted, he was outside leaning against his door, and glancing at his wrist after seeing me.

He slid into the front passenger's seat and said, "Get caught in traffic?"

I ignored the comment and said, "Chief LaMond stopped by this morning."

"That what made you late?"

No, your alternate reality did, I thought, but said, "Interested in why she came by the house?"

"Of course."

"Rachel Little was killed last evening."

He jerked his head in my direction so fast that I was afraid he'd pulled a muscle. "Who, what, why, how, where? Oh yeah, why'd you wait to tell me? What time did Cindy leave your house?"

That was enough questions to last the rest of the trip to Al's located on the outskirts of downtown Charleston.

I said, "Cindy left a little while ago, and if you'd like me to tell you what she shared, you'll have to hold the questions until I'm done. Think you can do that?"

"No, but I'll try."

That was the best I could get from him, so I started from the beginning, well almost the beginning. I left out she being soaked and asking if I had any food. Charles only interrupted me a dozen or so times before I found an empty parking space on the road two blocks off Calhoun Street and a block from Al's.

Al's was in a concrete block building it shared with a Laundromat. Both businesses had seen their better days before most high-school students had been born. It was still cloudy, but it appeared as bright as exploding fireworks as compared to the mineshaft-black darkness inside the restaurant. The only illumination was generated by Budweiser and Budweiser Light neon signs behind the bar.

In addition to near pitch darkness, we were greeted by Al Washington, who'd been sitting inside the door. He pushed out of the chair, stood on his eighty-five-year-old legs, and gave me a hug.

"It's been too long, Mr. Chris," he said before facing Charles, giving him a hug, and saying the same thing but substituted Charles for Chris.

"I agree," I said. "How're you doing?"

"Spend a lot of time hiding from the Grim Reaper and staying out of Blubber Bob's way."

I smiled. "I can understand, at least the part about avoiding Bob."

"Hey, old man!" boomed a loud voice from the back of the room, coming from Bob, or Blubber Bob according to Al. "Let those two troublemakers get back here so they can eat and get out before they scare more diners away."

Al patted me on the back and said, "Makes you feel welcome, don't it?"

I looked around and saw Charles and I were the fifth and sixth diner in the restaurant and said, "We must've scared away a bunch of diners."

"No, sir, Mr. Chris, you're getting here gave us the biggest lunch crowd in the last two weeks." He laughed, and added, "You may not want to let the owner know I told you."

"Your secret's good with me."

Being a customer-service-oriented owner, Bob came close to standing up to greet us. Only the table kept his stomach from getting out of his booth. To make up for not standing, he said, "About damn time you got here." He looked toward the grill and yelled, "Lawrence, get your ebony butt over here and take these guys' orders. They're nearly starving from waiting."

Charles and I sat on the opposite side of the table from Bob. Lawrence, Al's cook, who'd worked there for a decade or so for Al when he owned the business and now for Bob, arrived at the table before Bob could say anything else. He asked what he could fix us. I told him two of Al's famous cheeseburgers, two orders of fries, and two soft drinks.

Bob added, "Make that three orders of fries. I'm not going to sit here and wither away while these two wolf down their food. Better add a beer with those fries."

Bob had as much chance of withering away as I did of being crowned Miss Finland.

Lawrence wisely headed to the grill before Bob could lather more love on him.

From the jukebox, Tammy Wynette was bragging on standing by her man. Even though nearly all of Al's customers were African American, due to Bob's friendship with Al that'd spanned decades, he'd salted the jukebox with traditional country music, or according to Bob, the only kind of real music. The rest of the jukebox housed Motown hits from the late-1950s through the mid-1970s.

Bob said, "I see you two haven't been killed yet by whoever's rapidly decreasing the population of your quirky island."

Charles said, "Thanks, Bob. Your kind words warm my heart."

"Your bull manure spewing personality never fails to amaze me."

I said, "Other than wanting us to experience the best cheeseburgers in the southeast, why'd you call?"

"Did you ever think that I may've missed seeing two of my good friends and couldn't wait to rekindle our friendship?"

Charles and I harmonized on, "No."

Bob chucked and said, "Good. Wanted to make sure you hadn't gone senile or loony on me."

After a few more mushy statements, Lawrence arrived with our food, and Bob's extra order of fries. Bob stuffed two fries in his mouth and mumbled, "Since you're both still alive, guess you can tell me if you've caught the killer or killers yet."

"Not yet," Charles said.

"Then you'll thank me for using my warm personality, persuasive charm, and clue-gathering ability to help you solve the crimes."

If anyone else had said that, I would've asked what he or she was talking about. With Bob, silence was the quickest and best way to learn what he was getting at. I took a bite of burger before staring at Al's owner.

"Well," Bob said, "aren't you going to ask?"

"Nope."

"Okay, you twisted my arm. After we talked the other day when I told you I'd met Fritz Goss a while back, I made a couple of calls."

Charles leaned his elbows on the table and looked at Bob. "Who'd you call?"

"I told them I wouldn't divulge their names. They said if what they told me got back to Fritz, he could cause them a heap of hurt. Let's just say they knew more about the dark side of *El Fritzo* than any of us knew."

Charles said, "What'd they say?"

"Damn, Charles, you ever listen to anything all the way through without blurting out interruptions?"

I sat back and smiled, trying to stay out of the crossfire between Bob and Charles.

Instead of answering, Charles stuck a fry in his mouth. Apparently, that satisfied Bob because he said, "One of my anonymous sources said he was a client of Seward Wealth Management. His contact was Matthew III, your first victim, that was until he was meeting with Matthew in their offices. Fritz interrupted the meeting and said he needed to talk to Matthew, and he meant then. Matthew left and my source was left sitting there with his $7,000,000 portfolio in his lap for fifteen minutes. To say he was pissed would've been an understatement."

The sound of Sammi Smith singing "Help Me Make It Through the Night" filled the air. Bob stopped talking, looked toward the juke-box, and said, "I love that song." He then sighed.

I suppose it was okay if he interrupted himself, but I didn't ask.

The song ended, Bob sighed a second time, then said, "Matthew came back into the room and told my source something about the company's policy required Matthew to turn the account over to Fritz. My source tried to say he didn't want to switch, but Matthew said it was out of his hands. Matthew left and Fritz came in all smiles, apologizing for the change, but said that was how it had to be, company policy." He turned to Charles and said, "Don't interrupt, there's more."

Charles held both hands in front of him, palms facing Bob.

"One thing I forgot to tell you about my source. If I told him the North Pole was north of us, he'd find someone who'd disagree with me. Charles, he's a bigger pain than you can be. So, he finagled the names of three of his rich friends who trusted their money to Seward Wealth Management. Claims he called about fifty people to find out who dealt with the firm. Anyway, two of the three said they'd had their portfolios with Matthew III and Fritz reassigned them to himself. He told one of them that what he was telling him was confidential and not to tell anyone. Well, you can see how that went. He told me that Fritz said he would soon be terminating Matthew III."

"Firing him from his dad's company?" Charles said, after remaining silent beyond his comfort level.

Bob glared at him, turned to me, and said, "Yes. Guess when that was?"

I said, "Near the time Matthew was killed?"

"Three weeks. Sounds to me like Fritz's definition of terminated was more terminal than relieving him of his job."

Charles took a deep breath, probably calling up the courage to interrupt Bob, and said, "Because Matthew's dad wouldn't go along with Fritz's plan to fire him."

"That's what it looks like. There's another story my source shared. Said Fritz was embezzling a ton of money from a couple of clients."

I said, "He have proof?"

"Only whispers about it, and that's all I know." Bob looked toward the grill and yelled, "Lawrence, these skinny Caucasians need an extra helping of fries. They need energy to get home."

"Yes, Master Bob, right away," Lawrence said with more than an extra helping of sarcasm.

Bob smiled, looked at Charles and me, and said, "He's a great guy. Wouldn't know what I'd do without him."

I refrained from saying, "It shows."

From the jukebox Jack Greene added to the sounds in the room with "There Goes My Everything."

Bob waited for the song to end, then said, "There you go. I done solved another murder for you." He then turned to face Al sitting beside the door and yelled, "Hey, old man, you ordered the new sign saying *Al's Bar and Detective Agency*?"

"I'll get right on it," Al said, then laughed.

Bob mumbled, "Can't get good help these days."

Lawrence returned with our fuel to get home and quickly retreated to the kitchen.

Apparently, Bob was done solving the murder, and I made what I considered a wise decision not to ask him about the other two murders. I asked how Al's health was holding up. Bob painted a sad picture of the various issues Al was facing. I asked about Bob's wife Betty and was told she was in much better condition than Al but didn't elaborate. We finished the extra fries with minimal conversation.

I told Bob we'd better get home, he told us to pay for our meals and leave an extra-large tip for him to split with Lawrence. I thanked him for all the special attention he'd given to his two customers. He called me a smart-ass, again proving his customer service skills, and we left after goodbye hugs from Al.

35

Traffic was heavy after we left Al's and with a glimmer of sensitivity, Charles remained quiet while I maneuvered my way through vehicles going in all directions until I got to Folly Road.

Silence ended when he said, "Do I need to remind you my number one suspect has been Fritz Goss since we first learned about Matthew's death?"

"I remember."

"Now your buddy Bob confirmed it. You going to call Cindy now and tell her who killed the folks or are you going to make some excuse about waiting to call her later?"

"What am I going to tell her? Bob has an anonymous acquaintance who had Matthew as his contact and then Fritz took over for him. For that reason, Fritz killed Matthew?"

"Sure. That's what he said."

"If someone told me that, I'd say that Matthew may've had reason to murder Fritz and not the other way around."

"If you put it that way, but that's forgetting one point. An important one."

"What's that?"

"Matthew's dead, Fritz ain't."

"I understand, and Fritz may be the killer, but unless we have more to go on than the business dispute between the two, I'm not comfortable going to Cindy or Detective Adair with that."

"What about Fritz stealing from clients? Couldn't that be what Matthew was going to tell Noelle about on the date they never had?"

"Yes, but that rumor comes from an unreliable source."

We were passing Pet Helpers on Folly Road, when Charles said, "You know Carol Linville, the founder of Pet Helpers?"

"Talked to her a couple of times. Why?"

"Just saw the building and was wondering."

"Oh."

"Did you know Millard Fillmore founded a chapter of the American Society for the Prevention of Cruelty to Animals in his hometown of Buffalo, New York?"

That once again reinforced the fact that about the only things that could distract my friend from whatever we were talking about were animals and facts and quotes from U.S. Presidents. Combine the two and nothing could stop him from getting distracted.

"Fascinating."

"Who do you think killed them?"

"I shouldn't talk poorly about your suspect. My last two leading suspects have now been added to the list of victims."

"I don't think I'm going far out on a limb by saying the person who killed Rachel, and most likely Matthew and Foster is alive."

No wonder Charles considers himself a private detective, I thought, but said, "Now I don't have anyone I'd consider a suspect, much less a strong suspect."

"I'm sticking with Fritz."

"You may be right. The only others I know to add are Ron and Austin, but the only reason is because they're the only other people I know of who knew all three victims."

Charles said, "And you thought my suspect was weak. Don't forget, Noelle said someone owed Matthew a bundle of money. That person must be a suspect. And, didn't someone say Matthew owed somebody money."

"Rachel said it but didn't know who."

"That'd be two people who should be on the list."

"Yet we don't know who they are."

"There's that. Don't suppose you want to tell Cindy that at the same time you tell her about Fritz killing Matthew?"

I pulled into my friend's parking lot, rolled the windows down, shut off the motor, turned facing Charles, and said, "What else do we know?"

Charles rubbed his chin, looked toward his apartment door, then looked at me. "Millard Fillmore's favorite color was fuchsia."

I rolled my eyes before saying, "Perhaps I didn't word it well. What else do we know about the three murders that will help us get closer to the identity of the killer or killers?"

"If I knew anything helpful, think I would've shared Fillmore's favorite color?"

The phone rang before I kicked trivia-spouting Charles out of the car. Cindy LaMond's name appeared on the screen.

"Hi, Cindy."

As soon as I said her name, Charles started gyrating his arms, pointing to his ear, then at the phone, his subtle suggestion I put it on speaker. I did and he gave me a thumbs up.

"You taking hubby and me to Hall's Chophouse for supper tonight?"

"No. That why you called?"

"Was worth a try."

I waited for her to tell me the reason for the call.

She finally said, "Aren't you going to ask why I called?"

"No. Figured you'd tell me when you're ready."

"You drive a hard bargain. Okay, here it is. Just got the ballistic report back on the gun that killed Rachel Little. Want to guess what it said?"

"It was the same gun that killed Matthew."

"Wrong, have another guess?"

"Okay, it was the gun that killed Foster."

"Anybody ever tell you your guessing sucks?"

"Are you saying it wasn't the gun that killed either person?"

"Yep."

"Three killings. Three different guns?"

"Yep. Ain't that a hoot?"

"I wouldn't say a hoot, but it opens up about a thousand questions, doesn't it?"

"That's probably underestimating the number. It either means there are three killers or one killer who thinks guns are for a single use like toilet paper."

I would've preferred a different analogy, but moved past it and said, "Has Detective Adair said anything that would lead you to think there is more than one killer?"

"Not really. Seems to me although different weapons have been used, there are too many similarities in the deaths to think more than one person was responsible."

"Charles and I had lunch at Al's."

"And didn't invite me?"

"I knew it wouldn't compare with Hall's Chophouse, so didn't think you'd want to go."

"Smart aleck."

Charles was nodding his head but didn't say anything.

"Is it safe to say you're telling me about lunch for a reason other than making me jealous?"

"Bob Howard told us something about Fritz Goss he thought may be related to the deaths." I proceeded to share what Bob had told us. I was impressed that Charles kept quiet the entire time.

"That sounds more like a reason for Matthew to shoot Fritz rather than the other way around unless the embezzlement rumor was true, and Fritz learned that Matthew found out about it."

"That's what I thought but wanted you to know."

"I think that's more than Adair knows, so I'll share it with him. But don't worry, if he thinks it's the most stupid thing he's heard, I'll be sure and tell him it came from you."

"Thanks."

She probably didn't hear me since she'd ended the call.

I looked over at Charles and shrugged.

"I agree with that shrug. Three deaths, three guns, zero good suspects, and I'm beginning to get one headache."

He left me on that cheerful note.

36

Three victims, three guns. Regardless of how I tried to think about anything but the deaths the next morning, that fact dominated my thoughts. Actually, that thought battled with me thinking about what Bob Howard had said about Fritz Goss and how he'd yanked clients away from Matthew or the rumor about him stealing from clients. I still couldn't picture Fritz killing Matthew Seward, much less ending Foster Rodman's and Rachel Little's lives. Sure, he and Matthew could have had a strained working relationship, possibly intense anger issues with each other, but the leap to murder, or three murders, struck me as going too far.

Even if Fritz had killed Matthew and the two others, what could I possibly do to prove it? Why am I even thinking about it? Wasn't it the responsibility of law enforcement to solve the crimes? Yet, three murders, three guns popped up again. Nothing about that made sense.

The phone ringing saved me from pulling out hair I didn't have while trying to come to some logical conclusion.

I said, "Hello."

"This is your stalker."

I laughed and said, "Hi, Noelle."

"Is this a good time to talk?"

"I didn't know stalkers cared about things like that."

"I'm still working on my stalking technique."

"Then, yes, this is a good time."

"Remember I told you I first met Matthew at a New Year's Eve party at Austin Middleton's house?"

"Yes."

"Today at work, a project I was working on reminded me of that party and I started trying to remember everything I could about it. To be honest, I couldn't remember much. It was a pretty boring event unless you get excited about seeing a bunch of rich, white guys bragging on how much they could drink and remain vertical."

"And to think, nobody invited me."

I heard her laugh before saying, "I'll be sure and invite you if I get invited to another one. Bragging on how much fun I had wasn't the reason I called. I didn't remember much about the night except there was one guy there who seemed to be a friend of Matthew's. To be honest, I didn't remember even meeting him, but according to my notes, the man was talking with Matthew when Austin took me over to introduce me to Matthew."

"Your notes?"

"Did you forget that I'm obsessed with research for my book? I take notes about most everything. Anyway, after you and I talked, I went back to see if I noted anything about that night that I didn't mention to you. And I did."

"I'm impressed. Don't suppose the guy mentioned that he was planning on killing Matthew?"

"Of course not."

"What'd your notes say about meeting him?"

"He was talking to Matthew when Austin took me over." I heard what sounded like papers rustling in the background. "Okay, here's what I wrote, 'Austin introduced me to Matthew Seward III.' I'll leave out what I wrote next. It's about my first impression of Matthew. Anyway, I said, 'Introduced to Trace Spellman—5' 11", curly black hair, brown eyes, expensive clothes, talked fast—and was told by

Matthew that Trace was someone he did some friendly gambling with. Trace acted a little strange, possibly angry, when Matthew said that.' Then I wrote some more stuff about Matthew."

"That's interesting. Have any idea what you meant when you said Trace acted strange when Matthew said they did some friendly gambling?"

"No. Like I said, I didn't remember meeting him. Even after reading my notes, nothing came back about it."

"Was anything said about where Trace lives or what he does for a living?"

"Not that I recall."

"That could be helpful."

"Sorry I didn't put more in my notes. I was more impressed with Matthew. Tell you what I'll do, I'll go back through all my notes about Matthew and see if there is any mention of Trace."

"Good. I'll ask around and see if anyone knows this Trace Spellman character."

"Chris, thanks for listening. It's probably nothing, but who knows?"

"I appreciate your letting me know. While you're on the phone, any more dates with Virgil on the horizon?"

I heard her laugh again, before saying, "Yes, bye."

Noelle didn't know if Trace Spellman lived on Folly, but if anyone did, it'd be Councilmember Marc Salmon. While I didn't know Trace Spellman, there was a much better than average chance I knew where Marc Salmon would be, the same place I could fill my stomach with French toast.

"Good morning, Amber," I said as she greeted me at the Lost Dog Cafe's entry.

She smiled and said, "Morning, Chris. One?"

I looked over her shoulder and spotted Marc Salmon and Houston Bass seated at their regular table in the center of the room.

"Yes," I said and pointed to a table against the side wall.

Amber headed to the large coffee urn, and I headed to the councilmembers' table.

Marc saw me approach and said, "Well, if it isn't my favorite private detective."

"Marc, you're mistaking me for Charles."

Houston smiled and said, "That's not Marc's first mistake this morning. He's on the wrong side of the new ordinance I'm proposing. It's about short-term rentals and—"

Marc interrupted his tablemate. "Houston, Chris doesn't want to hear about our legislative differences."

I waited patiently while the two elected officials finished their sniping, then said, "Marc, I figured if anyone would know if someone lived on Folly it'd be you."

Flattery goes a long way with Councilmember Salmon.

Marc sat up straight and smiled. "Maybe not everyone," he said then shrugged.

Probably his effort at acting humble.

"Do you know Trace Spellman?"

Houston interrupted. "If he's registered to vote, Marc will know him."

Marc ignored Houston's comment and said, "Yes, he lives in one of those big houses on Shadow Race Lane. Got his own private walking pier over the marsh. Why?"

"His name came up in a conversation I was having with someone, and I didn't know him, but knew if anyone did, it'd be you. Other than where he lives, you know anything else about him?"

"Owns Class Realty."

"I don't recall seeing their signs over here."

"It's fairly new. Trace worked for Century 21 for years, made tons of money, then decided that wasn't enough and opened his own firm about a year ago."

I said, "Anything else?"

"He's married, wife works at a bank on James Island, he's in his 40s, seems friendly, but what realtor doesn't?" He said and smiled. "Anyway, he drives a new Lincoln SUV and doesn't hesitate to tell anyone who'll listen that he's one of the state's top realtors."

Houston said, "Marc probably knows the guy's shirt size, shoe size, and social security number."

Marc showed why he and Houston get along so well each morning. He ignored him and said, "Why do you want to know?"

"Like I said, someone mentioned him, and I was curious. He ever come in here?"

"Curious, right. Saw him in here a few times but not recently."

I wasn't ready to tell Marc why I was curious, so I said, "Better let you two continue your breakfast. Thanks for the information."

"Yes," Marc said, "we never get enough time to talk about how we can improve our city."

Yeah, I'm sure that's what they do in here nearly every morning, I thought, but repeated, "Thanks for the information," and headed to my table where my coffee was getting cold.

Amber saw me at the table, grabbed a plate from the window into the kitchen, poured a fresh cup of coffee, and headed my way.

"You're an angel," I said as she replaced my cold coffee and set the plate of French toast in front of me.

"Were they giving you a civics lesson?"

"Yes, telling me how much work the legislative branch of city government has to do and all the sacrifices they make for the betterment of Folly."

Amber laughed. "And to think, I left my violin at home."

I smiled. "Do you know Trace Spellman?"

"The realtor?"

"That's what Marc said."

"Don't know him outside of him coming in here. Seems like a friendly fellow. Maybe a little stuck on himself. Why?"

"Someone mentioned him, and I didn't know who he was. He come in by himself?"

"Comes in alone but he either sits with someone who's already here or someone comes in and joins him."

"Any familiar faces around?"

"A couple of them are in occasionally, but I don't know who they are. Whenever they're with Spellman they appear to be meeting, spreading paperwork out on the table, or doing something on laptops. May have to do with real estate since I sometimes see fact sheets like are at houses for sale." She glanced around the room and said, "I'd better get back to work. Let me know if you need anything else."

"Thanks, and I will."

My trip to the Dog had proved to be productive. I fed both my curiosity and my stomach. But it still didn't answer my question. Who killed the three people?

37

———————

On the walk home, I wondered why I was so curious about Trace Spellman. After all, the only connection he had with the murders was he was talking to Matthew Seward at a New Year's Eve party Noelle had attended. Hardly evidence that'd connect him to the deaths. I hated to admit it, but I suppose the reason for my interest simply was because in addition to Austin Middleton, Ron Dillon, and Fritz Goss, Trace was the only name I'd heard who had anything to do with the first victim.

He was still on my mind when I got home, so instead of trying to forget Trace, I called Bob Howard to see if he knew anything about him.

"Have I told you how much I hate driving in this damn Charleston traffic?" Bob said as his response to me saying, "Bob, this is Chris."

"Can't say you have, although it's been many years since you'd driven me anywhere. Want me to call back when you reach wherever you're going?"

I heard a horn blowing, and another profanity from the person on the other end of the phone, before he said, "Hell no, I can multitask.

Besides, if I get killed in the wreck I'm about to be in, I want you to suffer along with me."

"That's what friends are for. Do you know Trace Spellman?"

"Why, is he dead and you're trying to find out who killed him so the police could take the day off?"

"As far as I know, he's alive. Someone mentioned him this morning and since I heard he's a realtor, I thought you might know him."

"There are more than 1,700 real estate agents in Charleston. I'm rather brilliant and extraordinarily knowledgeable, if I say so myself, but even I can't know them all."

Two more sounds of a horn blasted through the speaker.

"I hope you're a brilliant driver. Sure you don't want me to call back?"

"Hell no, as soon as I run the guy in front of me off the road, I'll have a clear shot to work. Yes."

"Yes what?"

"Did you already forget what you asked?"

"You know Trace Spellman?"

"Not personally but know of him."

"What do you know?"

"You want the PR drivel or the rumors?"

"What do you think?"

"I think I'm going to grab that spot in the no parking zone, so I don't have as far to walk to get to Al's."

No, I didn't remind him it may be a *no parking zone* for a reason, but instead I said, "Rumors about Trace Spellman?"

"Chris, most of the people I still know in real estate are, how shall I say it, umm, old farts. They're older than dirt but not as useful."

"Your point?"

"The guy you're asking about is half their age, so they probably have little, if any, direct interactions with the younger realty hotshots, of which Mr. Spellman is one."

"But regardless, one or more of them have told you something about Spellman?"

"Hell no, I just wanted to make sure what kind of information you wanted about him. Let me make a couple of calls and get back with you."

I would've thanked him and told him I appreciated what he was doing. I saw little need to tell that to the dead phone, hopefully because Bob had hung up rather than been killed in a wreck.

A little after 1:00 p.m. the phone rang, and I was surprised to see Bob's name on the screen.

"That was quick," I said instead of *hello*.

"That's because I don't have all day to play Wikipedia for you. It's hard and time consuming running this fine dining and drinking establishment."

I was tempted to laugh but didn't want to deter the hardworking restaurant and bar owner from sharing whatever he'd learned about Spellman.

"I appreciate all your hard work," I said with a straight face.

"Your sarcasm can use some work. Anyway, I talked to two realtors I know who aren't senile or suffering from Alzheimer's, so they were the best contacts I still have. You ready to take notes?"

"Do I need to?"

"Hell yes, I may say something important."

"Okay, let me grab a pen." I didn't have to go far since I already had one in my hand, in case he did say something important. "Got it, what do you have?"

"First the PR hogwash. Mr. Spellman was in the top ten percent of Lowcountry realtors for two consecutive years when he was with Century 21. Mr. Bigshot specialized in beachfront properties since that's where the big bucks are. Then he told anyone who'd listen that he wanted to open his own shop. Long story short, he made the switch about a year ago and named his company Class Realty, whatever that means." He hesitated then said, "You may now praise me for learning all that."

"That's it?"

"No, that's the end of the PR hogwash."

"On to the rumors?"

"Damn, you're not nearly as dumb as you look."

"Thanks, coming from you, that's great."

"Still no better with the sarcasm."

I sighed. "Bob, what are the rumors?"

"My source says the management at Century 21 got so sick of Spellman's bragging, badmouthing their other agents, unethical practices, and overall obnoxiousness, they kicked him out of the company. That's big because he was their top producer. I also heard that he gambled away a lot of his commissions."

"Interesting. Anything else?"

"Crap, you think I'm a miracle worker?"

"So, that's it?"

"No, I am a miracle worker. Spellman's also rumored to be up to his Botoxed forehead in debt on his McMansion on Folly. Now that's it."

"I appreciate it, Bob."

"Appreciate it enough to tell me why all of a sudden you're curious about Mr. Spellman?"

"I heard he was a friend of Matthew Seward."

"Aha, now it's making sense. You're thinking Spellman killed Matthew, and probably the other unfortunate victims?"

"I have no idea. I just learned about his friendship with Matthew this morning."

"Then don't forget, when you're granting all those interviews with the media about how you solved the murders, tell them you couldn't have done it without your buddy Bob. Would talk longer, but I've got to get with Al to see if he's ordered the *Al's Bar and Detective Agency* sign." Bob's phone went dead after he said, "You're welcome."

38

I called Charles as soon as I got off the phone to share what I'd learned from conversations with Cindy, Noelle, and Bob.

"He answered with, "Coming around to my way of thinking that the killer is Fritz?"

"No. I wanted to share what I'd learned from a call from Noelle, what Marc Salmon told me, and my two calls with Bob Howard."

"When did all that happen? Why didn't you tell me you were going to talk with them? I could've helped. Two detectives' heads are better than one assistant detective, you know. Why didn't you call earlier? Why—"

Enough, I thought, and said, "All of that happened this morning. I got off the phone with Bob seconds before I called you."

"A bit cranky, are we?"

"Do you want to hear what I learned or wait until tomorrow when you can gripe about my not telling you closer to when I talked with them?"

"How about now?"

"Then, how about letting me talk, interruption free, if possible?"

"Crankeeeeeee."

"Want to hear it?"

"What're you waiting for?"

I shared what I'd learned from Noelle, my brief discussion with Marc, then my two calls from Bob. Charles only interrupted twice, which told me I should get cranky more often so he'd listen with minimal interruptions.

"You've had a busy morning. Do you know Trace?"

"All I know is what Marc told me. I don't think I've ever met him or know what he looks like. Do you know him?"

"Does he have a dog?"

"How would I know? And, what's that have to do with anything?"

"If he had a dog, I might've talked to him or his dog without knowing his name."

"Whatever."

"Since you mentioned him, does that mean you're adding him to your suspect list?"

"Don't you mean our suspect list?"

"No, my list has one name on it: Fritz Goss, the killer. I didn't hear you say anything that'd make Trace a suspect, other than one thing, that is."

"What's that?"

"When you said Century 21 fired him because of unethical practices."

I was impressed. Charles did occasionally listen to what I was saying.

"Why would that potentially put him on your list?"

"Don't know the highfalutin technical definition of unethical, but in my mind killing three people would be in it somewhere."

"All we know is Trace Spellman attended a party, was talking with Matthew, and was introduced to Noelle."

"Hey," Charles said, "you're the one with him on your list."

"True. He's definitely not a strong suspect but seems he's as good a suspect as Ron Dillon or Austin Middleton."

"See, you just made my point. None of those three are good suspects, so the only person who had a good enough reason to be killing people is Fritz Goss. Next time you talk to Cindy, let her know who the killer is."

"I'll keep that in mind."

"Good, now I've got to make a delivery for Dude."

I hadn't learned much from my call with Charles except he was convinced that Fritz Goss was the killer. Charles could be right, but it still didn't seem feasible. Unless there was a motive I was unaware of, he wouldn't be at the top of my list.

I didn't get to confuse myself more because the phone rang with Cindy's name on the screen.

"Morning, Cindy."

"Crap, you didn't have to remind me. This day must be sucky bad. This morning's already two days long."

"Sorry to hear it. Did you call to let me know about your sucky day, umm, morning?"

"No, guess who Detective Adair had a call from a little while ago."

"I have no idea."

"You wouldn't have guessed it anyway."

"So, who?"

"Matthew Seward II."

"Why'd he call?"

"Said he was going through some papers he'd left in the house on East Arctic and found one that wasn't his."

"Did it name his son's killer?"

"Adair said Matthew II told him the writing appeared to be his son's."

"What made it so special that he called Adair? His son lived in that house, so couldn't there have been several notes or papers or whatever left there? Grocery lists, to-do lists, letters, on-and-on."

"I asked Adair that. He said Matthew II said the paper he was calling about was in the wall safe and not with his son's other things."

"Was there anything else that belonged to Matthew III in the safe?"

"Yeah, he said Matthew had a couple of watches. Apparently, he had his everyday watch, an Apple one that's smarter than all of us combined, and a much more expensive one he wore on special occasions when he was trying to impress a client. The expensive one was in the safe. The sheet of paper and the watch were the only things belonging to Matthew in there."

"I have no idea how large the safe was or how much it contained, but it seems weird one sheet of paper and a watch were the only things in it belonging to the victim. And, if there was only one sheet of paper, why did Matthew II think it was important enough to tell Adair about it? Seems strange."

"None of it makes sense, does it?"

"Not to me."

Cindy said, "I asked Adair if the father said anything else about the contents of the safe or why he felt the need to let the police know about the paper. He said there wasn't anything else. He simply thought the paper may've been important. To be honest, he seemed bored with the subject. Adair said it didn't sound like it was anything important but asked Matthew II to scan it and send it to the Sheriff's Office."

"Did Adair ask Matthew II what he thought it meant?"

"Yes, he didn't know."

"After Adair got it, did he figure out its significance?"

"No, said it was what looked like initials and numbers beside them. It wasn't clear what the numbers meant but seemed to him that they were money amounts."

"Did the detective share a copy with you?"

"Yes."

"Cindy, why don't—"

She interrupted with, "To show you how brilliant a chief I am, let me guess what you were going to ask."

"Okay."

"You were going to ask me to send you a copy. How'd I do?"

"Amazing. You never cease to amaze me."

"The answer is no."

"Maybe I could help figure out what it is and what it means."

"That's true."

"So why not send it to me, or I could come by your office to get it."

"Nope."

"Why not?"

"Because if you'd get on your computer instead of begging me to let you have a copy, you'd see I sent it to you before I called."

"Oh, then thank you."

"You're welcome. Let me know when you know what it means."

I assured her I would.

Cindy was right. She'd sent me an email before she'd called. I downloaded and printed a copy of the attached document. From the yellow color of the paper, it appeared to be from a standard letter-sized writing pad. There was no heading on the sheet to give a hint of the meaning of what followed. On the left side of the paper, there were neatly printed letters on every other line, five sets in all. Next to each set of letters there were numbers, with some marked out.

The document read:

ML~~7000~~

R? ~~500~~~~300~~*475*

DP~~11000~~ ~~53500~~ *47200*

LA1700

SR~~1200~~

Nothing else was on the paper. I stared at the printed copy, carried it to the kitchen, grabbed a can of Diet Pepsi from the refrigerator, and sat at the table. Five more minutes of staring left me realizing I didn't know more about the document than I did when I saw it on the computer screen. If I had to guess, I'd say the numbers indicated money that was either owed to Matthew III or money he owed to someone. I didn't think it would be too big a leap to say the letters were initials of the people who owed Matthew or who Matthew owed.

If those assumptions were correct, the initials led nowhere in determining who killed the three people. None of the letters were the initials of the suspects we'd identified. The only initials that ended with the letter of the last name of any of our suspects were *ML* which could be Rachel Little although the first letter didn't correspond.

Unless Rachel was her first name and her middle name started with the letter *M* or vice versa, there was no connection to any of our suspects.

Even more frustrating, if my assumptions were correct about the letters representing peoples' initials, and the numbers reflecting money owed to Matthew or money he owed others, our suspect pool could increase from three people to eight.

Thanks a lot, Matthew III.

___

The next morning, I woke up with a splitting headache. On my way to the kitchen to fire up Mr. Coffee I grabbed three ibuprofen tablets from the bathroom. Ten minutes later, with the drugs addressing my headache and coffee slowly waking me up, I sat at the kitchen table trying to awaken my brain enough to sort through what I'd learned about the three deaths and their suspected killer or killers.

Charles was right. I was cranky, quick to jump on anything or anyone I found uncomfortable or didn't agree with my views. Over the years, I'd prided myself on handling criticism and uncomfortable discussions without attacking the person I had disagreements with. Lord knows, I'd gotten plenty of practice in my human relations career. Even after retiring and moving to Folly, I thought I'd handled difficult situations with a calm exterior even though inside I was furious or terrified. So, why the change?

I hated to admit it, but the thought that age catching up with me contributed to my discomfort and shortness with my friends. Yes, there had been three murders, but why would this senior citizen with no law enforcement training or responsibility want to get involved? I didn't know the victims other than from brief casual interactions. I was at least twice the age of each victim.

When I'd first moved here, I'd been dragged into murder investigations by some of my new friends. Sure, we'd successfully helped the police solve the crimes. After a while, it took less and less encouragement from others for me to get involved in solving crimes that Chief LaMond and a couple of detectives from the Charleston County Sheriff's Office rightly had said were none of my business. But most of those times, I either knew the victim or the alleged perpetrator more than through a brief encounter which inspired me to get involved or one or more of my friends had a relationship with the victim or alleged perpetrator. Should I have gotten involved? Absolutely not, but I did, even at great risk to myself and my friends.

My headache had eased, but my reluctance to get involved in the most-recent murders hadn't lessened. Could my internal conflict over being involved be the cause of what Charles called my crankiness? If true, it seems there are only one of two ways to return to being me, whatever that is. The first, and probably the right way would be to tell my friends who feel they have a role in catching the killer or killers to count me out. The other way, the most potentially dangerous way, the way those who are charged with solving crimes clearly resent is for me to continue digging and hoping to identify the person or persons responsible for the deaths.

I stared at the copy of the paper Matthew III had left in the safe and concluded the same thing I'd thought seconds after I first saw the document. If there were clues on it, I couldn't see them. And from what Cindy told me, neither had she nor had Detective Adair. This was even more reason to step aside.

I took my coffee, moved to the living room, and plopped down in the recliner. Instead of thinking about the deaths, I started thinking about what'd made me happier and more content after moving to Folly than anything I'd experienced in my first five decades living in Kentucky. Sure, being retired and not having to go to work five and often more days a week was a huge factor, but wouldn't that have been the same if I'd remained in the Commonwealth of Kentucky?

Living within a five-minute walk to the ocean, was another big plus, something I couldn't do living six-hundred miles from here. Being within a fifteen-minute drive to Charleston, one of the most beautiful and historic cities in the country, was another huge plus.

All of those things contributed to my happiness, but what did they do to my desire, no, my need to feel I've contributed something to society, contributed something that will live after I'm gone? I've answered that or similar questions several times over the last decade. The answer is so simple, it often slips my mind. Did that make sense? Probably not, but it was the truth. The answer can be summarized in one word: friendships.

Looking back, I'd developed more friendships since moving to Folly than in my time in Kentucky. I'm talking about true friendships, not simply situational friendships many of us accumulate throughout our jobs, neighbors, or organizations in which we participate. The friendships I'm talking about are with people who would do anything for me, and vice versa. I count as true friends Charles, Bob, Al, Burl, Cindy, William Hansel, Cal, Larry, and more recently, Virgil and Noelle. A few of them have risked their lives for me, and I for them.

I took a deep breath, slowly shook my head, as I realized before I'd left the kitchen, the smart thing would be to step aside and leave catching criminals to law enforcement. Now here I am in the living room, realizing true friendships contributed more to my approach to life than anything else. If I stepped aside, I would be letting down Noelle who had dated Matthew III, Charles who considered it his job to catch bad guys, and a few others who have provided answers to questions about the deaths.

My headache was now gone, attributable to ibuprofen or my decision to do whatever I could to learn the identity of the person or persons who murdered three people. My only hope is my devotion to my friends didn't get me killed.

I picked up the phone, tapped in Charles's number, and when he answered said, "Where do you want to meet me?"

"Why would we be meeting?"

"To hear what I learned about something Matthew II found in the

East Arctic Avenue house and to figure what we have to do next to catch a killer, or more than one killer."

"The Atlantic Office of Fowler Private Detective Agency."

"See you in fifteen minutes."

I WAS glad Charles had chosen the *Atlantic Office of Fowler Private Detective Agency*. It was only one of his imaginary offices for his imaginary agency, but it was the most scenic with an amazing view of much of the beach. The weather was perfect with a few puffy-white clouds dotting the blue sky and the temperature in the low 70s. Of course, my friend was already seated on a bench when I arrived.

I told him it was a beautiful day, he told me I was late. He would've complained more about me *being late* had he not been distracted by the sheet of paper in my hand.

He pointed to the paper and said, "Is that a written confession?"

"What do you think?"

"Suppose that means no. So, why'd you call this meeting?"

I handed him the paper, told him how I came to have it, and my initial thoughts about what the letters and numbers meant. He started scrutinizing the document as if it were an original copy of the Declaration of Independence. I took that time to watch a couple of gulls squawking about something only they understood, and a nearby angler staring at his fishing rod before searching for something in his red tackle box. At Charles's current pace, the fisherman could've rebaited his hook, caught a fish, and packed up to leave, before my friend finished staring at the document.

He finally turned to me and said, "It makes sense that you're right about the letters being people's initials. I think I'd even agree the numbers represent money." He nodded then continued, "Which leads me to say all we have to do now is figure out the names that go with the initials, and what the dollar amounts mean."

"And don't forget. We also need to see if the paper had anything to do with the three deaths. I can see Matthew leaving an expensive watch in the safe, but to leave one sheet of paper in there doesn't make sense unless it's important."

"Did Cindy have any idea what it meant?"

"Not that she mentioned and apparently neither did Detective Adair."

"See, that's more proof it's up to us to catch the killer or killers," Charles said and tapped his cane on the pier.

"That's easier said than done."

Charles pointed to the list of initials. "Are these initials of anyone we know or any of the people we know about who knew Matthew, or heck, anyone else that's been mentioned?"

"The only person we've talked about related to the deaths who has the first initial from this group is Rachel Little."

"Okay, if the *R* stood for Rachel, what's the question mark after it?"

"I don't know, but the only person we know about who has the last initial from this group is the *ML*, also Rachel Little."

"If one of the five is Rachel, she can't be both."

I was tempted to say, "Duh," but instead agreed with him. I then pointed out the initials of his top suspect Fritz Goss appear nowhere in the group.

"Are you saying if I'm right about the killer being Fritz, the list is meaningless since he doesn't appear?"

"Charles, all I'm saying is we don't know what it means. If you noticed, the *M* in *ML* could stand for Matthew himself."

"Since this is my Atlantic office of my detective agency, allow me to summarize. I, and from what you've said, you have no idea what the stuff on that piece of paper means."

"Excellent summary."

"Who do we know who may have some idea what it means?"

"Noelle could possibly recognize the initials belonging to someone Matthew mentioned on their dates. Then there are the two remaining members of Matthew's poker group."

"Austin Middleton and Ron Dillon."

"Yes."

"Any ideas how we can talk with each of them without looking like we're being nosy?"

That'd never stopped Charles from being nosy. I didn't know how to talk with the two poker buddies, but getting with Noelle would be much easier.

I said, "Let me call Noelle. I think I can meet with her and get her take on the lists."

Charles looked at my phone that I had on the bench beside me, and said, "What are you waiting for?"

"She's at work. I'll call this evening."

"Okay, if you want to delay catching the killer, I guess we'll have to live with it."

"Thanks."

"I think I'll do what I do best. After I adjourn this meeting, I'll wander around the island until I run into Austin or Ron, say howdy, then ask them about the names on the list."

"That sounds like a plan," I said, and thought, *a poor one.*

Charles nodded, smiled, tapped his cane on the pier, and said, "Meeting adjourned."

40

I waited until six o'clock to give Noelle time to get home from work. After five rings, I was afraid my call would rollover into voicemail. Instead, she said, "Hey, Chris, hold a sec." I heard a horn blow then Noelle returned. "Sorry about that. I had to get around a beer truck stopped in the middle of Folly Road."

"Want me to call back?"

"No, I'm fine now."

"I thought you'd be home."

"Yeah, me too. That was before my boss asked me to revise the copy on an ad for a gym I've been working on. I'm sure you didn't call to hear my sad story about having to change the copy in five ads I worked on for the last three weeks because the client didn't like me calling his gym a gym."

"What'd he want you to call it?"

"A large fitness studio."

"Sounds like a gym to me."

"Exactly. Aren't you glad you called?" She laughed. "Other than calling to ask what I spent this afternoon doing, was there another reason for your call?"

"I was going to see if you could meet for a few minutes so I could bounce something off you, but it sounds like you've had a busy enough day."

"I'm supposed to meet Virgil in an hour at Lowlife Bar. I'll arrive in about twenty minutes if you want to meet me there."

"Sounds good."

Lowlife Bar was in the 100 block of East Hudson Ave. and behind the Circle K convenience store. The bar is in the lower level of a three-story building and prides itself on being a casual beach bar serving a wide range of cocktails and varieties of food.

It was four blocks from the house, so I walked and was there ten minutes before Noelle indicated she'd arrive. I was greeted by Mick Kelly as I took one of the seats at the outside bar that opens to the interior dining room. I'd known him for several years and long before he was one of Lowlife's bartenders.

"Hey, Chris. What can I get you?"

"White wine."

Mick chuckled and said, "I can always count on you to order an exotic drink to challenge my mixology skills."

He managed to prepare my exotic concoction and deliver it before saying, "I hear you and Charles are going to catch the person who killed three of our citizens."

"You know better than to listen to rumors."

"Are you saying you're not meddling in what we pay Folly's finest to do?"

"Merely curious, my friend. Merely curious."

He laughed. "History tells me otherwise. So, with that out of the way, any good suspects?"

"Not really. Did you know any of the victims?"

"Foster Rodman was a regular. Came in nearly every day after work. Nice guy, quiet, seemed a little insecure."

"Why insecure?"

"Kinda shy, I guess. He never said it, but I had the impression that he was ashamed of his job."

"Why would he be ashamed of it. He worked at a tire store up Folly Road, didn't he?"

"Think it was because of the guys he played poker with. I don't know for sure, but think one owned his own company, another one was a bigshot in his family business. He didn't say this, mind you, but I figure he thought the others had money or came from money, and Foster didn't have much."

"Did you know Matthew Seward, the first man killed?"

Mick looked around like he wanted to see if anyone was listening, then leaned closer to me with his elbows rested on the bar. "Never met him but heard from a couple of people he liked to play big shot."

"Meaning?"

"Held parties at his big oceanfront house. Not necessarily to be friendly, but to show off what he owned, although I heard the place belonged to his parents."

"Anything else about him?"

"Heard he liked to play bank."

"Explain."

"He'd float loans to people who owed him money, like he didn't need to be repaid and was doing them a big favor. If you ask me, he wanted people to think he was rich."

"That's interesting. Do you remember who told you that?"

"Afraid not. I talk to tons of people in here. I'm lucky if I remember my own name by the time I get off work. Sorry."

"Did you know Rachel Little, the third victim?"

"Don't think so. I didn't recall ever hearing her name until I heard she'd been killed."

"How about Austin Middleton, Ron Dillon, or Trace Spellman?"

"Don't recall meeting any of them. I know that Dillon owns a plumbing company, seen their trucks around. One of the tenants upstairs uses them. I believe Spellman is a realtor, owns Class Realty."

"How do you know that?"

"He or someone from that company left business cards with us a couple of weeks ago. Was under the impression it's a new company and they're trying to drum up business by giving cards to every business over here."

"Anything else?"

He shook his head, smiled, and said, "Let's see if I have this right. You're asking a zillion questions because you're, umm, believe your words were *merely curious*?"

Noelle saved me from stumbling through an answer when she sat on the chair beside me. This was only the second time I'd seen her in her work clothes, this time consisting of navy-blue slacks, a light-blue blouse, and black dress shoes.

Mick turned his attention to the recent arrival and said, "Hey, Noelle. You sure you want to sit beside this old codger?"

She smiled at Mick and said, "I have a nosy senior citizen in my novel and like to observe Chris to see how a geezer acts."

I said, "You two do know I can hear you."

Mick said, "Whoops. I thought old people were hard of hearing." He laughed and asked Noelle if she wanted the regular.

She nodded and he headed to the far side of the bar.

"I see you survived your drive home."

"Barely. Traffic gets worse every year, even when I leave work this late. You don't have to deal with it."

"That's a plus for being retired, although being an *old codger* and a *geezer* are on the negative side of the scales."

"Is it safe to say, you didn't want to meet me to listen to two young-sters insult you, simply because you're older than we are?"

I took the copy of the page found in the safe at the Seward house, unfolded it, and slid it in front of Noelle. She looked at it then at me and said, "What am I looking at?"

I explained where the original had been and how it came to be in my possession.

She stared at it for another minute, and said, "If the main char-acter in my novel came across something like this while trying to learn who the killer was, he'd call it a clue."

"I think it'd fit the definition."

Mick set Noelle's drink in front of her. She took a sip of what looked like a frozen pina colada, but I wouldn't dare ask so I wouldn't be accused of being too old to know.

She took a second sip then said, "The difference between my novel and real life is in the novel, I would know what the clue means. I have no idea what this is or what it means. Do you?"

"That's why I wanted to meet. I have no idea but was hoping Matthew said something when you were dating that'd help me understand it. I'd guess the letters are initials of people's names. Do you recall if Matthew ever mentioned anyone who could match the initials?"

She looked down at the paper, shook her head, and said, "Matthew was a big name-dropper. It was like he thought the more names he could drop the more important people would think he was. I'm not saying he didn't mention someone on this list, but nothing is coming to mind."

"That's what I was afraid of. It was a long shot. Now another question, I recently heard Matthew often carried the debts of people who owed him money and didn't demand payment as soon as the person should've paid him."

She shook her head. "I know he did. I asked him about it once and he said some people didn't have much money. The way he said it, made me think what he really meant was he had plenty and didn't need to collect. In other words, pure ego." She smiled. "One more reason I didn't see us going anywhere with our relationship."

"Interesting," I said and pointed at the paper still in front of Noelle. "Do you think these numbers could be amounts people owed Matthew?"

"With the crossed-out numbers being amounts repaid or changes in the total owed?"

"Yes."

"Could be but he also liked working puzzles so this could mean anything."

I felt someone tap me on the back. I turned to see Virgil who said, "Christopher, are you replacing me as the person meeting the lovely, young Noelle this evening?"

I smiled. "No one can ever replace you."

Noelle smiled at Virgil and said, "Chris was keeping me company until my knight in shining armor arrived."

Virgil gave an exaggerated bow and said, "Noelle, it's no wonder why you're in advertising."

I turned to Vigil then to Noelle and said, "You've been helpful. I'll leave you two to—"

Virgil interrupted, "Nonsense, join us." He turned to Mick who'd returned to the bar and said, "Barkeep Mick, is there a vacant table inside where we might reconvene this gathering?"

I looked at Noelle who shrugged, then at Mick who said, "Give us a few minutes to clean one, then come in."

"You're a lifesaver," Virgil said and then turned to Noelle. "That's okay with you, isn't it?"

"Of course."

Virgil said, "Wonderful. What's that document the two of you were pondering when I arrived?"

Several people had gathered near us at the outside bar. I said, "I'll tell you when we get inside."

After four minutes of awkward conversation, our table was ready and we entered the rustic, eclectically decorated dining room. Noelle and I took our drinks with us, and Virgil asked Mick to get him an Edmund's Oast Bound by Time IPA, another drink I wasn't going to ask about although I assumed it was a beer since it had IPA in the name.

Noelle turned to Virgil. "How was your day?"

"Wonderful. Had a near record two toilets and two sinks to unstop. Made enough not only to cover my overdue rent, but my landlord gave me a fifty-dollar bonus. Drinks are on me."

"That's great," Noelle said.

I didn't detect any sarcasm in her voice and was pleased that she appeared to be comfortable with Virgil's financial status, overcoming his early concern about dating her.

"How was your day?" he said while looking at Noelle.

My day didn't appear to matter.

She shared much of what she told me before he'd arrived while Mick set Virgil's drink in front of him.

"Enough about work, what's the deal with that?" Virgil asked and pointed to the sheet of paper I'd folded and set beside my drink.

I shared what I'd already told Noelle as I handed him the document. Noelle added what she'd said about Matthew's penchant for name-dropping and solving puzzles and her interpretation of what it'd meant.

Mick returned and asked if we wanted anything to eat.

Virgil said, "How about a pimento cheese plate to give us something to nibble on?"

Neither Noelle nor I objected so Mick headed to the kitchen to place the order.

Virgil then said, "Your theories make sense. So then, who are the people with those initials?"

I said, "We don't know."

"That throws a wet blanket on solving the murders, doesn't it?"

Noelle and I agreed.

"That brings two things to mind, Christopher. Now, you know I'm not the great detective like you and Charles, so what I say might prove to be hogwash. Regardless, here it goes. It would appear whoever's initials are *DP* owed Matthew an excrement-pot full of money. Nearly fifty-thousand bucks if that's what the numbers mean. If true, he or she'd be my number one suspect for killing Matthew."

"That'd be the case in my novel. Excellent deduction, Virgil."

"Gee, thanks. Now my second thought may be out in left field, but what if the letters aren't initials of people, but if he was into puzzles, it could be some sort of code Matthew used to disguise the names of people who owed him money?"

I said, "Why would he do that? Apparently only he had access to the paper since it was in the safe in his house."

"Almost true, Christopher. Didn't his father have access?"

"Yes."

"Consider this," Virgil said, "Matthew III didn't want Matthew II, who obviously had access to the safe, to know who the people were.

Or Matthew II could've given someone else the combination so another person or several others could've had access."

"Like Fritz Goss," Noelle said. "After all, he was Matthew II's second in command, so he may've given the combination to him."

Virgil said, "That's good, Noelle."

I said, "Let's assume you're right, Virgil. Either of you any good at puzzles or figuring out what the codes could represent?"

"Not me," Noelle said.

Virgil said, "Me either."

Our pimento cheese plate arrived giving us a chance to do something we were good at, eating.

We spent the next fifteen minutes devouring the appetizer, talking in circles about what the code could've meant, and then talking about everything but the murders. I told them I needed to get home, and surprisingly, Virgil didn't ask why or try to get me to stay. I'd clearly overstayed my intrusion into their date.

Before I left, Virgil asked Mick if he could find a couple of sheets of paper. He managed to accomplish that task while hardly breaking a sweat. Virgil copied on each sheet the information off the paper I'd brought, handed Noelle one of the copies and put the other one in his pocket, then said this would give both a chance to either figure out what the letters meant or to find a cryptanalyst.

This time, I couldn't help but ask him what that meant. For the record it's a code breaker and not a Victorian word. I headed home on that enlightening note.

41

———————

It took me a long time to go to sleep last night after talking with Noelle and Virgil. Sleep was elusive between wondering if anything was said that'd help identify the killer or killers and dissecting the list of what appeared to be people's initials along with numbers that most-likely represent money either owed Matthew III or money he owed to the names the initials represented. Two cups of coffee this morning failed to fully awaken me, so I decided to take a walk and take advantage of what was predicted to be a pleasant spring morning.

After a stop at Bert's for coffee, cup number three, I walked a block to Center Street then toward the Folly River. I wasn't the only person thinking it was a good idea to walk along the island's center of commerce. The sidewalk in front of me was crowded so I crossed the street near the library. That's when I saw Sean Aker headed my way. He was in his early 50s, thin, with short curly hair. Today, he was casually dressed in tan khakis and a dark-green polo shirt.

"Morning, Chris," he said and smiled.

We shook and I said, "Heading to work?"

Sean was an attorney with an office over one of the island's gift shops adjacent to City Hall. He'd handled the paperwork when I opened Landrum Gallery and we'd been friends ever since. He lived on a forty-five-foot-long Chris-Craft Constellation given to him by a client as payment for legal assistance. The boat was in poor condition when he'd taken it in trade and in addition to being his home for years, it'd been his renovation project.

He looked at one of the benches in front of the library and said, "I was until you hijacked me and made me park my weary bod on that bench."

I followed him to the bench and sat beside him.

Sean was well-toned, athletic, and was an avid skydiver, scuba diver, and surfer.

"Why're you weary? You're in better shape than anyone I know, and younger than most."

"Let's just say, I had a long night," he said, chuckled, and looked at his watch.

"You late for something?"

"Marlene called fifteen minutes ago and said a potential client was due in the office in twenty minutes."

Marlene was Sean's receptionist and had a near-impossible task of controlling her boss with his penchant for being anywhere other than in his office.

"Don't let me keep you."

"I won't but will blame you if I'm not at my desk when the client arrives. Now, what's this I hear about you playing detective?"

"If you're talking about the three murder investigations, I'm not doing anything other than asking a few questions."

"Chris, I'm a highly trained, experienced attorney. That means I can detect bullshit as well as sling it. You can fool some of the people all the time, but you can't fool your buddy and attorney. So, have any good clues?"

That reminded me one of Matthew III's poker pals was an attorney.

"Do you know Austin Middleton?"

"Don't know him well but have met him. We talked briefly at a cocktail party I attended out East Arctic Avenue."

"It didn't happen to be at Matthew Seward's house, did it?"

Sean smiled. "It was."

I stared at him. "When were you going to tell me you knew Matthew?"

"It was more fun letting you flounder around trying to see what I knew about the victims."

"Thanks. Why were you invited? Did you know Matthew prior to the party?"

"I was on a potential client list Seward Wealth Management invited people from. To be honest, I hadn't even heard of it until I got the invite. I figured free food, free booze, so why not?"

"Do you know why you were on the list?"

"I only knew two other people there, and they were attorneys. We figured we were on the list because we were lawyers on Folly and James Island. Some people believe because we were attorneys, we had money." He smiled. "Little do they know."

"Was that the first time you met Matthew Seward III?"

"Yes."

"Okay, back to Austin. What's your impression?"

"Still wet behind the ears. He's about half my age and hasn't been practicing that long." Sean laughed. "The main impression I had was that he was mighty proud to tell everyone I saw introduced to him that he was a lawyer. I wasn't eavesdropping but heard him tell three others it's what he did for a living."

"Anything else about him?"

Sean smiled. "Like him saying he was going to kill three people?"

"That would help."

"Afraid not, but I could see him doing it if he had enough motive."

"Why say that?"

"After Matthew decided everyone was there, he clinked a spoon on his glass to get our attention. He had to do it several times. Free booze makes it difficult to get a group's attention. Anyway, Matthew started talking about his company, then went on and on about why it was wonderful, why we'd be idiots not to entrust our fortune with it, and a couple of other points that I failed to listen to. He then introduced the company's executive vice president, Fritz something or other, who started talking about the type of equities the company relied on. Matthew interrupted and said, the group had heard enough about the company and to let everyone get back to whatever they were doing before he started making remarks."

"Sean, what's that have to do with Austin Middleton?"

He nodded. "Sorry. Remember, I charge by the hour. Sometimes I have trouble ending my stories. Okay, Middleton. After Matthew cut Fritz off, I thought they were going to go toe to toe and slug it out. Hell, I was afraid a couple of other people there were going to get caught in the crossfire between those two."

"An actual fight?"

"Probably not coming to blows, but damn close. I wasn't close enough to hear what was said, but there was a back and forth between the two that was far from amicable. Then Austin, who I assumed was a friend of Matthew stepped between the two and pushed Fritz away from Matthew. I didn't hear what he said, but his expression said Fritz had better not mess with him."

"Interesting. Did anything happen after that?"

"No. Fritz left not ten minutes later," Sean said then looked at his watch again.

"You have to go?"

"Nah, it'd screw up Marlene's image of me if I got to the office before the client."

"Let me ask one more question. Charles thinks Fritz is the person who killed Matthew. Think that's possible?"

"He looked like he was ready to at the party. If he did, what would be his reason to kill the other two?"

"I have no idea."

"But you believe Fritz and Austin are strong suspects?"

"Yes, but you could as easily add Ron Dillon and possibly Trace Spellman."

"Dillon the plumber and Spellman the realtor?"

"Yes. You know either of them?"

"Don't know anything about Dillon, but Spellman just opened a new real estate agency. He dropped off a stack of cards in the office." He smiled. "Marlene had them in the trash before Spellman was down the stairs. She hates clutter in the office." He looked at his watch a third time. "Speaking of clutter, I'd better get over there and clutter up the place."

I thanked him for talking about Matthew Seward III and his party. He thanked me for keeping him out of his claustrophobic office.

42

The phone rang at five-thirty with Noelle's name on the screen.

"Good afternoon, Noelle."

"Bet you didn't think you'd be hearing from me this soon."

"It's always good hearing from you. Did you learn something about the initials and numbers at work?"

"Yes and no."

"Let's start with the yes."

"When I got to the office this morning, I asked if anyone liked working puzzles. I mostly struck out, but somebody said I should talk to Cletis. He's our graphics guru, a genius at designing ads for the print medium." She chuckled. "Can you believe his name is Cletis? His parents must've known he'd grow up to be a geek. Anyway, he's a nice guy but would rather stare at a computer all day than talk to humans. I managed to corner him after lunch and before he got back in front of his computer and tuned out the world." I heard what sounded like papers shuffling and Noelle continued, "I learned the trick to getting him talking was to ask him about breaking codes, figuring out puzzles, and other weird spy stuff. I wrote some things down, but don't have a clue what much of it means, so don't ask many questions."

"Deal."

"He said most codes are encrypted. That I did know, in fact, I thought all codes were encrypted, but I didn't want to throw him off his explanation. Anyway, he said it's usually done by substituting one letter for another or adding or subtracting one letter from whatever you're trying to decode, like if there's a letter *R* in whatever you're trying to decode, it could stand for the letter *Q* which is one letter before the *R*, or for the letter *S*, one letter after it. That make sense?"

"Yes."

"Good. He also mentioned complex algorithms, but to me, all algorithms are complex, so I didn't try to write down what he said about that. Incidentally, did you know *E* is the most commonly used letter in the English language?"

"I didn't. Does that happen to tell us who the killer is, or killers are?"

"No, just thought it interesting."

"Okay. Are you getting closer to telling me what you learned from your geek?"

"I hate to break it to you, but what I've already said is most of what I learned. After Cletis finished lecturing me on the ins and outs of code breaking, I gave him a copy of what you gave me. He glanced at it, said, "umm," and "aha," then said he'd like to study it more and would get back with me before I left the office."

"I assume he did, or you wouldn't have called."

"Wow, you broke my code," she said and laughed before continuing, "He handed it back, said he'd made a copy so he could study it more tonight, but told me not to get my hopes up."

"Did he learn anything from looking at it this afternoon?"

"He said the numbers appeared way too random to mean anything more than what was apparent. He did say, while he'd guess they indicated money, they could also represent rocks, M&M's, or anything that can be counted."

"In other words, don't assume they're dollars."

"That's how I decoded what he said."

"What about the letters?"

"That's where he lost me. I'll spare you hearing his long, convoluted, and downright confusing explanation. Mainly because I didn't understand it enough to write most of it down. The bottom line is with only five combinations of letters, there weren't enough to do much analysis. Something about even if you could break the encryption there were only enough letters to spell one word, possibly two, but not enough to be a decent-sized message. He said that's especially true since there was only one vowel in the letters, even if you add or subtract a letter from each you still only had one vowel, and on their own, there wasn't enough information to tie the letters to." She laughed. "Got all that?"

"Sort of. The bottom line is he wasn't helpful."

"Sure it was. Bet you never considered the numbers being candy that melts in your mouth, not in your hands."

"Cute. That slogan for M&M's is older than you."

She laughed again and said, "Don't forget, I'm in advertising. Slogans are my business."

"After all that, did Cletis say anything that would help get closer to the killer or killers?"

"He said the numbers probably speak for themselves and represent quantities of something, most-likely dollars, but unless we could associate the letters with anything we know about the deaths, there wasn't enough information to draw definitive conclusions."

"I appreciate you finding someone to look at the sheet. Sorry it didn't prove to be more informative."

"It gave me a chance to talk to Cletis. Until today, I doubt we'd spoken ten words, and that's in total."

"While I've got you, did Matthew ever mention a party at his house for prospective clients of Seward Wealth Management?"

"He didn't say anything about a specific party but did say the company held cocktail parties for different groups of prospective clients."

"Did he say what he meant about different groups or how many parties were held?"

"I asked about the kind of groups. He said he had separate parties for attorneys, real estate brokers, and a third group I can't recall. Basically, he said they were groups of professionals who'd have enough money to benefit from a wealth management group. He joked once that not many poor people needed his company. Why?"

I told her about my conversation with Sean Aker and what he'd said about the party he attended.

She said, "I'm not surprised Austin defended Matthew. His poker group was close. They had their differences, but if challenged, I have no doubt they'd take up for each other. Are you thinking that the conflict between Matthew and Fritz was strong enough for Fritz to kill Matthew?"

"Charles still thinks Fritz is the killer."

"Do you?"

"Don't have enough information to make that leap."

"Thanks, Cletis Junior."

That was the closest I'd ever come to being called a geek.

"Anything else from Cletis or about Matthew's cocktail parties?"

"Other than seeing Cletis smile for the first time since I've worked there, there wasn't anything else."

"Talking about smiles, did you and Virgil stay at Lowlife Bar much longer after I left?"

"About an hour. He's easy to talk to. There aren't many guys like that out there. It's refreshing."

"I agree."

43

I hadn't heard from Charles since our "meeting" on the Folly Pier. Since then, I'd met with Sean, Noelle and Virgil, plus this evening's call from Noelle. To say I'm probably in trouble would be like saying the blue whale is a big fish.

I might as well let the grief begin and dialed my friend's number. When he answered, I said, "Seven o'clock, The Washout."

"Sorry," he said, "I don't recognize your voice. Sounds a little like a friend I had way back, umm, about three days ago, but—"

I sighed and repeated, "Seven o'clock, The Washout." Then I tapped *end call*.

He didn't return the call, so I knew he'd be there.

The weekly cornhole tournament was in full swing in the restaurant's parking lot when I arrived a little before six-thirty knowing Charles would be arriving any minute.

Before I got to the door, Roger Rutledge called my name. If there's an event on Folly, Roger will be part of its planning, coordination, or simply attending. The cornhole event was one of his favorite activities.

"Hey, Roger. You have a good crowd out there."

"Good weather brings them out. Haven't seen you on any of the teams."

"I'm as good at cornhole as I am at pole vaulting."

"That's not a good enough excuse. We've got several who've never played before. I look forward to seeing you out here soon."

I'll consider it about the same time I'll consider skydiving, I thought, but instead said, "I'll think about it."

Charles arrived in time to save me from committing further to something I knew I'd probably never seriously consider.

"Roger, you recruiting Chris?"

"Trying to, you too, Charles."

Charles said, "That's something to think about."

Roger laughed. "That's a nice way to say no. At least consider it. Now I'd better get back to the folks who are playing."

Charles watched Roger join the group standing around the participants and said, "Want to get a team together and show those youngsters how to play?"

"No."

"Figured that's what you'd say. Are we going to stand out here or we going to get inside where you can buy me something to drink?"

I motioned for him to take the lead.

The patio was nearly full, and a band was setting up near the entry. Charles grabbed my arm and pointed toward the booths along the sidewalk side of the patio. "Look who's there."

I barely had time to see which booth he was pointing to, when he took off toward the table, the table occupied by Ron Dillon and Austin Middleton.

Charles was standing beside their table like a server taking their drink order. He said something to the two men, then turned to me, "Hey, Chris, look, it's Ron and Austin." He then returned his gaze to the two men peacefully enjoying their drinks—that was until Charles arrived.

"Ron, Austin, good to see you."

Ron looked at Austin, then at Charles before turning toward me. "Hi, Charles and Chris, right?"

"Good memory," Charles said then looked at the two vacant spaces at the table. "We interrupting something?"

Austin said, "Not really. Want to join us?"

Charles had nearly moved into the booth as he said, "If you don't mind."

If they minded, they'd need a forklift to move Charles out of the booth.

They were seated on opposite sides of the table, so I took the seat beside Ron.

As soon as we were seated, a server arrived, said she was Jenny, and asked if Charles and I wanted something to drink.

Charles said, "A Budweiser."

I responded with, "Glass of chardonnay."

Charles then turned to our tablemates and asked if they wanted another drink, or something to eat, before saying, "Chris is buying."

Fortunately, they said they were okay for now.

Jenny left and Charles turned to Ron and said, "What brings you two out? I thought the only time you got together was to play poker, and now that the other two are gone...."

Ron said, "This was one of the nights we played. I thought it'd be nice to get together each week to pay our respects to Matthew and Foster."

"Yeah," Austin said, "we can cuss and discuss all the highlights," he smiled and added, "and the lowlights from those poker nights."

"I can only imagine," Charles said.

That would be Charles, the person who'd never played poker.

Jenny returned with our drinks and again asked if we needed anything else.

Charles said, "You guys want something to eat? Think I could use some chicken nachos. We'll share with you."

Ron nodded and Austin said, "Sounds good."

"Charles said, "Jenny, better make that two orders."

She said she would.

I said, "Ron, Austin, believe the last time we talked, you were afraid you might be in danger since the only thing you knew

Matthew and Foster had in common was your poker games. You still worried?"

"That's another reason we get together," Ron said. "We can talk about anything else we may know or think we know that'll help us learn who may've killed them. It doesn't seem the police have done much."

I said, "I know the local police and the county Sheriff's Office are conducting an extensive investigation."

"Yeah," Austin said, "that detective from the Sheriff's Office came to my house the other night."

Charles said, "What'd he want?"

"Said he came to see if I remembered anything since the last time he interviewed me. Then he kept asking where I was when Matthew and the others were shot." He sighed. "If he thinks I killed them, that proves he doesn't have a clue."

Charles said, "Did you have good alibis?"

"Why, you think I did it?"

"No," Charles said, "of course not. Ron, did the detective talk to you again?"

He nodded. "Same day he talked with Austin. Same questions."

"So, he asked about your alibis?"

"Yes. They're no closer to the killer than they were when the three were killed."

"You may be right about them," Charles said. "But Chris and I have a good track record catching killers the police can't catch. We're on the case."

Thanks, Charles, I thought, but said, "The police are good. I wouldn't worry much about it."

Austin stared at me. "Yeah, right. That's easy for you to say. You're not the ones the killer might be after."

Ron said, "I've also heard what you said about being good at helping the police. You have any good suspects in Matthew and Foster's murders?"

"Don't forget Rachel," Austin said.

That reminded me how Ron had said Austin had a thing for Rachel.

Charles said, "We've got a couple of hot suspects. Actually, Chris thinks he knows, but I'm not certain. Don't be surprised if the killer's caught soon."

Our nachos arrived and Ron said, "Think I can use another margarita."

Me, too," Austin added.

Charles waited for Jenny to head for the bar, then said, "Either of you think Fritz Goss could've done it?"

Austin took a bite of the nacho then said, "I do."

Charles said, "Why?"

Austin and Fritz's interaction at one of Matthew's cocktail parties was one of the things I'd planned to tell Charles tonight. I wondered if Austin would share the incident.

"I only saw them together once, and that was at a party Matthew had at his house. They nearly got into a fistfight in front of everyone."

Jenny set the new drinks in front of Austin and Ron, and Charles said, "What happened?"

"Fritz thought Matthew was trying to show everyone he was in charge instead of Fritz. They had words, but nothing came of it that night, but it wouldn't surprise me if Fritz held a grudge, and, well, you know."

I said, "What do you think, Ron?"

"There was no love lost between the two, so I wouldn't be surprised if he did it."

"Then why bump off Foster and Rachel?" Charles asked.

Ron said, "All we can figure is they somehow learned about Fritz doing it, then he suspected they knew, and had to be, umm, eliminated." He grabbed a nacho, took a bite, then said, "Is he your only suspect, or the police's only suspect?"

Before Charles or I could respond, Austin said, "Think there could be more than one killer?" I heard they each were shot with a different gun."

I said, "The police are looking at all options."

Charles looked at Ron, then at Austin, and said, "We've narrowed it down to two people. Like I said before, Chris thinks it's one, I think it's someone else."

Austin said, "Other than Fritz, who else?"

"We'd better keep our list close to the vest, you understand."

"Yes," Austin said.

Ron said he agreed.

"While we're talking, got a question." Charles said as he pulled a familiar sheet of paper out of his rear pocket, unfolded it, then slid it in front of Austin.

Austin looked at it and said, "What am I looking at?"

"It belonged to Matthew. Wondering if it means anything to either of you."

"Are these people's initials?"

"Think so."

Austin looked back at the paper and said, "Who?"

Charles said, "Don't know. That's what we're trying to figure out."

Ron said, "Let me see it."

Austin handed it across the table. Ron looked at the paper and said, "What about the numbers. What do they mean?"

Charles said, "Money."

I didn't add, *or M&M's.*

Ron said, "Austin, I don't think I know anyone with these initials, do you?"

"Afraid not," and handed the paper back to Charles.

"That's okay, guys. Chris and I will figure it out."

"Good luck," Austin said. "I know I'll be glad when the killer is behind bars. It still scares the crap out of me."

"Guys," I said, "something else I heard is someone owed Matthew close to $50,000. Know anything about it?"

Ron said, "No."

Austin said, "Fifty grand, no. Matthew would occasionally win money from one of us or lend us some money if we were in a pinch. Instead of pushing us to repay it, he'd let it slide longer than would a bank or bookie." He laughed. "Think he thought it made him look wealthy."

That was similar to what Noelle had shared. I said, "Do you know anyone who owed him money?"

Austin and Ron had already finished their drinks and Austin said, "I did once. He lent me several thousand dollars so I could buy a car a client had to unload and offered to me well below book wholesale. It wasn't anywhere near $50,000 but he let me drag out paying him back for several months."

Charles said, "How about you, Ron?"

"Lost some nights of poker to him but no really big pots. Five, six thousand at the most."

I noticed Charles nearly choke when Ron said *five, six thousand.* He took a drink then said, "I know you guys are worried about the killer, but you won't have to be much longer. I'll be surprised if we don't identify the killer in the next few days."

"Hope that's true," Ron said.

Austin added, "I agree."

"I've got an early morning at work," Ron said. "Time to call it a night."

"Me too," Austin said.

"You can go ahead and leave," Charles said. "Chris will get the check."

It was my turn to choke, but I didn't.

Ron and Austin shook our hands, thanked us for the food and drinks, then headed to the exit.

Charles watched them go, and said, "Now, what'd you want to tell me that got me here?"

Thinking back on my meeting with Noelle and Virgil and the phone call from Noelle, about the only thing that was important enough to share was what Cletis told Noelle about the paper she shared with him. I could tell Charles was tired, since the only two things he asked about after I told him about Noelle's call were if she was sure her source couldn't tell who the initials belonged to and was Cletis really the guy's name.

On those insightful inquiries, we called it a night. I avoided running into Roger on the way out of The Washout.

On the way home, it struck me. Neither Ron nor Austin told us if they'd given Detective Adair decent alibis when he was interrogating them.

44

The next morning, a heavy rain was not only dampening everything on Folly but was dampening vacationers' walk on the beach or leisurely stroll along Center Street. This would be a good day to stay inside. I poured coffee, moved to the small kitchen table, and spread the copies of Matthew's mysterious document in front of me. I stared at it like I expected *CLUE* to appear in blinking red lights.

The blinking sign failed to appear, but I was reminded of awakening sometime overnight thinking about what Noelle had learned from her colleague Cletis. He'd told her there weren't enough letters or combination of letters on Matthew's sheet to draw any conclusions unless they could be associated with something, anything about the deaths. Even then, there might not be enough to learn if the initials were related to whatever they were being compared with. If I remembered anything else from my overnight thoughts, it'd escaped me like many overnight thoughts. The only thing I could think of now related to the death of Matthew III was the list of suspects Charles and I had identified.

I went into the office and grabbed a pad of paper, returned to the kitchen, and listed our initial group of suspects. The list included

Fritz Goss, Austin Middleton, Ron Dillon, and even though they were now deceased but had been alive when Matthew created the document, Foster Rodman, and Rachel Little. The only other person I knew who had a relationship with Matthew was Trace Spellman, so I added his name.

Now, instead of one sheet of paper to stare at I had two. Now what? A second cup of coffee will surely give me a clue to the clue, or so I rationalized. The coffee carafe was another cup lighter as I returned to the table.

The letters on the list were: *ML*, *R?*, *DP*, *LA*, and *SR*. If those letters represented initials of names, only two of the suspects, Foster Rodman and Rachel Little, had initials corresponding with those on the list, but only the second letters in the group of initials were the same as the first letter of their last names. The letters could represent three of the suspects if the initial followed by a question mark, *R?*, corresponded with one of the names. I stared at the question mark longer than I focused on the other initials. What could it represent? If it was someone's last name, wouldn't Matthew have known it?

After looking at the papers another fifteen minutes, I concluded two things. I had learned little if anything for my efforts, and I should never answer a help-wanted ad for a code breaker. I wasn't ready for a third cup of coffee, so I grabbed my mug and walked to my screened-in front porch. If anything, it was raining harder than it had been.

I returned to the kitchen table and once again tried to see any connection between the names of suspects and the initials or amounts on the paper. Only two of the suspects had their last initial represented on the list of initials, yet their first names didn't correspond to the first initials on the paper. What about switching the first and last initials? That may not be encryption, but it would confuse anyone who was trying to make sense of the sheet. Like me, for example.

I jotted down the names of our suspects whose last name was the first initial on Matthew's list and was shocked to see five of the six suspects were on my new list. That included Austin Middleton *ML*, Ron Dillon *DP*, Foster Rodman *R?*, Rachel Little *LA*, and Trace

Spellman *SR*. I'm no statistician, but wouldn't five of our six suspects appearing using this method be significant?

I was beginning to feel better about what I'd learned, or believe I'd learned. But after patting myself on the back, there still was a chance the letters and numbers had nothing to do with the suspects we'd identified. If I knew what the second letter represented, it would either give me added confidence that the names on the suspect list were the people on Matthew's note. So, what could the second letter represent? It's not the first name of the person whose last name corresponded with the first listed initial. It's also not the name they go by. I suppose it could be their middle name. But even if it were, how could I gain access to the middle name of each of the suspects? And even if I could gain access, what would that tell me. And, if it's not the initial of the suspects' middle name, each set of initials could correspond with countless other people.

I leaned back in the chair, took a deep breath, and said to myself, okay, the initials could be a clue. If they are, then what do the numbers represent? If I assumed the numbers are amounts of money owed Matthew, by far, the largest amount was beside *DP*. If my initial analysis was correct, the initials belonged to Ron Dillon. I then remembered something I'd heard that meant little at the time. Hadn't Noelle said Matthew told her that someone owed him nearly $50,000? I'd say $47,200 was close enough.

If my assumptions were correct, Ron Dillon owed Matthew Seward III $47,200. The others owed much smaller amounts ranging from the late Rachel Little owing $1,700, to Foster Rodman owing $475, to both Trace Spellman and Austin Middleton owing nothing. Assuming the names were correct, a rather weak assumption, and the amounts indicated dollars, Ron Dillon owed far and away the most. Was that enough to kill over? Assuming it was and Ron was guilty of shooting Matthew, why kill the other two? And that's assuming there was only one killer, a person using three handguns to commit the crimes.

Patting myself on the back earlier was premature—premature by a mile. Now what do I do? The wisest thing would be to call Cindy, outline my findings and assumptions, and wish her well putting it together and arresting Ron Dillon. Trying to take a step back, if someone brought to me what I was thinking and why, would it convince me of, well, of anything? Probably not, but would it provide enough information for the proper authorities to follow up on? Yes, that is if anyone took my admittedly weak conclusion seriously. If someone had brought it to me, I wouldn't.

I don't have enough evidence to prove my assumptions are correct. In fact, I don't have proof any of them are correct. How can I learn more about the initials and amounts listed? The easiest way to possibly learn more about the people I'm assuming the initials represent would be to Google them. Often, the full names of people can be found on one or several websites.

Rain continued to pelt the roof, so I couldn't head outside to try to be distracted by my incredible island enough to put all my confusing thoughts on the back burner. I reluctantly moved to the office and fired up my computer. The first name I entered was Austin Middleton. My experience with the Internet is it gives me way more information than I'm looking for. After entering Austin Middleton and receiving nearly a zillion hits, I then limited the search to *Austin Middleton, attorney, South Carolina*, and received five hits. Looking at each, I learned his name was Austin Simon Middleton, meaning the *L* on Matthew's paper didn't represent his middle name. An hour later after searching for information on the other four names that corresponded with the first initial on Matthew's chart, I learned the second initial did not represent any of their middle names. Another dead end, or with a more optimistic slant it reminded me of Thomas Edison's quote, "I have not failed. I've just found ten thousand ways that won't work."

The rain continued, and I was feeling like it was as bleak in my house as it was outside. I was frustrated, irritated, and anxious. I felt the initials revealed the last names of people I would consider the prime suspects in the three murders. The amounts led me to believe Ron Dillon had the most to lose if Matthew were still alive, but unless I could show that the second letter beside the first letter I assumed represented the suspects was somehow related to the suspect, I had nothing. Even if it tied the suspect to the initials, owing someone money didn't mean one of the others didn't have a reason to kill Matthew. That didn't even address the deaths of Foster Rodman and Rachel Little. Did they learn the identity of the killer and had to be eliminated as well, or could there be some other reason for their being murdered? Additionally, none of that addressed how many killers there were.

I stood, stretched, looked out the window noticing the rain had stopped. It still appeared to be as gloomy as I felt. Instead of returning to the table and the two sheets of paper, I opened the front door and moved to the porch to watch whatever little traffic there was. Most of the residents who worked had already made their way to their offices, businesses, or factories. Only a few vehicles were headed toward the east end of the island since the inclement weather had kept vacationers cooped up in their rental houses, condos, or hotel rooms.

As I stared at the lightly travelled road, I thought of something else that I had remembered during my awake period overnight. When Charles and I were talking with Ron and Austin neither of them had answered our questions about if they'd given Detective Adair alibis for the timeframe when the murders occurred. There was no way I'd ask the detective since he considered me a bother at a minimum and interfering with police investigations at the other extreme. Being accused of those things wouldn't bother me if they came from Chief LaMond, so I dialed her number.

"What do you want now?" she said by way of a friendly, professional salutation.

"Morning, Cindy. Got a question."

"Good. Meet me in Roasted in ten minutes and I may have an answer, the keyword being may."

She'd ended the call before I could respond.

45

Roasted was the coffee shop in the Tides Hotel, and Cindy was Folly's top law enforcement official seated at one of the two small tables in the shop.

She saw me in the doorway and pointed to the counter and said, "Go ahead and order. Penny's waiting for you to pay for my coffee."

Penny was Roasted's manager and had been for several years. After a couple of friendly exchanges with her, she took payment for both cups and said she'd bring mine to the table.

I joined Cindy who said, "You're getting off lucky. If I'd been at the Dog, the privilege of spending a few minutes with me would've cost you way more than coffee."

"Wow, how lucky can a guy be?"

"Your sarcasm doesn't go well with coffee. Remember, you're the one with the question."

I shrugged and said, "Charles and I were talking with Ron Dillon and Austin Middleton last evening at The Washout."

Cindy rolled her eyes. "Let me guess. You and your buddy were at The Washout minding your own business, when along came Dillon and Middleton. When they saw you, they got all excited and begged you and Charles to let them join you. How am I doing?"

"Close, but more like the other way around."

She grinned and said, "I'm shocked."

"Cindy, sarcasm doesn't go well with coffee."

She sighed. "And to think, I invited you."

"And I appreciate it," I said without any sarcasm.

"Okay, what's the question?"

"Both guys said Detective Adair had followed up with them after their first conversations after the death of Matthew Seward. I gathered from what they said he was asking if they had alibis for not only the time of Matthew's death, but for the other murders. After they told us that, either Charles or I, I'm not sure which, asked if they'd given Adair alibis. They changed the subject and never answered the question."

Cindy sighed. "I wouldn't answer if two guys I hardly knew asked me that question. Unless I missed it, again, what's your question?"

"Did Detective Adair tell you anything about questioning the two men?"

"How many times have I told you information between my office and the Sheriff's Office travels down a one-way street going from us to them?"

"I know. Was hoping this would've been an exception."

"Afraid not. What else did the guys tell you, or more specifically, what'd they tell you that was or could be related to the deaths?"

To tell, or not to tell, that is the question. Why not? Surely, Cindy won't scream or pull out her firearm and shoot me in a coffee shop in the middle of Folly's largest hotel.

"Charles showed them the paper you gave me showing initials and numbers, and asked if they knew anything about it, what the initials stood for, and what the numbers represented."

She lowered her head, shook it, then stared at me. "Chris, oh Chris, don't you know you can't take that wannabe detective near possible suspects."

"He would have asked even if I wasn't there."

"True. So, did they tell you anything worth sharing?"

I told her what I could remember about what they'd said about the initials and numbers, and my impression that nothing they said could help the police—with an emphasis on police—learn the identity of the killer or killers.

"What's your take on them?"

A young couple entered the coffee shop went to the shelves holding Tides Hotel caps and Koozies, then to the counter to order.

I leaned closer to Cindy so the newcomers couldn't hear and said, "I didn't get the impression either way about them but let me tell you what I was doing this morning."

"Swearing on a stack of Charleston Visitors Guides you would be a good boy and never meddle in police business again."

"Not exactly," I said, then proceeded to tell her how I'd been meddling in police business.

"You figured all that out from five sets of initials and a few numbers?"

"Yes, but I could also be 100% wrong about all of it."

"And you probably are wrong unless you can figure out what the second letter means in each combination, and it ties into the first initials. The fact is I could name several people on Folly with last names that share those initials."

"That's where I'm stumped."

"Don't feel bad. Stumped is how I spend most of my days as your Director of Public Safety. I have no idea if any of what you surmised is accurate but know how I can screw up your theory."

"How?"

"Ask Detective Adair if he's established the alibis for Ron Dillon and Austin Middleton. If Dillon has an ironclad alibi, your convoluted theory goes out the window." She picked up her phone and started scrolling through names.

I put my hand in front of her face. "You calling him now?"

"Why not? The room's empty except for you and Penny and she's good at not paying attention to what's being said in here. Better than a priest. And you're going to keep your trap shut." She tapped his number before I could say anything else.

"Hey, Detective, this is Chief LaMond. How're you today?"

I was impressed. She could begin a phone conversation with a civil, normal salutation, something I'd not received in the years I've known her.

She rolled her eyes, and said, "I'm fine. Yes, it was quite a downpour." She hesitated before saying, "Got a question. Have you established alibis for Dillon and Middleton, Matthew Seward's poker playing friends for the time of his death?" Another hesitation before she continued, "Neither of them? She tapped her fingers on the tabletop then said, "What about for the other two murders? She paused then said, "Sure, I'll wait." She put her hand over the phone's mic and whispered, "He's looking it up."

I nodded then waited for what seemed like an eternity. I wondered if he'd left his notes at home and was going for them.

Finally, Cindy said, "Yes, okay." One more pause before she said, "Okay, thanks." Another pause. "Not really, curious since I think they were on your suspect list. Talk to you later. Stay dry."

She returned the phone to the table, and I said, "Well?"

"That boy was full of no-good information, sort of what I expected from him."

"What's that mean?"

"Bottom line, neither Austin nor Ron had solid alibis. They could account for their time for some of the hours around the times of death, but with gaps enough so each could have murdered all three."

"Does he consider them viable suspects?"

"Yes, but he doesn't have anything to point to. Basically, the best he can do is they all knew Matthew, Foster, and Rachel. Beyond that, I don't think he has anything."

"What about you?"

"You tell anyone I said this, I'll make sure you never step foot on Folly again, hell, not a foot in South Carolina."

"My lips are sealed."

She looked over at Penny and said, "That goes for you, too, Penny."

"What's that, Chief?"

"Nothing, Penny." She turned to me and said, "Told you."

"You did, now what are you going to tell me that I've sealed my lips for?"

"Your convoluted theory that Ron Dillon is the killer makes more sense than anything the Sheriff's Office has. It also makes more sense than anything I have, which is nothing."

"What're you going to do about it?"

"I knoweth not."

46

After Cindy left to return to her office so she could, in her words "harass my officers like you harass me," I headed next door and up the wide staircase to the Folly Pier. I knew Cindy was right about how the initials could belong to many other people than to my list of suspects. It still seemed important that they also corresponded to the last initial of five people who knew Matthew. It was also likely that the second initial listed beside each of the combinations would help verify my theory. All I had to do was figure out what they meant. Nothing to it, right?

I slowly headed toward the far end of the Pier, talked briefly with a couple of anglers I knew, and watched a group of preschoolers laughing and splashing in the shallow surf. By the time I reached the end of the structure, I was more relaxed than I'd been in days.

I'd left Matthew's document at the house and had trouble remembering what the second letters were and how they combined with the first initials. What I did remember was the question mark beside the letter *R*. What did it signify?

Black clouds had moved in off the ocean, indicating that the rain that had left the area earlier may be returning, so instead of lingering on the Pier and listening to the soothing sound of the waves rolling ashore, I headed home.

The first thing I noticed in the kitchen was an empty table. Since I seldom ate or did much of anything else in the kitchen, that wouldn't have bothered me except Matthew's note and my note listing the suspects had been on the table before I left to meet Cindy.

I quickly went to my office in case I'd been mistaken about leaving the documents in the kitchen. They weren't there. Okay, stay calm and check the other rooms to see if anything appears disturbed. It never entered my mind that someone could still be in the house. Fortunately, no one was. I then returned to the kitchen and for the first time noticed the back door wasn't completely closed. Even if I'd failed to lock it earlier, I wouldn't have left it cracked open. If I hadn't suspected something was amiss, I wouldn't have noticed the quarter-inch gap between the door and the doorframe.

I opened the door and stepped on the small concrete pad that served as a step into the house. I looked around, noticed a folded sheet of paper by my foot, bent to pick it up, when I heard what sounded like two boards smacking together near the corner of the house. Two other things occurred at the same time. I heard glass breaking in the door less than a foot from me, and I felt a sharp pain in my left arm just below my shoulder. It felt like a knife had been plunged into my arm. I grabbed my arm and saw blood oozing out around my fingers.

My brain finally registered that the sound I'd heard from the side of the house was a gunshot.

I carefully walked back into the house, grabbed a dishtowel from the counter, and pressed it against my wound, hopefully to stop the bleeding, then gently picked up my phone with my right hand and pressed in 911. After telling the 911 dispatcher what'd happened and where I was, I took a deep breath, closed my eyes, and focused on slowing down my heart rate. I failed.

I realized not only was my arm throbbing more by the second, but I was shaking all over and felt like I was going to collapse. Instead of sitting in the kitchen, mere feet from the door and a possible killer, I slowly moved to the living room and flopped down in my recliner.

Less than a minute later, I heard a Folly Beach Public Safety cruiser siren blaring as the vehicle skidded to a halt in my drive, closely followed by a second cruiser. I carefully managed to get out of the chair and open the front door without collapsing to be met by Officer Rodney New. He had his hand on his firearm as he looked past me, then said, "Chris, you okay?"

"Not really."

He looked at the bloody towel I had pressed against my upper arm and said, "Let me help you to your recliner." He cautiously helped me in the chair while avoiding contact with my injured arm and added, "EMTs are on the way."

I adjusted my arm on the armrest, but no matter how I moved it, the pain continued.

Rodney knelt beside the chair and said, "Chris, you okay to talk?"

I nodded.

"What happened?"

I again adjusted my arm to try to lessen the pain before giving him a short version of what'd occurred.

"Did you see him, or I suppose her?"

"No, but the person had to be by the corner of the house closest to Bert's."

"You didn't see which way he left?"

I again said, "No, he probably went toward the street behind my house since he could've gone that way without me seeing him.

Officer Trula Bishop was the next to arrive. I'd known Trula for more than seven years. She had been a Folly Beach Public Safety Officer for several years and over that time we'd become friends. She'd helped me through a couple of jams when I stuck my nose where it had no business being. She'd also been Folly's first African American Public Safety Officer and initially had problems with a handful of less-tolerant citizens. The problems evaporated when they learned that she was competent, fair, pleasant, and a true asset to the police force. Officer New gave her a quick summary before he said he'd head out back to see if he could learn anything.

The low roar of one of Folly's fire engines was the next to arrive. Two firefighters who doubled as EMTs were next through the door. They nodded at me, glanced at the towel wrapped around my arm, then one of them put on gloves, and carefully unwrapped the towel. I turned my head away from my bloody arm as he began inspecting the wound.

Trula said, "Mr. Chris, you're in good hands. I'm going to step out back and see if Officer New has found anything."

The EMT got a gauze pad out of his medical kit, poured a liquid on it, and said, "Mr. Landrum, this is going to hurt."

He rubbed the pad on each side of my arm where the bullet had apparently entered and exited. He was right, it hurt. The other EMT remained standing and watching his colleague as he worked on me.

Another vehicle, siren blaring, stopped in my front yard and Cindy stormed through the front door, and said, "Chris, you okay?"

I assumed she would've noticed that I wasn't. "As good as I can be, I suppose."

She glared at the EMT working on my arm and said, "Taylor, what's the verdict?"

I'd seen the EMT/firefighter several times around town but didn't know his name was Taylor. He said, "Chief, he's lucky. The bullet didn't appear to hit anything vital. He still has circulation to his hand and his arm movements appear normal."

I wanted to add, "And it hurts like hell," but remained silent.

Cindy said, "Good."

Taylor added, "He'll still need stitches."

"Do what you can, and I'll run him over to the hospital."

"Chief," I said, "that's okay, I'll get there on my own."

She ignored my comment and turned to Taylor. "Think if I cuff him and throw him in the back of my vehicle, it'd hurt his arm too much?"

Taylor started to answer, and apparently decided Cindy was teasing. He smiled and said, "He'd survive."

Taylor had cleaned the wound, put some sort of gooey dressing on it, then tightly wrapped the arm with a roll of stretch gauze, before saying, "Chief, he's good to go."

She thanked Taylor and his partner who I hadn't seen before today and told them they could take off.

After they left, Cindy said, "You feeling okay?"

"Other than having been shot, having a pain in my arm, and knowing there's someone out there who wants me dead, I'm peachy."

"I understand. Feel good enough to show me where you were when it happened?"

Maybe it'd take my mind off the pain, that is, if I could get out of the recliner without collapsing.

"I'll try."

Cindy took my good arm and carefully helped me out of the chair then stood close to my side as I slowly headed into the kitchen and then to the back door.

I said, "I noticed papers about the murders I'd left on the table were gone, then saw the door ajar. I stepped out here, saw something by my foot and bent to pick it up. The next thing that happened was a gunshot from the corner of the house, the window breaking, and blood gushing out of my arm."

"You didn't see anyone?" She pointed to the corner where I'd heard the shot come from.

"No, he was gone. I assume headed around the side of the house and then to the road back there. If he'd gone in front of the house too many people could've seen him."

She looked around without leaving my side. I figured she thought I might collapse at any moment. I wasn't certain she was wrong.

Officer Bishop returned from the side of the house, nodded at me, then looked at Cindy. "Chief, we didn't find anything. It doesn't appear there are any doorbell cameras in the area, and we didn't see other security cameras. We also didn't see anyone who may've seen him. There are a lot of footprints along the street back there in the mud from today's rain. I doubt they'd tell us anything since there are so many."

"Okay, while you're here, take prints off the back door and find the bullet." She turned to me. "Did you leave it unlocked or anyone have a key?"

"Cindy, I thought it was locked, but wouldn't swear to it. It's not that hard to jimmy. And don't say it, I know you and Larry have been on me to get it replaced."

Cindy's husband has had to replace the window in my office several times over the years after people had broken it to gain access to the house, but this is the first time the person was courteous enough to use the door, even if he did break or pick the lock to get in.

She huffed then said, "Being from East Tennessee, I suspect you've heard me say this before, but replacing the lock now is like closing the barn door after the jackass has bolted."

Trula said, "I always heard that it was a horse that got out."

"Officer Bishop, the jackass I was referring to is this hardheaded man with a hole in his arm."

Trula did a good job of disguising a chuckle.

Cindy looked at me and said, "Got a question."

I shrugged.

"What in holy hell did you do to piss someone off enough to waste a bullet on you?"

"I don't know."

"On that enlightening note, it's time to get you to the emergency room and let the docs put more holes in your arm."

"I'm fine. I can get there on my own."

"Maybe, but this way I can make sure you don't get yourself in more trouble before you get that taken care of." She nodded toward my bandaged arm. We then stepped into the kitchen and she said, "You have anything in the fridge to drink other than beer or wine?"

"Don't know. I'm not thirsty."

"It's for me," she said and smiled, then opened the refrigerator and as a minor miracle, she found a six-pack of Diet Pepsis. She grabbed two, handed me one, continued to the front door. "Besides, you need to stay hydrated."

She helped me into the passenger side of her official pick-up truck then backed out of my front yard and headed toward Center Street.

We each took a sip and she said, "What was on the paper that saved your life?"

I'd already forgotten that I'd stuffed it in my pocket after returning to the house after being shot.

I took it out of my pocket, straightened it out and set it on the console. "It's my notes about the suspects I told you about."

She glanced down at it before looking at me and saying, "I assume it's what you noticed missing when you came into the kitchen before heading outside?"

"Yes, this plus the copy of Matthew's note you'd shared with me."

"You think someone broke in looking for those papers?"

"Maybe, but I'd assume the person figured I had more than that since the copy of Matthew's note came from you, so I would think the person would know the police had a copy."

"And don't forget, he or she tried to kill you."

That I would never forget. "True."

"What about your list of suspects?"

"If the person's name who broke in is on that list, he knows he's a suspect."

"You're sure there's nothing else missing?"

"I didn't notice anything."

"I know you've already told Officer Bishop and some of it to me, but are you up to repeating it?"

"Yes." I then told her everything from coming in the front door until I called 911.

The drive from Folly to the hospital on the outskirts of Charleston normally took from twenty minutes with no traffic to occasionally forty-five minutes or more with traffic backups. It took us fifteen minutes. That was easily explained by Cindy driving at least fifteen miles-per-hour over the posted limit and using her siren twice once we reached heavy traffic near the hospital.

Cindy aided me out of her vehicle and since she'd parked in a no-parking zone, she helped me for the short walk to the emergency room. Fortunately, the room was nearly empty, and she pointed to a chair near the door into the exam area, had me sit, and approached the receptionist like she was going to war against the entire medical community.

I couldn't hear what she was saying, but her hand gyrations and frown on her face, indicated Cindy was playing the police chief card. The receptionist picked up her phone and talked to someone, then said something to Cindy, who nodded.

Cindy came over and took the seat beside me.

"What'd you say to that poor woman? She looked like she was going to cry."

Cindy smiled. "It could've been something about a prisoner getting himself shot. That he needed to see a doc quickly since I had a short window of time to get him back to his cell. May've mentioned the word dangerous."

Before she finished the explanation, a young nurse pushed a wheelchair out from the door to the exam room, spotted Cindy and came over to us.

Cindy looked at me and said, "Your carriage arrives."

I managed without help to get from the chair into the wheelchair, and said, "You won't have to go in with me. I'll be fine."

"Sorry, but I do. I may've mentioned something about my prisoner being homicidal."

"Whatever," I said then was wheeled into an exam room. A second nurse arrived, took my vitals, then unwrapped the bandages from my arm. She gave the wound a bored look like she sees things much worse every day. She said the doctor would be in shortly. I knew from taking others to the emergency room over the years that in nurse speak shortly could be anywhere from a half hour to a half day.

I was surprised when a doctor entered the room. Surprised for two reasons. First, it'd only been ten minutes since the nurse had left the room. Second, because the doc was Tanesa Washington, Al Washington's daughter.

"Thought it was you when I saw the name on the computer," she said with a big smile.

Tanesa was one of nine children Al and his wife adopted and he'd raised as a single father after his wife died years ago. Tanesa was attractive, thin, and had an endearing smile, something that I was sure was welcomed by her numerous ER patients. We'd spent several hours together a few years ago when Al had serious health issues.

"Tanesa, it's great seeing you. Meet my jail guard Chief Cindy LaMond."

Tanesa shook Cindy's hand and said, "Chief, Dad has told me about you a few times over the years. Glad we finally meet, although I wish it'd been under more pleasant circumstances."

She then turned to me and said, "Hear you got in the way of a bullet. Let's take a look. This may pinch a little."

I'd also learned over the years that *pinch a little* was doc-speak for excruciating pain. While she was trying to be tender, once she started running her gloved hand over the area around the wound, it hurt, and that was an understatement.

She finished torturing me, and said, "You were lucky. It's a simple through-and-through wound; didn't hit any major blood vessels or bone. A few stitches and we'll get you out of here."

She left for a couple of minutes then returned with sutures and a curved needle that looked to me like a large fishhook. After a few stitches on each side of my arm, she said, "That ought to take care of it," and rewrapped my arm with clean gauze.

"Doc," Cindy said, "how about some pain meds?"

"Sure," Tanesa said, "I'll write him a script for antibiotics and pain meds."

Cindy said, "Not for him, for me. He's a constant pain in my posterior."

Tanesa laughed and said, "Sorry, you'll need a psychiatrist to help you overcome those pains."

Cindy smiled and said, "You're telling me."

An hour after the two ladies had made fun of the gunshot wound patient, we'd stopped at Walgreens to get my prescriptions filled and were pulling in my drive.

Cindy walked me into the house, checked the lock on the back door to make sure it still worked, checked each room to make sure I was safe. She made sure I took one of the pain pills and asked if she was going to have to tuck me in to make sure I got in bed. I assured her I could make it on my own.

Before Cindy left, she wrapped her arms around me, careful not to disturb my injured arm, hugged, and said, "Glad you're okay."

I walked her to the door, locked it after she'd left, thought how great it was to have such a wonderful friend, then slowly made my way to the bedroom.

All I could think about before falling into a drug-induced sleep, was why me? The police knew everything I knew about the deaths, even the list of suspects since I'd told Cindy about each of them days ago. What could I possibly know that earned me a bullet through my arm?

47

———

The next thing I knew, the bedside clock indicated it was three-fifteen, at least I thought that's what it said. The numbers were out of focus and moving around. I didn't know if it was a.m. or p.m., so I tried to look out the window to see if it was dark. I didn't know what the weather was outside, but I felt I was in a fog. I closed my eyes, tried not to move, then attempted to open my eyes again. This time I had better luck. It was dark so I assumed it was still the middle of the night.

I pushed to sit up and my left arm felt like someone had taken a chainsaw to it. That jarred me awake and introduced some reality into my brain. I then remembered why my arm was in such pain, which reminded me if it was three-fifteen in the morning, I was overdue for a pain pill.

The brain fog was lifting, so I concentrated on getting out of bed without putting weight on my injured arm. I sat on the side of the bed until I was confident I could stand and walk to the bathroom without collapsing. The house was eerily quiet and for a second I wondered if the person who'd shot me had slipped back in to finish the job. I then thought I was needlessly worrying, took a pain pill, and slowly returned to the bedroom.

By the time my head touched the pillow, something else came to mind—something that could prove I'd been right about the meaning of the letters on Matthew's note. If only I could remember what it was. Was it a dream? Was it something that came together during my awakening fog? The one answer I did know was I couldn't remember what it was and how it proved my theory about the initials. Sleep took pity on me and saved me from worrying more about something I couldn't remember.

The next time my eyes opened, the clock indicated it was seven-fifteen. Apparently, I was more alert than I'd been the last time I looked at the clock and couldn't tell if it was the middle of the night or the middle of the afternoon. It helped seeing sunbeams poking through the slats in my blinds. I'd survived the night.

This time, I gave careful thought to how to get out of bed without leaning heavily on my injured arm, further indication that I was more alert than earlier. I made it to the kitchen and managed to get Mr. Coffee doing its thing while only using my right arm. I poured a mug of coffee and carefully moved to a chair at the table. I glanced at the back door and saw the broken glass had been replaced by a piece of plywood. I smiled realizing that Cindy must've called her husband to board up the broken window when I was at the hospital. I then made the mistake of remembering what'd occurred yesterday. I shuttered thinking how close I'd come to being the fourth murder victim.

Then it hit me, the elusive thought I had overnight about what the unknown letters could mean, more accurately, what the question mark beside one of the initials could indicate. It wasn't my question, not the police's question, but Matthew's. That reminded me of something a couple of the poker players had said about questions they had when they were telling me about their games. Where did Foster Rodman live and what did he do for a living. Could that be the significance of the question mark beside the *R* which I thought stood for Rodman but as Cindy pointed out, it could stand for countless other names.

To test the theory, I needed to print a copy of Matthew's notes since the shooter took mine and to get my notes listing the suspects from the slacks I'd worn yesterday. Ten minutes later, I'd gone to my computer, printed the copy of what Cindy had shared, shuffled to the bedroom to get the copy of my notes, then returned to the kitchen table, all things I'd done many times without giving it a thought. The combination of pain pills and my throbbing arm made the short trip feel like I'd hiked the Appalachian Trail.

I took a deep breath as I looked at the two sheets of paper, but didn't get any further, since someone was knocking on the front door. My first thought was to ignore it, but curiosity got the better of me. I was glad I did.

My favorite Lost Dog Cafe server was standing on the porch holding a bag and offering a smile.

"Amber, what are you doing here? Shouldn't you be at work?"

"Carol, our owner, heard about what happened and said I'd better bring you some French toast so you wouldn't starve. She knows food is an alien concept to your kitchen."

I grudgingly admitted she was right and invited her in.

"Are you okay?" she said and stared at my bandaged arm.

"I will be." I motioned for her to lead the way to the kitchen. "How did Carol find out what happened?"

"Officer Bishop was in first thing this morning and told her." Amber smiled and added, "Then Marc Salmon told everyone in the restaurant before Charles stopped in and asked if I'd heard anything. He said he didn't know anything about it but heard Officer New telling someone something and heard your name mentioned combined with the word shot."

I smiled. "The rumor mill at its best. Would you like some coffee?"

"I would, but I need to get back. We're shorthanded this morning."

I told her I appreciated the kind gesture and was okay.

She carefully hugged me, smiled, and told me to enjoy breakfast.

I followed orders and enjoyed the French toast and was touched by the owner's kindness. One more reason I loved my years on Folly.

I could tell the pain pill I'd taken in the middle of the night was wearing off, but I wasn't a big fan of pills so I'd try to put off taking another one as long as I could. I pulled the two sheets of paper closer to study them while I ate. Assuming I was right about the question mark standing for where Foster lived or his occupation. He'd lived in an apartment on Center Street. What one initial could represent that? I could be wrong, but it seemed unlikely since addresses normally can't be identified by one initial. That left occupation. Foster worked in a tire store and since he'd told Amber he could get her tires at a good price, I assumed he was in sales, so the letter *S* would appear appropriate.

My new theory was that the first letter on Matthew's list represented the last name, so the *ML* I assumed was Austin Middleton. He was an attorney, so the *L* could stand for lawyer. That fit my theory. How about Ron Dillon? He owned a plumbing company so the *P* could stand for plumber. Now, I'm two for two. I had assumed the *LA* stood for Rachel Little, but the letter *A* had been a mystery. I smiled and said, "Yes!" She was an accountant so the letter *A* fit. Three for three. The final initials were *SR* and I'd assumed they were for Trace Spellman, the realtor so *SR* for Spellman realtor worked.

Any doubt I'd had about the names disappeared. All sets of letters on Matthew's note corresponded with our suspects. But all that proved was that they were on the list not who killed Matthew and the others. It also didn't answer why Matthew felt a need to disguise the names.

My phone rang before I had a chance to ponder the puzzle further.

I said, "Good morning, Charles."

"Are you alive?"

"What do you think?"

"Are you home?"

"Yes."

"Then open your front door."

I did and then repeated "Good morning," this time to my friend's face.

He handed me a paper bag and a cup of coffee from Bert's before saying, "Bert's best pastry. Figured you'd be hungry and wouldn't want to leave the house with a deranged murderer out to off you."

I motioned him in and let him follow me into the kitchen.

He saw the paper plate on the table with a few bites of French toast remaining on it and said, "Amber?"

"Yes."

"I'm hurt. You chose her over me."

I ignored his comment and said, "Great. You brought me lunch. I appreciate it."

He smiled then nodded toward my bandaged arm. "You okay?"

"I will be."

"Good. Who'd I con into buying me meals if you bit the dust?"

I translated that to mean he was thrilled I'd be okay.

"Want to see what I figured out?"

"That you like Amber more than you like me?"

I again ignored his comment and moved the two sheets of paper where he could see them.

He glanced at them and said, "So?"

I went through the two lists explaining what I'd concluded.

He listened with a minimal number of questions, which for Charles means fewer than 1,000.

I finished and he sighed before saying, "That all could be true, but you still didn't mention the killer."

"Fritz?"

"Yep."

If my arm didn't hurt so much, I'd apply it to his thick skull.

"Yes, Fritz may be guilty, but for me, Ron Dillon is still the best suspect."

"Because you think the 47,200 beside his name is money he owed Matthew?"

"Yes, we'd heard that someone owed him nearly $50,000, so it'd fit."

"I know. Tell you what, because you're injured, I'll go along with your theory, but still won't mark Fritz off my list."

"Thank you."

"So, now what do we do?"

"I'm going to share this with Cindy. She's leaning toward Ron Dillon, but wasn't convinced the *DP* initials represented him, and even if it did, it didn't prove he killed Matthew and the others. She also told me that neither Ron nor Austin had alibis for the times the people were killed."

"When were you going to tell me?"

"I've been rather busy. I'm telling you now."

"You're going to milk that hole in your arm a long time, aren't you?"

I smiled. "Yep."

"Figures," he said then looked at my phone. "Going to call her?"

Yes would be the only answer that'd work with Charles. Besides, I wanted her to know.

After dialing the Chief, I was rewarded with her voicemail. I left a brief message asking her to call when she got a chance. Charles huffed and puffed as if Cindy had intentionally failed to take my call because she knew he was here.

He said he had a delivery to make for Dude and since I looked so pitiful, he thought he'd better leave so I could crawl back into bed.

I didn't argue with him, although I didn't think I looked that pitiful.

He didn't hug me before he left, but did say, "Glad you're still alive."

Me, too.

48

———————

Fifteen minutes after Charles had left, there was another knock on the front door. I was beginning to wonder if I needed to hire a doorman.

I opened the door to find Cindy LaMond with a frown on her face and a white paper bag in her hand.

"Good morning, Cindy."

She cautiously pushed past me and said, "Why in the world would you open the door without knowing who's on the other side? In case you've forgotten, there's a killer out there with you in their sights. If I happened to be that person, you'd be dead."

"You're the only person I know who knocks and doesn't want the person to answer the door."

"You know what I mean."

I did and didn't think it was the time to tell her I'd already opened the door twice before she'd arrived. Instead, I said, "You're right. I need to be more careful."

"That's better." Her frown disappeared and she handed me the bag. "Donuts. Cops' favorite food group. Thought you needed the energy."

"Thank you." I urged her to have a seat in the living room. I didn't think she needed to go the kitchen and see the remnants of my previous two breakfast menu items.

She sat on the couch, glanced at my arm, and said, "How's it this morning?"

"Hurts, but better than it felt yesterday. Thanks for asking."

"I got your message and figured it'd be better to stop by than call. It also keeps me out of the office and a pile of reports the height of the Morris Island Lighthouse."

"Glad to help you avoid work."

"I figured you didn't call to confess to shooting yourself, so what's up?"

"First, thank you for having Larry fix the broken glass in my door."

"He was thrilled. Said it'd been way too long since he had to fix one of your broken windows. Think he was beginning to feel useless."

"You can tell him he's far from useless."

"He knows that. Heck, I told him the same thing about, umm, a decade ago. Are you going to tell me your theory or continue sucking up to my hubby?"

"This morning, something came to me that I believe shows the list of initials does represent the suspects I told you about. It supports my theory Ron Dillon is most likely the murderer, or at least the person who killed Matthew Seward."

"It took getting shot to figure all that out?"

I smiled. "Probably the pain meds."

"Great, I'm now going to have to listen to how a drug-addled geezer knows who killed Seward III."

"You ooze sympathy. Want to hear what I have or remind me of my senior status?"

"It beats being at the office, so let's hear it."

"Hang on," I said and headed to the kitchen to get the lists.

"If I were you, I wouldn't go out the back door. If you get killed, I'd have to eat the donuts and feel bad about gaining the thirty pounds they'd add to this lithe body."

"I won't open the back door."

I grabbed the two sheets of paper and returned to the living room. I handed the copies to Cindy and joined her on the couch so we could both see the papers.

She looked at the copy of Matthew's note. "What's with all the squiggles besides the initials?"

"The occupations of the people who are represented by the first initial of each combination."

"Okay, you've lost this East Tennessee country gal. What makes you think those letters are occupations?"

"Because of the question mark beside the letter *R* which I believe stands for Foster Rodman."

She looked down at the paper then at me. "I hope you don't think I understood a thing you just said. Try it again, and this time dumb it down for me."

I did, and after a handful of questions, she said, "I hate to admit it, but that sort of makes sense."

"Thank you. Not bad for a drug-addled senior citizen."

"I believe I said drug-addled geezer, but you're welcome. Now, let me throw another question or two, or more, at you."

"Hurl away."

"Let's say everything you showed me is true and Ron Dillon owed Matthew Seward III $47K. Where does it say he killed him?"

"It—"

"Whoa, geezer, there's more."

"Sorry."

"You're forgiven. Even if you're right and Dillon killed Seward to get out of paying the debt, did he kill Foster Rodman and Rachel Little? If he did, why, and why use a different gun with each murder? If he didn't kill the other two, who did?" She waved Matthew's notes in the air. "Why would Seward use this weird, confusing code instead of writing out the names or simply using their initials like normal people would, first initial first? It was locked away in his safe, so why the secrecy? Then...., umm, hell, that's enough for now."

I was tempted to tell her that she was law enforcement, so it was up to her and her colleagues to figure out the answers to those questions. She had a gun and probably would be tempted to use it on me if I said that. Instead, I said, "I honestly don't know, but I figured if we, that is, if you were certain the initials were the names of the most-likely suspects, it'd be easier to find answers to the other questions. It would at least give you a reason to talk to each of them again. You could also share this with Detective Adair, and he could possibly have ideas on how to proceed."

"True, and, oh yeah, one more question. Didn't Charles think Fritz Goss was the killer?"

"He still does."

"Good, it would've been way too easy to narrow the suspects to the two living members of Matthew's poker games."

"I can't prove any of what I said but thought it may help you and Adair."

She smiled at me and said, "It's a big help. It's way more than Adair or I have to tie anyone to the death or deaths. It doesn't prove it, but I agree with you that Ron Dillon at least killed Matthew, and most likely the other two."

"Thanks."

"Guess I'd better get out of here and call Adair. That's always a fun experience. Before I go, is there anything I can get you?"

"No, I'm fine."

She leaned over and hugged me and said, "I'm glad you're okay," stood and opened the door. "Be careful and before you open this again, see if you can see who's knocking first."

49

———————

I was relieved to have shared my theory with Cindy about Matthew's code, but she had a good point. While the code indicated that Ron Dillon probably owed Matthew a significant amount of money, it didn't prove he was a killer. To my knowledge, nobody had even indicated that Ron had a conflict with Matthew. Charles was right, the only conflict we'd heard between anyone and Matthew was with Fritz Goss. If Charles was right, how could I learn more about their relationship?

My arm was feeling better, and the weather was near-perfect. A walk may do me good, and if my arm started hurting or I didn't feel like continuing, I could head home. I left home and turned toward Center Street. I was in front of Bert's Market when a Dillon Plumbing van passed me heading the opposite direction. I couldn't see if Ron was its driver but reminded me of what I'd told Cindy earlier. In addition to trying to learn more about Fritz Goss's relationship with Matthew, I wondered if there was anything else I could learn about Ron Dillon's relationship with the deceased accountant, correction, accountants.

A half-block later, I was in front of Folly Beach Family Dentistry when the van that had passed me moments earlier, pulled off the road onto the brick sidewalk in front of the dental office.

If Ron was driving, this may be a good chance to learn more about his relationship with Matthew. I approached the passenger side window as it lowered.

"Chris, I thought that was you when I passed Bert's," Ron said and smiled. "Where're you headed?"

"Hi, Ron. Nowhere in particular. Out for a walk."

He looked at my arm. "What happened?"

"Just a cut, no big deal."

He smiled. "Good. Hop in. I wanted to tell you something I learned about Matthew's death. It has to do with his boss, Fritz Goss."

"That's okay, we can talk here," I said as I put my elbow on the passenger window frame.

I was surprised when he got out of the vehicle and walked around it to within a couple of feet from me.

I was between Ron and his van, so I couldn't step farther away from him.

"What'd you want to share about Matthew and Fritz?"

"Don't think it's important. Got a more pressing problem. I think you'd better hop in." His smile faded.

I glanced down to see his left hand holding a small caliber handgun—a handgun pointed at my chest.

"It's time you got in."

He opened the door, I took a quick glance around and didn't see anyone, nor a way to escape without further risking my life.

Ron moved a clipboard off the passenger seat and put it between the seat and the console. "Sorry for the mess. I don't usually have passengers." He gave me a sinister smile and transferred the handgun to his right hand and buckled my seatbelt with his left hand, before saying, "Leave it buckled while I walk around the van." He smiled again before adding, "You know it's dangerous not wearing a seatbelt."

The gun was never out of my sight as he walked around to his door and slid into the vehicle. He pulled back on the street and approached the traffic light at the intersection of Ashley Avenue and Center Street.

The light was green, and he continued through the intersection and west on Ashley Avenue.

He glanced at me and said, "You and your buddy don't give up, do you?"

I was afraid I knew what he meant, but now my only hope was to stall long enough to see how I could escape. Jumping out wasn't a viable option since he was going at least ten miles an hour over the twenty-five miles-per-hour island-wide limit. There's nothing I would like to see more than a Folly Beach patrol car stop him for speeding.

Ron suddenly slowed and pulled off the right side of the road, turned to me, and said, "Grab that roll of duct tape from behind my seat. While you're at it, don't get any funny ideas. I'm pretty good with one of these." He raised the gun a little higher so he wouldn't have any trouble hitting me if I tried anything stupid while reaching for the tape. "Suppose I should've said good at it, until I shot you in the arm instead of the head."

I didn't comment, instead I picked up the duct tape and returned to my seat.

"Now, wrap it around your wrist."

I did, then he reached over with his free hand and took the roll while telling me to push my palms together. He started rolling the tape around my wrists with one hand while keeping the gun pointed at me. He set the gun on his lap and with both hands wrapped the tape around my wrists several more times. He tore the tape and threw the roll in the back of the van.

He chuckled. "I've always wanted to do that after seeing it in movies." He then frowned. "Don't suppose you're going to comment on my wrapping job?"

He was right, instead of complimenting him, I said, "What now?"

"We're going for a boat ride. Don't worry, I'll be back later for your snoopy buddy."

Less than a mile farther up West Ashley Avenue, Ron turned right on 9th Street West, which told me he was serious about a boat ride as he parked in Sunset Cay Marina's parking lot. I'd been here a few times over the years and one thing I remembered was there were seldom many people around even though there were often forty boats docked here. Today was no exception. I didn't see anyone on any of the boats or on the docks. Not a good sign for my escape.

Ron glanced in the back of the van. Moved a tarp aside and grabbed what looked like a green beach towel. "I'm going to put this over your hands like you're carrying it. That should keep any wayward eyes from thinking anything is suspicious with you walking to the boat. Stay seated while I walk around to get you."

He was never more than a few feet away as he came around to the passenger door. Even if I could get out and run, where would I go?

He opened the door, stood back, and said, "Get out slowly. We're going to walk side by side. I don't have to tell you not to try anything funny, do I?" He slipped on a light jacket, put the handgun in the pocket but never took his hand off its grip.

"No," I said and grimaced from a stabbing pain in my wounded arm from the awkward position of my taped wrists.

We walked to the end of the dock, turned left, then right. We passed six boats before he said, "Your ride awaits," and pointed to a white boat with a wide black stripe along the side and a Sea Ray logo near the center. It appeared roughly twenty feet long.

The front passenger seat was stacked with brown boxes that, according to the renderings on the side of the containers, held PVC fittings. I had no idea why they were there. He helped me maneuver aboard onto the bench seat behind the front seats, probably to prevent me from falling into the Folly River attracting attention, rather than being courteous. It probably wouldn't have mattered since I still hadn't seen any sign of life nearby.

"Shove the junk out of your way and make yourself comfortable. We've got a long ride ahead of us."

He was right about the junk. It looked like he ran a plumbing business out of his boat. There was a cooler with a layer of dried mud on top of it, two life vests, several tools including a pipe wrench, two screwdrivers, two three-foot-long pieces of pipe, and a couple of other items I couldn't identify since they were partially covered with a blue tarp.

While I was looking around, he'd untied the boat and moved to the captain's seat. Less than a minute later, we were headed southwest on the Folly River then to the open sea. It was becoming clear his plan ended with me in the ocean with no hope of reaching land.

50

If I had any chance of getting out of this alive, I would have to stall long enough for either Ron to make a mistake, the Coast Guard to stop us for a routine inspection, or I found a way to get free from my restraints.

I leaned forward so he could hear me over the roar of the engine, and said, "Why me?"

He ignored my question, so I added, "We both know this isn't going to end well for me, so why not tell me what happened?"

"Good point," he said. "Why you? You have a reputation around town for being better at catching killers than are the cops. I saw that firsthand the other night at The Washout. Your buddy said you knew or thought you knew who killed Matthew. I saw in your eyes he was right." He smiled. "That's why I broke in your house to see if there was anything there that'd implicate me. You had those papers on the table with my name on one of them and the one you shared with Austin and me at The Washout. It didn't make sense, but it had the exact amount I owed Matthew right there on the paper. I didn't understand it, but knew it was a problem." He hesitated and looked to the left where we could see the west end of Folly.

"Then why shoot me?"

"You had the papers, so I figured you knew what they meant. That wouldn't do. I'd started back to your place to wait for you inside, then, well, you know what. Anyway, I was coming around the back of your house when you stepped outside. I wasn't at my best with my aim and caused that, what'd you call it, a *cut*?"

"So why'd you kill Matthew? I figured you owed him money, but that didn't prove anything about you shooting him."

He turned and looked in front of the boat, and I looked around to see if there was anything that'd cut through the duct tape. He turned back facing me, and said, "Yes, I owed him a bundle but other times I owed him he'd given me extra time to pay. Several extensions, in fact." He smacked his hand on the wheel. "Not this time, not even after I confided that my business was in a bind. I had several large receivables and was having difficulty collecting. Know what he said?"

"No."

"He gave me one of his sick-looking grins and said, 'Tough shit.' That's when I thought that'd look good carved on his tombstone."

"What happened?"

"I called him two days later and said I had his money and wanted to bring it to him. Like a fool, he said to come on over. I said I'd be right there. Guess you can guess what happened next."

"Instead of giving him the money, you gave him a bullet in the head."

"You got it. See, you can figure out all this murder stuff."

"What was the deal with the cocaine at his house?"

"Thought that'd be a nice touch. Make the cops think the murder had something to do with drugs and not about anything else."

I tried to keep looking at Ron as I felt around the rest of the bench seat to find something, anything that'd help me get free.

"Smart," I said even though that thought was far from my mind. "So, why kill Foster and Rachel?"

"Who said I killed them? They weren't even shot with the same gun, were they?"

"You still killed them."

"As you astutely pointed out a few minutes ago, this boat ride isn't going to end well for one of us." He smiled. "It ain't me." He glanced back to shore then said, "Yeah, I killed them."

"Why?"

A much larger oceangoing watercraft was off to our right, but not close enough to be paying attention to our smaller craft. Ron glanced at it and turned back to me.

"Over the years that we'd played poker, each of us lost to each other, sometimes a few hundred dollars, other times in the thousands. And, unfortunately in my case, many thousands, plus he'd loaned me thirty-grand six months ago to pay off some business debts. Anyway, one night after a few too many drinks, I told Foster about owing Matthew a bundle. After Matthew's death, good old Foster figured I was the one who shot him. Know what that idiot did then?"

Of course, I didn't and said so.

"He came to me and said for a measly five-grand, he'd forget about my crime. I've often wondered why it didn't enter his skull that if I killed Matthew, I wouldn't hesitate to kill him."

"Not wise on his part."

"Nope."

My hand finally found something that could possibly cut through the tape. A seven-inch long wire cutter with a one-inch blade was under the cooler. Now all I had to do was keep my hands out of Ron's line of sight and slowly cut through the thick tape. Easier said than done, but since it was my only hope, I had to try.

To keep him distracted, I said, "What about Rachel?"

"I hated to have to kill her. I really did. She said Matthew told her about my debt then after he was killed, she did the same thing Foster did."

"Tried to blackmail you?"

"No, but still accused me of killing him. That really pissed her off. She had this idea, wrong, but she still believed it, that Matthew would come back to her. That gal was crazy, unstable, and a threat to tell the police about me killing her ex-boyfriend. I really hated it, but she had to go."

I slid a couple inches to the right, so part of my body was blocked from his sight by his captain's chair. I then managed to get my right forefinger and thumb around the wire cutter's grip and held it with the cutting end facing the duct tape. My wounded arm felt like it was in a vice. Regardless how much it hurt, I had to keep him talking so he wouldn't pay attention to how I was leaning in the seat.

"Why different guns?"

"You have a lot of questions for someone in your fix."

"You have nothing to lose by talking about it."

"Know what I like watching on television?"

While he was asking, I slid the blades of the wire cutter over the duct tape and squeezed the grip. It was easy to see why they were wire cutters and not duct tape cutters. They barely cut through no more than a quarter inch of the tape. I had to keep him talking or this'd be my last day breathing.

I wasn't ready for that question, so guessed, "Crime shows."

"Bingo. See you're a natural at figuring things out. I've always liked watching police shows. Know what I learned early on from those educational programs."

"Forensic science techs can tell which gun bullets come from."

"Yes, if they have the gun to compare the bullet to. I knew the bullets would be analyzed, that's a no-brainer, even for a plumber. So, if the cops got suspicious of me and managed to search me or my house, shop, vans, boat, and found a gun, they'd know it fired the deadly rounds. That was one mistake I wasn't going to make. Luckily, I had two handguns, one I'd bought, and one Dad gave me years ago. If you're as good in math as you are in figuring out crimes, you'll know I needed to add three more. One for Rachel, this one for you, and the final one for your troublemaking buddy Charles." He held up the handgun that he'd placed on the other front seat, then added, "You wouldn't believe how easy it was to get the other guns."

I'd cut halfway through the tape. From twisting it around, my left arm hurt as much as it had after he shot me, but I endured the pain. It would be the least of my problems if I failed to get the tape off.

"What'd you do with the first three guns?" I asked, not really caring, but hoping to stall him from ending our ride together.

He pointed over the side of the boat. "That answer your question?"

It did, but much too quickly. I was still a quarter of an inch from cutting through the tape.

"Ron, you know you aren't getting away with killing me. Before you saw me this morning, I met with Chief LaMond and shared the information I learned from Matthew's notes. She knows you're the one who owed him the money and you're her prime suspect."

"So what? Like you said earlier, she may know I owed him money, but that doesn't prove I killed him. I don't have the weapon, no one saw me at his house when he was shot."

The wire cutter snipped the last of the tape making a clicking noise as it cut through. I hoped the sound of the boat's motor drowned out the noise. Now what? I had to keep him talking.

"Ron, you may be right, but she won't stop there. By now, she's told Detective Adair what I shared with her. I wouldn't be surprised if they aren't already looking for you."

"Maybe, but at least I won't have to deal with you."

He turned off the ignition and looked toward the horizon. The coast was nearly out of sight and no other watercraft were visible.

He picked up the gun. At the same time, I grabbed one of the three-foot-long sections of pipe off the floor.

He turned toward me and said, "I think it's time for you to stand up then either you can jump, or I can push you overboard. Your choice."

I chose a third option and swung the pipe at his head. He saw it coming and jerked to the right. The pipe hit his neck instead of his skull like I'd intended. He pitched forward but managed to catch himself before hitting the steering wheel. He still held the gun, screamed a profanity, and swung his gun hand in my direction.

I leaned back to get a better angle and again swung the pipe at his head. This time, I didn't miss. As soon as the pipe contacted his skull,

I thought I may've killed him. I didn't know if he was dead or alive, but there was no doubt he was out, at least for now.

I reached in front and picked up the handgun that'd landed on the seat and then slipped it into my pocket. Before I did anything else, I needed to find a way to secure Ron before he came to. That is, if he did. I moved the tarp that's been covering some of the other tools and no telling what else. There was a gray tool chest I hadn't seen before. I unlatched the top and opened the container. On top of more wrenches, there was a plastic package holding black 28" long zip ties. I pulled two out of the package, then pushed Ron's body to the side so I could pull both of his arms behind him. I may not have watched as many police shows as Ron but knew the best way to secure his hands were behind his back. I was glad he'd missed that episode. I yanked his arms around so both hands were close together and secured them with one of the restraints.

I took a deep breath, then began the arduous task of throwing the boxes of PVC fittings from the front passenger seat to the back, then moving Ron onto the other seat so I could get behind the wheel.

I moved to the captain's chair, wiped Ron's blood off the wheel, then took another zip tie and put it around his ankles then yanked it tight. It took way more time than it should have, but that was okay with me. That was time I wouldn't have been alive if I hadn't managed to free my hands.

51

Now what? I felt like I was in the middle of the Atlantic Ocean. Looking in three directions, I could've been. Fortunately, when I looked behind the boat I saw the coast, but it was too far away to discern details. In other words, I had no idea where I was, but knew what direction I needed to go.

I'd piloted boats slightly more times than I'd piloted F-35 fighter jets, so it took all my nautical skill to get the engine started, then turning the boat facing the Carolina coast rather than Ireland. After fifteen minutes, I recognized Folly Beach. About the same time, Ron moaned. It felt good knowing I hadn't killed him, although it was a greater feeling knowing I could probably make it home.

The closer I got to Folly, I realized I would severely challenge my piloting ability to return to the Sunset Cay Marina. I also could see how crowded the beach was near the Folly Pier and the Tides Hotel. Even after everything I'd been through I still had my phone in my pocket. I dialed Cindy's cell phone.

"What now?" she said lacking enthusiasm.

"What are you doing?"

"Falling asleep in the office. Why?"

"Good. Wake up and head down to the beach around 7th Street East."

"Is that where you are?"

"No."

"Then why should I be there?"

"So I can hand you a killer."

"Didn't you say you weren't there?"

"Not yet. You on your way?"

I heard a loud sigh, then, "Yes."

"You probably should order an ambulance, and possibly a couple of your firefighters, to join you." I ended the call before she asked more questions.

Ron was beginning to do more than moan. He tried to free his hands, gave up, then twisted his body toward me. Blood was dripping from his head onto his Dillon Plumbing shirt. His eyes appeared unfocused.

As I got closer to shore, I saw the red flashing lights from one of the city's fire engines between the houses near the public walkway to the beach. I also thought I saw Cindy's pickup truck but wasn't certain. There were also a couple of small groups watching a Sea Ray coming their way.

I then recognized Cindy standing on the beach side of the dunes. She raised her phone to her ear at the same time my phone rang. I smiled but was too busy to answer.

Fortunately, the people along the beach moved back from where I was headed. I suppose Ron's boat wouldn't be as good as new momentarily. I didn't care. My plan was simple. Ram the boat into the sand close to the water's edge and hand Ron over to the Folly Beach Department of Public Safety.

It was a good plan, until the boat caught a sandbar about twenty-five yards from shore. I was thrown into the steering wheel and Ron's head hit the windshield. We weren't going anywhere under the boat's power, so I turned off the ignition.

Cindy was now about a foot from the water. She shook her head and yelled, "If that was your attempt at a grand entrance, it sucked."

Two of the firefighter/EMTs moved up beside the Chief. She directed them to wade out and see if the man moaning in the passenger's seat needed their attention.

She then focused on me and said, "If you think I'm going to walk out there and meet you, you're crazy. Get on your water-wing floaties and slosh over here."

I did as ordered, minus the floaties, and joined Cindy on the beach. I heard the siren of an ambulance pulling off the road and Charles yelling, "Chris, you need more driving lessons if you did that." He pointed to the boat now holding two EMTs and Ron.

Another patrol car joined the group of emergency vehicles and Officer Trula Bishop joined us on the beach. She said, "Mr. Chris, you okay?"

"Thank you, Officer Bishop. I knew if I stood here long enough, someone would ask about me. I'm not okay, but much better now."

Cindy pointed to the boat and said, "I assume that's the killer you mentioned."

"Yes, goes by Ron Dillon. He's already wrapped up for you."

She wiped sweat from her forehead. "Join me in my air-conditioned vehicle. I'm not dressed for sunbathing."

Charles said, "Me, too?"

"Sure, why not. Officer Bishop, you might as well join us. I suspect Chris has quite a story to tell. But before you do, let the next two officers who show up know they won the chance to take care of the prisoner and figure out what to do with a beached Sea Ray."

My preference would have been to go home, take one, okay, maybe two pain pills, climb into bed and pull the covers over my head with my right arm and write this all off as a bad dream. Instead, I did my civic duty and told Cindy, Trula, and Charles, in Cindy's words *quite a story.*

ABOUT THE AUTHOR BILL NOEL

Bill Noel is the best-selling author of twenty-eight novels in the popular Folly Beach Mystery series. The award-winning novelist is also a fine arts photographer and lives in Louisville, Kentucky, with his wife, Susan, and his off-kilter imagination.

Angelica Cruz is the award-winning coauthor of four novels in the Folly Beach Mystery series.

Ms. Cruz lives near Elizabethtown, Kentucky, with her husband Hector, one dog, a bird, two cats, and four chickens.